**Robert Barr** (16 September 1849 – 21 October 1912) was a Scottish-Canadian short story writer and novelist. Robert Barr was born in Barony, Lanark, Scotland to Robert Barr and Jane Watson. In 1854, he emigrated with his parents to Upper Canada at the age of four years old. His family settled on a farm near the village of Muirkirk. Barr assisted his father with his job as a carpenter, and developed a sound work ethic. Robert Barr then worked as a steel smelter for a number of years before he was educated at Toronto Normal School in 1873 to train as a teacher. After graduating Toronto Normal School, Barr became a teacher, and eventually headmaster/principal of the Central School of Windsor, Ontario in 1874. While Barr worked as head master of the Central School of Windsor, Ontario, he began to contribute short stories—often based on personal experiences, and recorded his work. On August 1876, when he was 27, Robert Barr married Ontario-born Eva Bennett, who was 21. (Source: Wikipedia)

Literary works:
"The Face And The Mask" (1894)
In the Midst of Alarms (1894, 1900, 1912)
From Whose Bourne (1896)
One Day's Courtship (1896)
Revenge!
The Strong Arm
A Woman Intervenes (1896)
Tekla: A Romance of Love and War (1898)
Jennie Baxter, Journalist (1899)
The Unchanging East (1900)
The Victors (1901)
A Prince of Good Fellows (1902)
Over The Border: A Romance (1903)
The O'Ruddy, A Romance, with Stephen Crane (1903)

# LORD STRANLEIGH ABROAD, A CHICAGO PRINCESS & OVER THE BORDER

ROBERT BARR

PRINCE CLASSICS

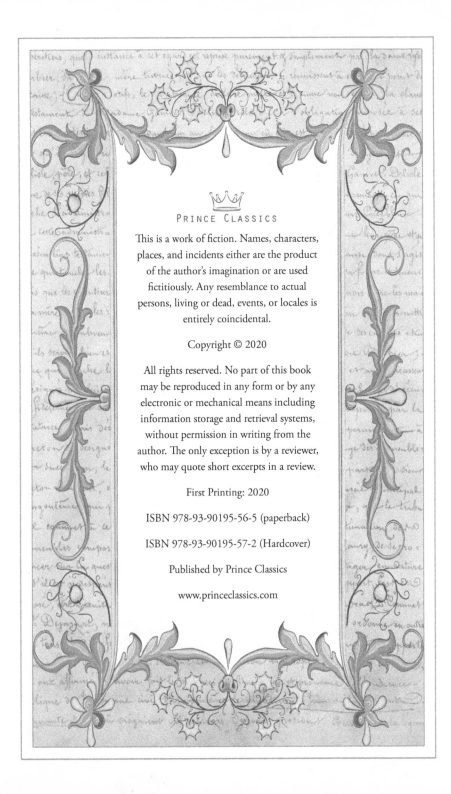

PRINCE CLASSICS

First Printing: 2020

ISBN 978-93-90195-56-5 (paperback)

ISBN 978-93-90195-57-2 (Hardcover)

Published by Prince Classics

www.princeclassics.com

# Contents

# LORD STRANLEIGH ABROAD,
## A CHICAGO PRINCESS
## &
## OVER THE BORDER

# LORD STRANLEIGH
# ABROAD

# I.—LORD STRANLEIGH ALL AT SEA.

A few minutes before noon on a hot summer day, Edmund Trevelyan walked up the gang-plank of the steamship, at that moment the largest Atlantic liner afloat. Exactly at the stroke of twelve she would leave Southampton for Cherbourg, then proceed across to Queenstown, and finally would make a bee-line west for New York. Trevelyan was costumed in rough tweed of subdued hue, set off by a cut so well-fitting and distinguished that it seemed likely the young man would be looked upon by connoisseurs of tailoring as the best-dressed passenger aboard. He was followed by Ponderby, his valet, whose usually expressionless face bore a look of dissatisfaction with his lot, as though he had been accustomed to wait upon the nobility, and was now doomed to service with a mere commoner. His lack of content, however, was caused by a dislike to ocean travel in the first place, and his general disapproval of America in the second. A country where all men are free and equal possessed no charms for Ponderby, who knew he had no equal, and was not going to demean himself by acknowledging the possibility of such.

Once on deck, his master turned to him and said—

"You will go, Ponderby, to my suite of rooms, and see that my luggage is placed where it should be, and also kindly satisfy yourself that none of it is missing."

Ponderby bowed in a dignified manner, and obeyed without a word, while Trevelyan mounted the grand staircase, moving with an easy nonchalance suited to a day so inordinately hot. The prospect of an ocean voyage in such weather was in itself refreshing, and so prone is mankind to live in the present, and take no thought of the morrow, that Trevelyan had quite forgotten the cablegrams he read in the papers on his way down from London, to the effect that New York was on the grill, its inhabitants sweltering—sleeping on the house-tops, in the parks, on the beach at Coney Island, or wherever a breath of air could be had. On the upper deck his slow steps were arrested by an exclamation—

"Isn't this Mr. Trevelyan?"

The man who made the enquiry wore the uniform of the ship's company.

"Ah, doctor, I was thinking of you at this moment. I read in the papers that you had been promoted, and I said to myself: 'After all, this is not an ungrateful world, when the most skilful and most popular medical officer on the Atlantic is thus appreciated.'"

"Ah, you put it delightfully, Trevelyan, but I confess I hesitated about adding, at my time of life, to the burden I carry."

"Your time of life, doctor! Why you always make me feel an old man by comparison with yourself; yet you'll find me skipping about the decks like a boy."

"If you'll take the right-hand seat at my table, I'll keep an eye on you, and prevent you from skipping overboard," laughed the doctor.

"Indeed, that was the boon I intended to crave."

"Then the seat is yours, Trevelyan. By the way, I read in the newspapers that Evelyn Trevelyan is none other than Lord Stranleigh; but then, of course, you can never believe what you see in the press, can you?"

"Personally, I make no effort to do so. I get my news of the day from Ponderby, who is an inveterate reader of the principal journals favoured by what he calls the 'upper classes.' But I assure you that Evelyn Trevelyan is a name that belongs to me, and I wear it occasionally like an old, comfortable-fitting coat."

"Ah, well, I'll not give you away. I'll see you at lunch between here and Cherbourg." And the doctor hurried away to his duties.

The young man continued his stroll, smiling as he remembered some of the doctor's excellent stories. He regarded his meeting with that friendly officer as a good omen, but hoped he would encounter no one else who knew him.

The next interruption of his walk proved to be not so pleasant. There came up the deck with nervous tread a shabbily-dressed man, who appeared from ten to fifteen years older than Stranleigh, although in reality there was no great disparity in their ages. His face was haggard and lined with anxiety, and his eyes had that furtive, penetrating glance which distinguishes the inveterate gambler. Stranleigh watched his oncoming with amazement.

The Hon. John Hazel had been a member of some of the most exclusive clubs in London; but whether or not Nature had endowed him with a useful talent, he had become notorious as a reckless cardsharper, quite unscrupulous when it came to obtaining money. No one knew this better than Lord Stranleigh, who had been so often his victim, yet had regarded his losses lightly, and forgiven the Hon. John time and again. But recently this younger son of an ancient and honourable house had committed the unpardonable sin—he had been found out, and had been permitted to resign from all his clubs but one, and from which he was expelled by a committee not so lenient. After that he disappeared. He was done for, so far as England was concerned, and he knew it.

"John, is this possible?" cried Lord Stranleigh, as the other approached.

Hazel stopped, his eyes veiling over, as though he held a hand at poker that was unbeatable.

"I haven't the pleasure of knowing you, sir," he said haughtily.

"I'm glad of that, because I'm Edmund Trevelyan at the moment, and was just hoping I should meet no one on board who would recognise me."

"I don't know Edmund Trevelyan, and have no wish to make his acquaintance," returned the other coldly.

"That's quite all right, and your wish does you credit. Trevelyan has no desire to force his friendship on any man. Nevertheless, Jack, time was when I helped you out of a hole, and, if occasion arose, I should be glad to do it again."

"You could have prevented my expulsion from the Camperdown Club, had you but cared to raise a finger," said the other hotly.

"Hazel, you are mistaken. I did all I could for you, as in other crises of the same nature. The committee proved to be adamant, and rather prided themselves on their independence, as if they were a group of blooming Radicals. The House of Lords isn't what it was, Jack, as, alas, you may learn, should you ever come into the title of your family, although many people stand between you and it at the present moment. Indeed, Jack, it has been on my conscience that my urgent advocacy prejudiced your case instead of helping it."

"Ah, well, that's all past; it doesn't matter now," said the other, with a sigh. "I have shaken the dust of England for ever from my feet."

"The mud, you mean."

"Oh, I admit I wallowed in the mud, but it was dust when I left London this morning. Ah, we're off! I must be going." And he moved away from the rail of the ship, where he had been gazing over the side.

"Going? Where?"

"Where I belong. I'm travelling third-class. The moment the steamer gets under way, I have no right on the cabin deck. Before she left, I took the liberty of a sightseer to wander over the steamship."

"My dear Jack," said his former friend, in a grave voice, "this will never do; you cannot cross the Atlantic in the steerage."

"I have visited my quarters, and find them very comfortable. I have been in much worse places recently. Steerage is like everything else maritime— like this bewilderingly immense steamer, for example—vastly improved since Robert Louis Stevenson took his trip third-class to New York."

"Well, it is a change for a luxury-loving person like my friend the Hon. John Hazel."

"It is very condescending of you to call me your friend. Nobody else would do it," replied the Hon. John bitterly.

"Condescension be hanged! I'm rather bewildered, that's all, and wish

16

for further particulars. Are you turning over a new leaf, then?"

"A new leaf? A thousand of them! I have thrown away the old book, with its blotches and ink-stains. I'm starting a blank volume that I hope will bear inspection and not shock even the rectitude of the Camperdown Committee."

"What's the programme?"

"I don't quite know yet; it will depend on circumstances. I think it's the West for me—sort of back-to-the-land business. I yearn to become a kind of moral cowboy. It seems the only thing I'm at all equipped for. I can ride well and shoot reasonably straight."

"I thought," said Stranleigh, "that phase of life had disappeared with Bret Harte. Is there any money in your inside pocket?"

"How could there be?"

"Then why not let me grub-stake you, which I believe is the correct Western term."

"As how, for instance?"

"I'll secure for you a comfortable cabin, and you will pay the damage when you strike oil out West, so, you see, there's no humiliating condescension about the offer."

"I'm sure there isn't, and it's very good of you, Stranleigh, but I can't dress the part."

"That's easily arranged. Ponderby always over-dresses me. His idea of this world is that there is London, and the rest of the planet is a wilderness. You could no more persuade him that a decent suit might be made in New York than that I am the worst-dressed man in London. You and I are about the same height and build. Ponderby will have in my mountainous luggage anywhere from twenty-five to forty suits never yet worn by me. I don't know on what principle he goes, but as the last time we went to America he took twenty-five new suits, and we crossed in a twenty-five thousand ton boat, he is likely to have at least forty-five suits for this forty-five thousand ton steamship, and he will feel as much pleasure in rigging you out as he took in the crowning of the new King."

"Very good of you, Stranleigh, but I cannot accept."

"I am pleading for Ponderby's sake. Besides, there's one practical point you have overlooked. If you attempt to land from the steerage—travelling under an assumed name, I suppose——"

"Like yourself, Stranleigh."

"No, I own the name 'Trevelyan.' But, as I was saying, if you attempt to land rather shabbily dressed and almost penniless, you will find yourself turned back as an undesirable alien, whereas you can go ashore from the first cabin unquestioned, save for those amazing queries the U.S.A. Government puts to one, the answers to which Ponderby will be charmed to write out for you."

Hazel without reply walked back to the rail, leaned his arms on it, and fell into deep thought. Stranleigh followed him.

"Give me your ticket," he said.

Hazel took it from his pocket and handed it over.

"Have you any luggage?"

"Only a portmanteau, which I placed in my bunk. It contains a certain amount of necessary linen."

"Wait here until I find out what there is to be had in the first cabin."

Stranleigh went down to the purser, and that overworked official threw him a friendly glance, which nevertheless indicated that his time was valuable.

"My name is Trevelyan," said the young man.

"Oh, yes, Mr. Trevelyan. You have our premier suite. How do you like your accommodation?"

"I haven't seen it yet. I have just discovered a friend, a rather eccentric man, who had made up his mind to cross the Atlantic in the steerage. One of those silly bets, you know, which silly young men make in our silly London clubs, and I have persuaded him out of it."

"Our steerage is supposed to be rather comfortable, Mr. Trevelyan."

"So he says, but I want his company on deck, and not on the steerage deck at that. Have you got anything vacant along my avenue?"

The purser consulted his written list.

"Nobody with him?"

"He's quite alone."

"All the larger cabins are taken, but I can give him No. 4390."

"I suppose, like your steerage, it is comfortable?" said Stranleigh, with a smile.

"It is, yet it's not a private hotel like your quarters."

"Oh, he'll not grumble. Will you send a steward to carry his portmanteau from the number indicated on this steerage ticket to his new room? Meanwhile, I'll have transferred to him his luggage that I brought from London."

The purser rapidly wrote out a new ticket, and took the difference in five-pound notes.

"Are you going to your quarters now?" the purser asked.

"Yes, I must give some instructions to my man."

"Then it will give me great pleasure to show you the way there," said the purser, rising and locking the door; and in spite of Stranleigh's protest against his taking the trouble, he led him to a series of rooms that would have satisfied a much more exacting person than his young lordship. When the purser had returned to his duties, Stranleigh said to Ponderby—

"The Hon. John Hazel is aboard, and his cabin is No. 4390. He had to leave London in a great hurry and without the necessary luggage."

19

Ponderby's eyes lit up with an expression which said—"I knew that would happen sooner or later." But he uttered no word, and cast down his eyes when he saw his master had noticed the glance. Stranleigh spoke coldly and clearly.

"How many new suits have you provided for me?"

"Thirty-seven, my lord."

"Very well. Clear out one or two boxes, and pack a dress-suit and two or three ordinary suits; in fact, costume the Hon. John Hazel just as you would costume me. Call a steward, and order the box to be taken to his room. Lay out for him an everyday garb, and get all this done as quickly as possible."

His lordship proceeded leisurely to the upper deck once more, and found Hazel just as he had left him, except that he was now gazing at the fleeting shore, green and village-studded, of the Isle of Wight.

"Here you are," said Stranleigh breezily, handing the Hon. John the cabin ticket.

There was a weak strain in Hazel's character, otherwise he would never had come to the position in which he found himself, and he now exhibited the stubbornness which has in it the infallible signs of giving way.

"I really cannot accept it," he said, his lower lip trembling perceptibly.

"Tut, tut! It's all settled and done with. Your room is No. 4390. You will find your bag there, and also a box from my habitation. Come along—I'll be your valet. Luncheon will be on shortly, and I want your company."

Stranleigh turned away, and Hazel followed him.

Cabin 4390 could not be compared with the luxurious suite that Stranleigh was to occupy, yet, despite the purser's hesitation to overpraise it, the cabin was of a size and promise of comfort that would have been found in few liners a decade ago. Ponderby was on hand, and saved his master the fag of valeting, and when finally the Hon. John emerged, he was quite his old jaunty self again—a well-dressed man who would not have done discredit even to the Camperdown Club.

"I have secured a place for you," said Stranleigh, "next to myself at the doctor's table. I flatter myself on having made this transfer with more tact than I usually display, for I am somewhat stupid in the main, trusting others to carry out my ideas rather than endeavouring to shine as a diplomatist myself. The purser—the only official aware of the change—thinks you made a bet to go over steerage, and will probably forget all about the matter. The question is, under what name shall I introduce you to the doctor?"

"What would you advise?" asked Hazel. "The name on my steerage ticket is William Jones."

"Oh, that's no good as a nom de guerre—too palpably a name chosen by an unimaginative man. I should sail under your own colours if I were you."

"Good! Then John Hazel I am, and so will remain. As a guarantee of good faith, I promise you not to touch a card all the way across."

"A good resolution; see that you keep it." And thus they enjoyed an appetising lunch together, and were regaled with one of the doctor's best salads.

They got away from Cherbourg before the dinner hour, and after that meal Stranleigh and Hazel walked together on the main deck, until the latter, admitting he was rather fagged after the exciting events of the day, went off to his cabin, and Stranleigh was left alone to smoke a final cigar. He leaned on the rail and gazed meditatively at the smooth sea.

It was an ideal evening, and Stranleigh felt at peace with all the world. There exists a popular belief that the rich are overburdened with care. This may be true while they are in the money-making struggle, but it is not a usual fault when the cash is in the bank or safely invested. Stranleigh occasionally lost money, but an immense amount had been bequeathed him, and he made many millions more than he had parted with, although he claimed this was merely because of a series of flukes, maintaining that, whenever he set to work that part of him known as his brains, he invariably came a cropper.

"You are Mr. Trevelyan, are you not?" said a very musical feminine voice at his elbow. Stranleigh turned in surprise, and seeing there a most charming young woman, he flung his partially consumed cigar into the sea.

"Yes," he replied, "my name is Trevelyan. How did you know?"

That rare smile came to his lips—a smile, people said, which made you feel instinctively you could trust him; and many ladies who were quite willing to bestow their trust, called it fascinating.

"I am afraid," said the girl, whose beautiful face was very serious, and whose large dark eyes seemed troubled—"I am afraid that I enacted the part of unintentional eavesdropper. I had some business with the purser—business that I rather shrank from executing. You came to his window just before I did, for I was hesitating."

"I am sorry," said Stranleigh, "if I obtruded myself between you and that official. Being rather limited in intelligence, my mind can attend to only one thing at a time, and I must confess I did not see you."

"I know you did not," retorted the girl. "There was no obtrusion. You were first comer, and therefore should have been first served, as was the case."

"I would willingly have given up my place and whatever rights I possessed in the matter, had I known a lady was waiting."

"I am sure of it. However, your conversation with the purser gave me a welcome respite, and, thinking over the crisis, I determined to consult you before I spoke to him; thus I have taken the unusual step of bringing myself to your notice."

"In what way can I assist you, madam?" asked Stranleigh, a return of his usual caution showing itself in the instant stiffening of manner and coldness of words.

"I learned you were exchanging, on behalf of a friend, a third-class ticket for a place in the cabin. I judged from this that you are a good-hearted man, and my attention was attracted when you introduced yourself to the purser as Trevelyan, because Trevelyan is my own name."

"Really?" ejaculated his lordship. "Have you relatives near Wychwood?

You are English, are you not?"

"I am English, and a distant connection with the family of Trevelyan, near Wychwood, none of whom, however, I have yet met, unless you happen to belong to that branch."

"I do," said Stranleigh. "And now tell me, if you please, what is your difficulty?"

"I wish to ask you if the steerage ticket you gave the purser was taken in part payment for the cabin ticket, or did you forfeit it altogether?"

"That I can't tell you," said Stranleigh, with a laugh. "I am not accustomed to the transaction of business, and this little arrangement had to be made quickly."

Although his lordship spoke lightly and pleasantly the girl appeared to have some difficulty in proceeding with her story. The large eyes were quite evidently filling with tears, and of all things in the world Stranleigh loathed an emotional scene. The girl was obviously deeply depressed, whatever the cause.

"Well," he said jauntily and indeed encouragingly, "we were talking of first and third-class tickets. What have you to say about them?"

"I speak of the steerage ticket only. If you haven't forfeited it, you have the right to demand its return."

"I suppose so. Still, it is of no particular use to me."

"No, but it would be vital to me. Coming down in the train from London, my purse was stolen, or perhaps I lost it when giving up my railway ticket. So I am now without either money or transportation voucher."

"Was it for cabin passage?"

"Yes."

"In that case you will have no difficulty; your name will be on the purser's list. Do you know the number of your state-room?"

"No, I do not, and, so far as my name goes, I can expect no help from that quarter, because the name I travel under is not Miss Trevelyan."

"Good gracious," cried Stranleigh, "there are three of us! This ship should be called Incognita. Was your money also in that purse?"

"Yes, all my gold and bank-notes, and I am left with merely some silver and coppers."

"Then the third-class ticket would not be of the slightest use to you. As I had to point out to another person on a similar occasion, you would not be allowed to land, so we will let that third-class ticket drop into oblivion. If you are even distantly related to the Trevelyan family, I could not think of allowing you to travel steerage. Are you alone?"

"Yes," she murmured almost inaudibly.

"Well, then, it is better that you should make all arrangements with the purser yourself. As I told you, I am not particularly good at business affairs. You give to him the name under which you purchased your ticket. You bought it in London, I suppose?"

"Yes," she murmured again.

"Mention to him the name you used then. He will look up his list, and allot you the state-room you paid for. It is probable he may have the power to do this without exacting any excess fare; but if such is not the case, settle with him for your passage, and take his receipt. The money will doubtless be refunded at New York. Here is a fifty-pound note, and you can carry out the transaction much better than I. But stop a moment. Do you remember how much you paid for the room?"

"Twenty-five pounds."

"That will leave you only the remaining twenty-five for New York, which is an expensive place, so we must make the loan a hundred pounds. Leave me your address, and if you do not hear from your people before that loan is expended, you may have whatever more you need. You will, of course, repay me at your convenience. I will give you the name of my New York agents."

The eyes had by this time brimmed over, and the girl could not speak. Stranleigh took from his pocket-book several Bank of England notes. Selecting two for fifty pounds each, he handed them to her.

"Good-night!" he said hurriedly.

"Good-night!" she whispered.

After dinner on the day the liner left Queenstown, Lord Stranleigh sat in a comfortable chair in the daintily furnished drawing-room of his suite. A shaded electric light stood on the table at his elbow, and he was absorbed in a book he had bought before leaving London. Stranleigh was at peace with all the world, and his reading soothed a mind which he never allowed to become perturbed if he could help it. He now thanked his stars that he was sure of a week undisturbed by callers and free from written requests. Just at this moment he was amazed to see the door open, and a man enter without knock or other announcement. His first thought was to wonder what had become of Ponderby—how had the stranger eluded him? It was a ruddy-faced, burly individual who came in, and, as he turned round to shut the door softly, Stranleigh saw that his thick neck showed rolls of flesh beneath the hair. His lordship placed the open book face downwards on the table, but otherwise made no motion.

"Lord Stranleigh, I presume?" said the stranger.

Stranleigh made no reply, but continued gazing at the intruder.

"I wish to have a few words with you, and considered it better to come to your rooms than to accost you on deck. What I have to say is serious, and outside we might have got into an altercation, which you would regret."

"You need have no fear of any altercation with me," said Stranleigh.

"Well, at least you desire to avoid publicity, otherwise you would not be travelling under an assumed name."

"I am not travelling under an assumed name."

The stout man waved his hand in deprecation of unnecessary talk.

25

"I will come to the point at once," he said, seating himself without any invitation.

"I shall be obliged if you do so."

The new-comer's eyes narrowed, and a threatening expression overspread his rather vicious face.

"I want to know, Lord Stranleigh, and I have a right to ask, why you gave a hundred pounds to my wife."

"To your wife?" echoed Stranleigh in amazement.

"Yes. I have made a memorandum of the numbers, and here they are—two fifty-pound notes. Bank of England. Do you deny having given them to her?"

"I gave two fifty-pound notes to a young lady, whose name, I understood, was Trevelyan—a name which I also bear. She informed me, and somehow I believed her, that her purse containing steamship ticket and money, had been lost or stolen."

A wry smile twisted the lips of the alleged husband.

"Oh, that's the story is it? Would you be surprised if the young lady in question denied that in toto?"

"I should not be astonished at anything," replied his lordship, "if you are in possession of the actual bank-notes I gave to her."

"She describes your having taken these flimsies from a number of others you carry in your pocket. Would you mind reading me the number of others you carry in your pocket. Would you mind reading me the number of the next note in your collection?"

"Would you mind reading me the numbers on the notes you hold?" asked Stranleigh, in cool, even tones, making no sign of producing his own assets.

"Not at all," replied the other; whereupon he read them. The notes were evidently two of a series, and the numbers differed only by a single unit. Stranleigh nonchalantly took out his pocket-book, and the intruder's eyes glistened as he observed its bulk. Stranleigh glanced at the number on the top bank-note, and replaced his pocket-book, leaning back in his easy chair.

"You are quite right," he said. "Those are the notes I gave to Miss Trevelyan."

"I asked why."

"I told you why."

"That cock-and-bull story won't go down," said the other. "Even the richest men do not fling money about in such reckless fashion. They do it only for a favour given or a favour expected."

"I dare say you are right. But come to the point, as you said you would."

"Is that necessary?"

"I don't know that it is. You want money—as large an amount as can be squeezed from a man supposedly wealthy. You use your good-looking wife as a decoy——"

"You are casting aspersion on a lady quite unknown to you!" cried his visitor, with well-assumed indignation.

"Pardon me, you seem to be casting aspersion on her whom you say is your wife. I don't know how these notes got into your hands, but I'd be willing to stake double the amount that the lady is quite innocent in the matter. She certainly is so far as I am concerned. If the lady is your wife, what is her name? She told me she was travelling under a different title from that written on the lost ticket."

"I am not ashamed of my name, if you are of yours. My name is Branksome Poole."

"Ah, then she is Mrs. Branksome Poole?"

"Naturally."

Stranleigh reached out and drew towards him a passenger list. Running his eye down the column of cabin passengers, he saw there the names: "Mr. and Mrs. Branksome Poole."

"Well, Mr. Poole, we come to what is the final question—how much?"

"If you give me the roll of Bank of England notes which you exhibited a moment ago, I shall say nothing further about the matter, and, understand me, there is no coercion about my request. You may accept or decline, just as you like. I admit that my wife and I do not get along well together, and although I consider I have a grievance against you, I am not assuming the injured husband rôle at all. If you decline, I shall make no scandal aboard ship, but will wait and take action against you the moment we arrive in New York."

"Very considerate of you, Mr. Poole. I understand that in New York the fountains of justice are perfectly pure, and that the wronged are absolutely certain of obtaining redress. I congratulate you on your choice of a battle-ground. Of course, you haven't the slightest thought of levying blackmail, but I prefer to spend my money on the best legal talent in America rather than trust any of it to you. It's a mere case of obstinacy on my part. And now, if you will kindly take your departure, I will get on with my book; I am at a most interesting point."

"I shall not take my departure," said Poole doggedly, "until we have settled this matter."

"The matter is settled." Stranleigh touched an electric button. An inside door opened, and Ponderby entered, looking in amazement at his master's visitor.

"Ponderby," said Lord Stranleigh, "in future I desire you to keep this outer door locked, so that whoever wishes to see me may come through your room. Take a good look at this gentleman, and remember he is not to be allowed within my suite again on any pretext. Meanwhile, show him into the corridor. Take him through your room, and afterwards return and lock this other door."

28

Then occurred an extraordinary thing. Ponderby, for the first time in his life, disobeyed his master's instructions. Approaching the seated Poole, he said—

"Will you go quietly?"

"I'll not go, quietly or otherwise," answered the man stubbornly.

Ponderby opened the door by which Poole had entered, then, seizing him by the collar, lifted him, led him to the door, and pitched him out of the room across the corridor. Returning, he closed, locked, and bolted the door.

"I beg your pardon, my lord," said the panting Ponderby to his amazed master, "but I dare not take him through my room. His wife is there. She appears to have followed him. Anyhow, she recognised his voice, and told me hurriedly why she came. I locked the door to the passage, for, as I heard her story, I felt it might be serious, and at least you ought to hear what she has to say before you acted. I hope you will excuse the liberty I have taken, my lord."

"Ponderby, as I have often told you, you are a gem! I will go into your room, but you must remain there while I talk to this lady. No more tête-à-tête conversations with the unprotected for me."

"I think she is honest, my lord, but in deep trouble."

"I am glad to have my opinion corroborated by so good a judge of character as yourself, Ponderby."

They went together to the valet's sitting-room, and there sat the woman, with her dark head bowed upon arms outstretched along the table, her shoulders shaking. She was plainly on the verge of hysterics, if, indeed, she had not already crossed the boundary line.

"Here is Mr. Trevelyan, madam," said Ponderby. "You wanted to speak with him."

She raised her head, dabbed her wet eyes nervously with her handkerchief, and made an effort to pull herself together. When she spoke, it was with rapid utterance, reeling off what she had to say as if it were a task learned by rote.

"I have at last come to the end of my tether, and to-night, if there is no prospect of freedom, I shall destroy myself. Before this I have often thought of suicide, but I am a cowardly person, and cling to life. Five years ago my father went out to America bent on a motor tour; he took me with him. Among other servants he engaged Charles Branksome, who had proved himself an expert chauffeur. He was English, and came to us well recommended. He intimated that he was of good family, but had his living to earn. He was handsome then, and had a most ingratiating manner. The person who called on you to-night bears little resemblance to the Branksome of five years ago. I had often gone motoring with him while in America, and I was young, and rather flighty: a foolish person altogether. Perhaps you read about it in the papers. I cannot dwell on the appalling mistake I made.

"We became very well acquainted, and at last he professed to have fallen in love with me, and I believed him. We were secretly married before a justice of the peace in America, and I was not long left in doubt as to the disaster that had befallen me. His sole desire was money. My father being wealthy, he hoped to get all he cared to demand. My father, however, is a very stubborn man, and, after his first shock on finding the episode made much of by the American papers, he refused to pay Branksome a penny, and returned forthwith to England. I never saw him again, nor could I get into communication with him. Two years after my mad act he died, and never even mentioned me in his will.

"My husband is a liar, a thief, a forger, a gambler, and a brute. He has maltreated me so that I have been left once or twice for dead, but finally he broke me to his will. He is known as a cheat in every gambling resort in Europe, and on the Atlantic liners. Lately I have been used as a decoy in the way of which you have had experience. Somehow he learned—indeed, that is his business—who were the rich travellers on this boat. He thought, as this was the newest and largest steamship on the ocean, its staff would not at first be thoroughly organised, and that he might escape detection. He pointed you out to me as you came on board, and said you were Lord Stranleigh, travelling as Mr. Trevelyan. The rest you know. He forced me to hand to him the money you had given, and told me it might be necessary for me to go on the witness-stand when we reached New York, but, as you were very wealthy, it is not likely you would allow it to go so far as that. His plan was to demand a very moderate sum at first, which was to be a mere beginning, and each exaction would be but a prelude for the next. He is old at the game, and is wanted now by the authorities in New York for blackmailing a very well-known millionaire."

"Do you know the name of the millionaire?"

She gave him the information.

"Very well, madam. In the first place, you must do nothing reckless or foolish. I shall see that this man is detained at New York on some pretext or other—in fact, I shall arrange for this by wireless. You should journey to one of the states where divorces are easily obtained. If you will permit me, I shall be your banker. Even if Branksome got free in New York, it will cost him dear, and his supplies are precarious. You should experience no difficulty in evading him with money in your possession. Do you agree?"

"Oh, yes!"

"That's settled, then. Ponderby, look into the corridor, and see that the way of escape is clear."

"I am sorry, my lord," she said, rising, "to cause you such trouble and inconvenience."

"No inconvenience at all," said Stranleigh, with his usual nonchalance, "and I never allow myself to be troubled."

Ponderby reported the way open, and the lady disappeared silently along the passage. Stranleigh betook himself to Room 4390, and had a long talk with the Hon. John Hazel, who, for the first time during the voyage, seemed to be enjoying himself.

Next morning the Hon. John paced up and down one deck after another, as if in search of someone. On an almost deserted lower deck he met the person whom he sought.

"I beg your pardon," said Hazel in his suavest manner, "but I am trying to find three men as tired of this journey as I am. I have never been on a voyage before, and I confess I miss London and the convenience of its clubs. A quiet little game of poker in the smoking-room might help to while away the time."

The keen eyes of Mr. Branksome Poole narrowed, as was a custom of theirs, and he took in the points of the man who addressed him.

"I am not much of a hand at poker," he said hesitatingly and untruthfully.

The Hon. John laughed.

"Don't mind that in the least," he said. "The requirement for this game is cash. I have approached several men, and they object to playing for money; but I confess I don't give a rap for sitting at a card-table unless there's something substantial on."

"I'm with you there," agreed the stout man, his eyes glistening at the thought of handling a pack of cards once more. His momentary hesitation had been because he feared someone might recognise him, for he felt himself quite able to cope with anyone when it came to the shuffle and the deal. They were a strangely contrasted pair as they stood there, the pleb and the patrician—the pleb grim and serious, the patrician carrying off the situation with a light laugh—yet it was hard to say which was the more expert scoundrel when it came to cards.

A little later four men sat down to a table. Hazel ordered a new pack of cards from the smoke-room steward, broke the seal, and pulled off the wrapper.

It is not worth while to describe the series of games: only the one matters. At first Poole played very cautiously, watching out of the tail of his eye for any officer who might spot him as one who had been ordered off the green, and so expose him for what he was. The consequence of this divided attention was soon apparent. He lost heavily, and finally he drew a couple of fifty-pound notes from his pocket-book. He fingered them for a moment as if loath to part with paper so valuable.

"Where's that steward?" he asked.

"What do you want?" demanded Hazel, as though impatient for the game to go on.

"Change for a fifty."

"I'll change it for you." And the Hon. John drew from his pocket a handful of gold and five-pound bank-notes, counted out fifty pounds, and shoved them across the table to Poole, who, still hesitating, was forced reluctantly to give up the big bank-note. Now Poole began to play in earnest, but still luck was against him, and soon the second fifty-pound note was changed, for they were playing reasonably high. Hazel, after glancing at the number on the note, thrust it carelessly into his waistcoat pocket alongside its brother, as if it were of no more account than a cigarette paper. Little did the pleb dream that he was up against a man of brains. Hazel now possessed the two bank-notes that could have been used in evidence against Lord Stranleigh, and he drew a sigh of satisfaction. Poole only saw that here was a man, evidently careless of money, possessing plenty of it, and extremely good-natured. He had already recognised him as an aristocrat, and expected that, whatever happened, he would treat it with a laugh, and perhaps leave the table, so the pleb now began some fine work. Two games were played in silence, and in the third it was the deal of Branksome Poole. Hazel watched him like a beast of prey, conscious of every crooked move, yet he did not seem in the least to be looking. He gazed at the cards dealt him, rose to his feet, and spread the hand face upward on the table.

"Sir, you are cheating," he said crisply.

"You lie!" roared Branksome Poole, turning, nevertheless, a greenish yellow, and moistening his parched lips. At the sound of the loud voice, a steward came hurrying in.

"Show your hand, if you dare!" challenged Hazel. "You have dealt yourself——" And here he named the concealed cards one after another. Poole made an effort to fling his hand into the rest of the pack, but Hazel stopped him.

"Show your hand! Show your hand!" he demanded. "These two

gentlemen will witness whether I have named the cards correctly or not. Steward, ask the chief officer to come here, or, if he is not on duty, speak to the captain."

The steward disappeared, and shortly returned with the chief officer, to whom Hazel briefly and graphically related what had happened.

"Will you come with me to the captain's room?" requested the chief officer.

Branksome Poole had been through the mill before, and he offered no resistance.

When the wireless came in touch with the American shore, a dispatch reached police headquarters in New York, informing them that Charles Branksome, wanted for blackmailing Erasmus Blank, the millionaire, was detained by the ship's authority for cheating at cards.

When the great vessel arrived at her berth, Mrs. Branksome Poole was quite unmolested as she took her ticket for the West. She was amply supplied with money, and among her newly-acquired funds were two fifty-pound notes which had been previously in her possession.

# II.—AN AUTOMOBILE RIDE.

When Lord Stranleigh of Wychwood came to New York under his family name of Trevelyan, he had intended to spend several weeks in that interesting metropolis, but newspaper men speedily scattered his incognito to the winds, and, what with interviewers, photographers, funny paragraphists and the like, the young lord's life was made a burden to him. Despite his innate desire to be polite to everyone, he soon found it impossible to receive even a tenth part of those who desired speech with him. This caused no diminution of interviews or special articles regarding his plans, and his object in revisiting America. The sensational papers alleged that he had untold millions to invest; that he had placed cash on all the available projects in Europe, and now proposed to exploit the United States in his insatiable desire to accumulate more wealth.

Stranleigh changed his quarters three times, and with each move adopted a new name. He endured it all with imperturbable good-nature, despite the intense heat, but Ponderby was disgusted with the state of affairs, and wished himself and his master back once more in that quiet village known as London.

"By Jove! Ponderby," said Stranleigh, "they say three moves are as bad as a fire, and the temperature to-day seems to corroborate this, for we are making our third move. Have you anything to suggest?"

"I should suggest, my lord," said Ponderby, with as much dignity as the sweltering day would allow, "that we return to London."

"A brilliant and original idea, Ponderby. Many thanks. Go down at once to the steamship office, and book the best accommodation you can get on the first big liner leaving New York."

Ponderby departed instantly, with a deep sigh of relief.

Stranleigh's life had been made more of a burden to him than was necessary through the indefatigable exertions of a fellow countryman, whose name was Wentworth Parkes. This individual brought with him a letter of introduction from the Duke of Rattleborough. Rattleborough was an acquaintance, but not a particular friend of Stranleigh's; nevertheless, a Duke overtops a mere Earl in social eminence, much as the Singer building overtops the structure next to it.

Wentworth Parkes told Stranleigh he had been in America for something more than a year. He had been very successful, making plenty of money, but expending it with equal celerity. Now he determined to get hold of something that contained princely possibilities for the future. This he had secured by means of an option on the Sterling Motor Company at Detroit, and the plant alone, he alleged, was worth more than the capital needed to bring the factory up to its full output. J. E. Sterling, he went on to explain, knew more about automobile designing than anyone else in the world, notwithstanding the fact that he was still a young man. He would undoubtedly prove to be the true successor of Edison, and everyone knew what fortunes had come to those who interested themselves in the products of the great Thomas Alva, who up to date had proved to be the most successful money-making inventor the world had ever seen, to which Lord Stranleigh calmly agreed. Well, J. E. Sterling was just such another, and all a man required to enter the combination, was the small sum of one hundred thousand dollars. This would purchase a share in the business which might be sold within a year or two for millions. Detroit was the centre of automobile manufacturing in America; a delightful city to live in; the finest river in the world running past its doors, with a greater tonnage of shipping than passed through the Suez Canal.

Mr. Parkes was a glib and efficient talker, who might have convinced anyone with money to spare, but he felt vaguely that his fluency was not producing the intended effect on Lord Stranleigh. His difficulty heretofore had been to obtain access to men of means, and now that he had got alongside the most important of them all, he was nonplussed to notice that his eloquence somehow missed its mark. Stranleigh remained scrupulously courteous, but was quite evidently not in the least interested. So shrewd a man as Parkes might have known that it is not easy to arouse enthusiasm in a London clubman under the most favourable auspices, and this difficulty is enormously increased when the person attacked is already so rich that any further access of wealth offers no temptation to him.

Parkes had come to believe that the accumulation of gold was the only thing the average man really cared about, so he failed, by moving against the dead wall of Stranleigh's indifference towards money, whereas he might have succeeded had he approached the sentimental side of the young man. Indeed, Mr. Wentworth Parkes seemed to catch a glimmering of this idea as his fairy visions of the future fell flat, so he reversed his automobile talk, and backed slowly out.

Conversation lagging, his lordship asked a few casual questions about the Duke of Rattleborough and other persons he knew in London, but if any of these queries were intended to embarrass his visitor, Stranleigh's failure was equal to that of Parkes himself. The latter answered all enquiries so promptly and correctly that Stranleigh inwardly chided himself for his latent distrust of the man who now, quick to see how the land lay, got his motor car in position once more, but took another direction. He mopped his forehead with his handkerchief, and drew a slight sigh.

"You see," he said, in a discouraged tone, "a person brought up as I have been, to do nothing in particular that is of any use to the world, finds himself at a great disadvantage in a hustling land like the United States, where the fellows are all so clever, and have been trained from their very boyhood to be alert business men. I have a good thing in this option, and if once I got upon my feet, I could soon build up a great and profitable business. My chief trouble is to convince any capitalist of this, and if he asks me whether or not the scheme will produce a fortune within six months or a year, I am forced to admit there is little chance of it. An American wishes to turn over his money quickly; a long look into futurity is not for him. He wishes to buy one railway on Monday, another on Tuesday, amalgamate them on Wednesday, and sell out the stock to the public at several millions profit on Thursday, then rake in the boodle on Friday, which proves an unlucky day for the investors. When I truthfully confess it will be a year before I get fairly under way, I am immediately at a discount. Capitalists won't listen any further."

Parkes saw that for the first time during the interview Lord Stranleigh began to show interest, reserved though it was.

"Do you know anything about cars?" asked his lordship.

"I can take apart any motor in the market, and put it together again, always leaving it a little better than when I found it."

"And this machine—invented by the Detroit man—does it fill the bill?"

"It's the best motor in the world to-day," asserted Parkes, with a return of his old confidence.

Stranleigh smiled slightly.

"I think," he said, "you have been very successful in catching the enthusiasm of America. You deal glibly with superlatives. Mr. Sterling is the most remarkable man on earth, Detroit the most beautiful city on the globe, and your motor-car beats the universe."

"Well, my lord, I don't disclaim the superlatives, but I insist on their truth. As I said, I deal in truth, and have suffered somewhat in pocket by doing so."

A slight shade of perplexity came into the young earl's face. There was something deferential in the tone used by Parkes when he enunciated the phrase "my lord," which Stranleigh did not like. Neither phrase nor tone would have been used by any person in his own circle of acquaintance addressing another in the same set. His former distrust was again aroused. As he remained silent, Parkes went on—

"You need not take my word for the automobile, which after all is the crux of the situation. I have one of them here in New York. I tested it very fully on the way from Detroit to this city, travelling in it the whole distance. Let me take you for a drive. You doubtless know all about a motor-car, for I was told in London that you owned at least a dozen of them."

"I daresay it's true. I'm not sure. Nevertheless, I am so unfortunate as to have only a slight knowledge of their mechanics. I have driven a good deal, but not being so energetic as Prince Henry of Prussia, I leave details to my chauffeurs."

"Very good. You are doubtless well acquainted with the merits of a car from the owner's point of view. Come out with me in this Detroit motor, and I will be your chauffeur, or you may drive the machine yourself, if you remember that in this country you keep to the right side of the road."

Thus the appointment was made, and was kept by Lord Stranleigh. At the end of his run, he said to Parkes—

"The car seems to be a satisfactory piece of construction, but I own two or three American cars in London, any one of which, I think, is equally good; in fact, as Mark Twain said about his Jumping Frog—'I see no points about this frog different from any other frog.' However, I will consider your proposal, and will let you know the result. Meanwhile, many thanks for a most interesting ride."

Stranleigh sauntered down town, and entered a cable office.

"Can I send a message to London, and leave a deposit here for the reply, that it may not cost my London friend anything?"

"Certainly, sir."

Stranleigh wrote—

"Duke of Rattleborough, Camperdown Club, London.

"A man calling himself Wentworth Parkes presented a letter of introduction from you to me. Please cable whether or not he is reliable."

Two days later, Stranleigh received a reply—

"Letter a forgery. Parkes was my valet for three years, then bolted, leaving a lot of little things behind him, but not if they were portable and valuable. Believe he is now abroad, though the London police are yearning for him.      Rattleborough."

Now began the persistent pursuit of Stranleigh, which culminated in his sending Ponderby down to the steamship office to buy tickets for England. The young man said nothing to anyone of the cablegram he had received, nor did he inform the police of London the whereabouts of their quarry. He rather pitied the poor wretch, as he called him, but he had no use for a thief and a liar, so he refused to hold further communication with him, or to make any explanation. Parkes, finding he could not gain admission to Stranleigh, took to sending letters by special messenger, first adopting an aggrieved tone, a reproachful suggestion of injured innocence running through his correspondence like a minor note in a piece of music; then he became the victim of an unscrupulous millionaire, asserting that Stranleigh had promised to finance the proposed company, and breathing threats of legal proceedings. Indeed, as the recipient read these later communications, he realised they were evidently written with a view to publicity in law courts, for there emanated from them sentiments of great patriotism. The United States, Stranleigh learned, would not put up with his villainy, as would have been the case with legal proceedings in decadent England, where judges were under the thumb of a debased aristocracy.

Stranleigh had no ambition to appear in the courts of either country, so he removed from one hotel to another, but apparently he was watched, for Parkes ran him down wherever he betook himself. Thus we come to the moment when the sedate but overjoyed Ponderby returned with the steamship tickets, which Stranleigh thrust into his pocket.

"Shall I pack up now, my lord?"

"I wish you would. The valet of the hotel will assist you. Prepare three boxes; one for yourself and two for me, filling mine with such clothing as I should take were I going to visit a friend in the country for a week or two. Place the other luggage in charge of the manager of the hotel, and say I will telegraph when I make up my mind where it is to be sent."

And then, to Ponderby's amazement, the young man left for Boston, and took passage in the steamer for St. John, New Brunswick.

"You see, Ponderby," said his lordship, when they got out into the ocean, "the estimable Parkes, if he is watching us, is already aware that you have booked for Southampton. He may possibly set the law in motion, and appear with some emissaries thereof aboard the liner before she sails, so we might be compelled to remain in this country which he so ardently loves."

"But the steamship tickets, my lord? They cost a lot of money."

"Quite so, my economical Ponderby, but remember for your consolation that when you step ashore from this boat, you will be under the British flag. You may telegraph to the company and tell them to sell the tickets, meanwhile sending them by post to New York. Here they are. Whatever money the company returns, is to be retained by you further to mitigate your disappointment. I have no doubt that in thus bolting for Canada you feel like a culprit escaping from justice, but we are only escaping from Parkes. Having pestered me as much about Detroit as he has done, that city will be the last place in which he is likely to look for me. We are making for Detroit, Ponderby, by the most roundabout route I could choose, seeing that the Panama Canal is not yet open, and thus I am unable to reach the autometropolis by way of San Francisco."

After passing through Canada, Lord Stranleigh settled himself very comfortably in a luxurious suite of rooms situated near the top storey of a luxurious hotel in the city of the Straits, under the assumed commonplace name of Henry Johnson. The windows of his apartment afforded wide and interesting views of skyscrapers and noble public edifices, with a wilderness of roofs extending towards the misty horizon to the west, north, and east, while to the south flowed the majestic river, its blue surface enlivened by stately steamers and picturesque sailing craft.

The gloomy valet did not share his master's admiration of the scene. Ponderby was heart and soul a Londoner, and although forced to admit that the Thames was grey and muddy, and its shipping for the most part sombre and uncouth, that tidal water remained for him the model of all other streams. He was only partially consoled by the fact that five cents brought him across to the Canadian shore, where he might inhale deep breaths of air that fluttered the Union Jack.

Stranleigh, confident that he had shaken off pursuit, enjoyed himself in a thoroughly democratic manner, sailing up stream and down, on one of the pearl white passenger boats, that carried bands which played the immortal airs of Sousa.

He began his second week in Detroit by engaging a motor to make a tour of the motor manufacturing district. He was amazed at the size and extent of the buildings, and recognised, among the names painted thereon, the designation of cars that were familiar to him. He had come to believe Parkes such an untruthful person, that he had taken a big discount from everything he said, and so was unprepared to find the reality far in advance of the description. However, he saw no sign bearing the name of the Sterling Motor Company, so asked his chauffeur to convey him thither. The chauffeur, pondering a moment, was forced to admit that he had never heard of the firm.

"Then be so good," requested Stranleigh, "as to drop into one of these offices and enquire. It is likely that someone will know the names of all other companies in the same line of manufacture."

"I don't doubt," said the chauffeur, "that they know all about it, but it wouldn't be business to direct a possible customer to a rival firm."

Stranleigh smiled.

"I have not been in this country so long as you have," he said, "but I think you will find an American business man ignores rivalry when he has an opportunity of doing an act of courtesy."

The chauffeur drew up at a huge factory and went inside. Returning very promptly, he informed his fare that they knew of no Sterling Motor Company, but there was in Woodbridge Street a young engineer named J. E. Sterling, who, they believed, made motor-cars.

"J. E. Sterling! That's the man I want. Where is Woodbridge Street?"

"Right away down town; next door, as you might say, to the river front."

"Very good; we'll go there. Just drive past Mr. Sterling's place, for if I do not like the look of it I shall not go in."

By and by they turned into Woodward Avenue, and raced down town at a speed which Stranleigh thought must surely exceed the legal limit, if there was one. Woodbridge Street proved to be crowded with great lumbering trucks, loaded with vegetables for the most part, and among these vehicles the chauffeur threaded his way cautiously. They passed a small, rather insignificant shop, above whose window was painted—

"J. E. Sterling. Motor Engineer. Repairs

promptly executed. Satisfaction guaranteed."

When the chauffeur came to a halt a little further on, Stranleigh said—

"The place doesn't look very inviting, but as Mr. Sterling guarantees satisfaction, I think it but right to call upon him. I sha'n't need you any more to-day."

The door being open, Stranleigh walked in unannounced. A two-seated runabout, evidently brand new, stood by the window, where it could be viewed by passers-by. Further down the room rested a chassis, over which two men, one middle-aged and the other probably twenty-five, were bending, with tools in their hands. They were dressed in grease-stained blue overalls, and they looked up as Stranleigh entered.

"I wish to see Mr. J. E. Sterling," he said.

"My name is Sterling," replied the younger man, putting down his tools, and coming forward.

"I understood," went on Stranleigh, "that there was a Sterling Motor Car Company."

"There will be," answered the young man confidently, "but that's in the sweet by and by. It hasn't materialised so far. What can I do for you?"

"Well, you can give me some information regarding J. E. Sterling. I want to learn if it tallies with what I have heard."

The young man laughed.

"It depends on who has been talking about me. I daresay you have been told things that might require explanation."

"I heard nothing but praise," his lordship assured him. "It was said you were the true successor of Thomas Alva Edison."

Sterling laughed even more heartily than before.

"I'm afraid they were getting at you. A man may be a creditable inventor, and a good, all-round engineer without being able to hold a candle to Edison. Are you looking for an automobile?"

"No; as I told you at first, I am looking for J. E. Sterling."

"I was going to say that I am not yet prepared to supply cars. I do repairing and that sort of thing, merely to keep the wolf from the door, and leave me a little surplus to expend in my business. My real work, however, is experimenting, and when I am able to turn out a machine that satisfies me, my next business will be to form a company, for one can't do anything in this trade without capital."

"The competition must be intense."

"It is, but there's always room for a first-rate article, and the production of a first-rate article is my ambition."

"Is that your work in the window?"

"Yes."

"Does it come up to your expectations?"

The young man's face grew serious; his brow wrinkled almost into a frown, and he remained silent for a few moments.

"Well, I can't exactly say that it does," he answered at last, "still, I think the faults I have found can be remedied with a little patience. On the other hand, I fear the improvement I have put in this car may not be as great as I thought when I was working at it."

Lord Stranleigh looked at the young man with evident approval; his frankness and honesty commended themselves to him.

"Do you mind showing me your improvement and explaining its function?"

"Not at all. You will remember, however, that this exhibition is confidential, for I have not yet patented the mechanism."

"I shall not mention to anyone what you show me. You asked me a moment ago if I wished to buy an automobile, and I said I did not. I have made a little money in my time, but mostly, it seems to me, by flukes. I do not pretend to be a business man, yet such is the conceit of humanity that I wish to invest some of my money to back my own judgment. If I lose the cash, it won't cripple me to any appreciable extent. On the other hand, should the investment prove satisfactory, I shall have more faith in my judgment than has hitherto been the case. In any event, I promise to assist you in the formation of your company."

"That's all right!" cried the young engineer, with enthusiasm. "My own judgment of men is frequently at fault, but somehow I'd stake my bottom dollar on you. Come over to the window, and I'll show you how the wheels go round."

The two men approached the car in the window, and as they did so a third person on the pavement outside stopped suddenly, and regarded them with evident astonishment. Neither of those inside saw him, but if one or the other had looked through the glass, he would have recognised the sinister face of Wentworth Parkes who, having satisfied himself as to the visitor's identity, turned away and retraced his steps.

Sterling lifted up a leather curtain which hung down in front from the passenger's seat and disclosed a line of three upright pegs, rising two or three inches from the floor of the car. They were concealed when the curtain was lowered.

"If you give the matter any thought," said Sterling, "you will discover that the passenger in an automobile is in rather a helpless position. His chauffeur may faint, or even die at his wheel from heart failure, as has been the case in several instances I know of, or he may be drunk, and therefore unreasonable or obstinate, driving the car with danger to all concerned, yet if his master attempt to displace him while the car is going at high speed, disaster is certain. Now, the centre peg here will stop the engine and put on the brakes. A pressure by the foot on the right-hand peg turns the car to the right; and on the left-hand to the left. In the ordinary car the passenger can

45

do nothing to save himself, but here he may stop the car dead, or, if he prefers it, may disconnect the steering wheel, and guide the car at his will."

"Why, I think that's an excellent device!" cried Stranleigh.

"I thought so, too, but there are disadvantages. The crises in which it could be brought to play are rare. As a general rule, a chauffeur is much more to be trusted than the owner, and if the owner happens to be a nervous man, he might interfere, with deplorable results."

"Yes," said Stranleigh, "it's like the pistol in Texas. You may not need it, but when you do you want it very badly. Has anyone else seen this contrivance?"

"No one except my assistant."

"Could you lend me this car to-morrow?"

"Certainly."

"Then place the car in charge of a competent chauffeur, who knows nothing of your safety device, and send it up to my hotel at eleven o'clock. Tell him to ask for Henry Johnson. I'll take a little trip into the country, where I can test the car on some unfrequented road."

"Better cross the river to Canada," said Sterling, with a smile. "Things are quiet over there."

"Very well," agreed Stranleigh. "You are a busy man, and I have taken up a considerable amount of your time. You must allow me to pay you for it."

The young man's face grew red underneath its spots of grease, and he drew back a step.

"You have spent your own time to an equal amount, so we'll allow one expenditure to balance the other."

"My time is of no account. I'm a loafer."

"I could not accept any money, sir."

The two looked at one another for a moment, and gentlemen understand each other even though one wears the greasy clothes of a mechanic.

"I beg your pardon," said Stranleigh, softly. "Now, let me ask you one question. Have you given an option on this business to anyone?"

Sterling glanced up in surprise.

"Why, yes, I did give an option to an Englishman. By the way, you're English, are you not?"

"I was born over there."

"This Englishman wasn't your sort. He was a most plausible talker, and as I told you, my judgment of men is sometimes at fault. I gave him an option for two months, but I think all he wanted was to get an automobile for nothing. He said he represented a syndicate of English capitalists, some of whom were in New York, and he borrowed the only car I had completed at that time. That was four months ago. Like the preacher after the futile collection, I wanted to get back my hat at least, but although I wrote letter after letter, I never received any answer. It wasn't worth my while to set the police on his track, so I tried to forget him, and succeeded until you spoke of an option just now."

"That agreement lapsed two months ago?"

"Yes."

"Then write out an option for me, good for a week. I'll pay you five hundred dollars down, to be forfeited if I fail to do what I promise."

"I'll give you the document with pleasure, but it is unnecessary to make a deposit."

"This is business, you know, Mr. Sterling. You are pretending you are as bad a business man as I am. I don't know much about the law of America, but I think you will find that unless a deposit is made, your instrument would be invalid in a court of law. There must be value received, I believe, when a bargain is made."

"All right," said Sterling, "but I'll give you back your money if you regret the deal."

He went to a desk in the corner, and wrote out the agreement, in which he acknowledged the receipt of five hundred dollars. Stranleigh selected from his wallet five bills for a hundred dollars each, and handed them over, then bidding farewell to the engineer, walked to his hotel, followed at a discreet distance by Mr. Wentworth Parkes.

Having located his quarry, Parkes retraced his steps to Woodbridge Street, deep in thought. His first resolution was to try bluster, but he abandoned that idea for two reasons, each conclusive in its way. His slight acquaintance with the engineer had convinced him that while much could be done with Sterling by persuasion, he would not yield to force, and secondly, the motor builder had no money. Whatever gold he was to acquire in his deal must come from Lord Stranleigh. It was, therefore, a mild and innocent lamb of a man who entered the machine shop of Woodbridge Street.

"Hello!" cried Sterling, who seemed taken aback by the encounter. "What have you done with my automobile, and why did you not answer my letters?"

"Your automobile is here in Detroit; a little the worse for wear, perhaps, but there is nothing wrong with it that you cannot put right in short order. As for letters, I never received any. I thought I had notified you of my changed address."

"As a matter of fact, you didn't."

"In that case, I apologise most humbly. The truth is, Mr. Sterling, I have been working practically night and day, often under very discouraging circumstances. Until quite recently there was nothing hopeful to tell, and the moment I struck a bit of good luck, I came on here in the car to let you know. You see, it was very difficult to interest capital in a proposition that apparently has no substantiality behind it. If you had possessed a big factory in going order, that I could have shown a man over, the company would have been formed long ago. It therefore surprised me exceedingly, when I passed your shop less than an hour ago, to see standing in this window, while you were explaining the car to him, the man on whom I chiefly depended. You must put it down to my credit that instead of coming in as I had intended, thus embarrassing him, and perhaps spoiling a deal by my interference, I passed on, waited until he came out, and followed him to his hotel."

Sterling was plainly nonplussed.

"I wish you had come in an hour earlier," he said. "You couldn't have interfered with a deal, because your option ran out two months ago."

"I know that," said Parkes regretfully, "but I thought the good work on my part would have made up for a legal lapse. Indeed, Mr. Sterling, if you will allow me to say so, I had such supreme faith in your own honesty, that I believed you would not hesitate to renew our arrangement."

"That's just the point," said Sterling. "Had you come in an hour sooner, you would have been in time. As it is, I have granted a new option to the man you saw here with me."

"What name did he give you? Trevelyan?"

"No; the name he mentioned was Henry Johnson."

Parkes laughed a little, then checked himself.

"He went under the name of Trevelyan in New York, but I know neither that nor Johnson is his true title. Well, is he going in with you, then?"

"He has asked for a week to decide."

Now Parkes laughed more heartily.

"I took him out in your motor in New York, and there also he asked for a week in which to decide. He seems to have taken the opportunity to come West, and try to forestall me."

"Oh, I don't believe he's that sort of man," cried Sterling, impatiently.

"Perhaps I do him an injustice. I sincerely hope so. Of course you're not compelled to show your hand, but I think, in the circumstances, you might let me know just how far you've got."

"Yes, I think you are entitled to that. I remember I was rather astonished when I learned he knew I had given a former option, but I shall be very much disappointed if he doesn't run straight. Still, I have been mistaken in men before. He took an option for a week, and paid me five hundred dollars down in cash, to be forfeited if he does not exercise it."

"Well, if the money is not counterfeit, that certainly looks like running straight. And meanwhile, what are you to do?"

"I am to do nothing, except send this car up to his hotel with a suitable chauffeur, at eleven o'clock to-morrow. He is going to test it along the Canadian roads."

"Was anything said about the amount of capital he was to put up?"

"Not a word; we didn't get that far."

Parkes took a few turns up and down the room then he said suddenly:

"Have you any particular chauffeur in mind?"

"No; I was just going out to make arrangements."

"You don't need to make any arrangements. I'll be your chauffeur, and can show off this car better than a stranger, who perhaps might be interested in some other automobile, and try to get your customer away. It's to my interest, having spent so much time on it, to see the deal put through. Besides, I know your man, and now that I have encountered him here in Detroit, he cannot deny that I sent him to your shop. I think he owes me at least a commission for bringing you together. I realise, of course, that I have no legal claim on either of you, yet I am sure, if the facts were proved, any court would allow me an agent's commission."

"I'll pay your commission," said Sterling.

"You haven't got the money, and he has."

"Very well; I will let you go as chauffeur, but I must inform him who you are."

Parkes shook his head.

"My dear Sterling, you are the most honest and impractical man I ever met. If you give him warning, he'll merely leave you in the lurch as he did me."

"Do you intend to disguise yourself?"

"Certainly not."

"Then he will recognise you at once."

"I understand that class of Englishman much better than you do. He will never see me, and I don't know that I shall call myself to his attention at all. My own idea is to let the deal go through, claiming only the privilege of being your adviser, and keeping altogether in the background. I can give you valuable hints about dealing with this sort of man. He will regard me as a servant, and unless I said to him: 'Lord Stranleigh of Wychwood, why did you bolt so suddenly from New York?' he would never have the least idea who was sitting beside him, and even then he would exhibit no surprise."

"Lord Stranleigh?" echoed Sterling in amazement.

"Yes; that's the man you're dealing with, and he's worth untold millions. I'll go up to this hotel now, and see him, if you prefer that I should do so."

"No; you may take him out to-morrow, but I advise you to say nothing to him about me or my business. Whatever arrangement we come to finally, you shall be recompensed for your share in the negotiations."

Parkes' prediction regarding Stranleigh's non-recognition of him proved accurate. The young man simply said—

"We will cross the ferry, and run up along the Canadian shore as far as Lake St. Clair."

The road continued along the river bank, with no fences on the left side. Although residences were fairly numerous, there was little traffic on the highway. The car was running at a moderate pace when the chauffeur suddenly diverted it towards the river, and with an exceedingly narrow margin escaped tumbling down the bank.

"I say," murmured Stranleigh, "I don't like that you know."

"There's worse to come," said the chauffeur menacingly. "You will promise to pay me a hundred thousand dollars, or I will dash you and the car over the edge into the river. If you consider your life worth that sum, speak quickly."

"Ah, it is you, Parkes? I hope you realise that you will dash yourself over at the same time?"

"I know that, but I'm a desperate man. Just get that through your head."

"You are aware that a promise given under duress is not binding?"

"Stow talk!" roared Parkes. "Say 'yes' or 'no.'"

"I say 'No!'" replied Stranleigh, so quietly that the other was unprepared for the prompt action which followed. Stranleigh flung his arms around the man, and jerked him backward from his wheel. His lordship was in good athletic condition; the ex-valet had looked too much on the wine when it was red, and on the highball when it sparkled in the glass. He felt helpless as a child.

"Now," said Stranleigh, "we will see who is the coward. I'll lay a wager with you that this car tumbles off the bank before five minutes are past."

Stranleigh with his heels was working the two outside pegs, and the car acted as if it were drunker than a lord, and almost as drunk as the valet.

"In God's name," cried the latter, "let me go. We shall be wrecked in a moment."

"No, we won't."

"I implore you, Lord Stranleigh!"

"I'll save your life, but will give you a lesson against attempted blackmail."

He steered to the edge of the bank, then pressed the middle peg, and stopped the car. Rising and carrying Parkes with him, he hurled him headlong over the slight earthy precipice into the water, which was shallow at that point. Parkes arose spluttering, and found Stranleigh had turned the car round, and with a smile on his face, was looking down at his dripping victim.

"You'll suffer for this!" cried Parkes, shaking his fist at him. "We're in a country, thank God, where we think very little of lords."

"Oh, I don't think much of lords myself, in any country," replied Stranleigh suavely, "and even less of their valets, notwithstanding I've a very good one myself. Now listen to my advice. I shall be in the United States before you can reach a telephone, and I don't see how you can get me back unless I wish to return. I advise you not to stir up the police. The Duke of Rattleborough cabled to me that a certain section of that useful body is anxious to hear of you. Call on Mr. Sterling, and whatever he thinks is just compensation for your introduction I will pay, but before you get the money, you must ensure both of us against further molestation in any way."

Stranleigh drove up to the shop on Woodbridge Street, and listened to the account Sterling gave of Parkes' visit and conversation, and his explanation of how he had come to allow him to drive the car.

"That's quite all right and satisfactory," said his lordship. "I never for a moment distrusted you. Still, I did get your name from Parkes, and I owe him something for that. What do you think would be a fair payment to make? I threw him into the river, but though it's clean, clear water, I expect no reward."

"If you'll allow me to pay him the five hundred dollars you gave me yesterday, I think the rogue will get much more than he deserves."

"Very good; I'll add another five hundred, but see that he signs some legal promise not to molest us further. I'll capitalise your company to the extent of any amount between a hundred thousand dollars and half a million."

# III.—THE GOD IN THE CAR.

Young Lord Stranleigh always proved a disappointment to a thorough-going Radical, for he differed much from the conventional idea of what a hereditary proud peer should be. He was not overbearing on the one hand, nor condescending on the other, being essentially a shy, unassuming person, easily silenced by any controversialist who uttered statements of sufficient emphasis. He never seemed very sure about anything, although undoubtedly he was a judge of well-fitting clothes, and the tailoring of even the remoter parts of America rather pleased him.

One thing that met his somewhat mild disapproval was undue publicity. He shrank from general notice, and tried to efface himself when reporters got on his track. In order, then, to live the quiet and simple life, his lordship modified a stratagem he had used on a previous occasion with complete success. He arranged that the obedient but unwilling Ponderby should enact the country gentleman of England, bent on enlarging his mind, and rounding out his experiences by residence in the United States. Ponderby wished to get back to the old country, but was too well-trained to say so. Lord Stranleigh, under the humble designation of Henry Johnson, set for himself the part of Ponderby's chauffeur, a rôle he was well fitted to fill, because of his love for motoring, and his expertness in the art. He dressed the character to perfection, being always particular in the matter of clothes, and was quite admirable in raising his forefinger deferentially to the edge of his cap, a salute whose effect Ponderby endangered by his unfortunate habit of blushing.

Accustomed to self-suppression though he was, Ponderby could not altogether conceal from Lord Stranleigh his dislike of the metamorphosis that was proposed. He had been born a servant and brought up a servant, with the result that he was a capable one, and posing as a gentleman was little to his taste. Of course, he would do anything Lord Stranleigh commanded, and that without consciously hinting disapproval, but the earl shrank from giving a command as much as he would have disliked receiving one. He was suave enough with the general public, but just a little more so in dealing with those who depended on him.

"Did you ever visit the ancient village of Burford, Ponderby?" he asked on this occasion.

"Burford in England, my lord?"

"Ponderby," pleaded Stranleigh, "kindly oblige me by omitting the appellation."

"Burford in England, sir?"

"That's better," said the earl with a smile, "but we will omit the 'sir' in future, also. I am a chauffeur, you know. Yes, I do mean Burford in Oxfordshire, nestling cosily beside the brown river Windrush, a village of very ancient houses."

"I have never been there." Ponderby swallowed the phrase "my lord" just in time.

"Then you have not seen the priory of that place; the ruins of a beautiful old English manor-house? It forms the background of a well-known modern picture by Waller—'The Empty Saddle.' The estate was purchased by Lenthall, Speaker of the House of Commons during the Long Parliament. Kings have put up at the Priory, the last being William the Third. Think of that, Ponderby! Royalty! I know how you will respect the house on that account. One of Lenthall's descendants was served by an ideal butler, who was happy, contented, well-paid; therefore, to all outward appearances, satisfied. One day he fell heir to three thousand pounds, which at present would be not quite fifteen thousand dollars, but at that time was a good deal more. Against his master's protests, he resigned his butlership.

"'I have always wished to live,' he confessed, 'at the rate of three thousand a year; to live as a gentleman for that period. I will return to you a year from to-day, and if you wish to engage me, I shall be happy to re-enter your service.'

"He spent his long-coveted year and the three thousand pounds, returning and taking up his old service again on the date he had set. Now,

Ponderby, there's a precedent for you, and I know how you love precedents. Remembering this historical fact, I have placed in the bank of Altonville fifteen thousand dollars to your credit. You cannot return to old England just yet, but you may enjoy New England. Already constituting myself your servant, I have taken a furnished house for you, and all I ask in return is that I may officiate as your chauffeur. I hope to make some interesting experiments with the modern American automobile."

And so it was arranged. Lord Stranleigh at the wheel saw much of a charming country; sometimes with Ponderby in the back seat, but more often without him, for the inestimable valet was quite evidently ill-at-ease through this change of their relative positions.

One balmy, beautiful day during the exceptionally mild Indian summer of that year, Stranleigh left Altonville alone in his motor, and turned into a road that led northward, ultimately reaching the mountains to be seen dimly in the autumn haze far to the north. It was a favourite drive of his, for it led along the uplands within sight of a group of crystal lakes with well-wooded banks on the opposite shore. The district was practically untouched by commerce, save that here and there along the valley stood substantial mills, originally built to take advantage of the water power from the brawling river connecting the lakes. Some of these factories had been abandoned, and were slowly becoming as picturesque as an old European castle. Others were still in going order, and doubtless the valley had once been prosperous, but lagging behind an age of tremendous progress, had lost step, as it were, with the procession. Lack of adequate railway connection with the outside world was the alleged cause, but the conservatism of the mill-owners, who, in an age of combination, had struggled on individually to uphold the gospel of letting well alone, a campaign that resulted in their being left alone, had probably more to do with bringing about adversity than the absence of railways. Some of the mills had been purchased by the Trusts, and closed up. One or two still struggled on, hopelessly battling for individualism and independence, everyone but themselves recognising that the result was a foregone conclusion.

Yet for a man who wished to rest, and desired, like the old-fashioned millers, to be left alone, this countryside was indeed charming. The summer visitors had all departed, missing the sublimest time of the year. Stranleigh had the road to himself, and there was no annoying speed limit to hamper the energy of his machine. Without any thought of his disconsolate valet moping about an unnecessarily large and well-furnished house, the selfish young man breathed the exhilarating air, and revelled in his freedom.

He passed a young couple, evidently lovers, standing on a grassy knoll, gazing across a blue lake at the wooded banks on the other side, seemingly at a fine old colonial mansion which stood in an opening of the woods, with well-kept grounds sloping down to the water's edge.

A man driving a car enjoys small opportunity for admiring scenery and architecture, so Stranleigh paid little regard to the view, but caught a fleeting glimpse of a beautiful girl, in whose expression there appeared a tinge of sadness which enhanced her loveliness; then he was past, with the empty road before him. He fell into a reverie, a most dangerous state of mind for a chauffeur, since a fall into a reverie on the part of a driver may mean a fall into a ravine on the part of the machine. The reverie, however, was interrupted by a shout, and then by another. He slowed down, and looking back over his shoulder saw that the young man was sprinting towards him at a record-breaking speed. Stranleigh declutched his automobile, and applying the brakes came to a standstill. The young man ran up breathlessly.

"You are the chauffeur of that Englishman in Altonville, are you not?" he panted, breathing hard.

"Yes."

"Are you going to meet him, or anything of that sort?"

"No; I'm out for my own pleasure."

"I'll give you a dollar if you take my wife and me back to Altonville."

Stranleigh smiled.

"I'll go, my chief; I'm ready," he murmured. "It is not for your silver bright, but for your winsome lady."

"My wife has sprained her ankle, and cannot walk," explained the young man.

"I am sorry to hear that," replied Lord Stranleigh. "Get in, and we will go back to her in a jiffy."

The young man sprang into the car, which the amateur chauffeur turned very deftly, and in a few moments they drew up close to the grassy bank where the girl was sitting. The young husband very tenderly lifted her to the back seat, and the polite chauffeur, after again expressing his regret at the accident, drove the car swiftly to Altonville, stopping at the office of the only doctor.

The young man rang the bell, and before the door was opened, he had carried the girl up the steps. Presently he returned, and found Stranleigh still sitting in the chauffeur's seat, meditatively contemplating the trafficless street. His late passenger thrust hand in pocket, and drew forth a silver dollar.

"I am ever so much obliged," he said, "and am sorry to have detained you so long."

"The detention was nothing. To be of assistance, however slight, is a pleasure, marred only by the fact of the lady's misadventure. I hope to hear that her injury is not serious, and then I shall be well repaid."

"You will not be repaid," returned the young man, with a slight frown on his brow, "until you have accepted this dollar."

Stranleigh laughed gently.

"I told you at the beginning that I was not working for coin."

The young man came closer to the automobile.

"To tell the truth," he said earnestly, "I fear that now we are in Altonville that pompous gentleman, your boss, may come along, and you will get into trouble. Masters do not like their motors used for other people's convenience."

"Don't worry about Mr. Ponderby. He is a very good-hearted person, and his pomposity merely a mannerism. I am waiting to take madame and yourself to your residence."

"It isn't much of a residence," laughed the young man rather grimly, "only a couple of rooms and a small kitchen, and is less than a hundred yards from this spot."

"Then I'll take you that hundred yards."

"I work in Fulmer's grist mill," explained the husband, "and business is not very good, so I had the day off. This is a time of year when we ought to be busy, but the trade is merely local. The huge concerns down east, and further west, do practically all the grinding nowadays."

The door opened, and the doctor appeared at the top of the steps.

"It's all right, Mr. Challis," he said encouragingly. "Mrs. Challis must stay indoors for a few days, and be careful to rest her foot. The cure may be tedious, but not painful, thanks to prompt treatment."

Challis brought out his wife, and Stranleigh took them to the two-storied frame house, of which they occupied part. When the young man came out to thank the chauffeur, he found the street empty.

A week later, Stranleigh's passengers heard the purr of an automobile outside the cottage. Challis opened the door in response to the chauffeur's knock.

"Good morning," said Stranleigh, shaking hands cheerfully. "What a lovely day! I am delighted to know that Mrs. Challis has completely recovered. I did not care to trouble you with repeated calls, but the doctor has been very kind, and has kept me informed of her progress. It is with his permission that I come to offer you a spin in the car. I'll take you anywhere you wish to go, and this invitation is extended with the concurrence of Mr. Ponderby, so you may enjoy the run to the full. My name's Johnson; not Jack, the celebrated, but Henry, the unknown."

Challis laughed.

"I'm delighted to meet you again," he said.

"Come in and see my wife. Her worry has been that she has never had the opportunity to thank you for your former kindness. Yes; I shall be glad of

59

a ride. I have been too much in the house lately."

"Another day off, eh?"

"All days are off days now," growled Challis. "The grist mill has shut down."

Mrs. Challis received the alleged Johnson with a graciousness that was quite charming. She thanked him in a manner so winning that Stranleigh sat there overcome with an attack of the shyness he had never been able to shake off. He could not help noticing the subtle melancholy of her beautiful face, a hint of which he had received in that brief first glance as he passed in the automobile. He attributed it then to her mishap, but now realised its cause was something deeper and more permanent. He was astonished later to find her so resolute in refusing his invitation. She wished her husband to go for a drive, but would not avail herself of that pleasure. In vain Stranleigh urged the doctor's dictum that it would be good for her especially as the day was so fine, and she had endured a week of enforced idleness indoors.

"Some other day perhaps," she said, "but not now," and he speedily recognised that her firmness was not to be shaken.

All her own powers of persuasiveness, however were turned upon her husband.

"You must go, Jim," she insisted. "I have kept you a prisoner for a week, and you need the fresh air much more than I do."

James Challis, protesting more and more faintly at last gave way, and the two men drove off together while Mrs. Challis fluttered a handkerchief from her window in adieu.

Challis had refused to sit in the back seat, and took his place beside the chauffeur.

"Where shall we go?" asked the latter.

"Drive to the place where you found us," said his passenger, and there they went. On the way thither, neither spoke, but at a sign from Challis,

Stranleigh stopped the car.

"You must not think," began the former, "that my wife did not wish to come. I know from the expression of her eyes that she did. Her reason for declining was one that I imagine any woman would consider adequate, and any man the reverse."

"I am an exception so far as the men are concerned," said Stranleigh, coming much nearer the truth than he suspected, "for I am sure that whatever motive actuated Mrs. Challis, it was commendable and right."

"Thank you," responded the other. "I am with you there. It is all a matter of clothes. My wife possesses no costume suitable for a motor excursion."

"In that case," cried Stranleigh impulsively, "the defect is easily remedied. I have saved a bit from the ample salary Mr. Ponderby allows me, and if I may offer you——"

"I could not accept anything," interrupted Challis.

"Merely a temporary loan, until the grist mill begins operations."

Challis shook his head.

"That mill will never grind again with the water that is past, nor the water that is to come. Fulmer has gone smash, and I could not accept a loan that I do not see my way to repay. Nevertheless, I appreciate fully the kindness of your offer, and if you don't mind, I will tell you how I got myself entangled, for there is no use in concealing from you what you must already have seen— that I am desperately poor, so much so that I sometimes lose courage, and consider myself a failure, which is not a pleasant state of mind to get into."

"Oh, I've often felt that way myself," said Stranleigh, "but nobody's a failure unless he thinks he is. You strike me as a capable man. You have youth and energy, and added to that, great good luck. I'm a believer in luck myself."

This commendation did not chase the gloom from the face of Challis.

"You have knocked from under me," he said, "the one frail prop on which I leaned. I have been excusing myself by blaming the run of horrid bad luck I have encountered."

Stranleigh shook his head.

"You can't truthfully say that," he rejoined quietly, "while you have had the supreme good fortune to enlist the affection of so clever and charming a wife."

The gloom disappeared from Challis's countenance as the shadow of a cloud at that moment flitted from the surface of the lake. He thrust forth his hand, and there being no onlookers, Stranleigh grasped it.

"Shake!" cried Challis. "I'll never say 'ill-luck' again! I wish she had come with us."

"So do I," agreed Stranleigh.

"I'd like her to have heard you talk."

"Oh, not for that reason. I'd like her to enjoy this scenery."

"Yes, and the deuce of it is, she practically owns the scene. Look at that house across the lake."

"A mansion, I should call it."

"A mansion it is. That's where my wife came from. Think of my selfishness in taking her from such a home to wretched rooms in a cottage, and abject poverty."

"I prefer not to think of your selfishness, but rather of her nobility in going. It revives in a cynical man like myself his former belief in the genuine goodness of the world."

"It all came about in this way," continued Challis. "I graduated at a technical college—engineering. I began work at the bottom of the ladder, and started in to do my best, being ambitious. This was appreciated, and I got on."

"In what line?" asked Stranleigh.

"In a line which at that time was somewhat experimental. The firm for which I worked might be called a mechanical-medical association, or perhaps 'surgical' would be a better term. We had no plant, no factory; nothing but offices. We were advisers. I was sent here and there all over the country, to mills that were not in a good state of health; dividends falling off, business declining, competition too severe, and what-not. I looked over the works, talked with managers and men, formed conclusions, then sent a report to my firm containing details, and such suggestions as I had to offer. My firm communicated with the proprietor of the works accordingly, and collected its bill."

"That should be an interesting occupation," said Stranleigh, whose attention was enlisted.

"It was. One day, I was sent up here to inspect the factory of Stanmore Anson, a large stone structure which you could see from here were it not concealed by that hill to the right. It has been in the Anson family for three generations, and had earned a lot of money in its time, but is now as old-fashioned as Noah's Ark. It was cruelly wasteful of human energy and mechanical power. It should have had a set of turbines, instead of the ancient, moss-grown, overshot waterwheels. The machinery was out of date, and ill-placed. The material in course of manufacture had to go upstairs and downstairs, all over the building, handled and re-handled, backward and forward, instead of passing straight through the factory, entering as raw material, and coming out the finished product. I reported to my firm that the establishment needed a complete overhauling; that it ought to have new machinery, but that if it was compulsory to keep the old machines at work, they should be entirely rearranged in accordance with the sketch I submitted, so that unnecessary handling of the product might be avoided. I set down the minimum expense that must be incurred, and also submitted an estimate covering the cost of turbines and new machinery, which I admit was large in the bulk, but really the most economical thing to do."

"I see. And the old man objected to the expense, or perhaps had not the necessary capital to carry out your suggestion? What sort of a person is he? Unreasonable, I suppose you consider him?"

"Strangely enough, I never met him in my life."

"And you married his daughter?"

"Had to. I was determined to take the girl away, whether I reformed the factory or not, and here you see where good luck and the reverse mingled. When I arrived at Mr. Anson's factory, the old man was in New York, for the purpose, as I learned, of raising a loan, or of selling the property, neither of which projects was he able to carry out."

"That was his misfortune, rather than his fault, wasn't it?"

"In a way, yes; still, the Trust had offered him a reasonable figure for his factory. He not only refused, but he fought the Trust tooth and nail, thinking that with low taxation, and country wages, he could meet the competition, which, of course, with the factory in its present state, he could not do. The fact that he was up against the Trust became well known, so that he could neither borrow nor sell. While in New York, he called several times on Langdon, Bliss, and Co., the firm that employed me. When my report came in and was read to him, I understand he fell into a tremendous rage, and characterised our company as a body of swindlers. Mr. Langdon ordered him out of the office.

"That was the first spoke in my wheel. Mr. Langdon was a capable man, always courteous and very calm when dealing with his fellows, so I am sure that my father-in-law must have been exceedingly violent when he provoked Langdon to vocal wrath. I judge that Langdon, when he recovered from his outbreak, regretted it extremely, and was inclined to blame me for rather muddling the affair of Anson's mill. I may say that I had been placed in rather a difficult position. The proprietor was absent, and had not taken his foreman into his confidence, therefore this foreman put difficulties in the way of investigation. The employees were suspicious, not knowing what this research by a stranger meant, so I went to Anson's house, hoping to find there someone with sufficient authority to enable me to get the information I must have.

"I met Mrs. Anson, a kindly woman, but realised in a moment that no authority had been delegated to her. She appeared afraid to suggest anything, but called in her only daughter to assist at our conference. The girl at once said she would accompany me to the mill, and did so. I shall never forget with what infinite tact and persuasiveness she won over the foreman, and it was quite evident that the workmen all knew and liked her, for her very presence appeared to dissipate distrust. I saw Miss Anson home, and it seemed, as my investigations progressed, many conferences became more and more necessary. You're a young man, and doubtless you know how it is yourself."

"As a matter of fact, I don't," interjected Stranleigh, "but I can guess."

"Well—your guess is right. We had no difficulty with Mrs. Anson, but both mother and daughter were uneasy about how the father would take it. I wrote him what I hoped was a straightforward letter, putting the case to him as man to man. He answered with a very brief and terse letter that left me no doubt regarding his opinion, but my own communication had arrived at an unfortunate time; the day after he had been ordered out of our office. He at once enclosed my letter to Mr. Langdon, saying in effect:—

"'This is the sort of man you sent like a wolf in sheep's clothing to my home.'"

"Langdon telegraphed, asking if this was true. I, of course, had to admit it was, with the result of instant dismissal. I never would have let either mother or daughter know about this, but my reticence was vain, for Mr. Anson wrote a stinging letter to his daughter saying she could do what she pleased about marrying me, but that he had secured my dismissal. It is strange," Challis murmured reflectively, speaking more to himself than to his companion, "it is strange that a father rarely recognises that when he comes to a difference with one of his children, he is meeting, in part at least, some of his own characteristics. I wonder if I shall ever be so unreasonable as——"

Stranleigh's eye twinkled as he remembered how firm the girl had been in refusing the automobile invitation, yet giving no explanation of that refusal.

"What Gertrude said to me was, holding her head very proudly: 'I have received my father's permission to marry you, and if you are ready for an immediate ceremony, I am willing.'

"We were married before the old man returned from New York."

"Has there been no further communication between Mr. Anson and yourself?"

"On my part, yes; ignored by him. It was Gertrude who wished to stay in Altonville. She knew a financial crisis was threatening her father, and she hoped that in some way I should be able to advise him. That was not to be. She requested permission to take away her belongings. This was refused. Everything she possessed, Mr. Anson said, had been purchased with his money. They remained at his home, and she was welcome to use them at his house, any time she chose to return, but having exchanged his care for that of another man, it was the other man's duty to provide what she needed. This ended our communication, and brings us to the present moment."

"Can you drive a car?" asked Stranleigh.

"Yes."

"The immediate question strikes me as being that of wearing apparel. I propose to return with at least a box full. I don't like to be baffled, and I wish Mrs. Challis to come out with us for a run. Will you exchange seats, and drive me down to the mill?"

"You're up against a tough proposition," demurred Challis.

"A proposition usually gives way if you approach it tactfully, as Miss Anson approached the manager. If you have never seen her father, he will not recognise you, so let us call at the mill."

"He would not recognise me, but the foreman would, also many of the men."

"We must chance that."

The two young men exchanged seats, and Challis at the wheel, with more caution than ever Stranleigh used, sent the car spinning down the slightly descending road by the margin of the lake, until they came to the water level. No word was spoken between them, but his lordship studied with keen scrutiny from the corner of his eye, the profile of the intent driver. He was immensely taken with the young man, and meditated on the story to which he had listened. The effect left on his mind by that recital surprised him. It was a feeling of sympathy with the old man who had acted so obstreperously, and gradually he placed this feeling to the credit of Challis, who had shown no rancour against his father-in-law, either in word or tone. Yes; he liked Challis, and was sorry for the elderly Anson, one evidently advanced in years, battling against forces that were too much for him, stubbornly using antiquated methods in a world that had out-grown them; the muzzle-loader against the repeating rifle. These two men should be pulling together.

"There's the factory," said Challis, at last, and Stranleigh, looking up, beheld further down the valley a three-storied structure, unexpectedly huge, built apparently for all the ages. There was no sign of activity about it; but the roar of waters came to their ears; idle waters, nevertheless, that were turning no wheels, the muffled sound of an unimpeded minor cataract.

"By Jove!" cried Stranleigh, jumping out as the car stopped.

Challis said nothing, but an expression of deep anxiety darkened his countenance. There were plastered here and there on the stone walls great white posters, bearing printing like the headings of a sensational newspaper, magnified several hundred times.

AUCTION SALE.

BY ORDER OF THE BANKRUPTCY COURT,

that desirable property known as Anson's Mill, fully equipped with machinery, in condition for immediate use, with never-failing water power, which at slight expense may be enormously increased; together with ten acres of freehold land; without reserve to the highest bidder; on the Seventeenth of November!

"A desirable property," said Challis, sadly, "which nobody desires except the Trust, and probably it cares nothing about it now."

"You forget that it is desired by Stanmore Anson."

"I am afraid that even he is tired of it by this time. I am sorry, but I feared it was inevitable."

Stranleigh looked up at him.

"Could you make this factory pay, if it were given into your charge?"

"Not in its present condition."

"I mean, of course, with your recommendations carried out. If the mill, free from all encumbrances, filled with modern machinery, rightly placed, were put under your management, could you make it pay?"

Challis did not answer for some moments. His brow was wrinkled in thought, and he seemed making some mental calculations.

"There would need to be a suitable amount of working capital——"

"Yes, yes; all that is understood. Could you make it pay?"

"I am almost sure I could, but there is that incalculable factor, the opposition of the Trust."

"Damn the Trust!" cried Stranleigh. "I beg your pardon; I should have said, blow the Trust! I thought I had lost the power of becoming excited, not to say profane. It must be the exhilarating air of America. The sale is a good way off yet, and I think it will be further off before I get through with it. If you will accept the management, and your father-in-law proves at all reasonable, I guarantee to find the necessary money."

"You mean that, Mr. Ponderby——"

"Exactly. I am his chief business adviser, as well as his only chauffeur. But we are forgetting the matter in hand. We must rescue the wardrobe of Mrs. Challis. Drive on to the mansion. You know the way, and I don't."

"I'm a warned-off trespasser, but here goes."

"You won't be called on to trespass very much. You're my chauffeur, pro tem. Perhaps you won't need to enter the house at all. I shall see Mrs. Anson before I meet her husband, if possible, and will try to persuade her to give me the wardrobe."

"She would not have the courage to do that without her husband's permission, and he will never give it."

"We'll see about that. Ah, the mill is not the only piece of property to be sold!"

They had turned into a well-shaded avenue, to the massive stone gate-pillars of which were attached posters similar to those at the mill, only in this case it was "This valuable, desirable and palatial residence," with the hundreds of acres of land attached, that were to be knocked down by the auctioneer's hammer.

"I might have known," commented Stranleigh, "that if Mr. Anson was bankrupt at his mill, he was also bankrupt at his house."

They drew up at the entrance. Stranleigh stepped down, and rang the bell, Challis remaining in the car. Shown into the drawing-room, the visitor was greeted by a sad-looking, elderly woman.

"Mrs. Anson," said the young man, very deferentially, "I expect your forgiveness for this intrusion on my part when I say that I am here in some sense as an ambassador from your daughter."

"From my daughter!" gasped the old lady in astonishment. "Is she well, and where is she?"

"She is very well, I am glad to say, and is living with her husband over in the village."

"In her last letter she said her husband was taking her to New York. There had been a—misunderstanding." The old lady hesitated for a moment before using that mild term. "On the day her letter was received, I went to the hotel at which they were stopping, and was told by the landlord they had gone, he did not know where. Do you tell me they have been living in Altonville all the time?"

"I think so, but cannot be sure. I met Mr. and Mrs. Challis for the first time only a week ago."

"I hope she is happy."

"She is," said Stranleigh confidently, "and before the day is done her mother will be happy also."

Mrs. Anson shook her head. She was on the verge of tears, which Stranleigh saw and dreaded. So he said hurriedly:

"You will select me what you think she should have at once, and I will take the box or parcel to Altonville in my car."

"When at last her father saw that everything we possessed must be sold," rejoined Mrs. Anson, "he packed up in trunks what belonged to Gertrude,

and as we could not learn where to send them, Mr. Asa Perkins, a friend of ours, who lives in Boston, lent us a room in which to store the things, and they are there now."

"How odd!" exclaimed Stranleigh. "I met Mr. Perkins just before he left his summer residence, and took the place furnished, acting for the present tenant. It is much too large for him, and some of the rooms are locked. Do you happen to have the key?"

"No; it is in the possession of the housekeeper. She is there still, is she not?"

"Yes; I took the house as it stood, servants and all."

"I'll write a note to the housekeeper, then. What name shall I say?"

"Please write it in the name of Mr. Challis. He's outside now, in my car."

"May I bring him in?" she asked, eagerly.

"Certainly," said Stranleigh, with a smile. "It's your house, you know."

"Not for long," she sighed.

"Ah,——" drawled Stranleigh, "Mr. Challis and I propose that this sale shall not take place. If I may have a short conversation with your husband, I think we shall come to terms."

An expression of anxiety overspread her face.

"Perhaps I had better not ask Jim to come in," she hesitated.

"Your husband does not know him, and I would rather you did not tell him who is with me. Just say that Henry Johnson and a friend wish to negotiate about the factory."

Stanmore Anson proved to be a person of the hale old English yeoman type, as portrayed by illustrators, although his ancestors originally came from Sweden. His face was determined, his lips firm, and despite his defeats, the lurking sparkle of combat still animated his eyes.

"Before we begin any conversation regarding a sale," he said, "you must answer this question, Mr. Johnson. Are you connected in any way, directly or indirectly, with the G.K.R. Trust?"

"I am not connected with it, directly or indirectly."

"You state that on your honour as a man?"

"No; I simply state it."

"You wouldn't swear it?"

"Not unless compelled by force of law."

"Then I have nothing further to say to you, sir."

The old man seemed about to withdraw, then hesitated, remembering he was in his own house. Stranleigh sat there unperturbed.

"You have nothing further to say, Mr. Anson, because two thoughts are sure to occur to you. First, a man whose word you would not accept cannot be believed, either on his honour or his oath. Second, the Trust doesn't need to send an emissary to you; it has only to wait until November, and acquire your factory at its own figure. No one except myself would bid against the Trust."

"That's quite true," agreed Anson. "I beg your pardon. What have you to propose?"

"I wish to know the sum that will see you clear and enable you to tear down those white posters at the gates, and those on the mill."

Stanmore Anson drew a sheet of paper from his pocket, glanced over it, then named the amount.

"Very good," said Stranleigh, decisively. "I'll pay that for the mill and the ten acres."

"They are not worth it," said Anson. "Wait till November, and even though you outbid the Trust, you'll get it at a lower figure."

"We'll make the mill worth it. You may retain the residence and the rest of the property."

"There is but one proviso," said the old man. "I wish to name the manager."

"I regret I cannot agree to that, Mr. Anson, I have already chosen the manager, and guarantee that he will prove efficient."

"I'll forego your generous offer of the house and property if you will allow me to appoint the manager."

"I am sorry, Mr. Anson, but you touch the only point on which I cannot give way."

"Very well," cried Anson, angrily, his eyes ablaze. "The arrangement is off."

Both young men saw that Stanmore Anson was indeed difficult to deal with, as his ancestors had been in many a hard-fought battle.

"Wait a moment! Wait a moment!" exclaimed Challis. "This will never do. It is absurd to wreck everything on a point so trivial. I am the man whom Mr. Johnson wishes to make manager. I now refuse to accept the position, but if the bargain is completed, I'll give Mr. Anson and his manager all the assistance and advice they care to receive from me, and that without salary."

"Be quiet, Challis!" cried Stranleigh.

"Challis! Challis!" interrupted the old man, gazing fiercely at his junior.

"Is your name Challis?"

"Yes, sir."

"You're not my son-in-law?"

"I am, sir."

"I did you a great injustice," admitted Anson. "No man has a right to deprive another of his livelihood. I have bitterly regretted it. It is you I wish appointed manager."

"Challis," said Stranleigh, "take the car, and bring your wife. Say her father wishes to see her."

Challis disappeared, and in an incredibly short space of time, during which Anson and Stranleigh chatted together, the door opened, and Gertrude Challis came in.

"Father," she cried, "Jim says he's going to scrap all the machinery in the factory. Shall we throw our differences on that scrap-heap?"

The old man gathered her to his breast, and kissed her again and again. He could not trust his voice.

# IV.—THE MAD MISS MATURIN.

"Would you like to meet the most beautiful woman in America?" asked Edward Trenton of his guest.

Lord Stranleigh drew a whiff or two from the favourite pipe he was smoking, and the faint suggestion of a smile played about his lips.

"The question seems to hint that I have not already met her," he said at last.

"Have you?"

"Of course."

"Where?"

"In every town of any size I ever visited."

"Oh, I daresay you have met many pretty girls, but only one of them is the most beautiful in America."

Again Stranleigh smiled, but this time removed his pipe, which had gone out, and gently tapped it on the ash tray.

"My dear Ned," he said at last, "on almost any other subject I should hesitate to venture an opinion that ran counter to your own experience, yet in this instance I think you wrong the great Republic. I am not very good at statistics, but if you will tell me how many of your fellow-countrymen are this moment in love, I'll make a very accurate estimate regarding the number of most beautiful women there are in the United States."

"Like yourself, Stranleigh, I always defer to the man of experience, and am glad to have hit on one subject in which you are qualified to be my teacher."

"I like that! Ned Trenton depreciating his own conquests is a popular actor in a new rôle. But you are evading the point. I was merely trying in my awkward way to show that every woman is the most beautiful in the world to the man in love with her."

"Very well; I'll frame my question differently.

Would you like to meet one of the most cultured of her sex?"

"Bless you, my boy, of course not! Why, I'm afraid of her already. It is embarrassing enough to meet a bright, alert man, but in the presence of a clever woman, I become so painfully stupid that she thinks I'm putting it on."

"Then let me place the case before you in still another form. Would your highness like to meet the richest woman in Pennsylvania?"

"Certainly I should," cried Stranleigh, eagerly.

Trenton looked at him with a shade of disapproval on his brow.

"I thought wealth was the very last qualification a man in your position would care for in a woman, yet hardly have I finished the sentence, than you jump at the chance I offer."

"And why not? A lady beautiful and talented would likely strike me dumb, but if she is hideously rich, I may be certain of one thing, that I shall not be asked to invest money in some hare-brained scheme or other."

"You are quite safe from that danger, or indeed from any other danger, so far as Miss Maturin is concerned. Nevertheless, it is but just that you should understand the situation, so that if you scent danger of any kind, you may escape while there is yet time."

"Unobservant though I am," remarked Stranleigh, "certain signs have not escaped my notice. This commodious and delightful mansion is being prepared for a house-party. I know the symptoms, for I have several country places of my own. If, as I begin to suspect, I am in the way here, just whisper the word and I'll take myself off in all good humour, hoping to receive an invitation for some future time."

"If that's your notion of American hospitality, Stranleigh, you've got another guess coming. You're a very patient man; will you listen to a little family history? Taking your consent for granted, I plunge. My father possessed a good deal of landed property in Pennsylvania. This house is the old homestead, as they would call it in a heart-throb drama. My father died a very wealthy man, and left his property conjointly to my sister and myself. He knew we wouldn't quarrel over the division, and we haven't. My activity has been mainly concentrated in coal mines and in the railways which they feed, and financially I have been very fortunate. I had intended to devote a good deal of attention to this estate along certain lines which my father had suggested, but I have never been able to do so, living, as I did, mostly in Philadelphia, absorbed in my own business. My sister, however, has in a measure carried out my father's plans, aided and abetted by her friend, Miss Constance Maturin. My sister married a man quite as wealthy as herself, a dreamy, impractical, scholarly person who once represented his country as Minister to Italy, in Rome. She enjoyed her Italian life very much, and studied with great interest the progress North Italy was making in utilising the water-power coming from the Alps. In this she was ably seconded by Miss Maturin, who is owner of forests and farms and factories further down the river which flows past our house. Her property, indeed, adjoins our own, but she does not possess that unlimited power over it which Sis and I have over this estate, for her father, having no faith in the business capacity of woman, formed his undertakings into a limited liability company where, although he owned the majority of stock during his life, he did not leave his daughter with untrammelled control. Had the old man known what trouble he was bequeathing to his sole heir, I imagine he would have arranged things a little differently. Miss Maturin has had to endure several expensive law-suits, which still further restricted her power and lessened her income. So she has ceased to take much interest in her own belongings, and has constituted herself adviser-in-chief to my dear sister, who has blown in a good deal of money on this estate in undertakings that, however profitable they may be in the future, are unproductive up to date. I am not criticising Sis at all, and have never objected to what she has done, although I found myself involved in a very serious action for damages, which I had the chagrin of losing, and which ran me into a lot of expense, covering me with injunctions and things of that sort. No rogue e'er felt the halter draw, with a good opinion of the law, and perhaps my own detestation of the law arises from my having frequently broken it. If this long diatribe bores you, just say so, and I'll cut it short."

"On the contrary," said Stranleigh, with evident honesty, "I'm very much interested. These two ladies, as I understand the case, have been unsuccessful in law——"

"Completely so."

"And unsuccessful in the projects they have undertaken?"

"From my point of view, yes. That is to say, they are sinking pots of money, and I don't see where any of it is coming back."

"Of what do these enterprises consist?"

"Do you know anything about the conservation controversy now going on in this country?"

"I fear I do not. I am a woefully ignorant person."

"My father had ideas about conservation long before the United States took it up. It is on these ideas that Sis has been working. You preserve water in times of flood and freshet to be used for power or for irrigation throughout the year. Her first idea was to make a huge lake, extending several miles up the valley of this river. That's where I got into my law-suit. The commercial interests down below held that we had no right to put a huge concrete dam across this river."

"Couldn't you put a dam on your own property?"

"It seems not. If the river ran entirely through my own property, I could. Had I paid more attention to what was being done, I might perhaps have succeeded, by getting a bill through the Legislature. When I tried that, I was too late. The interests below had already applied to the courts for an injunction, which, quite rightly, they received. Attempting to legalise the action, not only did I find the Legislature hostile, but my clever opponents got up a muck-raking crusade against me, and I was held up by the Press of this State as a soulless monopolist, anxious to increase my already great wealth by grabbing what should belong to the whole people. The campaign of personal calumny was splendidly engineered, and, by Jupiter! they convinced me that I was unfit for human intercourse. Tables of statistics were published to prove how through railway and coal-mine manipulation I had robbed everybody, and they made me out about a hundred times richer than I am, although I have never been able to get any of the excess cash. Sermons were preached against me, the Pulpit joining the Press in denunciation. I had no friends, and not being handy with my pen, I made no attempt at defence. I got together a lot of dynamite, blew up the partially-constructed dam, and the river still flows serenely on."

"But surely," said Stranleigh, "I saw an immense dam on this very river, when you met me at Powerville railway station the other day?"

Trenton laughed.

"Yes; that was Miss Maturin's dam."

"Miss Maturin's!" cried Stranleigh in astonishment.

"It was built years ago by her father, who went the right way about it, having obtained in a quiet, effective way, the sanction of legislature. Of course, when I say it belongs to Miss Maturin, I mean that it is part of the estate left by her father, and the odd combination of circumstances brought it about that she was one of my opponents in the action-at-law, whereas in strict justice, she should have been a defendant instead of a plaintiff. The poor girl was horrified to learn her position in the matter, and my sister was dumbfounded to find in what a dilemma she had placed me. Of course, the two girls should have secured the advice of some capable, practical lawyer in the first place, but they were very self-confident in those days, and Sis knew it was no use consulting her husband, while her brother was too deeply immersed in his own affairs to be much aid as a counsellor.

"Well, they kept on with their conservation scheme after a time, and both on this property and on Miss Maturin's, dams have been erected on all the streams that empty into the river; streams on either side that take their rise from outlying parts of the estate. They have built roads through the forest, and have caused to be formed innumerable lakes, all connected by a serviceable highway that constitutes one of the most interesting automobile drives there is in all the United States; a drive smooth as a floor, running for miles through private property, and therefore overshadowed by no speed limit."

"By Jove, Ned," exclaimed Stranleigh, "you must take me over that course."

"I'll do better than that, my boy. Constance Maturin is one of the best automobilists I know, and she will be your guide, for these dams are of the most modern construction, each with some little kink of its own that no one understands better than she does. There is a caretaker living in a picturesque little cottage at the outlet of every lake, and in each cottage hangs a telephone, so that no matter how far you penetrate into the wilderness, you are in touch with civilisation. From this house I could call up any one of these water-wardens, or send out a general alarm, bringing every man of the corps to the 'phone, and the instructions given from here would be heard simultaneously by the whole force. I think the organisation is admirable, but it runs into a lot of money."

"'But what good came of it at last,

Quoth little Peterkin,'"

asked Stranleigh. "Do these artificial lakes run any dynamos, or turn any spindles? Now tell me all about the war, and what they dammed each streamlet for."

"Ah, you have me there! The ladies have not taken me into their counsel: I've got troubles enough of my own. One phase of the subject especially gratifies me: their activities have in no instance despoiled the landscape; rather the contrary. These lakes, wooded to their brims, are altogether delightful, and well stocked with fish. A great many of them overflow, causing admirable little cascades, which, although not quite so impressive as Niagara, are most refreshing on a hot day, while the cadence of falling waters serves as an acoustic background to the songs of the birds; a musical accompaniment, as one might call it."

"Bravo, Ned; I call that quite poetical, coming as it does from a successful man of business. I find myself eager for that automobile ride through this forest lakeland. When do you say Miss Maturin will arrive?"

"I don't know. I expect my sister will call me up by telephone. Sis regards this house as her own. She is fond of leaving the giddy whirl of society, and settling down here in the solitude of the woods. I clear out or I stay in obedience to her commands. You spoke of a house-party a while ago. There is to be no house-party, but merely my sister and her husband, with Miss Maturin as their guest. If you would rather not meet any strangers, I suggest that we plunge further into the wilderness. At the most remote lake on this property, about seven miles away, quite a commodious keeper's lodge has been built, with room for, say, half a dozen men who are not too slavishly addicted to the resources of civilisation. Yet life there is not altogether pioneering. We could take an automobile with us, and the

telephone would keep us in touch with the outside world. Fond of fishing?"

"Very."

"Then that's all right. I can offer you plenty of trout, either in pond or stream, while in a large natural lake, only a short distance away, is excellent black bass. I think you'll enjoy yourself up there."

Stranleigh laughed.

"You quite overlook the fact that I am not going. Unless ejected by force, I stay here to meet your sister and Miss Maturin."

For a moment Trenton seemed taken aback. He had lost the drift of things in his enthusiasm over the lakes.

"Oh, yes; I remember," he said at last. "You objected to meet anyone who might wish you to invest good money in wild-cat schemes. Well, you're quite safe as far as those two ladies are concerned, as I think I assured you."

Ned was interrupted, and seemed somewhat startled by a sound of murmured conversation ending in a subdued peal of musical laughter.

"Why, there's Sis now," he said, "I can tell her laugh anywhere."

As he rose from his chair, the door opened, and there entered a most comely young woman in automobile garb, noticeably younger than Trenton, but bearing an unmistakable likeness to him.

"Hello, Ned!" she cried. "I thought I'd find you here," then seeing his visitor, who had risen, she paused.

"Lord Stranleigh," said Trenton. "My sister, Mrs. Vanderveldt."

"I am very glad to meet you, Lord Stranleigh," she said, advancing from the door and shaking hands with him.

"Why didn't you telephone?" asked her brother.

His sister laughed merrily.

"I came down like a wolf on the fold, didn't I? Why didn't I telephone? Strategy, my dear boy, strategy. This is a surprise attack, and I'd no wish that the garrison, forewarned, should escape. I am sure, Lord Stranleigh, that he has been descanting on the distraction of the woods and the camp, or perhaps the metropolitan dissipation of Philadelphia, depending on whether the yearning for sport, or his business in town was uppermost in his mind."

"My dear Sis," cried Ned with indignation, "that is a libellous statement. I never so much as mentioned Philadelphia, did I, Stranleigh? You can corroborate what I say."

"I'm not so sure about that," said Stranleigh, lightly. "Your attempt to drag me into your family differences at this point of the game is futile. I'm going to lie low, and say nothing, as Brer Rabbit did, until I learn which of you two is the real ruler of this house. I shall then boldly announce myself on the side of the leader. My position here is much too comfortable to be jeopardised by an injudicious partisanship."

"As for who's boss," growled Ned, "I cravenly admit at once that Sis here is monarch of all she surveys."

"In that case," rejoined Stranleigh, heaving a deep sigh of apparent relief,

"I'm on the side of the angels. Mrs. Vanderveldt, he did mention Philadelphia and his office there, speaking much about business interests, coal-mines, and what not, during which recital I nearly went to sleep, for I'm no business man. He also descanted on the lakes and the waterfalls and the fishing, and on trout and black bass, and would doubtless have gone on to whales and sea-serpents had you not come in at the opportune moment. Please accept me as your devoted champion, Mrs. Vanderveldt."

"I do, I do, with appreciation and gratitude," cried the lady merrily. "I've long wished to meet you, Lord Stranleigh, for I heard such glowing accounts of you from my brother here, with most fascinating descriptions of your estates in England, and the happy hours he spent upon them while he was your guest in the old country. I hope we may be able to make some slight return for your kindness to this frowning man. He is always on nettles when I am talking; so different from my husband in that respect."

"Poor man, he never has a chance to get a word in edgewise," growled Ned. "My soul is my own, I'm happy to say."

"Ah, yes," laughed the lady, "pro tem. But although I am saying so much for myself, I speak with equal authority for my friend Constance Maturin."

"Did you bring her with you, or is she coming later?" asked Trenton with some anxiety.

"She is here, dear brother, but I could not induce her to enter this room with me. Doubtless she wishes to meet you alone. She is a dear girl, Lord Stranleigh, and it will be my greatest joy to welcome her as a sister-in-law."

A warm flush was added to the frown on her brother's brow, but he made no remark.

"Gracious me!" cried the lady, laughing again "have I once more put my foot in it? Why Ned, what a fine confidential friend you are. If I were a young man, and so sweet a girl had promised to marry me, I should proclaim the fact from the house-tops."

"You wouldn't need to," groaned Ned, "if you had a sister."

"Never mind him," said Stranleigh, "you have betrayed no secret, Mrs. Vanderveldt. His own confused utterances when referring to the young lady, rendered any verbal confession unnecessary. I suspected how the land lay at a very early stage of our conversation."

"Well, I think he may congratulate himself that you do not enter the lists against him. You possess some tact, which poor Ned has never acquired, and now I'll make him sit up by informing him that Connie Maturin took a special trip over to England recently, in order to meet you."

"To meet me?" cried Stranleigh in astonishment.

"Yes, indeed, and an amazed girl she was to learn that you had sailed for America. She came right back by the next boat. She has a great plan in her mind which requires heavy financing. My brother here isn't rich enough, and I, of course, am much poorer than he is, so she thought if she could interest you, as the leading capitalist of England——"

"Good heavens, girl," interrupted Ned, the perspiration standing out on his brow, "do show some consideration for what you are saying! Why, you rattle on without a thought to your words. Lord Stranleigh just made it a proviso that——. Oh, hang it all, Sis; you've put your foot in it this time, sure enough."

The lady turned on him now with no laughter on her lips, or merriment in her tone.

"Why, Ned, you're actually scolding me. I promised Connie Maturin to help her, and my way of accomplishing anything is to go directly for it."

"Oh, heaven help me," murmured Ned, "the law courts have already taught me that."

"Mrs. Vanderveldt," said the Earl of Stranleigh, very quietly, "please turn to your champion, and ignore this wretched man, whose unnecessary reticence is finding him out."

The only person to be embarrassed by this tangle of concealments and revelations was Constance Maturin, who had indulged in neither the one nor the other. The Earl of Stranleigh found it difficult to become acquainted with her. She seemed always on her guard, and never even approached the subject which he had been given to understand chiefly occupied her thoughts.

On the day set for their automobile ride, Miss Maturin appeared at the wheel of the very latest thing in runabouts; a six-cylindered machine of extraordinary power, that ran as silently and smoothly as an American watch, and all merely for the purpose of carrying two persons. Stranleigh ran his eye over the graceful proportions of the new car with an expert's keen appreciation, walking round it slowly and critically, quite forgetting the girl who regarded him with an expression of amusement. Looking up at last, he saw a smile playing about her pretty lips.

"I beg your pardon," he said.

"I'm not sure that I shall grant it," she replied, laughing. "To be ignored in this callous fashion for even the latest project of engineering, is not in the least flattering."

"Not ignored, Miss Maturin," said Stranleigh, "for I was thinking of you, although I may have appeared absorbed in the machine."

"Thinking of me!" she cried. "You surely can't expect me to believe that! The gaze of a man fascinated by a piece of machinery is quite different from that of a man fascinated by a woman. I know, because I have seen both."

"I am sure you have seen the latter, Miss Maturin. But what I have just been regarding is an omen."

"Really? How mysterious! I thought you saw only an automobile."

"No, I was looking through the automobile, and beyond, if I may put it that way. I am quite familiar with the plan of this car, although this is the first specimen that I have examined. The car is yours by purchase, I suppose, but it is mine by manufacture. Your money bought it, but mine made it, in conjunction with the genius of a young engineer in whom I became interested. Perhaps you begin to see the omen. Some time ago I was fortunate enough to be of assistance to a young man, and the result has been an unqualified success. To-day perhaps I may be permitted to aid a young woman with a success that will be equally gratifying."

Stranleigh gazed steadily into the clear, honest eyes of the girl, who returned his look with a half-amused smile. Now she seemed suddenly covered with confusion, and flushing slightly, turned her attention to the forest that surrounded them. Presently she said—

"Do you men worship only the god of success? You have used the word three or four times."

"Most men wish to be successful, I suppose, but we all worship a goddess, too."

"I'm sorry," said Miss Maturin, "that Mrs. Vanderveldt mentioned my search for a capitalist. I have abandoned the quest. I am now merely your guide to the lakes. Please take a seat in this automobile of yours, Lord Stranleigh, and I will be your conductor."

The young man stepped in beside her, and a few moments later they were gliding, rather than running over a perfect road, under the trees, in a machine as noiseless as the forest. The Earl of Stranleigh had seen many beautiful regions of this world, but never any landscape just like this. Its artificiality and its lack of artificiality interested him. Nothing could be more businesslike than the construction of the stout dams, and nothing more gently rural than the limpid lakes, with the grand old forest trees marshalled round their margins like a veteran army that had marched down to drink, only to be stricken motionless at the water's edge.

It seemed that the silence of the motor-car had enchanted into silence its occupants. The girl devoted her whole attention to the machine and its management. Stranleigh sat dumb, and gave himself up to the full enjoyment of the Vallombrosic tour.

For more than half an hour no word had been spoken; finally the competent chauffeur brought the auto to a standstill at a view-point near the head of the valley, which offered a prospect of the brawling main stream.

"We have now reached the last of the lakes in this direction," she said quietly. "I think your automobile is admirable, Lord Stranleigh."

The young man indulged in a deep sigh of satisfaction.

"As a landscape gardener on a marvellous scale, you are without a competitor, Miss Maturin."

The girl laughed very sweetly.

"That is a compliment to nature rather than to me. I have merely let the wilderness alone, so far as road-making and dam-building would allow me."

"In that very moderation lies genius—the leaving alone. Will you forgive the inquisitiveness of a mere man whom you suspected at our outset of success-worship, if he asks what practical object you have in view?"

"Oh, I should have thought that was self-evident to an observant person like yourself," she said airily. "These lakes conserve the water, storing it in time of flood for use in time of scarcity. By means of sluices we obtain partial control of the main stream."

"You flatter me by saying I am observant. I fear that I am rather the reverse, except where my interest is aroused, as is the case this morning. Is conservation your sole object, then?"

"Is not that enough?"

"I suppose it is. I know little of civil engineering, absorbing craft though it is. I have seen its marvels along your own lines in America, Egypt, India, and elsewhere. As we progressed I could not help noticing that the dams built to restrain these lakes seemed unnecessarily strong."

A slight shadow of annoyance flitted across the expressive countenance of Constance Maturin, but was gone before he saw it.

"You are shrewder than you admit, Lord Stranleigh, but you forget what I said about freshets. The lakes are placid enough now, but you should see them after a cloud-burst back in the mountains."

"Nevertheless, the dams look bulky enough to hold back the Nile."

"Appearances are often deceitful. They are simply strong enough for the work they have to do. American engineering practice does not go in for useless encumbrance. Each dam serves two purposes. It holds back the water and it contains a power-house. In some of these power-houses

turbines and dynamoes are already placed."

"Ah, now I understand. You must perceive that I am a very stupid individual."

"You are a very persistent person," said the young woman decisively.

Stranleigh laughed.

"Allow me to take advantage of that reputation by asking you what you intend to do with the electricity when you have produced it?"

"We have no plans."

"Oh, I say!"

"What do you say?"

"That was merely an Anglicised expression of astonishment."

"Don't you believe me?"

"No."

They were sitting together on the automobile seat, deep in the shade of the foliage above them, but when he caught sight of the indignant face which she turned towards him, it almost appeared as if the sun shone upon it. She seemed about to speak, thought better of it, and reached forward

to the little lever that controlled the self-starting apparatus. She found his hand there before she could carry out her intention.

"I am returning, Lord Stranleigh," she said icily.

"Not yet."

She leaned back in the seat.

"Mr. Trenton told me that you were the most polite man he had ever met. I have seldom found him so mistaken in an impression."

"Was it a polite man you set out to find in your recent trip to Europe?"

As the girl made no reply, Stranleigh went on—

"My politeness is something like the dams we have been considering. It contains more than appears on the surface. There is concealed power within it. You may meet myriads of men well qualified to teach me courtesy, but when this veneer of social observance is broken, you come to pretty much the same material underneath. I seldom permit myself the luxury of an escape from the conventions, but on rare occasions I break through. For that I ask your pardon. Impressed by your sincerity, I forgot for the moment everything but your own need in the present crisis."

"What crisis?" she asked indignantly.

"The financial crisis caused by your spending every available resource on this so-called conservation policy. To all intents and purposes you are now a bankrupt. Mrs. Vanderveldt has contributed all she can, and both you and she are afraid to tell her brother the true state of the case. You fear you will get little sympathy from him, for he is absorbed in coal-mines and railways, and both of you have already felt his annoyance at the law-suit in which you have involved him. Hence your desperate need of a capitalist. A really polite man would be a more pleasant companion than I, but he is not worth that, Miss Maturin!"

Stranleigh removed his hand from the lever long enough to snap fingers and thumb, but he instantly replaced it when he saw her determination to start the machine.

"The man of the moment, Miss Maturin, is a large and reckless capitalist. I am that capitalist."

He released his hold of the lever, and sat upright. The sternness of his face relaxed.

"Now, Miss Maturin, turn on the power; take me where you like; dump me into any of those lakes you choose; the water is crystal clear, and I'm a good swimmer," and with this Stranleigh indulged in a hearty laugh, his own genial self once more.

"You are laughing at me," she said resentfully.

"Indeed I am not. Another contradiction, you see! I am laughing at myself. There's nothing I loathe so much as strenuousness, and here I have fallen into the vice. It is the influence of that brawling river below us, I think. But the river becomes still enough, and useful enough, when it reaches the great lake at Powerville, which is big enough to swallow all these little ponds."

The girl made no motion towards the lever, but sat very still, lost in thought. When she spoke, her voice was exceedingly quiet.

"You complimented Nature a while ago, intending, as I suppose, to compliment me, but I think after all the greater compliment is your straight talk, which I admire, although I received it so petulantly. I shall make no apology, beyond saying that my mind is very much perturbed. Your surmise is absolutely correct. It isn't that I've spent the whole of my fortune and my friend's fortune in this conservation scheme. It is because I have built a model city on the heights above Powerville. I was promised assistance from the banks, which is now withheld, largely, I suspect, through the opposition of John L. Boscombe, a reputed millionaire. To all intents and purposes Boscombe and I are the owners of Powerville and the mills there, but although this place was founded and built up by my father, I am a minority stock-holder, and powerless. Boscombe exercises control. Any suggestions or protests of mine are ignored, for Boscombe, like my father, has little faith—no faith at all, in fact—in the business capacity of a woman.

"I have tried, as I hinted, to enlist the co-operation of other capitalists, but experience has taught me that any appeal is futile that does not impinge directly upon cupidity. If there is the least hint of philanthropy in the project, every man of money fights shy of it."

"I am an exception," said Stranleigh, eagerly. "Philanthropy used to be a strong point with me, though I confess I was never very successful in its exercise. What humanitarian scheme is in your mind, Miss Maturin?"

Again she sat silent for some moments, indecision and doubt on her fair brow. Presently she said, as if pulling herself together—

"I will not tell you, Lord Stranleigh. You yourself have just admitted disbelief, and my plan is so fantastic that I dare not submit it to criticism."

"I suppose your new city is in opposition to the old town down in the valley? You alone are going to compete with Boscombe and yourself."

"That is one way of putting it."

"Very well, I am with you. Blow Boscombe! say I. I've no head for business, so I sha'n't need to take any advice. I shall do exactly what you tell me. What is the first move?"

"The first move is to set your brokers in New York at work, and buy a block of Powerville stock."

"I see; so that you and I together have control, instead of Boscombe?"

"Yes."

"That shall be done as quick as telegraph can give instructions. What next?"

"There will be required a large sum of money to liquidate the claims upon me incurred through the building of the city."

"Very good. That money shall be at your disposal within two or three days."

"As for security, I regret——"

"Don't mention it. My security is my great faith in Ned Trenton, also in yourself. Say no more about it."

"You are very kind, Lord Stranleigh, but there is one thing I must say. This may involve you in a law-suit so serious that the litigation of which Ned complains will appear a mere amicable arrangement by comparison."

"That's all right and doesn't disturb me in the least. I love a legal contest, because I have nothing to do but place it in the hands of competent lawyers. No personal activity is required of me, and I am an indolent man."

The second part of the programme was accomplished even sooner than Stranleigh had promised, but the first part hung fire. The brokers in New York could not acquire any Powerville stock, as was shown by their application to Miss Maturin herself, neither had their efforts been executed with that secrecy which Stranleigh had enjoined. He realised this when John L. Boscombe called upon him. He went directly to the point.

"I am happy to meet you, Lord Stranleigh, and if you'll excuse me, I'd like to say that you are more greatly in need of advice at this moment than any man in America."

"You are perfectly right, Mr. Boscombe. I am always in need of good advice, and I appreciate it."

"An application was made to me from New York for a block of stock. That stock is not for sale, but I dallied with the brokers, made investigations, and traced the inquiry to you."

"Very clever of you, Mr. Boscombe."

"I learn that you propose to finance Miss Constance Maturin, who is a junior partner in my business."

"I should not think of contradicting so shrewd a man as yourself, Mr. Boscombe. What do you advise in the premises?"

"I advise you to get out, and quick, too."

"If I don't, what are you going to do to me?"

"Oh, I shall do nothing. She will do all that is necessary. That woman is stark mad, Lord Stranleigh. Her own father recognised it when he bereft her of all power in the great business he founded. If she had her way, she'd ruin the company inside a year with her hare-brained schemes; love of the dear people, and that sort of guff."

"I am sorry to hear that. I noticed no dementia on the part of Miss

Maturin, who seemed to me a most cultivated and very charming young lady. You will permit me, I hope, to thank you for your warning, and will not be surprised that I can give you no decision on the spur of the moment. I am a slow-minded person, and need time to think over things."

"Certainly, certainly; personally I come to sudden conclusions, and once I make up my mind, I never change it."

"A most admirable gift. I wish I possessed it."

Lord Stranleigh said nothing of this interview to Constance Maturin, beyond telling her that the acquisition of stock appeared to be hopeless, as indeed proved to be the case.

"Boscombe must be a stubborn person," he said.

"Oh, he's all that," the girl replied, with a sigh. "He cares for one thing only, the making of money, and in that I must admit he has been very successful."

"Well, we've got a little cash of our own," said Stranleigh, with a laugh.

Miss Maturin and Mrs. Vanderveldt celebrated a national holiday by the greatest entertainment ever given in that district. The mills had been shut down for a week, and every man, woman and child in the valley city had been invited up to the new town on the heights. There was a brass band, and a sumptuous spread of refreshments, all free to the immense crowd. The ladies, for days before, visited everyone in the valley, and got a promise of attendance, but to make assurance doubly sure, an amazing corps of men was organised, equipped with motor cars, which scoured the valley from Powerville downwards, gathering in such remnants of humanity as for any reason had neglected to attend the show. Miss Maturin said she was resolved this entertainment should be a feature unique in the history of the State.

The shutting down of the mills had caused the water in the immense dam to rise, so that now the sluices at the top added to the picturesqueness of the scene by supplying waterfalls more than sixty feet high, a splendid view of which was obtainable from the new city on the heights. Suddenly it was noticed that these waterfalls increased in power, until their roar filled the valley. At last the whole lip of the immense dam began to trickle, and an ever augmenting Niagara of waters poured over.

"Great heavens!" cried Boscombe, who was present to sneer at these activities, "there must have been a cloud-burst in the mountains!"

He shouted for the foreman.

"Where are the tenders of the dam?" he cried. "Send them to lower those sluices, and let more water out."

"Wait a moment," said Constance Maturin, who had just come out of the main telephone building. "There can be no danger, Mr. Boscombe. You always said that dam was strong enough, when I protested it wasn't."

"So it is strong enough, but not——"

"Look!" she cried, pointing over the surface of the lake. "See that wave!"

"Suffering Noah and the Flood!" exclaimed Boscombe.

As he spoke, the wave burst against the dam, and now they had Niagara in reality. There was a crash, and what seemed to be a series of explosions, then the whole structure dissolved away, and before the appalled eyes of the sight-seers, the valley town crumpled up like a pack of cards, and even the tall mills themselves, that staggered at the impact of the flood, slowly settled down, and were engulfed in the seething turmoil of maddened waters.

For a time no voice could be heard in the deafening

uproar. It was Boscombe who spoke when the waters began to subside.

"This," he cried, "is murder!"

He glared at Constance Maturin, who stood pale, silent and trembling.

"I told you she was mad," he roared at Stranleigh. "It is your money that in some devilish way has caused this catastrophe. If any lives are lost, it is rank murder!"

"It is murder," agreed Stranleigh, quietly. "Whoever is responsible for the weakness of that dam should be hanged!"

# V.—IN SEARCH OF GAME.

The warm morning gave promise of a blistering hot day, as Lord Stranleigh strolled, in his usual leisurely fashion, up Fifth Avenue. High as the thermometer already stood, the young man gave no evidence that he was in the least incommoded by the temperature. In a welter of heated, hurrying people, he produced the effect of an iceberg that had somehow drifted down into the tropics. The New York tailor entrusted with the duty of clothing him quite outdistanced his London rival, who had given Lord Stranleigh the reputation of being the best-dressed man in England. Now his lordship was dangerously near the point where he might be called the best-dressed man in New York, an achievement worthy of a Prince's ambition.

His lordship, with nothing to do, and no companionship to hope for, since everyone was at work, strolled into the splendour of the University Club and sought the comparative coolness of the smoking room, where, seating himself in that seductive invitation to laziness, a leather-covered arm chair, he began to glance over the illustrated English weeklies. He had the huge room to himself. These were business hours, and a feeling of loneliness crept over him, perhaps germinated by his sight of the illustrated papers, and accentuated by an attempted perusal of them. They were a little too stolid for a hot day, so Stranleigh turned to the lighter entertainment of the American humorous press.

Presently there entered this hall of silence the stout figure of Mr. John L. Banks, senior attorney for the Ice Trust, a man well known to Stranleigh, who had often sought his advice, with profit to both of them. The lawyer approached the lounger.

"Hello, Banks, I was just thinking of you, reflecting how delightful it must be in this weather to be connected, even remotely, with the ice supply of New York."

Mr. Banks's panama hat was in one hand, while the other drew a handkerchief across his perspiring brow.

"Well, Stranleigh, you're looking very cool and collected. Enacting the part of the idle rich, I suppose?"

"No, I'm a specimen of labour unrest."

"Perhaps I can appease that. I'm open to a deal at fair compensation for you. If you will simply parade the streets in that leisurely fashion we all admire, bearing a placard 'Pure Ice Company,' I'll guarantee you a living wage and an eight hours' day."

"Should I be required to carry about crystal blocks of the product?"

"No; you're frigid enough as it is. Besides, ice at the present moment is too scarce to be expended on even so important a matter as advertisement."

Banks wheeled forward an arm chair, and sat down opposite his lordship. A useful feature of a panama hat is its flexibility. You may roll one brim to fit the hand, and use the other as a fan, and this Banks did with the perfection of practice.

"What's the cause of the unrest, Stranleigh?"

"Thinking. That's the cause of unrest all the world over. Whenever people begin to think, there is trouble."

"I've never noticed any undue thoughtfulness in you, Stranleigh."

"That's just it. Thinking doesn't agree with me, and as you hint, I rarely indulge in it, but this is a land that somehow stimulates thought, and thought compels action. Action is all very well in moderation, but in these United States of yours it is developed into a fever, or frenzy rather, curable only by a breakdown or death."

"Do you think it's as bad as all that?"

"Yes, I do. You call it enterprise; I call it greed. I've never yet met an American who knew when he'd had enough."

"Did you ever meet an Englishman who knew that?"

"Thousands of them."

Banks laughed.

"I imagine," he said, "it's all a matter of nomenclature. You think us fast over here, and doubtless you are wrong; we think you slow over there, and doubtless we are wrong. I don't think we're greedy. No man is so lavish in his expenditure as an American, and no man more generous. A greedy man does not spend money. Our motive power is interest in the game."

"Yes; everyone has told me that, but I regard the phrase as an excuse, not as a reason."

"Look here, Stranleigh, who's been looting you? What deal have you lost? I warned you against mixing philanthropy with business, you remember."

Stranleigh threw back his head and laughed.

"There you have it. According to you a man cannot form an opinion that is uninfluenced by his pocket. As a matter of fact, I have won all along the line. I tried the game, as you call it, hoping to find it interesting, but it doesn't seem to me worth while. I pocket the stakes, and I am going home,

in no way elated at my success, any more than I should have been discouraged had I failed."

Leaning forward, Mr. Banks spoke as earnestly as the weather permitted.

"What you need, Stranleigh, is a doctor's advice, not a lawyer's. You have been just a little too long in New York, and although New Yorkers don't believe it, there are other parts of the country worthy of consideration. Your talk, instead of being an indictment of life as you find it, has been merely an exposition of your own ignorance, a sample of that British insularity which we all deplore. I hope you don't mind my stating the case as I see it?"

"Not at all," said Stranleigh. "I am delighted to hear your point of view. Go on."

"Very well; here am I plugging away during this hot weather in this hot city. Greed, says you."

"I say nothing of the kind," replied his lordship calmly. "I am merely lost in admiration of a hard-working man, enduring the rigours of toil in the most

luxurious club of which I have ever been an honorary member. Let me soften the asperities of labour by ordering something with ice in it."

The good-natured attorney accepted the invitation, and then went on—

"We have a saying regarding any futile proposition to the effect that it cuts no ice. This is the position of the Trust in which I am interested. In this hot weather we cut no ice, but we sell it. Winter is a peaceable season with us, and the harder the winter, the better we are pleased, but summer is a time of trouble. It is a period of complaints and law-suits, and our newspaper reading is mostly articles on the greed and general villainy of the Trust. So my position is literally that of what-you-may-call-him on the burning deck, whence almost all but he have fled to the lakes, to the mountains, to the sea shore. Now, I don't intend to do this always. I have set a limit of accumulated cash, and when I reach it I quit. It would be high falutin' if I said duty held me here, so I will not say it."

"A lawyer can always out-talk a layman," said Stranleigh, wearily, "and I suppose all this impinges on my ignorance."

"Certainly," said Banks. "It's a large subject, you know. But I'll leave theory, and come down to practice. As I said before, you've had too much of New York. You are known to have a little money laid by against a rainy day, so everybody wants you to invest in something, and you've got tired of it. Have you ever had a taste of ranch life out West?"

"I've never been further West than Chicago."

"Good. When you were speaking of setting a limit to financial ambition, I remembered my old friend, Stanley Armstrong, the best companion on a shooting or fishing expedition I ever encountered. It is not to be wondered at that he is an expert in sport, for often he has had to depend on rod and gun for sustenance. He was a mining engineer, and very few know the mining west as well as he does. He might have been a millionaire or a pauper, but he chose a middle course, and set his limit at a hundred thousand pounds. When land was cheap he bought a large ranch, partly plain and partly foothills, with the eternal snow mountains beyond. Now, if you take with you an assortment of guns and fishing rods, and spend a month with Stanley Armstrong, your pessimism will evaporate."

"A good idea," said Stranleigh. "If you give me a letter of introduction to Mr. Armstrong, I'll telegraph at once to be sure of accommodation."

"Telegraph?" cried the lawyer. "He'd never get your message. I don't suppose there's a telegraph office within fifty miles. You don't need a letter of introduction, but I'll write you one, and give your name merely as Stranleigh. You won't have any use for a title out there; in fact, it is a necessary part of my prescription that you should get away from yours, with the consequences it entails. Not that you're likely to come across would-be investors, or any one with designs on your wealth. As for accommodation, take a tent with you, and be independent. When I return to my office, I'll dictate full instructions for reaching the ranch."

"Is it so difficult of access as all that?"

"You might find it so. When you reach the nearest railway station, which is a couple of days' journey from the ranch, you can acquire a horse for yourself, and two or three men with pack mules for your belongings. They'll guide you to Armstrong's place."

Stranleigh found no difficulty in getting a cavalcade together at Bleachers' station, an amazingly long distance west of New York. A man finds little trouble in obtaining what he wants, if he never cavils at the price asked, and is willing to pay in advance. The party passed through a wild country, though for a time the road was reasonably good. It degenerated presently into a cart-track, however, and finally became a mere trail through the wilderness. As night fell, the tent was put up by the side of a brawling stream, through which they had forded.

Next morning the procession started early, but it was noon before it came to the clearing which Stranleigh rightly surmised was the outskirts of the ranch. The guide, who had been riding in front, reined in, and allowed

Stranleigh to come alongside.

"That," he said, pointing down the valley, "is Armstrong's ranch."

Before Stranleigh could reply, if he had intended doing so, a shot rang out from the forest, and he felt the sharp sting of a bullet in his left shoulder. The guide flung himself from the saddle with the speed of lightning, and stood with both hands upraised, his horse between himself and the unseen assailant.

"Throw up your hands!" he shouted to Stranleigh.

"Impossible!" was the quiet answer, "my left is helpless."

"Then hold up your right."

Stranleigh did so.

"Slide off them packs," roared the guide to his followers, whereupon ropes were untied on the instant, and the packs slid to the ground, while the mules shook themselves, overjoyed at this sudden freedom.

"Turn back!" cried the guide. "Keep your hand up, and they won't shoot. They want the goods."

"Then you mean to desert me?" asked Stranleigh.

"Desert nothing!" rejoined the guide, gruffly.

"We can't stand up against these fellows, whoever they are. We're no posse. To fight them is the sheriff's business. I engaged to bring you and your dunnage to Armstrong's ranch. I've delivered the goods, and now it's me for the railroad."

"I'm going to that house," said Stranleigh.

"The more fool you," replied the guide, "but I guess you'll get there safe enough, if you don't try to save the plunder."

The unladen mules, now bearing the men on their backs, had disappeared. The guide washed his hands of the whole affair, despite the fact that his hands were upraised. He whistled to his horse, and marched up the trail for a hundred yards or so, still without lowering his arms, then sprang into the saddle, fading out of sight in the direction his men had taken. Stranleigh sat on his horse, apparently the sole inhabitant of a lonely world.

"That comes of paying in advance," he muttered, looking round at his abandoned luggage. Then it struck him as ridiculous that he was enacting the part of an equestrian statue, with his arm raised aloft. Still, he remembered enough of the pernicious literature that had lent enchantment to his early days, to know that in certain circumstances the holding up of hands was a safeguard not to be neglected, so he lowered his right hand, and took in it the forefinger of his left, and thus raised both arms over his head, turning round in the saddle to face the direction from whence the shots had come. Then he released the forefinger, and allowed the left arm to drop as if it had been a semaphore. He winced under the pain that this pantomime cost him, then in a loud voice he called out:

"If there is anyone within hearing, I beg to inform him that I am wounded slightly; that I carry no firearms; that my escort has vanished, and that I'm

going to the house down yonder to have my injury looked after. Now's the opportunity for a parley, if he wants it."

He waited for some moments, but there was no response, then he gathered up the reins, and quite unmolested proceeded down the declivity until he came to the homestead.

The place appeared to be deserted, and for the first time it crossed Stranleigh's mind that perhaps the New York lawyer had sent him on this expedition as a sort of practical joke. He couldn't discover where the humour of it came in, but perhaps that might be the density with which his countrymen were universally credited. Nevertheless, he determined to follow the adventure to an end, and slipped from his horse, making an ineffectual attempt to fasten the bridle rein to a rail of the fence that surrounded the habitation. The horse began placidly to crop the grass, so he let it go at that, and advancing to the front door, knocked.

Presently the door was opened by an elderly woman of benign appearance, who nevertheless regarded him with some suspicion. She stood holding

the door, without speaking, seemingly waiting for her unexpected visitor to proclaim his mission.

"Is this the house of Stanley Armstrong?" he asked.

"Yes."

"Is he at home? I have a letter of introduction to him."

"No; he is not at home."

"Do you expect him soon?"

"He is in Chicago," answered the woman.

"In Chicago?" echoed Stranleigh. "We must have passed one another on the road. I was in Chicago myself, but it seems months ago; in fact, I can hardly believe such a place exists." The young man smiled a little grimly, but there was no relaxation of the serious expression with which the woman had greeted him.

"What was your business with my husband?"

"No business at all; rather the reverse. Pleasure, it might be called. I expected to do a little shooting and fishing. A friend in New York kindly gave me a letter of introduction to Mr. Armstrong, who, he said, would possibly accompany me."

"Won't you come inside?" was her reluctant invitation. "I don't think you told me your name."

"My name is Stranleigh, madam. I hope you will excuse my persistence, but the truth is I have been slightly hurt, and if, as I surmise, it is inconvenient to accept me as a lodger, I should be deeply indebted for permission to remain here while I put a bandage on the wound. I must return at once to Bleachers, where I suppose I can find a physician more or less competent."

"Hurt?" cried the woman in amazement, "and I've been keeping you standing there at the door. Why didn't you tell me at once?"

"Oh, I think it's no great matter, and the pain is not as keen as I might have expected. Still, I like to be on the safe side, and must return after I have rested for a few minutes."

"I'm very sorry to hear of your accident," said

Mrs. Armstrong, with concern. "Sit down in that rocking-chair until I call my daughter."

The unexpected beauty of the young woman who entered brought an expression of mild surprise to Stranleigh's face. In spite of her homely costume, a less appreciative person than his lordship must have been struck by Miss Armstrong's charm, and her air of intelligent refinement.

"This is Mr. Stranleigh, who has met with an accident," said Mrs. Armstrong to her daughter.

"Merely a trifle," Stranleigh hastened to say, "but I find I cannot raise my left arm."

"Is it broken?" asked the girl, with some anxiety.

"I don't think so; I fancy the trouble is in the shoulder. A rifle bullet has passed through it."

"A rifle bullet?" echoed the girl, in a voice of alarm. "How did that happen? But—never mind telling me now. The main thing is to attend to the wound. Let me help you off with your coat."

Stranleigh stood up.

"No exertion, please," commanded the girl. "Bring some warm water and a sponge," she continued, turning to her mother.

She removed Stranleigh's coat with a dexterity that aroused his admiration. The elder woman returned with dressings and sponge, which she placed on a chair. Stranleigh's white shirt was stained with blood, and to this

Miss Armstrong applied the warm water.

"I must sacrifice your linen," she said calmly. "Please sit down again."

In a few moments his shoulder was bare; not the shoulder of an athlete, but nevertheless of a young man in perfect health. The girl's soft fingers pressed it gently.

"I shall have to hurt you a little," she said.

Stranleigh smiled.

"It is all for my good, as they say to little boys before whipping them."

The girl smiled back at him.

"Yes; but I cannot add the complementary fiction that it hurts me more than it does you. There! Did you feel that?"

"Not more than usual."

"There are no bones broken, which is a good thing. After all, it is a simple case, Mr. Stranleigh. You must remain quiet for a few days, and allow me to put this arm in a sling. I ought to send you off to bed, but if you promise not to exert yourself, you may sit out on the verandah where it is cool, and where the view may interest you."

"You are very kind, Miss Armstrong, but I cannot stay. I must return to Bleachers."

"I shall not allow you to go back," she said with decision.

Stranleigh laughed.

"In a long and comparatively useless life I have never contradicted a lady, but on this occasion I must insist on having my own way."

"I quite understand your reason, Mr. Stranleigh, though it is very uncomplimentary to me. It is simply an instance of man's distrust of a woman when it comes to serious work. Like most men, you would be content to accept me as a nurse, but not as a physician. There are two doctors in

Bleachers, and you are anxious to get under the care of one of them. No— please don't trouble to deny it. You are not to blame. You are merely a victim of the universal conceit of man."

"Ah, it is you who are not complimentary now! You must think me a very commonplace individual."

She had thrown the coat over his shoulders, after having washed and dressed the wound. The bullet had been considerate enough to pass right through, making all probing unnecessary. With a safety-pin she attached his shirt sleeve to his shirt front.

"That will do," she said, "until I prepare a regular sling. And now come out to the verandah. No; don't carry the chair. There are several on the platform. Don't try to be polite, and remember I have already ordered you to avoid exertion."

He followed her to the broad piazza, and sat down, drawing a deep breath of admiration. Immediately in front ran a broad, clear stream of water; swift, deep, transparent.

"An ideal trout stream," he said to himself.

A wide vista of rolling green fields stretched away to a range of foothills, overtopped in the far distance by snow mountains.

"By Jove!" he cried. "This is splendid. I have seen nothing like it out of Switzerland."

"Talking of Switzerland," said Miss Armstrong, seating herself opposite him, "have you ever been at Thun?"

"Oh, yes."

"You stopped at the Thunerhof, I suppose?"

"I don't remember what it was called, but it was the largest hotel in the place, I believe."

"That would be the Thunerhof," she said. "I went to a much more modest inn, the Falken, and the stream that runs in front of it reminded me of this, and made me quite lonesome for the ranch. Of course, you had the river opposite you at the Thunerhof, but there the river is half a dozen times as wide as the branch that runs past the Falken. I used to sit out on the terrace watching that stream, murmuring to its accompaniment 'Home, sweet Home.'"

"You are by way of being a traveller, then?"

"Not a traveller, Mr. Stranleigh," said the girl, laughing a little, "but a dabbler. I took dabs of travel, like my little visit to Thun. For more than a year I lived in Lausanne, studying my profession, and during that time I made brief excursions here and there."

"Your profession," asked Stranleigh, with evident astonishment.

"Yes; can't you guess what it is, and why I am relating this bit of personal history on such very short acquaintance?"

The girl's smile was beautiful.

"Don't you know Europe?" she added.

"I ought to; I'm a native."

"Then you are aware that Lausanne is a centre of medical teaching and medical practice. I am a doctor, Mr. Stranleigh. Had your wound been really serious, which it is not, and you had come under the care of either physician in Bleachers, he would have sent for me, if he knew I were at home."

"What you have said interests me very much, Miss Armstrong, or should I say Doctor Armstrong?"

"I will answer to either designation, Mr. Stranleigh, but I should qualify the latter by adding that I am not a practising physician. 'Professor,' perhaps, would be the more accurate title. I am a member of the faculty in an eastern college of medicine, but by and by I hope to give up teaching, and devote myself entirely to research work. It is my ambition to become the American Madame Curie."

"A laudable ambition, Professor, and I hope you will succeed. Do you mind if I tell you how completely wrong you are in your diagnosis of the subject now before you?"

"In my surgical diagnosis I am not wrong. Your wound will be cured in a very few days."

"Oh, I am not impugning your medical skill. I knew the moment you spoke about your work that you were an expert. It is your diagnosis of me that is all astray. I have no such disbelief in the capacity of woman as you credit me with. I have no desire to place myself under the ministrations of either of those doctors in Bleachers. My desire for the metropolitan delights of that scattered town is of the most commonplace nature. I must buy for myself an outfit of clothes. I possess nothing in the way of raiment except what I am wearing, and part of that you've cut up with your scissors."

"Surely you never came all this distance without being well provided in that respect?"

"No; I had ample supplies, and I brought them with me safely to a point within sight of this house. In fact, I came hither like a sheik of the desert, at the head of a caravan, only the animals were mules instead of camels. All went well until we came to the edge of the forest, but the moment I emerged a shot rang out, and it seemed to me I was stung by a gigantic bee, as invisible as the shooter. The guide said there was a band of robbers intent on plunder, and he and the escort acted as escorts usually do in such circumstances. They unloaded the mules with most admirable celerity, and then made off much faster than they came. I never knew a body of men so unanimous in action. They would make a splendid board of directors in a commercial company that wished to get its work accomplished without undue discussion."

The girl had risen to her feet.

"And your baggage?" she asked.

"I suppose it is in the hands of the brigands by this time. I left it scattered along the trail."

"But, Mr. Stranleigh, what you say is incredible. There are no brigands, thieves or road agents in this district."

"The wound that you dressed so skilfully is my witness, and a witness whose testimony cannot be impugned on cross-examination."

"There is a mistake somewhere. Why, just think of it; the most energetic bandit would starve in this locality! There is no traffic. If your belongings were scattered along the trail, they are there yet."

"Then why shoot the belonger of those belongings?"

"That's just what I must discover. Excuse me for a moment."

She passed through the house, and the young man heard a shrill whistle blown, which was answered by a call some distance away. The girl returned, and sat down again, her brow perplexed, and presently there came on to the platform a stalwart, good-natured looking man, dressed in what Stranleigh took to be a cowboy costume; at least, it was the kind of apparel he had read about in books of the Wild West. His head was covered with a broad-brimmed slouch hat, which he swept off in deference to the lady.

"Jim," she said, "did you hear any shooting out by the Bleachers trail about an hour ago?"

"No, Ma'am; I can't say that I did, except a rifle I shot off."

"That you shot off! What were you shooting at?"

"Well," said Jim, with a humorous chuckle, "I guess perhaps it was this gentleman."

"Why did you wish to murder me?" asked Stranleigh, with pardonable concern.

"Murder you, sir? Why, I didn't try to murder you. I could have winged you a dozen times while you were riding down to the house, if I'd wanted to. Where were you hit?"

"In the left shoulder."

"Then that's all right. That's what I aimed to do. I just set out to nip you, and scare you back where you came from."

"But why?" insisted the perplexed Stranleigh.

"You came along with a posse behind you, and I thought you were the sheriff, but I wouldn't kill even a sheriff unless I had to. I'm the peaceablest man on earth, as Miss Armstrong there will tell you."

"If that's your idea of peace," said Stranleigh, puzzled, "I hope next time I'll fall among warlike people."

Jim grinned. It was Miss Armstrong who spoke, and, it seemed to Stranleigh, with unexpected mildness, considering she knew so much of the Eastern States and Europe.

"I understand," she said, "but next time, Jim, it will be as well merely to fire the gun, without hitting anybody."

"Oh," explained Jim, in an off-hand manner, "our folk don't pay any attention to the like of that. You've got to show them you mean business. If this gentleman had come on, the next shot would have hit him where it would hurt, but seeing he was peaceable minded, he was safe as in a church."

"Is the baggage where he left it?"

"Certainly, Ma'am; do you wish it brought here?"

"Yes; I do."

"All right, Ma'am; I'll see to that. It's all a little mistake, sir," he said amiably, as he turned to Stranleigh. "Accidents will happen in the best regulated family, as the saying goes," and with a flourish of the hat he departed.

Miss Armstrong rose as if to leave the verandah. As she did so Stranleigh said in a tone of mild reproach:

"I confess I am puzzled."

"So am I," replied the girl, brightly. "I'm puzzled to know what I can offer you in the way of books. Our stock is rather limited."

"I don't want to read, Miss Armstrong, but I do want to know why there is such a prejudice here against a sheriff. In the land I came from a sheriff is not only regarded with great respect, but even with veneration. He rides about in a gilded coach, and wears magnificent robes, decorated with gold lace. I believe that he develops ultimately into a Lord Mayor, just as a grub, if one may call so glorious a personage as a sheriff a grub, ultimately becomes a butterfly. We'd never think of shooting a sheriff. Why, then, do you pot at sheriffs, and hit innocent people, out here?"

The girl laughed.

"I saw the Lord Mayor of London once in his carriage, and behind it were two most magnificent persons. Were they sheriffs?"

"Oh, dear no; they were merely flunkeys."

"Our sheriffs are elected persons, drawn from the politician class, and if you know America, you will understand what that means. Among the various duties of a sheriff is that of seizing property and selling it, if the owner of that property hasn't paid his debts."

"They act as bailiffs, then?"

"Very likely; I am not acquainted with legal procedure. But I must go, Mr. Stranleigh, for whatever the position of a sheriff may be, mine is that of

assistant to my mother, who is just now preparing the dinner, a meal that, further East, is called lunch. And now, what would you prefer to read? The latest magazine or a pharmaceutical journal?"

"Thank you, Miss Armstrong; I prefer gazing at the scenery to either of them."

"Then good-bye until dinner time," whereupon she disappeared into the house.

The meal proved unexpectedly good. There was about it an enticing freshness, and a variety that was surprising when the distance from the house to the nearest market was considered. Stranleigh could not remember any repast he had enjoyed so much, although he suspected that horseback exercise in the keen air had helped his appreciation of it. When he mentioned his gratification at so satisfactory a menu, the girl smiled.

"Plain living and lofty thought is our motto on the ranch," she said.

"This is anything but plain living," he replied, "and I consider myself no mean judge in such matters. How far away is your market town?"

"Oh, a market is merely one of those effete contrivances of civilisation. What you buy in a market has been handled and re-handled, and artificially made to look what it is not. The basis of our provender is the farm. All round us here is what economists call, in a double sense of the term, raw material. Farm house fare is often what it should not be because art belongs to the city while nature belongs to the farm. To produce a good result, the two must be united. We were speaking just now of Thun. If, leaving that town, you proceed along the left hand road by the lake, you will arrive at a large institution which is devoted entirely to the art of cookery. The more I progressed with my studies at Lausanne, the more I realised that the basis of health is good food, properly prepared. So I interrupted my medical studies for a time, entered that establishment, and learned to cook."

"Miss Armstrong, you are the most efficient individual I ever met."

"You are very complimentary, Mr. Stranleigh, because, like the various meals you have enjoyed in different parts of the world, you must have met a great many people. To enhance myself further in your eyes, I may add that I have brought another much-needed accomplishment to the farm. I am an expert accountant, and can manage business affairs in a way that would startle you, and regarding this statement of mine, I should like to ask you, hoping you won't think I am impertinent, are you a rich man?"

Stranleigh was indeed startled—she had succeeded in that—and he hesitated before he answered—

"I am considered reasonably well off."

"I am very glad to hear it, for it has been the custom of my father, who is not a good business man, to charge boarders two or three dollars a week when they come with their guns and fishing tackle. Now, we are in a unique position. We have the advantage of being free from competition. The hotels of New York are as thick as blackberries. They meet competition in its fiercest form, yet the prices they charge are much more per day than we charge for a month. I am determined that our prices shall be equal to New York prices, but I think it is only fair to let any customer know the fact before he is called upon to pay his bill."

"A very excellent arrangement," said Stranleigh, heartily, "and in my case there will be an additional account for medical services. Will that be on the basis of professional charges in London, New York, Vienna, Berlin, or Lausanne?"

"Not on the basis of Lausanne, certainly, for there an excellent doctor is contented with a fee of five francs, so if you don't object, I'll convert francs into dollars."

"My admiration for your business capacity is waning, Miss Armstrong. If this is to be an international matter, why choose your own country instead of mine? Transpose your francs into pounds, Professor. There are five francs in a dollar, but five dollars in a pound sterling. Let me recommend to you my own currency."

"A very good idea, Mr. Stranleigh," rejoined Miss Armstrong, promptly. "I shall at once take it into consideration, but I hope you won't be shocked when the final round-up arrives."

"I shall have no excuse for astonishment, being so honestly forewarned, and now that we are conversing so internationally, I'd like to carry it a little further. In Italy they call an accident a 'disgrazia,' and when you read in an Italian paper that a man is 'disgraced,' you realise that he has met with an accident. Then the account ends by saying that the patient is guaranteed curable in two days, or a week, or a month, as the case may be. How long, then, doctor, must I rest under this 'disgrace'?"

"I should say a week, but that's merely an off-hand guess, as I suppose is the case with the estimate of an Italian physician."

"I hope your orders won't be too strict. By the way, has my luggage arrived?"

"It is all in the large room upstairs, but if you have any designs upon it, you are disobeying orders."

"I must get at a portmanteau that is in one of the bundles."

"I will fetch what you want, so don't worry about that, but come and sit on the verandah once more."

Stranleigh protested, and finally a compromise was arrived at. Miss Armstrong would whistle for Jim, and he would do the unpacking. She saw a shade of distrust pass over Stranleigh's face, and she reassured him that Jim was the most honest and harmless man in the world, except, perhaps, where sheriffs were concerned.

"Now," she continued, when he had seated himself, "you have talked enough for one day, so you must keep quiet for the rest of the afternoon. I will do the talking, giving you an explanation of our brigandish conduct."

"I shall be an interested listener," said Stranleigh, resignedly. "But permit me, before silence falls, to ask what you may regard an impertinent question. Do you smoke?"

"Goodness, no!" she replied, with widely opened eyes.

"Many ladies do, you know, and I thought you might have acquired the habit during your travels abroad. In that case, I should have been delighted to offer you some excellent cigarettes from my portmanteau."

Jumping up, the girl laughed brightly.

"Poor man! I understand at last. You shall have the cigarettes in less than five minutes. Give me your keys, please."

"That particular piece of luggage is not locked. I am so sorry to trouble you, but after such a memorable dinner——"

"Yes, yes; I know, I know!" she cried, as she vanished.

"Interesting girl, that," murmured Stranleigh to himself, "and unusually accomplished."

He listened for a whistle, but the first break in the silence was the coming of Miss Armstrong, holding a box of cigars in one hand and a packet of cigarettes in the other.

"Then you didn't call for help, after all," said Stranleigh, a shade of reproach in his tone.

"Oh, it was quite easy. By punching the bundles I guessed what they contained, and soon found where the portmanteau was concealed. Now, light up," she continued, "lean back, and smoke. I'll do the talking. My father, as I've told you, is a very poor business man, and that is why I endeavoured to acquire some knowledge of affairs. He is generous and sympathetic, believing no evil of anyone, consequently he is often imposed upon to his financial disadvantage. Our position as father and daughter is the reverse of what is usual in such relationships. I attempt to guide him in the way he should go, and as a general thing he accepts my advice and acts upon it, but on the occasion of which I speak, I was at work in New York, and knew nothing of the disastrous contract into which he had entered, until it was too late.

"I always come West and spend the vacation on the ranch, and this time brought with me all the money I had saved, but it proved insufficient to cope with the situation. In his early days my father was a mining engineer. He was successful, and might have been a very rich man to-day if—— But that 'if' always intervened. Nevertheless, he accumulated money, and bought this ranch, determined to retire.

"The lower part of the ranch is good grazing ground, but the upper or western part is rocky, rising to the foothills. My father was not a success as a rancher, partly because we are too far from the markets, and partly because he chose as cowboys men who did not understand their business. I told you that my father is a sympathetic man. No one ever appealed to him in vain. He has always been very popular, but it seems to me that his friends are always poorer than himself. Thus it came about that miners who knew him, and were out of work, applied for something to do, and he engaged them as cowboys, until

113

he had half a dozen on his pay roll, and thus began the gradual loss of his money. These men were excellent as miners, but useless as cowboys, and there was no one here to teach them their duties, my father being himself a miner. It seemed, then, a dispensation of Providence that as he rambled over the western part of his property he struck signs of silver. He was not mistaken in his prospecting. He and the cowboys took hilariously to their old trade, and worked away at the rocks until all his money was gone."

"Did they find any real silver?" asked Stranleigh, interested.

"Oh yes, plenty of it," answered the girl. "It is evident they have opened a very rich mine."

"Then where is the difficulty?"

"The difficulty is the want of machinery, which there is no capital to purchase. My father tried to get that capital in this district, but there is very little ready money to be obtained out here. He enlisted the interest of Mr. Ricketts, a lawyer in Bleachers, and reputed the only rich man in the town. Ricketts came to the ranch with a mining engineer, and they examined the opening. Seemingly they were not impressed with the contents, and Ricketts advised my father to go East and form a company.

"My father explained his financial situation, and Ricketts, with apparent generosity, offered to lend him five thousand dollars on his note, to be paid on demand, with the ranch as security. Thus my father put himself entirely in the other's power.

Ricketts gave him the address of a lawyer in Chicago, who, he said, would be of assistance to him. The latest word we received from my father is that this lawyer, in one way or another, has got hold of all his money. Father telegraphed to Ricketts for help, which was refused. So he left Chicago on foot, determined to walk home, since he had not even money enough left to pay his fare home. Where he is at present, we have no idea, except that he is making for this ranch.

"Ricketts at once took action to sell the ranch. Apparently he is quite within his legal rights, but there are formalities to be gone through, and one

114

of these is the arrival of the sheriff to seize the property. That arrival the men, headed by Jim, are determined to prevent, and now, perhaps, you understand why you rode into danger when you came from Bleachers this morning.

"When I learnt of my father's predicament, I went out to Bleachers to see Mr. Ricketts, offering him what money I had brought from New York if he would hold his hand for a year. He refused, and from his conversation I realised he was determined to secure the ranch for himself, and I believe the whole transaction is a plot toward that end."

"Then the mine must be a valuable one?"

"I am sure it is; indeed, my father could make no mistake in that matter."

"Well, the position seems very simple after all. What you need, Miss Armstrong, is a change of creditors. You want a creditor who is not in a hurry for his money. In other words, if you could transfer that debt, you would be out of immediate danger. Would you allow me to go into Bleachers to-morrow, and see Mr. Ricketts?"

"Most decidedly not!"

"How much money did you bring with you from New York?"

"Two thousand dollars."

"I brought just twice that amount, so I think the affair may be arranged, and you can go to Ricketts to-morrow, and take up the note. I think perhaps you had better have five thousand five hundred dollars with you, as there will certainly be some interest and expenses to pay, for if the case is as you state it, Ricketts will be reluctant to part with the document. Is there another lawyer in Bleachers?"

"Yes."

"Well, get him to accompany you, and make formal tender of the money."

The girl had reddened while he was speaking, and now she said, in tones of distress—

"I fear you completely misunderstood my object in telling you of my difficulties. My object was not to borrow money, but to explain why Jim Dean shot at you."

"Oh, I understand perfectly why you spoke as frankly as you did, and I am very much obliged to you for doing so, but you must have no diffidence in accepting the money. It is purely a business transaction, and, as you say, you are a business woman. Therefore, as a matter of business, it would be folly to reject an offer that is to our mutual advantage. The security is ample."

"That is true, Mr. Stranleigh, but, you see, I have no power, no authority, to give this ranch as security; it belongs to my father."

"True; but you are not nearly so competent a business woman as you would have me believe. You will receive from Ricketts your father's promissory note. That you will hand to me, then I shall be your debtor for two thousand dollars. Those two thousand dollars I shall pay as soon as I get some money from New York, and your father will become my debtor for five thousand dollars. All perfectly simple, you see. In the first instance I trust you for three thousand dollars, and in the second instance you trust me for two thousand dollars. After I have paid you the two thousand dollars, I hold the note, and can sell you up whenever I please. I give you my word I won't do that, though even if I did you would be no worse off than you are now."

"Very well, Mr. Stranleigh; I will take the money."

It was several days later when Miss Armstrong returned from Bleachers. Her first interest was to satisfy herself of the patient's progress. He had been getting on well.

"You are an admirable physician, Miss Armstrong," he said. "Now let me know whether you are equally capable as a financier."

"I have failed completely," she answered, dejectedly. "Mr. Ricketts has refused the money."

"Did you take the other lawyer with you?"

"Yes."

"What did he say?"

"He said Ricketts had no right to refuse, but a different question has arisen. The guide who accompanied you to the ranch brought back news of the shooting. Ricketts guessed at once why you were shot at, and the sheriff has signed an affidavit, or some such instrument, to show that his life, and his men's lives, are in danger if they go to seize the property, so this complication has been overcome by some order from the legislature, and the personal seizure is waived. The sale is announced to take place in Bleachers two weeks from to-day. Mr. Timmins—that is the other lawyer—fears that Ricketts is within his rights in refusing the money at this stage."

"This is all very interesting, Miss Armstrong, but we have a fortnight to turn round in."

"Yes; that is so."

"I am delighted, for now I shall have the pleasure of trying a fall with the estimable Mr. Ricketts."

# VI.—THE BUNK HOUSE PRISONER.

As the wound in his shoulder healed, Stranleigh began to enjoy himself on the ranch. He was experiencing a life entirely new to him, and being always a lover of waving woods and rushing waters, even in the tamed state which England presents, he keenly appreciated these natural beauties in the wilderness, where so-called human improvements had not interfered with them. Without attempting to indulge in the sport for which he had come, he wandered about the ranch a good deal, studying its features, and at the same time developing an appetite that did justice to the excellent meals prepared for him. He visited Jim Dean, who had shot him, and tried to scrape acquaintance with his five aiders and abettors in that drastic act, but they met his advances with suspicion, naturally regarding him as a tenderfoot, nor were they satisfied that his long residence among them was as friendly as he evidently wished it to appear.

The men resided in a huge bunk house, which consisted of one room only, with a shack outside where the cooking was done. In the large room were a dozen bunks; half of them in a very dishevelled state, giving sleeping accommodation for the company, while the other half were ready in case of an accession of help, should the mine prosper.

The cabin was as securely built as a fortress, of the rugged stone which had been blasted from the rocks in opening the mine. The mine itself was situated about five hundred yards to the south of this edifice, but instead of being dug downwards, as Stranleigh expected, it extended westward on the level toward the heart of the mountain, so that a rudely built truck could carry out the débris, and dump it down the steep hill. To his æsthetic fancy this seemed a pity, because a short distance south from the opening of the mine, the river formed a cascade descending a hundred feet or more; a cascade of entrancing beauty, whose loveliness would be more or less destroyed as the mining operations progressed.

The rising sun illuminated the tunnel to its final wall, and Stranleigh found no difficulty in exploring it to the remotest corner. He passed the abandoned truck partly turned over beside an assortment of picks, shovels, hand-drills and the like. To his unpractised eye there was no sign of silver on walls, floor or ceiling. At the extreme end was piled up a quantity of what appeared to be huge cartridges.

Before entering the cavern he had noticed three or four of the miners standing in front of the bunk house, evidently watching him, but he paid no attention to them, and while he was inside, the roar of the cataract prevented him from hearing approaching footsteps. As he came out to the lip of the mine, he found Jim and three others waiting for him. Each had a rifle on his shoulder.

"Inspecting the property?" said Jim, casually.

"Yes," replied Stranleigh.

"What do you think of it?"

"My opinion would be of very little value. I know nothing of mining."

"The deuce you don't!" said Jim. "What are you doing with that lump of rock in your hand?"

"Oh, that," said Stranleigh, "I happened to pick up. I wanted to examine it in clear daylight. Is there silver in it?"

"How should I know?" replied Jim, gruffly. "I'm not a mining engineer. I only take a hand at the drill or the pick, as the case may be. But when you throw that back where you got it, throw it carefully, and not too far."

"I don't intend to throw it," said Stranleigh. "I'm going to take it down to the house."

"Oh, you think you're not going to throw it, but you are. We've just come up to explain that to you."

"I see. If it is compulsory, why shouldn't I throw it as far as I can?"

"Because," explained Jim, politely, "there's a lot of dynamite stored in the end of that hole, and dynamite isn't a thing to fool with, you know."

Stranleigh laughed.

"I rather fancy you're right, though I know as little about dynamite as I do about mines. But to be sure of being on the right side, I will leave the tossing of the stone to you. Here it is," whereupon he handed the lump of rock to Jim, who flung it carelessly into the mine again, but did not join in his visitor's hilarity.

"You seem to regard me as a dangerous person?"

"Oh, not at all, but we do love a man that attends to his own business. We understood that you came here for shooting and fishing."

"So I did, but other people were out shooting before I got a chance. A man who's had a bullet through his shoulder neither hunts nor fishes."

"That's so," admitted Jim, with the suavity of one who recognises a reasonable statement, "but now that you are better, what do you come nosing round the mine for? Why don't you go on with your shooting and your fishing?"

"Because Mr. Armstrong was to be my guide, and he, I regret to say, has not yet returned home. As he is tramping from Chicago to the ranch, no one knows when he will put in an appearance."

"Well, Mr. Stranleigh, we are plain, ordinary backwoods folks, that have no reason for loving or trusting people who come from the city, as you do. You say that shooting is your game. Now, we can do a bit of shooting ourselves, and I tell you plainly that if any stranger was found prowling around here, he'd have got a bullet in a more vital spot than you did. Do you understand me?"

"Your meaning, sir, is perfectly plain. What do you want me to do? Go away from here before Mr. Armstrong returns?"

"No; we don't say that, but we draw an imaginary line, such as they tell me the equator is, past this end of the farm house, and we ask you not to cross it westward. There's all the fishing you want down stream, but there's none up here by the waterfall, neither is there any game to shoot, so you see we're proposing no hardship if your intentions are what you say they are."

"Sir, you speak so beautifully that I must address you less familiarly than I am doing. My own name is Ned, but few take the liberty of calling me by that title. I don't know that I should like it if they did. You are already aware, perhaps, that I answer to the name of Stranleigh. May I enquire what your name is?"

"I'm James Dean."

"Ah, the Dean of the Faculty? You are leader of this band of brothers?"

"In a manner of speaking, yes."

"Are they unanimous in restricting my liberty on this ranch?"

"You bet!"

"You've no right to do such a thing, and besides, it is inhospitable. I came to this ranch properly accredited, with a letter of introduction to Mr. Armstrong. He happens to be away; if he had been here, and I had seen that my visit was unwelcome to him, I should instantly have taken my leave, but I refuse to have my liberty restricted by Mr. Armstrong's hired men."

"That's exactly where you're wrong, Mr. Stranleigh. In the first place, we're not hired men; we're Mr. Armstrong's partners, and we don't restrict your liberty on the ranch."

"A partner contributes his share to the expenses of the combination. I understand Mr. Armstrong bears the burden alone."

"We contribute our labour, which is cash in another form, therefore whether Mr. Armstrong is here, or whether he is away, we mean to defend our property. So when you cross the imaginary line I spoke of, you are trespassing, and no jury will convict a man who shoots a trespasser after he has been fully warned, as we warn you."

"Well, Mr. Dean, I admit that you have right on your side, even if there is not much wisdom at the back of it. There is just one more thing I should like to know. Why do you treat me as an enemy?"

"As a possible enemy," corrected Dean.

"As a possible enemy, then?"

"Because we don't like your actions, and we don't think much of you. You're a city man, and we don't trust any such."

"But Mr. Banks, who gave me the letter to your chief, is not only a city man, but a lawyer. He has been here, and spoke highly of his reception."

"That was before the mine was opened, and as for being a lawyer, we hate 'em, of course, but they're like rattlesnakes. In some seasons of the year they are harmless. The opening of the silver mine opened the rattlesnake season, and that's why this lawyer snake in Bleachers is trying to cheat Armstrong out of his ranch. He came over here with a mining engineer and learnt the whole value of the ground. How do we know you're not a mining engineer?"

"I regret to say I'm nothing so useful."

"And didn't you send Miss Armstrong into Bleachers to see that villain Ricketts? What connection have you with him?"

"None at all, Mr. Dean. I never saw Ricketts in my life, and never heard of him before the day you mistook me for the sheriff."

Dean glanced at his companions, who had taken no part in the colloquy, but who listened with an interest at once critical and suspicious. It was evident that their distrust could not be dissipated, or even mitigated, by strenuous talk, and for a moment Stranleigh was tempted to tell them that he had lent three thousand dollars to Miss Armstrong, in the hope that this money, added to her own, would gain some sort of concession from the obdurate lawyer. But he remembered that the girl was in constant communication with these men, and if she had not already informed them of his futile assistance, it was because she did not want them to know.

Dean pondered for a few moments before he spoke. He seemed to have gathered in the purport of his men's thoughts without the necessity for words. At last he said:

"May I take it you agree hereafter to attend to your own business?"

Stranleigh laughed.

"There would be no use in my making that promise, for I have never in my life attended to my own business. My business affairs are all looked after by men who are experts. They live in New York and in London, and although I make a decision now and then, I do that as seldom as possible. It fatigues me."

"So you are a loafer?"

"That's it exactly, Mr. Dean, and I freely give you my promise not to loaf about your silver mine."

"Are you so rich as all that?"

"You are not consistent, Mr. Dean. How can you ask me to attend to my business if you do not attend to yours? Whether I am rich or poor is none of your affair?"

"Quite true," agreed Jim, nonchalantly, "we will let it go at that."

Stranleigh, with a smile, bowed courteously to the group.

"I wish you a very good day," he said, and turning, strolled down to the house at a leisurely gait, quite in keeping with his self-declared character of loafer. His back offered an excellent target, but no man raised his rifle, and Stranleigh never looked over his shoulder, never hurried a step, but walked as one very sure of himself, and in no fear of attack.

"Stuck up cuss," said Jim to his comrades. "I'd like to take that chap down a peg. Let's get back to the bunk house and talk it over," so they, too, left the pit mouth, and returned to their cabin.

When the Earl of Stranleigh entered the house, he was accosted by Miss Armstrong, on whose fair face were traces of deep anxiety, which his lordship thought were easily accounted for by the fact that the homestead was to be sold in less than a fortnight.

"I have been anxious to see you, Mr. Stranleigh," she said. "Won't you come out on the verandah where we can talk?"

"With great pleasure, Miss Armstrong."

When they were seated, she continued—

"You have been talking with the men?"

"Yes; we had a little chat together."

"Did they tell you anything of their intentions?"

"No; except in so far as they were determined not to let me examine the mine."

"Ah; they have distrusted you from the first. Did you insist on visiting it?"

"I have visited it."

"Without asking one of them to accompany you?"

"I regarded them as hired men. They say they are your father's partners."

"So they are."

"Ah, well, if that is really the case, I must apologise to them. I thought when you ordered Dean to bring in my luggage, and he obeyed with such docility, that he was your servant. I intended to offer him some money for that service, but I suppose I must not."

"Certainly not. Those men will do anything for a friend, but nothing for one of whom they are suspicious. Their distrust, once aroused, is not easily removed. I am sure, however, you were tactful with them."

Stranleigh smiled ruefully.

"I am not so certain of that myself. I fear I failed in diplomacy."

124

"I do wish my father were here," she said, ignoring his last remark. "I am very much worried about the men."

"What do they know of your trouble with that man Ricketts?"

"They know all about it, and they now threaten to march into Bleachers in a body and, as we say, shoot up the town, including Ricketts, of course."

"When do they intend to do this?"

"On the day of the auction sale."

"Don't they understand that that would be futile?"

"It would cause an infinite amount of harm, and ultimately might result in their being wiped out themselves. Not that Bleachers could do such a thing, but because they would be pitting themselves against the United States Government, which is a mere name to those men, carrying no authority. All their lives have been spent in camps, where the only law is that of the mob. I have tried my best to influence them, but they regard me merely as a woman, and a woman from the East at that, who has no knowledge of practical affairs, so I have every reason for wishing my father were here."

"I should not trouble about that if I were you, Miss Armstrong. If they intended to carry out their resolution to-morrow, or next day, there might be reason for anxiety, but we have luckily plenty of time in which to act. The one immediate thing is to find your father. I'll undertake that task. He's travelling somewhere between here and Chicago, on foot. May I see the latest letter he wrote you?"

The girl brought it to him.

"Might I take this with me?"

"Yes. What do you intend to do?"

Stranleigh smiled.

"Oh, I never do anything. As I was telling your men, who wished me to mind my own business, I always have people to do that for me. I am a

125

great believer in the expert. Now, America seems to be the land of experts, and the man to deal with this case is Detective Burns, of New York. I shall get into touch with him by telegraph, and if he cannot attend to the matter himself, he will select the best substitute that is to be had, and as Burns and his men invariably track down anyone they want, even though he be seeking to elude them, it will be an easy task to find your father, who is tramping the straightest possible line between Chicago and this ranch. I shall give instructions for two or three hundred dollars to be handed to Mr. Armstrong, with directions to take the next train to Bleachers, as we need his presence here. I shall do nothing but send a telegram, and Mr. Burns will do the rest. Now, if you will assist me by ordering out my horse, I shall be ready to start within ten minutes. I'd order the horse myself, but I don't think your men would obey me."

In less than the time mentioned, Jim brought the horse to the door. All his men were standing in front of their cabin, looking on. They quite naturally

believed that their guest had taken alarm, and was making off to some district where he would be in less danger. When his lordship came downstairs and out to the front, Jim was overcome with astonishment. His lordship was accoutred amazingly, after the fashion of the English horseman. He had dressed himself in a riding costume such as an English gentleman would wear at home. Jim and his comrades had never seen such an outfit before, and they greeted his appearance with a roar of laughter.

Stranleigh sprang into his saddle with the agility of a cowboy, and smiling good-humouredly at his audience, raised his hat to them, and rode off.

As Stranleigh's horse entered the forest the young man began to ponder over the problem that confronted him. When the unfortunate Armstrong borrowed money from Ricketts, he had, of course, fully explained the situation. The lender had examined the property in company with a mining engineer, and this expert doubtless took away with him some ore to analyse at his leisure. Ricketts, being in possession of the engineer's estimate of the

126

pit's value, had probably formed a syndicate, or perhaps made arrangements with other capitalists, to see him through with the speculation. Undoubtedly Ricketts expected no competition when the estate was put up at auction, but if he was a shrewd man, as was almost certain to be the case, events had occurred which might stimulate thought regarding his position.

Miss Armstrong had ridden out to Bleachers, having in her possession five thousand dollars, the face value of the notes. Ricketts would wonder how she had obtained the money. She possessed only two thousand dollars on her first visit, as he knew from the fact that she had offered it to him for refraining from action until her father returned. Who could have given her the extra three thousand? Whoever had done so must have known the girl could offer no security for its repayment. He was therefore a rich man, or he could not afford to throw away a sum so considerable.

It was likely that such reflections as these had put Ricketts on the alert, and the sudden advent in Bleachers of a smartly costumed stranger, a stranger coming from the direction of the ranch, would almost certainly convince Ricketts that here was his opponent. In Bleachers, too, each inhabitant very probably knew every one else's business. That he could elude the astute Ricketts was therefore exceedingly doubtful, and Stranleigh already knew enough about the lawlessness of the district to believe that he might ride into considerable danger. In that sparsely-settled country, people were not too scrupulous in their methods of getting rid of an enemy.

He wondered how far down the line the next town was, for he was certain that any telegraphing he did from Bleachers would speedily be known to Ricketts. Would it be possible to deflect his course, and make for the next station eastwards? He possessed no map of the State, however, and there was little chance of meeting anyone, so there seemed nothing for it but to push on to Bleachers.

At this point his meditations were interrupted by the dimly heard sound of horses' hoofs on the trail behind him. He pulled up and listened. Pausing for a few minutes, he heard nothing more, and so went on again, with an uneasy feeling of being followed. He determined not to camp out when night overtook him, but to hurry on until he reached Bleachers. He had made a two days' journey to reach the ranch, but that was because the laden mules were slow. Before dark he would be on the high road, and after that he could not lose his way. After all, perhaps it was better to reach Bleachers at night, and trust to rousing up the people in the one tavern of the place.

It was after midnight when his task was accomplished, and having seen to the accommodation of a very tired and hungry horse, Stranleigh threw himself down, dressed as he was, upon the bed to which he was shown by a sleepy ostler. He had had quite enough equestrian exercise for one day.

Ten o'clock had struck next morning before he woke, and went down to breakfast. His mind had become clarified, and he knew now exactly what he meant to do. To avoid the cognizance of Ricketts was impossible; of that he was certain. His first object, then, was to draw a red herring across the trail, so he enquired from the hotel-keeper the whereabouts of Ricketts' office, and was directed to it.

He crossed the street and ascended a stair. Ricketts kept neither clerk nor office boy, so Stranleigh knocked at the door, was gruffly commanded to enter, and obeyed.

Silas A. Ricketts was seated at a large table strewn with books and legal-looking documents, and he stared in astonishment at the figure which presented itself. He, like the men on the ranch, had never seen such a costume before.

"Are you Mr. Ricketts?" asked his lordship.

"Yes, sir."

"My name is Stranleigh. I took the liberty of calling upon you to learn, if possible, the whereabouts of Mr. Stanley Armstrong."

"Why should I know anything of his whereabouts?" demanded Ricketts.

"Permit me to explain——"

"Now, before we go any further," interrupted the lawyer, "I want you to know that this is a business office, and I'm a business man. My time is valuable. I thought when you came in that you were a client. If you have come here for aimless gossip, I'm not your man. I have my own affairs to look after."

"You state the case very lucidly, Mr. Ricketts, and I congratulate your clients. My own time is far from precious, for I'm here after sport. How valuable is your time? How much does an hour's conference with you cost?"

"It all depends on the business transacted."

"I can't agree with you, Mr. Ricketts. An hour is an hour. I want to buy sixty minutes of your time and attention. What do you ask for it?"

"Five dollars!" snapped Ricketts.

Stranleigh drew forth a five-dollar bill, and placed it on the table.

"May I sit down?" he enquired. "No healthy man should be tired in the morning, but I endured a long horseback ride yesterday, and had an indifferent night's rest."

"Where did you come from?"

"I have been living for the past few days at Armstrong's ranch."

"Are you the man who was shot last week?"

"Yes; by mistake for your estimable sheriff I understand. You see, I came here from New York with a letter of introduction to Mr. Armstrong, being told that I might enjoy some good fishing and a little shooting, while Armstrong was described as a most admirable guide to these sports. I waited at the ranch day after day, hoping that Armstrong would return, but nobody seems to know yet where he is, or when he will return, so I came out here, hoping to get into telegraphic communication with him. I'm well enough now to take part in the chase, and I am loth to return to New York without having had any sport."

"I still don't understand why you come to me about the matter."

"I was told by his daughter that Armstrong had written to you. She

129

does not know in the least where he is, and so on the chance of your having received a recent letter, I have called to enquire."

"I see. Armstrong's letter to me was written from Chicago. It was a request for money. I had already loaned him a considerable sum and was unable to accede to his further demand. I answered to this effect, but have heard no more from him. It is likely that his own people have received word since the letter to me was written. Of course, you don't know the date of their last letter from him?"

"Yes, I do," said Stranleigh, "I have the letter with me. It contains all the data of which Miss Armstrong is possessed, and she gave me the letter to assist me in my search."

He drew the letter from his pocket, and showed the date to the lawyer, who consulted his file, and then said—

"It is just as I expected. That letter was written ten days later than the one I received. Sorry I am unable to give you any definite assistance, Mr. Stranleigh."

Stranleigh rose.

"I am sorry also. I suppose there wouldn't be much use in telegraphing to the address he gives in Chicago?"

"I see no object in that. The place is probably a boarding-house, and he's not there."

"Thank you, Mr. Ricketts. Good morning."

Stranleigh went slowly down the steep stairs, and reaching the sidewalk, almost fell into the arms of Jim Dean. Here, then, was the man who had been following him.

"Good morning, Mr. Dean."

"Morning," snarled Jim, briefly.

"I've just been up to see Mr. Ricketts, whom I think you mentioned the other day."

"So I supposed," agreed Dean.

"I expected to get some information from him about Mr. Armstrong, but he doesn't appear to know very much."

"Well, you're the first man I ever heard say that S. A. Ricketts doesn't know very much, but I think by and by you will find that others know a great deal."

"Perhaps they know a great deal that is not so; there's a lot of knowledge of that kind lying around loose."

"Very likely," remarked Jim, laconically, then turned on his heel and walked down the street, while Stranleigh went towards the depôt to enlist the services of a telegraph operator, and learn when the next train left for the east.

Stranleigh found the telegraph operator dozing in a wooden chair tilted back against the wall, his soft hat drawn over his eyes, his feet resting on a rung of the chair. It was a hot day, and the commercial inactivity of Bleachers called for very little exertion on the part of the telegraphist. The young man slowly roused himself as the door opened and shut. His unexpected customer nodded good morning to him.

"Could you oblige me with some forms?" asked the newcomer.

"Forms? Forms of what?" The operator's feet came down with a crash on the board floor as he rose from his chair.

"Well, telegraph blanks, perhaps I should have said."

"Oh, certainly."

The young man fished one out from a drawer, and flung it on the counter.

"This will do excellently for a beginning," said Stranleigh, "but you'd better let me have a dozen to go on with."

The young man was waking up. He supplied the demand, and with

131

ever-increasing amazement, watched his client write.

Stranleigh gave the New York detective particulars in great detail so far as he possessed them, asked him to spare no expense, and requested that Armstrong, when found, should be presented with two hundred dollars or more, as he required, with admonition to take the first train home, where his presence was urgently needed.

"Great Scott!" cried the operator, "is that all one message?"

"Yes," said Stranleigh.

"Where is it going?"

"I've written the address as plainly as I can. It's going to New York."

"I say, stranger," protested the telegraphist, "have you any idea what it costs to send a message across the Continent to New York?"

"No, I haven't, but I expect to be in possession of that information as soon as you have mastered my handwriting, and counted the words."

The operator was practically speechless when he reached the end of his enumeration, but after making a note on the pad, he was sufficiently recovered to remark—

"Say, stranger, you'll have to dig up a pretty big wad to pay for this. We don't give credit in a Western Union office."

"I shouldn't think of asking credit from a downtrodden monopoly," said Stranleigh, pulling out his pocket book, and liquidating his debt. "You ought to be happy if you get a percentage."

"Worse luck, I don't."

"Well, I think you're entitled to one. I've given a fee this morning and received no particular equivalent for it. Do you, being a useful man, object to accepting a five-dollar bill?"

"Not on your life!" assented the operator with great earnestness.

Stranleigh passed it over.

132

"I'm expecting a reply. At what time shall I call for it?"

"You don't need to call, Mr. Stranleigh. When it comes, I'll lock up the office, and find you if you're anywhere in town."

"I'm stopping over at the tavern."

"All right; you'll get it."

"Thanks. Good morning."

"See you later," said the now thoroughly-awakened operator, and Stranleigh proceeded to the railway station. He took the next train to the nearest town east, and there did some more telegraphing, but this time the message was in cypher, and it was addressed to his agent in New York. Translated, it read—

"Send me at once by express, registered and insured, twenty thousand dollars in currency, made up of five dollar, ten dollar, and hundred dollar bills."

The address was fully written out in plain English. He found there was time for a satisfactory lunch before the west-bound train arrived, and he partook of it in the chief hotel, whose accommodation was much superior to that of the Bleachers tavern.

On his return to headquarters, he called in at the telegraph office. The young man in charge, at once recognising him, announced—

"Nothing doing. The moment anything comes I'll take it over to the tavern. Say, is there anything secret about that telegram you sent?"

"No; why do you ask?"

"Well, Mr. Ricketts, a lawyer here, came in about ten minutes ago, and described you, and wanted to know if you had sent a telegram."

"What did you say to him?"

"I said nobody had sent a telegram, and that I knew nothing of you. He seemed powerful anxious, and offered me a dollar to let him know if you telegraphed anything. I went over to the tavern to tell you about it, but they said you hadn't been in since breakfast."

"I suppose you haven't many chances of picking up an extra dollar in Bleachers?"

"No; I haven't. Ricketts is always mighty curious about anyone who arrives here, but I never knew him offer a cent for information before."

"I'm very much obliged to you. You go right over to Ricketts' office and pick up his dollar, but don't say I gave you the advice. By the way, wouldn't you be breaking the rules of the Western Telegraph Company if you divulged the purport of any message that passed through your hands?"

A look of trouble, almost of fear, came over the young man's face.

"If a telegram is secret," he said, "the sender usually writes it in cypher."

"Quite so, but even in that case wouldn't you be punished if it became known that you had shown Mr. Ricketts a private despatch entrusted to your care?"

"Certainly," admitted the telegraphist, exhibiting more and more uneasiness, "but I have not shown your telegram to anybody, and what I told you was entirely in confidence."

"Oh, you need have no fear of my rounding on you. I am merely endeavouring to put you in possession of that dollar without getting your neck in a noose. Don't you see that you are placing yourself entirely at Mr. Ricketts' mercy?"

"But you," protested the frightened young man, "advised me to do so."

"Undoubtedly. I want you to get that dollar, but not to place yourself in jeopardy. From what I saw of Ricketts this morning, I should not like to be in his power, yet his dollar is just as good as any other man's dollar, and I want you to detach it from him with safety, and profit to yourself. Let me have another telegraph blank."

Stranleigh wrote rapidly—

"Pinkerton Detective Agency, Chicago.

"I want to be put into communication with Stanley Armstrong, who left Chicago on foot ten days ago, for the West, and I am willing to pay one hundred dollars for the job.

"Edmund Stranleigh.

"White's Hotel, Bleachers."

"There," said Stranleigh, passing over the sheet to the operator, "you show that to our inquisitive friend Ricketts, but don't send it over the line."

Stranleigh slept that night at White's Hotel, and shortly after breakfast next morning the telegraph clerk came across with a very satisfactory telegram from New York. The sender could not positively predict the finding of Armstrong, but anticipated no difficulty in the task.

Stranleigh paid his bill at the hotel, ordered out his horse, and trotted off towards the ranch. He saw no more of Ricketts, who, if on any trail, was following the wrong one.

Dusk had fallen as he was about to emerge into the clearing which in daylight would have afforded him a sight of Armstrong's house. Suddenly and stealthily he was surrounded by six armed men, and the voice of Jim Dean broke the stillness.

"Good evening, Mr. Stranleigh. I must ask you to get down from your horse."

"Willingly," replied the rider. "I confess I have had enough equestrian exercise for one day."

"We have supper ready for you at the bunk house."

"Why at the bunk house? I am perfectly satisfied with the fare that Mr. Armstrong's family provides."

"We'd like a little conversation with you, and the conversation must take place in private."

"In that case, Mr. Dean, you could hardly find a better spot than this."

135

"We're a kindly set of chaps, and couldn't think of keeping a hungry man out here."

"But I'm not very hungry. I took a pocketful of sandwiches with me from the tavern."

"Nevertheless, you are coming with us, either peaceably, or by force, whichever you choose."

"Oh, quite willingly, of course. I should be ungrateful if I gave you any unnecessary trouble, while accepting your hospitality. I may add that I am unarmed, so if you keep your guns in readiness you need fear no reprisal on my part."

"That's all right," responded Jim. "We're not easily scared, but are prepared to protect ourselves should you try any funny business."

"Is Peter going to take my horse to the farm?"

"Sure; your horse will be put in its old quarters, and will be well taken care of."

"Then I should be glad if Peter would oblige me by telling Miss Armstrong that I have arrived safely, and will give her an account of my journey when next I have the pleasure of meeting her."

"I'm afraid Peter can't carry any messages; indeed, it's not at all necessary. I've told Miss Armstrong that your horse will be brought back, and that I saw you off on the east-bound train, which is quite true. You've brought back the horse, and you did go east on the train. Miss Armstrong thinks you have become tired of waiting for her father, and that you've gone either to Chicago or New York."

"Am I to regard myself as your prisoner, then?"

"Prisoner is an ugly word, and we are not entitled to call ourselves gaolers, but if you wouldn't mind looking on it in that way, it's all the same to us."

"Well, truthful Jim, I'm your man in every sense of the word. Let us begin our amicable journey. I yearn for the bunk house."

"You will keep silent? No shouting or calling for help? There's no help to be had anyhow, and a noise would merely alarm the women."

"I recognise the necessity for silence, and I shall make no outcry. Indeed, my whole future conduct while with you will be governed by the strictest secrecy. When I get tired of the bunk house I shall merely cut all your throats while you are asleep, and will do it in the quietest and gentlest manner."

Jim laughed.

"I guess we can take care of our throats, but I'm much obliged for the suggestion, which may come in handy if you get funny, as I said before."

They reached the bunk house by a circuitous route. A fine fire of logs was blazing on the ample hearth, for even in summer a fire was good to look at when night came on, at that elevation.

When Stranleigh sat down to supper, he regretted more than ever the civilised fare of the farm house. The menu was rough, but plentiful, and they all sat together at the long table. A meal was a serious event, and they partook of it in silence. It was evident that the men were going to adopt full precautions, for while they supped one of them sat by the door, a rifle over his knees. He came in for the second course, and another took his place. After the table was cleared, they all sat round the big fire, and smoked.

Remembering that the best tobacco in the world came from the southeast of their country, the aroma of the weed they had chosen was not as grateful to Stranleigh's nostrils as might have been expected, so partly for good fellowship, and partly for his own protection, he presented each with a fine Havana cigar, such as would be welcomed in a London club, where pipes are not permitted. The men amiably accepted this contribution, but each put the cigar in his pocket against a future occasion, and went on with his pipe. Cheap as was the tobacco they were using, it was naturally scarce among men who had received no money for some months.

"I don't wish to appear unduly inquisitive," began their guest, "but now that we have all night before us, would you mind telling me why I am thus taken charge of by strangers on whom I have no claim?"

"There are several reasons," replied Jim, who was always the spokesman for the company, "and we are quite willing to mention them. You appear to be a person of some intelligence——"

"Thanks," interjected Stranleigh.

Jim went on, unheeding the interruption—"and so perhaps you know that we suspect you of being in cohoots with Ricketts."

"Does 'cohoots' mean co-partnership?"

"Something of that sort. You partly persuaded us that wasn't so, but I followed you to make sure. Perhaps you remember that I caught you coming out from Ricketts' office. You made for that office the moment you reached Bleachers."

"Pardon me, but I went first to the hotel."

"Yes; and you enquired there where Ricketts hung out."

"Certainly; but that's in my favour. It showed that so far from being in the employ of the lawyer, I didn't even know where he lived."

"It was a good bluff."

"It's very circumstantial evidence of my innocence. But for the sake of argument, I will admit that I am in 'cohoots,' as you call it, with the estimable Ricketts. What next?"

"The next thing is that you learnt from Miss Armstrong of our intention to go into Bleachers and shoot up the town, including Ricketts."

"That is true."

"You didn't like the plan and said so."

"That also is correct."

"You said it should be stopped, not knowing the ways of this country."

"Certainly. Desirable as may be the shooting up of Bleachers, the odds are too strongly against you."

"Oh, we'll chance that. But the next thing you do is to put your funny clothes on, get out your horse, and ride directly to Mr. Ricketts. You are an informer."

"An informer is always a despicable character, Mr. Dean. What's the next item in the indictment?"

"Don't you think that's enough? Men have been hanged for less. An informer is the most poisonous wretch in the world except a horse thief."

"Then I am in danger of being hanged?"

"You sure are."

"Isn't there any way in which I can compound my felony?"

"Well, I don't quite know what confounding a felony is, but you're the sleekest fellow I ever met, and if you think you can palaver us to let you go, you've made the mistake of your life."

"I shouldn't think of attempting such a thing. I am merely endeavouring to discover your state of mind. You're strong on muscle, Jim, and I admire your build, but I'm beginning to doubt whether your brain equals your frame. There was a time when your equipment would have been victorious, but those days are long since past. Nowadays it's brain that wins every time, and in every country. Physical force has had to give way before it. Jimmy, my boy, you're out of date."

"Brain isn't going to help you any," said Dean, evidently annoyed by these strictures on his mentality.

"Perhaps it won't, but if there was a corresponding brain in your head, I'd appeal to it, and probably win. Are all your men here as stupid as you, Jim?"

Jim rose up from his chair, a forbidding frown on his brow.

"Look here, stranger," he called out, "I've had enough of that line of

139

talk."

"Oh no, you haven't. Please sit down. This line of talk is only beginning, and I say, Jim, lay aside that pipe, and smoke the Havana cigar. It will put reason into your head if anything will."

Some of the company laughed, and Jim sat down, seeing that his opponent failed to show any fear at his captors' threatening attitude. He tried to change the course of the conversation into a less personal channel.

"You see, Mr. Stranleigh, we're short on tobacco, and I want to keep this cigar until to-morrow. I can tell by the smell it's a good one."

"That's all right," said Stranleigh, "I have plenty more of them down at the house, and when they are finished, I'll telegraph east for a fresh supply. If you will let me know your favourite brand of tobacco, I'll order a ton of it at the same time."

For a moment Jim's eyes twinkled, then they narrowed into their usual caution.

"Was that what you meant by confusing a penalty? Well, stranger, it doesn't go here. We ain't to be bought, even by a ton of tobacco."

"I hadn't thought of either buying or bribing you," said Stranleigh, "therefore we will get back to our original subject, the difference between brain and muscle. I see here on the table a pack of cards in a deplorably greasy condition. If you were playing a game with an opponent who was beating you, would you shoot him?"

"Yes," promptly replied Jim, "if I found he was cheating."

"Whereupon his friends would lynch you."

"A cheater hasn't any friends."

"Jim, I shouldn't like to sit down to a game with you. You would shoot first, and think afterwards, while I, being unarmed, should be at a disadvantage. That, indeed, is just what you are doing now. If you succeed in holding me here you will spoil my game. What I propose to do is not to attack Ricketts with a gun, but to learn his style of play, and beat him at it. Any confounded fool can shoot off a gun; there's no credit in that. It's a coward's trick."

"You say we'll spoil your game. You may bet your life we will. You daren't tell us what it is."

"Oh yes, I dare, because I have a trick that will quite delude you."

"I know you'll try to do that."

"Exactly. Well, my trick is to tell the truth. The situation is very simple. That morning when from the pit mouth you warned me off the premises, I found Miss Armstrong very much worried because she had learned of your intention to shoot up the town, and could not persuade you to abandon so foolish a project. It then became my duty to prevent you doing what you proposed."

"Do you think you can?"

"Of course; I knew it was no use attempting to reason with you, so the instant necessity was to get one man of common sense to counteract the stupidity of the bunk house. That I set out to do. I rode to Bleachers, called on Lawyer Ricketts, paid him five dollars down for whatever knowledge he could give me concerning the whereabouts of Mr. Armstrong. He could give me none that I did not already possess. He kept the five dollars, though. You saw me go off in the train. I merely went to the next town, to do some telegraphing that might be more or less secret from Ricketts. A detective agency will find Mr. Armstrong, and hand him two hundred dollars, asking him at the same time to make for home by the earliest train. Then, unless I'm much mistaken, Mr. Armstrong will see the idiocy of what you propose, and will prevent you from carrying out your scheme."

Jim pondered over this announcement for some minutes. At last he broke the silence.

"What you say may be true, but I don't believe a word of it. It's more likely Ricketts is your boss, and you went in to report to him and tell him what we intended to do. Then he'll see that Bleachers is prepared to meet us."

"Yes; that would be a simple way of turning the trick. There are good points about it, but it happens not to be my way, as you will learn in a few days when Mr. Armstrong returns."

Again Jim meditated for a while, and finally rose, walked to the further end of the room, and engaged for some minutes in earnest cogitation with his fellows, carried on in tones so low that Stranleigh could not hear. Resuming his seat, he spoke with deliberation—

"You want us to believe that you are a friend of Mr. Armstrong?"

"I don't care whether you believe it or not. I can hardly be a friend of Stanley Armstrong, because I've never seen him."

"Well, we'll put your good intentions to the test. When Mr. Armstrong gets here, he will have no money. Stony broke, that's what he is. Now, unless we shoot 'em up in Bleachers when they try to sell his place, Armstrong will lose it. We take it you are a rich man. Will you promise to lend him enough money to hold this ranch, and run the mine?"

"No; I won't," said Stranleigh, with decision.

"All right. Then you stay here until you cough up that cash. Even if Armstrong comes, he will never know you're here, because we shall tell him that you've gone East. Nobody else knows where you are, so there isn't any chance of a search being made."

"This is rank brigandage," remarked Stranleigh.

"I guess that's the right title, but a man who brags so much of his brains as you do, ought to see that if we're ready to shoot up a town, we won't stop at such a trifle as brigandage."

"That's so. And now, gentlemen, I'm tired after my long journey, and I think we've talked a great deal to very little purpose, so if you'll show me what bunk I am to occupy, I'll turn in."

"There are six unused bunks, Mr. Stranleigh, and you can take your choice. There's nothing mean about us."

Stranleigh made his selection, and rough as the accommodation was, he slept as soundly as ever he had done in his London palace, or his luxurious yacht.

Although the Earl of Stranleigh was naturally an indolent man, the enforced rest of the next few days grew very irksome. He had expected the guard set over him to relax as time went on, but this was not the case. The genial Jim saw to that, and it was soon evident to Stranleigh that Dean ruled his company with an iron hand. Such casual examination of the premises as he was able to make impressed him more and more with the difficulty of escape. Had the structure been built of logs, there might have been some hope, but the imperviousness of the thick stone walls was evident to the most stupid examiner. The place was lit in daytime by two slits, one at each gable, which were without panes, and narrow, so that they might as much as possible keep out the rain. No man could creep through, even if he could reach the height at which they were placed. During the day the stout door, fit to encounter a battering ram, was open, but a guard sat constantly at the sill, with a rifle across his knees. At night it was strongly locked. Stranleigh was handicapped by the fact that heretofore he had never been required to think out any difficult problem for himself. He had merely to give the order, and other people did his thinking for him, and when a plan was formed, there were others to carry it out, being well paid for doing so. Thus it happened that the means of escape were so obvious that a ten year old boy might have discovered them.

Each evening passed very pleasantly, for Stranleigh was a good story-teller, and had many interesting tales to relate. In spite of the fact that his gaolers were unanimous in their opinion that Stranleigh was a useless encumbrance upon earth, they began rather to like him. One night Stranleigh asked Jim if anything had yet been heard of Mr. Armstrong, and Dean, after hesitating a moment, replied that there was so far no news of him or from him.

"I'm sorry for Armstrong," said Stranleigh, more as if talking to himself than to anyone else. "Poor fellow, away from home all this time, and yet compelled to support six stalwart loafers without commonsense enough to do the obvious thing."

"What is the obvious thing?" asked Dean.

"Why, to work, of course. There's your mine; you've got plenty of dynamite to go on with, and yet you lounge about here not earning enough to keep yourselves in tobacco. If there is silver in that hole, you could by this time have had enough out to buy the ranch and furnish your own working capital. You say you are partners in the scheme, but you seem to be merely a blunderheaded lot of hired men, determined not to do any work."

Jim answered with acerbity—

"If you weren't a fool you'd know we'd gone already as far as hand work can go. We need a steam engine and a crusher."

"A steam engine?" echoed Stranleigh. "What on earth would you have to pay for coal, with railway haulage, and the cost of getting it out here from the line? Why, right there, rushing past you, is all the power you need. You've only to make a water-wheel, with a straight log, thrown across the falls as axle, and there you are. Pioneers have done that sort of thing since civilisation began, and here you don't need even to build a dam."

Jim was about to make an angry retort when the company were scattered by a roar and a heavy fall of soot on the log fire. The chimney was ablaze, but that didn't matter in the least, as the house was fireproof. In a short time the flames had died out, and the party gathered round the fire once more.

"Well," said Jim, "go on with your pretty advice."

Stranleigh replied dreamily, gazing into the fire.

"Oh, well, I think my advice doesn't amount to much, as you hinted. It is none of my affair. You are a most capable body of men, I have no doubt, only the fact has been concealed from me up to date. I find I am developing the vice of talking too much, so I'm going to turn in. Good-night!"

But the fall of soot had suggested to Stranleigh a method of escape.

# VII.—THE END OF THE CONTEST.

A wood fire is an evanescent thing, having none of the calm determination of coal combustion. A wood fire requires constant replenishing, and that in the bunk house did not receive this attention. When the men, tired with doing nothing, overcome by the lassitude enduring an empty day had caused, turned into sleep, the wood fire, left to itself, crumbled into a heap of ashes. The guarding of Stranleigh became more perfunctory as time passed. He proved to be a model prisoner, and usually the sentinel at the door fell into peaceful slumber as night wore on. On the particular evening Stranleigh chose for his attempt, Jim Dean sat on the chair against the door. Jim's jaw worked so much during the day, he talked so incessantly, emptying his mind of all it contained, that he was naturally exhausted when his turn for watching came. Each of the men slumbered more or less soundly at his post, but the confident Jim outdid them all, so Stranleigh selected him as the man destined to hold the empty bag.

It was two hours after midnight when his lordship slipped down from his bunk. The fire had long since gone out, and the stone chimney was reasonably cool. The climbing of that ample flue presented no difficulty to an athletic young man who in his time had ascended the Matterhorn. The inside of the chimney offered to the amateur sweep walls of rough stone, which projected here and there, forming an effective, if unequal ladder. He attained the top with such ease that he wondered he had remained so long a prisoner. Descending the roof silently, he let himself down to the top of the lean-to which acted as kitchen and supply store, and dropped from that elevation lightly to the ground. It was a night of clear moonlight, and Stranleigh smiled to think how nearly he must represent the popular idea of the devil, covered as he was with soot from head to foot.

He made directly down the hill to the farm house by the stream, and risked a few minutes of time in washing his face in the rapid current. He now took off his boots, the better to enact the part of burglar. The doors of the house, he knew, were never locked. First he secured his favourite magazine rifle and a large quantity of cartridges, then as, after all, he was entitled to the board he paid for, he penetrated softly to the kitchen. Here he secured a couple of loaves of bread and a cooked ham, together with some other things he wanted, including a supply of tobacco, and thus overloaded as he had rarely been in his life before, he stole softly outside, slipped his feet into his boots, and slowly climbed the hill to the silver cavern. Depositing within his goods and chattels, he examined his store carefully to learn whether there was anything more he needed to stand a siege.

Bright as was the moonlight outside, the cavern was pitch dark, so Stranleigh determined on another expedition to the house, and he brought back a bunch of candles and an armful of bedclothes.

"Now for the night's work," he said to himself, and having lit a candle, which he placed at the remote end of the cave, he began picking up stones, and with them building a wall across the mouth of the pit. No Roman wall was ever built with such care, and no Roman wall ever contained within itself such possibilities of wholesale obliteration, because the structure was intersticed with sticks of dynamite, which Stranleigh carried with the most cautious tenderness from the rear to the front of the cavern. When his task was completed the moon had gone down, and the misty, luminous grey of the eastern sky betokened the approach of dawn. The young man was thoroughly tired, and with a sigh of relief he stretched himself out on the bedclothes he had brought from the house.

The early sun shining on his face awakened him. He knew from experience that the bunk house men were not afflicted with the vice of early rising. There was no aperture in their habitation, unless the door was open, through which the sun might shine upon them. He was therefore not surprised that no one was visible anywhere near the sleeping quarters. So he breakfasted in peace, alternating slices of bread with slices of ham, thus constructing some admirable sandwiches.

A providential jug, which doubtless in its time had contained whisky, was one of the utensils left when the mine was abandoned. Stranleigh took this, and stepping over the dangerous wall, filled it three or four times at the rushing cataract, rinsing out all indication of its former use. He brought it back, filled with very clear and cold water. He could not help thinking as he returned what an excellent place the waterfall would be for the washing of dishes, if a person ran the risk of standing upon spray-drenched, slippery rock ledges.

Stranleigh sat down where he could see the enemy's quarters, and carefully examined his rifle, assured himself that the magazine was full, then with the weapon over his knees in the fashion adopted by his recent gaolers, watched the bunk house patiently, wishing he had a morning paper to while away the time.

The laggard sentinel was the first to rouse himself. The broad door opened, and Jim Dean, palpably bewildered, stepped out. With hand shading his eyes he minutely examined the landscape, slowly turning his head from left to right as he scrutinised the distant horizon and the ground intervening. Stranleigh, kneeling, rested his rifle on the top of the wall, and as Jim's left ear, a rather prominent feature, became fully visible, the young man fired.

Jim's action instantaneously verified the Indian romances of Stranleigh's youth. He sprang clear up into the air and clapped a hand upon his wounded ear. He was at that moment the most astonished man on the western hemisphere. His first instinct being to bolt for cover, he did so without pausing to close the door, which opened outwards, and this broad piece of woodwork now offered a much more prominent target than Jim's ear had done a moment before.

Stranleigh, exercising a care that seemed unnecessary with so big a target, fired out the cartridges of his magazine, then immediately restocked it, and shot away the second charge. Putting in a third load, he sat there with his customary nonchalance, awaiting the turn of events. In that clear atmosphere, and with his sharp vision, he saw that he had accomplished his intention, and had punctured the letter "S" on the panel of the open door.

Meanwhile, there was commotion in the bunk house. The first sharp report, accompanied by Jim's yell, woke every man within. The subsequent fusilade engendered a belief that the enemy was in possession of a Maxim gun, and brought every man to the floor, thankful that he was under better cover than if he stood behind the door, through the panel of which all the bullets had penetrated.

"How did he escape?" demanded one, addressing Jim, who was holding his left hand to his ear.

"I don't know," said the wounded man ruefully. "You can search me."

"Seems from that shooting that we'd better search outside. What in the fiend's name made him batter the door?"

"Sorry he left us, I suppose," muttered Dean, grimly. "Knocking because he wanted to come in again."

"How did he get his gun?"

"Hanged if I know," said the questioned man, impatiently.

"But you were on guard. You ought to know something about it."

"Look here," said Jim. "There's no use in talking. He got out some way, and he's got his gun some way. He's holding us up, and we must make terms with him."

"But where is he?"

"I tell you I don't know! The bullet came from the direction of the mine. Now, one of you boys throw up your hands, and go outside and hail him."

At this command, Jim met the first rebellion against his authority.

"Go outside yourself. It is you who have brought all this upon us. You shot him through the shoulder; you proposed capturing him, and it was you who fell asleep last night and let him escape."

Jim did not combat their charges.

"All right," he said. "I'll go out, and you sit here and shiver while I enjoy a little conversation with him."

Raising his hands above his head, Dean stepped across the threshold into the open, and stood like an oriental about to begin his prayers. He saw at once the wall that had been built during the night, and then caught sight of Stranleigh standing behind it. Pulling out a white handkerchief, and waving it, Dean proceeded towards the mine.

"Have you got a revolver?" shouted Stranleigh.

"No," answered Dean.

"Then put down your hands, and approach as a Christian should."

Jim obeyed.

"Now stand where you are," said Stranleigh, when the other was within four or five yards of the wall. "I see your ear is bleeding. That was rather a neat shot of mine, don't you think?"

"It was," admitted Dean, without enthusiasm.

"When you shot at my shoulder, you had a bigger mark."

"Oh, not so very much," growled Dean. "My ears are celebrated for their size."

"You'd better wrap it up in this handkerchief," commented Stranleigh, rolling it up in a ball, and flinging it towards Jim. The wounded man tied it round his voluminous ear.

"And now," said Stranleigh, "get through with your parley as soon as possible, then go to Miss Armstrong, who will very expertly attend to your hurt. But in order to win the privilege of surgical treatment, you must recognise that you are a prisoner."

"A prisoner?" echoed Dean.

"Certainly. You must give me your word you will say nothing to Miss Armstrong to show that I have had a hand in the game. Make whatever excuse you like for the disaster, and then get back to the bunk house, tell your fellows the condition of the game as far as we have gone. I will allow you five minutes

149

after your return to show those chaps the letter 'S' I have perforated in the door. They are a very unbelieving lot, and I wish to gain their affection and respect. Without hurting anybody I mean to prove that I am a dead shot. I'm well provisioned here, and prepared to stand a siege. Until Mr. Armstrong returns, not one of you will be allowed outside the châlet. Don't be misled by the fact that you outnumber me six to one. I hold a magazine rifle, possess an ample supply of ammunition, and have just given evidence of the rapidity with which reloading can be performed."

"Yes," said Dean, meditatively, "your position would be bull strong and hog tight, if you had a chum with you who could shoot as well as you do. But as it is, you've nobody to relieve you, and a man must sleep. It will only take one of us to defeat you. We've no magazine rifles and don't need none. I'll undertake the job myself."

"How do you propose to do it?"

"That would be telling," said Jim, craftily.

"Why not?" answered Stranleigh. "I'm placing my cards on the table. Why don't you do the same? I'm not yearning for war and bloodshed, but have inaugurated a sort of Hague tribunal. There were two things I determined to accomplish when I broke jail. I hope that wounded ear hasn't impaired your hearing, so that you may listen with attention. It's always as well to know what your enemy desires."

"I'm listening," said Jim.

"The first thing was to shoot you through the leg or the arm or the ear, choosing some spot that was not vital. This in return for your shooting me. One good turn deserves another, you know. That part of my programme I have accomplished."

"What's the other part?"

"The second is to keep you gentlemen in prison just as long as you kept me in prison. One good imprisonment deserves another. Now will you tell me what you intend to do?"

150

"No; I won't."

"That's mean of you, Jim; secretive, over-cautious and that sort of thing. I'm not so chary and so will give you the information. There are only two portions of the night during which you can come out unnoticed; before the moon rises and after it sets. You will steal out and take up a position where you can see the barricade when day begins to dawn. You'll need to chose a spot a long way off, because the explosion, when it comes, will wreck everything in the neighbourhood."

"What explosion?"

"The dynamite explosion. This wall is built of rock intersticed with those dynamite cartridges of yours. It is very likely you will obliterate the farm-house."

"I'll obliterate you, anyway."

"Quite so, but at a tremendous cost, because whatever the fate of Mr. Armstrong's residence, the doom of the bunk house is certain. You may be outside that danger, but you won't be free of another. You suppose, doubtless, that I shall be asleep in the cavern. As a matter of fact I shall be sleeping placidly under the stars, quite out of reach of the main disaster. Your first shot will awaken me. Now, it is by no means certain that your first shot will send off the dynamite. You may have to fire half a dozen times, and your best rifle is an old breech-loader. I use smokeless powder, and you don't. I could pepper away at you for half an hour and you'd never know where the bullets were coming from. The smoke from your rifle would give you away at once. When I fire at you next time, Jim, I shall aim at a more vital point, because, my dear boy, the person who sets off that dynamite is a murderer. So before you put your plan into operation, just consult your comrades and explain to them its disadvantages."

Dean stood there meditating for a few moments before he spoke.

"I'm very much obliged to you," he said at last, "for telling me what you mean to do. We'll change that plan a little, and come out of the bunk house together. We'll search the country for you, and so won't need to blow up the mine."

"That's a much more humane expedient, and will prevent unnecessary loss of life. I shall be lying quiet under whatever cover I can find. Your crowd will perambulate the locality, and I may remind you that you are no lightfooted Cinderellas. A herd of elephants would make less noise. I shall see you long before you see me, and I leave the result to your own imagination. And now, Jimmy, take the advice of a true friend. Your time to act was when you were snoring at that door and I was climbing the chimney. Once you allowed me to get my rifle, you had permitted opportunity to pass you, because I am a good shot, and I came West in order to shoot. When a person accustomed to downy beds of ease slumbers peacefully, as I did this morning, on hard and jagged rocks thinly disguised by a blanket, with my right ear against a dynamite cartridge, there's nothing the matter with his nerves, is there?"

"No; there isn't," said Dean, with conviction.

"Now, what you chaps want is not a battle, but an armistice. Leave well enough alone, I say, and accept the status quo. If you remain in the bunk house, you are as safe as in a Presbyterian church."

Jim did not reply, but deliberated, his open palm against his bandaged ear.

"Hurt?" asked Stranleigh.

"Yes, it does," admitted Jim, ruefully.

"Well, my shoulder hurt a good deal after you fired at me. Now, I'll tell you what I'll do, Jim. Next time I shoot at you, I'll take the other ear. You're determined to prove yourself a brigand, or a pirate, or something of that sort, and as pirates always wear earrings, that will put you in a position to adopt them. What do you say to my proposal for an armistice?"

"I can't answer for the rest of the boys without consulting them. If we need an armistice or a status quo, why, I suppose we ought to have them."

"All right. If your ear hurts, the sooner you get it attended to, the better. You go directly down to the house and see Miss Armstrong, and you can reflect upon the situation while she is dressing the wound. Deep thinking will take your mind from the pain. Then go up and consult the company. Come and let me know what they decide. Meanwhile, I'll guarantee that no one comes out of that bunk house without being shot at."

"Mr. Stranleigh, I'll do what you say, but I'll change the order. I'll go first to our shack, and warn the boys. That's only fair, for they're watching from that door, and if they see me going to the house they may think it's all right, and come outside. After talking with them, I'll visit Miss Armstrong, and then come back here to tell you what the boys say."

"Yes, Jim; that's a better plan than mine. But first give me your word that you will take no advantage of this respite until war. An armistice, you know, is a cessation of hostilities."

"You mean that there will be no shenanigan? I give you my word."

The wounded man made his way to the bunk house. Shortly afterwards Stranleigh saw him emerge, and go towards the homestead. After a longer interval he came slowly up towards the fortress, his ear neatly bandaged in white linen, which showed up, as one might say, like a small flag of truce.

"Well, what did Miss Armstrong say about the wounded ear?"

"She says it's about as serious as the sting of a bee, and won't hurt much longer than that would, and will be cured nearly as soon."

"That's first-rate, and relieves my conscience, which has been troubling me, because I'd much rather smite a man on the ear with my fist than with a bullet. For the same reason I hope you found your messmates undergoing a spasm of common sense."

"They agreed with me that it wasn't very healthy to take outdoor exercise for a while. If we decide to begin fighting again, we'll give you twelve hours' notice. Will that suit you?"

"I don't know that it does, quite. I want you to promise that you will not break loose either until Mr. Armstrong returns, or the auction is over."

"The boys wouldn't agree to that, Mr. Stranleigh. We're bound to attend

153

that auction."

Stranleigh sighed.

"Very good," he conceded. "I must content myself with what you offer. I accept your proposal, for I feel certain that Mr. Armstrong will return before the ranch is sold. So good-bye. Give my love to the boys."

Stranleigh watched the retreating figure until it disappeared into the bunk house. A moment later the perforated door was drawn shut, and then he rolled up the bedclothes into a bundle, and deposited it at the further end of the cavern. This done, he took his rifle under his arm, crossed the barricade, and strolled down to the farm-house. Miss Armstrong greeted him with surprise.

"I thought you had gone to New York," she said.

"I took the train east, but only to the next station from Bleachers."

"You've not been stopping at that wretched hotel in Bleachers ever since?"

"Oh no; I received a pressing invitation from some friends of mine to be their guest, with a prospect of a little shooting, so I've been staying with them ever since."

"Did you have a pleasant time?"

"Oh, excellent, and I heard more entertaining stories than ever I listened to in a similar period."

"Good shooting?"

"First rate. Limited in quantity, but of finest quality. Indeed, I may boast of a record; I hit everything I aimed at. Camp fare, however, left a good deal to be desired, so you may imagine how glad I am to return."

"I'm very pleased to have an opportunity of giving you something better. How would you like some nice broiled trout, freshly caught this morning?"

"Oh, heavenly!" cried Stranleigh, enthusiastically. "I haven't had anything but bread and salt pork since I saw you. Who caught the trout?"

"I did. I went down the river early this morning. I must have had a premonition that you would return, famished for trout, and I had quite an adventure, or rather, plunged into a mystery which I have not yet solved. I heard the sound of firing; first a single shot, then a fusilade. I could not tell from whence the sound came. I hurried home with my basket, but there was no one in sight. After a while Jim came in, very much crestfallen, it seemed to me, with his ear tied up clumsily in a handkerchief. He had been shot through the ear, and of course I came to his aid at once. With a woman's curiosity, I asked him how the accident happened. Now, one of Jim's infirmities is that he can only tell the truth when it suits his convenience."

"Many of us are like that," said Stranleigh.

"Well, this time it didn't suit his convenience."

"What did he say?"

"That the boys were having a sort of shooting match. I told him I had heard the firing, and feared that there had been a battle of some sort. He said it was the first shot that did for him. They had some bet on as to who could fire the quickest at a flying mark. In his hurry to get ready he had mishandled his gun, and sent a bullet through his ear. The other men had then fired almost simultaneously."

"Miss Armstrong, I fear you are too sceptical. Why shouldn't that be a true story?"

"Mr. Stranleigh, you quite underrate my intelligence.

The wound in Jim's ear was not caused by the gun he held. In the first place, his ear would have been blackened with gunpowder, and likely would have been partly torn off. Secondly, a mishandled gun would have fired upwards. The bullet that wounded him was fired from a distance by someone higher up than the spot where Jim stood. The wound was clean cut, slightly inclining downwards. Besides all that, Jim's bullet, coming from an old-fashioned rifle, would make a bigger hole. I know that, for you remember

I tended your shoulder, through which his bullet had gone."

"By Jove, Miss Armstrong, if Sherlock Holmes had a daughter, she would be just about your age. Was there anything else?"

"Yes; I looked at the handkerchief in which he had bound his ear. It was of a finer cambric than we have ever seen in this district, or indeed, than I have seen anywhere else. The corner was embroidered with a very delicately-worked crest."

"A crest?" said Stranleigh, rather breathlessly.

"I asked Jim where he had got this handkerchief. He seemed confused, but said he had always had it. Bought it once at a five-cent store in Denver."

Stranleigh could not refrain from laughing.

"You think it cost more than five cents?"

"Yes; I am sure it cost more than twenty-five."

"Perhaps he stole it?"

"Jim might shoot a man, but he'd never steal."

"I think that when you discover the owner of that handkerchief, you will have solved the mystery," remarked Stranleigh calmly.

"I think so, too," said the girl quietly. "Now I am going to cook your trout."

The three days following were among the most enjoyable Stranleigh had ever spent. He asked Miss Armstrong to show him the portion of the river in which she had caught those delicious trout. Heretofore, she had used a baited hook when fishing, landing her spoil with a trout pole, but now she was to be initiated in the delicate mysteries of fly fishing. Stranleigh remembered the story told of an English official sent to view the debateable land adjoining the far western boundary of Canada who reported the territory useless, because the fish wouldn't rise to the fly. He wondered what lure the official used, for here they rose readily enough, and fought like demons until Miss Armstrong deftly lifted them from the water in the new-fangled landing net, the like of which she had never seen before.

But in spite of the excellent sport he was enjoying, Stranleigh became more and more anxious as time went on. Nothing had been heard from Stanley Armstrong. The fisher began to fear that the detective had failed in his search. On the morning of the fourth day he dressed in his ordinary tweed suit. The riding costume attracted more attention than was altogether convenient. He put in his pocket an automatic revolver of the latest construction; light, accurate and deadly. The day of the auction was drawing uncomfortably near, and he was determined that his journey should not be interrupted, as his former ride had been. Aside from this, he expected to carry with him a large amount of money, and if any word of that got abroad, he knew a holdup was quite within the range of possibility. The coterie confined in the bunk house would doubtless learn that they were their own gaolers, and with that gang once free upon the landscape, he anticipated interruption which, if successful, would completely nullify his plans.

"Are you going fishing to-day?" asked Miss Armstrong, when he came downstairs. He had appeared unexpectedly soon that morning. The young woman was always an early riser.

"Fishing!" echoed Stranleigh. "Yes, in a manner of speaking. Isn't there a text which refers to fishers of men? I'm going fishing for your father. We should have had him here before this, but now the need of him becomes imperative. I imagine that a telegram awaits me in Bleachers. If not, I must communicate with New York, and wait for a reply."

Stranleigh walked up the hill to the bunk house, and rapped at the panel with the butt of his riding whip. Dean himself threw open the door, and he could not conceal his astonishment at seeing the young man standing there, apparently unarmed.

"Good morning, Jim," said Stranleigh cordially.

"I wish to enjoy a few minutes' conversation with the company before leaving for Bleachers."

"None of the company are out of their bunks yet, except myself, but I guess they're wide enough awake to hear what you say. Won't you come inside?"

"Thank you," said Stranleigh, stepping across the threshold; then, to the sleeping beauties—"The top of the morning to you! Early to bed and late to rise, makes a man healthy, wealthy, and wise. Has wisdom come to you since I left? Do you still intend to shoot up Bleachers on auction day?"

"You bet we do," said Dean.

Stranleigh seated himself upon the chair he had formerly occupied.

"How did you propose to get out?"

"By the same way you escaped," responded Dean with determination.

"What an inconvenient exit! I speak from sooty experience. Why not have gone by the doorway?"

"We didn't want to get shot," said Jim.

"There was no danger of that. I have been spending my days in fishing, and my nights in sound sleep."

"Do you mean to say," cried Jim, "that there's been nobody on guard?"

"No; you've been as free as air to go where you pleased."

Dean laughed heartily, and the others joined him. The joke was on them, but they seemed to enjoy rather than resent it.

"You were right about brain and muscle," observed Jim at last.

Stranleigh ignored the compliment.

"I've got a proposal to make to you men," he went on. "I'm off to Bleachers to do some telegraphing, trying to learn the whereabouts of Mr. Armstrong, who has not yet put in an appearance. The sale takes place day after to-morrow."

Stranleigh paused in his recital. He noticed a stealthy movement among the bunkers. He had observed that the first to sit up cast a longing glance at the rifles stacked in the corner, and it seemed to him that a simultaneous rush towards them was going to take place.

"As you know, gentlemen," he went on, "I have an objection to shooting as a settlement of any legal question, but if shooting has to be done, I am quite prepared for it, and the inhabitants of Bleachers will regret provoking me to a fusilade."

He took from his pocket the neat little automatic pistol.

"I don't suppose," he went on, "that you ever saw anything exactly like this. It will simply rain bullets, and I can re-load before any of those Bleachers men can get his hand to his hip pocket. Next to the Maxim gun, it's the most deadly object in existence." Casually he cast his eye along the bunks. Each man had withdrawn the leg that had been quietly reaching for the floor. Stranleigh still fondled his weapon.

"Just before you captured me, I had sent to New York for a considerable sum of money, which was to reach me by express. I thought it better to have no dealings with the bank, as I didn't wish Ricketts to learn what I was doing. I expect that sum of money is at this moment resting in the express office, and on the day of the sale I shall have more currency on my person than is perhaps quite safe to carry. I therefore wish to engage you as a bodyguard, if you agree to certain conditions. I shall expect you all in Bleachers day after to-morrow, and shall pay each of you fifty dollars for the day, and so that there may be no mistake, I tender you the money now. Do you agree?"

"What are the conditions?" asked Jim, cautiously.

"First, you will keep clear of the tavern, and not drink."

"That's easy. What next?"

"You will not shoot until I give the word of command, and until I have emptied my pistol."

Jim consulted with his fellows, then turned to Stranleigh.

"We agree," he said.

"Right you are." Stranleigh rose, took from his pocket-book six fifty-dollar bills, and laid them on the table.

"Look here," cried Dean, "we don't want any money for this job."

"I'm quite sure of that, but six honest men are as much entitled to their pay as is a dishonest lawyer like Ricketts. So good-bye, until I see you at Bleachers day after to-morrow."

Stranleigh went down to the house, mounted his horse, and rode away.

He had accomplished little more than half the distance when he perceived a horseman coming towards him. They approached one another with some caution. Stranleigh would have passed in silence had not the other accosted him.

"Hello, stranger!" he said. "You from the ranch?"

"Yes."

"Been stopping there?"

"Yes."

"How's everything? Folks all well?"

"Yes; they were when I left. Is there any chance that you are Mr. Armstrong?"

"That's my name."

"I'm very glad to meet you, sir. I'm Stranleigh, who telegraphed the detective to find you and hand you two hundred dollars, begging you to get home in a hurry."

"Well, Mr. Stranleigh, all that was done, and here I am, but as for paying back that two hundred dollars and expenses, I don't see how I am to do it. I'm broke."

"So I understand. Do you know your place is to be disposed of by forced sale day after to-morrow?"

160

"Yes; they've got me with my hands up."

"I don't think so. I'm going to attend that sale, and probably our friend Ricketts will regret the fact. Now, you turn your horse round and accompany me to the settlement. I've got some money coming by express, and being rather a stupid sort of person, it never occurred to me until half an hour ago that I'd need to be identified before I got my hands on that express package. So if you'll take my word that I am Stranleigh, we'll collar the currency and attend the sale. I have a letter of introduction to you from Mr. Banks, of New York, but I left it at your house."

"That's all right. I'll go surety that you're the man. I'd like mighty well to see a little money, even if it belongs to another fellow."

Armstrong turned his horse, who was not loth to set his face in the other direction, because he belonged to White's Tavern. As the two men jogged along together, Stranleigh explained the situation. Armstrong was silent for some time, evidently in a state of dejection.

"Well, Mr. Stranleigh," he said at last, "as you know, I am quite helpless. I haven't a cent to bless myself nor curse an enemy with. I'm no good as a business man, and the slick way in which those rascals in Chicago separated me from what cash I had would make you laugh at me if you knew how it was done."

"I shouldn't be inclined to laugh. We read in Scripture of the man who fell among thieves, and I imagine Chicago is a good place to find such cattle, although I believe there are a few of them further west. I think that Ricketts, in refusing the money when it was offered to him, exceeded his legal rights."

"Our sharpers out here," said Armstrong, "are always exceeding their legal rights, but they get rich all the same. I confess I haven't so much dependence on legality as a law-abiding citizen should have."

"Your men on the ranch seem to hold the same opinion. In spite of all I could say, they were determined to make a raid on Bleachers."

"Did you manage to stop them?" enquired Armstrong eagerly.

"I think I did," was the reply.

There had been a flash of hope in Armstrong's eyes, but it now died down to dejection again.

"I am sorry for that," he said.

Stranleigh gazed at him in astonishment.

"You don't mean to say that you approve of such violence?"

"Oh, well," said Armstrong nonchalantly, "when a man's in a corner, he'll do most anything, and at such times a little gun play is not out of place. I'll bet the boys would have stopped that sale."

"Doubtless, but what good would that do?"

"We should gain breathing space, and perhaps Ricketts wouldn't go on with his villainy."

"But it would land all your men in gaol."

"Don't you believe it. The sheriff would have to catch the boys first, and they know every ravine and stream and gully in the mountains, and every trail in the woods, and if Ricketts was sacrificed in the scrimmage, I, for one, wouldn't be chief mourner. These boys might not be much good in Chicago, but they are very useful out here. A scoundrel like Ricketts, who tries legally to steal a man's property, takes big chances and runs a lot of risks, and no one knows that better than himself. He has taken advantage of my being away from home."

"It's not too late yet to carry out your plan. Although your men hold to their resolve to visit Bleachers on the day of the sale, they have promised not to shoot until I give the word of command."

"They will be there, then, after all?" cried Armstrong, eagerly.

"Certainly; I have engaged them as bodyguard, because, as I told you, I shall have a considerable sum of money in my possession, and I don't wish to be detached from that cash, either by Chicago methods, or those of Bleachers.

I want the sale to go on without any disturbance."

"What's your plan?"

"I intend to buy the ranch."

"Do you imagine for a moment that you'll be allowed to?"

"How can they prevent me if I've got the cash in my pocket?"

"Why, first thing they'll do is to postpone the sale."

"Has Ricketts power to do that?"

"No; but the sheriff has, and the sheriff is Ricketts' man."

"Official bribery, eh? Are you personally acquainted with the sheriff?"

"Yes; I voted for him."

"Is he a man who would rather do right than wrong?"

"It depends how much money there is in either course."

"Then I think our path is reasonably clear. If Ricketts can bribe him to do wrong, we can bribe him to do right."

Armstrong shook his head doubtfully.

"It's not so easy as you think. He would take our money all right, but he might not deliver the goods. He wouldn't stay bought."

"That is a useful thing to know. We'll pay him half the money cash down, and the other half when he has delivered the goods. Would a hundred dollars be sufficient?"

"Oh, lord, yes! It gives Ricketts a pain when he parts with a ten-dollar bill, so it won't take very much money to compete with him."

"As you know the man, and as it's your ranch that is in jeopardy, you can carry out the negotiations better than a stranger like myself."

"That's so; if I have the cash. A hundred dollars would turn the trick."

"Better take five hundred dollars and be sure of it."

They stopped their horses and made the transfer of money where they stood, as being safer than in the tavern.

Arriving at Bleachers, they found the express office closed for the night, but next day his lordship, with Armstrong as his identifier, secured the package.

The land sale took place in the Agricultural Hall, the largest building in town. Stanley Armstrong's six armed followers arrived in good time, and quite unobtrusively seated themselves in a row on a bench at the rear of the hall. When Stranleigh, accompanied by Armstrong, came in, the half dozen shook hands with their chief, and expressed no more surprise at meeting him than if he had left them the week before. Large as the hall was, it speedily filled up, but Lawyer Ricketts, on entering, as he cast his eye over the assemblage, knew there were few moneyed men among the crowd gathered there, and so anticipated no serious opposition when the bidding began.

The lawyer was accompanied by two friends; strangers in Bleachers, who took their places beside him on the chairs provided near the auctioneer's desk. Ricketts was an important man, and quite entitled to reserved seats for himself and his friends. Last of all the sheriff entered, and mounted the platform, bowing graciously to the meeting, which was composed of constituents whose votes he would need next year. It was quite evident that the sheriff was a popular man, for there was a round of applause the moment he appeared.

He got down to business without any unnecessary loss of time, reading the documents giving the conditions of the sale, the item on which Stranleigh was relying being that no cheques would be accepted, or credit allowed. Payment must be cash down on the fall of the auctioneer's gavel. This the clever lawyer had insisted upon, to prevent all possibility of his being outbid by someone who desired time for payment. Thus he dug a pit for his own undoing.

Having finished this reading, the sheriff took a sip from the glass supposed to hold water, and promptly began—

164

"You all know the property, gentlemen, so I need not detain you by any lengthy description of it. How much am I offered for Armstrong's ranch?"

"Three thousand dollars," said Ricketts.

"Five thousand," promptly outbid the Earl of Stranleigh.

There was a buzz of interest in the crowd, as if some one had stirred up a nest of bees. They had not expected competition. Ricketts stood up and scrutinised the numerous faces turned towards him, endeavouring to discover from whom the bid came.

Then he sat down, and whispered to each of the men beside him. They nodded, and one of them stole quietly out through the door by which the sheriff had entered.

"He's gone for more money," said Stranleigh quietly to Armstrong.

"Five thousand dollars I am bid," went on the sheriff. "Is there any advance on five thousand dollars?"

His gavel hovered over the table.

"Six thousand," said Ricketts.

"Ten thousand," offered Stranleigh, realising that his opponent was playing for time.

"Ten thousand dollars!" echoed the sheriff, then, glancing at the lawyer; "It's against you, Mr. Ricketts."

The lawyer hesitated.

"Eleven thousand!" he said at last.

"Fifteen thousand," bid Stranleigh, promptly.

There were two anxious men in that hall. Stranleigh was wishing he had sent for a hundred thousand dollars. It was evident that Ricketts possessed good backing, but he had no means of knowing whether or

not these men had the necessary money actually in hand. Ricketts was the second anxious man, and he was now gazing with apprehension at the door through which his companion had disappeared. He was called to attention by the strident voice of the sheriff.

"Fifteen thousand dollars is the last bid. Going at fifteen thousand once; going at fifteen thousand twice——"

"Wait a moment, Mr. Sheriff: there's no hurry."

"The sale must go on, Mr. Ricketts."

"Certainly," replied the lawyer, "but it's your duty to get as much as you can for the property. We all sympathise very much with our neighbour, Mr. Armstrong, and whatever is paid over and above his debt to me, goes to him."

"I am aware of that, Mr. Ricketts, and your compassion for Mr. Armstrong does you credit. Still, as I have said before, the sale must go on, and unless there is another bid, I am compelled to knock the property down to the last offer. Fifteen thousand dollars I am bid, and for the third time——"

"Sixteen thousand," cried Ricketts, taking out a handkerchief, and mopping his brow.

The missing man now re-appeared, and took his place beside the lawyer. The three heads came closer together, and Stranleigh watched them with half-closed eyes, apparently indifferent.

"The bid is against you, sir," said the Sheriff. "By the way, what name, please?"

"Stranleigh."

"Well, Mr. Stranleigh, I'm waiting for your bid."

"Don't wait any longer, Mr. Sheriff. I'm anxious to know how much money Mr. Ricketts possesses at the present moment. The ranch belongs to him if he can hand over to you sixteen thousand dollars."

Down came the gavel on the table.

"Mr. Ricketts, the ranch is yours."

Mr. Ricketts rose to his feet.

"I ask for a postponement of this sale for a week from to-day."

"I have no objection," said the Sheriff, "as of course I shall earn another fee."

There was a laugh at this, then the Sheriff continued—

"But I cannot postpone the sale without the consent of Mr. Stranleigh. What do you say, Mr. Stranleigh?"

"A postponement would be very inconvenient to me, much as I should like to oblige Mr. Ricketts. I therefore refuse my consent."

"If the Sheriff is willing," roared Ricketts, "we will postpone without your consent, even if we have to turn you out by force."

"I shouldn't try that if I were you, Mr. Ricketts. There are six friends of mine sitting beside me, who are dead shots, and I don't think this crowd would stand in the way if the first gun were levelled at you. I ask that the sale go peacefully on, Mr. Sheriff."

"There must be a postponement! The Sheriff has control over this meeting!"

"I am counting on that," said Stranleigh, "and I am sure that the Sheriff will adhere strictly to the law. How much money have you collected, Mr. Ricketts?"

"That's none of your business."

"Perhaps not; and so to make everything easy and agreeable to all concerned, I bid seventeen thousand dollars for the property."

"Show your money," demanded Ricketts.

"You wouldn't show yours, so why should I show mine?"

"Knock it down to him, Sheriff. I don't believe he has the cash."

"Seventeen thousand I am offered. Going at seventeen thousand once; going at seventeen thousand twice; going at seventeen thousand third and last time. Going! Gone!"

Down came the mallet.

"I shall be obliged if you will hand over to me seventeen thousand dollars, Mr. Stranleigh."

"Certainly. With your permission, gentlemen!" and the crowd parted good-naturedly. Stranleigh counted out the money on the Sheriff's table.

Armstrong and his men went home directly the sale was over, but Stranleigh remained until all the legal business was finished, and the documents were in his possession. As he rode back to the ranch, he meditated upon the situation in which he found himself. The object of his trip to the West had been achieved. He had left New York tired of its noise, its heated pavements and other uncomfortable disadvantages. He had thought he would never care to see the metropolis again, but now he was yearning for the atmosphere of a large city; London for choice. He determined to bid farewell at once to the Armstrongs and the bunk house men, then turn his face eastwards.

Miss Armstrong was amazed to learn his decision.

"But you haven't had even one day's shooting!" she protested.

"Oh, I'll come for that another time," he assured her.

"Before you go away, my father would like to make some arrangement with you about this ranch."

"I shall be very glad to come to an agreement with him."

The girl sped up to the silver mine, where her father was superintending the removal of the dynamite to its proper place, a job requiring some little care. Armstrong accompanied his daughter down to the house, and greeted Stranleigh with eagerness.

"I am anxious to lease this place from you, Mr. Stranleigh, with the option of buying it later on. I am sure I can make money from the silver

168

mine."

"You must apply to the owner of the ranch, Mr. Armstrong."

"The owner!" echoed Armstrong, in some alarm.

"You haven't sold the ranch since I saw you, I hope?"

"No; but like most other men, I am in debt, and I intend to use this property in payment of my obligation."

Armstrong was taken aback by this declaration. Turning to Miss Armstrong, Stranleigh took from his pocket a long, well-filled envelope.

"These, Professor, are all the legal documents necessary to make you the owner of the ranch, including deed and what-not. I am quite incapable of understanding the red tape wound round the transaction, but I am assured it is all right. I tender this in payment of my medical bill."

"Oh," cried the girl, softly. Then she smiled. "As the sensational plays have it, this is too much!"

"Not a bit of it," returned Stranleigh. "You have no idea of the appalling charges made by specialists in New York and London. Besides, this includes payment of Jim's bill. You cured Jim's ear as well as my shoulder, and I am responsible for Jim. His ear is the only shooting I have had since I came to the ranch."

The girl again began to protest, but Stranleigh interrupted.

"As you are so loth to receive the property, I shall burden it with some conditions. Your father will ask you to mortgage this land to raise money for him. You must refuse that. Keep the ranch in your own name. You have just seen how much trouble has been caused by Ricketts getting his claws on the place. Your father has got, or will get, something between ten and twelve thousand dollars from the proceeds of the sale. Will you put that money into your daughter's hands, Mr. Armstrong?"

"I suppose I'll have to if you say so," rather grudgingly conceded the rancher.

"Yes; I say so, because she is a good business woman. Now, Miss Armstrong, you own the ranch, and with this money at your disposal, you should be able to prove conclusively whether there is profitable ore in that mine. When you are ready to demonstrate that fact, write to me, and I'll get together the capital you need for the energetic development of the mine. And now I must be off. Will you bid good-bye for me to my friends, the bunk house men?"

"Certainly; where shall I write to you when there is news of the mine to send?"

"Mr. Banks of New York always has my address."

The girl held forward her hand.

"Good-bye to you, Lord Stranleigh of Wychwood," she said.

For the first time in his life, his lordship neglected to take the proffered hand of a lady.

"Are you making a guess, or stating a certainty, Miss Armstrong?"

"I guess it's a certainty. I saw in a New York paper that Earl Stranleigh of Wychwood was coming into this district to shoot. Then from Jim's ear I unbound a handkerchief with a crest and a monogram on it."

Stranleigh laughed, and took the hand still outstretched to him.

THE END.

# A CHICAGO PRINCESS

# CHAPTER I

WHEN I look back upon a certain hour of my life it fills me with wonder that I should have been so peacefully happy. Strange as it may seem, utter despair is not without its alloy of joy. The man who daintily picks his way along a muddy street is anxious lest he soil his polished boots, or turns up his coat collar to save himself from the shower that is beginning, eager then to find a shelter; but let him inadvertently step into a pool, plunging head over ears into foul water, and after that he has no more anxiety. Nothing that weather can inflict will add to his misery, and consequently a ray of happiness illumines his gloomy horizon. He has reached the limit; Fate can do no more; and there is a satisfaction in attaining the ultimate of things. So it was with me that beautiful day; I had attained my last phase.

I was living in the cheapest of all paper houses, living as the Japanese themselves do, on a handful of rice, and learning by experience how very little it requires to keep body and soul together. But now, when I had my next meal of rice, it would be at the expense of my Japanese host, who was already beginning to suspect,—so it seemed to me,—that I might be unable to liquidate whatever debt I incurred. He was very polite about it, but in his twinkling little eyes there lurked suspicion. I have travelled the whole world over, especially the East, and I find it the same everywhere. When a man comes down to his final penny, some subtle change in his deportment seems to make the whole world aware of it. But then, again, this supposed knowledge on the part of the world may have existed only in my own imagination, as the Christian Scientists tell us every ill resides in the mind. Perhaps, after all, my little bowing landlord was not troubling himself about the payment of the bill, and I only fancied him uneasy.

If an untravelled person, a lover of beauty, were sitting in my place on that little elevated veranda, it is possible the superb view spread out before him might account for serenity in circumstances which to the ordinary individual would be most depressing. But the view was an old companion of mine; goodness knows I had looked at it often enough when I climbed that weary hill and gazed upon the town below me, and the magnificent harbor of Nagasaki spreading beyond. The water was intensely blue, dotted with shipping of all nations, from the stately men-of-war to the ocean tramps and the little coasting schooners. It was an ever-changing, animated scene; but really I had had enough of it during all those ineffective months of struggle in the attempt to earn even the rice and the poor lodging which I enjoyed.

Curiously, it was not of this harbor I was thinking, but of another in far-distant Europe, that of Boulogne in the north of France, where I spent a day with my own yacht before I sailed for America. And it was a comical thought that brought the harbor of Boulogne to my mind. I had seen a street car there, labelled "Le Dernier Sou," which I translated as meaning "The Last Cent." I never took a trip on this street car, but I presume somewhere in the outskirts of Boulogne there is a suburb named "The Last Cent," and I thought now with a laugh: "Here I am in Japan, and although I did not take that street car, yet I have arrived at 'Le Dernier Sou.'"

This morning I had not gone down to the harbor to prosecute my search for employment. As with my last cent, I had apparently given that idea up. There was no employer needing men to whom I had not applied time and again, willing to take the laborer's wage for the laborer's work. But all my earlier training had been by way of making me a gentleman, and the manner was still upon me in spite of my endeavors to shake it off, and I had discovered that business men do not wish gentlemen as day-laborers. There was every reason that I should be deeply depressed; yet, strange to say, I was not. Had I at last reached the lotus-eating content of the vagabond? Was this care-free condition the serenity of the tramp? Would my next step downward be the unblushing begging of food, with the confidence that if I were refused at one place I should receive at another? With later knowledge, looking back at that moment of mitigated happiness, I am forced to believe that it was the effect of coming events casting their shadows before. Some occultists tell us that every action that takes place on the earth, no matter how secretly done, leaves its impression on some ethereal atmosphere, visible to a clairvoyant, who can see and describe to us exactly what has taken place. If this be true, it is possible that our future experiences may give sub-mental warnings of their approach.

As I sat there in the warm sunlight and looked over the crowded harbor, I thought of the phrase, "When my ship comes in." There was shipping enough in the bay, and possibly, if I could but have known where, some friend of mine might at that moment be tramping a white deck, or sitting in a steamer chair, looking up at terrace upon terrace of the toy houses among which I kept my residence. Perhaps my ship had come in already if only I knew which were she. As I lay back on the light bamboo chair, along which I had thrown myself,—a lounging, easy, half-reclining affair like those we used to have at college,—I gazed upon the lower town and harbor, taking in the vast blue surface of the bay; and there along the indigo expanse of the waters, in striking contrast to them, floated a brilliantly white ship gradually, imperceptibly approaching. The canvas, spread wing and wing, as it increased in size, gave it the appearance of a swan swimming toward me, and I thought lazily:

"It is like a dove coming to tell me that my deluge of misery is past, and there is an olive-branch of foam in its beak."

As the whole ship became visible I saw that it, like the canvas, was pure white, and at first I took it for a large sailing yacht rapidly making Nagasaki before the gentle breeze that was blowing; but as she drew near I saw that she was a steamer, whose trim lines, despite her size, were somewhat unusual in these waters. If this were indeed a yacht she must be owned by some man of great wealth, for she undoubtedly cost a fortune to build and a very large income to maintain. As she approached the more crowded part of the bay, her sails were lowered and she came slowly in on her own momentum. I fancied I heard the rattle of the chain as her anchor plunged into the water, and now I noticed with a thrill that made me sit up in my lounging chair that the flag which flew at her stern was the Stars and Stripes. It is true that I had little cause to be grateful to the country which this piece of bunting represented, for had it not looted me of all I possessed? Nevertheless in those distant regions an Englishman regards the United States flag somewhat differently from that of any nation save his own. Perhaps there is an unconscious feeling of kinship; perhaps the similarity of language may account for it, because an

Englishman understands American better than any other foreign tongue. Be that as it may, the listlessness departed from me as I gazed upon that banner, as crude and gaudy as our own, displaying the most striking of the primary colors. The yacht rested on the blue waters as gracefully as if she were a large white waterfowl, and I saw the sampans swarm around her like a fluffy brood of ducklings.

And now I became conscious that the most polite individual in the world was making an effort to secure my attention, yet striving to accomplish his purpose in the most unobtrusive way. My patient and respected landlord, Yansan, was making deep obeisances before me, and he held in his hand a roll which I strongly suspected to be my overdue bill. I had the merit in Yansan's eyes of being able to converse with him in his own language, and the further advantage to myself of being able to read it; therefore he bestowed upon me a respect which he did not accord to all Europeans.

"Ah, Yansan!" I cried to him, taking the bull by the horns, "I was just thinking of you. I wish you would be more prompt in presenting your account. By such delay errors creep into it which I am unable to correct."

Yansan awarded me three bows, each lower than the one preceding it, and, while bending his back, endeavored, though with some confusion, to conceal the roll in his wide sleeve. Yansan was possessed of much shrewdness, and the bill certainly was a long standing one.

"Your Excellency," he began, "confers too much honor on the dirt beneath your feet by mentioning the trivial sum that is owing. Nevertheless, since it is your Excellency's command, I shall at once retire and prepare the document for you."

"Oh, don't trouble about that, Yansan," I said, "just pull it out of your sleeve and let me look over it."

The wrinkled face screwed itself up into a grimace more like that of a monkey than usual, and so, with various genuflections, Yansan withdrew the roll and proffered it to me. Therein, in Japanese characters, was set down the long array of my numerous debts to him. Now, in whatever part of the world a man wishes to delay the payment of a bill, the proper course is to dispute one or more of its items, and this accordingly I proceeded to do.

"I grieve to see, Yansan," I began, putting my finger on the dishonest hieroglyphic, "that on the fourth day you have set down against me a repast of rice, whereas you very well know on that occasion I did myself the honor to descend into the town and lunch with his Excellency the Governor."

Again Yansan lowered his ensign three times, then deplored the error into which he had fallen, saying it would be immediately rectified.

"There need to be no undue hurry about the rectification," I replied, "for when it comes to a settlement I shall not be particular about the price of a plate of rice."

Yansan was evidently much gratified to hear this, but I could see that my long delay in liquidating his account was making it increasingly difficult for him to subdue his anxiety. The fear of monetary loss was struggling with his native politeness. Then he used the formula which is correct the world over.

"Excellency, I am a poor man, and next week have heavy payments to make to a creditor who will put me in prison if I produce not the money."

"Very well," said I grandly, waving my hand toward the crowded harbor, "my ship has come in where you see the white against the blue. To-morrow you shall be paid."

Yansan looked eagerly in the direction of my gesture.

"She is English," he said.

"No, American."

"It is a war-ship?"

"No, she belongs to a private person, not to the Government."

"Ah, he must be a king, then,—a king of that country."

"Not so, Yansan; he is one of many kings, a pork king, or an oil king or a railroad king."

"Surely there cannot be but one king in a country, Excellency," objected Yansan.

"Ah, you are thinking of a small country like Japan. One king does for such a country; but America is larger than many Japans, therefore it has numerous kings, and here below us is one of them."

"I should think, Excellency," said Yansan, "that they would fight with one another."

"That they do, and bitterly, too, in a way your kings never thought of. I myself was grievously wounded in one of their slightest struggles. That flag which you see there waves over my fortune. Many a million of sen pieces which once belonged to me rest secure for other people under its folds."

My landlord lifted his hands in amazement at my immense wealth.

"This, then, is perhaps the treasure-ship bringing money to your Excellency," he exclaimed, awestricken.

"That's just what it is, Yansan, and I must go down and collect it; so bring me a dinner of rice, that I may be prepared to meet the captain who carries my fortune."

# CHAPTER II

AFTER a frugal repast I went down the hill to the lower town, and on inquiry at the custom-house learned that the yacht was named the "Michigan," and that she was owned by Silas K. Hemster, of Chicago. So far as I could learn, the owner had not come ashore; therefore I hired a sampan from a boatman who trusted me. I was already so deeply in his debt that he was compelled to carry me, inspired by the optimistic hope that some day the tide of my fortunes would turn. I believe that commercial institutions are sometimes helped over a crisis in the same manner, as they owe so much their creditors dare not let them sink. Many a time had this lad ferried me to one steamer after another, until now his anxiety that I should obtain remunerative employment was nearly as great as my own.

As we approached the "Michigan" I saw that a rope ladder hung over the side, and there leaned against the rail a very free-and-easy sailor in white duck, who was engaged in squirting tobacco-juice into Nagasaki Bay. Intuitively I understood that he had sized up the city of Nagasaki and did not think much of it. Probably it compared unfavorably with Chicago. The seaman made no opposition to my mounting the ladder; in fact he viewed my efforts with the greatest indifference. Approaching him, I asked if Mr. Hemster was aboard, and with a nod of his head toward the after part of the vessel he said, "That's him."

Looking aft, I now noticed a man sitting in a cushioned cane chair, with his two feet elevated on the spotless rail before him. He also was clothed in light summer garb, and had on his head a somewhat disreputable slouch hat with a very wide brim. His back was toward Nagasaki, as if he had no interest in the place. He revolved an unlit cigar in his mouth, in a manner quite impossible to describe; but as I came to know him better I found that he never lit his weed, but kept its further end going round and round in a little circle by a peculiar motion of his lips. Though he used the very finest brand of cigars, none ever lasted him for more than ten minutes, when he would throw it away, take another, bite off the end, and go through the same process once more. What satisfaction he got out of an unlighted cigar I was never able to learn.

His was a thin, keen, business face, with no hair on it save a tuft at the chin, like the beard of a goat. As I approached him I saw that he was looking sideways at me out of the corners of his eyes, but he neither raised his head nor turned it around. I was somewhat at a loss how to greet him, but for want of a better opening I began:

"I am told you are Mr. Hemster."

"Well!" he drawled slowly, with his cigar between his teeth, released for a moment from the circular movement of his lips, "you may thank your stars you are told something you can believe in this God-forsaken land."

I smiled at this unexpected reply and ventured:

"As a matter of fact, the East is not renowned for its truthfulness. I know it pretty well."

"You do, eh? Do you understand it?"

"I don't think either an American or a European ever understands an Asiatic people."

"Oh, yes, we do," rejoined Mr. Hemster; "they're liars and that's all there is to them. Liars and lazy; that sums them up."

As I was looking for the favor of work, it was not my place to contradict him, and the confident tone in which he spoke showed that contradiction would have availed little. He was evidently one of the men who knew it all, and success had confirmed him in his belief. I had met people of his calibre before,—to my grief.

"Well, young man, what can I do for you?" he asked, coming directly to the point.

"I am looking for a job," I said.

"What's your line?"

"I beg your pardon?"

"What can you do?"

"I am capable of taking charge of this ship as captain, or of working as a man before the mast."

"You spread yourself out too thin, my son. A man who can do everything can do nothing. We specialize in our country. I hire men who can do only one thing, and do that thing better than anybody else."

"Sir, I do not agree with you," I could not help saying. "The most capable people in the world are the Americans. The best log house I ever saw was built by a man who owned a brown-stone front on Fifth Avenue. He simply pushed aside the guides whose specialty it was to do such things, took the axe in his own hands, and showed them how it should be accomplished."

Mr. Hemster shoved his hat to the back of his head, and for the first time during our interview looked me squarely in the face.

"Where was that?" he inquired.

"Up in Canada."

"Oh, well, the Fifth Avenue man had probably come from the backwoods and so knew how to handle an axe."

"It's more than likely," I admitted.

"What were you doing in Canada?"

"Fishing and shooting."

"You weren't one of the guides he pushed aside?"

I laughed.

"No, I was one of the two who paid for the guides."

"Well, to come back to first principles," continued Mr. Hemster, "I've got a captain who gives me perfect satisfaction, and he hires the crew. What else can you do?"

"I am qualified to take a place as engineer if your present man isn't equally efficient with the captain; and I can guarantee to give satisfaction as a stoker, although I don't yearn for the job."

"My present engineer I got in Glasgow," said Mr. Hemster; "and as for stokers we have a mechanical stoker which answers the purpose reasonably well, although I have several improvements I am going to patent as soon as I get home. I believe the Scotchman I have as engineer is the best in the business. I wouldn't interfere with him for the world."

My heart sank, and I began to fear that Yansan and the sampan-boy would have to wait longer for their money. It seemed that it wasn't my ship that had come in, after all.

"Very well, Mr. Hemster," I said, "I must congratulate you on being so well suited. I am much obliged to you for receiving me so patiently without a letter of introduction on my part, and so I bid you good-day."

I turned for the ladder, but Mr. Hemster said, with more of animation in his tone than he had hitherto exhibited:

"Wait a moment, sonny; don't be so hasty. You've asked me a good many questions about the yacht and the crew, so I should like to put some to you, and who knows but we may make a deal yet. There's the galley and the stewards, and that sort of thing, you know. Draw up a chair and sit down."

I did as I was requested. Mr. Hemster threw his cigar overboard and took out another. Then he held out the case toward me, saying:

"Do you smoke?"

"Thank you," said I, selecting a cigar.

"Have you matches?" he asked, "I never carry them myself."

"No, I haven't," I admitted.

He pushed a button near him, and a Japanese steward appeared.

"Bring a box of matches and a bottle of champagne," he said.

The steward set a light wicker table at my elbow, disappeared for a few minutes, and shortly returned with a bottle of champagne and a box of matches. Did my eyes deceive me, or was this the most noted brand in the world, and of the vintage of '78? It seemed too good to be true.

"Would you like a sandwich or two with that wine, or is it too soon after lunch?"

"I could do with a few sandwiches," I confessed, thinking of Yansan's frugal fare; and shortly after there were placed before me, on a dainty, white, linen-and-lace-covered plate, some of the most delicious chicken sandwiches that it has ever been my fortune to taste.

"Now," said Mr. Hemster, when the steward had disappeared, "you're on your uppers, I take it."

"I don't think I understand."

"Why, you're down at bed-rock. Haven't you been in America? Don't you know the language?"

"'Yes' is the answer to all your questions."

"What's the reason? Drink? Gambling?"

Lord, how good that champagne tasted! I laughed from the pure, dry exhilaration of it.

"I wish I could say it was drink that brought me to this pass," I answered; "for this champagne shows it would be a tempting road to ruin. I am not a gambler, either. How I came to this pass would not interest you."

"Well, I take it that's just an Englishman's way of saying it's none of my business; but such is not the fact. You want a job, and you have come to me for it. Very well; I must know something about you. Whether I can give you a job or not will depend. You have said you could captain the ship or run her engines. What makes you so confident of your skill?"

"The fact is I possessed a yacht of my own not so very long ago, and I captained her and I ran her engines on different occasions."

"That might be a recommendation, or it might not. If, as captain, you wrecked your vessel, or if, as engineer, you blew her up, these actions would hardly be a certificate of competency."

"I did neither. I sold the yacht in New York for what it would bring."

"How much money did you have when you bought your yacht?"

"I had what you would call half a million."

"Why do you say what I would call half a million? What would you call it?"

"I should call it a hundred thousand."

"Ah, I see. You're talking of pounds, and I'm talking of dollars. You're an Englishman, I suspect. Are you an educated man?"

"Moderately so. Eton and Oxford," said I, the champagne beginning to have its usual effect on a hungry man. However, the announcement of Eton and Oxford had no effect upon Mr. Hemster, so it did not matter.

"Come, young fellow," he said, with some impatience, "tell me all about yourself, and don't have to be drawn out like a witness on the stand."

"Very well," said I, "here is my story. After I left Oxford I had some little influence, as you might call it."

"No, a 'pull,' I would call it. All right, where did it land you?"

"It landed me as secretary to a Minister of the Crown."

"You don't mean a preacher?"

"No, I mean the Minister of Foreign Affairs, and he put me into the diplomatic service when he found the Government was going to be defeated. I was secretary of legation at Pekin and also here in Japan."

I filled myself another glass of champagne, and, holding it up to see the sparkles, continued jauntily:

"If I may go so far as to boast, I may say I was entrusted with several

186

delicate missions, and I carried them through with reasonable success. I can both read and write the Japanese language, and I know a smattering of Chinese and a few dialects of the East, which have stood me in good stead more than once. To tell the truth, I was in a fair way for promotion and honor when unfortunately a relative died and left me the hundred thousand pounds that I spoke of."

"Why unfortunately? If you had had any brains you could have made that into millions."

"Yes, I suppose I could. I thought I was going to do it. I bought myself a yacht at Southampton and sailed for New York. To make a long story short, it was a gold mine and a matter of ten weeks which were taken up with shooting and fishing in Canada. Then I had the gold mine and the experience, while the other fellow had the cash. He was good enough to pay me a trifle for my steam yacht, which, as the advertisements say, was 'of no further use to the owner.'"

As I sipped my champagne, the incidents I was relating seemed to recede farther and farther back and become of little consequence. In fact I felt like laughing over them, and although in sober moments I should have called the action of the man who got my money a swindle, under the influence of dry '78 his scheme became merely a very clever exercise of wit. Mr. Hemster was looking steadily at me, and for once his cigar was almost motionless.

"Well, well," he murmured, more to himself than to me, "I have always said the geographical position of New York gives it a tremendous advantage over Chicago. They never let the fools come West. They have always the first whack at the moneyed Englishman, and will have until we get a ship canal that will let the liners through to Chicago direct. Fleeced in ten weeks! Well, well! Go on, my son. What did you do after you'd sold your yacht?"

"I took what money I had and made for the West."

"Came to Chicago?"

"Yes, I did."

"Just our luck. After you had been well buncoed you came to Chicago.

187

I swear I'm tempted to settle in New York when I get back."

"By the West I do not mean Chicago, Mr. Hemster. I went right through to San Francisco and took a steamer for Japan. I thought my knowledge of the East and of the languages might be of advantage. I was ashamed to return to England when I found I could make no headway here. I tried to bring influence to bear to get reinstated in the diplomatic service, but my brand of statesman was out of office and nothing could be done. I lived too expensively here at first, hoping to make an impression and gain a foothold that was worth having, and when I began to economize it was too late. I took to living in the native quarter, and descended from trying to get a clerkship into the position of a man who is willing to take anything. From my veranda on the hill up yonder I saw this boat come in, like a white-winged sea-gull, and so I came down, got into a sampan, and here I am, enjoying the best meal I've had for a long time. 'Here endeth the first lesson,'" I concluded irreverently, pouring out another glass of champagne.

Mr. Hemster did not reply for some moments. He was evidently ruminating, and the end of his cigar went round and round quicker and quicker.

"What might your name be?" he said at last.

"Rupert Tremorne."

"Got a handle to it?"

"A title? Oh, no! Plain Mr. Tremorne."

"I should say, off-hand, that a title runs in your family somewhere."

"Well; I admit that Lord Tremorne is my cousin, and we have a few others scattered about. However, there's little danger of it ever falling upon me. To tell the truth, the family for the last few years has no idea where I am, and now that I have lost my money I don't suppose they care very much. At least I have seen no advertisements in the papers, asking for a man of my description."

"If you were secretary to the Minister of whatever you call it, I don't know but what you'd do for me. I am short of a private secretary just at the present moment, and I think you'd do."

Whether it was the champagne, or the sandwiches, or the prospect of getting something to do, and consequently being able to pay my way, or all three combined, I felt like throwing my hat into the air and uttering a war-whoop; but something of native stolidity counterbalanced the effect of the stimulant, and I was astonished to hear myself reply very quietly:

"It would be folly for a man who had just applied for the position of stoker to pretend he is not elated at being offered a secretaryship. It is needless to say, Mr. Hemster, that I accept with alacrity and gratitude."

"Then that's settled," said the millionaire curtly. "As to the matter of salary, I think you would be wise to leave that to me. I have paid out a good deal of money recently and got mighty little for it. If you can turn the tide so that there is value received, you will find me liberal in the matter of wages."

"I am quite content to leave it so," I rejoined, "but I think I ought in honesty to tell you, if you are expecting a shrewd business man as your secretary who will turn the tide of fortune in any way, you are likely to be disappointed in me. I am afraid I am a very poor business man."

"I am aware of that already," replied Hemster. "I can supply all the business qualifications that are needed in this new combination. What I want of you is something entirely different. You said you could speak more languages than your own?"

"Yes, I am very familiar with French and German, and have also a smattering of Spanish and Italian. I can read and write Japanese, speaking that language and Chinese with reasonable fluency, and can even jabber a little in Corean."

"Then you're my man," said my host firmly. "I suppose now you would not object to a little something on account?"

"I should be very much obliged indeed if you have confidence enough in me to make an advance. There are some things I should like to buy before

I come aboard, and, not to put too fine a point to it, there are some debts I should like to settle."

"That's all right," commented Hemster shortly, thrusting his hand deep in his trousers pocket, and bringing out a handful of money which he threw on the wicker table. "There ought to be something like two hundred dollars there. Just count it and see, and write me a receipt for it."

I counted it, and, as I did so, thought he watched me rather keenly out of the corner of his eye. There was more than two hundred dollars in the heap, and I told him the amount. The Japanese brought up a sheet of paper headed with a gorgeous gilt and scarlet monogram and a picture of the yacht, and I wrote and signed the receipt.

"Do you know anything about the stores in town?" he asked, nodding his head toward Nagasaki.

"Oh, yes!"

"They tell me Nagasaki is a great place for buying crockery. I wish you would order sent to the yacht three complete dinner sets, three tea sets, and three luncheon sets. There is always a good deal of breakage on a sea-going yacht."

"Quite so," I replied. "Is there any particular pattern you wish, or any limit to the price?"

"Oh, I don't need expensive sets; anything will do. I'm not particular; in fact, I don't care even to see them; I leave that entirely to you, but tell the man to pack them securely, each in a separate box. He is to bring them aboard at half-past five this afternoon precisely, and ask for me. Now, when can you join us?"

"To-morrow morning, if that will be soon enough."

"Very well; to-morrow morning at ten."

I saw that he wished the interview terminated, as, for the last few minutes, he had exhibited signs of uneasiness. I therefore rose and said,—

rather stammeringly, I am afraid:

"Mr. Hemster, I don't know how to thank you for your kindness in——"

"Oh, that's all right; that's all right," he replied hastily, waving his hand; but before anything further could be spoken there came up on deck the most beautiful and stately creature I had ever beheld, superbly attired. She cast not even a glance at me, but hurried toward Mr. Hemster, crying impetuously:

"Oh, Poppa! I want to go into the town and shop!"

"Quite right, my dear," said the old man; "I wonder you've been so long about it. We've been in harbor two or three hours. This is Mr. Rupert Tremorne, my new private secretary. Mr. Tremorne, my daughter."

I made my bow, but it seemed to pass unnoticed.

"How do you do," said the girl hastily; then, to her father, "Poppa, I want some money!"

"Certainly, certainly, certainly," repeated the old gentleman, plunging his hand into his other pocket and pulling out another handful of the "necessary." As I learned afterward, each of his pockets seemed to be a sort of safe depository, which would turn forth any amount of capital when searched. He handed the accumulation to her, and she stuffed it hastily into a small satchel that hung at her side.

"You are going to take Miss Stretton with you?" he asked.

"Why, of course."

"Mr. Tremorne is cousin to Lord Tremorne, of England," said the old gentleman very slowly and solemnly.

I had been standing there rather stupidly, instead of taking my departure, as I should have done, for I may as well confess that I was astounded at the sumptuous beauty of the girl before me, who had hitherto cast not even a look in my direction. Now she raised her lovely, indescribable eyes to mine, and I felt a thrill extend to my finger-tips. Many handsome women have I seen in my day, but none to compare with this superb daughter of the West.

"Really!" she exclaimed with a most charming intonation of surprise. Then she extended a white and slim hand to me, and continued, "I am very glad to meet you, Mr. Tremorne. Do you live in Nagasaki?"

"I have done so for the past year."

"Then you know the town well?"

"I know it very well indeed."

At this juncture another young woman came on deck, and Miss Hemster turned quickly toward her.

"Oh, Hilda!" she cried, "I shall not need you to-day. Thanks ever so much."

"Not need her?" exclaimed her father. "Why, you can't go into Nagasaki alone, my dear."

"I have no intention of doing so," she replied amiably, "if Mr. Tremorne will be good enough to escort me."

"I shall be delighted," I gasped, expecting an expostulation from her father; but the old gentleman merely said:

"All right, my dear; just as you please."

"Rupert, my boy!" I said to my amazed self; "your ship has come in with a vengeance."

# CHAPTER III

A STAIRWAY was slung on the other side of the yacht from that on which I had ascended, and at its foot lay a large and comfortable boat belonging to the yacht, manned by four stout seamen. Down this stairway and into the boat I escorted Miss Hemster. She seated herself in the stern and took the tiller-ropes in her hands, now daintily gloved. I sat down opposite to her and was about to give a command to the men to give way when she forestalled me, and the oars struck the water simultaneously. As soon as we had rounded the bow of the yacht there was a sudden outcry from a half-naked Japanese boy who was sculling about in a sampan.

"What's the matter with him?" asked Miss Hemster with a little laugh. "Does he think we're going to desert this boat and take that floating coffin of his?"

"I think it is my own man," I said; "and he fears that his fare is leaving him without settling up. Have I your permission to stop these men till he comes alongside? He has been waiting patiently for me while I talked with Mr. Hemster."

"Why, certainly," said the girl, and in obedience to her order the crew held water, and as the boy came alongside I handed him more than double what I owed him, and he nearly upset his craft by bowing in amazed acknowledgment.

"You're an Englishman, I suppose," said Miss Hemster.

"In a sort of way I am, but really a citizen of the world. For many years past I have been less in England than in other countries."

"For many years? Why, you talk as if you were an old man, and you don't look a day more than thirty."

"My looks do not libel me, Miss Hemster," I replied with a laugh, "for I am not yet thirty."

"I am twenty-one," she said carelessly, "but every one says I don't look more than seventeen."

"I thought you were younger than seventeen," said I, "when I first saw you a moment ago."

"Did you really? I think it is very flattering of you to say so, and I hope you mean it."

"I do, indeed, Miss Hemster."

"Do you think I look younger than Hilda?" she asked archly, "most people do."

"Hilda!" said I. "What Hilda?"

"Why, Hilda Stretton, my companion."

"I have never seen her."

"Oh, yes, you did; she was standing at the companion-way and was coming with me when I preferred to come with you."

"I did not see her," I said, shaking my head; "I saw no one but you."

The young lady laughed merrily,—a melodious ripple of sound. I have heard women's laughter compared to the tinkle of silver bells, but to that musical tintinnabulation was now added something so deliciously human and girlish that the whole effect was nothing short of enchanting. Conversation now ceased, for we were drawing close to the shore. I directed the crew where to land, and the young lady sprang up the steps without assistance from me,—before, indeed, I could proffer any. I was about to follow when one of the sailors touched me on the shoulder.

"The old man," he said in a husky whisper, nodding his head toward the yacht, "told me to tell you that when you buy that crockery you're not to let Miss Hemster know anything about it."

"Aren't you coming?" cried Miss Hemster to me from the top of the wharf.

194

I ascended the steps with celerity and begged her pardon for my delay.

"I am not sprightly seventeen, you see," I said.

She laughed, and I put her in a 'rickshaw drawn by a stalwart Japanese, got into one myself, and we set off for the main shopping street. I was rather at a loss to know exactly what the sailor's message meant, but I took it to be that for some reason Mr. Hemster did not wish his daughter to learn that he was indulging so freely in dinner sets. As it was already three o'clock in the afternoon, I realized that there would be some difficulty in getting the goods aboard by five o'clock, unless the young lady dismissed me when we arrived at the shops. This, however, did not appear to be her intention in the least; when our human steeds stopped, she gave me her hand lightly as she descended, and then said, with her captivating smile:

"I want you to take me at once to a china shop."

"To a what?" I cried.

"To a shop where they sell dishes,—dinner sets and that sort of thing. You know what I mean,—a crockery store."

I did, but I was so astonished by the request coming right on the heels of the message from her father, and taken in conjunction with his previous order, that I am afraid I stood looking very much like a fool, whereupon she laughed heartily, and I joined her. I saw she was quite a merry young lady, with a keen sense of the humour of things.

"Haven't they any crockery stores in this town?" she asked.

"Oh, there are plenty of them," I replied.

"Why, you look as if you had never heard of such a thing before. Take me, then, to whichever is the best. I want to buy a dinner set and a tea set the very first thing."

I bowed, and, somewhat to my embarrassment, she took my arm, tripping along by my side as if she were a little girl of ten, overjoyed at her outing, to which feeling she gave immediate expression.

195

"Isn't this jolly?" she cried.

"It is the most undeniably jolly shopping excursion I ever engaged in," said I, fervently and truthfully.

"You see," she went on, "the delight of this sort of thing is that we are in an utterly foreign country and can do just as we please. That is why I did not wish Hilda to come with us. She is rather prim and has notions of propriety which are all right at home, but what is the use of coming to foreign countries if you cannot enjoy them as you wish to?"

"I think that is a very sensible idea," said I.

"Why, it seems as if you and I were members of a travelling theatrical company, and were taking part in 'The Mikado,' doesn't it? What funny little people they are all around us! Nagasaki doesn't seem real. It looks as if it were set on a stage,—don't you think so?"

"Well, you know, I am rather accustomed to it. I have lived here for more than a year, as I told you."

"Oh, so you said. I have not got used to it yet. Have you ever seen 'The Mikado?'"

"Do you mean the Emperor or the play?"

"At the moment I was thinking of the play."

"Yes, I have seen it, and the real Mikado, too, and spoken with him."

"Have you, indeed? How lucky you are!"

"You speak truly, Miss Hemster, and I never knew how lucky I was until to-day."

She bent her head and laughed quietly to herself. I thought we were more like a couple of school children than members of a theatrical troupe, but as I never was an actor I cannot say how the latter behave when they are on the streets of a strange town.

"Oh, I have met your kind of man before, Mr. Tremorne. You don't

196

mind what you say when you are talking to a lady as long as it is something flattering."

"I assure you, Miss Hemster, that quite the contrary is the case. I never flatter; and if I have been using a congratulatory tone it has been directed entirely to myself and to my own good fortune."

"There you go again. How did you come to meet the Mikado?"

"I used to be in the diplomatic service in Japan, and my duties on several occasions brought me the honor of an audience with His Majesty."

"How charmingly you say that, and I can see that you believe it from your heart; and although we are democratic, I believe it, too. I always love diplomatic society, and enjoyed a good deal of it in Washington, and my imagination always pictured behind them the majesty of royalty, so I have come abroad to see the real thing. I was presented at Court in London, Mr. Tremorne. Now, please don't say that you congratulate the Court!"

"There is no need of my saying it, as it has already been said; or perhaps I should say 'it goes without saying.'"

"Thank you very much, Mr. Tremorne; I think you are the most polite man I ever met. I want you to do me a very great favor and introduce me to the higher grades of diplomatic society in Nagasaki during our stay here."

"I regret, Miss Hemster, that that is impossible, because I have been out of the service for some years now. Besides, the society here is consular rather than diplomatic. The Legation is at the capital, you know. Nagasaki is merely a commercial city."

"Oh, is it? I thought perhaps you had been seeing my father to-day because of some consular business, or that sort of thing, pertaining to the yacht."

As the girl said this I realized, with a suddenness that was disconcerting, the fact that I was practically acting under false pretences. I was her father's humble employee, and she did not know it. I remembered with a pang when her father first mentioned my name she paid not the slightest attention to it; but when he said I was the cousin of Lord Tremorne the young lady had favored me with a glance I was not soon to forget. Therefore, seeing that Mr. Hemster had neglected to make my position clear, it now became my duty to give some necessary explanation, so that his daughter might not continue an acquaintance that was rapidly growing almost intimate under her misapprehension as to who I was. I saw with a pang that a humiliation was in store for me such as always lies in wait for a man who momentarily steps out of his place and receives consideration which is not his social due.

I had once before suffered the experience which was now ahead of me, and it was an episode I did not care to repeat, although I failed to see how it could be honestly avoided. On my return to Japan I sought out the man in the diplomatic service who had been my greatest friend and for whom I had in former days accomplished some slight services, because my status in the ranks was superior to his own. Now that there was an opportunity for a return of these services, I called upon him, and was received with a cordiality that went to my discouraged heart; but the moment he learned I was in need, and that I could not regain the place I had formerly held, he congealed in the most tactful manner possible. It was an interesting study in human deportment. His manner and words were simply unimpeachable, but there gathered around him a mantle of impenetrable frigidity the collection of which was a triumph in tactful intercourse. As he grew colder and colder, I grew hotter and hotter. I managed to withdraw without showing, I hope, the deep humiliation I felt. Since that time I had never sought a former acquaintance, or indeed any countryman of my own, preferring to be indebted to my old friend Yansan on the terrace above or the sampan-boy on the waters below. The man I speak of has risen high and is rising higher in my old profession, and every now and then his last words ring in my ears and warm them,—words of counterfeit cordiality as he realized they were the last that he should probably ever speak to me:

"Well, my dear fellow, I'm ever so glad you called. If I can do anything for you, you must be sure and let me know."

As I had already let him know, my reply that I should certainly do so must have sounded as hollow as his own smooth phrase.

Unpleasant as that episode was, the situation was now ten times worse, as it involved a woman,—and a lovely woman at that,—who had treated me with a kindness she would feel misplaced when she understood the truth. However, there was no help for it, so, clearing my throat, I began:

"Miss Hemster, when I took the liberty of calling on your father this morning, I was a man penniless and out of work. I went to the yacht in the hope that I might find something to do. I was fortunate enough to be offered the position of private secretary to Mr. Hemster, which position I have accepted."

The young lady, as I expected, instantly withdrew her hand from my arm, and stood there facing me, I also coming to a halt; and thus we confronted each other in the crowded street of Nagasaki. Undeniable amazement overspread her beautiful countenance.

"Why!" she gasped, "you are, then, Poppa's hired man?"

I winced a trifle, but bowed low to her.

"Madam," I replied, "you have stated the fact with great truth and terseness."

"Do you mean to say," she said, "that you are to be with us after this on the yacht?"

"I suspect such to be your father's intention." Then, to my amazement, she impulsively thrust forth both her hands and clasped mine.

"Why, how perfectly lovely!" she exclaimed. "I haven't had a white man to talk with except Poppa for ages and ages. But you must remember that everything I want you to do, you are to do. You are to be my hired man; Poppa won't mind."

"You will find me a most devoted retainer, Miss Hemster."

"I do love that word 'retainer,'" she cried enthusiastically. "It is like the magic talisman of the 'Arabian Nights,' and conjures up at once visions of a historic tower, mullioned windows, and all that sort of thing. When you were made a bankrupt, Mr. Tremorne, was there one faithful old retainer who refused to desert you as the others had done?"

"Ah, my dear young lady, you are thinking of the romantic drama now, as you were alluding to comic opera a little while ago. I believe, in the romantic drama, the retainer, like the man with the mortgage, never lets go. I am thankful to say I had no such person in my employ. He would have been an awful nuisance. It was hard enough to provide for myself, not to mention a retainer. But here we are at the crockery shop."

I escorted her in, and she was soon deeply absorbed in the mysteries of this pattern or that of the various wares exposed to her choice. Meanwhile I took the opportunity to give the proprietor instructions in his own language to send to the yacht before five o'clock what Mr. Hemster had ordered, and I warned the man he was not to mix up the order I had just given him with that of the young lady. The Japanese are very quick at comprehension, and when Miss Hemster and I left the place I had no fear of any complication arising through my instructions.

We wandered from shop to shop, the girl enthusiastic over Nagasaki, much to my wonder, for there are other places in Japan more attractive than this commercial town; but the glamor of the East cast its spell over the young woman, and, although I was rather tired of the Orient, I must admit that the infection of her high spirits extended to my own feelings. A week ago it would have appeared impossible that I should be enjoying myself so thoroughly as I was now doing. It seemed as if years had rolled from my shoulders, and I was a boy once more, living in a world where conventionality was unknown.

The girl herself was in a whirlwind of glee, and it was not often that the shopkeepers of Nagasaki met so easy a victim. She seemed absolutely reckless in the use of money, paying whatever was asked for anything that took her fancy. In a very short time all her ready cash was gone, but that made not the slightest difference. She ordered here and there with the extravagance of a queen, on what she called the "C. O. D." plan, which I afterward learned was an American phrase meaning, "Collect on delivery." Her peregrinations would have tired out half-a-dozen men, but she showed no signs of fatigue. I felt a hesitation about inviting her to partake of refreshment, but I need not have been so backward.

"Talking of comic operas," she exclaimed as we came out of the last place, "Aren't there any tea-houses here, such as we see on the stage?"

"Yes, plenty of them," I replied.

"Well," she exclaimed with a ripple of laughter, "take me to the wickedest of them. What is the use of going around the world in a big yacht if you don't see life?"

I wondered what her father would say if he knew, but I acted the faithful retainer to the last, and did as I was bid. She expressed the utmost delight in everything she saw, and it was well after six o'clock when we descended from our 'rickshaw at the landing. The boat was awaiting us, and in a short time we were alongside the yacht once more. It had been a wild, tempestuous outing, and I somewhat feared the stern disapproval of an angry parent. He was leaning over the rail revolving an unlit cigar.

"Oh, Poppa!" she cried up at him with enthusiasm, "I have had a perfectly splendid time. Mr. Tremorne knows Nagasaki like a book. He has taken me everywhere," she cried, with unnecessary emphasis on the last word.

The millionaire was entirely unperturbed.

"That's all right," he said. "I hope you haven't tired yourself out."

"Oh, no! I should be delighted to do it all over again! Has anybody sent anything aboard for me?"

"Yes," said the old man, "there's been a procession of people here since you left. Dinner's ready, Mr. Tremorne. You'll come aboard, of course, and take pot-luck with us?"

"No, thank you, Mr. Hemster," I said; "I must get a sampan and make my way into town again."

"Just as you say; but you don't need a sampan, these men will row you back again. See you to-morrow at ten, then."

Miss Hemster, now on deck, leaned over the rail and daintily blew me a kiss from the tips of her slender fingers.

"Thank you so much, retainer," she cried, as I lifted my hat in token of farewell.

# CHAPTER IV

**I WAS** speedily rowed ashore in a state of great exaltation. The sudden change in my expectations was bewilderingly Eastern in its completeness. The astonishingly intimate companionship of this buoyant, effervescent girl had affected me as did the bottle of champagne earlier in the day. I was well aware that many of my former acquaintances would have raised their hands in horror at the thought of a girl wandering about an Eastern city with me, entirely unchaperoned; but I had been so long down on my luck, and the experiences I had encountered with so-called fashionable friends had been so bitter, that the little finicky rules of society seemed of small account when compared with the realities of life. The girl was perfectly untrained and impulsive, but that she was a true-hearted woman I had not the slightest doubt. Was I in love with her? I asked myself, and at that moment my brain was in too great a whirl to be able to answer the question satisfactorily to myself. My short ten weeks in America had given me no such acquaintance as this, although the two months and a half had cost me fifty thousand dollars a week, certainly the most expensive living that any man is likely to encounter. I had met a few American women, but they

all seemed as cold and indifferent as our own, while here was a veritable child of nature, as untrammelled by the little rules of society as could well be imagined. After all, were these rules so important as I had hitherto supposed them to be? Certainly not, I replied to myself, as I stepped ashore.

I climbed the steep hill to my former residence with my head in the air in every sense of the word. Many a weary journey I had taken up that forlorn path, and it had often been the up-hill road of discouragement; but to-night Japan was indeed the land of enchantment which so many romantic writers have depicted it. I thought of the girl and thought of her father, wondering what my new duties were to be. If to-day were a sample of them then truly was Paradise regained, as the poet has it. I had told Mr. Hemster that I needed time to purchase necessary things for the voyage, but this would take me to very few shops. I had in store in Nagasaki a large trunk filled with various suits of clothing, a trunk of that comprehensive kind which one buys in America. This was really in pawn. I had delivered it to a shopkeeper who had given me a line of credit now long since ended, but I knew I should find my goods and chattels safe when I came with the money, as indeed proved to be the case.

It was a great pleasure to meet Yansan once more, bowing as lowly as if I were in truth a millionaire. I had often wondered what would happen if I had been compelled to tell the grimacing old fellow I had no money to pay him. Would his excessive politeness have stood the strain? Perhaps so, but luckily his good nature was not to be put to the test. I could scarcely refrain from grasping his two hands, as Miss Hemster had grasped mine, and dancing with him around the bare habitation which he owned and which had so long been my shelter. However, I said calmly to him:

"Yansan, my ship has come in, as I told you this morning; and now, if you will bring me that bill, errors and all, I will pay you three times its amount."

Speechless, the old man dropped on his knees and beat his forehead against the floor.

"Excellency has always been too good to me!" he exclaimed.

I tried to induce good old Yansan to share supper with me; but he was too much impressed with my greatness and could do nothing but bow and bow and serve me.

After the repast I went down into the town again, redeemed my trunk and its contents, bought what I needed, and ordered everything forwarded to the yacht before seven o'clock next morning. Then I went to a tea-house, and drank tea, and thought over the wonderful events of the day, after which I climbed the hill again for a night's rest.

I was very sorry to bid farewell to old Yansan next morning, and I believe he was very sorry to part with his lodger. Once more at the waterside I hailed my sampan-boy, who was now all eagerness to serve me, and he took me out to the yacht, which was evidently ready for an early departure. Her whole crew was now aboard, and most of them had had a day's leave in Nagasaki yesterday. The captain was pacing up and down the bridge, and smoke was lazily trailing from the funnel.

Arrived on deck I found Mr. Hemster in his former position in the cane chair, with his back still toward Nagasaki, which town I believe he never glanced at all the time his yacht was in harbor. I learned afterward that he thought it compared very unfavorably with Chicago. His unlighted cigar was describing circles in the air, and all in all I might have imagined he had not changed from the position I left him in the day before if I had not seen him leaning over the rail when I escorted his daughter back to the yacht. He gave me no further greeting than a nod, which did not err on the side of effusiveness.

I inquired of the Japanese boy, who stood ready to receive me with all the courtesy of his race, whether my luggage had come aboard, and he informed me that it had. I approached Mr. Hemster, bidding him good-morning, but he gave a side nod of his head toward the Japanese boy and said, "He'll show you to your cabin," so I followed the youth down the companion-way to my quarters. The yacht, as I have said, was very big. The main saloon extended from side to side, and was nearly as large as the dining-room of an ocean liner. Two servants with caps and aprons, exactly like English housemaids, were dusting and putting things to rights as I passed through.

My cabin proved ample in size, and was even more comfortably equipped than I expected to find it. My luggage was there, and I took the opportunity of changing my present costume for one of more nautical cut, and, placing a yachting-cap on my head, I went on deck again. I had expected, from all the preparedness I had seen, to hear the anchor-chain rattle up before I was equipped, and feared for the moment that I had delayed the sailing of the yacht; but on looking at my watch as I went on deck I found it was not yet ten o'clock, so I was in ample time, as had been arranged.

I had seen nothing of Miss Hemster, and began to suspect that she had gone ashore and that the yacht was awaiting her return; but a glance showed me that all the yacht's boats were in place, so if the young woman had indulged in a supplementary shopping-tour it must have been in a sampan, which was unlikely.

The old gentleman, as I approached him, eyed my yachting toggery with what seemed to me critical disapproval.

"Well," he said, "you're all fitted out for a cruise, aren't you? Have a cigar,"—and he offered me his case.

I took the weed and replied:

"Yes, and you seem ready to begin a cruise. May I ask where you are going?"

"I don't know exactly," he replied carelessly. "I haven't quite made up my mind yet. I thought perhaps you might be able to decide the matter."

"To decide!" I answered in surprise.

"Yes," he said, sitting up suddenly and throwing the cigar overboard. "What nonsense were you talking to my daughter yesterday?"

I was so taken aback at this unexpected and gruff inquiry that I fear I stood there looking rather idiotic, which was evidently the old man's own impression of me, for he scowled in a manner that was extremely disconcerting. I had no wish to adopt the Adam-like expedient of blaming the woman; but, after all, he had been there when I went off alone with her, and it was really not my fault that I was the girl's sole companion in Nagasaki. All my own early training and later social prejudices led me to sympathize with Mr. Hemster's evident ill-humour regarding our shore excursion, but nevertheless it struck me as a trifle belated. He should have objected when the proposal was made.

"Really, sir," I stammered at last, "I'm afraid I must say I don't exactly know what you mean."

"I think I spoke plainly enough," he answered. "I want you to be careful what you say, and if you come with me to my office, where we shall not be interrupted, I'll give you a straight talking to, so that we may avoid trouble in the future."

I was speechless with amazement, and also somewhat indignant. If he took this tone with me, my place was evidently going to be one of some difficulty. However, needs must when the devil drives, even if he comes from Chicago; and although his words were bitter to endure, I was in a manner helpless and forced to remember my subordinate position, which, in truth, I had perhaps forgotten during my shopping experiences with his impulsive daughter. Yet I had myself made her aware of my situation, and if our conversation at times had been a trifle free and easy I think the fault—— but there—there—there——I'm at the Adam business again. The woman tempted me, and I did talk. I felt humiliated that even to myself I placed any blame upon her.

Mr. Hemster rose, nipped off the point of another cigar, and strode along the deck to the companion-way, I following him like a confessed culprit. He led me to what he called his office, a room not very much larger than my own, but without the bunk that took up part of the space in my cabin; in fact a door led out of it which, I afterward learned, communicated with his bedroom. The office was fitted up with an American roll-top desk fastened to the floor, a copying-press, a typewriter, filing-cases from floor to ceiling, and other paraphernalia of a completely equipped business establishment. There was a swivelled armchair before the desk, into which Mr. Hemster dropped and leaned back, the springs creaking as he did so. There was but one other chair in the room, and he motioned me into it.

"See here!" he began abruptly. "Did you tell my daughter yesterday that you were a friend of the Mikado's?"

"God bless me, no!" I was surprised into replying. "I said nothing of the sort."

"Well, you left her under that impression."

"I cannot see, Mr. Hemster, how such can be the case. I told Miss Hemster that I had met the Mikado on several occasions, but I explained to her that these occasions were entirely official, and each time I merely accompanied a superior officer in the diplomatic service. Although I have spoken with His Majesty, it was merely because questions were addressed to me, and because I was the only person present sufficiently conversant with the Japanese language to make him a reply in his own tongue."

"I see, I see," mused the old gentleman; "but Gertie somehow got it into her head that you could introduce us personally to the Mikado. I told her it was not likely that a fellow I had picked up strapped from the streets of Nagasaki, as one might say, would be able to give us an introduction that would amount to anything."

I felt myself getting red behind the ears as Mr. Hemster put my situation with, what seemed to me, such unnecessary brutality. Yet, after all, what he had said was the exact truth, and I had no right to complain of it, for if there was money in my pocket at that moment it was because he had placed it there; and then I saw intuitively that he meant no offence, but was merely repeating what he had said to his daughter, placing the case in a way that would be convincing to a man, whatever effect it might have on a woman's mind.

"I am afraid," I said, "that I must have expressed myself clumsily to Miss Hemster. I think I told her,—but I make the statement subject to correction,—that I had so long since severed my connection with diplomatic service in Tokio that even the slight power I then possessed no longer exists. If I still retained my former position I should scarcely be more helpless than I am now, so far as what you require is concerned."

"That's exactly what I told her," growled the old man. "I suppose you haven't any suggestion to make that would help me out at all?"

"The only suggestion I can make is this, and indeed I think the way seems perfectly clear. You no doubt know your own Ambassador,—perhaps have letters of introduction to him,—and he may very easily arrange for you to have an audience with His Majesty the Mikado."

"Oh! our Ambassador!" growled Mr. Hemster in tones of great contempt; "he's nothing but a one-horse politician."

"Nevertheless," said I, "his position is such that by merely exercising the prerogatives of his office he could get you what you wanted."

"No, he can't," maintained the old gentleman stoutly. "Still, I shouldn't say anything against him; he's all right. He did his best for us, and if we could have waited long enough at Yokohama perhaps he might have fixed up an audience with the Mikado. But I'd had enough of hanging on around there, and so I sailed away. Now, my son, I said I was going to give you a talking to, and I am. I'll tell you just how the land lies, so you can be of some help to me and not a drawback. I want you to be careful of what you say to Gertie about such people as the Mikado, because it excites her and makes her think certain things are easy when they're not."

"I am very sorry if I have said anything that led to a misapprehension. I certainly did not intend to."

"No, no! I understand that. I am not blaming you a bit. I just want you to catch on to the situation, that's all. Gertie likes you first rate; she told me so, and I'm ever so much obliged to you for the trouble you took yesterday afternoon in entertaining her. She told me everything you said and did, and it was all right. Now Gertie has always been accustomed to moving in the very highest society. She doesn't care for anything else, and she took to you from the very first. I was glad of that, because I should have consulted her before I hired you. Nevertheless, I knew the moment you spoke that you were the man I wanted, and so I took the risk. I never cared for high society myself; my intercourse has been with business men. I understand them, and I like them; but I don't cut any figure in high society, and I don't care to, either. Now, with Gertie it's different. She's been educated at the finest schools, and I've taken her all over Europe, where we stayed at the very best hotels and met the very best people in both Europe and America. Why, we've met more Sirs and Lords and Barons and High Mightinesses than you can shake a stick at. Gertie, she's right at home among those kind of people, and, if I do say it myself, she's quite capable of taking her place among the best of them, and she knows it. There never was a time we came in to the best table d'hôte in Europe that every eye wasn't turned toward her, and she's been the life of the most noted hotels that exist, no matter where they are, and no matter what their price is."

I ventured to remark that I could well believe this to have been the case.

"Yes, and you don't need to take my word for it," continued the old man with quite perceptible pride; "you may ask any one that was there. Whether it was a British Lord, or a French Count, or a German Baron, or an Italian Prince, it was just the same. I admit that it seemed to me that some of those nobles didn't amount to much. But that's neither here nor there; as I told you before, I'm no judge. I suppose they have their usefulness in creation, even though I'm not able to see it. But the result of it all was that Gertie got tired of them, and, as she is an ambitious girl and a real lady, she determined to strike higher, and so, when we bought this yacht and came abroad again, she determined to go in for Kings, so I've been on a King hunt ever since, and to tell the truth it has cost me a lot of money and I don't like it. Not that I mind the money if it resulted in anything, but it hasn't resulted in anything; that is, it hasn't amounted to much. Gertie doesn't care for the ordinary presentation at Court, for nearly anybody can have that. What she wants is to get a King or an Emperor right here on board this yacht at lunch or tea, or whatever he wants, and enjoy an intimate conversation with him, just like she's had with them no-account Princes. Then she wants a column or two account of that written up for the Paris edition of the "New York Herald," and she wants to have it cabled over to America. Now she's the only chick or child I've got. Her mother's been dead these fifteen years, and Gertie is all I have in the world, so I'm willing to do anything she wants done, no matter whether I like it or not. But I don't want to engage in anything that doesn't succeed. Success is the one thing that amounts to anything. The man who is a failure cuts no ice. And so it rather grinds me to confess that I've been a failure in this King business. Now I don't know much about Kings, but it strikes me they're just like other things in this world. If you want to get along with them, you must study them. It's like climbing a stair; if you want to get to the top you must begin at the lowest step. If you try to take one stride up to the top landing, why you're apt to come down on your head. I told Gertie it was no use beginning with the German Emperor, for we'd have to get accustomed to the low-down Kings and gradually work up. She believes in aiming high. That's all right ordinarily, but it isn't a practical proposition. Still, I let her have her way and did the best I could, but it was no use. I paid a German Baron a certain sum for getting the Emperor on board my yacht, but he didn't deliver the goods. So I said to Gertie: 'My girl, we'd better go to India, or some place where Kings are cheap, and practise on them first.' She hated to give in, but she's a reasonable young woman if you take her the right way. Well, the long and the short of it was that we sent the yacht around to Marseilles, and went down from Paris to meet her there, and sailed to Egypt, and, just as I said, we had no difficulty at all in raking in the Khedive. But that wasn't very satisfactory when all's said and done. Gertie claimed he wasn't a real king, and I say he's not a real gentleman. We had a little unpleasantness there, and he became altogether too friendly, so we sailed off down through the Canal a hunting Kings, till at last we got here to Japan. Now we're up against it once more, and I suppose this here Mikado has hobnobbed so much with real Emperors and that sort of thing that he thinks himself a white man like the rest. So I says to Gertie, 'There's a genuine Emperor in Corea, good enough to begin on, and we'll go there,' and that's how we came round from Yokohama to Nagasaki, and dropped in here to get a few things we might not be able to obtain in Corea. The moment I saw you and learned that you knew a good deal about the East, it struck me that if I took you on as private secretary you would be able to give me a few points, and perhaps take charge of this business altogether. Do you think you'd be able to do that?"

"Well," I said hesitatingly, "I'm not sure, but if I can be of any use to you on such a quest it will be in Corea. I've been there on two or three occasions, and each time had an audience with the King."

"Why do you call him the King? Isn't he an Emperor?"

"Well, I've always called him the King, but I've heard people term him the Emperor."

"The American papers always call him an Emperor. So you think you could manage it, eh?"

"I don't know that there would be any difficulty about the matter. Of course you are aware he is merely a savage."

211

"Well, they're all savages out here, aren't they? I don't suppose he's any worse or any better than the Mikado."

"Oh, the Mikado belongs to one of the most ancient civilizations in the world. I don't think the two potentates are at all on a par."

"Well, that's all right. That just bears out what I was saying, that it's the correct thing to begin with the lowest of them. You see I hate to admit I'm too old to learn anything, and I think I can learn this King business if I stick long enough at it. But I don't believe in a man trying to make a grand piano before he knows how to handle a saw. So you see, Mr. Tremorne, the position is just this. I want to sail for Corea, and Gertie, she wants to go back to Yokohama and tackle the Mikado again, thinking you can pull it off this time."

"I dislike very much to disagree with a lady," I said, "but I think your plan is the more feasible of the two. I do not think it would be possible to get the Mikado to come aboard this yacht, but it might be that the King of Corea would accept your invitation."

"What's the name of the capital of that place?" asked Mr. Hemster.

"It is spelled S-e-o-u-l, and is pronounced 'Sool.'"

"How far is it from here?"

"I don't know exactly, but it must be something like four hundred miles, perhaps a little more."

"It is on the sea?"

"No. It lies some twenty-six miles inland by road, and more than double that distance by the winding river Han."

"Can I steam up that river with this yacht to the capital?"

"No, I don't think you could. You could go part way, perhaps, but I imagine your better plan would be to moor at the port of Chemulpo and go to Seoul by road, although the road is none of the best."

"I've got a little naphtha launch on board. I suppose the river is big enough for us to go up to the capital in that?"

"Yes, I suppose you could do it in a small launch, but the river is so crooked that I doubt if you would gain much time, although you might gain in comfort."

"Very well, we'll make for that port, whatever you call it," said Hemster, rising. "Now, if you'll just take an armchair on deck, and smoke, I'll give instructions to the captain."

# CHAPTER V

WE had been a long time together in the little office, longer even than this extended conversation would lead a reader to imagine, and as I went through the saloon I saw that they were laying the table for lunch, a sight by no means ungrateful to me, for I had risen early and enjoyed but a small and frugal breakfast. I surmised from the preparations going forward that I should in the near future have something better than rice. When I reached the deck I saw the captain smoking a pipe and still pacing the bridge with his hands in his pockets. He was a grizzled old sea-dog, who, I found later, had come from the Cape Cod district, and was what he looked, a most capable man. I went aft and sat down, not wishing to go forward and became acquainted with the captain, as I expected every moment that Mr. Hemster would come up and give him his sailing-orders. But time passed on and nothing happened, merely the same state of tension that occurs when every one is ready to move and no move is made. At last the gong sounded for lunch. I saw the captain pause in his promenade, knock the ashes out of his pipe into the palm of his hand, and prepare to go down. So I rose and descended the stairway, giving a nod of recognition to the captain, who followed at my heels. The table was laid for five persons. Mr. Hemster occupied the position at the head of it, and on his right sat his daughter, her head bent down over the tablecloth. On the opposite side, at Mr. Hemster's left, sat the young lady of whom I had had a glimpse the afternoon before. The captain pushed past me with a gruff, "How de do, all," which was not responded to. He took the place at the farther end of the table. If I have described the situation on deck as a state of tension, much more so was the atmosphere of the dining-saloon. The silence was painful, and, not knowing what better to do, I approached Miss Hemster and said pleasantly:

"Good-morning. I hope you are none the worse for your shopping expedition of yesterday."

The young woman did not look up or reply till her father said in beseeching tones:

"Gertie, Mr. Tremorne is speaking to you."

Then she glanced at me with eyes that seemed to sparkle dangerously.

"Oh, how do you do?" she said rapidly. "Your place is over there by Miss Stretton."

There was something so insulting in the tone and inflection that it made the words, simple as they were, seem like a slap in the face. Their purport seemed to be to put me in my proper position in that society, to warn me that, if I had been treated as a friend the day before, conditions were now changed, and I was merely, as she had previously remarked, her father's hired man. My situation was anything but an enviable one, and as there was nothing to say I merely bowed low to the girl, walked around behind the captain, and took my place beside Miss Stretton, as I had been commanded to do. I confess I was deeply hurt by the studied insolence of look and voice; but a moment later I felt that I was probably making a mountain of a molehill, for the good, bluff captain said, as if nothing unusual had happened:

"That's right, young man; I see you have been correctly brought up. Always do what the women tell you. Obey orders if you break owners. That's what we do in our country. In our country, sir, we allow the women to rule, and their word is law, even though the men vote."

"Such is not the case in the East," I could not help replying.

"Why," said the captain, "it's the East I'm talking about. All throughout the Eastern States, yes, and the Western States, too."

"Oh, I beg your pardon," I replied, "I was referring to the East of Asia. The women don't rule in these countries."

"Well," said the staunch captain, "then that's the reason they amount to so little. I never knew an Eastern country yet that was worth the powder to blow it up."

"I'm afraid," said I, "that your rule does not prove universally good. It's

215

a woman who reigns in China, and I shouldn't hold that Empire up as an example to others."

The captain laughed heartily.

"Young man, you're contradicting yourself. You're excited, I guess. You said a minute ago that women didn't rule in the East, and now you show that the largest country in the East is ruled by a woman. You can't have it both ways, you know."

I laughed somewhat dismally in sympathy with him, and, lunch now being served, the good man devoted his entire attention to eating. As no one else said a word except the captain and myself, I made a feeble but futile attempt to cause the conversation to become general. I glanced at my fair neighbor to the right, who had not looked up once since I entered. Miss Stretton was not nearly so handsome a girl as Miss Hemster, yet nevertheless in any ordinary company she would be regarded as very good-looking. She had a sweet and sympathetic face, and at the present moment it was rosy red.

"Have you been in Nagasaki?" I asked, which was a stupid question, for I knew she had not visited the town the day before, and unless she had gone very early there was no time for her to have been ashore before I came aboard.

She answered "No" in such low tones that, fearing I had not heard it, she cleared her throat, and said "No" again. Then she raised her eyes for one brief second, cast a sidelong glance at me, so appealing and so vivid with intelligence, that I read it at once to mean, "Oh, please do not talk to me."

The meal was most excellent, yet I never remember to have endured a half-hour so unpleasant. Across the table from me, Miss Hemster had pushed away plate after plate and had touched nothing. When I spoke to her companion she began drumming nervously on the tablecloth with her fingers, as if she had great difficulty in preventing herself giving expression to an anger that was only too palpable. Her father went on stolidly with his lunch, and made no effort to relieve the rigor of the amazing situation. As soon as the main dish had been served and disposed of, the captain rose, and, nodding to the company, made for the companion-way. Once there he turned on his heel and said:

"Mr. Hemster, any orders?"

Before her father could reply, the young lady rose with an action so sudden and a gesture of her right hand so sweeping that the plate before her toppled and fell with a crash to the floor. I noticed Mr. Hemster instinctively grasp the tablecloth, but the girl marched away as erect as a grenadier, her shapely shoulders squared as if she was on military parade, and thus she disappeared into the forward part of the ship. Miss Stretton looked up at her employer, received a slight nod, then she, with a murmur of excuse to me, rose and followed the mistress of the ship. I heard a loud, angry voice, shrill as that of a peacock, for a moment, then a door was closed, and all was still. Mr. Hemster said slowly to the captain:

"I'll be up there in a minute and let you know where we're going. We've got all the time there is, you know."

"Certainly, sir," said the captain, disappearing.

There was nothing to say, so I said nothing, and Mr. Hemster and I sat out our lonely meal together. He seemed in no way perturbed by what had taken place, and as, after all, it was no affair of mine, even if my unfortunate remark regarding the Mikado had been the cause of it, I said inwardly there was little reason for my disturbing myself about it. Although the old gentleman showed no outward sign of inward commotion, he nevertheless seemed anxious that our dismal meal should draw to a speedy close, for he said to me at last:

"If you wish for coffee, you can have it served to you on deck."

"Thank you," said I, glad to avail myself of the opportunity to escape. As I mounted the companion-way I heard him say in firmer tones than I had known him to use before:

"Tell my daughter to come here to me,"—a command answered by the gentle "Yes, sir," of the Japanese boy.

I moved the wicker chair and table as far aft as possible, to be out of

217

earshot should any remarks follow me from the saloon. I saw the captain on the bridge again, pacing up and down, pipe in mouth and, hands in pockets. Even at that distance I noticed on his face a semi-comical grimace, and it actually seemed to me that he winked his left eye in my direction. The coffee did not come, and as I rose to stroll forward and converse with the captain I could not help hearing the low determined tones of the man down in the saloon, mingled now and then with the high-pitched, angry voice of the woman. As I hurried forward there next came up the companion-way a scream so terrible and ear-piercing that it must have startled every one on board, yet nobody moved. This was followed instantly by a crash, as if the table had been flung over, which of course was impossible, as it was fastened to the floor. Then came the hysterical, terrifying half-scream, half-sob of a woman apparently in mortal agony, and instinctively I started down the companion-way, to be met by Miss Stretton, who stretched her arms from side to side of the stairway. The appealing look I had noticed before was in her eyes, and she said in a low voice:

"Please don't come down. You can do no good."

"Is anybody hurt?" I cried.

"No, nobody, nobody. Please don't come down."

I turned back, and not wishing to see the captain or any one else at that moment, sat down in my chair again. The sobs died away, and then Mr. Hemster came up the companion-way with a determined look on his face which seemed to me to say, "Women do not rule after all." Once on deck he shouted out to the captain the one word:

"Corea!"

# CHAPTER VI

THE shouting of those three syllables was like the utterance of a talismanic word in an Arabian legend. It cleft the spell of inactivity which hung over officers and crew as the sweep of a scimitar cuts through the web of enchantment. The silence was immediately broken by the agitated snorting of a pony-engine, and the rattle of the anchor-chain coming up. Then the melodious jingling of bells down below told the engineer to "stand by." As the snort of the engine and the rattle of the chain ceased, the crew mustered forward and began to stow the anchor. Another jingle below, and then began the pulsating of the engines, while the sharp prow of the yacht seemed slowly to brush aside the distant hills and set them moving. To a seasoned traveller like myself there is something stimulating in the first throb of an engine aboard ship. It means new scenes and fresh experiences. Farewell Nagasaki and starvation; yes, and sometimes despair. Yet I had a warm corner in my heart for the old commercial city, with its queer little picturesque inhabitants, whose keen eye for business was nevertheless frequently softened by sentiment.

The man whose sharply uttered words had called up commotion out of the stillness sank somewhat listlessly into his customary armchair, and put his feet, crossed, on the rail. There was something in his attitude that warned me he did not wish his privacy intruded upon, so I leaned over the opposite rail and steadfastly regarded the receding city. The big yacht moved smoothly and swiftly over the waters of Nagasaki Bay, which at that moment glittered dazzlingly in the sunlight. The craft was evidently well engined, for the vibration was scarcely perceptible, and somehow it gave one the consciousness that there was a reserve of power which might be called upon in a pinch. Once clear of Nagasaki Bay the captain laid her course due west, as if we were to race the declining sun. I surmised that a safe rather than a quick voyage was his object, and that he intended to strike through the Yellow Sea and avoid threading the mazes of the Corean Archipelago.

Long before the gong sounded for dinner we were out of sight of land.

As I went down the companion stairs I must admit that I looked forward to the meal with some degree of apprehension, hoping the atmosphere would be less electric than during luncheon. I need have harboured no fear; Mr. Hemster, the captain, and myself sat down, but the ladies did not appear during the meal. Mr. Hemster had little to say, but the jovial captain told some excellent stories, which to his amazement and delight I laughed at, for he had a theory that no Englishman could see the point of any yarn that ever was spun. Mr. Hemster never once smiled; probably he had heard the stories before, and in the middle of dinner (such seemed to be the captain's impolite habit) the story-teller rose and left us. He paused with his foot on the first step, as he had done before, turned to the owner, and said:

"No particular hurry about reaching Corea, is there?"

"Why?" asked Hemster shortly.

"Well, you see, sir, I don't want to run down and sink one of them there little islands in the Archipelago, and have a suit for damages against me; so, unless you're in a hurry I propose to run a couple of hundred miles west, and then north this side of the hundred-and-twenty-fifth meridian."

"Washington or Greenwich?" asked the owner.

"Well, sir," said the captain with a smile, "I'm not particular, so long as there's a clear way ahead of me. I once sailed with a Dutchman who worked on the meridian of Ferro, which is the westernmost point of the Canary Islands. When I am in home waters of course I work by Washington, but the charts I've got for this region is Greenwich, and so I say the hundred-and-twenty-fifth."

"That's all right," replied Hemster seriously. "I thought you were too patriotic a man to use any meridian but our own, and then I thought you were so polite you were using Greenwich out of compliment to Mr. Tremorne here. You pick out the meridian that has the fewest islands along it and fewest big waves, and you'll satisfy me."

The owner said all this quite seriously, and I perceived he had a sense of humour which at first I had not given him credit for.

220

The captain laughed good-naturedly and disappeared. Mr. Hemster and I finished our dinner together in silence, then went on deck and had coffee and cigars. Although he proffered wine and liqueurs he never drank any spirits himself. I was able to help him out in that direction, as he once drily remarked.

It was one of the most beautiful evenings I had ever witnessed. There was no breeze except the gentle current caused by the motion of the yacht. The sea was like glass, and as night fell the moon rose nearly at the full. Mr. Hemster retired early, as I afterward learned was his custom, but whether to work in his office or to sleep in his bed I never knew. He seemed to have no amusement except the eternal rolling of the unlit cigar in his lips. Although there was a good library on board I never saw him open a book or display the slightest interest in anything pertaining to literature, science, or art. This is a strange world, and in spite of his undoubted wealth I experienced a feeling of pity for him, and I have not the slightest doubt he entertained the same feeling toward me.

I went forward after my employer left me, and asked the captain if outsiders were permitted on the bridge, receiving from him a cordial invitation to ascend. He had a wooden chair up there in which he sat, tilted back against the after rail of the bridge, while his crossed feet were elevated on the forward one, and in this free and easy attitude was running the ship. Of course there was nothing calling for exceeding vigilance, because the great watery plain, bounded by the far-off, indistinct horizon, was absolutely empty, and the yacht jogged along at an easy pace, which, as I have said, gave one the impression that much power was held in reserve. I sat on the forward rail opposite him, and listened to his stories, which were often quaint and always good. He had been a fisherman on the banks of Newfoundland in his early days, and his droll characterization of the men he had met were delicious to listen to. From the very first day I admired the captain, whose name I never learned, and this admiration increased the more I knew of him. I often wonder if he is still following the sea, and indeed I can never imagine him doing anything else. He was able, efficient, and resourceful; as capable a man as it was ever my fortune to meet.

My interest in the captain's stories came to an abrupt conclusion when I saw a lady emerge from the companion-way, look anxiously around for a moment, and then begin a slow promenade up and down the after deck. I bade good-night to the captain, and descended from the bridge. The lady paused as she saw me approach, and I thought for a moment she was about to retreat. But she did not do so. I had determined to speak to Miss Hemster on the first opportunity as if nothing had occurred. Ill-will is bad enough in any case, but nowhere is it more deplorable than on shipboard, because people have no escape from one another there. I was resolved that so far as I was concerned there should not be a continuance of the estrangement, which must affect more or less each one in our company, unless it was the captain, who seemed a true philosopher, taking whatever came with equal nonchalance.

As I neared the lady, however, I saw she was not Gertrude Hemster, but Hilda Stretton.

"It is a lovely evening, Miss Stretton," I ventured to say, "and I am glad to see you on deck to enjoy it."

"I came up for a breath of fresh air," she replied simply, with no enthusiasm for the loveliness of the night, which I had just been extolling. I surmised instinctively that she preferred to be alone, and was inwardly aware that the correct thing for me to do was to raise my yachting-cap and pass on, for she had evidently come to a standstill in her promenade, to give me no excuse for joining it. But, whether or not it was the glamour of the moonlight, her face was much more attractive than it had seemed when, for the first time, I had had a glimpse of it, and, be that as it may, I say this in excuse for my persistence. When has a young man ever been driven from his purpose by the unresponsiveness of the lady he is bold enough to address?

"If you do not mind, Miss Stretton, I should be very much gratified if you would allow me to join your evening saunter."

"The deck belongs as much to you as it does to me," was her cold rejoinder, "and I think I should tell you I am but the paid servant of its actual owner."

I laughed, more to chase away her evident embarrassment than because there was anything really to laugh about. I have noticed that a laugh sometimes drives away restraint. It is the most useful of human ejaculations, and often succeeds where words would fail.

"A warning in exchange for your warning!" I exclaimed as cheerfully as I could. "I, too, am a paid servant of the owner of this yacht."

"I did not expect to hear the cousin of Lord Tremorne admit as much," she replied, thawing somewhat.

"Well, you have just heard the cousin of his lordship do so, and I may add on behalf of Lord Tremorne that if he were in my place I know his candour would compel him to say the same thing."

"Englishmen think themselves very honest, do they not?" she commented, somewhat ungraciously, it seemed to me, for after all I was trying to make conversation, always a difficult task when there is veiled opposition.

"Oh, some Englishmen are honest, and some are not, as is the case with other nationalities. I don't suppose a dishonest Englishman would have any delusions about the matter, and perhaps if you pressed him he would admit his delinquency. I hope you are not prejudiced against us as a nation; and, if you are, I sincerely trust you will not allow any impression you may have acquired regarding myself to deepen that prejudice, because I am far from being a representative Englishman."

We were now walking up and down the deck together, but her next remark brought me to an amazed standstill.

"If you possess the candour with which you have just accredited yourself and your people, you would have said that you hoped I was not prejudiced against your nation, but you were certain, if such unfortunately

was the case, the charm of your manner and the delight of your conversation would speedily remove it."

"Good gracious, Miss Stretton," I cried, "do you take me for a conceited ass?"

The lady condescended to laugh a little, very low and very sweetly, but it was an undeniable laugh, and so I was grateful for it.

"You mistake me," she said. "I took you for a superior person, that was all, and I think superior persons sometimes make mistakes."

"What mistake have I fallen into, if you will be so good as to tell me?"

"Well, as a beginning, Mr. Tremorne, I think that if I was an English lady you would not venture to accost me as you have done to-night, without a proper introduction."

"I beg your pardon. I considered myself introduced to you by Miss Hemster to-day at luncheon; and if our host had not so regarded it, I imagine he would have remedied the deficiency."

"Mr. Hemster, with a delicacy which I regret to say seems to be unappreciated, knowing me to be a servant in his employ, did not put upon me the embarrassment of an introduction."

"Really, Miss Stretton, I find myself compelled to talk to you rather seriously," said I, with perhaps a regrettable trace of anger in my voice. "You show yourself to be an extremely ignorant young woman."

Again she laughed very quietly.

"Oh!" she cried, with an exultation that had hitherto been absent from her conversation; "the veneer is coming off, and the native Englishman stands revealed in the moonlight."

"You are quite right, the veneer is coming off. And now, if you have the courage of your statements, you will hear the truth about them. On the other hand, if you like to say sharp things and then run away from the consequences, there is the saloon, or there is the other side of the deck. Take your choice."

"I shall borrow a piece of English brag and say I am no coward. Go on."

"Very well. I came down from the bridge after a most friendly and delightful talk with the captain, having no other thought in my mind than to make myself an agreeable comrade to you when I saw you on deck."

"That was a very disingenuous beginning for a truthful lecture, Mr. Tremorne. When you saw me, you thought it was Miss Hemster, and you found out too late that it was I; so you approached me with the most polite and artful covering of your disappointment."

We were walking up and down the deck again, and took one or two turns before I spoke once more.

"Yes, Miss Stretton, you are demoniacally right. I shall amend the beginning of my lecture, then, by alluding to an incident which I did not expect to touch upon. At luncheon Miss Hemster received my greeting with what seemed to me unnecessary insolence. We are to be housed together for some time aboard this yacht; therefore I came down to greet her as if the incident to which I have alluded had not taken place."

"How very good of you!" said Miss Stretton sarcastically.

"Madam, I quite agree with you. Now we will turn to some of your own remarks, if you don't mind. In the first place, you said I would not address an English lady to whom I had not been properly introduced. In that statement you were entirely wrong. Five years ago, on an Atlantic liner, I, without having been introduced, asked the Countess of Bayswater to walk the deck with me, and she graciously consented. Some time after that, the deck steward being absent, her Grace the Duchess of Pentonville, without a formal introduction to me, asked me to tuck her up in her steamer chair; then she requested me to sit down beside her, which I did, and we entered into the beginning of a very pleasant acquaintance which lasted during the voyage."

"Dear me!" said Miss Stretton, evidently unimpressed, "how fond you are of citing members of the nobility!"

"Many of them are, or have been, friends of my own; so why should I not cite them? However, my object was entirely different. If I had said that Mrs. Jones or Mrs. Smith were the people in question, you might very well have doubted that they were ladies, and so my illustration would have fallen to the ground. You said English ladies, and I have given you the names of two who are undoubtedly ladies, and undoubtedly English, for neither of them is an American who has married a member of our nobility."

If ever fire flashed from a woman's eyes, it was upon this occasion. Miss Stretton's face seemed transformed with anger.

"Sir!" she flashed, "that last remark was an insult to my countrywomen, and was intended as such. I bid you good-night, and I ask you never to speak to me again."

"Exactly as I thought," said I; "the moment shells begin to fly, you beat a retreat."

Miss Stretton had taken five indignant steps toward the companion-way when my words brought her to a standstill. After a momentary pause she turned around with a proud motion of her figure which elicited my utmost admiration, walked back to my side, and said very quietly:

"Pardon me; pray proceed."

"I shall not proceed, but shall take the liberty of pausing for a moment to show you the futility of jumping to a conclusion. Now, try to comprehend. You said, English ladies. My illustration would have been useless if the Countess and the Duchess had been Americans. Do you comprehend that, or are you too angry?"

I waited for a reply but none came.

"Let me tell you further," I went on, "that I know several American women who possess titles; and if any man in my presence dared to hint that one or other of them was not a lady I should knock him down if I could, and if no one but men were about. So you see I was throwing no disparagement on your countrywomen, but was merely clenching my argument on the lines you yourself had laid down."

"I see; I apologize. Pray go on with the lecture."

"Thank you for the permission, and on your part please forgive any unnecessary vehemence which I have imported into what should be a calm

226

philosophical pronouncement. When you accuse an Englishman of violating some rule of etiquette, he is prone to resent such an imputation, partly because he has an uneasy feeling that it may be true. He himself admits that nearly every other nation excels his in the arts of politeness. It is really not at all to his discredit that he fondly hopes he has qualities of heart and innate courtesy which perhaps may partly make up for his deficiency in outward suavity of manner. Now, madam, etiquette is elastic. It is not an exact science, like mathematics. The rules pertaining to decimal fractions are the same the world over, but the etiquette of the Court differs from the etiquette of the drawing-room, and dry-land etiquette differs from the etiquette on board ship."

"I don't see why it should," interrupted Miss Stretton.

"Then, madam, it shall be my privilege to explain. Imagine us cast on a desert shore. If, for instance, our captain were less worthy than he is, and ran us on the rocks of Quelpaerd Island, which is some distance ahead of us, you would find that all etiquette would disappear."

"Why?"

"Why? Because we should each have to turn around and mutually help the others. Whether I had been introduced to you or not, I should certainly endeavour to provide you with food and shelter; whereas if I contracted one of the island's justly celebrated fevers, your good heart would prompt you to do what you could for my restoration. Now a ship is but a stepping-stone between the mainland of civilization and the desert island of barbarism. This fact, unconsciously or consciously, seems to be recognized, and so the rules of etiquette on board ship relax, and I maintain, with the brutal insistance of my race, that I have not infringed upon them."

"I think that is a very capital and convincing illustration, Mr. Tremorne," confessed the lady generously.

Now, look you, how vain a creature is man. That remark sent a glow of satisfaction through my being such as I had not experienced since a speech of my youth was applauded by my fellow-students at the Union in Oxford.

Nevertheless, I proceeded stubbornly with my lecture, which I had not yet finished.

"Now, madam, I am going to give you the opportunity to charge me with inconsistency. I strenuously object to the application of the term 'servant' as applied to yourself or to me. I am not a servant."

"But, Mr. Tremorne, you admitted it a while ago, and furthermore said that your distinguished cousin would also have confessed as much if in your place."

"I know I said so; but that was before the veneer fell away."

"Then what becomes of the candour of which you boasted? Has it gone with the veneer?"

"They are keeping each other company on the ocean some miles behind us. I have thrown them overboard."

Miss Stretton laughed with rather more of heartiness than she had yet exhibited.

"Well, I declare," she cried; "this is a transformation scene, all in the moonlight!"

"No, I am not Mr. Hemster's servant. Mr. Hemster desires to use my knowledge of the Eastern languages and my experience in Oriental diplomacy. For this he has engaged to pay, but I am no more his servant than Sir Edward Clark is a menial to the client who pays him for the knowledge he possesses; and, if you will permit me the English brag, which you utilized a little while since, I say I am a gentleman and therefore the equal of Mr. Silas K. Hemster, or any one else."

"You mean superior, and not equal."

"Madam, with all due respect, I mean nothing of the sort."

"Nevertheless, that is what is in your mind and in your manner. By the way, is your lecture completed?"

"Yes, entirely so. It is your innings now. You have the floor, or the deck rather."

"Then I should like to say that Silas K. Hemster, as you call him, is one of the truest gentlemen that ever lived."

"Isn't that his name?"

"You were perfectly accurate in naming him, but you were certainly supercilious in the tone in which you named him."

"Oh, I say!"

"No, you don't; it is my say, if you please."

"Certainly, certainly; but at first you try to make me out a conceited ass, and now you endeavour to show that I am an irredeemable cad. I have the utmost respect for Mr. Hemster."

"Have you? Well, I am very glad to hear it, and I wish to give you a firmer basis for that opinion than you have been able to form from your own observation. Mr. Hemster may not be learned in books, but he is learned in human nature. He is the best of men, kind, considerate, and always just. He was a lifelong friend of my father, now, alas, no more in life. They were schoolboys together. It was inevitable that Mr. Hemster should become very wealthy, and equally inevitable that my father should remain poor. My father was a dreamy scholar, and I think you will admit that he was a gentleman, for he was a clergyman of the Episcopal Church. He was not of the money-making order of men, and, if he had been, his profession would have precluded him from becoming what Mr. Hemster is. Although Mr. Hemster grew very rich, it never in the least interfered with his friendship for my father nor with his generosity to my father's child. If I cared to accept that generosity it would be unstinted. As it is, he pays me much more than I am worth. He is simple and honest, patient and kind. Patient and kind," she repeated, with a little tremor of the voice that for a moment checked her utterance,—"a true gentleman, if ever there was one."

"My dear Miss Stretton," I said, "what you say of him is greatly to the credit of both yourself and Mr. Hemster; but it distresses me that you should intimate that I have failed to appreciate him. He has picked me up, as I might say, from the gutters of Nagasaki without even a line of recommendation or so much as a note of introduction."

"That is what I said to you; he is a judge of men rather than of literature and the arts; and it is entirely to your credit that he has taken you without credentials. You may be sure, were it otherwise, I should not have spent so much time with you as I have done this evening. But his quick choice should have given you a better insight into his character than that which you possess?"

"There you go again, Miss Stretton. What have I said or done which leads you to suppose I do not regard Mr. Hemster with the utmost respect?"

"It is something exceedingly difficult to define. It cannot be set down as lucidly as your exposition of etiquette. It was your air, rather than your manner at luncheon time. It was a very distant and exalted air, which said as plainly as words that you sat down with a company inferior to yourself."

I could not help laughing aloud; the explanation was absolutely absurd.

"Why, my dear Miss Stretton, if I may call you so, you never even glanced at me during luncheon time; how, then, did you get such extraordinary notions into your head?"

"One did not need to glance at you to learn what I have stated. Now, during our conversation you have been frightened—no, that is not the word—you have been surprised—into a verbal honesty that has been unusual to you. Please make the confession complete, and admit that in your own mind you have not done justice to Mr. Hemster."

"Miss Stretton, the word you have been searching for is 'bluff.' I have been bluffed into confessions, before now, which in my calmer moments I regretted. You see I have been in America myself, and 'bluff' is an exceedingly expressive word. And, madam, permit me to say that in this instance the bluff will not work. You cannot get me to admit that either by look or tone I think anything but what is admirable of Mr. Hemster."

"Oh, dear, oh, dear!" cried the girl in mock despair. It was really wonderful how unconsciously friendly she had become after our tempestuous discussion. "Oh, dear, oh, dear! how you are fallen from the state of generous exaltation that distinguished you but a short time ago. Please search the innermost recesses of your mind, and tell me if you do not find there something remotely resembling contempt for a man who accepted you—appalling thought!—without even a note of introduction."

"Very well, my lady, I shall make the search you recommend. Now we will walk quietly up and down the deck without a word being said by either of us, and during that time I shall explore those recesses of my mind, which no doubt you regard as veritable 'chambers of horrors.'"

We walked together under the bridge, and then to the very stern of the ship, coming back to the bridge again. As we turned, the lady by my side broke the contract.

"Oh!" she cried with a little gasp, "there is Miss Hemster!"—and I saw the lady she mentioned emerge from the companion-way to the deck.

"Damnation!" I muttered, under my breath, forgetting for an instant in whose presence I stood, until she turned her face full upon me.

"I—I beg your pardon most sincerely," I stammered.

"And I grant it with equal sincerity," she whispered, with a slight laugh, which struck me as rather remarkable, for she had previously become deeply offended at sayings much milder than my surprised ejaculation.

231

# CHAPTER VII

WE were sailing due west, so that the full moon partly revealed the side face of the figure approaching us, and I venture to assert that the old moon, satellite of lovers, never shone upon anything more graceful than the vision we now beheld. Man as I was, I knew intuitively that she was dressed with a perfection far beyond my powers of description. The partly revealed face wore an expression of childlike simplicity and innocence, with all of a mature woman's exquisite beauty. No frowns now marred that smooth brow; the daintily chiseled lips were animated by a smile of supreme loveliness.

"What a perfectly enchanting night!" she cried, as she came to a standstill before us. "But don't you think it is a trifle chilly?"—and a slight shiver vibrated her frame. "But I suppose you have been energetically walking, and therefore have not noticed the change of temperature. Oh, Hilda, darling, would you mind running down to my room and bringing up that light fleecy wrap, which I can thrown over my shoulders?"

"I will bring it at once," replied Miss Stretton, hastening toward the companion-way. Just as she reached the head of the stair a ripple of tinkling laughter added music to the night.

"Dear me, how stupid I am!" cried Miss Hemster, "Why, Hilda, I have it here on my arm all the time! Don't bother, darling!"

Miss Stretton paused for a moment, then said, "Good-night!" and disappeared down the stairway.

Man is a stupid animal. I did not know at the moment, nor did I learn until long after,—and even then it was a lady who told me,—that this was a sweet dismissal, as effective as it was unperceived by myself.

Miss Hemster busied herself with the fleecy wrap, whose folds proved so unmanageable that I ventured to offer my aid and finally adjusted the fabric upon her shapely shoulders. We began walking up and down the deck, she regulating her step to mine, and, in the friendly manner of yesterday afternoon, placing her hand within my arm.

However, she did not hop and skip along the deck as she had done on the streets of Nagasaki, although I should have thought the smooth white boards offered an almost irresistible temptation to one who had shown herself to be bubbling over with the joy of youth and life. Notwithstanding the taking of my arm, she held herself with great dignity, her head erect and almost thrown back, so I expected to be treated to a new phase of her most interesting character. I was finding it somewhat bewildering, and hardly knew how to begin the conversation; but whether it was the springing step, or the smoothness of the deck, or both combined, it struck me all at once that she must be a superb dancer, and I was about to make inquiry as to this when she withdrew her hand rather quickly after we had taken two or three turns up and down the deck in silence, and said:

"You are not taking advantage of the opportunity I have been kind enough to present to you."

"What opportunity?" I asked in amazement.

"The opportunity to apologize to me."

"To apologize?" cried I, still more at a loss to understand her meaning. "Pray, for what should I apologize?"

She said with great decision and some impatience:

"How terribly dense you Englishmen are!"

"Yes, I admit it. We are celebrated as a nation for obtuseness. But won't you take pity on this particular Englishman, and enlighten him regarding his offence. What should I apologize for?"

"Why, you told my father you were not a friend of the Mikado!"

"Certainly I told him so. I am not a friend of the Mikado; therefore why should I claim to be?"

"Oh!" she cried, with a fine gesture of disdain, "you are trying to do the George Washington act!"

233

"The George Washington act!" I repeated.

"Certainly. Of course you don't see that. He could not tell a lie, you know."

"Ah, I understand you. No, I am doing the Mark Twain act. I can tell a lie, but I won't."

"Not even for me?" she asked, looking up at me with that winning smile of hers.

"Ah, when you put it that way I fear I shall be unable to emulate the truthfulness of either George or Mark."

"Now that isn't so bad," she said, taking my arm again, which gave me the hope that I had been at least partially restored to favour.

"You certainly intimated to me yesterday that you were a friend of the Mikado."

"Then I am to blame; for with equal certainty I had no right to do so."

"You said you had seen him several times and had spoken with him."

"Yes, but that does not constitute a claim upon His Majesty's consideration."

"Why, you have only seen me two or three times, and I am sure you know I'm a friend of yours."

"Madam, I am delighted to hear you say so. If the Mikado had made a similar statement, I should claim him as a friend before all the world."

"Then there was another thing you said, and I suppose you'll go back on that, too. You said you were a partisan of mine, or, since you are such a stickler for accuracy, an adherent—I think that was the word—yes, you were my adherent, or retainer, or something of the sort, such as we read of in old-fashioned novels, and when you said so, poor little trustful girl that I am, I believed you."

"Indeed, Miss Hemster, you had every right to do so. Should occasion arise, you will find me your staunch defender."

"Oh, that's all very pretty; but when it comes to the test, then you fail. You heard what my father said. You must have known I meant you to claim friendship with the Mikado. Poor father's as transparent as glass, and he surely made it as plain as this funnel that I wished you to claim friendship with the head of the Japanese nation. So, after all your beautiful promises, the moment you get a chance to back me up, you do so by going back on me."

"My dear Miss Hemster, why did you not give me a hint of your wishes? If, when we were in Nagasaki, you had but said that you wished me to proclaim myself the Emperor's brother, I should have perjured myself on your behalf like a gentleman."

"It happened that I was not on deck when you came aboard, and so did not see you. But I do think, if you hadn't forgotten me entirely, you would have learned at once from my father's talk what I wished you to say."

"Yes, I see it all now, when it is too late; but as you have remarked, and as I have admitted, I am extremely dense, and unless a thing is as plain as the funnel—to use your own simile—I am very apt to overlook it. Sometimes I don't see it even then. For instance, when you are walking by my side, I am just as likely to run into the funnel as to walk past it."

She laughed most good naturedly at this observation, and replied:

"Oh, you do say things very charmingly, and I will forgive you, even if you refuse to apologize."

"But I don't refuse to apologize. I do apologize—most abjectly—for my stupidity."

"Oh, well, that's all right. Perhaps, when everything's said and done, it was my own fault in not giving you warning. Next time I want you to stand by me, I'll have it all typewritten nice and plain, and will hand the paper to you twenty-four hours ahead."

"That would be very kind of you, Miss Hemster; and, besides, you would then possess documentary evidence of the stupidity of an Englishman."

"Oh, we don't need to have documentary evidence for that," she replied brightly; "but I tell you I was mad clear through when I knew what you had said to my father. I raised storm enough to sink the yacht."

"Did you?"

"Didn't I? Why, you knew I did."

"I hadn't the slightest suspicion of it."

"Oh, well, you are denser than I thought. And I have been worrying myself all the afternoon for fear you were offended by the way I told you to take your seat at the table."

"Offended? I shouldn't have had the presumption to think of such a thing. Indeed, it was very kind of you to indicate my place. Such instructions are usually given by the steward."

She bestowed a sly, sidelong glance upon me, and there was a somewhat uncertain smile at the corners of her pretty lips.

"Is that a little dig at me?" she asked.

"Nothing of the sort. It was a mere statement of fact."

"Sometimes I think," she said meditatively, more to herself than to me, "that you are not such a fool as you look."

I was compelled to laugh at this, and replied with as much urbanity as I could call to my command:

"I am overjoyed to hear that statement. It seems to prove that I am making progress. Such evidence always encourages a man."

"Oh, well," she said, with a shrug of impatience, "don't let's talk any more about it. I didn't want to go to Corea, and I did want to return to Yokohama; so here we are going to Corea. Don't you think I am a very good-natured girl to let bygones be bygones so easily?"

"You certainly are."

"Then that's settled. Tell me what Miss Stretton was talking to you

236

about."

I was somewhat taken aback by this extraordinary request, but replied easily:

"Oh, we had not been walking the deck very long, and we discussed nothing of extreme importance so far as I can remember."

"What did she say about me?"

"I assure you, Miss Hemster, your name was not mentioned between us."

"Really? Then what on earth did you talk about?"

"When I have the good fortune to be in your presence, Miss Hemster, I confess it seems impossible that I should talk about anyone else than yourself, nevertheless I should not presume to discuss one lady with another."

The girl jerked away her arm again, and turned to me with a flash in her eyes that was somewhat disconcerting.

"Look here, Mr. Tremorne," she cried, "if you've got anything to say against me, I want you to say it right out like a man, and not to hint at it like a spiteful woman."

"What have I said now?" I inquired very humbly.

"You know quite well what you have said. But if you imagine I am as stupid as you admit yourself to be, you'll get left!"

"My dear madam," I ventured; "one of the advantages of having a thick skin is that a person does not take offence where no offence is meant."

"There you go again! You know very well that you were driving at me when you said that you refused to discuss one lady with another; because, if you meant anything at all, you meant that I was trying to do what you couldn't bring yourself to do; and when you talk of 'lady' and 'lady' you are in effect putting Miss Stretton on an equality with me."

"I should never think of doing so," I replied, with a bow to the angry person beside me.

"Is that another?" she demanded. "Oh, you know very well what I mean. Do you consider Miss Stretton a lady?"

"My acquaintance with her is of the shortest, yet I should certainly call her a lady."

"Then what do you call me?"

"A lady also."

"Well, if that isn't putting us on an equality, what is?"

"I said, madam, that I did not put you on an equality. That was done by a celebrated document which

you often fling in our faces. I refer to the Declaration of Independence, which, if I remember rightly, begins—'All men are created equal,' and I suppose, as the humourist puts it, that the men embrace the women."

"Miss Stretton is my paid servant," insisted Miss Hemster, evading the point; "and, as was said in the opera of 'Pinafore,' when one person has to obey the orders of another, equality is out of the question."

"I didn't think that made any difference in the United States."

"But this isn't the United States."

"I beg your pardon, but this is the United States. We are on the high seas, aboard a steamer that is registered in New York, and so this deck is just as much a part of your country as is New York itself, and the laws of the United States would justify the captain in putting me in irons if he thought my conduct deserved such treatment."

"Then you refuse to tell me what you and Miss Stretton were discussing!"

"My dear madam, if Miss Stretton asked me what you and I were discussing, I should certainly refuse to inform her. Should I not be justified in doing so? I leave it to yourself. Would you be pleased if I repeated our conversation to Miss Stretton?"

"Oh, I don't know that I should mind," replied Miss Hemster mildly, the storm subsiding as quickly as it had risen; "I have no doubt she told you that her father was a clergyman, and that my father had borrowed five hundred dollars from her father to get his start in life. And she doubtless hinted that her father was the founder of our fortune."

"I assure you, Miss Hemster, that she said nothing at all about five hundred dollars or any other sum. She spoke mostly of your father, and she spoke very highly of him."

"She certainly had every right to do so. My father gave her what education she has and supported her ever since."

I made no comment upon this statement, and my companion veered round a bit and said brightly:

"Oh, I see you don't like me to talk like that, and perhaps I shouldn't, but Hilda Stretton is as sly as they make them, and I've no doubt she came on deck just to size you up, while you would never suspect it."

"I venture to think you do the young lady an injustice, Miss Hemster. I am sure she would have preferred to walk the deck alone, although she was too polite to say so. I rather fear I forced my company upon her."

"Oh, yes, oh, yes; I understand all about that. Such is just the impression Hilda Stretton would like to make upon a man. Now I am honest. I came on deck purposely to have a talk with you."

"Then I am very much flattered."

"Well, you ought to be, and I may say this for you, that you don't talk to me in the least as other men do. Nobody has ever dared to contradict me."

"Have I done so? You shock me, for I certainly did not intend to contradict you."

"Why, you have done nothing else, and I don't think it's gentlemanly at all. But we'll let that go. Now I wish to talk about yourself."

"Well, I think we might choose a more entertaining topic."

"We'll talk about Lord Tremorne then."

"Hang Lord Tremorne!"

"Ah, Miss Stretton and you were discussing him then?"

"Indeed we were not, but I am rather tired of the gentleman. Yet he is a very good fellow, and I ought not to say 'Hang him!' even if I am on the high seas. I am sure I wish him nothing but good."

"If he were to die, would you become Lord Tremorne?"

"Bless me, no!"

"Who stands between you?"

"His three sons, who are very healthy specimens of humanity, I am glad to say."

"Isn't there ever any possibility of your becoming Lord Tremorne, then?"

"Oh, there's a possibility of anything, but no probability. I may say quite truthfully that no one would be so sorry as I if the probability occurred."

"Don't you want to have a title?"

"I wouldn't give twopence for it."

"Really? I thought every one in England wanted a title?"

"Dear me, no! There are men in England, plain Mr. This or That, who wouldn't change their appellation for the highest title that could be offered them."

"Why?"

"Oh, they belong to fine old families and look upon the newer aristocracy as upstarts."

"It seems funny to talk of old families, for all families are the same age. We all spring from Adam, I suppose."

"Doubtless, but I believe the College of Arms does not admit such a contention."

"Don't you think family pride a very idiotic thing?"

"Oh, I don't know. To tell you the truth, I haven't thought very much about it, though I don't see why we should parade the pedigree of a horse and be ashamed of the pedigree of a man."

"It isn't the same thing. A horse may have notable ancestors, whereas I am told that most of your aristocracy sprang from thieves and outlaws."

"As far as that goes, some of them are still in the pirate profession, those who belong to the public companies, for example,—bogus companies, I mean. I suppose, after all said and done, that the pedigree of even the oldest family in Europe is as nothing to that of the Eastern Kings, for this King of Corea that we are going to see traces his ancestry about as far back as did Pooh-Bah."

"Do you think there will be any trouble in getting to see his Corean Majesty?" Miss Hemster asked with a shade of anxiety in her tone.

"I am not at all sure, for the etiquette of the Corean Court is very rigid. A horseman must dismount when he is passing the Palace, although it is but a ramshackle conglomeration of shabbiness. Every one admitted to the Presence must prostrate himself before the King."

"Well, I shan't do it," said the girl confidently.

"I hope to obtain a relaxation of the rule in the case of a Princess like yourself, Miss Hemster. If his Majesty should graciously touch your hand, the law of Corea demands that ever afterward you must wear a badge as token of the distinction conferred upon you."

"Oh, I shall just wear another ring with the arms of Corea on it,—that is, if Corea has arms,"—said Miss Hemster with vivacity. "I am sure it is very good of you to take all this trouble for us. And now I must bid you good-night and thank you for the very pleasant walk we have had together."

With that my lady withdrew her bright presence and disappeared down the companion-way.

241

# CHAPTER VIII

I AWOKE next morning after a sweet and dreamless sleep that was almost inspiring. Months and months had passed since I slept in a European bed, and, although necessity had accustomed me to the habit of a Japanese mat upon the floor and a block of wood for a pillow, I must confess that the bed of the West still seemed to me a very paradise of luxury. There were more patent contrivances about that yacht than I have ever seen in such small compass before. Of course it had electric lights everywhere. There was a water-condensing machine, an ice-making machine, and all the usual fittings that now go to the construction of a luxurious steamer for sailing in warm latitudes. There was a bathroom which was Oriental in its splendour and Occidental in its patent fittings. One could have any sort of bath that one desired. By simply turning a handle on a dial the great marble basin became filled with water at any temperature indicated by the figures at which you set the pointer, from boiling-hot to ice-cold. This was indeed a delight, and when I came to it from my room in dressing-gown and slippers I found the Japanese boy there with a cup of delicious tea such as can be had only in the immediate vicinity of China. On a dainty plate whose figure

work was only partially obscured by a filmy lace napkin were some finger-lengths and finger-widths of buttered toast. "Rupert, my boy," I said to myself, "you have indeed fallen upon your feet!"

I now knew that I was going to have the pleasantest voyage of my life. The clouds which yesterday threatened to obscure my acquaintance with Miss Hemster had cleared away, and although I had surmised that the young woman was somewhat quick to take offence when one approached the confines of either ridicule or criticism, yet I was well aware that no man has a right to inflict conversation that is distasteful upon any woman, and I thought I had sufficient power over my speech to prevent further errors in that direction. A most unaccustomed sense of elation filled me, and, as I tossed about my wardrobe, I came across a pair of Oxford bags that I had not worn for years. As they were still spotlessly white, I put them on, with a blazer which gave to the world the somewhat glaring colors of my college, and, thus gloriously arrayed with cap on head, I almost imagined myself about to stroll along the High, once more an extremely young man.

My costume made quite a sensation at the breakfast-table, and caused great laughter on the part of our worthy captain, who said the only thing it reminded him of was a clown in Barnum's circus. Miss Hemster was good enough to compliment the outfit, and, after the meal was over, did me the honour of strolling up and down the deck for nearly an hour, after which she disappeared below. Silas K. Hemster occupied his customary place on deck in the wicker armchair, and after his daughter had deserted me I stood beside him for a few moments, endeavouring to engage him in conversation, but soon saw that he preferred his own thoughts, for which preference, to be sure, I could find no fault with him, for anything I had to say was neither novel nor entertaining. I was about to go below and select a book from the rather extensive library when there met me at the head of the companion-way the notes of the very subdued playing of one of Chopin's most charming nocturnes. I paused for a moment at the head of the stair, then descended softly, saying to myself that Miss Hemster was a most accomplished musician.

Perhaps I have not stated that at the farther end of the saloon from the foot of the stairs stood an excellent piano, and at the stairway end an equally fine American organ. As I descended I soon saw that the musician was Miss Stretton, who sat with her back toward me, playing with a touch I have seldom heard equalled even by professionals. I am very fond of music, so I slipped quietly into a chair and listened to those divine harmonies divinely played. Miss Stretton went on from nocturne to nocturne, and I felt somewhat guilty at thus surreptitiously listening, but resolved that the moment she gave a sign of ceasing I would steal quietly up the stair again without revealing my presence.

Down the passage facing me, that formed a highway from the saloon to the suites occupied by the ladies, I saw Miss Hemster come out of her room, and, by the same token, she must have seen me. She advanced a few steps, then stood still, apparently listening to the music, finally turned, and

243

re-entered her apartment with a distinct, emphatic slam of the door. I paid no attention to this, but then was the time for me to steal on deck again if I had had any wisdom in my head, which I so frequently must admit I have not. Miss Stretton, absorbed in the music, presumably had not heard the slam of the door, but a little later Miss Hemster emerged again, and this time came straight down the passage and through the saloon, with a swish, swish of silken skirts that sounded eloquent in anger. I have never heard silk skirts rustle since then without remembering the occasion I am endeavouring to describe; yet never before or since have I heard the hiss of silk that actually swore, if I may be permitted the use of such an expression.

The young woman marched past me with head erect, and a gleam in her eyes such as I had seen on one occasion before, but this time fixed and anything but transient, as the other flash had been. I rose respectfully to my feet as she passed, but she cast not even a glance at me, merely pausing for a second at the foot of the stairs to catch up the train of her magnificent gown, then up the steps she went at a run. Now I had consciously given the girl no cause of annoyance, but, the music having ceased suddenly, I turned around and saw Miss Stretton regarding me with something like dismay in her eyes.

"How long have you been here?" she asked.

"Oh, only for a few minutes," I replied. "Pray go on, Miss Stretton. I am very fond of music, and not for years have I been privileged to hear it so well played."

"It is very kind of you to say that," murmured Hilda Stretton, "but I think I have played enough for one morning."

"At least finish the selection you were just now engaged upon," I begged.

"Some other time, please," she said in a low voice; and I did not urge her further, for I saw she was frightened.

"Very well," I replied, "I shall take that as a promise."

She inclined her head as she came down the room, and went up the stairs, disappearing also on deck, leaving me wondering what all this disquietude was about. I thought of going on deck myself, but, feeling slightly resentful at the treatment accorded me by Miss Hemster, I walked forward, sat down on the piano-stool, and began to drum a few of the catchy London tunes that ran through my head. I was playing "Knocked 'em in the Old Kent Road" with little idea of how excellent an overture it would prove for the act about to be commenced, and was thinking of the Strand, and the Tivoli, and Chevalier, and Piccadilly Circus, and the Empire, and Leicester Square, and the Alhambra, when I was startled by a woman's appealing voice crying just above a whisper:

"Oh, don't, Gertie; please don't!"

I turned my head and saw, coming down the stairway, Gertrude Hemster followed by Hilda Stretton. The latter was evidently almost on the verge of tears, but the face of the former was shocking to behold. I could not have believed that a countenance so beautiful was capable of being transformed into a visage that might have stood model for a picture of murderous wrath.

"Will you stop your foolish pounding on my piano?" she cried, with a tremendous emphasis on the first personal pronoun.

"Madam, I have stopped," I replied, giving a soft answer that failed to have the supposed effect.

"I guess you think you own the yacht and all it contains, don't you? Now, I beg to inform you that we don't allow employees to conduct themselves as if they were in a bar-room or a drinking-saloon."

As she said this, she strode once up and down the length of the room.

"Madam," said I, "I beg your pardon, and shall never touch your piano again. My only excuse is that I have been so accustomed to public liners, where the piano is free to all, that for the moment I forgot myself."

At this juncture Miss Stretton was so injudicious as to touch the other on the elbow, apparently trying to guide her into the passage that led to her room, but Miss Hemster whirled around like an enraged tigress, and struck her companion a blow that would have landed on her cheek had not the victim suddenly and instinctively raised an arm to protect her face. Then with the viciousness of a harridan of Drury Lane Miss Hemster grasped the shrinking girl by the shoulders, and shook her as a terrier does a rat, finally forcing her down into a seat by the side of the table. One girl's face was as white as paper, and the other's nearly purple with rage. I had intended to go up on deck, but paused for two reasons. First I was afraid of injury to Miss Stretton, and secondly the struggle took place, if struggle it could be called when one was entirely passive, in the midst of the only route open to me.

"You dare to interfere, you little fool," shrieked Miss Hemster. "You that are the cause of all the trouble, with your silly little ditties—tinkle-tinkle-tinkle-tinkle—and I'll box your ears for you if you dare stir!"

"Madam," said I, "you are possibly so ignorant as not to know that you were listening to Chopin's most subtle harmonies."

This had exactly the effect I desired, which was to turn her away from the trembling girl whom she had so harshly misused.

"Ignorant, you puppy! Have you the gall to apply such language to me, looking, as you do, like a monkey on a stick; like a doll that one can buy at the bargain counter."

This graphic description of my Oxford blazer was so striking that in spite of the seriousness of the case I did the one thing I should not have done,—I laughed. The laugh was like a spark to a powder-mine, and what made the crisis worse was that the old gentleman in his armchair on deck, hearing the shrieking voice, came down, his face haggard with anxiety.

"Gertie, Gertie!" he cried. I would not like to say the young lady swore, but she came so near it that there was but tissue paper between the expression she used and that which an angry fish-wife would have employed. With the quickness of light she sprang at a large Japanese vase which temporarily decorated the center of the table. This she heaved up, and with the skill of a football player flung it squarely at me. Now, I have had some experience on the football field myself, and I caught that vase with a dexterity which would have evoked applause had any enthusiast of the game happened to be present.

I suppose my placing of this huge vase on the top of the piano was the last straw, or perhaps it was her father coming forward, crying in a grief-shaken voice, "Oh, Gertie, Gertie, my child, my child!"

I was so sorry for him that I passed him and would have gone on deck out of the way, but my purpose was checked by a startling incident. The young woman had whisked open a drawer. I heard it come clattering to the floor, for she had jerked it clear from its place; then there was a scream. Turning quickly around I met the blinding flash of a pistol, and heard behind me the crash of a splintering mirror. The sound of the revolver in that contracted space was deafening, and even through the smoke I saw that my young friend was about to fire again. I maintain it was not fear for my own life that caused instant action on my part, but this infuriated creature, who seemed to have become insane in her anger, faced three helpless, unarmed people, and whatever was to be done had to be done quickly. I leaped through the air, and grasped her two wrists with an energetic clutch I daresay she had never encountered before.

"Drop that revolver!" I cried.

"Let go my wrists, you beast," she hissed in my face. For answer I raised her arms and brought them down with a force that would have broken her fingers with the weight of the revolver if she had not let it go clattering to the floor.

"You beast, you beast, you beast!" she shrieked at me, as well as her choking throat would allow utterance. I swung her around a quarter-circle, then pushed her back, somewhat rudely I fear, until she sank down into a chair.

"Now, sit there and cool," I cried, giving her a hearty shake, so that she should know how it felt herself. "If you don't keep quiet I'll box your ears."

I don't defend my action at all; I merely state that I was just as angry as she was, and perhaps a little more so.

"You brute, let go of my wrists! I'll kill you for this! Hilda, call the captain and have this man put in irons. Father, how can you stand there like

247

a coward and see a beastly ruffian use me in this way?"

"Oh, Gertie, Gertie!" repeated the father without moving.

She now burst into a passionate flood of tears, and I released her wrists, ready, however, to catch them again if she made any motion to reach the revolver.

During this fierce if brief contest,—it took less time in happening than it requires in telling,—Miss Stretton had been seated in the chair upon which the angry woman had thrust her, and she gazed at us in open-eyed terror. The old man stood half leaning against the table, steadying himself with his hands. Miss Hemster's fit of weeping was as dramatic as everything else she did. It began with a burst of very angry and genuine tears, and this storm passed through a gamut of more or less varying emotions until it subsided into a hysterical half-sobbing, half-gasping wail which resembled the cry of the helpless child who had been tyrannized over. It was bogusly pathetic, but I saw it went straight to the old man's heart and wrung it with very real agony, and this mean advantage which I knew she was taking of the father's deep love for her increased my scornful contempt for the creature. His grief was actual enough, and she was quite consciously playing upon it, although,—wonderful actress that she was,—she pretended an utter abandon of heart-breaking sorrow.

As for me, I undoubtedly felt myself the brute she had named me, and even at that moment,—much more so later,—was shocked to find in my own nature depths of primeval savagery which had hitherto been unsuspected. Seeing, however, that the worst of the storm was over, and that the young woman would make no more attempts at gun-firing, I replaced the drawer in position and threw into it its scattered former contents. Then I picked up the revolver, saying:

"I will keep this, for there is nothing more dangerous than such an instrument in the hands of a woman who can't shoot."

The effect of this remark on the drooping figure was instantaneous. She abruptly raised her tear-sodden face, which now became crimson with a new wave of anger.

"You gaping baboon," she cried, "I can shoot a great deal better than you can!"

I paid no heed to her, but, advising Mr. Hemster to lock up any other firearms he might have on board, abruptly left the saloon.

# CHAPTER IX

I WALKED the deck alone, the revolver stuck between my hip and my gaudy sash, as if I were a veritable pirate, and doubtless my appearance was not dissimilar to some of those nautical heroes who have been terrors of the sea. A pirate more dissatisfied with himself never trod a quarter-deck. If there had been a plank at hand I would willingly have walked it. It was no comfort that I despised the girl, for I despised myself a thousand times more. What right had I to interfere? Why had I not bowed to her when she ordered me away from the piano, and come at once on deck, without proffering any of my foolish explanations? The whole disgraceful row had arisen through my contemptible efforts to justify a situation which allowed of no justification. The piano was hers, as she truly said, and I had no more right to touch it than I had to wear her jewellery. My sole desire at first was to get ashore as soon as anchor was dropped, and never again see either father or daughter. But a few moments' reflection showed me the quandary into which I had brought myself. I was already indebted to the old gentleman, not only for the money he had advanced to me, but for his kindness from the very first, which I had repaid by an interference in his family affairs that made me loathe myself. Never before had I felt so acutely the sting of poverty. Not even in my starvation days at Nagasaki had my lack of means borne so heavily upon me. It was utterly impossible for me to refund a penny of the pounds he had so generously bestowed upon me. The only requital in my power was that of honest service to him, and now I had made my stay on the yacht impossible, when, had I retained a modicum of sanity at the proper moment, I might have withdrawn with no loss of dignity. Now my own self-respect was gone, and I had more than justified every bitter taunt she flung at me.

So, in a very hopeless state of misery and dejection, I walked up and down the deck until Mr. Hemster himself came quietly up the companion-way and took his usual place in his wicker chair, setting his heels upon the rail in front of him, and biting off the end of a cigar. He gave me no greeting, but this also was usual with him, and so it meant nothing one way or another.

However, I had at last made up my mind on a course of action, so I strode over to where he sat, and he looked up at me with what I took to be more of apprehension than censure in his gaze. It was no matter of wonder to me that he must be seriously doubting his wisdom in taking on board without recommendation a stranger who had just proved himself such a brawler.

"Mr. Hemster," said I, "an apology is a cheap method of trying to make amends for what is inexcusable; but I should like to tell you, and I should like you to believe, how sorry I am for my conduct of a short time since. I regret to say it is impossible for me to return the money you have advanced. When I first had the pleasure of meeting you, I stated to you quite truthfully that I was at the end of my resources, and of course my prospects have not improved in the mean time, except in so far as your own favour is concerned, and that, I quite realize, I have forfeited. From this time until we sight land, I shall live forward with the crew in the forecastle, and shall not again come aft except in obedience to your orders. When we reach Corea I am entirely at your disposal. If you wish me to carry out the project you have in hand, I shall do so to the best of my ability; if not, I give you my word I will refund to you the money as soon as I can earn it."

"Sit down," he said very quietly, and when I had done so he remained silent, gazing over the rail at the distant horizon for what seemed to me a very long time. Then he spoke, never raising his voice above the level at which he always kept it.

"You are a little excited just now," he said, "and take an exaggerated view of the matter. Do you think any one on deck heard that pistol-shot?"

"I don't know; I rather imagine not. No one seemed at all on the alert when I came up."

"Well, it sounded as if it would raise all creation down below, but perhaps it didn't make such a racket up here. Now, if you went forward and lived with the crew, what would be the effect? They would merely say we made it impossible for you to live aft. I suppose by rights I shouldn't mind what my crew thinks or says; but I do mind it. We are in a way a small democracy afloat, one man as good as another. If the firing were heard on deck, then the captain will be joking about it at luncheon time, and we'll know. If it wasn't, the least said about it the better. If you don't like to come to meals, I haven't a word to say; you can have them served in your own room. As for the money I advanced, that doesn't amount to anything. I am sure you are just the man I want for what there is to do, and when that's done it will be me that's owing you money. I'm a good deal older than you, and I have found that in business a man must keep his temper, or he's going to give all his adversaries a great advantage over him, and things are cut so close nowadays that no one can afford to give points to his rival. I've had to control my temper or be a failure, so I controlled it. My daughter hasn't had to do that. Instead of blaming her, you should blame me. It's my temper she's got."

"My dear Mr. Hemster, I assure you I am blaming neither of you; I am blaming myself."

"Well, that's all right. It's a good state of Christian feeling and won't do you any harm. Now you said that when we land you are willing to do anything I ask. Are you willing to do that before we go ashore?"

"Yes, Mr. Hemster, any command you may lay upon me I shall execute without question."

"Oh, I won't lay a command on you at all; but I ask as a favour that you go below, knock at my daughter's door, and tell her you are sorry for what has happened. Put it any way you like, or don't do it at all if you don't want to. After all, she is a woman, you know. You and I are men, and should stand the brunt, even if we are not entitled to it, and it may make things go a little smoother, perhaps."

We are supposed to be an unemotional race, but I confess that the old man's mild words touched me deeply, and made it next to impossible for me to reply to him. But, even so, my own judgment told me that a life of this desire to make things go smoothly had resulted in building up a character in his daughter which took an obstreperous advantage of the kindly old gentleman's strong affection for her. I arose without a word, thrust forward my hand to him, which he shook somewhat shamefacedly, glancing nervously around, fearing there might be onlookers. I entirely appreciated his reserve, and wished for a moment that I had not acted upon my impulse, to his visible embarrassment. I went instantly to the saloon, along the passage, and knocked at the door of Miss Hemster's apartment. She herself opened the door, with what seemed to me to be her usual briskness; but when I looked at her, I saw her drooping like a stricken flower, head bent, and eyes on the floor. Scarcely above a whisper, she asked with tremor-shaken voice:

"Did you wish to see me?"

"Yes, Miss Hemster," I replied, nerving myself to the point. "I wish, since you are good enough to receive me, to apologize most abjectly for my rudeness to you this morning."

She replied in a sad little voice, without looking up:

"I do not really mind in the least how much you play the piano, Mr. Tremorne."

This was so unexpected a remark, so ludicrously aside from the real point at issue between us, so far from touching the hideousness of my culpability, that I looked at the girl, wondering whether or not she was in earnest. I had not come to get permission to play the piano. Her attitude, to which no other word than "wilted" so appropriately applied, continued to be one of mute supplication or dependence. Yet in the semi-darkness I fancied I caught one brief glance at my face. Then she leaned her fair head against the jam of the door and began to cry very softly and very hopelessly.

I stood there like the awkward fool I was, not knowing what to say; and finally she completed my desolation by slowly raising her two arms up toward my face. Since our contest she had removed the striking costume she then wore, and had put on a white lace fleecy garment that was partly dressing-gown, partly tea-gown, decorated with fluttering blue ribbon. This had very wide sleeves which fell away from her arms, leaving them bare and rounded, pure and white. Her two slender, shapely hands hung in helpless fashion from the wrists like lilies on a broken stem. The slow upraising of them seemed to me strange and meaningless, until the light from the inner room fell upon her wrists, and then the purport of her action became stunningly clear to me. Around that dainty forearm, delicately fashioned for the tenderest usage, showed red and angry the marks of my brutal fingers, silent accusers held up before my very eyes. Distraught as I was with self-accusation, I could not help admiring the dramatic effectiveness of the slow motion and resulting attitude. The drooping girl, with her soft, clinging draperies, her sad face so beautiful, her contour so perfect, and those soft appealing hands upraised,—hands that I could not forget had been placed with impulsive friendliness in mine on the streets of Nagasaki,—and all this accompanied by the almost silent symphony of quivering sobs that were little louder than sighs tremulously indrawn, formed a picture that has never been effaced from my memory. I had rather a man's clenched fist had struck me to the ground than that a woman's open palm should be so held in evidence against me. I regard that moment as the most unbearable of my life, and with a cry almost of despair I turned and fled. For once language had become impossible and utterly inadequate.

As I beat this precipitate retreat, was it my over-wrought imagination, or was it actual, that I heard an indignant word of expostulation, followed by a low sweet ripple of laughter. Had there been some one else in the room during this painful interview? I staggered like a drunken man up to the deck, and then endeavoured to walk it off and cease thinking.

Mr. Hemster said nothing to me that day, nor I to him, after I came on deck again. For an hour I strode the deck with an energy which, if applied in the right direction, would have driven the yacht faster than she was going. When the gong sounded for luncheon I went down to my own room and was served there. After the meal I did not go up on deck again, but sat on the sofa gloomily smoking. Later I got a novel from the library, and tried to interest myself in it, but failed. I felt physically tired, as if I had done a hard day's work, and, unsentimental as it is to confess it, I fell asleep on the sofa, and slept until the gong for dinner aroused me.

Dinner I also enjoyed in solitary state in my own apartment, then, under the brilliant cluster of electric lights, tried the novel again, but again without success. The nap in the afternoon made sleep improbable if I turned in, so I scarcely knew what to do with myself. I rather envied Silas K. Hemster's reticence, and his seeming dislike for intercourse with his fellows. He was the most self-contained man I had ever met, preferring the communion of his own thoughts to conversation with any one. At this crisis of indecision the way was made plain for me by the youth from Japan. There came a gentle tap at my door, and on opening it the Japanese boy said respectfully:

"Sir, Miss Stretton would like to speak with you on deck."

# CHAPTER X

I HAD flung my much-maligned blazer into a corner, and now I slipped on an ordinary tweed coat. I found the deck empty with the exception of Miss Stretton, who was walking up and down in the moonlight, as she had done the night before, but this time she came forward with a sweet smile on her lips, extending her hand to me as if we had been old friends long parted. There was something very grateful to me in this welcome, as I was beginning to look upon myself as a pariah unfit for human companionship. Indeed, I had been bitterly meditating on striking into the Corean wilderness and living hereafter as one of the natives, about the lowest ambition that ever actuated the mind of man.

"Have you sentenced yourself to solitary imprisonment, Mr. Tremorne?"

"Yes. Don't you think I deserve it?"

"Frankly, I don't; but as you did not appear at either luncheon or dinner, and as the Japanese boy who brought my coffee up here told me you were keeping to your room, I thought it as well to send for you, and I hope you are not offended at having your meditation broken in upon. Prisoners, you know, are allowed to walk for a certain time each day in the courtyard. I do wish I had a ball and chain for your ankles, but we are on board ship, and cannot expect all the luxuries of civilization."

Her raillery cheered me more than I can say.

"Miss Stretton, it is more than good of you to receive an outcast in this generous manner."

"An outcast? Please don't talk rubbish, Mr. Tremorne! Somehow I had taken you for a sensible person, and now all my ideas about you are shattered."

"I don't wonder at it," I said despondently.

"Yes, I know you are in the Slough of Despond, and I am trying to pull you out of it. When I remember that men have ruled great empires, carried on important wars, subdued the wilderness, conquered the ocean, girdled the earth with iron, I declare I wonder where their brains depart to when they are confronted with silly, whimpering, designing women."

"But still, Miss Stretton, to come from the general to the particular, a man has no right to ill-treat a woman."

"I quite agree with you; but, as you say, to come to this particular incident which is in both our minds, do you actually believe that there was ill-treatment? Don't you know in your own soul that if the girl had received treatment like that long ago she would not now be a curse to herself and to all who are condemned to live within her radius?"

"Yet I cannot conceal from myself that it was none of my business. Her father was present, and her correction was his affair."

"Her correction was any one's affair that had the courage to undertake it. What had you seen? You had seen her strike me, and thrust me from her as if I were a leper. Then you saw this girl with the temper of the—the temper of the—oh, help me——"

"Temper of the devil," I responded promptly.

"Thank you! You saw her take up a deadly weapon, and if she has not murdered one of the three of us, we have to thank, not her, but the mercy of God. You did exactly the right thing, and the only thing, and actually she would have admired you for it had it not been that you came down to her door and prostrated yourself for her to trample over you."

"Good heavens, Miss Stretton! were you inside that room?"

"It doesn't matter whether I was or not. I know that she twisted you around her little finger, and took her revenge in the only way that was possible for her."

"Ah, but you don't know the depth of my degradation. She showed me her wrists, marked by the fingers of a savage, and that savage was myself."

"Pooh! pooh! pooh!" cried Miss Stretton, laughing. "Do you think those marks indicate pain? Not a bit of it. Your grasp of her wrists did not injure her in the least, and, short of putting handcuffs on them, was the only method at your disposal to prevent her perhaps killing her father, a man worth a million such as she, and yet neither he nor you have the sense to see it. I can inform you that Miss Gertrude's arm is sore to-night, but not where you clasped it. She hurt herself more than she injured me when she struck me. Look at this,"—and she drew back her sleeve, disclosing a wrist as pretty as that of Miss Hemster, notwithstanding the fact that one part was both bruised and swollen. "That is where I caught her blow, and can assure you it was given with great force and directness. So, Mr. Tremorne, if you have any sympathy to expend, please let me have the benefit of it, and I will bestow my sympathy upon you in return."

"Indeed, Miss Stretton, I am very sorry to see that you are hurt. I hoped you had warded off the blow slantingly, instead of getting it square on the arm like that."

"Oh, it is nothing," said the girl carelessly, drawing down her sleeve again, "it is merely an exhibit, as they say in the courts, to win the sympathy of a man, and it doesn't hurt now in the least, unless I strike it against something. I ask you to believe that I would never have said a word about the girl to you if you had not seen for yourself what those near her have to put up with. You will understand, Mr. Tremorne, I am but a poor benighted woman who has had no one to talk to for months and months. I cannot unburden my soul to Mr. Hemster, because I like him too well; and if I talk to the captain he will merely laugh at me, and tell funny stories. There is no one but you; so you see, unfortunate man, you are the victim of two women."

"I like being the victim of one of them," said I; "but am I to infer from what you have said that, as you don't speak to Mr. Hemster because you like him, you speak to me because you dislike me?"

"What a far-fetched conclusion!" she laughed.

"Certainly not. I like you very much indeed, and even admired you until you used the word 'abjectly' down in that passage. That is a word I detest; no one should employ it when referring to himself."

"Then you were in Miss Hemster's room after all."

"I have not said so, and I refuse to admit it. That is hereafter to be a forbidden topic, and a redeemed prisoner in charge of his gaoler must not disobey orders. If it were not for me, you would now be in your room moping and meditating on your wickedness. I have wrestled with you as if I were a Salvation lass, and so you should be grateful."

"Never was a man wallowing in despondency more grateful for the helping hand of a woman enabling him to emerge."

"It is very generous of you to say that, when it was the helping hand of a woman that pushed you into it."

"No, it was my own action that sent me there. I doubt if a man ever gets into the Slough of Despond through the efforts of any one else. A lone man blunders blindly along, and the first thing he knows he is head over ears in the mud,—and serve him right, too."

"Why serve him right?"

"Because he has no business being a lone man. Two heads are better than one; then, if one is making for the ditch, the helping hand of the other restrains."

"Since when did you arrive at so desperate a conclusion, Mr. Tremorne?"

"Since I met you."

"Well, it is a blessing there was no one to restrain you to-day, or otherwise somebody might have been shot. There is something to be said for lack of restraint upon occasion."

"Miss Stretton, if I had had a sensible woman to advise me, I am certain I would never have lost my money."

"Was it a large amount?"

"It was a fortune."

"How one lives and learns! I have often heard that women squander fortunes, but never yet that a woman helped to preserve one."

"It is better for a man's wife to squander a fortune than to allow a stranger to do it."

"Oh, I am not so sure. The end seems to be the same in both cases. I suppose you have in your mind the woman who would have given you good advice at the proper time."

"Yes, I have."

"Then why don't you ask her now, or is it too late?"

"I don't know that she would have anything to do with me; however, it is very easy to find out. Miss Stretton, will you marry me? I have nothing particular to offer you except myself, but I think I've reached the lowest ebb of my fortunes, and any change must be toward improvement."

"Good gracious, is this actually a proposal?"

"If you will be so generous as to regard it as such."

The young lady stopped in her promenade, and leaned back against the rail, looking me squarely in the face. Then she laughed with greater heartiness than I had yet heard her do.

"This is most interesting," she said at last, "and really most amazing. Why, you must have known me for nearly two hours! I assure you I did not lend you a helping hand out of the Slough of Despond to imprison you at once in the Castle Despair of a penniless marriage. Besides, I always thought a proposal came after a long and somewhat sentimental camaraderie, which goes under the name of courtship. However, this explains what I have so often marvelled at in the English papers; a phrase that struck me as strange and unusual: 'A marriage has been arranged and will take place between So-and-So and So-and-So.' Such a proposal as you have just made is surely an arrangement rather than a love affair. Indeed, you have said nothing about love at all, and so probably such a passion does not enter into the amalgamation. If you were not so serious I should have thought you were laughing at me."

"On the contrary, madam, I am very much in earnest, and it is you who are laughing at me."

"Don't you think I've a very good right to do so? Why, we are hardly even acquainted, and I have no idea what your Christian name is, as I suppose you have no idea what mine is."

"Oh, Hilda, I know your name perfectly!"

"I see you do, and make use of it as well, which certainly advances us another step. But the other half of my proposition is true, and I remain in ignorance of yours."

"When unconsciously I went through the ceremony of christening, I believe my godfathers and godmothers presented me with the name of Rupert."

"What a long time you take in the telling of it. Wasn't there a Prince Rupert once? It seems to me I've heard the phrase 'the Rupert of debate,' and the Rupert of this, and the Rupert of that, so he seems to be a very dashing fellow."

"He was. He dashed into misfortune, as I have often done, but there all likeness between us ends."

"It seems to me the likeness remains, because the present Rupert is dashing into the misfortune of a very heedless proposal. But do not fear that I shall take advantage of your recklessness, which is the more dangerous when you remember my situation. I sometimes think I would almost marry the Prince of Darkness to get out of the position I hold, for I am told he is a gentleman, who probably keeps his temper, and I am coming to the belief that a good temper is a jewel beyond price. However, I'm exaggerating again. I do not really need to stay here unless I wish it, and I remain for the sake of Mr. Hemster, who, as I told you last night, has always been very kind to me, and for whom I have a great respect and liking. Besides, I am not nearly so helpless as perhaps you may imagine. If I went home I could make a very good living teaching music in the States. So you see I do not need to accept the Prince of Darkness should he offer his hand."

"You mean, when he has offered his hand?"

261

She laughed at this, and went on merrily:

"No, 'if;' not 'when.' I shall always cherish the proposal of Prince Rupert, and when the Prince of Darkness makes advances I shall probably tell him that he is not the first Highness so to honour me. When the sunlight comes to take the place of the moonlight, we shall laugh together over this—I can't call it sentimental episode, shall we term it, business arrangement? Now, would you mind accepting a little advice on the subject of matrimony?"

"I'll accept your advice if you'll accept me. Turn about is fair play, you know. Let us finish one transaction before we begin another."

"Transaction is a charming word, Mr. Tremorne, nearly as good as arrangement; I am not sure but it is better. I thought the transaction was finished. You are respectfully declined, with thanks, but, as I assured you, I shall always cherish the memory of this evening, and, now that the way is clear, may I tender this advice, which I have been yearning for some hours to give you. You won't reply. Well, on the whole I think your attitude is very correct. You could hardly be expected to jump joyously from one transaction to another, and I really feel very much flattered that you have put on that dejected look and attitude, which becomes you very much indeed and almost makes me think that the precipitancy of my refusal equals the headlong impetuosity of your avowal. A wiser woman would have asked time for consideration."

"Pray take the time, Miss Stretton; it is not yet too late."

"Yes, it is. What is done, is done, and now comes my advice. You said two heads are better than one. That is true generally, but not always, so I shall present you with an aphorism in place of it, which is that two purses are better than one, if either contains anything. If one purse is always empty, and the other is bursting full, the truth of my adage cannot be questioned. I surmise that your purse and mine are almost on an equality, but I can assure you that Miss Hemster's portemonnaie is full to repletion."

"That has nothing to do with me," I answered curtly.

"Oh, but it may have, and much. I noticed when you came down to luncheon yesterday that you are very deeply in love with Miss Hemster."

"My dear Miss Hilda,—I claim the right to call you that,—when one remembers that you never took your eyes from your plate at luncheon I must say that you have most extraordinary powers of observation. You thought I was high and mighty toward Mr. Hemster, which was not the case, and now you assert that I was in love with Miss Hemster, which is equally beside the fact."

"Of course you are bound to say that, and I may add that although I am offering you advice I am not asking confidences in exchange. I assert that you fell in love with Miss Hemster during your charming ramble through Nagasaki; falling in love with a haste which seems to be characteristic of you, and which totally changes the ideas I had previously held regarding an Englishman."

"Yes, a number of your notions concerning the men of my country were entirely erroneous, as I took the liberty of pointing out to you last night."

"So you did, but actions speak louder than words, and I form my conclusions from your actions. Very well, propose to Miss Hemster; I believe she would accept you, and I further believe that you would prove the salvation of the girl. Her father would make no objection, for I see he already likes you; but in any case he would offer no opposition to anything that his daughter proposed. His life is devoted, poor man, to ministering to her whims and caprices, so you are certain of the parental blessing, and that would carry with it, as I have pointed out, the full purse."

"You spoke of the Prince of Darkness just now, Miss Stretton, so I will appropriate your simile and say that if there were an unmarried Princess of Darkness I would sooner try my luck with her than with Miss Hemster."

"Oh, nonsense! Miss Hemster is a good-hearted girl if only she'd been rightly trained. You would tame her. I know no man so fitted to be the modern Petruchio, and I am fond enough of the drama to say I would like to see a modern rendering of 'The Taming of the Shrew.'"

"She'll never be tamed by me, Miss Stretton."

"She has been, Mr. Tremorne, only you spoiled your lesson by your apology. You must not make a mistake like that again. If you had stood your ground, preserving a distant and haughty demeanour, with a frown on your noble brow, pretty Miss Gertrude would soon have come around to you, wheedling, flattering, and most exquisitely charming, as she well knows how to be. You could then have caught her on the rebound, as the novels put it, just, in fact, as I have managed to catch you to-night. You will be very thankful in the morning that I refused to retain my advantage."

"I shall never be thankful for that, Miss Hilda, and it is equally certain that I shall never propose to Miss Hemster. If I were a speculative adventurer I'd venture to wager on it."

"Most men who see her, propose to her; therefore you must not imagine that Gertrude has not been sought after. I should not be at all certain of your success were it not that every man she has hitherto met has flattered her, while you have merely left the marks of your fingers on her wrists and have threatened to box her ears. This gives you a tremendous advantage if you only know how to use it. I have read somewhere that there is a law in Britain which allows a husband to punish his wife with a stick no bigger than his little finger. I therefore advise you to marry the girl, take something out of the full purse and buy back the ancestral acres, then go into the forest and select a switch as large as the law allows. After that, the new comedy of 'The Taming of the Shrew,' with the married pair living happily ever afterward. You should prove the most fortunate of men, in that you will possess the prettiest, richest, and most docile wife in all your island."

"I am not a barrister, Miss Stretton, therefore can neither affirm nor deny the truth you have stated regarding the law of the stick. If, however, a belief in that enactment has led you to reject my proposal, I beg to inform you that I have no ancestral acres containing a forest; therefore I cannot possess myself of a twig of the requisite size without trespassing on some one else's timber. So you see you need have no fear on that score."

"I am not so sure," replied Hilda, shaking her pretty head, "I imagine there must be a Wife-Beaters' Supply Company in London somewhere, which furnishes the brutal Britisher at lowest rates with the correct legal apparatus for matrimonial correction. I tremble to think of the scenes that must have been enacted in the numerous strong castles of Britain which have had new copper roofs put on with the money brought over by American brides. Girls, obstreperous and untrained, but wealthy beyond the dreams of avarice, have gone across, scorning the honest straightforward American man, who in my opinion is the most sincere gentleman of all the world. These rich but bad-tempered jades have disappeared within the castle, and the portcullis has come down. Have we ever heard a whimper from any one of them? Not a whisper even. If they had married American men there would have been tremendous rows, ending with divorce cases; but not so when they have disappeared into the castle. You never hear of an American woman divorcing a lord, and Lord knows some of those lords are the riff-raff of creation. History gives us grim pictures of tragical scenes in those old strongholds, but I shudder to think of the tragedies which must occur nowadays when once the drawbridge is up, and the American girl, hitherto adored, learns the law regarding flagellation. The punishment must be exceedingly complete, for the lady emerges cowed and subdued as the Kate that Shakespeare wrote about. And how well that great man understood a wilful and tyrannical woman! Oh, you needn't look shocked, Mr. Tremorne. Haven't you an adage on that benighted island which says 'A woman, a dog, and a walnut-tree; the more you beat them the better they be?'"

"Great heavens, girl, what an imagination you have! You should really write a novel. It would be an interesting contribution toward international love affairs."

"I may do so, some day, if music-teaching fails. I should like, however, to have the confession of one of the victims of an international matrimonial match."

"Which victim? The English husband or the American wife?"

"The wife, of course. I think I shall wait until you and Miss Hemster are married a year or two, and then perhaps she will look more kindly on me than she does at present, and so may tell me enough to lend local colour to

265

my book."

"I can give you a much better plan than that, Miss Stretton. Hearsay evidence, you know, is never admitted in courts of law, and by the same token it amounts to very little in books. I am given to understand that, to be successful, an author must have lived through the events of which he writes, so your best plan is to accept my offer; then we will purchase a moated grange in England, and you can depict its horrors from the depths of experience."

"Where are we to get the money for the moated grange? I haven't any, and you've just acknowledged that you are penniless."

"I forgot that. Still, moated granges are always going cheap. They are damp as a general rule, and not much sought after. We could possibly buy one on the instalment plan, or even rent it if it came to that."

Miss Stretton laughed joyously at the idea, held out her hand, and bade me a cordial good-night.

"Thank you so much, Mr. Tremorne for a most interesting evening, and also for the proposal. I think it very kind of you, for I suppose you suspect I haven't had very many. I think we've each helped the other out of the Slough of Despond. So good-night, good-night!"

266

# CHAPTER XI

**I** WAS awakened next morning by the roar of the anchor-chain running out, and found the yacht at a standstill, with the vibration of the machinery temporarily at an end. On looking out through the porthole I recognized the town of Chemulpo, which had grown considerably since I last saw it. Beyond stood the hills of Corea, rising wave upon wave, as if the land had suffered a volcanic eruption.

Mr. Hemster and I had breakfast alone together, after which we went on deck.

"Now," said he, "the captain has brought us safely here without running down an island, and the next move in the game is yours. What do you propose to do?"

"I shall go ashore at once, engage ponies and an escort, change a quantity of silver money into ropes of sek, then I shall make my way as quickly as possible to the capital."

"What are ropes of sek?" asked Mr. Hemster.

"They are bronze, iron, or copper coins, which are strung on ropes of straw by means of a square hole in the middle. They are the most debased currency on earth, and are done up in strings of five hundred cash. Sek is useful in dealing with the natives, but when I come to the capital I shall need silver and gold. When I have made arrangements at Seoul I shall return to Chemulpo and let you know the result."

"You told me I could not take the 'Michigan' up the river,—what do you call it,—the Han?—and you were doubtful about the advisability of using the naphtha launch."

"No, the yacht would be sure to run aground before you had gone very far, and as for the naphtha launch, the Han is rather a treacherous and very crooked piece of navigation, and if you had to stop half-way we might be farther from the capital than we are now, with a worse road ahead of us, and no chance of getting ponies or escort. I strongly advise you to stay where you are till I return, and meanwhile I'll find out more about the river than I know now."

To this Mr. Hemster agreed, and, being well provided with the sinews of war, I went ashore. Chemulpo proved to be quite a commercial town, and there was no difficulty in my getting everything I wanted. I was shocked but not surprised to find that the Prime Minister, whom I formerly knew, and on whose help I had somewhat counted, had been deposed and beheaded, while all his relatives, male and female, had been eliminated from human knowledge by death, slavery, or exile. However, even if this man had remained in office, my best plea with him would have been money, and as I was well provided with this necessity I foresaw no obstacle to my purpose. Having had an early start, and pushing on with more energy than my escort relished, in spite of my promises of recompense, I reached the capital before the great bell rang and the gates were closed.

I had some thought of calling on the British representative, and if I had done so would doubtless have enjoyed better accommodation for the night than fell to my lot; but as, the last time I saw him, I was, like himself, a servant of our Government, I could not bring myself to acknowledge that I was now merely the hired man of an American millionaire, as his daughter had so tersely put it.

Next day I very soon bribed my way to the presence of the then Prime Minister, and was delighted to find in him a certain Hun Woe, whom I had previously known in a very much more subordinate capacity. After our greetings I went straight to the point, and told Hun Woe that I represented a gentleman and his daughter, now at Chemulpo, who wished the honour of a private conference with the Emperor. I also mentioned casually that there was a certain amount of money in this for the Prime Minister if he could bring about the interview. Hun Woe, with many genuflections, informed me that the delight of serving me would more than recompense him for any trouble he was likely to incur, ending his protestations of deep friendship and regard by inquiring how much of the needful the gentleman in Chemulpo would be prepared to place on the table. I replied by naming a sum about one quarter of the amount I was willing to pay. The Prime Minister's eyes glittered, and he made various shrugs of the shoulders and motions with his hands, during the time that he politely intimated to me his

rise in the world since last I met him. A cash dividend which would have been ample in those days, he gently hinted, was little less than an insult at the present time. So far as he was himself concerned, he added, his services were freely at my disposal, and none of the silver would stick to his fingers; but, as I must be aware, the Court at Seoul was a most grasping and avaricious body, and he should need to disburse freely before my object could be accomplished.

I sighed and shook my head, rising to leave, regretting it was not to be my good fortune to add to the wealth of an old friend, whereupon Hun Woe begged me to be seated again, and, after many declarations of affectionate esteem, was good enough to name a sum which he thought might be sufficient to cover all expenses; and as this came to less than half of what I was willing to dispose of, we speedily reached an agreement. This haggling at the outset was necessary, not only to save Hemster his hardly earned money, but also to satisfy the official that he was driving a shrewd bargain. I accordingly paid the sum in prompt cash to Hun Woe, and then informed him that if everything went off to the satisfaction of my employer a further bonus would be awarded him, depending in size on the celerity and satisfactory nature of the interview. This delighted the honest Premier, and I must admit that he conducted the business with an energy and despatch which was as gratifying as it was unexpected.

East or West, money is a great lubricator, and, as I have said, I was well provided. That very afternoon Hun Woe secured me an audience with His Imperial Majesty, and for the third or fourth time in my life I stood before the ruler of Corea. I do not know whether he recognized me or not, but it was quite evident that the scent of gold was in the air, and the Emperor did not leave it long in doubt that he intended to acquire as much as might be available of it. By way of introduction, and to show that I was prepared to do the proper thing, I placed a heavy bag of the seductive metal on the shabby deal table before him, begging His Majesty to accept it as an earnest of more to follow. He poured it out on the table, and gloated over it with a miser's eagerness. He had not improved in appearance since last we met. The seams of dissipation had cut deeply into the royal countenance, and his little crinkling pig eyes were even more rapacious and cruel than I remembered them to be.

The proposal to come aboard the yacht was at once dismissed as impracticable. His Majesty would not venture away from his capital, and, above all, he would not risk his precious person on board of anybody's steamship, so, on the whole, it was just as well that Mr. Hemster had not essayed the navigation of the river Han. However, His Majesty was good enough to inform me that although he would not trust his royal person to the care of the infidels, yet he would make up for that by giving so generous a suitor a suite of rooms in the Palace itself, and my principal would therefore have the honour of being the guest of Corea, as one might say. I imagined that this would look as well in the columns of the "New York Herald" as if the Emperor had gone on board the yacht. I fancied that a few lines, something to the following effect, would read very acceptably in the Sunday papers of Chicago, under the head of Society Notes:

"Mr. Silas K. Hemster, of this city, and Miss Hemster, occupy a suite of rooms in the royal Palace of Seoul, as guests of the Emperor of Corea."

So, all in all, I was more than satisfied with the speedy and gratifying outcome of my mission to the Corean capital. After retiring from the royal presence I congratulated the Prime Minister upon his method of conducting negotiations and gave him a further payment on account, so that he would not be tempted to falter in well-doing; and as for Hun Woe himself he looked upon me as the most valuable visitor that had set foot in Corea for many years. I distributed backsheesh somewhat indiscriminately among the underlings of the Palace, and early next morning left the royal precincts on my return to Chemulpo, which port I reached without any mishap. Possibly never before in the history of Seoul had business been so rapidly transacted.

I found Mr. Hemster, as usual, sitting on deck in his accustomed chair, as if he had no interest in the negotiations I had been conducting. He listened quietly to my account of the various interviews, and received without comment the bribery bill I presented to him. He did not appear to be so tremendously impressed as I had expected with the royal invitation to visit the Palace, and said he would have preferred to take up his quarters at the chief hotel in the place, but when I told him there was not a hotel in the city fit for a white man to sleep in, he made no demur to the Imperial proposal. It seemed he had visited Chemulpo during my absence, and in consequence of what he heard there he now made some inquiry regarding the safety of a stay in the capital. I told him that as a rule the Coreans were a peaceable people unless incited to violence by the authorities, and as long as we were willing to bribe the authorities sufficiently they would take care that the influx of the newly acquired affluence would not be interfered with. So he asked me to go to Chemulpo and make arrangements for the transport of the party next morning.

I had not seen Miss Hemster on the day I left for Seoul, but she welcomed my return with her former girlish enthusiasm, just as if nothing particular had happened. She seemed to have entirely recovered from her disappointment in not getting to see the Emperor of Japan, and was now effusively enthusiastic over our coming journey. The young woman more than made up for her father's lack of interest in the royal invitation, and I was asked question after question regarding the Palace at Seoul, which I feared would disappoint her when she saw it, because of its dilapidations and general lack of impressiveness. However, a palace was a palace, she averred, and she further pronounced the opinion that the news of their residence there would make Chicago "sit up" when it was cabled over. Miss Stretton sat silent with downcast eyes during this cross-examination, her intelligent face as inscrutable as that of the old millionaire himself.

I did not get a word with her that evening, and, as it was drawing late, I had to return to Chemulpo to make arrangements for the trip the following day, and so stayed ashore that night.

We had a beautiful day for our expedition, and rather a jolly trip of it,—almost, as Miss Hemster said, as if it were a picnic. At Miss Hemster's request I rode by her side, with Miss Stretton sometimes with us, but more often in front, with the old gentleman, who jogged moodily on, absorbed in his own meditations, saying nothing to anybody. Miss Hemster chatted very gaily most of the day, but as evening drew on she became tired of talk and began to look anxiously for the gate of Seoul. When at last we passed through it she expressed great contempt for the city of shanties, as she called it, giving somewhat petulant expression to her disgust at the disillusionment for which I had unsuccessfully endeavoured to prepare her. Of course by the time we reached the Palace the ladies were tired out, and, if we had had the slightest notion of what was before us, anxiety would have been added to fatigue.

# CHAPTER XII

WE were more comfortable in the royal apartments than might have been expected. Mr. Hemster had brought his own cook with him, together with the Japanese boy to wait on us, and he had also taken the precaution to bring a week's provisions, so that in spite of the primitive arrangements of the kitchen placed at our disposal we fared very much as usual so far as the cuisine was concerned. The officials made no complaint at this reflection on their hospitality; in fact, they rather relished our foresight, because, as Hun Woe admitted with great simplicity, it enabled them to charge our keep to the royal exchequer and yet incur no expense in providing for us. A system which admits of collection and no disbursements is heavenly to a Corean official. We were probably at the outset the most popular party that had ever lodged in the royal Palace.

Our first dilemma arose, not through any interference from the officers of the Court, but because of certain objections which Miss Gertrude Hemster herself promulgated. The Prime Minister did us great honour in offering to coach us personally regarding the etiquette that surrounds the approach to the throne. It seemed that both Emperor and Empress were to receive us in state, and the moment we came in sight of their Majesties we were to turn our faces aside, as if dazzled by the magnificence before us and the glory conferred upon us march a dozen steps to the left, turn again, march a dozen steps to the right, bowing extremely low at each evolution, advancing, with great caution and humility, never more than two steps forward at a time, approaching the throne by a series of crab-like movements and coming very gradually forward, zigzag fashion, until we stood with heads humbly inclined before the two potentates. My translation of all this caused great hilarity on the part of Miss Hemster, and she quite shocked the genial Prime Minister by giving way to peal after peal of laughter. After all, he was a dignified man and did not regard the ceremony as a joke, which appeared to be the way it presented itself to the young lady.

"I'm not going through any of that nonsense," she exclaimed. "Does he think I intend to make a Wild West show of myself? If he does, he's mistaken. I'll proceed right up to the Emperor and shake hands with him, and if he doesn't like it he can lump it. You translate that to him, Mr. Tremorne."

I intimated respectfully to the young woman that Court etiquette was Court etiquette, and that everything would be much more simple if we fell in with the ways of the country. This marching and counter-marching was no more absurd than our own way of shaking hands, or the Pacific Island method of salutation by rubbing noses.

"'When in Rome do as the Romans do,'" I suggested; but this expostulation had no effect whatever upon the determined young person, who became more and more set in her own way from the fact that her father quietly agreed with me. Furthermore, when she learned that there were no chairs in the Royal reception-room, she proclaimed that her Japanese attendant must carry a chair for her; because, if the Royal pair were seated, she insisted on being seated also. I was to tell "His Nibs,"—by which expression she referred to the smiling Prime Minister,—that she belonged to sovereign America, and therefore was as much an Empress in her own right as the feminine Majesty of Corea.

"Miss Hemster," said I, "I don't know whether what you wish can be accomplished or not; but in any case it is sure to cause considerable delay, and, furthermore, it will probably cost your father a very large sum of money."

I speedily saw that I would better have preserved silence. The young lady drew herself up with great dignity and flashed upon me a glance of withering indignation.

"Will you oblige me by minding your own business?" she asked harshly. "Your duty is to obey orders, and not to question them."

To this, of course, no reply was possible, so I contented myself by bowing to her, and, turning to Hun Woe, who stood smiling first at one and then at the other of us, not understanding even the drift of our conversation, but evidently growing somewhat uneasy at the tone it was taking, I translated to him as well as I could what Miss Hemster had said, softening the terms as much as possible, and laying great stress on her exalted position in her own country, of which land the Prime Minister was enormously ignorant.

Hun Woe became extremely grave; and his smile, unlike that in the advertisement, at once "came off."

"If the strenuous Empress of China," said I, "arrived at Seoul on a visit, she would certainly be received by His Majesty as an equal, and would not need to go through the ceremony of advance which you have so graphically described. Now this Princess," I continued, "holds herself to be of a rank superior to the Empress of China, and is considered of higher status by her own countrymen."

The Prime Minister very solemnly shook his head and seemed much disquieted.

"Her father," I continued earnestly, and in a measure truthfully, "maintains a much larger fleet than China possesses, and his private war-ship, now in the waters of Corea, is grander than anything that empire ever beheld, much less owned. His territories are vast. Thousands of people,—yes, millions,—pay tribute to him. He has waged commercial war against those who dared to dispute his authority, and has invariably defeated them. His revenue exceeds that of the kingdom of Corea twice over, so is it likely,—I put it to you as man to man,—that such a potentate will consent to the dozen steps this way, and the dozen steps that? His only daughter is the Crown Princess, and will be heiress to all his powers and emoluments. I pray you, therefore, put this matter in its right light before His Majesty of Corea, and I can assure you, if you succeed, your own income will be largely augmented."

This speech undoubtedly impressed the Premier, who bowed low to Mr. Hemster and his daughter time and again as I went on. The girl's anger had subsided as quickly as it had risen, and she watched us both intently, seeming at first to doubt that I translated accurately what I had been so curtly ordered to say; but as our conversation went on the increasing deference of the Prime Minister showed that I was at least doing my best. The old gentleman, too, regarded us shrewdly from under his bushy eyebrows, but seemed rather tired of the game, as if it were not worth such a pow-wow. He evidently wished to get the whole thing over as quickly as possible, and return to the comforts of his yacht, and in this I entirely sympathized with him.

The Prime Minister replied that he would present the new facts before His Majesty, and averred that if they had the same effect upon the Emperor of Corea as they had produced upon the Prime Minister the impediment would be speedily removed. He assured me I could count on his utmost endeavours to find a solution for the unexpected exigency, and I was well aware that my tale would not decrease in the retelling. With many and most profound obeisances to the two Western grandees, the Prime Minister took his departure, and I accompanied him outside, where I made him a payment on a gold basis.

The Royal audience had been appointed for two o'clock of the afternoon on the day succeeding our arrival at Seoul, but this new question that had arisen caused the ceremony to be postponed, much to my annoyance, for I knew the habitual delay of these people, especially where money was in question, and I feared that the inconvenient assumption of dignity on the part of the young woman might land us in trouble of which neither she nor her father had the least appreciation. I communicated my fears of delay and complications to the old gentleman when I got him alone, hoping he might use his influence with his daughter to modify what seemed to me her ill-timed assertion of high rank; but Mr. Hemster, though a resourceful man in every other direction, always proved a broken reed so far as his daughter was concerned, and he pathetically admitted his inability to curb either her actions or her words.

"All we can do, Mr. Tremorne," he said, "is to fork over the cash. Don't you spare it. I can see very well you are handling this situation as expertly as a ward politician. You're all right. If you can talk to this here King as you talked to his Prime Minister, I think you'll fix up the thing in five minutes, and remember this is a game of bluff in which there is no limit. I don't restrict you in the cash you spend, so go ahead."

And this indeed proved to be the way out of the muddle, although I explained to him that too lavish distribution of cash was not without its own danger. But at this juncture a message arrived to the effect that the Prime Minister wished to see me, and I at once departed to learn what had been the outcome of his mediation. I found that he had made little progress, but by a curious coincidence he put forth the same suggestion previously offered by Mr. Hemster. He had arranged a conference for me with the King, and advised me, as Mr. Hemster had done, to lay it on thick. Hun Woe was somewhat encouraged by the orders he had received from his royal master in regard to my audience. The King would receive me entirely alone; not even his Prime Minister was to be present. From this condition Hun Woe surmised I was to be successful in my quest, and I was well aware that this unwitnessed reception of me was as much contrary to Corean customs as was the proposal Miss Hemster had made.

I saw his Majesty in one of the private apartments of the Palace, and speedily realized that he did not care a rap what honours belonged to Mr. Hemster. The sinister, shifty eyes of his Majesty were filled with greed. Never was there such a picture of avarice presented to me as the countenance of the King showed. His claw-like hands had been withdrawn from the voluminous bell sleeves of his robe of red silk and yellow gold, and were twitching nervously on the table before him. His tremulous attitude of uneasy eagerness reminded me of the Miser in the "Chimes of Normandy." Impatiently he waved aside the recital touching the claims of my employer to the most-favoured-monarch treatment, and gasped out the Corean equivalent for "How much, how much?"

A tangible object-lesson is better than talk even in the Orient; so, bringing my eloquence to an abrupt conclusion, I drew from my pocket another bag of gold, similar in weight to the one I had previously presented to him, and, seeing he was impatient for touch as well as for sight, undid the string and poured the stream of shining metal discs before him on the table. He thrust his vibrant hands among the coins, and gave utterance to a low guttural sound of satisfaction which resembled the noise made by a pig thrusting its snout into a trough of slops, rather than any exclamation I had ever before heard from human lips. I assured him that no word of all this would be spoken by me, and promised that as soon as the conference was safely over on the terms that Miss Hemster and her father had laid down, a similar amount would be privately paid to his Royal self in an equally secret manner; and so my mission terminated in a glorious success, and it was arranged that the reception should take place the next day at two o'clock. The process was costly, but effective; and effectiveness, after all, was the main thing.

I reported my victory to Mr. Hemster and his daughter, and almost immediately after this the Prime Minister came in to offer his congratulations. The good man had seen his royal master for a few moments, and was evidently delighted that everything was going on so smoothly. It meant money in his pocket, and he was becoming rich with a celerity which left stock-exchange speculations far in the rear. He had received his commands regarding next day's reception, and the Emperor had been pleased to order that the audience should take place in the same room where I had seen him, with none of the nobles of the Court present except the Prime Minister. This was a good example of his Majesty's craftiness. The Premier already knew that the etiquette of the Court was to be put aside for the occasion; but the monarch had no desire for further witnesses, and was evidently not going to set a precedent in the realm of Corea that might produce inconvenient consequences thereafter.

I had had little opportunity of talking with Miss Stretton since the night of our walk on deck,—the night of the proposal, as I called it to myself, as amidst all these negotiations I kept continually thinking of it. Without exactly avoiding me, Miss Stretton never seemed to be alone, and although very rarely I caught a glance of her eye I had no opportunity of private speech with her. She kept very much in the background and was more than usually quiet and thoughtful.

We had dinner early that night, somewhere about six o'clock, for there were neither candles nor lamps in the Palace, and if we waited until nightfall we had to "grope," as Mr. Hemster termed it. In spite of the success of her plans, Miss Hemster was distinctly snappy at dinner, if I may use such a term regarding a person so beautiful. She shut me up most effectually when I ventured a little harmless general conversation, and I think she made Miss Stretton feel more than usual the bitterness of a dependent's bread. Mr.

Hemster said nothing. I could see the poor old gentleman was hankering for a daily paper, and from my soul I felt sorry for him as he listened with the utmost patience to the querulous fault-findings of his lovely daughter.

Toward the end of dinner something that was said did not please the young lady, and she rose abruptly and left the table, with a gesture of queenly disapproval of us all. Anger appeared to fill her as electricity fills an accumulator, and until the battery was discharged we never knew who would suffer the next shock. When the young woman's ill-temper had been aroused by my opposition earlier in the day, perhaps we would have spent a pleasanter evening if it had been allowed to run its course. But as it was checked by her interest in the negotiations it now filtered out in very palpable discontent. When Miss Stretton arose to leave I took the liberty of begging her to remain.

"I should like very much," I said, "to show you the light on Nam-san."

"And what is the light on Nam-san?" she asked, pausing with her hand on the back of the chair.

"Beacons are lighted all along the coast of Corea, on the mountain tops," I replied, "so that peak calls to peak, as it were; and the last one to be lit is that on Nam-san, which is the name of the highest mountain near Seoul. They kindle it at eight o'clock, and its blazing up shows that the kingdom of Corea is safe and at peace with the world."

"Very well," said Miss Stretton after a pause; "I will return here about ten minutes to eight."

She was as good as her word, and we took a stroll together in the great courtyard of the Palace, which is a city within a city. The gates of the Palace grounds were now closed and guarded, and we could not have got out into Seoul if we had wished to do so. But it was all very still and pleasant in the broad square surrounded by the low, strangely roofed buildings that constituted the Palace. We saw the beacon light flash out and then die away. I cannot remember that we talked much, but there was a calm and soothing sense of comradeship between us that was very comforting. She told me, when I had tried to warn her against expecting too much on seeing the

Emperor next day, that she did not intend to accompany our party, and I suspected that she had been ordered to remain away. Moreover I could see that she was very tired of it all, and, like Mr. Hemster, wished herself back in her own country.

# CHAPTER XIII

SHORTLY before two o'clock the next day the Prime Minister came for us, and conducted us directly to the Presence Chamber, instead of taking us to the small wooden building, containing a table and some chairs, where visitors usually had to wait until the Emperor's messenger arrived with orders permitting an advance to the throne-room. Our little procession consisted of four persons,—Mr. Hemster, Miss Hemster, the Prime Minister, and myself. Hun Woe was visibly uneasy, and I was well aware that, in spite of the money paid him, he would much rather have been absent from the ceremony. In Eastern lands it is extremely dangerous for a Vizier to witness a Sultan's humiliation, and the Prime Minister well knew that although the Emperor had permitted the deference due to him to be temporarily annulled through payment of gold, he might nevertheless consider it desirable to eliminate the onlooker, so that no record of this innovation were left on the earth.

The room into which we were conducted was but indifferently lighted. It was oblong in shape, and a low divan ran across the farther end of it. Four very ordinary wooden chairs had been placed midway between the door and the divan.

Both the Emperor and the Empress were seated, Oriental fashion, on huge cushions, and were decked out in a fashion that might be termed tawdry gorgeousness. I do not know whether the strings of colored gems that hung around the Empress were real or imitation, but they were barbaric in size and glitter and number. The Empress, whom I had never seen before, sat impassive, with eyes half closed, as if she were a statue of the feminine Buddha. During the whole of the exciting interview she never moved or showed the slightest sign of animation.

The Emperor's ferret-like eyes glanced shiftily over the advancing party, which came forward, as I might say, in two sections, the three white people upright, and the Premier bending almost double, working his way toward the divan by zigzag courses, giving one the odd notion that he was some sort of wild beast about to spring upon the Emperor when he arrived at a proper position for the pounce.

The twinkling eyes of the Emperor, however, speedily deserted the rest of our party, and fixed themselves on Miss Hemster, who moved toward him with graceful ease and an entire absence of either fear or deference. She instantly made good the determination she had previously expressed, and, gliding directly up to him, thrust forward her hand, which the Emperor seemed at a loss what to do with. His eyes were fastened on her lovely countenance, and there broke on his lips a smile so grim and ghastly that it might well have made any one shudder who witnessed it. The bending Prime Minister uttered a few words which informed the Emperor that the lady wished to shake hands with him, and then his Majesty took his own grimy paws from out of the great bell sleeves in which they were concealed, and with his two hands grasped hers. Never did so sweet a hand disappear in so revolting a clutch, and the young woman, evidently shocked at the contact, and doubtless repelled by the repulsiveness of the face that leered up at her, drew suddenly back, but the clutch was not relaxed.

"Let me go!" she cried breathlessly, and her father took an impulsive step forward; but before he reached her the Emperor suddenly put forth his strength and drew the young woman tumbling down to the divan beside him, grimacing like a fiend from the bottomless pit. Little he recked what he was doing. With a scream Miss Hemster sprang up, flung out her right arm, and caught him a slap on the side of his face that sounded through the hall like the report of a pistol. The Prime Minister, with a shuddering cry of horror, flung himself on his face, and grovelled there in piteous pretence of not having seen this death-earning insult which the Western woman had so energetically bestowed on the Eastern potentate. Hun Woe's open palms beat helplessly against the wooden planks, as if he were in the tremors of dissolution. The active young woman sprang back a pace or two, and, if a glance could have killed, the look with which she transfixed his Imperial Majesty would have brought extinction with it.

As for the Emperor, he sat there, bending slightly forward, the revolting grimace frozen on his face, and yet his royal head must have been ringing with the blow he had received. The Empress sat stolid, as if nothing had happened, and never moved an eyelid. Then his Majesty, casting a look of contempt at the huddled heap of clothes which represented the Prime Minister, threw back his head and gave utterance to a cackling laugh which was exceedingly chilling and unpleasant to hear. Meanwhile the young lady seated herself emphatically in one of the chairs, with a sniff of indignant remonstrance.

"There," she said, "I flatter myself I have taught one nigger a lesson in good manners. He'll bear the signature of my fingers on his cheeks for a few hours at least."

"Madam," I said solemnly, "I beg you to restrain yourself. Your signature is more likely to prove a death-warrant than a lesson in etiquette."

"Be quiet," she cried angrily to me, turning toward me a face red with resentment; "if there is no one here to protect me from insult I must stand up for myself, and you can bet your bottom dollar I'll do it. Do you think I am afraid of an old hobo like that?"

The Emperor watched her with narrowing eyes as she was speaking, and it really seemed as if he understood what she said; for again he threw back his head and laughed, as if the whole thing was a joke.

"Madam," said I, "it isn't a question of fear or the lack of it, but merely a matter of common sense. We are entirely in this man's power."

"He daren't hurt us," she interrupted with a snap, "and he knows it, and you know it."

"I beg your pardon, Miss Hemster, I know a great deal more of these people than you do. No Westerner can predict what may happen in an Eastern Court."

"Westerners are just as good as New Yorkers, or Londoners either, for that matter," cried the gentle Gertrude, holding her head high in the air.

"You mistake me, Miss Hemster; I am speaking of Europeans as well as of Americans. This Emperor, at a word, can have our heads chopped off before we leave the room."

"Oh, you're a finicky, babbling old woman," she exclaimed, tossing her head, "and just trying to frighten my father. The Emperor knows very well that if he laid a hand on us the United States would smash his old kingdom in two weeks."

"If you will pardon me, madam, the Emperor is quite ignorant. If he should determine to have us executed, not all the United States or Britain and Europe combined could save us. He has but to give an order, and it will be rigidly obeyed if the heavens fell the moment after. If you are anxious to give the Emperor your opinion of him, all I beg of you is that you wait until we're out of this trap, and then send it to him on a picture post-card. Whatever action the Powers might subsequently take would be of no assistance to us— when we are executed."

During this heated conversation the Prime Minister had partly risen to his hands and knees, although he kept his head hanging down until it nearly touched the floor. The Emperor had been watching Miss Hemster's animated countenance, and he seemed greatly to enjoy my evident discomfiture. Even though he understood no word of our language, he saw plainly enough that I was getting the worst of the verbal encounter. Now the gradual uprising of the Prime Minister drew his attention temporarily to this grovelling individual, and he spoke a few words to him which at once raised my alarm for the safety of those in my care. His Majesty had evidently forgotten for the moment that I understood the Corean tongue. Hun Woe now rose to his feet, kept his back at an angle of forty-five degrees, and, without turning around, began to retreat from the Imperial presence. I at once stepped in his way, and said to the Emperor that this command must not go forth, whereupon the Majesty of Corea was good enough to laugh once more.

"What are you talking about?" demanded Miss Hemster. "You must translate everything that is said; and, furthermore, you must tell him that he has to apologize to me for his insult at the beginning."

"All in good time, Miss Hemster."

"Not all in good time," she cried, rising from her chair. "If you don't do that at once, I'll go and slap his face again."

284

"Please believe me, Miss Hemster, that you have already done that once too often. I assure you that the situation is serious, and you are increasing the danger by your untimely interference."

Before she could reply, a roar of laughter from the Emperor, who wagged his head from side to side and rocked his body to and fro in his glee, drew my attention to the fact that I had been outwitted. The Prime

Minister, taking advantage of my discussion with Miss Hemster, had scuttled silently away and had disappeared. I fear I made use of an exclamation to which I should not have given utterance in the presence of a lady; but that lady's curiosity, overcoming whatever resentment she may have felt, clamoured to know what had happened.

"His Majesty," said I, "gave orders to the Prime Minister doubly to guard the Palace gates, and see that no communication reached the outside from us. It means that we are prisoners!"

All this time I had not the least assistance from the old gentleman, who sat in a most dejected attitude on one of the wooden chairs. I had remained standing since we entered the room. Now he looked up with dismay on his countenance, and I was well enough acquainted with him to know that his fear was not for himself but for his daughter.

"Will you tell the Emperor," he said, "that we are armed, and that we demand leave to quit this place as freely as we entered it?"

"I think, Mr. Hemster," said I, "that we had better conceal the fact that we have arms,—at least until the Prime Minister returns. We can keep that as our trump card."

"Will you please do exactly what my father tells you to," snapped the young woman sharply.

"Hush, Gertrude!" said Mr. Hemster. Then, addressing himself to me: "Sir," he added, "do whatever you think is best."

I now turned to the Emperor, and made the speech of my life. I began by stating that Corea had been face to face with many a crisis during its history,

285

but never had she been confronted with such a situation as now presented itself. Mr. Hemster, besides being King, in his own right, of the provision market in Chicago, was one of the most valued citizens of the United States, and that formidable country would spend its last sen and send its last man to avenge any injury done to Mr. Hemster, or the Princess, his daughter. I asserted that the United States was infinitely more powerful than Russia, China, and Japan added together, with each of whom he had hitherto chiefly dealt. This alone would be bad enough, but the danger of the situation was augmented by my own presence. His Majesty might perhaps be good enough to remember that the last time I had had the pleasure of meeting him I was an Envoy of a country which had probably fought more successful battles than any other nation in existence. Great Britain was also in the habit of avenging the injuries inflicted on her subjects; and so, if the Emperor was so ill-fated as to incur the displeasure of these mighty empires, whose united strength was sufficient to overawe all the rest of the earth, he would thus bring about the extinction of himself and of his nation.

I regret to say that this eloquence was largely thrown away. His Majesty paid but scanty attention to my international exposition. His fishy eyes were fixed continually on Miss Hemster, who now and then made grimaces at him as if she were a little schoolgirl, once going so far as to thrust out her tongue, which action seemed to strike the Emperor as exceedingly comic, for he laughed uproariously at it.

When I had ceased speaking the Emperor replied in a few words, but without ever taking his eyes from the girl. I answered him,—or, rather, was answering him,—when Miss Hemster interrupted impatiently:

"What are you saying? You must translate as you go on. I wish you would remember your position, Mr. Tremorne, which is that of translator. I refuse to be kept in the dark in this way."

"Gertie, Gertie!" remonstrated her father. "Please do not interfere. Mr. Tremorne will tell us what is happening all in good time."

And now the Emperor himself, as if he understood what was being said, commanded me to translate to them the terms he had laid down.

286

"I shall try to remember my position, Miss Hemster," I replied; "and, as his Majesty's ideas coincide with your own, I have pleasure in giving you a synopsis of what has passed."

Then I related my opening speech to the Emperor, which appeared to commend itself to Mr. Hemster, who nodded several times in support of my dissertation on the national crisis.

"The Emperor," I continued, "has made no comment upon what I have laid before him. He tells us we are free to go,—that is, your father and myself,—as long as we leave you here. Not to put too fine a point to it, he offers to buy you, and says he will make you the White Star of his harem, which he seems to think is rather a poetical expression."

"Well, of all the gall!" exclaimed Miss Hemster, raising her hands and letting them fall helplessly into her lap again, as if this gesture should define the situation better than any words she had at her command. "You inform His Nibs that I am no White Star Line, and you tell this mahogany graven image that my father can buy him and his one-horse kingdom and give them away without ever feeling it. When he talks of buying, just inform him that in the States down South we used to sell better niggers than him every day in the week."

I thought it better to tone down this message somewhat, and in doing so was the innocent cause, as I suspect, of a disaster which has always troubled my mind since that eventful time. I said to the Emperor that American customs differed from those of Corea. Miss Hemster, being a Princess in her own rank, of vast wealth, could not accept any position short of that of Empress, and, as there was already an Empress of Corea, the union he proposed was impossible. I reiterated my request that we be allowed to pass down to the coast without further molestation.

This statement was received by the Emperor with much hilarity. He looked upon it merely as an effort on my part to enhance the price of the girl, and expressed his willingness to turn over to her half the revenues of the kingdom. He seemed to imagine he was acting in the most lavishly generous manner, and I realized the hopelessness of the discussion, because I was face to face with a man who had never been refused anything he wished for since he came to the throne. His conceited ignorance regarding the power of other countries to enforce their demands made the situation all the more desperate.

At this juncture the crouching Prime Minister returned, made his way slowly, by means of acute angles, to the foot of the throne, and informed the Emperor that the guards of the Palace had been doubled, and had received instructions to allow no living thing to enter or leave the precincts of the Court. I now repeated to Hun Woe the warning I had so fruitlessly proffered to the Emperor, but I doubt if the satellite paid much more attention than his master had done. While in the presence he seemed incapable of either thought or action that did not relate to his Imperial chief. He intimated that the audience was now finished and done with, and added that he would have the pleasure of accompanying us to our rooms. It seemed strange, when we returned, to find Miss Stretton sitting in a chair, placidly reading a book which she had brought with her from the yacht, and the Japanese boy setting out cups for tea on a small table near her. Miss Stretton looked up pleasantly as we entered, closing her book, and putting her finger in it to mark the place.

"What a long time you have been," she said; "the conference must have proved very successful."

Miss Gertrude Hemster paced up and down the room as if energetic action were necessary to calm the perturbation of her spirit. As the other finished her remark she clenched her little fist and cried:

"I'll make that Emperor sit up before I've done with him!"

I thought it more advisable to refrain from threats until we were out of the tiger's den; but the reticent example of Mr. Hemster was upon me, and I said nothing. Nevertheless the young woman was as good as her word.

# CHAPTER XIV

THE Hemsters had fallen into the English habit of afternoon tea, and, having finished the refreshing cup, I excused myself and went outside to learn how strict the cordon around us was kept. I found that the Prime Minister had done his work well. The gates were very thoroughly guarded, and short of force there seemed to be no method of penetrating into the city. I tried bribery, desiring to get a short note through to the British Consul-General, and, although my bribe was willingly accepted, I found later that the missive was never sent.

Rambling around the vast precincts of the Palace, trying to discover any loophole of escape, I came upon our escort and the ponies which had brought us from the port to the capital. These had been gathered up in the city and taken inside. I could not decide at the moment whether this move on the part of our gaolers strengthened or weakened our position. The escort was composed of a very poor set of creatures who would prove utterly valueless if the crisis developed into a contest. They were all huddled together under a shed, and were very evidently in a state of hopeless panic. They knew intuitively that things were going badly with us, and it needed no prophet to foretell that they would instantly betray us if they got the chance, or cut our throats if they were ordered to do so. I deeply regretted now that we had not stayed longer at Chemulpo until we had gathered together an escort composed entirely of Japanese. Two Japanese followers were among our crowd, and they now stood apart with the imperturbable nonchalance of their race. I was aware that I could depend upon them to the death; but the rest were the very scum of the East, cowardly, unstable as water, and as treacherous as quicksand. I spoke a few words of encouragement to the Japanese, patted the ponies, and then returned to Mr. Hemster. I told him I had endeavoured to send a note to the British representative in Seoul, and to my amazement found that he did not approve of this move.

"The fact is, Mr. Tremorne, we have acted like a parcel of fools, and if this thing ever gets out we shall be the laughing-stock of the world. I don't want either the American or the British Consul to know anything of our position. God helps those who help themselves. I don't want to boast at all, but I may tell you I'm a dead shot with a revolver, and I have one of the best here with me, together with plenty of cartridges. This expertness with a gun is a relic of my old cowboy days on the plains, and if these here Coreans attempt to interfere with me, somebody is going to get hurt. You have another revolver, and if you are any good with it I guess we'll have no difficulty in forcing our way through this flock of sheep. Have you learned whether your two Japanese can shoot or not? If they can, I've got revolvers here for them, and it seems to me that four of us can put up a bluff that will carry us through this tight place. If it wasn't that we have women with us, I wouldn't mind the encounter in the least. As it is, we'll have to do the best we can, and I propose that we start to-morrow as soon as the gates are opened."

"All right, Mr. Hemster, I believe your diagnosis of the case is correct. I can trust the Japanese, and I think I may say you can trust me."

A little later in the day, the Prime Minister, accompanied by an imposing following, came to me, and with much circumlocution made formal proposal of marriage to Miss Hemster on behalf of the Emperor of Corea. The misguided man appeared to think that this smoothed away all difficulty, and that the only question now to be settled was the amount of money the honoured lady's father would pay down as dowry. Hun Woe fatuously ventured to hope that it would be large in proportion to the elevation in station which awaited the young lady. I replied that Mr. Hemster considered himself equal in rank, and greatly superior in wealth and power, to the Emperor of Corea; that he was now practically held prisoner in the Palace; therefore, if negotiations were to continue, he must be set free, and allowed to return to his own battleship, in which I should be happy to carry on the discussion in a manner which I hoped would prove satisfactory to all parties concerned.

The Prime Minister replied that what I proposed was impossible. The Emperor was completely infatuated with Miss Hemster, and only as a great concession,—due, Hun Woe said, to his own pleadings, which he hoped would be remembered when settlements were made,—did his Majesty consent to a marriage. The Prime Minister continued with many professions of friendship for myself, urging me therefore, as he pretended to have urged the Emperor, to put myself in a reasonable frame of mind. He had never known the Emperor so determined in any course of action before, and lack of compliance on the part of our company would do no good, and might lead to irretrievable disaster. The Emperor had resolved, if his offer were refused, to seize the young lady, and to behead her father, myself, and the whole party who accompanied her. He therefore trusted humbly that I would not thwart his efforts toward an amicable understanding.

I said he must surely have mistaken his instructions; the barbarous programme he had proposed would shock the civilized world. He answered, with a shrug of his shoulders, that the civilized world would never hear of it. I averred he was mistaken in this, telling him I had already communicated with my Consul, and his reply to this was to pull from his sleeve the hasty note I had written and bribed the man at the gate to deliver. This man, he said, had at once brought the communication to him, and he hoped I would acknowledge the fruitlessness of further opposition.

I quickly saw that we were in a predicament, and that it would need all my diplomacy to find a means of egress. However, I determined first to impress upon Hun Woe the dangers of the plan he had outlined. If the Emperor did what he proposed to do, that would bring upon Corea the irretrievable disaster of invasion by both the United States and England. It was not possible to keep assassinations secret. Mr. Hemster's great steamship was at this moment awaiting him at Chemulpo. If no one returned, the captain of that boat had orders to communicate at once with both the British and the American authorities. I endeavored to flatter Hun Woe by telling him that an official of his great learning and intelligence must realize what the result would be. The good man sighed, but in the presence of his entourage apparently had not the courage to admit that Corea would come badly out of the encounter. In fact, he said that the Emperor could defend his country against the combined forces of the world; but whether he believed this or not, I should hesitate to say.

I now changed my tactics, and told the Prime Minister that I was

291

merely Ambassador for Mr. Hemster, and that I would inform him of the offer the Emperor had made. It was more than likely, I asserted, that the proposal would be extremely gratifying to him; so we would postpone further consideration until he had time to think over the matter. I further suggested that we should have another interview with the Emperor at the same hour next day, and with this the Prime Minister joyously concurred. To assist the negotiations he told me that the Emperor had referred to my objection of an existing Empress, but means would be found to divorce that august lady, and this he wished me to place before Mr. Hemster and his daughter. He seemed to imagine that thus had been removed the last obstacle to the proposed union, and I said I would put all this in the most favourable light before Mr. Hemster. The conference which had begun so tempestuously therefore ended in a calm that was extremely gratifying to the Prime Minister, who quite evidently hoped that everybody would be reasonable, that the flow of gold should not cease, and that the contest might end happily. So, with many gestures and expressions of deep regard for myself and my companions, the distinguished party withdrew.

I was anxious to see Mr. Hemster alone, so that I might communicate to him the result of my interview with the Prime Minister, but this intention was frustrated. Gertrude Hemster had nothing whatever to occupy her mind, and the adage informs us that mischief is provided for all such persons. She was already aware that this gorgeous deputation had waited upon me, and it required all her father's persuasion to keep her from breaking in upon us and learning what was going on. The curiosity of woman has before now wrecked many promising undertakings, and this threatened to be the fate of Mr. Hemster's plan. The young lady was frank enough to say that she believed me to be playing a double game; not interpreting correctly the message of the Emperor or the sayings of the Prime Minister. She refused to incur the risk of a forced exit from the Palace, and was sure that if the Emperor was rightly spoken to we would all be allowed to march to the port with a royal escort and the honours of war. She insisted that if I were not a coward I would myself brave the dangers of the exit, go to the American Consulate, and there get an interpreter who would be official, and also bring the Consul himself. She was not going to be frightened out of Seoul by a mud-colored heathen like the Emperor, and if only we had treated him as she had done, there would have been no trouble.

I must admit that I agreed with the girl so far as calling in the aid of the American Consul was concerned, and I told her I was quite willing to force the gate and make a run for it to the little spot of the United States which existed in Seoul. But her father could be a determined man when he liked, and this time he put down his foot, declaring firmly that he would not have the news of this fiasco get abroad if he could help it. Curiously enough, Mr. Hemster seemed to have more fear of the yellow press of America than of the yellow man of Corea. His daughter, however, feared neither, and seemed in fact to relish the publicity which this episode might give to her. Whether it was bravery or recklessness on her part, I could not get her to see that we were in any serious danger; but this did not matter, for on appeal to her father to postpone the proposed exodus he proved adamant, and for once the young lady was forced to acquiesce.

I took the pair of extra pistols, and, with ample ammunition, sought out the two Japanese members of our party. I found that both of them had served in the Japanese army and were quite capable of handling firearms with effect. I then told them to say nothing to their Corean comrades, but, as soon as the gates were open in the morning, to bring ponies for the whole party to our door. The manner in which they carried out this order showed their alertness to the exigencies of the situation.

When we all emerged in the morning,—we four white people, our Chinese cook and Japanese serving-boy,—ten ponies were at our door, two of them being loaded down with heavy strings of cash which we had not found occasion to use, because our dealings had been entirely with higher classes and so we had had to employ silver and gold. But only one Japanese man was there. When I asked him where the other fellow was, he replied he was holding a revolver over the huddled heap of Coreans so that they would not give the alarm. As soon as we were mounted, he said he would call his comrade, who would instantly respond.

This proved a very wise precaution, and gave us some valuable minutes before the Palace was roused. We had arrived at the gates ere the sleepy guards realized what was upon them, and the first warning the Palace received of our attempt was the wild firing of the useless muskets which the guards possessed. We had determined not to shoot, hoping that the guards would give way when they found we were resolved to emerge; but their reckless firing, which luckily did no harm to any of our party, made any further attempt at silence unnecessary, and lucky it was for us that we were free to fire, because Mr. Hemster whipped out his revolver at once and shattered the hand of a man who attempted to close the gates. This wounded creature set up such a howl that the guards immediately threw down their arms and fled, leaving the way clear before us.

Now we were in the main street of Seoul, and if it had not been for Mr. Hemster's prohibition I would strongly have advised making directly for the Consulate of either one nation or the other. However, his orders were to press on to the western gate before the alarm should extend through the city. This we did. Now that we were clear of the royal gates, the guards seemed to have resumed their firearms and were evidently determined to make the Emperor believe that they had been extremely valorous, for a regular fusillade greeted our departure down the main street of Seoul. Whatever commotion the firing may have aroused in the Palace, it certainly had an extraordinary effect upon the city itself, for it caused the population to pour in thousands from the narrow lanes with which this human warren is intersected. There seemed a danger that we might be stopped by the mere pressure of the crowd, so I gave the word to whip up our steeds, and we dashed along, regardless of whom we knocked over.

Just as we reached the gate on the Chemulpo road the great bell began to ring, the bell which every night at sunset orders the closing of the gates. The big doors were being slowly closed as we approached, and here my two Japanese again gave striking proof of their value. They dashed forward, and, in spite of the ringing of the bell, ordered the guards to fling wide the portal, but upon the guards showing some hesitation, the foremost Japanese at once shot one of them in his tracks, whereupon the rest fled. We squeezed through, and the Japanese proposed we should close the gates completely, so that the crowd might be kept in, but this proved impossible, because they could be fastened only on the inside, and we had no means of assuring ourselves that the gates would remain shut. There was therefore nothing for it but a race for Chemulpo, twenty-six miles away. Before we had gone a dozen yards the pressure of the crowd opened the gates wide, and the howling mob poured through like a resistless torrent.

I now re-arranged my party, asking Mr. Hemster to take the lead, while the two Japanese and myself fought a retreating battle with the multitude that followed us. The Corean man is a stalwart individual with sturdy legs that are almost untiring in a race. While cowards individually, they become dangerous in the mass, and I continually urged our people to gallop as hard as they could, with the double purpose of exhausting all but the most strenuous in our pursuit, and of preventing the outskirts of the mob on either hand from outflanking us. For the first three miles or so our revolver-shots kept them at a respectful distance, but after five or six miles had been accomplished, and the crowd showed no signs of fatigue, while our ammunition began to run low, I realized that I must do something to save the rest from capture.

Leaving the two Japanese as an efficient rearguard, I galloped forward to Mr. Hemster, and gave him details of my plan, which I had some difficulty in getting him to accept. In fact he did accept it only on my assurance that there was no real danger to myself. Bidding a hasty farewell to the ladies, I dropped again to the rear. Each of the Japanese had tethered to his horse's bridle a rope attached to a pony carrying our strings of cash. I untied these ponies, and attached them to my own mount, ordering the Japanese to take the van once more; and, as they were residents of Chemulpo, and therefore knew the road perfectly, I told them to lead the party as quickly as they could into safety, promising them a large additional reward for doing so.

The rest now galloped on, leaving me standing in the middle of the road, with three horses under my charge. The bellowing mob seemed nonplussed by this movement, and, apparently fearing a trap of some kind, came to a halt. There was not bravery enough among them even to attack one man at close quarters, although they might have overwhelmed him by simply moving in bulk upon him. Each of the two led-horses carried something like twenty thousand sek, strung in ropes of five hundred each, so knotted that the cash is divided into sections of a hundred each. I took my pocket-knife and cut off the first knot, and, grasping the two ends of the string, flung it lasso-wise around my head, and then let go the cut end, causing the hundred cash to shoot into the air like the bursting of a sky-rocket. These people, after all, were merely like children with two dominant qualities, a love of cruelty, and an unlimited avarice,—possibly avarice has the greatest hold upon their affections, and this belief was the basis of my adventure.

Now ensued the strangest battle that ever was fought by mankind, a struggle which Mr. Hemster himself should have appreciated because he had engaged in it time and again in his own country, a battle in which one man with money stood against the bulk of the people. When the shower of a hundred cash was flung above the heads of the mob there ensued one of the wildest struggles it has ever been my fate to witness. I cut the second knot, and flung the second lot of cash far to the left, to check the advance of the crowd that way, which it very effectually did. Then the third knot was severed, and the third lot of coins went spinning through the air to the right. Even before the first string was gone, my party had long since disappeared toward the west. Of course this congregation of heathens could have availed themselves at once of my whole available stock by merely pressing forward, but this thought either never occurred to them, or they were too cowardly to put it into practice. As soon as the flung cash was secured and the scattered stock picked up, two and two fighting for the possession of one miserable coin, a shout arose from them which was the cry of Oliver Twist for "more." And so I played David against that Goliath of a crowd until I began to fear that my arm which whirled the sling would become helpless through exhaustion.

My idea had been, of course, to put the whip to my horse and make for the port after my party, but very soon this project proved to be impossible. I was standing on a slight elevation in the road, and, in spite of my throwing the coins right and left, the two wings of this tatterdemalion army gradually enfolded me, and before my fortune was more than half scattered I found myself completely outflanked and surrounded. But no one made a dash; there was left a respectable circular clear space about me, the circumference of which was never nearer than twenty or thirty feet from where I stood. Moreover I was thankful to see that even those to the west, who had a free way toward Chemulpo, did not attempt to break toward the coast. They were all too eager to get a share of the spoil to mind what became of the rest of the party, and by the time we had been an hour or more at this flinging of largesse every individual of them knew that pursuit was hopeless, and by the same token I knew also that the least danger threatening me was being carried back to Seoul. The crowd had become riotously good natured, but I knew their changeableness too well to consider myself safe on that account. They were as like as not to take me back to Seoul in a hundred pieces. I began to think seriously of the future when I came to the last string of cash on the pony beside me. There was still twenty thousand on the other nag; but, when that was gone, this mob, which had no sense of gratitude, were as like to cut my throat as not. So when I came to the last hundred sek on the first pony, scattered like grape-shot through the air, I took advantage of the struggle that ensued to remount my own nag. There was at once a howl of rage at this, especially from those to the west of me, who expected me to attempt escape in that direction. They stiffened up, and shook fists and sticks at this supposed intention on my part to cheat them of their just dues. Never since the Corean kingdom was founded had there been such a distribution of wealth as was now taking place. Heretofore the office-holders had accumulated everything in sight, and naturally the populace was indignant that this enchanting scattering of money should cease while there was still a horseload of it within reach. I raised my right hand for silence, and then raised my voice and addressed them:

"Gentlemen," said I, "the next hurling of coin takes place at the gates of Seoul. If you are good enough to march quietly with me, I shall relieve the tedium of the way by an occasional contribution. So, my braves, let us get back to the capital."

Capital was what they were after, and so with a howl, which was their nearest approach to a cheer, we set off for Seoul. Tired as my arm was, I occasionally distributed five hundred cash before and behind me, also to the right and left, keeping steadily on, however, until the city was in sight. Then to my dismay, I saw that the great gate was closed. The mob ahead of me had noticed the barred gate before I did, and set up a wail like a lot of lost children. Instantly the cash distribution was forgotten, and panic seized them. They were locked out, and no one knew what might be happening inside. The tolling of the big bell still boomed through the air, but only occasionally, bearing some resemblance to a funeral knell. Because the gate was shut these people had not reasoning powers enough to surmise that the other gates were shut also, and in a magic way the huge mob began to dissolve and disappear, scampering over rocks and stones to find out whether the whole city was hermetically sealed or not. There was a group of people on the wall above the gate, and someone had shouted that the northern port was open. This statement was undoubtedly false, but the official who cried it evidently thought it was safer to dismiss the mob as he could. In a few minutes I found myself practically alone, and then was amazed beyond measure to hear a voice from above the gate call down to me:

"For Heaven's sake, Tremorne, is that you?"

# CHAPTER XV

**I** LOOKED up, and saw leaning toward me Wallace Carmichel, the British Consul-General in Seoul, an efficient man whom I had not met for five years, when he was in the Embassy at Pekin. At once there flashed through my mind Mr. Hemster's desire that I should not mention our plight to the Consuls of either his country or my own, so I resolved on the instant to keep to myself, if possible, the mission that had brought me to the capital. Indeed within the last few minutes the whole situation had changed. I had no desire to return to Seoul, and only retreated because I was compelled to do so; but now the way was perfectly clear between me and Chemulpo on turning my horse around. Yet Carmichel would think it exceedingly strange if I could not give some excuse for marching up to the gate of Seoul and marching down again, like the historical general on the hill. I wished he had remained at his Consulate, yet there he was, beaming down upon me, so I took momentary refuge in airy persiflage.

"Hullo, Carmichel, how goes it? Has the early-closing movement been adopted in Seoul? It isn't Saturday afternoon, is it?"

"No, it isn't," he replied, "and if you'll take the advice of an old friend, you'll turn your horse's head, and make straight back for Chemulpo. I think we're in for a rather nasty time here, if you ask me."

"I do ask you. What's wrong?"

I was anxious to learn whether he knew anything of the escape of our party in the early morning; but even if he had been told about it, the Coreans are such unmitigated liars that it is not likely he would have believed them if he had not himself seen the procession, and I very much doubted if he had done so, for Carmichel was never afflicted with the early-rising habit. I was, however, wholly unprepared for his amazing reply.

"The Empress of Corea was assassinated last night," he said. "I imagine they don't want the news to spread. The Palace is closed, and all the gates of the city were shut before I was up this morning. The Court entourage is trying to pretend that the Empress died a natural death, but I have it on as good authority as anything can be had in this mendacious place that the Empress was literally cut to pieces."

"Good God!" I cried. "Can that be true?"

"Anything may be true in this forsaken hole. I heard you had left the service. Came into a fortune, eh? Lucky devil! I wish I were in your shoes! This is worse than China, and that was bad enough. I suppose you are here on private business. Well, take a friend's advice and get back. Nothing can be done here for a while, any how."

"I'll take your advice, Carmichel. Is there any message I can carry for you to Chemulpo?"

"No, you may tell them what's happened."

"Are you in any danger, do you think?"

"I don't think so. Of course, one can never tell what may turn up in this beastly place. I've got the Consulate well guarded, and we can stand a siege. I heard that there was a mob approaching the town, and so came up to see what it was all about. Where are you stopping at Chemulpo?"

"I have been yachting with a friend of mine, and his craft is in the harbour there."

"Well, if you've no business in Seoul, I advise you to get back to the yacht. You'll be safer on the sea than in Corea."

"I believe you!"

"How did you come to be in the midst of that Bank Holiday gang, Tremorne?" asked the Consul, his curiosity evidently rising.

"Oh, they overtook me, so we came along together."

"It's a wonder they didn't rob you of all you possess."

"I forestalled that by scattering something like twenty thousand sek among them. I thought I'd be all right when I came to the gate, but was rather taken aback to find it closed."

"Twenty thousand sek! And I suppose you don't mind throwing it away any more than a handful of ha' pence! Lucky beggar! And yachting around the world with a millionaire friend, I expect. Well, life's easy for some people," said the Consul-General with a sigh.

I laughed at him, and wondered what he would have said had he known the truth.

"Sure you don't want me to send a guard up from Chemulpo for you?"

"No, I don't think our consulate will be the storm-center here. I rather imagine the tornado will rage around the residence of our Japanese friends. The Coreans say that a Japanese killed one of the guards here this morning at the gate, but the Japanese Minister insists that all of his countrymen in the city are accounted for, and that this allegation of murder is a lie, which I have not the least doubt it is. I heard a lot of promiscuous firing this morning before I was up, but it seemed to me all in the direction of the Palace. They are eternally raising some shindy here, and blaming it on decent people. I'm sorry to see you turn back, Tremorne, but a man who isn't compelled to stay here is wise to avoid such diggings. If you return you'll call on me, won't you?"

"Oh, certainly," said I, gathering up the reins. "So long, Carmichel, and be as good to yourself as you can."

Saying this I turned toward Chemulpo, and reached it very late that night. The journey was one of the most disagreeable I had ever taken, for my right arm—I suppose through the straining of the muscles—became utterly helpless and very painful. It swelled so, especially at the shoulder, that I feared I should have to cut the sleeve of my coat. David was more fortunate than I, because he did his business with one shot: my giant required continual shooting, and now I was suffering for it. If I had been attacked, I should have found myself completely helpless; but fortunately

the way was clear, and with my three steeds I came through without mishap. Before going on board I searched out my two Japanese, and found, as I expected, that Mr. Hemster had rewarded them with a liberality that took their breath away. He had paid them for the three horses, which he looked upon as lost, and now I turned the nags over to them, together with the twenty thousand sek that was on one of them; so the brave, resourceful little men had no complaint to make regarding lack of recognition.

I had not intended to go aboard the yacht that night, but Mr. Hemster had made the Japs promise to show a flare if any news came of me, and in the morning he was going to organize an expedition for my rescue. As soon as I encountered my Japs one of them ran for a torch and set it afire. It was at once answered by a rocket from the yacht, and before I had finished my conversation with him I heard the measured beat of the oars in the water, and found that in spite of his fatigue the kindly old man himself had come ashore for me. He tried to shake hands, but I warded him off with my left arm, laughing as I did so, and told him my right would not be in condition for some time yet. As we rowed out to the yacht I told him all that had happened, and informed him about the murder of the Empress, which news my Japanese friends were commissioned to proclaim in Chemulpo, as I had promised the British Consul. Mr. Hemster was much affected by this news, and I saw plainly that he considered his ill-fated expedition to have been the probable cause of this unfortunate lady's taking off.

I was nearly famished when we reached the steamer, for I had had nothing since early morning but a ham sandwich I had put in my pocket. The bag of provisions intended for consumption on the way had been carried by the Chinese cook, and at the moment of parting I had thought nothing of the commissariat, which was extremely poor generalship on my part, and an omission which caused me sorrow later in the day.

Sitting in the boat after my exertions left me so stiff and unwieldy that one of the sailors had to help me up the side, and, stepping on deck, I staggered, and would have fallen if he had not caught me. The waning moon had risen, but the light was not strong. I saw a shadowy figure make for the companion-way, then stop with a little cry, and run forward to where I stood.

"You are wounded, Mr. Tremorne!" she cried.

"No, Miss Stretton, I am all right, except my arm, and its disablement is rather a joke than otherwise."

"He is wounded, is he not, Mr. Hemster?" appealed the girl, as the old man came up the gangway.

"Tut, tut, child! You should have been in bed long ago! He isn't wounded, but he's nearly starved to death through our taking away all the provisions with us when we deserted him."

"Oh, dear!" she cried. "Then you didn't find the bag."

"What bag?" I asked.

"When we were having lunch Mr. Hemster remembered that you were unprovided for, so we raised a cairn of stones by the wayside and left a bag of provisions on top of it, hoping you would recognize it, for Mr. Hemster felt sure you would win through somehow or other. You would be extremely flattered, Mr. Tremorne, if you knew what faith he has in you."

I laughed and told her I was glad to hear it.

"Tut, tut!" said the old man. "Don't stand idly chattering here when there's a first-rate supper spread out for you down below. Away you go. I must have a word with the captain, for we are off to Nagasaki within ten minutes, so I shall bid you both good-night."

I took it very kindly of the old gentleman to leave us thus alone, and I have no doubt he thought of his own younger days when he did so. I wickedly pretended a greater weakness than I actually felt, and so Miss Stretton kindly supported me with her arm, and thus we went down the stairway together, where, as the old gentleman had said, I found one of the most delicious cold collations I had ever encountered, flanked by a bottle of his very finest champagne. I persuaded Miss Stretton to sit down opposite me, which, after some demur about the lateness of the hour, she consented to do, for I told her my right arm was absolutely helpless, and the left almost equally awkward.

"So," I said, "you must prove yourself a ministering angel now."

"Ah, that," she said, "is when pain and anguish wring the brow. As

303

I understand it, pain and anguish wring the arm. Please tell me how it happened."

Under the deft manipulation of the Japanese boy, the champagne cork came out with a pop, and, as if it were a signal-gun, there immediately followed the rattle of the anchor-chain coming up, and almost before my story was begun, we heard the steady throb-throb of the engine, and it sent a vibration of thankfulness through my aching frame.

"You do look haggard and worn," she said; "and I think I must insist on regarding you rather in the light of a hero."

"Oh, there was nothing heroic in flinging cheap cash about in the reckless way I did. I was never in any real danger."

"I think we have all been in danger, more or less, since we entered those Palace gates. Although I said nothing I could see from your face what you were thinking."

"Yes, I know of old your uncanny proclivities in mind-reading. Now that every pulsation of the engine is carrying us farther away from that plague-spot of earth, there is no harm in saying that I spent some days and nights of deep anxiety, and that, I assure you, not on my own account."

"I quite believe you," said the young lady, raising her eyes for a moment, and gazing down on the tablecloth again. Then she looked brightly up once more, and said archly:

"I hope it won't make you conceited, but I walked the deck to-night with fear tugging at my heart. I don't think I ever was so glad in my life as when I saw the flare, as had been arranged, and knew you were safe. When I heard you talking to Mr. Hemster in the boat, your voice floated over the water very distinctly, and I think I breathed a little expression of gratitude."

"Hilda," said I, leaning across the table, "it is very kind of you to say that."

Here, to my annoyance, the Japanese boy came into the saloon, although I had told him I had no further need for him that night. He approached us, and said respectfully, and I am sure somewhat unwillingly:

"Miss Hemster's compliments, sir, and she wishes you would stop chattering here all night long, so that people could get to sleep."

Miss Stretton sprang to her feet, a crimson flush coming into her face.

"Thank Miss Hemster for me," said I to the Japanese, "and inform her that we will finish our conversation on deck."

"No, no!" cried Hilda peremptorily; "it is terribly late, and it is too bad of me keeping you talking here when you should be resting. I assure you I did not intend to remain on deck after I had learned of your safe arrival."

"I know that, Hilda. It was when you saw me stagger that, like the kind-hearted girl you are, you came forward. Now, do come up on deck with me, if only for five minutes."

"No, no," she repeated in a whisper.

Forgetting the condition of my arm, I made an effort to encircle her. She whisked herself silently away, but, hearing the groan that involuntarily escaped me when the helpless arm struck the table and sent an electric spasm of pain to my shoulder, she turned rapidly toward me with pity in her face. Then, springing forward, she raised her lips to mine for one infinitesimal fraction of a second, and almost before the rest of that moment of bliss was passed I found myself alone in the empty saloon.

# CHAPTER XVI

LATE as it was, I went up on deck, and it was lucky for me I did so, for I met our bluff old captain, who, when he learned of the disablement of my arm, said genially that he had a Cape Cod liniment good for man or donkey, and I was welcome to it in either capacity. He ordered me down to my stateroom, and followed later with the bottle. His own gnarled hands rubbed the pungent-smelling stuff on my arm, and he told me I'd be next to all right in the morning, which prophecy came true.

I am sorry that in these voyages to and from Corea we met absolutely no adventures, picked up no shipwrecked crew, and met no cyclone, so I am unable to write down any of those vivid descriptions that I have always admired in Mr. Clark Russell.

Next morning was heavenly in its beauty and its calm. Nagasaki was the last civilized address which would receive telegrams, letters or papers for Mr. Hemster, and the old gentleman was anxious to reach there as soon as possible. As I have remarked before, he was constantly yearning for a daily paper. The captain informed me that he had engaged a "heathen Chinee" as pilot, and so was striking direct from Chemulpo to Nagasaki, letting the islands take care of themselves, as he remarked.

I walked the deck, watching eagerly for the coming of Hilda Stretton, but instead there arrived Gertrude Hemster, bright, smiling, and beautiful. I was just now regretting lack of opportunity to indulge in Clark-Russellism, yet here was a chance for a descriptive writer which proved quite beyond my powers. The costume of Miss Hemster was bewildering in its Parisian completeness. That girl must have had a storehouse of expensive gowns aboard the yacht. I suppose this was what a writer in a lady's paper would call a confection, or a creation, or something of that sort; but so far as I am concerned you might as well expect an elucidation of higher mathematics as an adequate delineation of that sumptuous gown. All I can say is that the tout ensemble was perfect, and the girl herself was radiant in her loveliness. She approached me with a winning smile like that of an angel.

"I want you to know how I appreciate your bravery. I shall never forget,—no, not if I live to be a thousand years old,—how grand and noble you looked standing up alone against that horde of savages. I was just telling Poppa that the very first reporter he meets, he must give a glowing account to him of your heroism."

I have always noted that when Miss Hemster was in extreme good humour she referred to the old gentleman as Poppa; on other occasions she called him Father. The project of giving away my adventures to the newspapers did not in the least commend itself to me.

"Good-morning, Miss Hemster," I said, "I am extremely pleased to see you looking so well after a somewhat arduous day."

"It was rather a trying time, wasn't it?" she replied sweetly, "and if I look well it's because of the dress, I think. How do you like it?" and she stepped back with a sweeping curtesy that would have done credit to an actress, and took up an attitude that displayed her drapery to the very best advantage.

"It is heavenly," I said; "never in my life have I seen anything to compare with it,—or with the wearer," I added.

"How sweet of you to say that!" she murmured, looking up at me archly, with a winning, bird-like movement. A glorified bird-of-paradise she seemed, and there was no denying it. With a touching pathetic note in her voice she continued,—very humbly, if one might judge,—"You haven't been a bit nice to me lately. I have wondered why you were so unkind."

"Believe me, Miss Hemster," I said, "I have not intended to be unkind, and I am very sorry if I have appeared so. You must remember we have been thrown into very trying circumstances, and as I was probably better acquainted with the conditions than any one of our party I always endeavoured to give the best advice I could, which sometimes, alas, ran counter to your own wishes. It seemed to me now and then you did not quite appreciate the danger which threatened us, and you also appeared to have a distrust of me, which, I may tell you, was entirely unfounded."

"Of course it was," she cried contritely, "but nevertheless I always had the utmost confidence in you, although you see I'm so impulsive that I always say the first thing that comes into my head, and that gives people a wrong idea about me. You take everything so seriously and make no allowances. I think at heart you're a very hard man."

"Oh, I hope not."

"Yes, you are. You have numerous little rules, and you measure everybody by them. I seem to feel that you are mentally sizing me up, and that makes me say horrid things."

"If that is the case, I must try to improve my character."

"Oh, I'm not blaming you at all, only telling you the way it strikes me. Perhaps I'm altogether wrong. Very likely I am, and anyhow I don't suppose it does any good to talk of these things. By the way, how is your arm this morning?"

"It is all right, thank you. The captain's liniment has been magical in its effect. It was very stupid of me to get my arm in such a condition, and there is less excuse because I used to be a first-rate cricket bowler; but somehow yesterday I got so interested in the game that I forgot about my muscles."

"Is it true that the Empress has been murdered?"

"Yes, I had the news from the British Consul, and I have no doubt of its accuracy."

"How perfectly awful to think that only the day before yesterday we saw her sitting there like a graven image; indeed she scarcely seemed alive even then. What in the world did they kill the poor woman for?"

"I do not know," I replied, although I had strong suspicions regarding the cause of her fate. The next statement by Miss Hemster astonished me.

"Well, it served her right. A woman in that position should assert herself. She sat there like a Chinese doll that had gone to sleep. If she had made them stand around they would have had more respect for her. Any woman owes it to her sex to make the world respect her. Think of a sleepy creature like that holding the position of Empress, and yet making less than nothing of it."

"You must remember, Miss Hemster, that the status of woman in Corea is vastly different from her position in the United States."

"Well, and whose fault is that? It is the fault of the women. We demand our rights in the States, and get them. If this creature at Seoul had been of any use in the world she would have revolutionized the status of women,—at least within the bounds of her own kingdom."

I ventured to remark that Oriental ideas of women were of a low order, and that, as the women themselves were educated to accept this state of things, nothing much should be expected of them.

"Oh, nonsense!" cried Miss Hemster strenuously; "look at the Empress of China. She makes people stand around. Then there was Catherine of Russia, and goodness knows Russia's far enough behind in its ideas! But Catherine didn't mind that; she just walked in, and made herself feared by the whole world. A few more women like that in the Orient would bring these heathen people to their senses. It serves this Corean Queen right when you think of the opportunity she had, and the way she misused it, sitting there like a great lump of dough strung around with jewels she could not appreciate, like a wax figure in a ten-cent show. I have no patience with such animals."

I thought this judgment of Miss Hemster's rather harsh, but experience had taught me not to be rash in expressing my opinion; so we conversed amicably about many things until the gong rang for luncheon. I must say that hers was a most attractive personality when she exerted herself to please. At luncheon she was the life of the party, making the captain laugh outrageously, and even bringing a smile now and then to her father's grave face, although it seemed to me he watched her furtively under his shaggy eyebrows now and then as if apprehensive that this mood might not last,—somewhat fearful, I imagine, regarding what might follow. I could not help noticing that there was a subtle change in the old gentleman's attitude toward his daughter, and I fancied that her exuberant spirits were perhaps forced to the front, to counteract in a measure this new attitude. I thought I detected now and then a false note in her hilarity, but perhaps that may have been a delusion of my imagination, such as it is. After the captain had gone, toward the end of the meal, her father seemed to be endeavouring silently to attract her attention; but she rattled on in almost breathless haste, talking flippantly to Miss Stretton and myself alternately, and never once looking toward the head of the table. I surmised that there was something beneath all this with which I was not acquainted, and that there was going on before me a silent contest of two wills, the latent determination of the father opposed to the unconcealed stubbornness of the daughter. I sympathized with the old man, because I was myself engaged in a mental endeavour to cause Hilda Stretton to look across at me, but hitherto without success. Not a single glance had I received during the meal. At last the old gentleman rose, and stood hesitating, as if he wished to make a plunge; then, finally, he interrupted the rattle of conversation by saying:

"Gertrude, I wish to have a few words with you in my office."

"All right, Poppa, I'll be there in a minute," she replied nonchalantly.

"I want you to come now," he said, with more sternness in his voice than I had ever heard there before. For one brief moment I feared we were going to have a scene, but Miss Gertrude merely laughed joyously and sprang to her feet, saying, "I'll race you to the office then," and disappeared down the passage aft almost before her sentence was ended. Mr. Hemster slowly followed her.

Hilda Stretton half rose, as if to leave me there alone, then sat down again, and courageously looked me full in the face across the table.

"He is too late," she whispered.

"Too late for what?" I asked.

"Too late in exerting parental authority."

"Is he trying to do that?"

"Didn't you see it?"

"Well, if that was his endeavour, he succeeded."

"For the moment, yes. He thinks he's going to talk to her, but it is she who will talk to him, and she preferred doing it this time in the privacy of the room he calls his office. A moment more, and he would have learned her opinion of him before witnesses. I am very glad it did not come to that, but the trouble is merely postponed. Poor old gentleman, I wish I could help him! He does not understand his daughter in the least. But let us go on deck and have coffee there."

"I was just going to propose that," I cried, delighted, springing to my feet. We went up the stair together and I placed a little wicker table well forward, with a wicker chair on each side of it, taking a position on deck as far from the companion-way as possible, so that we should not be surprised by any one coming up from below. The Japanese boy served our coffee, and when he was gone Hilda continued her subject, speaking very seriously.

"He does not understand her at all, as I have said. Since she was a baby she has had her own way in everything, without check or hindrance from him, and of course no one else dared to check or hinder her. Now she is more than twenty-one years of age, and if he imagines that discipline can be enforced at this late hour he is very much mistaken."

"Is he trying to enforce discipline?"

"Yes, he is. He has foolishly made up his mind that it will be for the girl's good. That, of course, is all he thinks of,—dear, generous-hearted man that he is! But if he goes on there will be a tragedy, and I want you to warn him."

"I dare not interfere, Hilda."

"Why not? Haven't you a very great liking for him?"

"Yes, I have. I would do almost anything in the world for him."

"Then do what I tell you."

"What is it?"

"See him privately in his office, and tell him to leave his daughter alone. Warn him that if he does not there will be a tragedy."

311

"Tell me exactly what you mean."

"She will commit suicide."

This statement, solemnly given, seemed to me so utterly absurd that it relieved the tension which was creeping into the occasion. I leaned back in my chair and laughed until I saw a look of pained surprise come into Hilda's face, which instantly sobered me.

"Really, Hilda, you are the very best girl in the world, yet it is you who do not understand that young woman. She is too thoroughly selfish to commit suicide, or to do anything else to her own injury."

"Suicide," said Hilda gravely, "is not always a matter of calculation, but often the act of a moment of frenzy,—at least so it will be in Gertrude Hemster's case if her father now attempts to draw tight the reins of authority. He will madden her, and you have no conception of the depth of bitterness that is in her nature. If it occurs to her in her next extravagant tantrum that by killing herself she will break her father's heart, which undoubtedly would be the case, she is quite capable of plunging into the sea, or sending a revolver bullet through her head. I have been convinced

of this for some time past, but I never thought her father would be so ill-advised as to change the drifting line of conduct he has always held in regard to her."

"My dear Hilda, you are not consistent. Do you remember an occasion, which to tell the truth I am loth to recall, when you said if her father treated her as I had done her character would be much more amiable than it now appears to be?"

"I don't think I said that, Mr. Tremorne. I may have hinted that if her father had taken a more strenuous attitude in the past, he would not have such a difficult task before him in the present, or I may have said that a husband might tame the shrew. The latter, I believe, would lead to either a reformation or the divorce court, I don't quite know which. Or perhaps even then there might be a tragedy; but it would be the husband who would suffer, not herself. A man she married might control her. It would really be an interesting experiment, and no one can predict whether it would turn out well or ill; but her father cannot control her because all these years of affectionate neglect are behind him, years in which he was absorbed in business, leaving the forming of her character to hirelings, thinking that because he paid them well they would do their duty, whereas the high salary merely made them anxious to retain their positions at any cost of flattery and indulgence to their pupil."

"Then, Hilda, why don't you speak to him about it? You have known him for more years than I have days, and I am sure he would take it kindlier from you than from me."

"To tell you the truth, I have spoken to him. I spoke to him last night when we were both waiting for that flare from the shore at Chemulpo. I could not tell whether my talk had any effect or not, for he said nothing, beyond thanking me for my advice. I see to-day that it has had no effect. So now I beg you to try."

"But if you failed, how could I hope to succeed?"

"I'll tell you why. In the first place because you are the cause of this change of attitude on the part of Mr. Hemster."

"I the cause?"

"Certainly. He has undoubtedly a great liking for you, in spite of the fact that he has known you so short a time. In some unexplainable way he has come to look at his daughter through your eyes, and I think he is startled at the vision he has seen. But he does not take sufficient account of the fact that he is not dealing now with a little girl, but with a grown woman. I noticed the gradual change in his manner during our stay at the Palace, and it became much more marked on the way back to Chemulpo, after we had left you alone battling with the savages of Seoul. You have said you were in no real danger, but Mr. Hemster did not think so, and he seemed greatly impressed by the fact that a comparative stranger should cheerfully insist on jeopardizing his life for the safety of our party, and to my deep anxiety his demeanour toward his daughter was at first severe and then harsh, for he

313

roundly accused her of being the cause of our difficulties. I shall pass over the storm that ensued, merely saying that it took our whole force to prevent Miss Hemster from returning to Seoul."

"Great Heavens!" I exclaimed, "surely that was mere pretence on her part; sheer bravado."

"Not altogether. It was grim determination to do the thing that would immediately hurt her father, and I do not know what would have happened if she had escaped from us. It had the instant effect of subduing him, bringing him practically to his knees before her. So she sulked all the way to Chemulpo, and I expected that the brief assumption of authority had ended; but while we were rowing out to the yacht he spoke very sharply to her, and I saw with regret that his determination was at least equal to hers. Therefore I spoke to him after she had gone to her room, and he said very little one way or the other. Now he appears to think that as he has got her safely on his yacht once more he can bend her to his will, and I am terrified at the outlook."

"Well, it doesn't look enticing, does it?"

"No, it doesn't, so won't you please talk with him for his own sake?"

"I'd rather face the Emperor of Corea again, or his amiable subjects in mass meeting assembled, but I'll do it for your sake. Oh, yes, and for his sake, too; I would do anything I could to make matters easy for Mr. Hemster."

"Thank you so much," said the girl simply, leaning back in her chair with a sigh of contentment. "Now let us talk of something else."

"With all my heart, Hilda. I've been wanting to talk of something else ever since your very abrupt departure last night. Now am I over-confident in taking your last brief action there as equivalent to the monosyllable 'Yes'?"

The girl laughed and coloured, visibly embarrassed. She darted a quick glance at me, then veiled her eyes again.

"The brief action, as you call it, seems rather impulsive now in the glare of daylight, and was equivalent to much more than the monosyllable 'Yes'. Three times as much. It was equivalent to the trisyllable 'Sympathy.' I was merely expressing sympathy."

"Was that all?"

"Wasn't that more than enough? I have thought since, with shame, that my action was just a trifle over-bold, and I fear you are of the same opinion, although too kind-hearted to show it."

"My whole thought was a protest against its brevity."

"But brevity is the soul of wit, you know."

"Yes, Hilda," said I, leaning forward toward her, "but not the soul of kissing. If my right arm had not temporarily lost its power you had never escaped with the celerity you did. 'Man wants but little here below,' and I want that little monosyllable rather than the large trisyllable. Make me for ever happy by saying you meant it."

"For ever is a long time," she answered dreamily, her eyes partially closed.

*"Miss Stretton, will you oblige me by going downstairs; I wish to talk to Mr. Tremorne."*

The words, sharp and decisive, cut like a knife, and, starting to my feet in amazement, I saw that Gertrude Hemster stood before us, her brow a thundercloud. Turning from her beautiful but forbidding countenance to see the effect of her peremptory sentence upon my dear companion, I found the chair empty, and the space around me vacant as if she had vanished into invisibility through the malign incantation of a sorceress.

# CHAPTER XVII

"**WILL YOU** be seated, Miss Hemster?" I said with such calmness as I could bring to my command.

"No, I won't," she snapped, like the click of a rifle.

I don't know why it is that this girl always called forth hitherto unsuspected discourtesy which I regret to admit seems to lie very deep in my nature. I was bitterly angry at her rude dismissal of Hilda Stretton.

"Oh, very well; stand then!" I retorted with inexcusable lack of chivalry, and, that my culpability should be complete, immediately slammed myself emphatically down into the chair from which I had just risen. As I came down with a thump that made the wicker chair groan in protest, the look the lady bestowed upon me must have resembled that of the Medusa which turned people into stone.

"Well, you are polite, I must say," she exclaimed, with a malicious swish of her skirts as she walked to and fro before me.

"You so monopolize all politeness on board this yacht," was my unmannerly rejoinder, "that there is none of it left for the rest of us."

She stopped in her rapid walk and faced me.

"You're a brute," she said deliberately.

"You expressed that opinion before. Why not try something original?"

"Do you think that is a gentlemanly remark to make?" she asked.

"No, I don't. Some years of vagabondage coupled with more recent events have destroyed all claim I ever possessed to being a gentleman."

"You admit, then, you are the scum of the earth."

"Oh, certainly."

Suddenly she flounced herself down in the chair Hilda had occupied, and stared at me for a few moments. Then she said in a voice much modified:

"What were you and Miss Stretton discussing so earnestly when I came up?"

"Didn't you hear?"

"No. I am no eavesdropper, but I know you were talking of me."

"Ah, then you didn't hear."

"I told you I didn't, but I tell you what I suspect."

"Then your suspicions are entirely unfounded, Miss Hemster."

"I don't believe it, but I'll say this for you; however much of a beast you may be, you are rather unhandy at a lie; so if you wish to convince me that you are speaking the truth, you must tell me, without taking time to consider, what you were talking about if you were not talking of me."

All this was uttered at lightning speed.

"I need no time for consideration to answer that question. We were talking of ourselves."

"What were you saying? Come now, out with it if you dare. I can see by your face you are trying to make up something."

"Really, you underestimate my courage, Miss Hemster. I was asking Hilda Stretton to do me the honour of marrying me, and she was about to reply when you cut short a conference so absorbing that we had not noticed your approach."

This explanation seemed to be so unexpected that for a moment the young woman sat breathless and expressionless. Then she gradually sank back in her chair with closed eyes, all colour leaving her face.

Now, I am well aware of the effect the words just written will have on the mind of the indulgent reader. She will think I'm trying to hint that the girl, despite her actions, was in love with me. I beg to state that I am no such conceited ass as the above paragraph would imply. My wife has always held that Gertrude Hemster was in love with me, but that is merely the prejudiced view of an affectionate woman, and I have ever strenuously combated it. The character of Gertrude Hemster has for long been a puzzle to me, and I can hardly expect the credence of the reader when I say that I have toned down her words and actions rather than exaggerated them. But my own theory of the case is this: Miss Hemster had an inordinate love of conquest and power. I think I should have got along better with her if I had proposed to her and taken my rejection in a broken and contrite spirit. That she would have rejected me, I am as positive as that I breathe. I am equally certain that, while she would have scorned to acknowledge me as a favoured lover, she was nevertheless humiliated to know that I had given preference to one upon whom she rather looked down,—one whom she regarded as a recipient of her own bounty,—and the moment I made my confession I was sorry I had done so, for Hilda's sake.

It has also been hinted,—I shall not say by whom,—that I was on a fair way of being in love with Gertrude Hemster if everything had progressed favourably. I need hardly point out to the reader the utter erroneousness of this surmise. I do not deny that during the first day of our acquaintance I was greatly attracted by her, or perhaps I should say wonderfully interested in her. I had never met any one just like her before, nor have I since for that matter. But that I was even on the verge of being in love with her I emphatically deny. I have no hesitation in confessing that she was the most beautiful woman I have ever seen, when it pleased her to be gracious. She would certainly have made a superb actress if Fortune had cast her rôle upon the stage. But, as I have said, I never understood this woman, or comprehended her lightning changes of character. I do not know to this day whether she was merely a shallow vixen or a creature of deep though uncontrolled passion. I therefore content myself with setting down here, as accurately as possible, what happened on the various occasions of which I speak, so that each reader may draw her own conclusions, if indeed there are any conclusions to be drawn, and I do this as truthfully as may be, at the risk of some misunderstanding of my own position, as in the present instance.

The silence which followed my announcement was at last broken by a light sarcastic laugh.

"Really, Mr. Tremorne," she said, "it is not very flattering to me to suppose that I am interested in the love affairs of the servants' hall."

I bowed my acknowledgment of this thrust.

"My statement, Miss Hemster, was not made for your entertainment, or with any hope that it would engage your attention, but merely as an answer to your direct question."

"So two penniless paupers are going to unite their fortunes!"

"Penniless, only relatively so; paupers, no."

"Nothing added to nothing makes how much, Mr. Tremorne?"

"Madam, I am an Oxford man."

"What has that to do with it?"

"Much. Cambridge is the mathematical university. I never was good at figures."

"Perhaps that's why you threw away your money."

"Perhaps. Still, the money I threw away yesterday belonged to your father."

"Is that to remind me of the debt I am supposed to owe you?"

"You owe me nothing. If anybody owes me anything I am certain Mr. Hemster will discharge the debt with his usual generosity."

"Oh, you are counting on that, are you?"

"We have Biblical assurance, Miss Hemster, of the fact that the labourer is worthy of his hire. My hire is all I expect, and all I shall accept."

"Well, it is my hope that your term of employment will be as short as possible; therefore I ask you to resign your position as soon as we reach Nagasaki. Your presence on this ship is odious to me."

"I am sorry for that."

"Then you won't resign?"

"I say that I am sorry my presence on this ship is odious to you."

"You can at once solve the problem by resigning, as I have suggested."

"I dispute your right to make suggestions to me. If you want me to leave the yacht, ask your father to discharge me."

"There is always a certain humiliation in abrupt dismissal. If you do not go voluntarily, and without telling my father that I have asked you to resign, I shall put Hilda Stretton ashore at Nagasaki with money enough to pay her passage home."

"How generous of you! First-class or steerage?"

Her face became a flame of fire, and she clenched her hands till the nails bit the pink palms.

"You sneaking reptile!" she cried, her voice trembling with anger; "you backbiting, underhand beast! What lies have you dared tell my father about me?"

"You are under some strange misapprehension, Miss Hemster," I replied, with a coolness which earned my mental approbation, fervently hoping at the same time that I might continue to maintain control over my deplorable temper; "you have jumped at a conclusion not borne out by fact. I assure you I have never discussed you with your father, and should not venture to do so."

I remembered the moment I had spoken that I had just promised another lady to do that very thing. What everybody says must be true when they state that my thoughts are awkward and ungainly, rarely coming up to the starting-point until too late. I fear this tardy recollection brought the colour to my face, for the angry eyes of the girl were upon me, and she evidently misread this untimely flushing. She leaned across the little wicker table and said in a calm, unruffled voice, marked with the bitterness of hate:

"You are a liar."

320

I rose to my feet with the intention of leaving her, but she sprang up with a nimbleness superior to my own, and before I was aware of what she was about she thrust her two hands against my breast and plumped me unexpectedly down into my chair again. It was a ludicrous and humiliating situation, but I was too angry to laugh about it. Standing over me, she hissed down at me:

"You heard what I said."

"Perfectly, and I am resolved that there shall be no further communication between us."

"Oh, are you? Well, you'll listen to what I have to say, or I'll add 'coward' to 'liar.' Either you or Hilda Stretton has been poisoning my father's mind against me. Which was it?"

"It was I, of course."

"Then you admit you are a liar?"

"'All men are liars,' said the Psalmist, so why should I be an exception?"

"You are very good at quoting the Bible, aren't you? Why don't you live up to it?"

"I should be the better man if I did."

"Will you resign at Nagasaki, then?"

"I shall do exactly what your father orders me to do."

"That is precisely the answer I should have expected from a mud-wallower who came to us from the gutter."

"You are mistaken. I lived up on a hill."

"Well, I give you warning, that if you don't leave this yacht you will regret it."

"I shall probably regret the tender memories of your conversation, Miss Hemster; but if you think to frighten me I beg to point out that it is really yourself who is in danger, as you might know if experience taught the class of persons it is said to teach. You have called me a brute and a beast and all the rest of it, and have partly persuaded me that you are right. Now the danger to you lies in the fact that you will go just a step too far on one of these occasions, and then I shall pick you up and throw you overboard. Now allow me to say that you have about reached the limit, likewise to inform you that I shall not resign."

I now arose, confronting her, and flung the wicker chair to the other side of the deck. Then, taking off my hat, I left her standing there.

# CHAPTER XVIII

I AM tired of my own shortcomings, and I have no doubt the reader is also, if she has read this far. I shall therefore make no attempt to excuse my language toward Gertrude Hemster. The heated conversation in which we indulged had, however, one effect upon my future course. I resolved not to say a word to her father against his treatment of her. Whatever the old gentleman had said to her, it could not have been cruder or ruder than the language which I had myself employed. Therefore I felt it would be ludicrous for me to act the part of censor or adviser. I had shown my own unfitness for either of those rôles. Besides this, I had been convinced that Hilda Stretton was entirely mistaken in thinking that the young woman would commit suicide or do any injury to herself. My summing up of her character led me to the belief that although she would be quite willing to inflict pain upon others, she would take good care not to act to her own discomfort. Seizing the first opportunity that presented itself, I told Miss Stretton my determination, and, while she did not agree with me, she made no effort to induce me to forego my resolution.

The bustle pertaining to our safe arrival at Nagasaki drove all other subjects from my mind, and I was inclined to think that my recent troubles and quarrels arose through the well-known activity of Satan to provide employment for idle hands. We were now busy enough. There had accumulated at Nagasaki a mass of letters and a bundle of cablegrams for Mr. Hemster which required his immediate attention, and in his disposal of these messages I caught a glimpse of the great business man he really was. However lax he might have proved in his conduct toward his only daughter, he showed himself a very Napoleon in the way he faced the problems presented to him, settling momentous affairs thousands of miles away by the dispatch of a code word or two.

In all this, so far as my abilities permitted, I was his humble assistant, and I found myself filled with admiration and astonishment at his powers of concentration and the brilliancy of his methods. The little naphtha launch was kept running backward and forward between the yacht and the telegraph office, and during the long day that followed our arrival at Nagasaki that roll-top desk was a centre of commercial activity vastly different in its efficiency from the lazy routine to which I had been accustomed in the diplomatic service. My own nervous tension kept me going until the long day had passed, and the time seemed as but a few minutes. At the end I was as tired as if I had spent twelve hours continuously on the football field, and for the first time in my life I realized how men are burnt up in their pursuit of the mighty dollar. My natural inclination was to doubt whether the game was worth the candle, but during the progress of the game there was no question, for it held on the alert every faculty a man possessed, and I could well believe that it might exert a fascination that indulgence in mere gambling could never equal.

Silas K. Hemster himself was like a man transformed; the eyes which I had hitherto considered dull and uninteresting became aglow with the excitement of battle. His face was keen, stern, and relentless; I saw he was an enemy who gave no quarter and expected none. His orders to me were sharp and decisive, and I no more thought of questioning them than of offering unsought advice regarding them. He was like an exiled monarch come again to his throne; for the first time in our brief acquaintance I had seen the real Hemster, and the sight had given me a feeling of my own inane inadequacy in the scheme of things here below. When at last the day was done, his face relaxed, and he leaned back in his swivel chair, regarding me with eyes that had taken on their old kindliness. He seemed enlivened rather than exhausted by the contest, as if he had taken a sip of the elixir of youth.

"Well, my boy," he said, "you're tired out. You look as if you had been running a race."

"That is exactly what I've been doing, sir."

The old gentleman laughed.

"Let's see," he mused ruminatingly, "did we have lunch or not?"

"You consumed a sandwich which I placed on your desk, Mr. Hemster, and I bolted another during one of my rushes for the dispatch-boat."

Again he laughed.

"I had forgotten," he said, "but we will enjoy our dinner all the more when we sit down to it. Confess that you're used up."

"Well, sir, I don't feel just as active as I did in the morning."

The old gentleman shook his head with a slow motion that had something of pity in it.

"You English have no aptitude for business. It shows the decadent state of Europe that Britain has held supremacy on that continent for so long."

"I should be sorry, sir, if you took me for a typical example of the English business man. I doubt if in any respect I am a credit to my country, still I am not such an idiot as to suppose I shine as a man of affairs. My training has been against me, even if I had any natural aptitude for commerce, which I doubt. Still, we are supposed to possess some creditable captains of industry on our little island."

"Supposed! That's just it, and the supposition holds good until they are up against something better. Now, if you were in Chicago, and you wished me to join you in a deal while I was cruising on the coast of Japan, what would you do?"

"I should write you a letter explaining the project I had to put before you."

"Quite so. You wouldn't go to the expense of cabling the whole thing, would you?"

"If the scheme was important enough I might go to that cost."

The old gentleman held in his hand two or three cable messages which I had not seen, also a letter or two.

"Now, here is a man," he said, "who has hit upon a plan I have often thought of myself. He has, he tells me, made a combination which possesses considerable strength, but in order to be impregnable he needs my co-operation. He cables the points very concisely, and puts his case with a good deal of power; but that cablegram is merely an advance agent for himself, expensive as it is. His object is to hold me at Yokohama until he can arrive. He actually crosses the continent to San Francisco, and takes the first steamer for Japan. I received his cablegram at Yokohama, but did not wait for him. I sent off a word or two myself to Chicago, asking confidential information which I have now received. Just before we left for Corea I got a telegram from this man in Yokohama, asking me to wait for him at Nagasaki, which I did not do, because I wished to impress on the energetic individual that I was not anxious to fall in with his plan, and I knew that, having come so far, he would not return without seeing me. Meanwhile I determined to find out whether his combination is as strong as he said it was, and this information is now in my possession. Also, I wished on my own account to make a combine so formidable that whether I gave my adherence to the one or the other my weight would tip the beam in favour of the one I joined. This combination also has been completed, and I hold the balance, of course. Our friend who has come over from Japan probably does not know that there is any opposition to his scheme, and no one in the world except yourself and myself and a man in Chicago knows I have anything to do with the other combine. You see I am just yachting for pleasure and for health, and am reluctant to touch business at all. At least, that is the information which I intend to be imparted to our friend, who is now impatiently awaiting me at the Nagasaki Hotel. You might think that I should invite him to come aboard my yacht and talk the matter over, or that I should go ashore and visit him, which he asks me to do; but I shall do neither. You see I want Mr. John C. Cammerford to realize that he is not nearly so important in the commercial affairs of America as he supposes himself to be."

"John C. Cammerford!" I cried in amazement. "I think I have met him in New York, though it may not be the same man."

"Well, the name is not a common one, and if you know him, all the better. I now instruct you to call on him first thing to-morrow morning. You will notice that I have trusted you fully in this matter by giving you information which must not leak through to Cammerford. You will tell him, however, that his combination is not the only one in the United States, and if I'm to join his he must prove to me that it is stronger than the opposition. He must give you a list of the firms he has combined, and he will have to show you the original documents pertaining to the options he has received. I want to know how long his options last. They will probably have at least six months' life, or he could never have taken this journey to see me. If he satisfies you that his combination is genuine, and that his options have still several months to run, then I shall consent to meet him. If he cannot do this, or if he refuses to do it, I shall send a few cables which will certainly upset his apple-cart before he reaches San Francisco. You will not promise anything on my behalf, and I should have no objection if he imagines that my lack of eagerness in meeting him is caused by the fact that the other combination appears to me the stronger."

"Would you mind my sending to him your card instead of my own? He might possibly refuse to meet me if I sent in the name of Tremorne."

"That's all right. Use my card if you wish. The main point is that you get as much information as possible, and give as little in return as may be. There's the dinner gong, and I'm quite ready to meet whatever's on the table. Come along."

Next morning after breakfast I went ashore, and, arriving at the Nagasaki Hotel, sent up Mr. Hemster's card to Mr. John C. Cammerford, and was promptly admitted to his presence. He occupied what I took to be the finest suite of rooms in the hotel, and had a large table placed near the principal window of his sitting-room, so that his back was to the light, which shone full on the face of any visitor who called upon him. It was quite evident to me that Mr. Cammerford hoped to impress Silas K. Hemster with the fact that he was carrying on great affairs right here in Japan similar to those that occupied his attention in Chicago. The table was littered with papers, and Cammerford sat busily writing as if every moment was of importance. All his plans for the impression of a visitor fell to pieces like a house of cards when the astonished man saw who was approaching him. He sprang to his feet with a cry of dismay and backed toward the window. From his position I could

327

not very well read the expression on his face, but it seemed to be one of fear.

"I'm expecting another man," he cried, "you have no right here. Get out."

"I beg your pardon, Mr. Cammerford, I have a right here, and I have come to talk business."

"What are you following me for? Why are you here?" he cried.

"I am here as the representative of Silas K. Hemster, of Chicago, and with his permission I sent up his card to you."

Gradually his self-possession returned to him, but he took care to keep the table between himself and me. He indulged in a little cynical laugh.

"You took me by surprise, Mr. Tremorne. I—I thought perhaps you intended trying to collect—a—a little account of your own."

"No, I came entirely on Mr. Hemster's behalf. Have I your permission to be seated?"

"Certainly. Sit down, sit down," and, saying this with an effort at bluff geniality, he placed himself in the chair he had so abruptly vacated.

"I thought, as I said before," he added, with another uneasy laugh, "that you had some notion of collecting a little money from me. The last time we met you held a very mistaken view of the business matter in which we had been associated. I assure you now—you wouldn't listen then—that everything done was strictly legal, and no one was more sorry than I that the deal did not prove as successful as we had both hoped."

"You cover me with confusion, Mr. Cammerford. I have no remembrance that I ever disputed the legality of the transaction, and I deeply regret that I seem to have permitted myself at the time to use harsh language which you are quite justified in deploring. If it is any comfort to you, I beg to assure you that I look upon the half-million dollars as irretrievably lost, and at this hour yesterday had no more idea you were in Japan than you had that I was, if you did me the honour to think of me."

Cammerford gazed doubtfully across the table at me, as if he feared there was something sinister behind all this show of submission.

"It was you, then, who sent up Mr. Hemster's card?"

"Yes. He asked me to see you."

"Why couldn't he come himself? Is he ill?"

"No, he never was in better health," I answered; "but he is exceedingly busy. I am by way of being his confidential man, and if you can prove to me that the claims you have made are real, I shall have much pleasure in arranging an interview between you."

"Oh, that's how the land lies, is it? What do you know of my proposals to Mr. Hemster?"

"I have read all your letters and telegrams relating to the matter this morning; in fact, I have them in my pocket now."

"Mr. Hemster seems to repose great trust in you.

That is rather unusual with him. I suppose you have some document to prove that you are empowered to deal?"

"As a matter of fact I am not empowered to deal. I am merely the avant coureur of Mr. Hemster. I sent you up his card, and here are your own letters, telegrams, and cablegrams. I was told to inform you that since you have left America another combination which Mr. Hemster considers nearly if not quite as strong as your own has been put through, and Mr. Hemster has been invited to join. He is well acquainted with the person who has effected the second combination, but, as you have just intimated, Mr. Hemster is not a man to allow personal considerations to deflect him from the strict business path. If you can show that your combination is the stronger, I can guarantee that you will have opportunity of speaking with Mr. Hemster. If not, he sails away to-morrow in his yacht, and deprives himself of the pleasure of meeting you, as you happen to be an entire stranger to him."

"How am I to show him all this if he refuses to see me?"

"You are to convince me of two things by exhibiting the original documents: first, that these firms mentioned in your letters have given you options; and second, the length of the options,—the date on which they expire, in fact."

"And if I refuse?" said Cammerford, seemingly puzzled and displeased at the trend of our conversation.

I rose to my feet and bowed to him.

"If you refuse," I said, "that ends my mission. Good-morning to you."

"Wait a bit, wait a bit," cried Cammerford, "sit down, Mr. Tremorne. This requires a little thought. Please don't go; just sit down for a moment. I don't see how Mr. Hemster can expect me to show my whole hand to one who, begging your pardon, is a comparative stranger, and one who will have nothing to do with our transaction. Secrecy is the very soul of such a deal as I am trying to put through. What guarantee have I that you will not cable to New York or Chicago full particulars of what I am asked to tell you."

"None whatever, Mr. Cammerford."

"Well, that's not business."

"Quite so. Then I shall report your opinion to Mr. Hemster."

"What's his object? Why doesn't he come and see me himself?"

"I think I may go so far as to say that he wishes to know whether or not it is worth his while to meet you. You see, Mr. Cammerford, you are a stranger to him. He was good enough to hint that if I reported favourably on your scheme, he would wait over a day or two and go into the matter with you. As I have said, he is exceedingly busy. I left him immersed in letters and cablegrams, and all day yesterday we were over head and ears in matters of rather large importance. If you had been his Chicago acquaintance who formed the other combine, I imagine he would have seen you; as it is, he has sent me."

"Well, now, look here, Tremorne," cried Cammerford, with a fine assumption of honest bluffness, "let us talk as man to man. We're not school-boys or sentimental girls. You know as well as I do that there is not one chance in ten million for my seeing old Hemster if the choice in the matter lies with you. You are exceedingly polite, and speak as sweetly as molasses, but I wasn't born yesterday, and am not such a darned fool as to suppose you are going to put in a good word for me."

"You are quite right, Mr. Cammerford; I shall put in no good word for you that I can possibly keep out. Nevertheless I shall report fairly to Mr. Hemster exactly what you place before me."

"Oh, that's all guff. You'll knife me because you've got the chance to do it. I quite admit it will be done with smooth talk, but it will be effective nevertheless."

"If you believe that, Mr. Cammerford, I shall make no endeavour to convince you of the contrary. You will act, of course, as best serves your own interest. Personally I do not care a halfpenny whether the great beef combine is formed in the interest of the dear public, or goes to smash through the non-agreement of its promoters. I fancy you cannot float such a trust and leave Mr. Hemster out, but you know more about that than I. Now it's your next move. What are you going to do?"

Cammerford leaned across the table, showing me his crafty eyes narrowing as he seemed trying to find out what my game really was. I knew exactly where his error lay in dealing with me. He could not believe that I was honestly trying to serve my employer, and so he was bound to go wrong in any assumption formed by taking such false premises for granted.

"See here, Tremorne, I'm going to talk straight business to you. Whatever may be our pretences, we are none of us engaged in this for our health; we want to make money. I want to make money; Hemster wants to make money; don't you want to make money?"

"Certainly," I replied, "that's what I'm here for."

"Now you're shouting," exclaimed Cammerford, an expression of great relief coming into his face. He thought that at last he had reached firm ground.

331

"I confess, then," he went on, "that it is supremely important I should meet Hemster, and he should be favourably disposed toward me. It is not likely I should have taken a journey clear from New York to Nagasaki if there wasn't a good deal at stake. You see, I'm perfectly frank with you. You've got the drop on me. Just now my hands are right up toward the ceiling, and I'm willing to do the square thing. Did you know whom you were going to meet when you left the yacht?"

"Yes, I did."

"Mr. Hemster mentioned my name to you?"

"Yes, he did."

"Did you tell him anything of our former dealings?"

"No, I did not."

"He does know you lost half a million in the States a while since?"

"Oh, yes, he knows that, but he doesn't know you're the man who got it."

"Hang it all, Tremorne; don't put it that way. I'm not the man who got it; I lost money as well as you did."

"Oh, I beg your pardon; I thought we were talking frankly and honestly to each other. Well, be that as it may, Mr. Hemster knows I lost the money, but he doesn't know you're the man who was so unfortunate as to be in the business with me."

"Well now, Tremorne, I'll tell you what I'll do. You say nothing of this former company of ours, and if you will report favourably on what I have to tell you so that old Hemster will come and see me, or allow me to go to him, I'll give you two hundred thousand dollars cash as soon as our deal is completed."

"I refuse it."

"You don't trust me?"

"No, I do not, but I refuse it nevertheless. I should refuse it if you offered me the money here and now."

Cammerford leaned back in his chair.

"You want to go the whole hog?"

"I don't know what you mean," said I.

"You want the whole five hundred thousand or nothing. Well, I tell you at once I can't afford to give that much. I'll raise fifty thousand dollars, and make the total amount two hundred and fifty; but I can't go a cent more, and there is no use trying to bluff me."

"I am not trying to bluff you, Mr. Cammerford. I should refuse the bribe if you made it five hundred thousand."

"Oh, it's not a bribe at all, it's—well, whatever you like to call it. Restitution if you prefer to put it that way."

"It doesn't matter what it is called, I have come for the purpose of hearing what you have to say regarding the great beef combine. If you have nothing to say I shall leave, because, as I told you, Mr. Hemster has a good deal of work on his hands, and I'm trying to help him."

"Well," said Cammerford, in a hopeless tone of voice, "you are the darndest fool I ever met in my life."

"You are not the first person who has said as much, Mr. Cammerford, although not in precisely the same language. Now, for the last time, give me a list of the names of those who are behind you."

"I'll do that if you will promise me not to say anything to old Hemster about our former relations."

"I regret that I cannot make you any such promise, Mr. Cammerford. It is my duty to lay before Mr. Hemster everything you place before me, and it is also my duty to warn him that I consider you as big a scoundrel as you consider me a fool."

"That's plain talk," said Cammerford, scowling.

"I intend it to be. Now, without further loss of time, let me see your documents."

For some minutes Cammerford maintained silence, a heavy frown on his brow, and his eyes fixed on the carpet beneath the table. At last he muttered, "Well, I'm damned!"—and, taking a bundle of papers from before him, he slipped off the elastic band, picked out one after another which he perused with care, then handed them across the table to me, watching me very narrowly as he did so. I took the papers one by one and read them over, making a note with my pencil now and then in my pocket-book. They proved to be exactly what he had said they were in his letter to Mr. Hemster. I pushed them back toward him again, saying:

"I see by some of these documents that the option is for six months, but others make no mention of the time. Why is that?"

"Because we have bought the businesses and the options are ours for ever."

"Have you anything to prove that?"

Without further reply he selected several other papers and presented them to me. These also were satisfactory.

"I shall report to Mr. Hemster that your position appears to be quite as strong as you stated it to be, and so I wish you good-morning, Mr. Cammerford."

"Hold your horses a minute," he cried, seeing me about to arise. "As you have asked me a whole lot of questions, I'd like you to answer a few of mine. Who's in this other combine?"

"I know nothing of it, except that it is in existence."

"Do you imagine it's a bluff?"

"I tell you I don't know. I should think Mr. Hemster is not a man to engage in bluff."

"Oh, isn't he? That shows how little you know of him. Have you been with him ever since he left Chicago?"

"No."

"How long have you been in his employ?"

"That is a private matter, Mr. Cammerford, which concerns no one but myself and Mr. Hemster. Besides, to tell you the truth, I came here to receive information, not to impart it; so it is useless to question me further."

"Oh, one more won't do any harm," said Cammerford, rising when I had risen; "do you think old Hemster will consent to see me?"

"I am almost certain that he will."

"Through your recommendation, eh?"

"No, I shall strongly advise him not to see you."

"Well, I'm damned if I understand your game. It's either too deep or too mighty shallow for me."

"It doesn't occur to you, Mr. Cammerford, that there's no game at all, and therefore there can be neither depth nor shallowness. You are troubling your mind about what does not exist."

"Then I am forced to take refuge in my former assumption, not at all a flattering one, which is that you're a fool."

"I think that's the safest position to assume, Mr. Cammerford; so, finally, good-bye."

I left the man standing at the head of the stairs, his hands on the banister, gazing after me with an expression of great discontent.

# CHAPTER XIX

WHEN I arrived at the landing I saw the little naphtha launch making a trip from the yacht to the shore. As it swung to the steps I noticed that Gertrude Hemster was aboard with her new companion, a Japanese lady, said to be of extremely high rank, whom the girl had engaged on the first day of our arrival at Nagasaki, when her father was so deeply immersed in business. The old gentleman told me later that his daughter had taken an unfortunate dislike to Miss Stretton, and had very rapidly engaged this person, who, it was, alleged, could speak Chinese, Japanese, Corean, and pidgin English.

In spite of what her father had said, I thought the engaging of this woman with so many lingual advantages was rather a stroke aimed at myself than an action deposing Hilda Stretton. I suppose Miss Hemster thought to give proof that I was no longer necessary as interpreter on board the yacht. I doubted the accomplishments of the Japanese high dame, thinking it impossible to select such a treasure on such short notice, and so the evening before had ventured to address her in Corean; but she answered me very demurely and correctly in that language, with a little oblique smile, which showed that she knew why I had spoken to her, and I saw that I had been mistaken in slighting her educational capacities.

I went down the steps and proffered my escort to the young woman, but she was so earnestly engaged in thanking the crew of the naphtha launch that she quite ignored my presence. She sprang lightly up the steps and walked away to the nearest 'rickshaw, followed by the toddling Japanese creature. The boat's crew, who were champions of Miss Hemster to a man, each embued with intense admiration for her, as was right and natural, may or may not have noticed her contemptuous treatment of me; but after all it did not much matter, so I stepped into the launch and we set out for the yacht.

I found Mr. Hemster immersed in his papers as usual. Apparently he had never been on deck to get a breath of fresh air since his steamship arrived in the harbour.

"Well," he said shortly, looking up; "you saw Mr. Cammerford?"

"Yes."

"Did he give down or hold up?"

"He seemed very much startled when he saw me, and I had some difficulty in getting him to discuss the matter in hand."

"Was he afraid you had come to rob him, or did he think he had got me in a corner?"

"No. He knew who it was that approached him, but I should have told you, Mr. Hemster, that this is the man who got my five hundred thousand dollars some years ago, and he was under the mistaken impression that I had come to wring some part of it back from him."

"Ah, he thought you were camping on his trail, did he? What did you do?"

"I explained that I was there merely as your representative. He made some objection at first to showing his hand, as he called it; but finally, seeing that he could not come at his desired interview with you unless he took me into his confidence, he did so, although with extreme reluctance."

"Yes, and what were your conclusions?"

"My conclusions are that his letter to you was perfectly truthful. He has the following firms behind him on a six months' option, and these others have sold their businesses to him outright. His position, therefore, is all that he asserted it to be," and with this I placed my notes before my chief.

"You are thoroughly convinced of that?"

"Yes, I am; but of course you will see the papers he has to show, and may find error or fraud where I was unable to detect either."

"All right, I shall see him then."

"There is one thing further, Mr. Hemster. He offered me two hundred thousand dollars, then two hundred and fifty thousand, if I would conceal from you the fact that he had formerly defrauded me."

"Yes, and what did you say?"

"I refused the money, of course."

The old gentleman regarded me with an expression full of pity.

"I am sorry to mention it, Tremorne, but you are a numskull. Why didn't you take the money? I'm quite able to look after myself. It doesn't matter in the least to me whether or not the man has cheated everyone in the United States. If he cheats me as well, he's entitled to all he can make. 'The laborer is worthy of his hire,' as the good Book says."

As I had used this quotation to his daughter, I now surmised that she had told her father something of our stormy conversation.

"Quite true, Mr. Hemster, but the good Book also says, 'Avoid the very appearance of evil,' and that I have done by refusing his bribe."

"Ah, well, you don't get anything for nothing in this world, and I think your duty was to have closed with his offer so long as you told me the truth about the documents I sent you to search."

"He is a man I would have nothing whatever to do with, Mr. Hemster."

"There's where you are wrong. If he happens to possess something I want, why in the world should I not deal with him. His moral character is of no interest to me. As well refuse to buy a treatise on the English language because the bookseller drops his 'h's.' I am very much disappointed in your business capacity, Mr. Tremorne."

"I am sorry I don't come up to your expectations, sir; but he is a man whom I should view with the utmost distrust."

"Oh, if you are doing business with him, certainly. I view everyone with distrust and never squeal if I'm cheated. Tell me about this deal with Cammerford in which you lost your money."

I related to him the circumstances of the case, which need not be set down here. When I had finished Mr. Hemster said slowly:

"If you will excuse me, Mr. Tremorne, never say that this man swindled you. Such an expression is a misuse of language. Everything done was perfectly legal."

"Oh, I know that well enough. In fact he mentioned its legality during our interview this morning. Nevertheless, he was well aware that the mine was valueless."

"What of that? It wasn't his business to inform you; it was your business to find out the true worth of the mine. You are simply blaming Cammerford for your own carelessness. If Cammerford had not got the money, the next man who met you would; so I suppose he sized you up, and thought he might as well have it, and, to tell you the truth, I quite agree with him. Now, if I told you this bag contained a thousand dollars in gold, would you accept my word for it without counting the money?"

"Certainly I would."

The old gentleman seemed taken aback by this reply, and stared at me as if I were some new human specimen he had not met before.

"You would, eh?" he cried at last. "Well, you're hopeless! I don't know but you were right to refuse his bribe. The money would not do you the least good if you got it again."

"Oh, yes, it would, Mr. Hemster. I should invest it in Government securities, and risk not a penny of it in any speculation."

"I don't believe you'd have that much sense," demurred the old gentleman, turning again to his desk. "However, you have served me well, even if you have served yourself badly. I will write a letter to Cammerford and let him know the terms on which I will join his scheme."

"You surely don't intend to do that, Mr. Hemster, without seeing the documents yourself?"

"Oh, have no fear; you must not think I am going to adopt your business

339

tactics at my age. Run away and let Hilda give you some lunch. I shall not have time for anything but the usual sandwich. My daughter's gone ashore. She wants lunch at the Nagasaki Hotel, being tired of our ship's fare. I'll have this document ready for you to take to Cammerford after you have eaten."

Nothing loth, I hurried away in search of my dear girl, of whom I had caught only slight glimpses since her sudden dismissal by Gertrude Hemster. I was glad to know that we should have the ship practically to ourselves, and I flatter myself she was not sorry either. Lunch was not yet ready, so I easily persuaded her to come upon deck with me, and there I placed the chairs and table just as they had been at the moment when Miss Hemster had come so unexpectedly upon us.

"Now, Hilda," I began when we had seated ourselves, "I want an answer to that question."

"What question?"

"You know very well what question; the answer was just hovering on your lips when we were interrupted."

"No, it wasn't."

"Hilda, there was an expression in your eyes which I had never seen before, and if your lips were about to contradict the message they sent to me——"

"Seemed to send to you," she interrupted with a smile.

"Was it only seeming, then?"

"Oh, I don't know. I'm very much disappointed with myself. I don't call this a courtship at all. My idea of the preliminaries to a betrothal was a long friendship, many moonlight walks, and conversations about delightful topics in which both parties are interested. I pictured myself waiting eagerly under some rose-covered porch while the right person hurried toward me,— on horseback for choice. And now turn from that picture to the actuality. We have known each other only a few days; our first conversation was practically a quarrel; we have talked about finance, and poverty, and a lot of repulsive

340

things of that sort. If I were to say, 'Yes,' I should despise myself ever after. It would appear as if I had accepted the first man who offered."

"Am I the first man, Hilda? I shall never believe it."

"I'm not going to tell you. You ask altogether too many questions."

"Well, despite your disclaimer, I shall still insist that the right answer was on your lips when it and you were so rudely chased away."

"Well, now, Mr. Tremorne——"

"Rupert, if you please, Hilda!"

"Well, now, Prince Rupert, to show you how far astray you may be in predicting what a woman is about to say, I shall tell you exactly what was in my mind when the thread of my thought was so suddenly cut across. There were conditions, provisos, stipulations, everything in the world except the plain and simple 'Yes' you seemed to anticipate."

"Even in that case, Hilda, I am quite happy, because these lead to the end. It cannot be otherwise, and all the provisos and stipulations I agree to beforehand, so let us get directly to the small but important word 'Yes!'"

"Ah, if you agreed beforehand that would not be legal. You could say you had not read the document, or something of that kind, and were not in your right mind when you signed it."

"Then let us have the conditions one by one, Hilda, if you please."

"I was going to ask you to say no more at present, but to wait until I get home. I wanted you to come to me, and ask your question then if you were still in the same mind."

"What an absurd proviso! And how long would that be? When shall you reach your own home?"

"Perhaps within a year, perhaps two years. It all depends on the duration of Mr. Hemster's voyage. Of course it is quite possible that at any minute he may make up his mind to return. I could not leave him alone here, but once he is in Chicago he will become so absorbed in business that he would never miss me."

"There is an uncertain quality about that proviso, Hilda, which I don't at all admire."

"Now, you see how it is," she answered archly; "my very first proposition is found fault with."

"On the contrary, it is at once agreed to. Proceed with the next."

"The next pertains more particularly to yourself. I suppose you have no occupation in view as yet, and I also suppose, if you think of marrying, you do not expect to lead a life of idleness."

"Far from it."

"Very well. I wish that you would offer your services to Mr. Hemster. I am sure he has great confidence in you, and as he grows older he will feel more and more the need of a friend. He has had no real friend since my father died."

"You forget about yourself, Hilda."

"Oh, I don't count; I am but a woman, and what he needs near him is a clear-headed man who will give him disinterested advice. That is a thing he cannot buy, and he knows it."

"I quite believe you, but nevertheless where is the clear-headedness? He has just asserted that I am a fool."

"He surely never called you that."

"Well, not that exactly, but as near as possible to it, and somehow, now that I am sitting opposite to you, I rather think that he is right, and I have been quixotic."

"Now I come to another condition," Hilda said with some perceptible hesitation. "It is not a condition exactly, but an explanation. I have often wondered whether I acted rightly or not in the circumstances, and perhaps your view of the case may differ from the conclusion at which I arrived. The one man with whom I should most naturally have consulted in a business difficulty—Mr. Hemster himself—was out of the question in this case, so I tried to imagine what my father would have had me do, and I acted accordingly, but not without some qualms of conscience then and since. I fear I did not do what an independent girl should have done, but now that we have become so friendly you shall be my judge."

"You will find me a very lenient one, Hilda; in fact the verdict is already given: you did exactly right whatever it was."

"Sir, you must not pronounce until you hear. We approach now the dread secret of a woman with a past. That always crops up, you know, at the critical moment. I think I told you my father and Mr. Hemster were friends from boyhood; that they went to school together; that their very differences of character made the friendship sincere and lasting. My father was a quiet, scholarly man, fond of his books, while Mr. Hemster cared nothing for literature or art, but only for an outdoor life and contest with his fellow men. It is difficult to imagine that one so sedate and self-restrained as Mr. Hemster now seems to be should have lived the life of a reckless cowboy on the plains, riding like a centaur, and shooting with an accuracy that saved his life on more than one occasion, whatever the result to his opponents. Nevertheless, in the midst of this wild career he was the first, or one of the first, to realize the future of the cattle business, and thus he laid the foundation of the colossal fortune he now possesses. I can imagine him the most capable man on the ranch, and I believe he was well paid for his services and saved his money, there being no way of spending it, for he neither drank nor gambled. While yet a very young man an opportunity came to him, and he had not quite enough capital to take advantage of it. My father made up the deficit, and, small as the amount was, Mr. Hemster has always felt an undue sense of obligation for a loan which was almost instantly repaid. When my father died he left me practically penniless so far as money was concerned, but with a musical education which would have earned me a comfortable living. Shortly after my father's death the manager of our local bank informed me that there had been deposited to my order one hundred thousand dollars' worth of stock in Mr. Hemster's great business. Now the question is, Should I have kept that, or should I have returned it to Mr. Hemster?"

"I beg your pardon, Hilda, but there is no question there at all. Your father, by reason of his most opportune loan, was quite honestly entitled to a share in the business the creation of which his money had made possible."

"But the sum given to me was out of all proportion to the amount lent. It is even more out of proportion than the figures I have mentioned would lead you to suppose, for the interest paid is so great that such an income could not be produced by four or five times the face value of the stock. Then Mr. Hemster was under no obligation to have given me a penny."

"Surely a man may be allowed to do the right thing without being legally bound to do it. I hope you accepted without hesitation."

"Yes, I accepted, but with considerable hesitation. Now, I think Mr. Hemster would be greatly annoyed if he knew I had told you all this. His own daughter has not the slightest suspicion of it, and I imagine her father would be even more disturbed if she gathered any hint of the real state of affairs. Indeed, I may tell you that she has dismissed me since this Japanese Countess came."

"Then we are in the same plight, for the young lady ordered me to resign."

"And are you going to?"

"Not likely. She didn't engage me, and therefore has no standing in the contract. But, to return to ourselves, which is always the paramount subject of interest, this dread secret, as you called it, puts an entirely different complexion on our relations. You must see that. Here have I been suing you under the impression that you were a helpless dependent. Now you turn out to be an heiress of the most pronounced transatlantic type. You once accused me of being dull in comprehension."

"I never did."

"Well, people do accuse me of that; nevertheless I am brilliant enough to perceive that this is a transformation scene, and that the dreams which I have indulged in regarding our relationship are no longer feasible."

Hilda clasped her hands and rested her elbows on the wicker table, leaning forward toward me with an expression half quizzical, half pathetic.

"I never called you dull, Mr. Tremorne——"

"Rupert, if you please."

"——but I did think you slightly original, Rupertus. Now, your talk of all this making a great difference is quite along the line of conventional melodrama. I see you are about to wave me aside. 'Rich woman, begone,' say you. You are going out into the world, registering a vow that until you can place dollar for dollar on the marriage altar you will shun me. Now I have read that sort of thing ever since I perused 'The Romance of a Poor Young Man,' but I never expected to encounter in real life this haughty, inflexible, poor young man."

"Rich woman, there are many surprises here below, and of course you cannot avoid your share of them. However, I shall not so haughtily wave you aside until you have answered that important question with a word of three letters rather than one of two. I cannot refuse what is not proffered. So will you kindly put me in a position to enact a haughty poor young man by saying definitely whether you will marry me or not?"

"I reply, 'Yes, yes, yes, yes,' and a thousand other yes's, if you wish them. Now, young man, what have you to say?"

"I have this to say, young woman, that your wealth entirely changes the situation."

"And I maintain it doesn't, not a particle."

"I will show you how it does. I was poor, and I thought you were poor. Therefore it was my duty, as you remarked, to go out into the world and wring money from somebody. That, luckily, is no longer necessary. Hilda, we may be married this very day. Come, I dare you to consent."

"Oh!" she cried, dropping her hands to her side and leaning back in her creaking chair, looking critically at me with eyes almost veiled by their long lashes, a kindly smile, however, hovering about her pretty lips. "You are in a hurry, aren't you?"

"Yes, you didn't expect to clear the way so effectively when you spoke?"

Before she could reply we were interrupted by the arrival of Mr. Hemster, who carried a long sealed envelope in his hand. He gazed affectionately at the girl for a moment or two, then pinched her flushed cheek.

"Hilda, my dear," he said, "I never saw you looking exactly like this before. What have you two been talking about? Something pleasant, I suppose."

"Yes, we were," replied Hilda pertly; "we were saying what a nice man Silas K. Hemster is."

The old gentleman turned his glance toward me with something of shrewd inquiry in it.

"Hilda," he said slowly, "you mustn't believe too much in nice men, young or old. They sometimes prove very disappointing. Especially do I warn you against this confidential secretary of mine. He is the most idiotically impractical person I have ever met. Would you believe it, my dear, that he was to-day offered two hundred and fifty thousand dollars if he would merely keep quiet about something he knew which he thought was his duty to tell me, and he was fool enough to refuse the good and useful cash?"

"Please tell Miss Stretton, Mr. Hemster, that the good and useful cash bore the ugly name of bribe, and tell her further that you would have refused it yourself."

"Oh, I don't know about that. I don't want the girl to think me quite in my dotage yet. Such a sum is not picked up so easily every day on the streets of Nagasaki, as I think you found out a while ago."

"It may be picked up on board a yacht," said Hilda archly, smiling up at him.

"Ah, you're getting beyond me now. I don't know what you mean,

Hilda," and he pinched her cheek again.

"And now, Mr. Tremorne, I am sorry to send you away again without lunch, but business must be attended to even if we have to subsist on sandwiches. How old a man is this Cammerford?"

"About forty, I should think."

"Does he strike you as a capable individual?"

"Naturally he does. He has proved himself to be much more capable than I am."

"Oh, that's no recommendation. Well, I want you to take this letter to him; it is my ultimatum, and you may tell him so. He must either accept or refuse. I shall not dicker or modify my terms. If he accepts, then bring him right over to the yacht with you; if he refuses, you tell him I will have him wiped out before he can set foot in San Francisco." He handed me the sealed envelope.

"You see you were in at the beginning of this business, so I'd like you to be on hand at the finish. I'm sorry to make an errand-boy of you, Tremorne, but we are a little distant from the excellent messenger service of Chicago."

I rose at once, placed the envelope in my inside pocket, and said:

"I shall do my best, Mr. Hemster, although, as you have remarked, I seem to be little more than a messenger-boy in the negotiations."

"Oh, not at all; you're ambassador, that's what you are; a highly honourable position, and I feel certain that as you are not particularly fond of Cammerford your manner will go far toward showing him his own insignificance. When he once realizes how powerless he is, we'll have no further difficulty with him."

I laughed, received a sweet smile from Hilda and a kindly nod from Hemster, then turned to the gangway and was in the ever-ready naptha launch a moment later.

Cammerford was not expecting me, so I had to search for him, and at last ran him down at the equivalent of the American bar which Nagasaki possesses for the elimination of loneliness from the children of the Spread Eagle.

"Have a drink with me, Tremorne," cried Cammerford, as genially as if we were the oldest possible friends.

"Thanks, no!" I replied. "I'd sooner meet the muzzle of a revolver than imbibe the alleged American drinks they furnish at this place. You see, I know the town; besides, I've come on business."

"Ah, is the old man going to see me, then?"

"That will depend on your answer to his letter which I have here in my pocket. May I suggest an adjournment to your rooms in the hotel?"

"Certainly, certainly," muttered Cammerford hastily, evidently all aquiver with excitement and anxiety.

When we reached his apartments he thrust out his hand eagerly for the letter, which I gave to him. He ripped it open on the instant, and, standing by the window, read it through to the end, then, tossing it on the table, he threw back his head and gave utterance to a peal of laughter which had an undercurrent of relief in it.

"I was to tell you," said I, as soon as I could make myself heard, "that this document is by way of being an ultimatum, and if you do not see fit to accept it——"

"Oh, that's all right, my dear boy," he cried, interrupting me. "Accept it? Of course I do, but first I must tender an abject apology to you."

"There is no necessity, Mr. Cammerford," I protested, "I hope that is not a proviso in the communication?"

"No, my dear boy, it is not. I offer the apology most sincerely on my own initiative. Actually I took you for a fool, but you are a damned sight shrewder man than I am. I told you when you were here that I could not get on to your game, but now I see it straight as a string, and I wonder I was such a chump as not to suspect it before. Tremorne, you're a genius. Of course your proper way of working was through the old man with that cursed high-bred air of honesty which you can assume better than any one I ever met. That kind of thing was bound to appeal to the old man because he's such an unmitigated rogue himself. Yes, my dear boy, you've played your cards well, and I congratulate you."

"I haven't the least idea what you are driving at," I said.

"Do you mean to tell me you don't know what is in this letter?"

"The letter was delivered to me sealed, and I have delivered it sealed to you. I have no more notion what it contains than you had before I handed it to you."

"Is that really a fact? Well, Tremorne, you're a constant puzzle and delight to me. This world would be a less interesting place if you were out of it. It is an ever-recurring problem to me whether you're deep or shallow; but if you are shallow I'll say this, that it cuts more ice than depth would do. Well, just cast your eyes over the last paragraph in that letter." He tossed across the final sheet to me, and I read as follows:

"The condition under which I shall treat with you is this: You will place at once in the Bank of Japan, to the order of Rupert Tremorne, the five hundred thousand dollars you borrowed from him, together with interest compounded for three years at six per cent. If, as is likely, you are not in a position to hand over such a sum, you may pay half the amount into the Bank of Japan here, and cable to have the other half similarly placed in the First National Bank of Chicago. The moment I receive cable advice from my confidential man of business in Chicago that the money is in the bank there, or the moment you show me the whole amount is in the bank here, I shall carry out the promises I have made in the body of this letter.

"Yours truly,

"Silas K. Hemster."

The look of astonishment that doubtless came into my face must have appeared genuine to Cammerford as he watched me keenly across the table. I handed the letter back to him.

"I assure you I know nothing of this proviso."

"In that case," said Cammerford airily, "I hope you will have no objection to paying me back the money when once you have received it. I trust that your silk-stockinged idea of strict honesty will impel you toward the course I have suggested."

"I am very sorry to disappoint you, Mr. Cammerford, but circumstances have changed since I saw you last, and, if you don't mind, I'll keep the money."

Cammerford laughed heartily; he was in riotous good humour, and I suppose his compensation in this trust-forming business would be so enormous that the amount paid into the bank seemed trifling by comparison.

"I should be glad," said I, rising, "if you would pen a few words to Mr. Hemster accepting or declining his offer."

"Of course I will, dear boy," he replied, taking the latest pattern of fountain pen from his waistcoat pocket; "you are the most courteous of messengers, and I shall not keep you two shakes." Whereupon he rapidly scrawled a note, blotted it, sealed it, and handed it to me.

He arose and accompanied me to the door, placing me under some temporary inconvenience by slapping me boisterously on the shoulder.

"Tremorne, old man, you're a brick, and a right-down deep one after all. I'm ever so much obliged to you for lending me your money, although I did not think it would be recalled so soon, and I did not expect the interest to be so heavy. Still, I needed it at the time, and put it where it has done the most good. So long, old fellow. You will imagine yourself a rich man to-morrow."

"I imagine myself a rich man to-day, Mr. Cammerford."

# CHAPTER XX

On reaching the yacht I went directly to the old gentleman's office and handed him Cammerford's letter, which he tore open, read, and tossed on the desk.

"Mr. Hemster," said I, while an emotion which I had not suspected myself of possessing caused my voice to tremble a little; "Mr. Hemster, I don't know how I can thank you for what you have done for me to-day."

"Oh, that's all right, that's all right!" he said gruffly, as if the reference annoyed him. "What you need is a guardian."

"I think," said I, "I have secured one."

The old gentleman glanced up at me quickly.

"Is that so? Well, if the land lays as I have suspected, I congratulate you. Yes, and I congratulate Hilda also. As for a guardian, you have chosen a good one, and now don't begin to thank me over again, but go and tell her all about it."

Thus dismissed, I went to the saloon, and there found the lady of whom I was in search, and persuaded her to come up on deck with me. In spite of the vexatious interruption to which we had been forced to submit at this spot, I had become attached to the locality of the two chairs and the wicker table.

"I like this place," said I, "for its associations, and yet I am certain, the moment we begin to talk, Mr. Hemster will order me overboard, or his daughter will tell you to go down below."

"There is no immediate danger," answered Hilda. "Mr. Hemster is busy, and his daughter has not returned from Nagasaki; I suspect, however, that you should be down in the office helping your chief, rather than up here frivolously gossiping with me."

"I am obeying orders in being up here. My chief, as you call him, told me to search you out and tell you all about it."

"All about what?"

"Did you tell Mr. Hemster anything of our conversation after I left?"

"Not a word. Poor dear, his mind was occupied with other matters. He talked about you, and fished,—in, oh, such an awkward way,—to find out what I thought of you. He gave me much good counsel which I shall ever treasure, and he warned me to beware of fascinating young men, and not allow myself to become too deeply interested. Indeed I yearned to let him know that his caution was already too late; but, not being sure whether that would ease his mind or cause it greater anxiety, I held my peace. I wish you would tell him. Perhaps I should do it myself, but I cannot find the exact words, I am afraid."

"I'll tell him with great pleasure. No, to be honest, I have already told him."

"Really, and what did he say?"

"Oh, he said I needed a guardian, and I informed him I had already secured one. He twigged the situation in a moment, congratulated me on my choice, and ordered me to come and tell you all about it."

"Tell me all about what? I've asked you that before."

"Why, about the money with which we are to start housekeeping. Mr. Hemster estimates that it will amount to something more than half a million."

Hilda sat back in her chair with a remote resemblance to a frown on her pretty brow.

"That was what you were discussing with Mr. Hemster, was it?" she said primly.

"Of course. Don't you think it most important?"

"I suppose it is."

"He certainly thought so, and looked on me as very fortunate coming into such a tidy sum so easily."

"Easily! Did he, indeed?"

"Yes, he's awfully pleased about it, and so am I."

"I am delighted to hear it."

"He said you would be, and he regards me as more than lucky, which, to tell the truth, I acknowledge that I am. You see it was such a complete surprise. I hadn't expected anything at all, and to find myself suddenly the possessor of such a sum, all because of a few words, seemed almost too good to be true."

Hilda was leaning back in her chair; there was no question about the frown now, which was visible enough, and, as I prattled on, the displeasure in her speaking eyes became deeper and deeper.

"All because of a few words!" she murmured, as if talking to herself.

"Certainly. Plain, simple, straightforward words, yet look what an effect they had. They practically make me an independent man, even rich, as I should count riches, although I suppose Mr. Hemster wouldn't consider the amount very important."

"Probably not, but you seem to look upon the amount as very, very important,—even of paramount importance, I should say."

"Oh, not of paramount importance, of course, but nevertheless I shall always regard this day as the most fortunate of my life."

"Really? Because of the money, I suppose?"

"Now, Hilda," I protested, "you must admit that money is exceedingly necessary."

"I do admit it. So Mr. Hemster was more pleased about your getting the money than anything else?"

"Oh, I don't say that, but he certainly was delighted with my luck, and what true friend wouldn't be? I am sure my people at home will be overjoyed when they hear the news."

"Because of the money?" reiterated Hilda, with more of irritation in her tone than I had ever heard there before.

"Why not? Such a lump of gold is not won every day."

"By a few simple words," suggested Hilda tartly.

"Exactly. If you choose the psychological moment and use the right words they form a great combination, I can tell you, and success is sure to follow."

"Deserving man! I think those that called you a fool were mistaken, don't you?"

"Yes, I rather imagine they are, and in fact that has been admitted."

"So you and Mr. Hemster have been discussing this money question down in your office?"

"Yes, at first, of course. I began about the money at once, and thanked him sincerely for what he had done."

"You were quite right; if it had not been for him there would have been no money to make you so jubilant."

"That's exactly what I told him. 'Mr. Hemster' said I, 'if it had not been for your action I should never have got a penny.'"

"Well," said Hilda, with a little break in her voice that went right to my heart and made me ashamed of myself, while the moisture gathered in her eyes, "and so you and Mr. Hemster at last got to me, and began to discuss me after the money question had been exhausted. Really, I suppose I should be thankful to have received so much attention. I wish I had known that gold occupied so large a space in your thoughts, and then I should have entered more accurately into particulars. I told you the amount was two or three times the face value of the stock, but it is what you say, over half a million, and now if you don't mind I shall go downstairs for a while."

"I do mind. I want to speak to you, Hilda."

"I would rather not talk any more just now. If you are wise you will say nothing until I have had time to think it all over."

"But I never claimed to be wise, Hilda. Sit down again, I beg of you. Indeed you must, I shall not let you go at this juncture."

The flash in her eyes chased away the mist that had veiled them.

"Sir," she cried, "you are only making matters worse. If you have any care for me, say no more until I see you again."

"Hilda," said I, "I can make it all right with you in five minutes. What will you bet?"

"If you are jesting, I am tired of it. Can't you see I don't want to talk. Don't you understand you have said enough? Do be content. I wish I hadn't a penny of money, and that I had never told you."

I now became aware that I was on the horns of a dilemma; I had gone too far, as a stupid man will who thinks he is on the track of a joke. The dear girl was on the verge of tears, and I saw that if I suddenly proclaimed the jest her sorrow would turn into anger against me, and my last state might be worse than my first. I had got this joke by the tail, and the whole dilemma arose through not knowing whether it was safer to hang on or let go. I quickly decided to hang on. I trusted to escape by reason of our national reputation for unreadiness, and determined to stand to my guns and proclaim that all along I had been speaking of my own fortune and not of hers. My obtuseness she would pity and forgive, but ill-timed levity and trifling with her most cherished feelings on this day of all others might produce consequences I dared not face.

"Hilda," I said, with what dignity I could bring to my command, "you actually seem sorry at my good fortune. I assure you I expected you would rejoice with me. When I spoke to you this morning I was to all intents and purposes a penniless man, and yet, as Mr. Hemster himself informed you, I had but an hour before refused two hundred and fifty thousand dollars as a bribe. That money was but half of the fortune which this man Cammerford had previously looted from me. Now, through a few simple words in the letter Mr. Hemster wrote to him, this man is going to refund the whole half million, with interest for three years at six per cent. Therefore, my darling, imagine the delight with which I learned of this great stroke of good luck. No living person could assert here or hereafter that I was an impecunious fortune-hunter, although equally, of course, no person could have convinced you that your money weighed a particle with me when I asked you to honour me as you have done. And now, really perhaps I am too sensitive, but it seems to me that you do not take the news so kindly as I had expected."

She swayed a moment, then sank helplessly down into the armchair again.

"Rupert," she said, looking across at me with a puzzled pathos in her eyes that made me ashamed of myself; "Rupert, what are you talking about? Or am I dreaming? What half million is this you are referring to? I told you that my fortune was two or three times the hundred thousand, but I supposed you had found out its real value. Now you seem to have been speaking of something else."

"Hilda," I cried, with a horror that I hope was well simulated,—Lord forgive me for the necessity of using it,—"Hilda, you never supposed for a moment that I was referring to your money?"

Her troubled face seemed fixed on something intangible in the distance, as if her mind were trying to recall our conversation, that she might find some point in what I had said to account for the mistake she supposed herself to have made. The double meaning of my words was apparent enough, but of course every sentence I had uttered applied to her money equally well with my own. Now that enlightenment had come, her supposed error became obtrusively plain to her. She turned her puzzled face to me, and her expression melted into one of great tenderness as she reached forward her two hands and laid her palms on the back of mine, which rested on the wicker table.

"Rupert," she said in a low voice, "will you forgive me? I have deeply misjudged you."

"Hilda," said I, "would you have forgiven me if I had been in the wrong?"

"I would, I would, I would," she cried, and it was plain that she meant it, yet I did not dare to risk a full confession. What brutes we men are after all, and how much we stand in need of forgiveness every day of our lives!

"Tell me all about this newly found treasure," she said, and now I launched out on fresh ground once more, resolving never to get on such thin ice again after so narrow an escape. As we talked, the indefatigable little naphtha launch came alongside, and Gertrude Hemster appeared at the gangway, followed by her miniature Countess. Miss Hemster was good enough to ignore us entirely, and, after a few words to her new companion, disappeared down the companion-way. The Countess toddled up to where we sat, and, addressing Hilda, said in her high-keyed Japanese voice:

"Mees Stretton, the mistress desires your attendance immediately," and with that she toddled away again. Hilda rose at once.

"Don't go," I commanded; but she smiled, and held out her hand to me.

"Isn't it funny," she said; "you and I together are equal to one millionaire, yet we have to dance attendance when called upon, but, unlike others in bondage, we don't need to cry, 'How long, O Lord! how long?' do we?"

"Not on your life, Hilda, as they say in the Wild West. The day of jubilee is a-coming my dear," and, in spite of her trying to slip away, I put my arm around her and drew her toward me.

"Oh, the captain is looking at us," she whispered in alarm.

"The captain is a good friend of ours, and has done the same in his time, I dare say," and with that I———. Hilda swung herself free and fled, red as a rose. On glancing up at the bridge I noticed that the captain had suddenly turned his back on us. I always did like that rough man from Cape Cod, who would haunt the bridge during his waking hours whether the ship had steam up or not.

# CHAPTER XXI

NEXT day was the most eventful I had spent on the yacht in spite of all that had gone before, for a few moments were filled with a peril which we escaped, as one might say, by a miracle, or more accurately by the prompt and energetic action of a capable man whom I shall always regard with deep affection. If Cape Cod has turned out many like him, it is a notable section of a great country.

Somewhat early in the morning I paid my third visit to the Nagasaki Hotel and brought John C. Cammerford with me to the yacht. He told me he had placed the full amount to my credit in the Bank of Japan, and said he did not need to do any cabling to America. Mr. Hemster was closeted with him in his office until the luncheon gong rang, and the amiable Cammerford was a guest at our table, referring to me several times as his old friend, and recounting stories that were more humourous than accurate about my adventures with him in the Adirondack Mountains and the fishing districts of Canada. I gathered that all the stories he had ever heard of Englishmen he now fastened on me, relating them with great gusto as having come within his own cognizance. Therefore I was delighted to be able to inform him that one of his anecdotes had appeared in Punch in the year 1854, which he promptly denied, whereupon I proposed a modest little wager that was accepted by him under the supposition that I could not prove my assertion. But we happened to have in the library two volumes of Punch for that year, which I had frequently thumbed over, and I now confounded him by their production. I don't think he minded the money so much as the slight cast on what he supposed to be a genuine American joke. About three o'clock the good man left us in a high state of exultation, carried away by the useful naphtha launch.

We were all on deck about four o'clock in the afternoon when the event happened to which I have referred. Hilda and I were sitting in our chairs by the wicker table, quite boldly in the face of all, for our engagement was now public property. Gertrude Hemster and the little Japanese noblewoman were walking up and down the other side of the deck, and from the snatches of conversation wafted to us it really seemed as if Miss Hemster were learning Japanese. She had passed the ignoring phase so far as I was concerned, and had reached the stage of the icily polite and scrupulously courteous high dame, so that I quite looked forward to an intimate interview with her later on if this change continued. The old gentleman occupied his customary armchair with his feet on the rail, and it is a marvellous thing to record that during all the excitement he never shifted his position. He said afterward that it was the captain's duty to deal with the crisis, and he had absolute confidence in the captain. This confidence was not misplaced.

The harbor of Nagasaki is usually crowded with shipping, and steamers are continually arriving or departing, consequently they attract but little attention, for they are generally capably managed. Of course a yacht swinging at anchor with no steam up is absolutely helpless if some vessel under way bears down upon her. We were lying broadside on to Nagasaki. I was so absorbed in my conversation with Hilda that I did not notice our danger until the captain put a megaphone to his lips and vehemently hailed an oncoming steamer. Looking up, I saw a huge, black, clumsy craft steaming right down upon us, and knew in a moment that if she did not deflect her course she would cut us in two amidships. The captain, who recognized the nationality of the vessel, although I did not, roared down to me:

"What is the Chinese for 'Sheer off?'"

I sprang to my feet. "Fling me the megaphone," I cried. He instantly heaved it down to me, and a moment later I was roaring through it a warning to the approaching steamer. But to this not the slightest attention was paid, nor indeed could I see anyone aboard. The black brute came on as if she were an abandoned ship without captain or crew. She appeared to grow up out of the waters; looming tremendous in size above us, and it did seem as if nothing under Heaven could save us. However, good luck and the resources of our captain did that very thing. The good luck assumed the shape of a tug which came tearing past our stern. The captain by this time was on deck with a coil of rope with a bowline on its end. Not a word did he say to the flying tug, but he swung the rope so unerringly that the loop came down like a flying quoit right on the sternpost of the little vessel. In a flash the captain had the end he held twisted twice around a huge iron cleat at our side.

"Lie down, you women, at once," he roared, bracing his feet against the cleat and hanging back upon the end of the rope.

Hilda obeyed instantly, but Miss Hemster, with the Countess clinging to her, stood dazed, while I sprang forward and caught her, breaking the fall as much as was possible, all three of us coming down in a heap with myself underneath. The rope had tightened like a rod, and had either to break, jerk the tug backward out of the water, or swing us around, which latter it did, taking the yacht from under us with a suddenness that instantly overcame all equilibrium, and in a jiffy we were at right angles to our former position, while the black hulk scraped harmlessly along our side. Even now no one appeared on the deck of the Chinese steamer, but after running a hundred yards nearer the city she slowly swerved around, heading outward again, and I thought she was about to escape; but instead of that she came to a standstill a quarter of a mile or so from our position and there coolly dropped anchor.

I helped the ladies to their feet again, inquiring if they were hurt, and Miss Hemster replied with a sweet smile that, thanks to me, she was not. The Countess showed signs of hysterics with which I could not deal, therefore I turned my attention to Hilda, who by this time had scrambled up, looking rather pale and frightened. Mr. Hemster's chair had been swung with a crash against the bulwarks, and he had been compelled to take his feet down from the rail, but beyond that he kept his old position, chewing industriously at his unlit cigar. The captain was in a ludicrously pitiable position because of a red-hot Cape Cod rage and his inability to relieve his feelings by swearing on account of the ladies being present. Hilda noticed this and cried with a little quivering laugh:

"Don't mind us, captain; say what you want to, and it is quite likely we will agree with you."

The captain shook his huge fist at the big steamer now rounding to her anchorage.

"You can say what you please," he shouted; "that was no accident; it was intended. That damned,—I beg your pardon, ladies,—that chap tried to run us down, and I'll have the law of him, dod-blast-him,—excuse me, ladies,—if there's any law in this God-forsaken hole!"

Mr. Hemster very calmly shoved his chair back to its former position, and put his feet once more on the rail, then he beckoned to the captain, and when that angry hero reached his side he said imperturbably, as if nothing had happened:

"Captain, there's no use swearing. Besides, so capable a man as you never needs to swear. In that half minute you earned ten thousand dollars, and I'll make it more if you don't think it enough."

"Nonsense," protested the captain, "it's all in the day's work: a lucky throw of the rope, that's all."

"Now I see that you want to swear at somebody," Mr. Hemster went on, "and suppressed profanity is bad for the system; so I suppose you'll prefer to swear at the person mostly to blame. Get into the launch with Mr. Tremorne here, who will translate for you, because our oaths, unlike our gold, are not current in every country. Go over to that black monstrosity; get aboard of her; find out what their game is, and swear at whoever is responsible. When we know their object we can take action, either by law, or by hiring some pirate to run her down and see how she likes it herself. I want to get at the bottom of this business."

The upshot was that the captain and I got into the naphtha launch and made directly for the Chinese steamer. We went around her twice, but saw not a soul on board, neither was there any ladder alongside by which we could ascend, or even a rope; so, after calling in vain for them to throw us a line, the captain, with an agility I should not have expected of his years and bulk, caught hold of the anchor-chain and worked himself up over the bow. His head appearing over the rail must have been a stupefying surprise to the crew, whom he found lying flat on their faces on deck. I followed the captain up the anchor-chain route, though in somewhat less effective fashion, until I was at the captain's heels. He had thrown one leg across the rail, when he

361

whipped out a revolver and fired two rapid shots, which were followed by howls of terror. The crew had sprung to their feet and flashed out knives, but his quick revolver-shots stopped the attack even before it was rightly begun. We both leaped over the rail to the deck. The cowardly crew were huddled in a heap; no one had been killed, but two were crippled and crawled moaning on the deck; the rest had ceased their outcry and crouched together with that hopeless air of resignation to take stolidly whatever fate had in store for them, which is characteristic of the lower-class Chinese. They expected instant death and were prepared to meet it with nonchalance.

"Where is your captain?" I asked them in their own tongue.

Several of them made a motion of their head toward a low deck-house aft.

"Go and bring him," I said to one who seemed rather more intelligent than the rest. He got on his feet and went into the deck-house, presently emerging with a trembling man who admitted he was the captain.

"What did you mean," I asked him, "by trying to run us down?"

He spread out his hands with a gesture that seemed to indicate his helplessness, and maintained that it was all an accident.

"That is not true," I insisted, but nothing could budge him from his statement that the steering-gear had gone wrong and he had lost control of the ship.

"Why didn't you stop the engines when you saw where you were going?" I asked.

He had become panic-stricken, he said, and so had the crew. The engineer had run up on deck, and there was no one to shut off steam. I knew the man was lying, and told our captain so, whereupon he pressed the muzzle of his revolver against the other's forehead.

"Now question him," he said.

I did so, but the captain simply relapsed into the condition of his crew, and not another word could I get out of him.

"It's no use," I said to our captain, "these people don't mind being shot in the least. You might massacre the whole lot, and yet not get a word of truth out of any one of them previous to their extinction. Nevertheless, until you kill them they are in some wholesome fear of firearms, so if you keep the drop on the captain and his men I'll penetrate this deck-house and see what it contains."

"I wouldn't do that," said our captain, "they're treacherous dogs, I imagine, and, while afraid to meet us in broad daylight on deck here, they might prove mighty handy with the knife in the darkness of that shanty. No, send the captain in and order him to bring out all his officers, if he's got any."

This seemed practical advice, so, asking our captain to remove his revolver from the other's forehead, I said to the latter:

"How many officers have you?"

He answered that there were five.

"Very well, go and bring them all out on deck here."

He gave the order to one of the crew, who went into the deck-house and presently came out with five discouraged-looking Chinese ship's officers. There was nothing to be made out of this lot; they simply stood in a row and glowered at us without answering. Whenever I put a question to them they glanced at the captain, then turned their bovine gaze upon me, but never once did one of them open his mouth.

"Now, captain," said I, "I propose that we herd this whole mob, officers and men, into the forecastle. The windlass, anchor-tackle, and all that will impede them, if they endeavour to take concerted action. You stand here on the clear deck with your two revolvers and keep an eye on them. The captain and officers will probably imagine you understand Chinese, too, so they will give no orders. Then I shall penetrate into the deck-house, for I am convinced that we have not yet come upon the responsible man. I don't believe this fellow is the captain at all."

To all this my comrade agreed, although he still demurred at my entering the deck-house. I ordered the men forward and then lined the alleged captain and his officers along the rail near them, and, while my captain stood by with a revolver in each hand, I, similarly equipped, went down three steps into the low cabin. It was a dangerous move if there had been anyone of courage within, for there were no windows, and what little light penetrated the place came in through the open door, and that was now largely shut out by the bulk of my body. Knowing that I was rather conspicuously silhouetted against the outside glare and formed an easy mark for either pistol or knife, I stepped down as quickly as possible and then stood aside. I thought at first the place was empty, but as my eyes became accustomed to the gloom I saw that a bench ran around three walls and in the further corner was a huddled figure which I knew.

"Ah, Excellency Hun Woe!" I cried, covering him with the revolver, "it is to you then we were to have been indebted for our death."

The wretch flung himself on his face at my feet, moaning for mercy. A Corean never has the nonchalance of a Chinaman when danger confronts him.

"Get up from the floor and sit down where you were," I said; "I want to have some conversation with you." Then I went to the door again and cried to the captain:

"It's all right. There is no one here but the Prime Minister of Corea, and I think I begin to see daylight so far as this so-called accident is concerned. I want to have a few minutes' talk with him, so, unless you hear a pistol-shot, everything is going well."

"Good enough," cried the genial captain, "you play a lone hand for all it's worth, and I'll hold up these hoodlums while you pow-wow."

"Now, Hun Woe," I cried, turning to him, "what is the meaning of this dastardly trick?"

"Oh, Excellency," he moaned, "I am the most miserable of men."

"Yes, you are. I admit that, and, furthermore, unless you tell the truth you are in some danger of your life at this moment."

"My life," he went on,—and I knew he spoke truly enough,—"is already forfeited. My family and my kinsmen are all in the hands of the Emperor. Their heads will fall if I do not bring back the white woman whom the Emperor has chosen for his mate."

"But how in Heaven's name would it have brought back the white woman if you had run us down and drowned us all?"

"We have expert swimmers aboard," he said, "divers brought for the purpose, who would have saved the white woman, and indeed," he added hurriedly, "would have saved you all, but the white woman we would have brought back with us."

"What a hairbrained scheme!" I cried.

"Yes, Excellency, it is not mine. I but do what I am ordered to do. The Emperor wished to sink the war-vessel of the American King so that he might not invade our coasts."

"Is it true that the Empress has been murdered?"

"Ah, not murdered, Excellency; she died of a fever."

"She looked anything but feverish when I saw her the day before," I insisted.

"We are all in God's hands," said the Prime Minister with a shrug of resignation, "and death sometimes comes suddenly."

"It does indeed in Seoul," I commented, whereupon the Prime Minister groaned aloud, thinking probably of his own impending fate and that of his wife, children, and kinsfolk.

"Excellency," he went on with the courage of desperation, "it is all your fault. If you had not brought that creature to Seoul, I would have been a happy man to-day. I have always been your friend, and it is said your country stands by its friends; but that, I fear, is not true. You can help me now, but perhaps you will not do it."

"I admit it is largely my fault, although, like yourself, I was merely the Prime Minister on our side of the affair. Nevertheless, if there is anything I can do to help you, Hun Woe, I shall be very glad to do it."

He brightened up perceptibly at this, and said eagerly, as if to give further spur to my inclination:

"If you do, I will make you a rich man, Excellency."

Nothing showed the desperate nature of his case more conclusively than this offer of money, which is always a Corean's very last card.

"I do not want a single sek from you, Hun Woe; in fact I am willing to give away many thousands of them if it will aid you. Tell me what I can do for you. I will even go so far as to return with you to Seoul and beg or bribe the Emperor's clemency."

"That would indeed be useless," demurred the Prime Minister; "His Majesty would promise you anything and take what money you liked to give him; but my body would be dismembered as soon as you were gone, and all my kinsfolk killed or sent to slavery."

I knew this to be an accurate presentation of the case.

"What, then, can I do for you?" I asked.

He lowered his voice, his little eyes glittering.

"There is but one thing to do, and that is to get the white woman on board this ship."

"To kidnap her? That is impossible; you cannot do it here in Japan, and you could not do it even if the ship were lying in Chemulpo roadstead. It is a dream of foolishness, and if your Emperor had any sense he would know it could not be done."

"Then," wailed Hun Woe, "my line is extinguished, and the deaths of myself and of my relatives lie at your door, who brought the accursed white woman to Seoul."

His lamentations disturbed me deeply, because, for a wonder, he spoke the truth.

"I'll tell you what I will do, Hun Woe, which will be far more effective than your ridiculous project of kidnapping the young lady. Has not your Emperor the sense to see, or have you not the courage to tell him, that if you succeeded in getting Miss Hemster to Seoul you would bring down on yourselves the whole force of America, and probably of England as well? Either country could blot Seoul, Palace and all, off the face of the earth within half an hour of surrounding it, and they would do it, too, if needs be. You know I speak the truth; why did you not explain this to the Emperor?"

"His Majesty would not believe me; his Majesty cares for nothing but the white woman; so any other plan but that of getting her is useless."

"No, it isn't. So far as you are concerned, Hun Woe, it would be useless for me to appeal to either the English or the American authorities. They will never interfere unless one of their own citizens is in jeopardy, but I can trust the Japanese. I am sure Mr. Hemster will lend me his yacht, and I will take a party of fearless Japanese with me to the capital and to the Palace. There will be no trouble. I shall return with your family and your kinsmen, escort them down to Chemulpo, and I shall deliver them to you here in Nagasaki. So long as you remain in Nagasaki you are safe."

This brave offer brought no consolation to the Prime Minister of Corea: he shook his head dolefully, and told me what I already knew, that a man who fled from Corea to Nagasaki had been nearly murdered here by Coreans, then, thinking himself more safe under the British flag, he had escaped to Shanghai, where he was followed and killed in cold blood, his mutilated remains being taken to Seoul, and there exhibited. All his relatives and his family had already preceded him into the unknown.

"Nothing will suffice," groaned the Prime Minister, "but the white woman,—may curses alight on her head!"

"Do not be so downhearted; my scheme is quite practicable, while yours is not. Mr. Hemster is the most generous of men, and I am certain he will see you and your family safe across the Pacific to the United States, and there I will guarantee no Corean will ever follow you. You have money enough if you can get your hands on it. Perhaps you have some here with you now."

"Yes," he replied simply, "I have my whole fortune on board this ship."

"There you are. I see you did not intend to return to Corea if you could not get the white woman."

"It was not that. I brought my fortune to give it away in bribes."

"And that's why you offered me a bribe?"

"Yes, Excellency," he replied with childlike candour.

"Well, Hun Woe, take my advice. I think I shall be able to get you all clear away. You are in command here, and these Chinese would rather die than split on you, so perhaps, instead of taking Mr. Hemster's yacht, we had better stick to this vessel, and I will bring my band of Japanese aboard. However, keep up your courage until I have seen Mr. Hemster, and then I will let you know what I am prepared to do. As this ship is now empty you had better spend your time and money in Nagasaki filling her with coal. We will go to Corea, get your family and relatives aboard, and then you can sail direct for San Francisco. It is a wild project, but with a little courage I make no doubt it can be carried out, and if you haven't money enough I can help you. Indeed, now that I have considered the matter, I shall not ask Mr. Hemster for his yacht at all. This ship is the very thing. All you need is plenty of coal and plenty of provisions, and these you can get at Nagasaki without attracting the least attention. Mr. Hemster could not accommodate you all on his yacht even if he consented to do so. Yes, cheer up, my plan is quite feasible, while yours is impossible of execution. You can no more get the girl than you can get the moon for the Emperor of Corea."

So, telling the Prime Minister that I would call upon him next day and discuss particulars, I left him there, asked the captain to release the patient crew and their officers, threw a rope ladder down the side, and so descended to our waiting naphtha launch, the crew of which had been rather anxious at the long silence following the two rapid shots; but they had obeyed orders and stood by without attempting to board.

# CHAPTER XXII

Sɪʟᴀs Hemster was sitting in his wicker chair on deck just as I had left him, so I drew up another chair beside him and sat down to give him my report. He listened to the end without comment.

"What a darned-fool scheme," he said at last. "There wasn't one chance in a thousand of those chumps picking any of us out alive if they had once destroyed the yacht. Do you think they will attempt it again?"

"Well, it seems as if I had discouraged old Hun Woe, but a person never can tell how the Oriental mind works. He stated that the precious plan emanated from the Emperor, who wished at a blow to destroy your fleet, as it were, and capture your daughter; but it is more than likely the scheme was concocted in his own brain. He is just silly enough to have contrived it, but I rather imagine our good captain overawed the officers and crew to such an extent that they may be chary of attempting such an outrage again. When two of us had no difficulty in holding up the whole company, they may fear an attack from our entire crew. Still, as I have said, no one can tell what these people will do or not do. The Prime Minister himself, of course, is in a bad way, and I should like to enable him to escape if I could."

"You intend, then, to carry out the project you outlined to him?"

"I certainly do, with your permission."

"Well, not to flatter you, Tremorne, I think your invasion of Corea at the head of a band of Japanese is quite as foolhardy as his attempt to run down the yacht."

"Oh, no, Mr. Hemster; the Coreans are a bad people to run away from, but if you face them boldly you get what you want. They call it the Hermit Kingdom, but I should call it the Coward Kingdom. A squad of determined little Japs would put the whole country to flight."

"Well, you can do as you like, and I'll help you all I'm able. Of course you're not responsible for the plight of the Prime Minister; I'm the cause of the mix-up, and if you want the yacht you just take it, and I'll stay here in Nagasaki with the womenfolk till you return; but if I had my way I'd clear out of this section of the country altogether."

"Why not do so, Mr. Hemster. I have entirely given up the notion of taking the yacht, because the Chinese steamer will be much less conspicuous and will cause less talk in Chemulpo than the coming back of the yacht. Of course the Emperor will have spies down at the port, and it will seem to them perfectly natural for the black ship to return. Meanwhile, before his Majesty knows what has happened, I shall be up in Seoul and in the Palace with my Japanese, and I think I shall succeed in terrorizing the old boy to such an extent that in less than ten minutes we shall be marching back again with Hun Woe's whole family and troop of relatives. 'Once aboard the lugger' they are safe, for Corea has no ship to overtake them, and the whole thing will be done so suddenly that the Chinese steamer will be half-way across the Pacific, or the whole way to Shanghai, before the Coreans have made up their minds what to do. I shall leave with the ship, and have them drop me at Nagasaki or Shanghai, or whatever port we conclude to make for. Then I can rejoin the yacht at any port we agree upon."

"You appear to think you'll have no trouble with your expedition, then?"

"Oh, not the slightest."

"Well, you know, we had trouble enough with ours."

"Yes, but this is a mere dash of twenty-six miles there and twenty-six miles back. We ought to be able to do it within a day and a night, and if old Hun Woe attends rightly to his coaling and his provisioning, all Corea cannot stop him. I think he is badly enough frightened not to omit any details that make for his safety."

"Very well, we'll stay right here till you return. I suppose that old Chinese tub will take some time worrying her way to Corea and back again, although I'll confess she seemed to come on like a prairie fire when she was heading for us. Now I guess everybody is just a little tired of life on shipboard. I've noticed that when a lot of people are cooped up together for a while things don't run on as smoothly as they might sometimes, so I'll hire a floor in the principal hotel here and live ashore until we see your Chinese steamer come into the harbour again. I suppose the captain will prefer to live on the yacht, but the rest of us will sample hotel life. I'm rather yearning for a change myself; besides I think my daughter would be safer ashore than on board here, for one can't tell, as you said, what these hoodlums may attempt; and as long as they're convinced she's on the yacht we're in constant danger of being run down, or torpedoed, or something. Now, you wouldn't mind telling my daughter what you've told me about the intentions of this here Prime Minister? She's rather fond of wandering around town alone, and I guess she'd better know that until this Chinese steamer sails away she is in some danger."

"I suggest that she shouldn't go sightseeing or shopping without an escort, Mr. Hemster."

"Well, a good deal will depend on what Gertie thinks herself, as perhaps you have found out while you've been with us."

He sent for his daughter, and I placed a third chair for the girl when she arrived. She listened with great interest to my narration of the events on board the Chinese steamer, and I added my warning that it was advisable for her not to desert the frequented parts of Nagasaki, and never to make any expedition through the town without one or more masculine persons to protect her. She tossed her head as I said this, and replied rather cuttingly:

"I guess I'm able to take care of myself."

I should have had sense enough to let it go at that, but I was much better aware of her peril then even her father was, for I knew Nagasaki like a well-thumbed book; so I said it was a regular labyrinth into whose mazes even a person intimately acquainted with the town might get lost, and as the Prime Minister had plenty of money at his command, he had the choice of all the outscourings of the nations here along the port, who would murder or kidnap without a qualm for a very small sum of ready cash.

"There is no use in saying anything more, Mr. Tremorne," put in

371

her father, definitely; "I'll see to it that my daughter does not go abroad unprotected."

"Well, Poppa," she cried, "I like the hotel idea first rate, and I'm going there right away; but I want a suite of rooms to myself. I'm not coming down to the public table, and I wish to have the Countess and my own maid with me and no one else."

"That's all right," said her father, "you can have what you like. I'll buy the whole hotel for you if you want it."

"No, I just wish a suite of rooms that will be my own; and I won't have any visitors that I don't invite specially."

"Won't you allow me to visit you, Gertie?" asked the old gentleman with a quizzical smile.

"No, I don't want you or any one else. I'm just tired of people, that's what I am. I intended to propose going to the hotel anyhow. I'm just sick of this yacht, and have a notion to go home in one of the regular steamers. I'm going right over to the hotel now and pick my own rooms."

"Just as you please," concurred her father. "Perhaps Mr. Tremorne will be good enough to escort you there."

"I have told you that I don't want Mr. Tremorne, or Mr. Hemster, or Mr. Anybody-else. If I must have an escort I'll take two of the sailors."

"That will be perfectly satisfactory. Take as many trunks as you want, and secure the best rooms in the hotel."

Shortly afterward Miss Hemster, with her maid and the Countess, left the yacht in the launch, the mountain of luggage following in another boat. The launch and the boat remained an unconscionably long time at the landing, until even Mr. Hemster became impatient, ordering the captain to signal their return. When, in response to this, they came back, the officer in charge of the launch told Mr. Hemster that his daughter had ordered them to remain until she sent them word whether or not she had secured rooms to her satisfaction at the hotel. Meanwhile she had given the officer a letter to her father, which he now handed to the old gentleman. He read it through two or three times with a puzzled expression on his face, then handed it to me, saying:

"What do you make of that?"

The letter ran as follows:

"DEAR POPPA:

"I have changed my mind about the hotel, and, not wanting a fuss, said nothing to you before I left. As I told you, I am tired to death of both the yacht and the sea, and I want to get to some place where I need look on neither of them. The Countess, who knows more about Japan than Mr. Tremorne thinks he knows, has been kind enough to offer me her country house for a week or two, which is situated eight or nine miles from Nagasaki. I want to see something of high life in Japan, and so may stay perhaps for two weeks; and if you are really as anxious about my kidnapping as you pretend, you may be quite sure I am safe where I am going,—much more so than if I had stayed at the hotel at Nagasaki. I don't believe there's any danger at all, but think Mr. Tremorne wants to impress you with a feeling of his great usefulness, and you may tell him I said so if you like. Perhaps I shall tire of the place where I am going in two or three days; it is more than likely. Anyhow, I want to get away from present company for a time at least. I will send a message to you when I am returning.

"Yours affectionately,

"Gertie."

This struck me as a most ungracious and heartless communication to a father who was devoting his life and fortune to her service. I glanced up at the old gentleman; but, although he had asked my opinion on this epistle, his face showed no perturbation regarding its contents. I suppose he was accustomed to the young woman's vagaries.

The letter seemed to me very disquieting. It had been written on board the yacht before she left, so perhaps the country house visit had been in her mind for some time; nevertheless there were two or three circumstances which seemed to me suspicious. It was an extraordinary thing that a Countess should take what was practically a servant's position if she possessed a country house. Then, again, it was no less extraordinary that this Japanese woman should be able to speak Corean, of which fact I had had auricular demonstration. Could it be possible that there was any connection between the engaging of this woman and the arrival of the Chinese steamer? Was the so-called Countess an emissary of the Corean Prime Minister? A moment's reflection caused me to dismiss this conjecture as impossible, because Miss Hemster had engaged the Countess on the day she arrived at Nagasaki, and, as our yacht was more speedy than any other vessel that might have come from Corea, all idea of collusion between the Corean man and the Japanese woman seemed far fetched. Should I then communicate my doubts to Mr. Hemster? He seemed quite at his ease about the matter, and I did not wish to disturb him unnecessarily. Yet he had handed me the letter, and he wished my opinion on it. He interrupted my meditations by repeating his question:

"Well, what do you make of it?"

"It seems to me the letter of one who is accustomed to think and act for herself, without any undue regard to the convenience of others."

"Yes, that's about the size of it."

"Has she ever done anything like this before?"

"Oh, bless you, often. I have known her to leave Chicago for New York and turn up at Omaha."

"Then you are not in any way alarmed by the receipt of this?"

"No, I see no reason for alarm; do you?"

"Who is this Countess that owns the country house?"

"I don't even know her name. Gertie went ashore soon after we came into the harbour and visited the American Consul, who sent out for this woman, and Gertie engaged her then and there."

374

"Isn't it a little remarkable that she speaks Corean?"

"Well, the American Consul said there wasn't many of them could; but Gertie, after being at Seoul, determined to learn the language, and that's why she took on the Countess."

"Oh, I see. She stipulated, then, for one who knew Corean?"

"Quite so; she told me before we left Chemulpo that she intended to learn the language."

"Well, Mr. Hemster, what you say relieves my mind a good deal. If she got the woman on the recommendation of the American Consul, everything is all right. The coming of the Prime Minister, and the fact that this Countess understands Corean, made me fear that there might be some collusion between the two."

"That is impossible," said Mr. Hemster calmly. "If the Corean Minister had come a day or two before the Countess was engaged, there might have been a possibility of a conspiracy between them; but convincing proof that such is not the case lies in the fact that the Prime Minister would not then have needed to run us down, which he certainly tried to do."

I had not thought of this, and it was quite convincing, taken in the light of the fact that Miss Hemster had frequently acted in this impulsive way before.

We resolved not to leave the yacht that night, even if we left it at all, now that Miss Hemster had taken herself into the interior. Whatever she thought, or whatever her preferences were, I imagine her father liked the yacht better than a hotel.

Hilda and I went on deck after dinner and remained there while the lights came out all over Nagasaki, forming a picture like fairyland or the superb setting of a gigantic opera. We were aroused by a cry from one of the sailors, and then a shout from the bridge.

"That Chinese beast is coming at us again!"

Sure enough the steamer had left her moorings, rounded inside toward the city, and now was making directly toward us without a light showing.

"Get into the boats at once," roared the captain.

I hailed Hemster, who was below, at the top of my voice, and he replied when I shouted: "Come up immediately and get into the small boat."

By the time he was on deck I had Hilda in one of the boats, and Mr. Hemster was beside her a moment later. Two sailors seized the oars and pushed off. The next instant there was a crash, and the huge black bulk of the Chinese steamer loomed over us, passing quickly away into the night. I thought I heard a woman scream somewhere, but could not be quite sure.

"Did you hear anything?" I asked Hemster.

"I heard an almighty crashing of timber. I wonder if they've sunk the yacht."

The captain's gruff voice hailed us.

"They've carried away the rudder," he said, "and shattered the stern, but not seriously. She will remain afloat, but will have to go into dry-dock to-morrow."

# CHAPTER XXIII

THE Chinese steamer, if indeed it were she, although we could not be sure in the darkness, had sent us to the hotel when we had made up our minds not to go. We in the boat hovered near the yacht long enough for the captain to make a hurried examination of the damage. The wreck certainly looked serious, for the overhang of the stern had been smashed into matchwood, while the derelict rudder hung in chains like an executed pirate of a couple of centuries agone. It was impossible at the moment to estimate with any degree of accuracy the extent of the disaster. The captain reported that she was not leaking, and therefore her owner need have no fear that she would sink during the night. The rudder had certainly been carried away, and probably one of the propellers was damaged. In any case the yacht would have to go into dry-dock; so, being satisfied on the score of immediate safety, Mr. Hemster gave orders to pull ashore, and thus we became guests of the Nagasaki Hotel.

Next morning the Chinese steamer was nowhere in sight, so it was reasonably certain she had been the cause of our misfortune. The yacht rode at its anchorage, apparently none the worse so far as could be seen from the town. Before noon the craft was in dock, and we learned to our relief that her propellers were untouched. She needed a new rudder, and the rest was mere carpenter work which would be speedily accomplished by the deft Japanese workmen. Mr. Hemster had his desk removed to a room in the hotel, and business went on as before, for there were still many details to be settled with Mr. John C. Cammerford before he proceeded toward San Francisco. I think we all enjoyed the enlarged freedom of residence on shore, and the old gentleman said that he quite understood his daughter's desire to get away from sight of sea or ship. It struck me as remarkable that he was not in the slightest degree alarmed for the safety of his daughter, nor did he doubt for a moment her assertion that she was going to stop at the country house of the Countess. On the other hand I was almost convinced she had been kidnapped, but did not venture to display my suspicions to her father, as there seemed no useful purpose to be served by arousing anxiety when my fears rested purely on conjecture. Of course I consulted confidentially with Hilda, but a curious transformation had taken place in our several beliefs. When she spoke of the probability of the girl's committing suicide or doing something desperate, I had pooh-poohed her theory. We had each convinced the other, and I had adopted her former view while she had adopted mine. She had heard no scream on the night of the disaster, and regarded it as a trick of my imagination.

But what made me more uneasy was the departure of the Prime Minister. His fears for himself and family were genuine enough, and he was not likely to abandon a quest merely because his first effort had failed. It meant death to him if he returned to Seoul without the girl, so, if he had not captured her, it seemed incredible that he should return the same night without a single effort to accomplish his mission. The second,—and, as far as he knew, successful,—essay to sink the yacht, must have been to prevent pursuit. He was probably well aware that the yacht was the fastest steamer in the harbour, and, if it were not disabled, would speedily overhaul him. He also knew that his officers and crew were no heroes, and that with half-a-dozen energetic Japanese in addition to our own crew we could capture his steamer on the high seas without the slightest effort being put forth to hinder us. He had now a clear run to Chemulpo, and, however resolute we were, there was no possibility of our overtaking him. I had offered him my assistance, which he had accepted in a provisional sort of way, yet here he had disappeared from the scene without leaving word for me, and apparently had returned to the land where his fate was certain if he was unsuccessful. Of course, he might have made for Yokohama or Shanghai, but I was convinced, after all, that he cared more for the safety of his family than for his own, and indeed, if he was thinking only of himself, he was as safe in Nagasaki as elsewhere. I could therefore come to no other conclusion than that the girl was aboard the Chinese steamer and was now a prisoner on her way to Seoul, but of this I could not convince Hilda Stretton, and Mr. Hemster evidently had no misgivings in the matter.

Obviously the first thing to do was to learn the antecedents of the so-called Japanese Countess, and with this intent I called at the American

Consulate. The official in charge received me with the gracious good-comradeship of his nation, and replied with the utmost frankness to my questions. He remembered Miss Hemster's visit of a few days before, and he assured me that the Countess was above suspicion. As for her knowledge of Corean, that was easily accounted for, because her late husband had been a Japanese official at Seoul a dozen years or so ago, and she had lived with him in that city. Corea, indeed, had been in a way the cause of the Countess's financial misfortunes. Her husband, some years before he died, had invested largely in Corean enterprises, all of which had failed, and so left his wife with scarcely anything to live upon except the country house, which was so remote from Nagasaki as to be unsalable for anything like the money he had expended upon it. Exactly where this country house was situated the United States Consul professed himself ignorant, but said he would endeavour to find out for me, and so genially asked me to take a drink with him and call a few days later.

This conversation did much to dissipate my doubts. Of course, without Mr. Hemster's permission I could not tell the Consul the full particulars of the case, or even make any reference to them. So far as that courteous official knew, I was merely making inquiries on behalf of Mr. Hemster about the woman engaged to be his daughter's companion, and about the country house which the girl had been invited to visit. The Consul assured me that everything was right and proper, and that Miss Hemster would get a glimpse of the inner life of the Japanese not usually unfolded to strangers, and thus my reason was convinced, although my instinct told me there was something unaccountable in all this. The scream I had heard simultaneously with the crashing of the collision might of course have been the shrill shriek of one of the Chinese sailors, but at the time it had sounded to me suspiciously like the terrified exclamation of a woman. Then, again, the action of the Prime Minister remained as unaccountable as ever, unless my former theory proved correct. However, I got the name of the Countess, which none of us who remained had known before, and I promised to return and learn the situation of the country house. My visit, on the whole, was rather reassuring; for, after all, there was little use in attaching too much importance to the actions of any Corean, even though he were Prime Minister of that country; so the problem began to appear to be a self-conjured one, and I gradually came to recognize that I had been troubling myself for nothing.

The week that followed was one of the most delightful in my existence. The captain was superintending the repairs on the yacht, and the intricacies of Mr. Hemster's business activity were such that I could not be of much assistance to him; so there was practically nothing to do but to make myself agreeable to that dear girl, Hilda, to whom I showed whatever beauties Nagasaki possessed, and surely no one knew the town better than I did. She took a vivid interest, not only in the place, but also in my own somewhat doleful experience there in former and less happy times, not yet remote, the recital of which experiences rendered the present all the more glorious by contrast.

On our tenth day ashore Hilda told me that the old gentleman was beginning to worry because he had heard nothing from his daughter, and Hilda herself expressed some uneasiness because of the long silence. This aroused all my old doubts, and I called a second time on the American Consul. He told me that the information I sought had been in hand several days. The villa was called "The House of the Million Blossoms," and it was situated nearly ten miles from Nagasaki. He produced a sketch map, drawn by himself, which he said would guide me to the place, so I resolved to visit it without saying a word to anyone.

I found the villa of the Blossoms without the least difficulty, and a most enchanting spot it appeared to be. Situated inland, at the bottom of a sheltered valley, through which ran a trickling stream, the place had evidently been one of importance in its day; but now the entrance lodge showed signs of dilapidation, and the plantation itself was so marvellously overgrown as to be almost a wilderness, with foliage too thick for me to see anything of the house itself. The custodian of the lodge received me with great urbanity but no less firmness. He confessed that the ladies were there, but added that he had strict orders to allow no one to enter or even to approach the house. I asked him to take my card to the stranger lady, and, although at first he demurred, I overcome his reluctance by an urbanity which I flatter myself was a stage imitation of his own, and, what was more to the purpose, I induced him to accept a present in the coinage of the realm. Nevertheless he securely barred the gate and left me outside, showing that his trust in my good faith was either very weak, or that his politeness was confined to the flowery language of his country. After a long absence he returned, and handed to me a folded sheet of note paper which I recognized as belonging to the stationery of the yacht. It bore these words in English, and in Miss Hemster's handwriting:

> "I wish to remain here in seclusion, and I consider it very impertinent of you to have sought me out. I am perfectly happy here, which I was not on board the yacht, and all I wish is to be left alone. When good and ready I will write to the yacht and to the Nagasaki Hotel. Until that time it is useless for you to intrude."

This was definite enough, and I turned away angry with myself for having played the busybody, not knowing enough to attend to my own affairs. I had intended to tell the young woman of the accident to the yacht, making that in some way the excuse for my visit; but in the face of such a message I forgot all about the information I desired to impart, and so returned in a huff to Nagasaki. This message set at rest all thoughts of kidnapping, although it left my honoured friend Hun Woe's precipitate departure as much a mystery as ever.

On my arrival at the hotel I showed the note to Hilda, who averred there could be no doubt about its genuineness, and she asked my permission to give it to Mr. Hemster to allay his rapidly arising anxiety, which mission it certainly performed as completely as it had snubbed me.

Next day the yacht was floated and appeared none the worse for the collision. The captain took her out to the anchorage, and so we waited several days to hear from the girl, but no word came. Finally her father wrote a letter to her, beseeching some indication of her plans, and this was sent by messenger to the House of the Million Blossoms. The old gentleman had become exceedingly tired of Nagasaki, and very evidently did not know what to do with himself. The messenger returned, but brought no answer. He said the man at the gate had taken in the letter, and brought out the verbal message that the lady would write when she was ready to do so. This was the reverse of satisfactory, and Mr. Hemster roamed about disconsolately like a lost spirit. Hilda said he told her that his daughter had never before remained in the same mind for two days together, and this prolonged country house visit caused him great uneasiness. He now became infused with the kidnapping idea, not fearing that she had been taken away to Corea, but believing that the Japanese were holding her prisoner, perhaps with the idea of a ransom later on. Finally Mr. Hemster determined to visit the House of the Million Blossoms himself, and he insisted on Hilda's accompanying us, which she did with some reluctance. Never did she believe that this was other than one of the girl's prolonged caprices to make us all anxious, hoping to laugh at us later on for being so.

At the gateway we were met by the same imperturbable guardian, who was as obdurate as ever. He would take in any message, he said, but would not permit us to enter even the grounds. Mr. Hemster sent a letter he had written at the hotel, and in due time the keeper came out with a signed note, somewhat similar to the one I had received. It said:

"DEAR FATHER:

"Do not worry about me; I am perfectly happy and wish to remain here a few days longer.

"Your affectionate daughter,

"G."

After reading this he passed it on to Hilda and me in silence. He got into his 'rickshaw without a word, and we entered ours. The men tottered along until we were out of sight of the lodge, and then Mr. Hemster called a halt. He sprang out, and, approaching me, said:

"Well, Tremorne, what do you make of it?"

The voice in which his question was put quivered with anguish, and, glancing at his face, I saw it drawn and haggard with an expression that betokened terror.

"Oh, there's nothing to make of it, Mr. Hemster, except that the young lady, for some reason unknown to me, desires to make you anxious and has succeeded."

"Tremorne," he said, unheeding this attempted consolation, "look at this note. It was not written to-day, but weeks ago. It was written on board the yacht, and so was the one you received, although I did not notice that at the time. This was written with a stub pen, the same that she used in sending me the first letter; but this pen she did not take away with her, nor the ink. My poor girl has been deluded into writing those letters by some one who had a subtle end to serve. I cannot fathom the mystery, but I am certain she is not in that house."

I sprang down from my 'rickshaw.

"I'll soon settle that point," I cried, "I will crush through the boundary hedge, and break in the door of the house. If there are any ladies within they will soon make an outcry, which will reveal their presence. You wait for me here."

To this he at once agreed, and with some difficulty I got into the thick plantation, through which I made my way until I came to the house, the first look at which convinced me it was empty. There is something of desolate loneliness about a deserted house which instantly strikes a beholder.

There was no need for me to break in, for one of the windows was open, and, tip-toeing up on the broad veranda, so that there would be no chance of the custodian hearing me, I entered a room through this window, and the whole silent house was at my disposal.

The interior would have struck a European unacquainted with Japan as being unfurnished, but I saw that it remained just as the Countess had left it. On a small table, standing about a foot from the floor, I saw a note similar to the one that had been handed to me when I first inquired at the gate, also three long slips of Japanese paper on which were written instructions in the Japanese language. I read them with amazement. The first said:

"This letter is to be given to a young man who calls, and who speaks Japanese and English."

On the next slip:

"This letter is to be given to an old man who speaks nothing but English."

The third slip bore:

"This is to be given to a young woman who speaks nothing but English."

There was also a minute description of Mr. Hemster, Miss Stretton, and myself, so that the man at the gate could make no mistake, which indeed he had not done. Hilda had not asked for a letter, therefore the remaining note had not been delivered.

Whoever concocted the plot had expected a search to be made for the House of the Million Blossoms, and of course knew that its situation could easily be found. I put all the documents into my pocket, and now went out by the public exit, greatly to the amazement of my urbane friend at the gate. I fear I may be accused of adopting Western methods, but the occasion seemed to me too serious for dilly-dallying. I pulled Mr. Hemster's revolver from my pocket and pointed it at the man's head.

"Now, you scoundrel," I said in his own tongue, "when did those women leave here? Answer me truly, or I shall take you prisoner to Nagasaki, where you will have to face the authorities."

I showed him the written instructions I had captured inside the house, and he saw at once that the game was up.

"Excellency!" said he, still politely enough, "I am but a poor man and a hireling. Many days ago a messenger brought me these instructions and three letters. No lady has been in this house for some years; the instructions were written by my mistress, the Countess, and I was compelled to follow them."

I saw that the man spoke the truth, and proceeded to cross-examine him on the motives which he imagined actuated this extraordinary complication; but he had told me all he knew, and was apparently as much in the dark regarding the motive as I was myself. I left him there, and hurried along the road over the hill to the spot where I had left Mr. Hemster and Hilda. Here I explained the conspiracy so far as I had discovered it, but the record of my investigation naturally did nothing to calm the fears of my employer, whose shrewdness had given a clue to the real situation at the House of the Million Blossoms. There was nothing to do but get back to Nagasaki as speedily as possible, and lay the case before the authorities. Hemster seemed suddenly to have become in truth an old man. We went directly to the hotel, and the clerk met us in the passage-way.

"Mr. Hemster," he said, "this telegram came for you about two hours ago."

The old gentleman tore open the envelope, read the dispatch, then crushed the paper in his hand.

"Just as I thought," he said. "She is in Seoul and has found some way of communicating with me. Poor little girl, poor little girl."

The father's voice broke momentarily, but he at once pulled himself together again.

"Tremorne, tell the captain to get the yacht under way. We will go on board immediately. We shall want an escort from Chemulpo to Seoul; can we depend on getting them at the port as we did before, or had we better bring them from Nagasaki?"

"I think, sir," said I, "that it would be well to take a dozen from here. They are men I can trust, and I shall have them aboard the yacht before steam is up."

"Very well," he said, decisively, "see to it."

I sent a messenger to the captain, then devoted all my energies to the selecting of my twelve men, taking care that they were properly armed and provided with rations. I sent them aboard one by one or two by two in sampans, so that too much attention might not be attracted toward our expedition.

This task accomplished, I hurried back to the hotel, and found Mr.

Hemster and Hilda waiting for me. Cammerford was there also, talking in a low voice very earnestly with the old gentleman, who stood with his eyes bent on the ground, making no reply to the other's expostulations beyond shaking his head now and then. Hilda and I went on ahead to the landing, the two men following us. To my surprise Cammerford stepped into the launch and continued talking to the silent man beside him. When we reached the yacht Mr. Hemster without a word mounted the steps to the deck. Hilda followed, and Cammerford stood in the launch, a puzzled expression on his face. After a momentary hesitation he pushed past me, and ran up the steps. I also went on deck, and by the time I reached there my chief was already in his wicker chair with his feet on the rail, and a fresh unlit cigar in his mouth. Cammerford went jauntily up to him and said with a laugh that seemed somewhat forced:

"Well, Mr. Hemster, I propose to continue this discussion to Corea."

"Just as you please," replied the old man nonchalantly. "I think we can make you very comfortable on board."

# CHAPTER XXIV

**Now** it was full speed ahead and a direct line for Corea. Once in the open sea, we struck straight through the Archipelago and took our chances of running down an island, as the captain had said. There was no dawdling this time, for the engines were run to the top of their power. As was the case with our former voyages in these waters, the weather was perfect and the sea smooth.

Our dinner that night was on the whole a silent festival. The jovial captain did not come down, and Mr. Hemster sat moodily at the head of the table, absorbed in thought and doubtless tortured with anxiety. Cammerford was the only member of the party who endeavoured to make a show of cheerful demeanour. His manner with women was one of deferential urbanity, and, as he never ventured to joke with them, he was justly popular with the sex. I quite envied him his power of pleasing, which was so spontaneous that it seemed a natural and not an acquired gift. The man appeared to possess an almost hypnotic power over his fellow-creatures, and although I believed him to be one of the most untrustworthy rascals alive, yet I felt this belief crumbling away under the magnetic charm of his conversation.

The old gentleman at the head of the table was evidently immune so far as Cammerford's fascination was concerned. I surmised that there had come a hitch in the negotiations between them. There was no trace of uneasiness in Cammerford's attitude, and his voice was as mildly confident as ever. No one would guess that he was practically a self-invited guest at this board. Our host was completely taciturn, but the unbidden guest never risked a snub by addressing a direct question to him, although he airily included Mr. Hemster with the rest of us within the area of his polite discourse. Hilda was scarcely more responsive than Mr. Hemster and seemed troubled because he was troubled, and as I possessed an instinctive dislike for Cammerford it will be seen that he had a most difficult rôle to play, which he enacted with a success that would have done credit to Sir Henry Irving himself. If there was indeed, as I suspected, a conflict between the elder man and the younger, I found myself wondering which would win, but such a quiet atmosphere of confidence enwrapped the latter that I began to fear Mr. Hemster had met his match, in spite of the fact that he held all the trump cards. Cammerford represented the new school of financiers, who juggled with billions as a former generation had played with millions. My sympathies were entirely with Mr. Hemster, but if I had been a sporting man my bet would have been laid on Cammerford. I mention this as an instance of the hypnotic power I have referred to. I knew that Cammerford could not form his gigantic trust and leave Mr. Hemster out; therefore, as I say, the elder man held the trumps. Nevertheless the bearing of Cammerford indicated such reserved assurance that I felt certain he would ultimately bend the old man to his will, and I watched for the result of this opposition of forces with the eagerness with which one awaits the climax of an exciting play on the stage.

After dinner Hilda came on deck for half an hour or thereabouts, and we walked up and down together. The excitement of the day and the uncertainty that lay ahead of us had told heavily on the poor girl, and I had not the heart to persuade her to remain longer on deck. She was rather depressed and admittedly weary of the life we were leading. So I took cowardly advantage of this and proposed we should get married at the American Consulate as soon as the yacht returned to Nagasaki. Then, I said, we could make our way to Yokohama and take passage on a regular liner for San Francisco.

To this proposal she made no reply, but walked demurely by my side with downcast eyes.

"Think of the glories of Chicago at this moment!" I cried enthusiastically, wishing to appeal to the home feeling. "Dinner finished; the roar of the traffic in the streets; the brilliancy of the electric light; the theatres open, and the gay crowds entering therein. Let us make for Chicago."

She looked up at me with a wan little smile, and laughed quietly.

"You do need a guardian, as Papa Hemster says. I suppose it is about noon in Chicago at the present moment, and I don't see why the theatres should be open at that hour. It is the roar of the wheat pit, and not of the traffic you are hearing. I fear your visit to Chicago was of the briefest, for your picture is not very convincing. Still, I confess I wish I were there now, if you were with me." Then with a slight sigh she added, "I'll accept that guardianship at Nagasaki. Good-night, my dear," and with that she whisked away and disappeared before I was aware of her meditated escape.

I lit a fresh cigar and continued my promenade alone. As I walked aft I caught snatches of the musical monotone of Cammerford's voice. Ever since dinner time he had been in earnest conversation with Mr. Hemster, who sat in his usual chair at the stern of the boat. So far as I am aware, Mr. Hemster was leaving the burden of the talk to the younger man, who, from the tone of his voice, seemed in deadly earnest. At last Mr. Hemster got up and threw his cigar overboard. I heard him say:

"I told you, Mr. Cammerford, that I would not discuss this matter further until I reached Nagasaki. The papers are all in my desk under lock and key in the room at the hotel, and that room is closed and sealed. I'll say no more about this scheme until I am back there."

"And when you are back there, Mr. Hemster, what action are you going to take?"

"Whatever action seems to be best for my own interests, Mr. Cammerford."

"Well, from most men that reply would be very unsatisfactory. However, I am glad to say I trust you completely, Mr. Hemster, and I know you will do the square thing in the end."

"I'm glad you think so," said the old man curtly, as he went down the stairway. Cammerford stood there for a few moments, then strode forward and joined me.

"May I beg a light of you?" he asked, as if he were conferring a favour.

I don't care to light one cigar from another, so I struck a match and held it while he took advantage of the flame.

"Thanks. Now, Tremorne, I want to talk with you as to a friend. We

389

were friends once, you know."

"True; the kind of friend the celebrated phrase refers to, perhaps."

"What phrase?"

"'God protect me from my friends,' or words to that effect."

He laughed most genially.

"That's one on me," he said. "However, I look on our score as being wiped out. Can't you let bygones be bygones?"

"Oh, yes."

"You see you are in a way responsible. I have turned over the money to you. Granted I was forced to do so. I claim no merit in the matter, but I do say a bargain is a bargain. I showed you the old man's letter to me, in which he said if I did thus and so by you, he would join me in the big beef combine. You remember that, don't you?"

"Naturally, I shouldn't soon forget it, or forget the generosity of Mr. Hemster in writing it."

"Oh, generosity is cheap when you are doing it at somebody else's expense. Still, I don't complain of that at all. What I say is this: I've kept my part of the contract strictly and honestly, but now the old man is trying to euchre me."

"I remember also, Mr. Cammerford, that you said Mr. Hemster was a rogue or dishonest, or something of like effect."

"Well, so he is."

"In that case, why do you object to being euchred by him?"

"Well, you see, I had his promise in writing, and I thought I was safe."

"You have it in writing still, I presume. If he does not live up to what he has written, you probably have your recourse at law, for they say there is no wrong without a remedy."

390

"Oh, that's all talking through your hat. It isn't a lawsuit I'm after, but the co-operation of Mr. Hemster. What chance would I have against a man of his wealth?"

"I'm sure I don't know. What is it you wish from me? Advice?"

"I wanted to explain the situation that has arisen, and I wish to know if you have anything to suggest that will lead the old man to do the square thing?"

"I have no suggestion to make, Mr. Cammerford."

"Supposing he does not keep his promise, don't you think it would be fair that the money I expended on the strength of it should be returned to me?"

"It does seem reasonable, I admit."

"I am glad to hear you say so, and to tell the truth, Mr. Tremorne, it is just the action I should expect of you."

"What action?"

"The returning of the money, of course."

"Bless my soul, you don't suppose I'm going to return a penny of it, do you?"

"Ah, your honesty is theory then, not practice."

"My dear sir, my honesty is both theory and practice. The money is mine. I made you no promises regarding it. In fact, I refused to make any promise when you offered me half the amount. If I had made any engagements I should have kept them."

"I see. I take it then you do not regard yourself as bound by any promises the old man made on your behalf?"

"Certainly not. I knew nothing of the matter until you showed me his letter."

"Your position is perfectly sound, Mr. Tremorne, and I unreservedly withdraw the imputation I put upon your honesty a moment since. But the truth is that this amount represents a very serious loss to me. It was a sprat thrown out to catch a whale, or, rather, a whale thrown out to catch a shoal of whales. But if I lose the whale and do not catch my shoal, then I have done a very bad piece of business by coming East. Through this proposed combine I expected to make several millions. Now, if you will join in with me, and put your half-million into the pool, I'll guarantee that before a month you have doubled it."

"You gave me a chance like that once before, Mr. Cammerford."

The man laughed heartily as if I had perpetrated a very amusing joke.

"Oh, yes, but that was years ago. We have both learned a good deal since."

"I certainly have, Mr. Cammerford. I have learned so much that I will not part with a penny of the money; not a red cent of it, as we say out West. That sum is going to be safely salted down, and it's not going to be salted in a corned-beef tub either. I don't mind telling you that I intend to get married upon it at the American Consulate at Nagasaki before a week is past."

"Really? Allow me to congratulate you, my boy. I surmised that was the way the land lay, and I quite envy you your charming young lady."

"Thanks!"

"But you see, Mr. Tremorne, that makes your money doubly safe. I noticed that Mr. Hemster is as fond of Miss Stretton as he is of his own daughter, and if you give me the half million, he'll see to it that you make a hundred per cent on it."

"I don't at all agree with you, Mr. Cammerford. To speak with brutal frankness, if I trusted you with the money which you once succeeded in detaching from me,—if I trusted you with it again,—he would merely look upon me as a hopeless fool, and I must say I think he would be right."

John C. Cammerford was a man whom you couldn't insult: it was not business to take offence, so he took none, but merely laughed again in his free-hearted way.

"The old man thinks I don't see what his game is, but I do. He is playing for time. He expects to hold me out here in the East, dangling this bait before me, until it is too late for me to do anything with my options. Now, he is going to get left at that game. I have more cards up my sleeve than he imagines, but I don't want to have any trouble with him: I want to deal with him in a friendly manner for our mutual benefit. I'll play fair if he plays fair. It isn't too much to ask a man to keep his word, is it!"

"No, the demand doesn't appear excessive."

"Very good. Now, I wish you would have a quiet talk with him. I can see that he reposes great confidence in you. You have admitted that my request is an honest one, so I hope you won't mind just presenting my side of the case to him."

"It is none of my business, Mr. Cammerford. I could not venture to take such a liberty with Mr. Hemster."

"But you admit the old man isn't playing fair?"

"I admit nothing of the sort: I don't know his side of the story at all. He may have reasons for declining to deal with you, which seem to him conclusive."

"Granted. But nevertheless, don't you think he should return the money given on the strength of his promise?"

"Really I would rather not discuss the matter any further, Mr. Cammerford, if you don't mind. I overheard you telling him at the head of the companion-way that you trusted him completely. Very well, then, why not continue to do so?"

Cammerford gave a short laugh that had little of mirth in it: his politeness was evidently becoming worn threadbare, and I imagine he was inwardly cursing my obstinacy. There was silence between us for several minutes, then he said sharply:

"Is this yarn about the kidnapping of his daughter all guff?"

"Who told you about it?" I asked.

"Oh, he did: gave that as the reason he didn't wish to talk business."

"The story is true, and I think the reason is valid. If you take my advice, you will not talk business with him in the face of his prohibition until his mind is at rest regarding his daughter."

"Well, I guess I'll take your advice; it seems to be the only thing I'm going to get out of you. I thought the daughter story was only a yarn to bluff me from coming aboard the yacht."

"It wasn't, and furthermore, I don't think you showed your usual perspicacity in not accepting Mr. Hemster's intimation that he didn't want to be bothered at this particular time."

"Oh, well, as to that," said Cammerford, confidently, "the old man has been making a monkey of me for some weeks now, and the whole matter might have been settled in as many hours if he had cared to do so. He isn't going to shake me off so easily as he thinks.

I'll stick to him till he keeps his promise, and don't you forget it."

"All right, I'll endeavour to keep it in mind."

"You won't be persuaded to try and lure him on to the straight and narrow path of honesty, Mr. Tremorne?"

"No, I'm not sure that he's off it. I have always found him treading that path."

"I see. Well, good-night. When do we reach that outlandish place,— whatever its name is?"

"We ought to arrive at Chemulpo some time to-morrow night."

"Chemulpo, is it? Well, I wish it was Chicago. So long."

"Good-night," I responded, and with that he left the world to darkness and to me.

# CHAPTER XXV

WE came to anchor a little after ten the next night. Mr. Hemster was naturally very impatient, and wished to proceed at once to the capital, but the customs authorities refused to let us land until daylight. Cammerford talked very valiantly of forcing our way ashore and going to Seoul in the darkness in spite of all opposition, and indeed the old gentleman was rather in favour of such a course; but I pointed out that our mission might be one of great delicacy, and that it was as well not to use force unless we were compelled to do so.

"Even in New York," said I, "we should not be allowed to proceed up the harbour after sunset, no matter how anxious we might be to land."

This was not thought to be a parallel case, but the old gentleman suggested that, as he wished no undue publicity, it would be better to wait until daylight and make our landing with as little ostentation as possible. I tried bribery, but for once it was ineffective, and in spite of the fact that I incurred the contempt of the energetic Cammerford, I counselled less hurry and more speed, though there was nothing to do but turn in and get a night's sleep in preparation for the toilsome journey in the morning.

I was on deck at daylight and found my Japs had all disappeared except their leader. He explained to me that he thought it best to get them ashore during the night unobtrusively in sampans. They would be waiting for us, he said, two or three miles beyond the port on the Seoul road. Now our Excellencies might disembark, he added, without attracting any attention. I complimented the little man on his forethought, and, sure enough, we found our company just where he said we would.

The next surprise was that Cammerford also had disappeared. I went down to his stateroom, but found his bed had not been slept in. The Japs had seen nothing of him, neither had any of the crew, so our unbidden guest had departed as he came.

Hilda was evidently most reluctant to take the journey. She told me she had seen enough of Seoul to last her a lifetime, but as she found that Mr. Hemster was most anxious for her to accompany us, she did what she always had done, and sacrificed her own inclinations in deference to the wishes of others.

We had got nearly half way to Seoul when I saw with alarm a large party, apparently of Corean soldiers, marching westward. They were easily ten to one as compared with our escort, yet I had not the slightest doubt our Japs would put them all to flight if they attempted to bar our way. Taking two of the Japs with me, I galloped on ahead to learn the intentions of the cavalcade in front. They paused in their march on seeing us coming up, and their leader galloped forward to meet me. To my surprise I saw it was the Prime Minister himself.

"Well, you old scoundrel," I cried, "your head is still on your shoulders unfortunately. What's the meaning of this movement of troops. Do you think you're going to stop us?"

"Oh, no, Excellency, no. I have come to greet you, and offer you the profound regard of the Emperor himself."

"Now, just try to speak the truth for once; it won't hurt you. You know very well that you had no word of our coming."

"Pardon, most Gracious Excellency, but your white ambassador arrived as soon as the gates were open this morning."

"Our white ambassador! Oh, that's Cammerford, very likely. So he has reached the capital, has he?"

"Yes, Excellency, and has received the honour due."

"That ought to be a gorgeous reception. And did he send you to meet us?"

"No, Excellency, it was the white Princess."

"Ah, you villain, you did kidnap her after all. Now if any harm has come to her, off goes your head, and down goes your pasteboard city."

"Ah, Excellency," said the Prime Minister with a wail of woe, "it was indeed depths of wickedness, but what was I to do? If I did not bring her to Seoul, not only was my head lost, but the heads of all my kin; and now, alas, the Emperor says that if she goes not willingly away he will yet execute me, and all my family as well. Excellency, it was an unlucky day

when the white Princess came to the Palace. The Emperor is in fear of his life, and terror reigns in every corner. Yet she would not go until the King, her father, brought his warship to Chemulpo, and she demanded to be escorted by the whole court with the honours of an Empress from the capital to the sea. She was going to make the Emperor himself come, but he bowed his forehead in the dust, a thing unknown these ten thousand years in Corea, and so she laughed at him and allowed him to remain in the Palace. She has made a mock of his Majesty and his ancestors."

"Serves him jolly well right," said I, beginning to get an inkling of how the case stood. "Her ancestors fought for liberty, and it is not likely she is going to be deprived of hers by any tan-bark monarch who foolishly undertakes the job. Is the lady still at the Palace, Hun Woe?"

"No, Excellency, she is on her way hither, escorted by the Court, and riding proudly with her white ambassador. Indeed," he continued, looking over his shoulder, "I can see them now, coming over the brow of that hill. She was so anxious to meet her father that she would not await your coming."

"All right, Hun Woe, you line up your troops on each side of the road, and see that they bow low when the Princess passes. I shall return and acquaint the King, her father, with the state of the poll."

So saying I wheeled my horse, galloped back, and informed the old gentleman that everything was all right. He heaved a deep sigh of relief, and I fancied his eyes twinkled somewhat as I related what particulars I had gathered of the reign of terror in Seoul since his daughter's enforced arrival.

By the time I had finished my recital the cavalcade to the rear had passed between the lines of prostrate soldiers. The old gentleman moved forward to meet his daughter, and she came galloping on her pony and greeted him with an affectionate abandon that was delightful to see, although when she flung her arms round his neck she nearly unhorsed him. Her reception of the rest of us was like that of a school-girl out on a lark. She seemed to regard her abduction as the greatest fun that ever was, and was bubbling with laughter and glee. She kissed the sedate Hilda as if she were an only sister, reproaching herself that even for a moment she had preferred that little beast of a Countess, as she called her, to so noble a treasure as Miss Stretton. To me she was as gracious as if I were her dearest friend.

"And now, Poppa," she cried, "shall I make this circus come with us to Chemulpo? I can do what I please with them; they belong to me."

"I don't think we want that crowd tagging after us, Gertie," said her father without enthusiasm.

"Then, Mr. Tremorne," she said, "will you order them home again, and tell 'em to be good for ever after. And oh! I want you to ask the Prime Minister if I didn't make that old Emperor kow-tow to me."

"He has already admitted that you did, Miss Hemster."

"Then that's all right: I thought they'd try to deny it."

I bade an affectionate farewell to Hun Woe, who was as glad to be quit of me as I was to be rid of him, and we have never seen each other since.

I don't remember ever taking part in a jollier excursion than that which now set forth towards Chemulpo, which place we reached before sunset.

Miss Hemster related her adventures with a gusto and enjoyment that I never saw equalled. Even her father smiled now and then at the exuberant humour of her declamation. It seemed that the Countess was in the pay of the Corean Government, probably as a spy. The Prime Minister had telegraphed her to win the confidence of Miss Hemster if she could, and so the Countess had made application to the American Consul and succeeded even beyond her fondest hopes. There had been no intention of going to the House of the Million Blossoms, but she had proposed instead to Miss Hemster a round of visits among the nobility of Japan, or at least whatever section of them lived near Nagasaki. As this round was to take some time, and as the Countess proclaimed that it must be done in strict secrecy, she outlined the writing of the different letters which her caretaker at the villa would hand to whoever called, if an investigation was made, as the wily Countess thought was highly probable, and this scheme proved peculiarly attractive to Miss Hemster and was accordingly carried out, and the young lady laughed till tears came into her eyes when I told her how I had been deceived by the receipt of my letter.

After landing from the yacht the Countess took Miss Hemster and her maid to a tea house situated on the shore of the bay, and from the moment they drank tea there, Miss Hemster and her maid remembered nothing more until they found themselves on board the Chinese steamer.

"Did you know about the attempted sinking of the yacht?" I asked.

"I wasn't sure," she said. "I was in a sort of daze: I seemed to have awakened when they began to take up the anchor, but I was stupid and headachy. Then there came a crash, and I screamed fit to kill, but those Chinese brutes put us into the cabin, and after that of course there was no escape. We did not land at Chemulpo, but somewhere along the coast. It was a fearful ride into Seoul, but after that I had my revenge; I made the old Emperor and his Court stand around, I tell you, for I had a revolver and plenty of cartridges in my trunk, and once I got them the situation belonged to me."

"And where are your trunks, Gertie?" asked her practical father.

"Oh, they're stored in Chemulpo. The Emperor wanted me to leave, but I wouldn't until you came and I was provided with a proper escort. He wanted me to go back on the same old Chinese tub, but I told him I'd a steamer of my own coming."

We got the trunks and set sail for Nagasaki once more. The voyage was a dream of delight. Never did I see Miss Gertrude Hemster, or any one else for that matter, so admirably charming and considerate of everyone around her. Mr. Cammerford proved a most devoted cavalier, and this gave Hilda and me opportunity for converse which we did not neglect. Gertrude Hemster cheered her father's heart by telling him that she was tired of king-hunting and wanted to get back to Chicago. When we arrived at Nagasaki I made arrangements for our marriage at the American Consulate. Miss Hemster was most fascinatingly sweet to Hilda when she heard the news. We all went together to the consulate, Cammerford asking permission to join our party. When we arrived, Cammerford, who seemed to be taking a great deal upon himself, said politely to the Consul:

"I should think a real American wedding takes precedence over an international affair, but at any rate I bespoke your services first."

The Consul smiled and said such was indeed the case; then, to the amazement of Hilda and myself, Gertrude, with a laugh, took the outstretched hand of John C. Cammerford and stood before the official, who married them according to the laws of the land to which they belonged.

"What do you think of this combine, Mr. Hemster?" said Cammerford with his most engaging smile, holding out his hand to his newly made father-in-law.

The old man took it and said quietly:

"Whoever makes Gertie happy makes me content."

Next came the turn of Hilda and myself.

THE END

# OVER THE BORDER

TO

FREDERICK A. STOKES

WITH WHOM MY LITERARY LIFE HAS BEEN PLEASANTLY
ASSOCIATED

SINCE I BEGAN TO WRITE BOOKS.

# BOOK I.—THE GIRL.

## CHAPTER I.—ASSERTION.

The end of October had been more than usually fine, and now the beginning of November was following the good example set by its predecessor. In the Home Park, the only part of the extensive grounds surrounding Hampton Court Palace that was well wooded, the leaves had not entirely left the branches, and the turf beneath was green and firm, as yet unsodden by autumnal rain.

Along one of the forest aisles there walked a distinguished party, proceeding slowly, for the pace was set by a disease-stricken man whose progress was of painful deliberation. He was tall and thin; his body was prematurely bent, though accustomed to be straight enough, if one might judge by the masterful brow, now pallid with illness, or by the glance of the piercing eye untamed even by deadly malady. That he was not long for this earth, if Nature had her way, a scrutinizer of that handsome, powerful face might have guessed; yet he was singled out for destruction even before his short allotted time, for at that moment his enemies, hedged in secrecy behind locked doors, were anxiously planning his ruin. They were wise in their privacy, for, had a whisper of their intentions gone abroad, the Earl of Strafford would have struck first and struck hard, as, indeed, he intended to do in any case.

Thomas Wentworth, Earl of Strafford, was accompanied by an imposing train. On either side of him, accommodating their slow steps to his, were some of the highest in the land, who waited on his words and accorded him a deference more obsequious than that with which they might have distinguished the King himself; for all knew that this shattered frame was more to be dreaded than the most stalwart personage who that day trod English soil.

Behind this noble circle followed a numerous band of attendants, alert for beck or call, each having place according to his degree. A huntsman was surrounded by dogs kept in thrall by fear of the whip. Falconers with hooded hawks attested a favorite sport of the Earl, who loved to have the birds near him even though he made no trial of their flight. And here he walked the grounds of the King as if he owned them; as though he were permanent master instead of transient guest. Here he rested for the moment, hoping to recover some remnant of health by the placid Thames, after his troublous journey from Ireland, which turbulent country lay numb under his strong hand, soon to be vocal enough when the hounds were upon him. No echo of London's clamour came to this green paradise. He knew the mob was crying out against him, as in truth the whole country cried; but he heeded not the howl, despising his opponents. Better for him had he been more wary or more conciliatory.

Among those now in his company was young De Courcy, one of the numerous band of Frenchmen smilingly received at Court because the consort of Charles had a predilection for her countrymen,—a preference unshared by any save her husband. The French contingent thought little of the scowls of the English so long as those in authority smiled on them and the smile brought profit. They were regarded as titled mercenaries; spies probably, anxious to feather their own nests at the expense of the Treasury; possibly the propagating agents of a Church of which England had a deep distrust; certainly possessing an overweening influence at Court, dividing still further the unfortunate King from his suspicious people. It might have been imagined that so thoroughly English, so strenuous a man as Strafford, the last to be deluded by suave manners or flattery, although he had an insatiable appetite for cringing deference, yet uninfluenced by it (as witness his crushing of Lord Montmorris in Ireland), would have shown scant friendship for frivolous French nobles; but it was a fact that he bore from young De Courcy a familiarity of address that he would have suffered from none other in the kingdom. Courtiers find a ready reason for every action, and they attributed Strafford's forbearance to the influence De Courcy possessed with the Queen, for his lordship was well aware that his sovereign lady showed small liking for the King's most powerful minister. Strafford was too keen a politician not to make every endeavour to placate an enemy who at all hours had access to the private ear of his master, on whose breath depended his own elevation. Therefore it may well be that he thought it worth while to conciliate one of the haughty lady's favourites.

The conversation under the trees was lightly frivolous, despite the seriousness of the time. Strafford was not one to wear his heart on his sleeve, and if he was troubled that the King insisted on his presence in London, refusing to him permission to return to Ireland, where he was safe,—the wielder of the upper hand,—his manner or expression gave no hint of his anxiety. A cynical smile curved his bloodless lips as he listened to the chatter of De Courcy, not noticing the silence of the others, who disdained a conversational contest with the voluble Frenchman.

"I give your lordship my assurance," insisted the young man, "that his Majesty was much perturbed by the incident. All Scots are superstitious, and the King has Scottish blood in his veins."

"As to superstition, I have never learned," said Strafford, speaking slowly, "that the French are entirely free from some touch of it."

"That's as may be," continued De Courcy airily, "but her Majesty, who is French, advised the King to think nothing more of the encounter, so she regards but lightly any predictions of doom from an old gipsy hag."

"There were no predictions of doom, and no gipsy hag. The case was of the simplest, now exaggerated by Court gossip," amended the Earl.

"My lord, I have it almost direct from the King himself."

"Your 'almost' will account for anything. It was merely a piece of youthful impertinence which should have been punished by one of the park rangers, had any been present. The King had honoured me with his company in the park. We were alone together, discussing problems of State, when there suddenly sprang out before us a smiling, froward girl, who cried, 'Merry gentlemen, I will predict your fortunes if in return you tell me where I may find the Earl of Strafford.' His Majesty looked at me, and the hussy, quick to take a hint, evidently saw that I was the person sought. In any case the King's remark must have confirmed her suspicion. 'Your predictions are like to prove of small value,' said his Majesty, 'if you ask such a question. Here you have two men before you. Choose the greater.' Whereupon the wench seized my hand before I was aware, and the King laughed."

"It was an uncourtierlike proceeding," said De Courcy. "That young woman will not advance in a world which depends on the smile of the mighty for promotion."

"The choice shows her a true prophet," muttered one of the nobles; but Strafford, paying no heed, went on with his account.

"The words which followed were more diplomatic than the action. 'You are the King's best friend,' she said, examining the palm she had taken. Then his Majesty cried, 'What do you read in my hand?' 'You are the King's worst enemy,' said the pert hussy. This nonplussed Charles for the moment, who replied at last, 'I think you are more successful with my comrade. Read all you find in his palm, I beg of you.' Then the gipsy, if such she was, went glibly on. 'Your fate and that of the King are interwoven. If you overcome your enemies, the King will overcome his. If you fall, the King falls. Your doom will be the King's doom; your safety the King's safety. At the age you shall die, at that age will the King die, and from the same cause.' His Majesty laughed, somewhat uneasily I thought, but said jauntily, 'I have the advantage of you, Strafford, for you may die at any moment, but I am given seven years to live, being that space younger than you.' I was annoyed at the familiarity of the creature, and bade her take herself off, which she did after making vain appeal for some private conversation with me."

"Was she fair to look upon? In that case I do not wonder at your indignation. To learn that a handsome and young woman was searching for you in the lonely forest, to meet her at last, but in company of a King so rigid in his morals as Charles, was indeed a disappointment. You had been more favoured with any other monarch of Europe beside you. Had you no chance of getting one private word with her; of setting time and place for a more secluded conference?"

A slight frown ruffled the broad, smooth brow of the statesman, but it vanished on the instant, and he shrugged his shoulders nonchalantly.

"I but gave you a brief account of a very simple incident that you were inclined to make much of. You have now the truth, and so may dress the retailing of it in the guise that best pleases you. I make no doubt 'twill be fanciful enough when next I hear it."

"Were it any other monarch than Charles, I should say he was annoyed to find his minister so favoured; but in his mind the prediction will take more space than thought of the prophet, be she never so young or so fair. But all good wishes go toward you, my lord. It is my prayer that when next you meet the woodland sylph you are alone in the forest."

As if to show how little profit follows the prayer of a French exquisite, there stepped out from behind a thick tree in front of them the person of whom they spoke. She was tall and slender, with dancing eyes of midnight blackness, which well matched the dark, glossy ringlets flowing in profusion over her shapely shoulders. Her costume betokened the country rather than the Court, yet its lack of fashionable cut or texture was not noticed in a company of men, and the almost universal gaze of admiration that rested on her showed that in the eyes of the majority she was well and tastefully garbed.

"My lord of Strafford," she said in a sweet clear voice, "I crave a word with you in private."

De Courcy laughed provokingly; the others remained silent, but turned their regard from the interloper to the Earl, whose frown of annoyance did not disappear as it had done before. Strafford spoke no word, but his underlings were quick to interpret and act upon his black look. Two attendants silently took places beside the girl, ready to seize her did his lordship give a sign. The huntsmen let loose the dogs that had been snarling at the newcomer. They made a dash at her, while she sprang nimbly to the tree that had concealed her, having first whisked from the scabbard of an astonished attendant the light sword with which he was supposed to guard himself or his master.

"Call off your hounds, you villain!" she cried in a voice that had the true ring of command in it; indeed, to many there the order had a touch of the

411

Earl's own tones in anger. "I ask not for my own escape from scath, but for theirs. I'd rather transfix a man than hurt a dog. You scoundrel, you shall feel the sting of this point if you do not instantly obey."

The thin shining blade darted here and there like an adder's tongue, and as painfully. Yelp after yelp showed its potency, and the dogs, quick to learn that they were overmatched, abated their fury and contented themselves with noisy outcry at a safe distance from the semicircle of danger, jumping sideways and backward, barking valorously, but keeping well clear of the rapier. At a glance from the Earl the huntsman whipped them back into their former places.

"Yes, lash them, you whelp, but it's over your own shoulders the cord should go, had I the ordering, thou meanest of the pack."

"Madam," said the Earl of Strafford sternly, "I would have you know that none give orders here but me."

"In that you are mistaken, my lord. You have just heard me give them, and furthermore have seen them obeyed. But aside from the ordering of either you or me, I understand this to be the King's park." Again De Courcy laughed.

"She hit you there, my lord," he had the temerity to say.

Strafford paid no attention to his gibe, but gazed darkly at the fearless intruder.

"What do you want?" he asked.

"I have told you, my lord. I wish a word in your private ear."

"Speak out what you have to say."

"'T is to be heard by none but the Earl of Strafford; no, not even by the King himself; for, you should know, were it other fashion, I would have spoken when last I encountered you."

"I have no secrets from the King."

"Nor need this be one. 'T is yours to proclaim to the world at your

412

pleasure. But first it is for your ear alone. Send that painted popinjay to the rear with the dogs. The others are gentlemen and will retire of their own accord when they learn a lady wishes to speak privily with you."

It was now the turn of the English nobles to laugh, which they did merrily enough, but De Courcy seemed less pleased with the rude suggestion. He fumbled at his sword-hilt, and muttered angrily that if any present wished to make the girl's reference his own, a meeting could be speedily arranged to discuss the question. Strafford, however, had no mind for any by-play. His glance quelled the rising difference; then he said harshly to the young woman,—"What do you here in the King's park, lacking permission, as I suspect?"

"Indeed," cried the girl with a toss of the head, "they say, where I come from, that everything seemingly possessed by the King belongs actually to the people, and being one of the people I come to my own domain asking permission of none."

"You are young to speak treason."

"'T is no treason of mine. I but repeat what others say."

"Still, how came you here?"

"Easily. Over the wall. I was refused access to you by any other means, so I took the method that suggested itself."

"You were feigning yesterday to be a gipsy. Who are you?"

"That is what I wish to tell your lordship when I get the opportunity. As for yesterday, I feigned nothing. I but retold what an old gipsy once said to me regarding the King and Lord Strafford. I wished to engage your attention, but, like the underlings of this palace, you turned me away."

"Your persistence shall be rewarded, but with this proviso. If the news you make so much of is not worth the telling, then shall you expiate your impudence in prison. If you fear to accept the risk, you had better begone while there is yet time, and let us see no more of you."

"I accept the hazard freely, my lord."

The Earl of Strafford said no more, but turned to his followers, who at once withdrew to the background, except De Courcy, who, not having forgiven the insult placed upon him, and unconscious that his reluctance to quit the spot was giving point to the girl's invective, cried angrily,—"Beware, Lord Strafford. There may be more in this than appears on the surface. She has shown herself expert with a stolen blade. That blade is still in her hand."

The Earl smiled coldly; he was unused to disobedience even where it concerned his own safety.

"'Tis but fair," he said, "that I should take some risk to equal hers. I'll chance the stroke. Your prayer was that I should meet this damsel alone in the forest. Do not, I beg of you, prevent fulfilment of your devout petition by further tarrying."

But before this was spoken the girl had flung the borrowed rapier far into the forest glade, then waved her disencumbered hand to the departing Frenchman, saying mockingly,—"Farewell, popinjay. The treacherous ever make suggestion of treachery." To the Earl she added, "My lord, I am entirely unarmed."

"What have you to say to me?" replied Strafford severely, bending his dark gaze upon her.

"Sir,"—her voice lowered so that none might by any chance overhear,—"Sir, I am Frances Wentworth, your lordship's eldest daughter."

## CHAPTER II.—RECOGNITION.

The Earl lowered upon the girl, and the black anger upon his brow might have warned a more intrepid person than even she appeared to be that there was peril in trifling. When at last he spoke, his voice was harsh and menacing.

"What do you expect to gain by a statement so preposterous?"

"I expect to gain a father."

The girl's answer trod quick upon the heels of the question, but her colour changed from red to pale, and from pale to red again, and her hurried

414

breathing hinted of some knowledge of her hazard, which nevertheless she faced without flinching.

"My eldest daughter, say you? My eldest daughter is Ann, aged thirteen, a modest little maid. I take you to be older, and I should hesitate to apply to you the qualification I have just coupled with her name."

"I am sixteen, therefore her senior. Thus one part of my contention is admitted. If she is modest, it doth become a maid, and is reasonably to be expected, for she hath a mother's care. I have had none. If you detect a boldness in my manner, 't is but another proof I am my father's daughter."

Something resembling a grimace rather than a smile disturbed the white lips of Strafford at this retort. He bent his eyes on the ground, and his mind seemed to wander through the past. They stood thus in silence opposite each other, the girl watching him intently, and when she saw his mouth twitch with a spasm of pain, a great wave of pity overspread her face and brought the moisture to her eyes; but she made no motion toward him, held in increasing awe of him.

"Boldness is not a virtue," he muttered, more to himself than to her. "There's many a jade in England who can claim no relationship with me."

This remark, calling for no response, received none.

"Sixteen years of age! Then that was in——"

The Earl paused in his ruminations as if the simple mathematical problem baffled him, the old look of weariness and pain clouding his downturned face.

"The year 1624," said the girl promptly.

"Doubtless, doubtless. 1624. It is long since; longer than the days that have passed seem to indicate. I was a young man then, now——now——I am an aged wreck, and all in sixteen years. And so in you, the spirit of youth, the unknown past confronts me, demanding——demanding what?"

"Demanding nothing, my lord."

"Humph. You are the first then. They all want something. You think I

415

am an old dotard who is ready, because you say you want nothing, to accept your absurd proposal. But I am not yet fifty, nor as near it as these fell maladies would have me appear; and a man should be in his prime at fifty. Madam, it will require more convincing testimony to make me listen to you further."

"The testimony, irrefutable, stands here before you. Raise your eyes from the ground, my lord, and behold it. If, scrutinizing me, you deny that I am your daughter, I shall forthwith turn from you and trouble you no more."

Strafford slowly lifted his gloomy face, prematurely seamed with care, and his heavy eyes scanned closely the living statue that confronted him. The sternness of his features gradually relaxed, and an expression near akin to tenderness overspread his face.

"Any man might be proud to claim you, my girl, no matter how many other reasons for pride he possessed. But you have not come here merely because someone flattered the Earl of Strafford by saying you resembled him."

"No, my lord. I am come to return to you this document which once you presented to my mother."

She handed him a paper, which he read with intent care. It ran thus:

*"I have, in little, much to say to you, or else one of us must be much to blame. But in truth I have that confidence in you, and that assurance in myself, as to rest secure the fault will never be made on either side. Well, then; this short and this long which I aim at is no more than to give you this first written testimony that I am your husband; and that husband of yours that will ever discharge these duties of love and respect toward you which good women may expect, and are justly due from good men to discharge them; and this is not only much, but all which belongs to me; and wherein I shall tread out the remainder of life which is left to me———"*

Strafford looked up from his perusal, blank amazement upon his countenance.

"How came you by this paper?"

"I found it among the documents left by my grandfather, who died a year ago. It was sent by you to my mother."

"Impossible."

"Do you deny the script?"

"I do not deny it, but 't was written by me eight years since, and presented to my third wife, whom I married privately."

"Your third wife? Who was she?"

"She was Mistress Elizabeth Rhodes, and is now Lady Strafford."

"Then she is your fourth wife. You will see by your own inditing that this letter was written in March, 1624."

The date was unmistakably set down by the same hand that had penned the bold signature, "Thomas Wentworth," and the bewilderment of the Earl increased as he recognized that here was no forgery, but a genuine letter antedating its duplicate.

"Is it possible," he murmured to himself, "that a man has so little originality as to do practically the same thing twice?" Then aloud to the girl he said:

"Who was your mother?"

"I had hoped the reading of this document would have rendered your question unnecessary. Has a man such gift of forgetting, that the very name of the woman he solemnly married has slipped his memory as easily as the writing of the letter she cherished?"

"She was Frances, daughter of Sir John Warburton," murmured the Earl.

"His only daughter, as I am hers, my lord."

"But when Sir John wrote me coldly of her death, he made no mention of any issue."

"My grandfather always hated you, my lord. It is very like that he told you not the cause of my mother's death was her children's birth."

"Children?"

"Yes, my lord. My twin brother and myself."

An ashen hue overspread the Earl's face, and the hand that held the letter trembled until the fateful missive shook like one of the autumn leaves on the tree above it. Again his mind wandered through the past and conjured up before him the laughing face of his supposedly only son, whose position was thus unexpectedly challenged by a stranger, unknown and unloved. A daughter more or less was of small account, but an elder son promised unsuspected complications. The ill favour with which he had at first regarded the girl returned to his troubled countenance, and she saw with quick intuition that she had suddenly lost all the ground so gradually gained. Cold dislike tinctured the tone in which the next question was asked.

"If, as you say, you have a brother, why is he not here in your place; you in the background, where you properly belong?"

"Sir, I suppose that her good name is thought more of by a woman than by a man. She wishes to be assured that she came properly authenticated into this world, whereas a man troubles little of his origin, so be it he is here with some one to fight or to love. Or perhaps it is that the man is the deeper, and refuses to condone where a woman yearns to forgive. My brother shares our grandfather's dislike of you. He thinks you cared little for our mother, or you would not have been absent during her last days when——"

"I knew nothing of it. The times then, as now, were uncertain, requiring absorbed attention from those thrown willingly or unwillingly into public affairs. What can a boy of sixteen know of the duties thrust upon a man in my situation?"

"Sixteen or not, he considers himself even now a man of position, and he holds your course wrong. He says he has taken up the opinions you formerly held, and will do his best to carry them to success. He is for the Parliament and against the King. As for me, I know little of the questions that disturb the State. My only knowledge is that you are my father, and were you the wickedest person in the world I would come to you. A man may have many daughters, but a daughter can have but one father; therefore am I here, my lord."

Like the quick succession of shade and sunshine over the sensitive surface of a lovely lake, the play of varying emotions added an ever-changing beauty to the girl's expressive face; now a pitiful yearning toward her father when she saw he suffered; then a coaxing attitude, as if she would win him whether he would or no; again a bearing of pride when it seemed she would be denied; and throughout all a rigid suppression of herself, a standing of her ground, a determination not to give way to any rising sentiment which might make the after repulse a humiliation; if a retreat must come it should be carried out with dignity.

The Earl of Strafford saw nothing of this, for his eyes were mostly on the ground at his feet. That his mind was perturbed by the new situation so unexpectedly presented to him was evident; that he was deeply suspicious of a trap was no less clear. When he looked up at her he found his iron resolution melting in spite of himself, and, as he wished to bring an unclouded judgment to bear upon the problem, he scrutinized the brown sward at his feet. Nevertheless he was quick to respond to any show of sympathy with himself, even though he was unlikely to exhibit appreciation, and he was equally quick to resent the slightest lack of deference on the part of those who addressed him. If the girl had made a thorough study of his character she could not have better attuned her manner to his prejudices. Her attitude throughout was imbued with the deepest respect, and if the eye refused to be advocate for her, the ear could not close itself to the little thrill of affection that softened her tone as she spoke to him. He raised his head abruptly as one who has come to a decision.

"November is the stepmother of the months, and the air grows cold. Come with me to the palace. In a world of lies I find myself believing you; thus I am not grown so old as I had feared. Come."

The girl tripped lightly over the rustling leaves and was at his side in an instant, then slowed her pace in unison with his laboured mode of progression.

"Sir, will you lean upon my shoulder?"

"No. I am ailing, but not decrepit."

They walked together in silence, and if any viewed them the onlookers were well concealed, for the park seemed deserted. Entering the palace and arriving at the foot of a stairway, solicitous menials proffered assistance, but Strafford waved them peremptorily aside, and, accepting now the support he had shortly before declined, leaned on his daughter's shoulder and wearily mounted the stair.

The room on the first floor into which he led her overlooked a court. A cheerful fire burned on the hearth and cast a radiance upon the sombre wainscoting of the walls. A heavy oaken table was covered with a litter of papers, and some books lay about. Into a deep arm-chair beside the fire Strafford sank with a sigh of fatigue, motioning his daughter to seat herself opposite him, which she did. He regarded her for some moments with no pleased expression on his face, then said with a trace of petulancy in the question:

"Did your grandfather bring you up a lady, or are you an ignorant country wench?"

She drew in quickly the small feet out-thrust to take advantage of the comforting fire, and the blaze showed her cheek a ruddier hue than heretofore.

"Sir," she said, "the children of the great, neglected by the great, must perforce look to themselves. I was brought up, as you know, without a mother's care, in the ancient hall of a crusty grandfather, a brother my only companion. We played together and fought together, as temper willed, and he was not always the victor, although he is the stronger. I can sometimes out-fence him, and, failing that, can always outrun him. Any horse he can ride, I can ride, and we two have before now put to flight three times our number among the yokels of the neighborhood. As to education, I have a smattering, and can read and write. I have studied music to some advantage, and foreign tongues with very little. I daresay there are many things known to your London ladies that I am ignorant of."

"We may thank God for that," muttered her father.

"If there are those in London, saving your lordship, who say I am not a lady, I will box their ears for them an they make slighting remarks in my presence."

"A most unladylike argument! The tongue and not the hand is the Court lady's defence."

"I can use my tongue too, if need be, my lord."

"Indeed I have had evidence of it, my girl."

"Queen Elizabeth used her fists, and surely she was a lady."

"I have often had my doubts of it. However, hereafter you must be educated as doth become a daughter of mine."

"I shall be pleased to obey any commands my father places on me."

The conversation was interrupted by a servant throwing open the door, crying:

"His Majesty the King!"

The girl sprang instantly to her feet, while her father rose more slowly, assisting himself with his hands on the arms of the chair.

## CHAPTER III.—MAJESTY.

There was more of hurry than of kingly dignity in the entrance of Charles. The handsome face was marred by an imperious querulousness that for the moment detracted from its acknowledged nobility.

"Strafford," he cried impatiently, "I have been kept waiting. Servants are at this moment searching palace and park for you. Where have you been?"

"I was in the forest, your Majesty. I am deeply grieved to learn that you needed me."

"I never needed you more than now. Are you ready to travel?"

Strafford's gloomy face almost lighted up.

"On the instant, your Majesty," he replied with a sigh of relief.

"That is well. I trust your malady is alleviated, in some measure at least;

still I know that sickness has never been a bar to duty with you. Yet I ask no man to do what I am not willing to do myself for the good of the State, and I shall be shortly on the road at your heels."

"Whither, your Majesty?" asked the Earl with falling countenance, for it was to Ireland he desired to journey, and he knew the King had no intention of moving toward the west.

"To London, of course; a short stent over bad roads. But if you are ailing and fear the highway, a barge on the river is at your disposal."

"To London!" echoed the Earl, something almost akin to dismay in his tone. "I had hoped your Majesty would order me to Ireland, which I assure your Majesty has been somewhat neglected of late."

"Yes, yes," exclaimed the King brusquely, "I know your anxiety in that quarter. A man ever thinks that task the most important with which he intimately deals, but my position gives me a view over the whole realm, and the various matters of State assume their just proportions in my eyes; their due relations to each other. Ireland is well enough, but it is the heart and not the limbs of the empire that requires the physicians' care. Parliament has opened badly, and is like to give trouble unless treated with a firm hand."

The hand of the Earl appeared anything but firm. It wavered as it sought the support of the chair's arm.

"Have I your Majesty's permission to be seated? I am not well," Strafford said faintly.

"Surely, surely," cried the King, himself taking a chair. "I am deeply grieved to see you so unwell; but a journey to London is a small matter compared with a march upon Dublin, which is like to have killed you in your present condition."

"Indeed, your Majesty, the smaller journey may well have the more fatal termination," murmured the Earl; but the King paid no attention to the remark, for his wandering eye now caught sight of a third in the conference, which brought surprised displeasure to his brow. The girl was standing behind the high back of the chair in which she had been seated, in a gloomy angle where the firelight which played so plainly on the King and Strafford did not touch her.

"In God's name, whom have we here? The flippant prophet of the forest, or my eyes deceive me! How comes this girl in my palace, so intimate with my Lord Strafford, who seemed to meet her as a stranger but yesterday?"

The slumbering suspicion of Charles was aroused, and he glanced from one to the other in haughty questioning.

"I never met her until I encountered her in the forest when I had the honour to accompany your Majesty. To-day, as I walked with De Courcy and others, there came a second accosting from her, as unexpected as the first. The girl craved private speech with me, which I somewhat reluctantly granted. The upshot is, she brings me proof, which I cannot deny, that she is my eldest daughter."

"Your eldest daughter!" cried the King, amazed. "Is your family then so widely scattered, and so far unknown to you, that such a claimant may spring up at any moment?"

"I was married privately to the daughter of Sir John Warburton. Circumstances separated me from my wife, and although her father curtly informed me of her death he said nothing of issue. There was a feud between us,—entirely on his part,—I had naught against him. It seems he has been dead this year past, and my daughter, getting news of her father among Sir John's papers, comes thus southward to make inquiry."

"You fall into good fortune, my girl. Your extraordinary claim is most readily allowed."

Frances, finding nothing to say, kept silence and bowed her head to the King, whom she had regarded throughout with rapt attention.

"Where got you your gift of prophecy? Is prescience hereditary, and has your father's mantle already fallen on your shoulders? He is my best friend, you said, and I my worst enemy. God's truth, Madam, you did not lack for boldness, but the force of the flattery of your father is lessened by my knowledge of your relationship, hitherto concealed from me."

"Your Majesty, it has hitherto been concealed from myself," said the Earl wearily.

"Has the girl no tongue? It wagged freely enough in the forest. Come, masquerader, what have you to say for yourself?"

"Your Majesty, I humbly crave your pardon. The words I used yesterday were not mine, but those of a gipsy in the north, who told me I was the daughter of the Earl of Strafford at a time when such a tale seemed so absurd that I laughed at her for connecting my name of Wentworth with one so exalted as the Earl of Strafford. Later, when I received proof that such indeed was the case, her words returned to me. I had no right to use them in your august presence, but the entourage of the Lord Strafford prevented my meeting him; thus, baffled, I sought to intercept him in the forest, and was willing to use any strategy that might turn his attention toward me, in the hope of getting a private word with him."

"I knew you had a tongue. Well, it matters little what you said; your mission seems to have been successful. Do not think I placed any weight upon your words, be they gipsy-spoken or the outcome of a spirit of mischief. My Lord Strafford, you will to London then?"

"Instantly, your Majesty."

"I will consult with you there to-morrow. And have no fear; for on my oath as a man, on my honour as a king, I will protect you."

The King rose and left the room as abruptly as he had entered it.

For some moments Strafford lay back in his chair, seemingly in a state of collapse. The girl looked on him in alarm.

"Sir, is there anything I can do for you?" she asked at length.

"Call a servant. Tell him to order a coach prepared at once, and see that it is well horsed, for I would have the journey as short as possible."

"My lord, you are in no condition of health to travel to London. I will go to the King and tell him so."

"Do that I requested you, and trouble me not with counsel. There is enough of woman's meddling in this business already."

Frances obeyed her father's instructions without further comment, then came and sat in her place again. The Earl roused himself, endeavouring to shake off his languor.

"What think you of the King?" he asked.

"He is a man corroded with selfishness."

"Tut, tut! Such things are not to be spoken in the precincts of a Court. No, nor thought. He is not a selfish monarch, other than all monarchs are selfish, but——discussion on such a theme is fruitless, and I must be nearing my dotage to begin it. I am far from well, Frances, and so, like the infirm, must take to babbling."

"Do you fear Parliament, my lord? How can it harm you when you have the favour of the King?"

"I fear nothing, my girl, except foolish unseen interference; interference that may not be struck at or even hinted against. Did they teach you the history of France in your school?"

"No, my lord."

"Then study it as you grow older; I'll warrant you'll find it interesting enough. Ruined by women. Ruined by women. Seven civil wars in seventeen years, and all because of viperish, brainless women. Well, we have one of the breed here in England, and God help us!"

"You mean the Queen, my lord?"

"Hush! Curses on it, will you be as outspoken as another of your sex is spiteful and subtle? Mend your manners, hussy, and guard your tongue. Could you not see you spoke too freely to the King a moment since?"

"Sir, I am sorry."

"Be not sorry, but cautious."

Strafford fell into a reverie, and there was silence in the room until the servant entered and announced that the coach was ready, whereupon his master rose unsteadily.

"Sir," said the girl, "will you not eat or drink before you depart?"

"No." Then, looking sharply at his daughter, he inquired, "Are you hungry?"

"Yes, my lord."

"Bring hither some refreshments, whatever is most ready to hand, and a measure of hot spiced wine. I had forgotten your youth, Frances, thinking all the world was old with me."

When the refection came, she ate but sparingly, despite her proclamation, but coaxed him to partake and to drink a cup of wine. He ordered a woman's cloak brought for her, which, when she had thrown it over her shoulders, he himself fastened at her throat.

"There," he said, when the cloak enveloped her, "that will protect you somewhat, for the night grows cold."

Strafford himself was wrapped in warm furs, and thus together they went down the stairs to the court, now dimly lighted. A cavalier, who seemed to have been standing in wait for them, stepped out from the shadow of the arches, and Frances recognized the French spark whom she had so frankly characterized earlier in the day.

"My lord," protested De Courcy jauntily, "you have your comrades at a disadvantage. You have captured the woodland nymph, and, I hear, propose spiriting her away to London. I do protest 't is most unfair to those who are thus left behind."

"Sir," said Strafford, with severity, pausing in his walk, "I would have you know that the lady to whom you refer is the Lady Frances Wentworth, my eldest daughter, ever to be spoken of with respect by high and low. Native

426

and foreign shall speak otherwise at their distinct peril."

The Frenchman pulled off his bonnet with an impressive sweep that brushed its ample feather lightly on the stones. He bent his body in a low obeisance that threatened, were it not so acrobatically accomplished, to pitch him forward on his nose.

"If I congratulate your lordship on finding so rare a daughter, rather than offer my felicitations to the lady in the attainment of so distinguished a father, it is because I am filled with envy of any man who acquires a companionship so charming. My lady, may I have the honour of escorting you to the carriage?"

The girl shrank closer to her father and made no reply. On the other hand the father offered no objection, but returned—rather stiffly, it is true— the bow of the foreigner, and De Courcy, taking this as an acceptance, tripped daintily by the girl's side, chattering most amiably.

"I hear on the highest authority that our sovereign lady is tired of Hampton, and that we are all to be on the march for London again; to-morrow, they tell me. London delights me not. 'T is a grimy city, but if, as I suspect, a new star of beauty is to arise there, then 't will be indeed the centre of refulgence, to which worshippers of loveliness will hasten as pilgrims to a shrine. I take it, my lord, that you will introduce your daughter to the Court, and hide her no longer in the cold and envious northland?"

"My daughter has already been presented to his Majesty, and doubtless will take the place at Court to which her birth entitles her."

"And to which her grace and charm no less lay claim. I hope to be present when the lady is greeted by the Queen we both adore. The meeting of the Lily of France with the Rose of England will be an occasion to be sung by poets; would that I were a minstrel to do justice to the theme."

Their arrival at the carriage, with its four impatient horses, postillion-ridden, saved Strafford the effort of reply had he intended such. He seated himself in the closed vehicle, and his daughter sprang nimbly in beside him, ignoring the proffered aid of De Courcy, who stood bowing and bending with much courtesy, and did not resume his bonnet until the coach lurched on its lumbering way, preceded and followed by a guard of horsemen, for the Earl of Strafford always travelled in state.

Nothing was said by either until the jingling procession was well clear of the park, when the girl, with a shudder, exclaimed:

"I loathe that scented fop!"—then, seeming to fear a reproof for her outspoken remark, added, "I know I should not say that, but I cannot see what you have in common with such a creature that you are civil to him."

To her amazement her father laughed slightly, the first time she had heard him do so.

"When we travel, Frances, safe out of earshot, you may loathe whom you please, but, as I have warned you, 't is sometimes unsafe to give expression to your feelings within four walls. I may find little in common with any man, least of all with such as De Courcy, whom I take to be as false as he is fair; but there is slight use in irritating a wasp whom you cannot crush. Wait till he is under my hand, then I shall crush ruthlessly; but the time is not yet. He has the ear of the Queen, and she has the ear of her husband."

"Sir, what reason have you to suspect that the Queen moves against you?"

"One reason is that I am this moment journeying east when I would be travelling west. In truth, my girl, you seem resolved unconsciously to show you are your father's daughter with that uncurbed tongue of yours, for a lack of lying is like to be my undoing. If I had told the King I must to London, 't is most like we were now on our way to Dublin."

"But it may be the King himself who thus orders you contrarywise."

"I know the King. He is not, as you think, selfish, but ever gives ear to the latest counsellor. He is weak and thinks himself strong; a most dangerous combination. With trembling hand he speaks of its firmness. Now, a weak monarch or a strong monarch matters little; England has been blessed with both and has survived the blessing; but a monarch who is. weak and strong by

428

turns courts disaster. 'War with the Scots,' says the King. He will smite them with a firm hand. Very good; a most desirable outcome. But our captains, promoted by a woman's whisper and not by their own merit, trust to the speed of their horses rather than the ingenuity of military skill, and so escape the Scots. Our army is scattered, and there is panic in Whitehall. I am called, for God's sake, from Ireland, and I come scarce able, through illness, to sit my horse. I gather round me men of action and brain, and send Madam's favourites to the rear, where they will gallop in any case as soon as the enemy shows front. What is the result? A portion of our Scottish friends are cut up, and those whose legs are untouched are on the run. Very good again. The dogs are rushing for their kennels. What happens? An added title for me, you might suppose. Not so. A censure comes post haste from London. 'Leave the Scots alone, the King is negotiating with them.' In the face of victory he embraces defeat. A peace is made that I know nothing of; all their demands are granted, as if they had environed London! I am left like a fool, with a newly inspired army and no enemy. They termed it 'negotiating' in London, but I call it 'surrender.' If you intend to submit, keep the sword in its sheath and submit. If you draw the sword, fight till you are beaten, then submit when there is nothing else to do. God's name! they did not need to hale me from Ireland, where I had wrenched peace from chaos, to encompass a disgraceful retreat! Even De Courcy could have managed that with much greater urbanity than I."

"And you think the Queen is responsible?"

"Who else? Her generals were disgraced and whipped like dogs. Unvaliant in the battle-field, they are powerful in the ante-chamber, and their whines arise in the ears of the Lily of France, who would rather see her husband wrecked than saved by me. But I was never one to hark back on things that are past. My duty was to save the King from future errors. One more grave mistake lay open to him, and that was the summoning of Parliament at such a moment. It was a time for action, not for words. 'If you meant to concede, why did you not concede without bloodshed?' was a question sure to be asked; a question to which there could be no answer. Very well. I accepted in humbleness the censure that should have been placed on other shoulders, and sent back by the courier who brought it a message imploring the King to call no Parliament until we had time to set our house in order and face Lords and Commons with good grace. I then arranged my command so that if the Scots broke forth again they would meet some examples of military science, and not view only the coat-tails of the Queen's favourite generals. No reply coming from the King, I mounted my horse, and, with only one follower, set forth for London. Pushing on through darkness on the second night of my journey, I heard the galloping of a horse behind me, and drew rein, fully expecting that the greedy Scots, asking more than could be allowed, had taken to the field again. 'Good friend,' I cried, 'what news, that you ride so fast?' 'Great news,' he answered, breathless. 'A Parliament is summoned, and as I am an elected member I ride in haste. Please God, before the month is done we have Strafford's head in our hands and off his treacherous shoulders.'"

The girl gave utterance to a little cry of terror.

"Oh, 't was nothing but some braggart countryman, knowing not to whom he spoke so freely, and big in the importance of his membership, dashing on to London, thinking the world rested on his speed; and thus I learned how my advice had been scorned. When I met the King he was all panic and regret. He had conjured up the Devil easily enough, but knew not how to allay him. He bewailed his mistakes and called himself the most unfortunate of monarchs, eager to please, yet constantly offending. He was in a contrite mood, but that soon changed. 'T is my head they want,' I said. 'Do with it as you please. If it is useless to you, toss it to them; if useful, then send me to Ireland, where I shall be out of the way, yet ready to afford you what service lies in my power.' He swore he would concede them nothing. He was done with unappreciated complaisance, and now it was to be the firm hand. They should learn who was ruler of the realm. He gave me permission to return to my post. I was his only friend; his truest counsellor. That was yesterday. You heard him speak to-day. It is still the firm hand, but I must to London. There indeed exists a firm hand, but it is concealed, and so directed by hatred of me that it may project the avalanche that will overwhelm us all."

"And what will you do in London?" asked his daughter in an awed whisper.

"God knows! Had I the untrammelled ordering of events, I would strike terror into Parliament, as I struck terror into the Scots or the Irish, but——but if, after that, there was a similar sneaking underhand surrender, why then the countryman would have my head, as he hoped. I fear there are troublous times before us. This alternate grip of the firm hand, and offering of open-palmed surrender, each at the wrong time, is like the succeeding hot and cold fits of an ague; 'T will rend the patient asunder if long continued. Frances, be ever a womanly woman. Never meddle with politics. Leave sword and State to men."

Tired with long converse and the jolting of the vehicle, Strafford sank into a troubled sleep, from which he was at last awakened by the stopping of the carriage in front of his town house.

## CHAPTER IV.—PROPOSAL.

Frances Wentworth crossed the threshold of her father's house with more trepidation than she had experienced on entering the palace of the King at Hampton Court. Here probably awaited a stepmother with her children, and Frances doubted the cordiality of the approaching reception. The ever-increasing fear of her father, a sentiment felt by nearly all those who encountered him, mingled with hatred, usually, on their part, but with growing affection on hers, prevented the putting of the question whether or no Lady Strafford was now in London. Their journey together had been silent since he ceased the exposition of the difficulties which surrounded him,—a man whom all England regarded as being paramount in the kingdom, yet in reality baffled and almost at bay. Looking back over the day now drawn to its close, she marvelled at her own courage in approaching him as she had done, light-heartedly and confident. Were her task to be re-enacted her mind misgave her that she would not possess the temerity to carry it through, with her new knowledge of the man. Yet if Strafford were hated in the three kingdoms, he seemed to be well liked in that little despotism, his home, where servants clustered round, for each of whom he had a kind word. Whether they knew of his coming or not, the house was prepared for his reception, fires blazing, and a table spread in the room to which he conducted his daughter. Outside, the night was cold and damp, and the inward warmth struck gratefully upon the senses of the travellers.

"Mrs. Jarrett," said the Earl to his housekeeper, who looked with wonder at the new-comer he had brought, "have you aught of woman's trappings that will fit my daughter here?"

"Your daughter, my lord?"

"Yes, and as you will be consumed by curiosity until you know how it comes so, I will add that she is newly found, having lived till now with her grandfather in the North, and is the child of my second wife, Frances Warburton, married by me some seventeen years since. Any further particulars my daughter herself will supply, if you question shrewdly, as I doubt not you will; but postpone inquiry, I beg of you, until to-morrow. Meanwhile robe her as best you may with the materials at hand, and that quickly, for I wish her company at supper."

Frances was then spirited away to the apartment assigned to her, and when presently she reappeared she was costumed more to her father's liking than had hitherto been the case. They sat down together to the meal that had hastily been prepared for them.

"To-morrow, if I remember aright what you said, is your birthday."

"Yes, my lord."

"Is it difficult for you to say 'Father'? My other children pronounce the word glibly enough. When you and I first met, and even since then, you seemed not backward in speech."

"Sir, I find myself more afraid of you than I was at the beginning."

Strafford smiled, but answered: "I assure you there is no need. I may be an implacable enemy, but I have the reputation of being as staunch a friend. So to-morrow is your birthday, saddened by the fact that it is also the date of your mother's death. That is a loss for which a man in my onerous position cannot even partially atone, but it is a loss which you perhaps have not keenly felt. It seems heartless to speak thus, but the fact remains that we cannot deeply deplore the departure of what we have never enjoyed. One thing I

432

can covenant; that you shall not hereafter know the lack of money, which is something to promise in a city of shops."

"I have never known the lack of it, my lord."

"Have you indeed been so fortunate? Well, there again you bear a resemblance to your father. Sir John was reputed comfortably off in the old days, and I infer he harboured his wealth, a somewhat difficult task in times gone by. Are you then his heir?"

"One of two, my lord."

"Ah, yes! I had momentarily forgotten the brother who favours his grandfather rather than his sire. I am like to be over-busy to-morrow to attend the mart of either mercer or goldsmith, and if I did, I should not know what to purchase that would please you. But here are all the birthday presents of London in embryo, needing but your own touch to bring forth the full blossom of perfect satisfaction. Midas, they say, transmuted everything he fingered into gold, and it is the province of your sex to reverse the process. Buy what catches your fancy, and flatter your father by naming it his gift."

He held forward a very well filled purse, through whose meshes the bright gold glittered.

"Sir, I do not need it, and you have been very kind to me as it is."

"Nonsense! We all desire more than we can obtain. It is my wish that you take it; in any case it is but part payment of a debt long running and much overdue."

Fearing again to refuse, she accepted the proffered purse with evident reluctance, now standing opposite her father, who said:

"I am very tired and shall not rise early to-morrow. Do not wait breakfast for me. Good-night, daughter."

"Good-night, father."

Although he had said the last conventional words of the day, he still stood there as if loath to retire, then he stooped and kissed her on the lips, ruffling her black, wayward, curly hair so like his own in texture, colour, and freedom from restraint, and patting her affectionately on the shoulder.

"You will not be afraid of me from this time forward, child?" he asked. "Indeed, Frances, I grow superstitious as I become older, and I look on your strange arrival as in some measure providential. There is none of my own kind to whom I can speak freely, as I did to you in the carriage; my daughters—my other daughters—are too young. My Lady Strafford takes much interest in her garden, and dislikes this London house and this London town, for which small blame is to be imputed to her. In you, a man's courage is added to a woman's wit, and who knows but my daughter may prove the reinforcement I lacked in my baffling fight with the unseen. Do you speak French, my girl, or are you as ignorant of the language of that country as of its history?"

"I speak it but haltingly, sir, though I was taught its rudiments."

"We must amend that. It is to our tongue what the thin rapier is to the broadsword. Good lack! there was a time when one language served the English, yet great deeds were done and great poems written; but that time is past now. I must get you a master. I have likely used the broadsword overmuch, but who knows? You may be the rapier by my side."

"I hope I shall not disappoint you, sir, though I am but a country maid, with some distrust of this great city and its Court."

"City and Court are things we get speedily accustomed to. Well, again good-night, sweetheart, and sleep soundly. I see those fine eyes are already heavy with slumber."

But sleep came not so quickly as he surmised to the eyes he had complimented. The day had been too full of rapid change and tense excitement. The strange transformation of the present, and the dim, troubled vista of the future which opened out to her, cherished thought and discouraged slumber. Was it possible that she was thus to be transplanted, was to stand by the side of the greatest man in England, his acknowledged daughter, his welcome aid? God grant she might not fail him, if he had real need of her. And so she planned the days to come. She would be as subtle as the craftiest. She

434

would cover all dislikes as the cloak had covered her, and her lips should smile though her heart revolted. Her tongue must measure what it said, and all rural bluntness should disappear. She slipped from these meditations into a hazy, bewildering conflict; her father, somehow, was in a danger that she could not fathom, she lacking power to get to him, restrained by invisible bonds, not knowing where he was, although he called to her. Then it seemed there was a turmoil in the street, a cry for help, a groan, and silence, and next Mrs. Jarrett was moving about the room and had drawn curtains that let in a grey, misty daylight.

"Is my father yet arisen?" she cried.

"Oh, good lack! no, your ladyship, nor will he for hours to come."

The girl's head fell back on her pillow, and she said dreamily, "I thought there had been trouble of some sort, and men fighting."

"Indeed, your ladyship, and so there was, a rioting going on all the night. I think the citizens of London are gone mad, brawling in the street at hours when decent folk should be in their beds. 'T is said that this new Parliament is the cause, but how or why I do not know."

Although the Earl of Strafford did not quit his chamber until noontide, he was undoubtedly concerned with affairs that demanded attention from the greatest minister of State. There were constant runnings to and fro, messengers despatched and envoys received, with the heavy knocker of the door constantly a-rap. It was two hours after mid-day when Strafford sent for his daughter, and she followed his messenger to the library, where she found her father in his chair beside a table, although he was equipped for going forth from the house. There had been seated before him De Courcy, but the young man rose as she entered and greeted her with one of his down-reaching bows which set her a-quake lest he should fall forward on his face.

"My child," said the Earl, "I am about to set out for Parliament, and it may be late before I return. Yet I think you shall sup with me at seven if all goes well and debate becomes not too strenuous; but do not wait in case I should be detained. I counsel you not to leave the house to-day, for there seem to be many brawlers on the streets. Any shopman will be pleased to wait upon you and bring samples of his wares, so send a servant for those you wish to consult. My friend De Courcy, here, begs the favour of some converse with you, and speaks with my approval."

Strafford looked keenly at the girl, and her heart thrilled as she read the unspoken message with quick intuition. He had some use for De Courcy, and she must be suave and diplomatic. Thus already she was her father's ally; an outpost in his vast concerns now committed to her. The young man saw nothing of this, for he had eyes only for the girl. The broad rim of his feathered hat was at his smirking lips, and his gaze of admiration was as unmistakable as it was intent.

"Sir, I shall obey you in all things, and hope to win your commendation," said Frances with inclination of the head.

"You are sure of the latter in any case, my child," replied Strafford, rising. "And now, De Courcy, I think we understand each other, and I may rely upon you."

"To the death, my lord," cried the young man, with another of his courtly genuflections.

"Oh, let us hope 't will not be necessary quite so far as that. I bid you good-day. To-morrow at this hour I shall look for a report from you. For the moment, good-bye, my daughter."

No sooner was the Earl quit of the room, and the door closed behind him, than De Courcy, with an impetuous movement that startled the girl, flung himself at her feet. Her first impulse was to step quickly back, but she checked it and stood her ground.

"Oh, divine Frances!" he cried, "how impatiently I have waited for this rapt moment, when I might declare to you——"

"Sir, I beg of you to arise. 'T is not seemly you should demean yourself thus."

"'T is seemly that the whole world should grovel at your feet, my lady

436

of the free forest; for all who look upon you must love you, and for me, who have not the cold heart of this northern people, I adore you, and do here avow it."

"You take me at a disadvantage, sir. I have never been spoken to thus. I am but a child and unaccustomed. Only sixteen this very day. I ask you———"

"Most beauteous nymph! How many grand ladies of our Court would give all they possess to make such confession truly. Aye, the Queen herself. I do assure you, sweetest, such argument will never daunt a lover."

"I implore you, sir, to arise. My father may return."

"That he will not. And if he did, 't would pleasure him to see my suit advancing. I loved you from the first moment I beheld you; and though you used me with contumely, yet I solaced my wounded heart that 't was me you noticed, and me only, even though your glance was tinged with scorn."

Notwithstanding a situation that called for tact, she was unable to resist a touch of the linguistic rapier, and her eyes twinkled with suppressed merriment as she said, "You forget, sir, that I also distinguished the keeper of the hounds with my regard;" but, seeing he winced, she recollected her position and added, "In truth, I was most churlishly rude in the forest, and I am glad you spoke of it, that I now have opportunity to beg your pardon very humbly. I have learned since then that you stand high in my dear father's regard, and indeed he chided me for my violence, as 't was his duty to do by a wayward child." The gallant was visibly flattered by this tribute to his amour propre. He seized her hand and pressed his lips to it, the tremor which passed over her at this action being probably misinterpreted by his unquenchable vanity. The tension was relieved by a low roar from the street, a sound that had in it the menace of some wild beast roused to anger. It brought to the girl a reminiscence of her disturbed dreams.

"Good heaven! What is it?" she exclaimed, snatching away her hand and running to the window. Her suitor rose to his feet, daintily dusted the knees of his silken wear with a film of lace that did duty for a handkerchief, and followed her.

The street below was packed with people howling round a carriage that seemed blocked by the press. The stout coachman, gorgeous in splendid livery, had some ado to restrain the spirited horses, maddened and prancing with the interference and the outcry. Cudgels were shaken aloft in the air, and there were shouts of "Traitor!"

"Tyrant!" and other epithets so degrading that Frances put her hands to her ears in horrified dismay.

"Whom are they threatening so fiendishly?" she whispered.

"That is your father's carriage," answered De Courcy.

Before she could make further inquiry there came up to them the cold, dominating tones of her father's voice, clear above that tumult,—

"Strike through!"

The stout coachman laid about him with his whip, and the curses for the moment abandoned the head of Strafford to alight on that of the driver. The horses plunged fiercely into the crowd. The cruel progress changed the tenor of the cries, as if a wailing stop of a great organ had suddenly taken the place of the open diapason. The press was so great that those in front could not make for safety, and the disappearing coach was greeted with screams of terror and was followed by groans of agony. Men went down before it like ripe grain before a sickle.

"Oh! oh! oh!" moaned the girl, all color leaving her face.

"It serves the dogs right," said De Courcy. "How dare they block the way of a noble, and the chief Minister of State."

"I—I cannot look on this," lamented Frances, shrinking back to the table, and leaning against it as one about to faint, forgetting her desire to avoid further demonstration from her companion, in the trepidation which followed the scene she had witnessed.

"Indeed they were most mercifully dealt with, those scullions. The King of France would have sent a troop of horse to sabre them back into their kennels. 'Strike through!' cried his lordship, and, by God! 't is a good phrase, most suitable motto for a coat of arms, a hand grasping a dagger above it. 'Strike through!' I shall not forget it. But 't was a softer and more endearing theme I wished to——"

"Sir, I beseech your polite consideration. I am nigh distraught with what I have seen, and am filled with a fear of London. 'T is not the courtly city I expected to behold. I am not myself."

"But you will at least bid me hope?"

"Surely, surely, all of us may hope."

"Why, 't was the last and only gift left in Pandora's casket, and London were grim indeed to be more bereft than the receptacle of that deceitful woman. May I make my first draught on Madam Pandora's box by hoping that I am to see you at this hour tomorrow?"

"Yes—to-morrow—to-morrow," gasped the girl faintly.

## CHAPTER V.—EXACTION.

A 'drizzling rain had set in and had driven the crowds from the streets. Frances drew a chair to the window of the library and sat there meditating on the strange events in which she was taking some small part, so different from the tranquil happenings of the district she had known all her life. She had imagined London a city of palaces facing broad streets, fanciedly, if not literally, paved with gold; a town of gaiety and laughter: and here was the reality, a cavernous, squalid, gloomy, human warren, peopled with murky demons bent on outrage of some sort, ill-natured and threatening. As the day waned, she saw that in spite of the rain the mob was collecting again, its atoms running hither and thither, calling to each other; bedraggled beings labouring under some common excitement. And now its roar came to her again, farther off than before,—a roar that chilled her while she listened, and the wave of sound this time seemed to have a fearful note of exultation in it. She wondered what had happened, and was anxious for her father if he were at the mercy of it. Mrs. Jarrett came into the room, followed by a man-servant, and also by one of her father's secretaries, as the woman whispered to the girl:

"My lady, we must close the shutters and bar them tightly, for the ruffians are threatening again, and may be here in force at any moment, to stone the windows, as they have done before."

The secretary seated himself at the table and was arranging papers. The man-servant opened the windows, from which Frances drew back, and now the cries came distinctly to her. "Death to Strafford!"

"Down with the tyrant!" "To the block with the King's Earl!" were some of the shouts she heard lustily called forth.

"Oh! I fear my father is in danger. Do you think they have him in their power, that they exult so?"

Good Mrs. Jarrett, anxiety on her own honest face, soothed her young mistress, and the secretary came forward.

"Be not troubled, Madam," he said. "While they cry 'To the block' it shows they have not possession of his lordship's person, but hope to stir up rancour to his disfavour. While they shout for process of law, his lordship is safe, for the law is in his hands and in those of the King, whose behests he carries out."

This seemed a reasonable deduction, and it calmed the inquirer, although there remained to her disquietude the accent of triumph in the voice of the mob.

"Death to Strafford!" was the burden of the acclaim; but now one shouted, "Justice on Strafford!"—though his meaning was clearly the same as the others. There was no dissenting outcry, and this unanimous hatred so vehemently expressed terrified at least one listener. Why was her father so universally detested? What had he done? Stern he was, undoubtedly; but just, as his reception of herself had shown, and courteous to all to whom she heard him speak; yet the memory of that phrase "Strike through!" uttered with such ruthless coldness, haunted her memory, and she heard again the shrieks of those trampled under foot. It was an indication that what he had to do he did with all his might, reckless of consequence. If any occupied his path, the obstructor had to stand aside or go down, and such a course does not make for popularity.

The windows being now shuttered and barred securely, and the tumult muffled into indistinct murmur, lights were brought in. Mrs. Jarrett urged the girl to partake of some refreshment, but Frances insisted on waiting for her father. The secretary, seeing her anxiety, said:

"Mr. Vollins went out some two hours ago to learn what was taking place, and I am sure if anything serious had happened he would have been here before now with tidings."

"Who is Mr. Vollins?"

"His lordship's treasurer, Madam."

As the words were uttered, the door opened, disclosing John Vollins, the expression of whose serious, clean-shaven face gave little promise of encouragement.

"What news, Mr. Vollins? The mob seems rampant again," spoke up the secretary.

"Disquieting news, or I am misled. The rumour is everywhere believed that his lordship was arrested in Parliament this afternoon, and is now in prison."

"Impossible! 'T would be a breach of privilege. In Parliament! It cannot be. Did you visit the precincts of Parliament?"

"No man can get within a mile of it, the mass of people is so great. It seems as if all London were concentrated there, and one is swept hither and thither in the crush like a straw on the billows of the sea. Progress is out of the question except in whatever direction impulse sways the mob. There are so many versions of what is supposed to have happened that none can sift the truth. It is said that Parliament, behind closed doors, impeached his lordship, and that when he demanded entrance to his place he was arrested by order of the two Houses acting conjointly."

"But even if that were true,—and it seems incredible,—the King can liberate him at a word."

"They say even the King and Court have fled, and that hereafter Parliament will be supreme; but one cannot believe a tithe of what is flying through the streets this night. The people are mad,—stark mad." Mrs. Jarrett hovered about the young lady in case an announcement so fraught with dread to all of them should prove too much for her; but Frances was the most collected of any there. "If that is all," she said calmly, "'T will be but a temporary inconvenience to my father which he will make little of. He has committed no crime, and may face with fortitude the judgment of his peers, certain of triumphant acquittal. He is in London by command of the King, his master, and his Majesty will see to it, should all else fail, that he suffers not for his obedience."

This conclusion was so reasonable that it had the effect of soothing the apprehensions of all who heard it, and, young as she was, Frances seemed to assume a place of authority in the estimation of those present, which was to stand her in good stead later in the evening.

The headless household, barricaded in, with frequent testimony of public execration in the ominous impact of missiles flung against doors and shutters outside, went about its accustomed way in an anxious, halfhearted manner, continually on the qui vive. As the girl wandered aimlessly about the large house, nothing gave her so vivid a sense of insecurity as the dim figure of the secretary seated in the ill-lighted hall, with his cheek against the front door, listening for any hint of his master's approach, ready to undo bar and bolt with all speed and admit him at the first sign of necessity; ready, also, to defend the portal should the door be broken in by the populace, a disaster which the blows rained against it sometimes seemed to predict, followed by breathless periods of nonmolestation. The secretary's sword lay across his knee, and, like a phantom army, backs against the wall, stood in silence, similarly armed, the menservants of the household. The one scant twinkling light had been placed on a table, and a man sat beside it, his pale face more strongly illumined than any other of that ghostly company, radiant against a background of darkness. He was prepared to cover the light instantly, or to blow it out, at a signal from his leader the secretary, seated in the chair by the strong oaken door.

It was after nine o'clock, during a lull in the tempest, that there was a rap at the door.

"Who is there?" asked the secretary through the grating.

"A messenger from the Court," was the reply. Frances had come up the hall on hearing the challenge.

"What name?" demanded the secretary.

"De Courcy. Open quickly, I beg of you. The mob has surged down the street, but it may return at any moment."

"Open," said Frances with decision, and the secretary obeyed.

De Courcy came in, unrecognizable at first because of the cloak that enveloped him. The door was secured behind him, and he flung his cloak to one of the men standing there. His gay plumage was somewhat ruffled, and the girl never thought she would be so heartily glad to see him.

"Is it true that my father is sent to the Tower?" were her first words.

"No, Mademoiselle; but he is in custody, arrested by order of Parliament, and at this moment detained in the house of James Maxwell, Keeper of the Black Rod, who took his sword from him and is responsible for his safety. 'T is said he will be taken to the Tower to-morrow; but they reckon not on the good will of some of us who are his friends, and they forget the power of the King. Mon Dieu! What a night, and what a people! One walks the streets at the risk of life and garments. I was never so mauled about, and despaired of reaching this door. I've been an hour outside screeching 'Death to Strafford!' with the rest of them, else I were torn limb from limb."

Frances frowned, but said:

"What were the circumstances of my father's arrest? What do they charge against him?"

"God knows what the indictment is; chiefly that he is Strafford, I think.

443

He entered the House of Lords this afternoon, and walked with customary dignity to his place, but was curtly ordered to withdraw until he was sent for, as the Commons were at that moment enunciating their formula against him. He withdrew in the face of this loud protest, and at last, being recalled, stood before them; was commanded to kneel, which with some hesitation he did, while the articles to his disparagement were read from the Woolsack. He was then dismissed, and, once in the outer room again, the Black Rod demanded his sword, and so conducted him, under restraint, to a carriage; no man of all then present capping to him, although they had been obsequious enough when he entered. A scurvy lot!"

"Were you among them?"

"Not I; I give you the account as 't was told to me, but had I been in that contemptible company, my hat would have gone lower than ever before."

"You have not seen my father, then; he has sent no message by you?"

"I have not seen him, but I come to crave a few words with you in private."

"Sir, you must excuse me. I am so tense with anxiety about my father, I can think of naught else."

"'T is on that subject I wish to discourse. He has set in train a series of events in which I hoped to aid him, but it is like to go awry through this most unlooked-for arrest. That is why I was here this morning, and the commission was to have been completed to-morrow. Did he say anything to you about it?"

"You heard all he said to me to-day. I saw him for but a moment, and that in your presence."

"I had hoped his lordship made a confidant of you, so my mission were the easier of accomplishment."

"If it has to do with his welfare, I am ready to confer with you. Come with me to the library." But before they could quit the hall, they were aware that another was taking advantage of the lull in the street to seek entrance to the mansion. Frances paused to learn the result. This time it was an envoy from Strafford himself, and he brought a letter addressed to "Mistress Frances Wentworth." She opened and read the note with eager anticipation, forgetting, for the moment, all who were standing there.

Sweetheart:

"You have heard before this what hath befallen me; yet trust thou in the goodness of God that my enemies shall do me no hurt. I am troubled that you should be in London at this time, where I can be of no help to you. It would please me to know that you were safe in the home where you have lived until this present time. Think not that you can assist me other than by obeying, for I trust in God and the King, and in the assurance that I am innocent of the charges malice hath brought against me. Therefore be in no way alarmed, but betake yourself straightway to the North, there to wait with your brother, as heretofore, until I send a message for you, which I hope to do right speedily. Travel in comfort and security, and take with you such of my household as will secure both.

"My treasurer, John Vollins, will give you all money you require, and this letter is his assurance to fulfil your wishes in this and every respect. Trust in God; give way to no fear; but bear yourself as my daughter.

"Your loving father,

"Strafford."

The young woman folded the letter without a word, except to the secretary, to whom she said:

"My father writes in good confidence, seeing no cause for alarm, having assurance of his innocence and faith in God and the King."

Then she led the way to the library, followed by De Courcy, hat in hand. Vollins arose and left them together, whereupon the Frenchman, with some slight hesitation, possibly remembering a different plea on that spot a few hours before, began his recital.

"This morning his lordship, your honoured father, requested my assistance in a business which he thought I was capable of bringing to a satisfactory conclusion. It concerned a highly placed personage, whom it is perhaps improper for me to name, and perhaps unnecessary for me to particularize further. His lordship's intention was to present this exalted lady with some gift which she would value for its intrinsic worth no less than its artistic quality, and, as he professed himself no judge of such, preferring to depend upon the well-known taste of my nation in delicate articles of merit, also so far complimenting me as to believe that I could, in suitable manner and phrase, present this token to the gracious accepter of it, he desired my intervention, and I promised so to pleasure him to the best of my poor abilities. On leaving you this morning I made selection of the gift, and furthermore gave hint to the recipient of its intended presentation,—a hint, I may say, which was received with palpable delight. Judge, then, my consternation when I heard of the Earl's arrest, for he had promised to pay me the money to-morrow."

The young man paused, his listener pondering with her eyes on the floor. She had such a deep distrust of him, and was so well aware of the prejudice, that she struggled against it, praying for an unbiased mind. Yet much that he had said coincided with certain things she knew,—her father's desire that the Queen should cease from meddling in affairs of State to his disadvantage and theirs; his seeming friendship for De Courcy, although he despised him; his intention that she should be civil to him; his disclaimer of all knowledge regarding what a woman valued in a gift when he presented her with a full purse the night before,—all these fitted with the Frenchman's story. The suppliant, scrutinizing her perplexed brow, seemed to fear that his chance of getting the money was vanishing, as he continued on the line most likely to incline her to favour his present demand.

"Of course, I should not have troubled you in this matter did I not think that if the arrangement your father wished to make was important this morning, it is ten times more important to-night. Indeed, his liberty may depend upon it. I am well aware that it is open to me to say to the lady, 'Lord Strafford is in prison, and is unable to carry out his generous intentions,' but I fear the deep disappointment will outweigh the force of the reasoning. Your charming sex is not always strictly logical."

"What was the sum agreed upon?" asked Frances, looking suddenly up.

"A thousand pounds in gold."

The question had been sprung upon him, and he had answered without thought, but as he watched her resolute face a shade of disappointment passed over his own, as if of inward regret that he had not made the amount larger, should her determination prove his ally.

"I shall see that you get the money, if not to-night, at the time promised."

She sent for Vollins and placed the case before him. The treasurer stood by the table, with inscrutable face and listened in silence, his somewhat furtive look bent on the Frenchman.

"Has Monsieur De Courcy some scrap of writing in which my lord signifies that so considerable a payment is to be made?"

"My dear fellow, this relates to business that is not put in writing between gentlemen," said the foreigner hastily.

"I am not a gentleman, but merely the custodian of his lordship's purse. I dare not pay out gold without his lordship's warrant over his own signature."

De Courcy shrugged his shoulders and spread out his hands, as though he had washed them of responsibility.

"Mr. Vollins," pleaded the girl eagerly, "my father's life and liberty may depend on this disbursement. I will be your warrant. I have money of my own in the North, many times the sum I request you to pay. Should my father object, I will refund to you the thousand pounds; indeed I will remit it to you in any case, and my father need know nothing of this transaction, therefore you cannot be held in scath." Vollins shook his head.

"I must not do it," he said. "His lordship is a very strict man of business and will hold me to account. He would forgive you, Madam, but would be merciless with me did I consent to so unheard of a proposal. I dare not count out a thousand pounds to the first man who steps from the street and asks for it, giving me his bare word."

"Do you dispute my word, sir?" demanded De Courcy, bristling.

"Assuredly not. I am but putting a case, as his lordship would undoubtedly put it to me were I to consent,—and what would be my answer?"

"But you have my word as well, Mr. Vollins," urged the girl.

"Madam, I beseech you to consider my position. I am but a servant. The money is not mine, or you were welcome to it. Yet why all this haste? His lordship can undoubtedly be communicated with tomorrow, and then a word or line from him is sufficient."

"You have an adage, sir, of striking while the iron is hot; the iron may be cool enough by the time your scruples of legality are satisfied," warned De Courcy.

"His lordship can be communicated with; you are quite right, Mr. Vollins," cried Frances, remembering. "He has communicated with me. I ask you to read this letter, and then to pay the thousand pounds required of you."

Vollins read the letter with exasperating slowness, and said at last:

"There is nothing here authorizing me to pay the gentleman a thousand pounds."

"True, there is not. But my father says you are to pay me what moneys I require. I require at this moment a thousand pounds in gold."

"The money is for your safe conduct to the North."

"You have read my father's letter more carelessly than I supposed, by the time you took. He says you are to fulfill my wishes in this and every respect. Do you still refuse me?"

"No, Madam. But I venture to advise you strongly against the payment."

"I thank you for your advice. I can certify that you have done your duty fully and faithfully. Will you kindly bring forth the gold?"

Vollins weighed the five bags of coin with careful exactitude and without further speech. De Courcy fastened them to his belt, then looked about him for his cloak, which he at last remembered to have left in the hall. Vollins called upon a servant to fetch it, taking it from him at the door. The Frenchman enveloped himself, and so hid his treasure. The cautious Vollins had prepared a receipt for him to sign, made out in the name of Frances Wentworth, but De Courcy demurred; it was all very well for the counting-house, he said, but not in the highest society. The Earl of Strafford would be the first to object to such a course, he insisted. Frances herself tore the paper in pieces, and said that a signature was not necessary, while Vollins made no further protest. She implored De Courcy, in a whispered adieu, to acquit faithfully the commission with which her father had entrusted him, and he assured her that he was now confident of success, thanking her effusively for the capable conduct of a difficult matter of diplomacy. Then, with a sweeping gesture of obeisance, he took his courteous departure.

Mr. Vollins deferentially asked Frances to sign a receipt which he had written, acknowledging the payment of a thousand pounds, and to this document she hurriedly attached her signature.

## CHAPTER VI.—ORDEAL.

Frances made her way to the North as her father had directed, and everywhere found the news of his arrest in advance of her; the country ablaze with excitement because of it. The world would go well once Strafford was laid low. He had deluded and misled the good King, as Buckingham did before him. Buckingham had fallen by the knife; Strafford should fall by the axe. Then the untrammelled King would rule well; quietness and industry would succeed this unhealthy period of fever and unrest.

The girl was appalled to meet everywhere this intense hatred of her father, and in her own home she was surrounded by it. Even her brother could not be aroused to sympathy, for he regarded his father not only as a traitor to his country, but as a domestic delinquent also, who had neglected and deserted his young wife, leaving her to die uncomforted without even a message from the husband for whom she had almost sacrificed her good name, bearing uncomplaining his absence and her father's wrath. During the winter Frances saw little of her brother. Thomas Wentworth was here and there riding the country, imagining, with the confidence of extreme youth, that he was mixing in great affairs, as indeed he was, although he was too young to have much influence in directing them. The land was in a ferment, and the wildest rumours were afloat. Strafford had escaped from the Tower, and had taken flight abroad, like so many of his friends who had now scattered in fear to France or to Holland. Again it was said the King's soldiers had attacked the Tower, liberated Strafford, and the Black Man was at the head of the wild Irish, resolved on the subjugation of England. Next, the Queen had called on France for aid, and an invasion was imminent. So there was much secret preparation, drilling and the concealing of arms against the time they should be urgently needed, and much galloping to and fro; a stirring period for the young, an anxious winter for the old, and Herbert Wentworth was in the thick of it all, mysteriously departing, unexpectedly returning, always more foolishly important than there was any occasion for. Yet had he in him the making of a man who was shortly to be tried by fire and steel, when greater wisdom crowned him than was at present the case.

One by one the sinister rumours were contradicted by actual events; no French army crossed the Channel; the Irish did not rise; the grim Tower held Strafford secure in its iron grasp. Parliament seemed hesitating to strike, piling up accusations, collecting proof, but staying its hand. Everyone was loyal to the King, so grievously misled. The King could do no wrong, but woe to the Minister who could and did. So, this exciting winter passed and springtime came, ringing with news of Strafford's approaching trial. A stern resolve to be finally rid of him, proof or no proof, was in the air, tinctured with the fine silken hypocrisy that all should be done according to the law; that the axe should swing in rhythm with a solemn declaration of judgment legally rendered. And there was no man to say to the hesitating King, "When that head falls, the brain of your government is gone."

Since the letter she had received on the night of his arrest, the daughter heard no word from the father. Had he again forgotten, or were his messages intercepted? She did not know and was never to know. She had written to him, saying she had obeyed him, but there was no acknowledgment that her letter had reached its destination. Thus she waited and waited, gnawing impatience and dread chasing the rose from her cheeks, until she could wait no longer. Her horse and the southern road were at her disposal, with none to hinder, so she set forth for London, excusing herself for thus in spirit breaking her father's command, by the assurance that he had not forbidden her return. She avoided her father's mansion, knowing that Lady Strafford and her children were now in residence there, and went to the inn where she had formerly lodged. She soon learned that it was one thing to go to London, and quite another to obtain entrance to Westminster Hall, where the great trial, now approaching its end, was the fashionable magnet of the town. No place of amusement ever collected such audiences, and although money will overcome many difficulties, she found it could not purchase admission to the trial through any source that was available. Perhaps if she had been more conversant with the ways of the metropolis the golden key might have shot back the bolt, but with her present knowledge she was at her wit's end.

Almost in despair, a happy thought occurred to her. She wrote a note to John Vollins, her father's treasurer, and asked him to call upon her, which the good man did at the hour she set.

"Your father would be troubled to know you are in London, when he thinks you safe at home," he said.

"I could not help it, Mr. Vollins. I was in a fever of distraction and must have come even if I had walked. But my father need never know, and you remember he wrote that you were to help me.' I wish a place in Westminster Hall and cannot attain it by any other means in my power than by asking you."

"It is difficult of attainment. I advise you not to go there, for if his lordship happened to catch sight of you in that throng, who knows but at a critical moment it might unnerve him, for he is a man fighting with his back to the wall against implacable and unscrupulous enemies."

"Could you not get me some station where I might look upon my father unseen by him?"

"Seats in the Hall are not to be picked or chosen.. If a place can be come

451

by, it will be because some person who thought to attend cannot be present."

"Do you think that where there are so many faces a chance recognition is possible? I should be but an atom in the multitude."

"Doubtless his seeing you is most unlikely. I shall do my best for you, and hope to obtain an entrance for to-morrow."

And so it came about that Frances was one of the fashionable audience next day, occupying the place of a lady who had attended the trial from the first, but was now tired of it, seeking some new excitement, thus missing the most dramatic scene of that notable tragedy. Frances found herself one of a bevy of gaily dressed ladies, all of whom were gossiping and chattering together, comparing notes they had taken of the proceedings, for many of them had dainty writing-books in which they set down the points that pleased them as the case went on. It seemed like a gala day, animated by a thrill of eager expectancy; a social function, entirely pleasurable, with no hint that a man stood in jeopardy of his life. Although the body of the hall was crowded, draped benches at the upper end were still untenanted, except that here and there sat a man, serving rather to emphasize the emptiness of the benches than give token of occupancy.

The lady placed at Frances's right, observing that the girl was a stranger and somewhat bewildered by the unaccustomed scene, kindly made explanation to her.

"On those benches will sit the Lords, who are the judges; on the others the Commons, who are the accusers. They have not yet taken their stations."

"Will the King be present?"

"Technically, no; actually, yes. The Throne, which you see there, will be vacant throughout, but the King may be behind that latticed screen above it, where he can see but cannot be seen. The King must not interfere at a State trial, but he may overset its verdict, and he will, if it should go against the Earl, which is not likely."

"I—I do not see my——I do not see the Earl of Strafford."

"He is not here yet, and will not arrive until the Houses sit."

The girl listened to the hum of conversation going on round her, and caught understandable scraps of it now and then. She was in an entirely new atmosphere, for here every one seemed in favour of Strafford, thought him badly used, and was certain he would emerge triumphant from the ordeal. Then let his enemies beware! Feminine opinion was unanimous that all those who were concerned in this trial against his lordship would bitterly regret the day they had taken such action. The spirits of Frances rose as she listened. The invariable confidence by which she was environed had its inspiring effect on her depressed mind. She no longer thought the gathering heartlessly frivolous, as at first she had resentfully estimated it. She was in the midst of enthusiastic champions of her father, and realized now, as never before, the great part he played in the world.

Suddenly there was a movement in the upper part of the Hall, and Lords and Commons filed in to their places. A silence fell on the audience, maintained also in dignified state by the judges, but to the section occupied by the Commons was transferred the rustle of talk which had previously disturbed the stillness of the auditorium. Men bustled about, whispering to this member of Parliament or that. Papers and notes were exchanged, while by contrast their Lordships seemed like inanimate statues.

Once again the centre of attention changed. The Hall resounded with the measured tramp of armed men. Two rows of soldiers took their stand opposite each other, leaving a clear passage between, and slowly up this passage, with four secretaries and some halfdozen others behind him, came a bowed and pallid figure, dressed in black, a single decoration relieving the sombreness of his costume, which hung, loosely unfitting, about a frame that had become gaunt since its wear began.

"That is the Earl of Strafford," whispered the lady on the right, but the remark fell upon unlistening ears. How changed he was! No trace now of that arrogance of which she had caught chance glimpses during her brief acquaintance with him; a broken man who had but a short time to live, whatever might be the verdict of this court. Sentence of death was already passed on him by a higher tribunal, and all this convocation might do was to forestall its execution. He stood in his place for a moment, and bowed to his judges, but gave no sign that he had knowledge of the existence of his accusers, and the girl began to doubt if the old arrogance had, after all, entirely departed from him. Then, leaning heavily on the arm of one of his secretaries, he sank into his seat and closed his eyes, as if the short walk from the barge to the hall of judgment had been too much for him. As he sat thus there stole down to him a boy leading two children. Strafford's eyes opened, and he smiled wanly upon them, put an arm around the boy's neck, and fondled the girls to his knee, both of whom were weeping quietly.

"Who—who are those?" gasped Frances, yet knowing while she asked, and feeling a pang, half jealousy, half pain, that she must hold aloof unnoticed.

"They are his son and his two daughters. The third daughter is not here."

"The third!" she' cried in surprise. "Does he then acknowledge a third?"

"The third is an infant too young to know what is going on. Hush! We must not talk."

The girl's eagerness fell away from her; she reclined back in her seat and sighed deeply. The preliminaries of the day passed her like a dream, for she knew nothing of the procedure, but at last her attention was aroused, for she saw her father on his feet, and before she was aware he began to speak, the voice at first cold and calm, penetrating the remotest corner of that vast room, in argument that even she recognized as clear, logical, and dispassioned as if he were setting forth the case of another. He was listened to with the most profound respect by enemies and friends alike. He seemed to brush away the charges against him as if they were very cobwebs of accusation. As he went on, he warmed more to his theme, and by and by the girl, leaning intently forward, drinking in every word, knew that she was listening to oratory such as had never before greeted the ears of England, and probably never would again. A breathless tension held the audience spellbound, and it seemed impossible that his direst foe could remain unmoved. The belief in his acquittal now became a certainty, and it was every moment more and more evident that this acquittal would also be a triumph. He stood, one man

454

against three kingdoms thirsting for the blood, yet turning the crisis to the dumfounding of his enemies by the overwhelming force of eloquence. Not a chord on the harp of human sentiment and passion was left unsounded. The deft hand swept every string and fascinated his hearers. When he spoke of his children, pleading more for them than for himself, they weeping at his knee, his own voice broke into a sob more touching even than his living words. From the eyes of Frances gushed the pent-up tears. And she was not alone in her emotion, for the flutter of lace at the eyes of fair ladies broke like white blossoms everywhere. And yet——and yet she became reluctantly convinced that her father in this crisis had entirely forgotten her, and when he spoke of his children, remembered only those that had been all their lives about his knees. She was but the daughter of a day!

Recovering himself, the speaker went on to his peroration. "And now, my lords, I thank God, I have been, by His blessing, sufficiently instructed in the extreme vanity of all temporal enjoyments, compared to the importance of our eternal duration. And so, my lords, even so, with all humility and with all tranquillity of mind, I submit clearly and freely to your judgments. And whether that righteous doom shall be to life or death, I shall repose myself, full of gratitude and confidence, in the arms of the Great Author of my existence. Te Deum laudamus, te Dominum confitemur."

The Latin phrase pealed forth like the solemn tone of a chant, and the speaker subsided into his chair almost in a swoon, for physical weakness had at last overcome the indomitable spirit.

On none of the vast visible throng had the effective oration exercised greater power than upon an unseen listener. The awed stillness was suddenly broken by a splintering crash, and the startled audience, looking up, saw the frail lattice work of the alcove shattered, and the King standing there like a ghost enframed by jagged laths. Stern determination sat on that handsome countenance; a look which said as plainly as words, "This man shall not die!" His hands clutched the broken framework beneath him, and he moistened his lips as if to give utterance to the words his expression foreshadowed. But before he could speak, a tall, angular figure sprang out from among the Commons and held up a sinewy hand. His face was ablaze with anger; his stentorian voice dominated the Hall, envenomed with hatred, striking the ear with terror as does the roar of a tiger.

"The might of England, in Parliament assembled, gives judgment untrammeled and unafraid. The King is not here. The King cannot be here. The Throne is vacant, and must remain vacant until justice is done."

As the last words rang out, the long index finger, shaken menacingly, pointed at the empty chair. There was defiance of King or Minister in words, and tone and gesture; a challenge to the Throne. The pale face of the King became ghastly white, his hand trembled, and fragments of the lattice-work fell from beneath it. Irresolution took the place of former determination, and he glanced pitifully from right to left, as if seeking human support, of which, in the amazed stillness, there was no indication. Then the fine white hand of an unseen woman showed for a moment on his arm like a snow-flake, and Charles, with one look of haunting compassion on the prisoner, disappeared from sight. The phantom picture had vanished from its ragged frame without a sound, and blank darkness occupied its place. Truly the King was not present, conjured away by the strenuous hand of the fierce combatant on the stage, and the soft hand of the woman behind the scenes.

"Who is that man?" whispered Frances, gazing in frightened fascination on the rude interrupter.

"That is John Pym, the chief prosecutor and deadly personal enemy of Lord Strafford."

As the girl gazed at this dominating individuality, all the froth of confidence in her father's acquittal, whipped up by the chatter of conversation at the beginning, evaporated. There stood the personified hatred of England against the Earl of Strafford. No wavering in accent or action there, but a determined man, knowing what he wanted and bent on having it. To her excited imagination the resolute face took on the semblance of a death-mask, and the clenched hand seemed to grasp the shaft of an axe. It was as if the headsman had suddenly stood forth and claimed his own, and a chill as of the grave, swept over the audience with a shudder in its wake.

A low wailing cry went sobbing across the silence; a cry that tugged at

Strafford's heart when he heard it. What memory did it stir in his troubled mind? A reminiscence of something that had escaped him, crowded out by matters of more pressing moment.

"What is that?" he asked anxiously.

"It is nothing, my lord," answered Vollins, stepping between his master and the commotion among the women. "A lady has fainted, that is all. They are taking her out."

## CHAPTER VII.—APPEAL.

Once out in the open air, Frances Wentworth came again into control of herself, ashamed that, for the moment, her emotions had overwhelmed her. She had no desire to re-enter Westminster Hall, even if the doorkeepers would have permitted her, so she wandered slowly back to the inn which was her temporary home. In the evening John Vollins came to see her, and offered money which she told him she did not need. He gave some account of Pym's speech, and said that the Commons had not asked the Lords for judgment, which was taken by Strafford and his friends as an indication that they knew the weakness of the evidence and feared the effect of his lordship's speech in his own defence. The refusal to ask for judgment was regarded as a good omen, and for some days Frances felt the revival of hope, when she could forget the grim figure of John Pym, but the Commons speedily disillusioned the Straffordian party. A bill of attainder was brought in, and they showed their determination to have the head of the unfortunate Earl by act of Parliament, if not by legal procedure. At last the bill, passing its third reading, was sent up to the House of Lords. There were many who said the Lords would never assent to it; that the Commons should have asked for judgment at the close of the trial; that if they could not hope to have the verdict as they wanted it then, it was not likely the Lords would allow themselves to be cozened by a side wind now. These predictions were quickly falsified. The Lords gave their consent to the bill of attainder, and nothing stood between Strafford and the block but a scrawl from the King's pen.

The Lords, it was said by those who defended them, had been coerced by the populace. The mob had gathered again and had clamoured around the House of Peers, crying for justice on Strafford; now they transferred their loud-throated exclamations to Whitehall, for success with the nobles foreshadowed success with the King.

It was late on Saturday night when John Vollins made his way to the inn at some jeopardy to himself, for the streets were wild with joy at the action of the Lords. He told Frances that her father's life depended solely on the firmness of the King. If Charles signed on Monday, Strafford was to be led to the block on Wednesday. Vollins was in deep gloom over the prospect. The Earl, he said, had some time previously written to the King, absolving him from all his promises, offering his life freely if the taking of it would advantage his Majesty in dealing with his obstreperous subjects.

"But the King is trebly perjured if he signs. He cannot sign," cried Frances.

Vollins shook his head.

"If all the Lords in England are held in terror by the people's clamour, and so let the greatest of their number slip through their fingers to the axe, how can one weak man be expected to withstand the concentration of the popular will brought against him? 'T is blinded folly to look for it."

"But the people dare not coerce a King."

"Dare they not? Go down to Whitehall and you will find them doing it. This very day they have all but stormed the palace."

"I will see the King, throw myself at his feet and implore him to keep his word. I was present when he bade my father take this fateful journey to London, and when he promised full protection. A King's word should stand against the world, for he is the source of truth and honour in a nation."

"You cannot get to see him. Every entrance to the palace is strongly guarded. Highly placed friends of my lord, friends when all others had fallen away from him, have sought admission to the royal presence in vain. He has refused to see the Earl of Bristol, whose son, Lord Digby, spoke out against the conclusiveness of the evidence, and his Majesty has let it be spread abroad that he gives no approval of Lord Digby's plain words, and so the people cry 'God save the King!' and revile Lord Digby."

The girl stood aghast at this intelligence, remembering the scene at the trial, when royalty in the person of Charles Stuart, and the people in the person of John Pym, opposed their wills to each other. Then royalty had faded from the sight of men, and the strong champion of the people held his ground alone and triumphant. "Trust in God and the King," wrote the prisoner. What a conjunction! Almighty power, and a bending reed! "Nevertheless, I will see the King," she said.

On Sunday the immensity of the swaying crowd, shouting and moving like a slow resistless flood through the streets, daunted her. There was no employment that day to keep any one within doors, and it seemed as if that labyrinth of human warrens called London had emptied itself into the narrow thoroughfares. She hesitated like a timid swimmer on the brink of a raging torrent, yet if she was to win access to the King she must trust herself to the current, which had this advantage, it set toward the direction in which she wished to go. If the streets could be compared to sluggish streams, the broad avenue or square of Whitehall might be likened to the lake into which they emptied. It was a packed mass of humanity, surging to and fro, as if influenced by mysterious tides, but making no progress. Way through it in any given direction might well seem an impossibility; but an alert atom, by constantly watching opportunity, could edge here and there, through chance openings, and, by a constant devotion to a given direction, ultimately attain any chosen point. Thus the girl, buffeted about, often well-nigh exhausted and breathless, came by the entrance to the palace that stood next the banqueting-house. The gates, however, were tightly closed, and guarded on the outside by a double row of soldiery, who stood the hustling of the mob with great good humour, being evidently cautioned not to exasperate the populace by any hostile act. The crowd itself seemed good-natured enough, although constant fighting took place here and there along its choking surface; but the great bulk of those present appeared to be out on a larking holiday, although they all riotously lent breath to the unceasing roar, calling for justice on Strafford. Occasionally there were shouts for the King, and demands that he should speak to them, but the windows of Whitehall Palace were blank and gave no sign of human occupancy.

Suddenly Frances found herself in new danger through one of those unexplainable heaves of the many-throated beast at whose mercy she stood.

"To the gates!" went up a shout. "We will make the King hear," and a great human wave, overwhelming the soldiers, struck against the shuddering portal. The mere pressure of the multitude was deadly and irresistible. There were shrieks and appeals for forbearance, but the unreasoning mass behind pressed on, unheeding, cheering, and shoving. A crash of rending timbers, and the gates flew inward; then the mob, as if frightened at what it had done, paused, giving the soldiers time to collect themselves and help the wounded. There was as yet no malice in the crush; it was more like a conglomeration of irresponsible children, bent on mischief of any kind, but temporarily scared at the breaking of something. This fact seemed to be recognized by a man in authority who came through the gate and with some difficulty secured a precarious footing on one of the stone pillars which stood in a row between the pathway and the road, thus giving him a position which towered over the heads of the assemblage. He held up a hand for a hearing, and the crowd cheered him, not in the least knowing who he was or why he was there. Comparative silence followed the cheer, and the nobleman spoke.

"My good people," he said, "there is little use in the breaking of gates that the King may hear you; for the King has heard, and is taking the requests of his faithful subjects into his august consideration."

"Where is the King?" demanded an auditor.

"His Majesty is in the banqueting-house, where, as you know, he is in touch with his people. 'T is a prayerful subject he has to meditate on, and I beg of you not to disturb his devotions by further——"

"Is the Queen at her devotions too? In that hall she began masked revels on a Sunday, and six good men were done to death for protesting against the desecration, each life more valuable than the wicked Earl's. Let the King say that he will sign, and we will disperse!"

460

These and other cries more or less to the purpose baffled the orator, and the air quivered with denunciations of Strafford. The man on the stone post had cast his eyes behind him several times, as if to see what progress was being made with the readjustment of the gate, and from this his hearers quickly divined that he was but deluding them to gain time, which was more than likely his purpose, so the shout went up to move through the breach and surround the hall. Meanwhile reinforcements had been summoned from within, and a hand-to-hand fight ensued with the encroachers. Frances, panting and nigh worn out in the struggle, nevertheless saw her opportunity. There were few women in the throng, and such as came near them the soldiers sought to protect. She attempted appeal to the officer, but that harassed dignitary could harken to none, and thrust her rudely but effectually through the opening, saying,—"You will find egress at one of the other gates. Take care of yourself. I cannot help you."

Breathing a sigh of thankfulness, she cowered and ran along the end of the banqueting-hall, turned at the corner, then down the side, entering an archway that let her into a passage. She knew that she must turn to her right, but where after that she had not the slightest notion. The tumult at the gate was so frightful that she expected every moment to hear the victorious assaulters at her heels. Her joy at finding herself thus unexpectedly within the precincts of the palace, unimpeded, caused her to overlook the fact that this was scarcely a propitious moment in which to implore the King to disregard the lusty giant rudely beating at his doors. A frightened waiting-maid came hurrying along the corridor, and to her she directed inquiry regarding the entrance to the banqueting-hall.

"Turn to the right and up the stair."

"Take me there, I beg of you."

"I cannot. I bear a message."

"But I bear a message to the King, so yours must wait."

At this the maid turned and conducted her to the door of the hall, saying to the man at arms,—"This lady has a message for his Majesty."

461

The first thing that struck her on entering the great painted chamber was that the nobleman on the stone outside had not spoken the truth when he said the King heard the demands of his people. A growl as of an angry lion penetrated the closed windows, but the words spoken were not to be distinguished.

The King was sitting at a massive table, his head in his hands. Behind him were grouped a number of bishops in their robes, and it certainly seemed that his Majesty was engaged in devotional exercises, as had been stated by the orator. But if this were the case they were of a strangely mixed order, for behind the lady who was talking volubly to the King, stood two Capuchin monks with folded arms. Excepting the bishops none of the English nobility were present, but several Frenchmen, among whom she recognized De Courcy, held aloof from the cluster at the table, so the girl quite correctly surmised that the lady bearing the whole burden of the conversation was no other than the Queen herself, and that these foreigners were members of her train.

Her Majesty spoke sometimes in French, sometimes in English, the latter with broken accent, and her eloquence was rather puzzling to follow, for the flow of her conversation was of extreme rapidity. Palpably she supposed herself talking in English, but whenever she came to a difficulty in the choice of a word she made no attempt to surmount it by any effort of thought, but swam swiftly round it on the easy current of her native tongue. Translated, her discourse ran thus:

"My God! These good men have made it perfectly plain; for, as they say,—and who shall question the dictum of the Church in such matters,—you have two consciences, the conscience of the Prince and the conscience' of the man; and where the consciences come into conflict that of the Prince must of necessity rule, as is the axiom in all civilized Courts. Is it right that you, a King, should jeopardize yourself in a useless effort to save one condemned by his peers, because your private conscience as a man urges you to keep a promise which he himself has relieved you from, holding you guiltless before God and the nations, and further advised by these good men, lords of their Church, that such action would not make toward peace of the realm. It is not a subject to be hesitated upon for a moment, the good of the ruler being paramount always——"

"Oh, my lord, the King, listen not to such sophistry, be it from the lips of priest or woman. The given word is the man, and he stands or falls by it. If the foresworn peasant be a cringing craven, ten thousand times worse is the perjured Prince. You pledged your faith to Lord Strafford, and now, in his just Heaven, God demands the fulfilment of your word."

The dishevelled girl had flung herself at the feet of the frightened monarch, who started back, gazing wildly about him, shaking as one struck with palsy, so startling and unexpected had been the interruption. Red anger flushed the face of the no less amazed Queen, speechless with indignation at the words and the tone of them, addressed to her exalted husband. The sage bishops were astounded at the lack of diplomacy on the part of the petitioner, who had thus rudely thrown herself counter to the expressed wishes of the highest lady in the land; but Frances, with an instant intuition more subtle than theirs, saw that the Queen was an enemy not to be cajoled by deference or flattery, so she determined that the war between them should be open and above board.

The King had reason for agitation greater than the surprise that had made breathing statues of those about him. The accents that disturbed him were the accents of Strafford himself, softened as they were by the lips that uttered them. The boldness of the address was Strafford's, and, until he saw that a woman knelt before him, it almost seemed that the dominant spirit of the prisoner had burst the bonds of the Tower and sped hither to reproach him for meditated treachery.

Frances, gathering breath, took advantage of the silence her sudden advent had caused.

"Why is Lord Strafford in a dungeon to-day? Because, trusting your word, he obeyed your command at Hampton. Why was he put on trial? Because, faithfully, he carried out his King's behests. Why was he condemned to death? Because he stood true to the King. If he deserve death, then so do you, for you are the master and he the servant. Has God stricken you and your counsellors with blindness, that you cannot see in the destruction of

463

Strafford the throwing away of the shield which guards your breast, leaving you naked to your enemies? Surrender bastion, and the castle falls."

"God of Heaven!" cried the quivering Queen. "What country of the mad is this, where the meanest of subjects may so address a monarch! Strip the mantle from her back and scourge her rebellious flesh to the kennel whence she comes."

"No, no!" gasped Charles, staggering to his feet and sweeping with a gesture of his hand the documents which lay before him on the table, so that they fluttered to the floor. "Christ have mercy upon me! She speaks the truth; happy is the Prince who hears it and heeds it. I have passed my word to Strafford, and it shall be kept. I will not sign,—no, though the heavens fall. Rise, my girl! You have my promise,—the promise of a Stuart,—and it shall be fulfilled."

Charles graciously assisted the girl to her feet with the same courtesy he would have shown to the first lady of the Court.

The rage of the Queen now passed all bounds of restraint. "And this before me, your wife! You weigh the word of this bedraggled creature of the streets above that of the royal House of France, and Queen of this turbulent realm! By God, you deserve to be hooted by your loathsome mob. Who is this strumpet?" De Courcy whispered a word into her ear.

"What! The bastard of that profligate Strafford! Jesu, to what a pass this Christian Court has come!"

"Madam," said Frances with frigid dignity, "you misname me. I have the honour to be Lord Strafford's lawful daughter, acknowledged by him as such in presence of his Majesty the King."

"'T is true, 't is true," murmured Charles, visibly quailing before the increasing wrath of his wife, adding in piteous appeal, "God's wounds, have I not enough to bear without the quarreling of women."

"The quarreling of women! Dare you couple me in the same breath with such as she? Is there none in my train to whip forth this impudent wench into the wretched rabble that has spewed her into our presence. The quarreling of women! A slattern that wishes to divert, from her reputed father's head to yours, the anger of the gutter. Listen to it, my lord, listen to it."

All this was shrieked forth with gestures so rapid and amazing that the eye could scarce follow the motion of her hands. Now she flew to the window and fumbled with its fastening, too greatly excited to succeed with the opening. Several of the French gallants stumbled over each other in their haste to aid her, but the lady's impatience could not wait for them. She lifted her clenched hand and smote the diamond panes, which went shivering down beneath the fierce impact of the blow. Glass or lead or both cut the imperious hand and wrist, and the blood trickled down the fair rounded arm. The breach she made was like the letting in of waters; the roar outside became instantly articulate, and waves of meaning flooded the great apartment.

"To the block with Strafford. Death to the people's oppressor!" was the cry, and the tortured King shrank from it as from the lash of a whip.

"Harken to the wolves!" shrieked the Queen. "It is your blood or Strafford's! Which, which, which?"

Then, perhaps because of the hurt which she scarcely seemed to feel, her mood changed as quickly as her anger had risen, and she melted into tears, glided to her husband, and threw her arms about his neck.

"Oh Charles, Charles," she moaned, "it is my love for you that would coerce you. You have not been to blame, misled by an obstinate Minister who would sacrifice an indulgent master to buy his own safety. A King is not to be bound as other men. The claim of your wife and children rise superior to that of any subject, for you have sworn to protect them." Charles stood by the wall which was eight years later to be broken for his own final exit, his eyes filled with tears, caressing the woman who clung to his breast. He saw that the girl was about to address him again and said hastily,—"Go, go! You but pile distraction on distraction. Fear not; for the word of a King goes with you."

"No, no!" sobbed the Queen. "For my sake withdraw it."

Two of the bishops now stepped forward, and with gentle urgency used their persuasion on the girl to withdraw. "God keep your Majesty firm," she cried, "and so deal with you as you deal with my father." But the last sight she was to have of her ruler, as the good men pushed her to the door, was far from inspiring. His cheeks were womanishly wet, and wavering irresolution was stamped upon his brow. The twining wounded arms of his wife had reddened the white scarf at his throat with the royal, passionate blood of France.

## CHAPTER VIII.—EXECUTION.

On Monday there were ever-increasing rumours through the town that Charles had signed the bill which would send his chief Minister to the block, qualified by statements equally vague that he had done nothing of the sort; but as night drew on, the rising jubilation of the crowds in the streets gave point to the more sinister report. In the evening, his usual time of calling, the sombre Vollins came to the inn, chiefly, as he said, to urge the girl to quit the turbulent city, where she could accomplish nothing, and where she might be in danger were it once guessed that she bore any relationship to the condemned man; but to this good counsel the girl would not listen. What she demanded impatiently was news, news, news, and this, with exasperating deliberation, Vollins gave forth. It was quite true that the bill was signed, not by the King's hand, but by the hands of four Commissioners whom he had appointed for that purpose. The House of Lords, and even the House of Commons, was amazed at this betrayal, said Vollins, and the effect of the announcement had been seen on the populace itself; for, after certainty came home to the people, they had dispersed quietly to their houses, and the streets were almost empty.

The girl was mute with dismay, but Vollins pointed out that the case was in reality no worse than it had been on Saturday or Sunday. By the exercise of his prerogative the King could at any moment free his Minister or mitigate the sentence, notwithstanding the fact that the Commission had signed the bill of attainder in his name. Vollins had always been distrustful of the King, but his pessimism was not increased by the hurrying events of the last few days; rather, he saw signs of encouragement where Frances found only blank despair. The signing had had the immediate effect of stilling the outcry of the public, yet it in no way increased Strafford's danger. The action was merely typical of the King's roundabout methods of accomplishing his objects. The people were notoriously fickle and could not keep up the shouting indefinitely; indeed there were already signs that they were tired of it. It was more than likely that Charles would reprieve the Earl, possibly at the last moment, and have him shipped off to France or Holland before London knew what had been done. Or, it might be, Strafford would escape when Charles saw that Lords, Commons, and people were in grim earnest. The Tower was on the waterside, and the prisoner would not be the first who had slipped away by boat the night before an intended execution. Such a plan would be peculiarly acceptable to the mind of the King, for he had given way to the expressed will of his subjects and could not be held responsible for the avolation of the convicted man. The Tower was impregnable and cared nothing for clamour.

Tuesday seemed to bear out these surmises. Frances determined to see the King once more, and learn from his own lips the fate of her father; but when she reached Whitehall she found some commotion there, for Charles was taking his departure from the palace, and people said he was on his way to the House of Lords, and that it was likely he had determined to let Strafford go. Even although this suspicion was prevalent among those assembled, there seemed to be no popular resentment of it, and the crowd loudly cheered Charles as he rode away surrounded by his jingling guards—truly a remarkable change in public sentiment since Sunday. She went from Whitehall to the Tower, viewing the stronghold from various points, but not venturing near it. At first she had some thought of asking admission that she might see her father; but she was almost certain a refusal was all she might expect, and there was ever the fear she would arouse inquiry by making any application, and so frustrate plans already formed for his rescue. Vague visions passed through her mind of prisoners escaping through the devotion of friends sacrificing themselves, or concocting ingenious schemes that resulted in liberty; but as she looked at the forbidding, strong fortress, her dreams were confronted by a very stern reality, and the conviction was impressed upon her that there was nothing to be gained in lingering about the Tower. After all, the word of the King was sufficient to open the gates, could he but pluck up courage to speak it. He was bound in honour to say the word, and Frances saw that her only chance of helpfulness lay in urging him to keep his promise.

In the evening she learned authoritatively the object of the King's visit to the House of Lords. He had pleaded earnestly for the life of his Minister, promising, if he were released, never again to employ him even in the meanest capacity. He implored them at least to grant a reprieve until Saturday, and this was so small a favour for a King to ask that Vollins was sure it would be granted, and that many things might happen in the intervening days. The confidence of a man so generally despairing as Vollins, in the certainty of a short reprieve, and in the ultimate safety of Lord Stratford, did much to bring the girl to a like belief, but she resolved, nevertheless, to see the King next day if she could win her way into Whitehall Palace.

Wednesday saw no excitement on the streets; people were going soberly about, each on his own affairs, and the reprieve had provoked no outburst, which in itself was a hopeful sign. Frances had grown to fear the hue and cry of the mob even more than she feared the indecision of the King. If he were left unterrified, all his tendency was toward mercy and the keeping of his oath.

There was no crowd to distract the attention of the guard at the palace gates opening on Whitehall, and they absolutely refused to grant her admission without an order. She turned to the captain of the guard and asked how such an order could be obtained, and that official, apparently struck by her youth and beauty, as well as her evident distress, said that if she knew any about the Court who might be sent for, and who proved willing to vouch for her, he would allow her to pass; but the rule at the gate was strict, because of past disturbances, and he had no option but refusal unless she went in under the convoy of some one in authority. Frances pondered a few moments, and hesitated, but her need was great, and she could not choose when it came to finding security. At last she said with reluctance,—"I am acquainted with Monsieur De Courcy. Is he within?"

"I do not know, but 't will be speedily ascertained." With that he invited her to a seat in the guardhouse, and sent a messenger for De Courcy, knowing there would be prompt response when the Frenchman learned that a beautiful lady awaited him, and in this he was not mistaken. De Courcy came, as debonair and as well groomed as usual, twirling his light moustache, and doffing his hat with a grand air when he saw who his petitioner was.

"I wish to see his Majesty again," said Frances, rising; "but they detain me at the gate, and I have no one to vouch for me unless you will be so kind, though I am sorry to trouble you."

"To pleasure me, Mademoiselle, you must mean. 'T is an ungallant country, as I have always said, when they keep so fair a maid a-waiting. Such a boorish act is not conceivable in France. Most honoured am I to be your sponsor, and it gratifies me to tell you that the King is at present disengaged. I beg you to accompany me."

The friend of the Queen did not even trouble to make any explanation to the captain of the guard, and he was too powerful a courtier to have anything he did questioned by the underlings. It was palpable that the officer had small liking for him, but wholesome fear of his influence in high places.

As the two crossed the yard together, the young man said with the greatest affability,—"Would you prefer to see the King alone, or in company?"

"Oh, alone, if it be possible."

"Quite possible. I shall delight in arranging a private interview, and am sure his Majesty will not refuse my request. If you do not wish to meet any of the Court, I can take you to him by a private route where we are almost certain to encounter none."

"I shall be deeply indebted to you."

They threaded their way through devious and labyrinthian passages, turning now to the right, now to the left, sometimes ascending a few steps, and sometimes a narrow stairway, until at last the guide came to a door which he pushed open.

"If you will wait here for a moment, I will go and fetch the King." He bowed gracefully as she passed through the doorway, entering a square room, the walls of which were decorated by groups of swords and rapiers of various sorts; a veritable armory. A table occupied the centre, and there were several chairs, with a lounge against the wall. A door opened upon an inner room.

De Courcy, instead of taking his departure, stepped in quickly after the girl, closed the door, and turned the key in the lock. With the grating of the key came the first suspicion to the mind of Frances that her guide was treacherous. Much as she had always distrusted him, it seemed incredible that, knowing her to be the daughter of the Earl of Strafford, anything disastrous might befall her here in the very palace of the King, the sworn protector of his people. The leer on De Courcy's face and his words speedily disillusioned her.

"If you will be seated, my dear, we may have some converse, interesting and entertaining to us both. You can scarcely imagine my joy at seeing so lovely a visitor in my poor apartments."

"Sir, you said you would bring the King. A gentleman keeps his word."

"Oh, the King in good time, my pretty one. Charles is but a doleful companion just now, and we are well quit of him. As for a man's word, the fashion seems to be the breaking of it, example being set us poor gentlemen in the highest places. For instance, our last discussion related to marriage, but times have changed since that day, and you will not be so cruel as to expect me to carry out the good domestic intentions I then expressed."

"Sir, I am very glad I shall hear no more of them."

"Truly? Then so much the better. I expected tears and reproaches, but am pleased you are not given to complaining. By my honour, I love you the more for it. So, then, I'll steal a kiss from those ripe lips to seal the new compact we are to make, and I warn you that a scream is not likely to be heard from this chamber."

"I need not your warning. You shall neither hear me scream nor see me weep."

"By Saint Denis, I like your spirit. Some scream, and some weep, but they all end by clinging."

"Sir, a warning for your warning. Approach not another step nearer me. Stand aside, rather, and allow me quittance of this place as freely as I ignorantly came hither."

470

"And if I cannot consent?"

"Then 't will be the worse for you."

"God's truth, but you spur an inclination already highly mettled. Still would I treat you with all courtesy. You are a nameless woman, and many of the highest dames in England are proud to call me their friend."

"That I believe to be as untrue as your saying I am a nameless woman."

"Nevertheless, one is as true as the other. Your father never acknowledged you."

"He has been burdened with more important affairs, but he will do so when he is free."

During this dialogue the participants had been constantly changing their positions, De Courcy advancing and Frances retreating, keeping the table between them. The girl's design was plain enough; she desired to hold him in conversation, gradually shifting her position, until she got between him and the door, when a sudden dash might give her freedom. But he easily fathomed this design and laughed as he checkmated it. At her last words, however, he drew himself upright, a look of genuine amazement overspreading his face.

"When he is free!" he echoed. "Powers of Heaven! Then you have not come to reproach the King, but to plead with him!"

"Why should I reproach him?"

"It would surely be useless enough, but feminine. Why? Because Gregory Brandon, with one good stroke, severed the King's word and Strafford's neck on Tower Hill this morning."

The girl's face went white as the kerchief about her throat, and, swaying half an instant, she leaned against the table for support. Something in the brutal method of the announcement convinced her of its truth more surely than if he had spoken with all the solemnity of which he might be capable. Yet she struggled not to believe.

"You are lying to me," she gasped.

"Far from it, my little lady. How could I imagine you did not know? You are surely the only person in London who is ignorant of it. Why is everything so quiet near Whitehall, where the generous citizens have been so solicitous about us of late? Merely because the centre of interest has changed to the other end of the town, and a rare show was put on the stage for all good people to see, free of cost to themselves, unless they have the brains to know of what they are bereft by Strafford's death, which is most unlikely." As he spoke he had been edging toward her, catlike, but she paid no heed to him. Then with a spring he caught her wrists, but she did not move or make any effort to free herself. She looked dully at him, as if wondering why he acted so.

"You will be pleased to withdraw yourself, sir, and let me go. My heart is broken."

She spoke with forced calmness, but there was a tremor in her tone that cast doubt on her former assertion regarding the tears.

"Your heart is not broken, and if it was I'd mend it for you. Absurd! Why, you knew the man for scarce a day, and that time is full short for the growth of any large affection."

"I shall never love any as I have loved him."

"Tush! How little you know of yourself. You are a very goddess of love, and I will——"

He released one wrist and endeavored to slip his disengaged arm about her waist. This seemed to rouse the girl from her stupor, for she suddenly thrust him back, and, taking him unaware, sent him sprawling; then she sprang for the door. But he was as nimble as she, for, quickly recovering himself, he held her tight before she could turn the key.

"Sir, you forget who I am. Release me at once, and molest me no further."

"Divinest of the fair, I swear to you——"

She whisked herself free of him, and, darting to the other side of the room, whipped down a thin rapier from the wall.

"You will be well advised to put an end to this fooling. I am now in no humour for it, and with you, never. If you have not the gift to see it, I would have you know that I detest you and despise you, and have done so since first I saw you."

"Ah, my little lady Termagant, you say as much now; but when the world knows you paid a thousand pounds for a lover there will be many envious persons who wish to be despised as much."

"You ruffian and thief! Well did Vollins estimate your honesty. But stand aside from that door, or your stealing will profit you little."

"Indeed!" cried De Courcy with a laugh, as he possessed himself of a similar weapon to that which threatened him. "'T is already squandered, and I am in sore need of a further instalment. Are you for a duel, then?"

"If you are coward enough to lift blade to a woman."

"I meet kiss with kiss, and steel with steel; always ready for either. Guard yourself, Madam."

His pretended antagonism was but a feint to throw her off the guard he advised her to maintain, for, being one of the best swordsmen of his time, he knew by her holding of the blade that she was ignorant of its practice. He brushed her sword aside, dropped his own, and sprang in upon her, grasping again her helpless wrists, her arms pinioned thus transversely across her body, her right hand still clinging to the useless hilt, with the blade extending past her shoulder and behind her. His sneering, grinning face so close to hers that his breath fanned her cheek, he pressed her back and back against the wall, the sword bending and bending behind her until the blade snapped off some six inches from the hilt and fell ringing to the floor.

"There, sweetest of Amazons, you are stingless now, and naught but the honey is to be gathered."

The very ease with which he had overcome her hoodwinked him to his danger. The proud dominant blood of the Wentworths flushed her face with an anger that steeled every nerve in her lithe body. As, with a victorious laugh, he released her wrists and slipped his arms around her, she struck him twice with lightning swiftness, first across the brow, then down the face. Nothing could well be more terrible than the weapon she had used, for the jagged iron tore his flesh like the stroke of a tiger's claw. The red cross showed for a brief moment, then was obliterated in a crimson flood.

"Cowardly poltroon, wear the brand of Cain!"

He had warned her not to scream, but now his own cries filled the room as he staggered back, his hands to his face. Yet, grievously wounded as he was, he seemed resolved she should not escape him, and, after the first shock, groped blindly for her. She flung the broken weapon to the further side of the room, and the noise of its fall turned him thither, striking against the table, and then against a chair. She tip-toed cautiously to the door, turned the key, and threw it open before he could recover himself, for he had lost all sense of direction and could see nothing. She took the immediate risk of drawing the key from the door, to ward off the greater danger of pursuit, and calmly locked him in. If screams were as ineffectual as he had insisted, he would take little good from his battering of the door for some time to come. Frances now threaded her way through the maze of passages, meeting no one, for the gloom of death pervaded the palace, at least in the direction she had taken.

She dared not hurry, in spite of the urging of her quickly beating heart, but must proceed leisurely, as if she had a perfect right to be where she was, should any inquisitive servant encounter her. At last, with a deep breath, she emerged upon the great courtyard and so came to the gate. The officer bowed to her, and she paused for a moment to thank him for his kindness to her in the earlier part of the day.

"Is it true—that—that Lord Strafford——" She could get no further.

"Yes, my lady, and grieved we all are that it should be so. This morning on Tower Hill. The Lords refused a reprieve even until Saturday." Frances bent her head and struggled with herself to repress undue emotion, but, finding that impossible, turned abruptly and walked fast down Whitehall.

"Her bright eyes, bless her!" said the officer to a comrade, "are not the only ones dimmed with tears for this morning's work."

474

On reaching the inn Frances thought of waiting for the faithful Vollins, but she had not the heart to meet him, nor the inclination to rest another night in the city now so hateful to her. She wrote a letter which was forwarded to him by a messenger, but said nothing of her visit to Whitehall, telling him his estimate of De Courcy had been correct, promising to send the thousand pounds to be replaced in her father's treasury as soon as she reached her home in the North, and asking pardon that his counsel had been declined.

Two hours later Frances was on her way to the North. She paused on Highgate Hill and looked back on the Babel she had left, vast and dim in the rising mist of the mild spring evening. "Oh, cruel city! Oh, faithless man! The bloodthirst of London may be whetted and not quenched, perjured King of England!" She bowed her head to her horse's mane and wept helplessly.

# BOOK II.—THE MAN.

## CHAPTER I.—COINCIDENCE.

William Armstrong rode his splendid black steed like one more accustomed to the polishing of saddle-leather than to the wearing out of the same material in the form of boots. Horse and man were so subtly suited, each to each, that such another pair might well have given to some early artist the first idea of a centaur. Armstrong was evidently familiar with the district he traversed, for he evinced no surprise when, coming to the crown of a height, he saw in the valley below him a one-storied stone building, whose outhouses and general surroundings proclaimed it a solitary inn, but the horse, less self-contained, and doubtless more fatigued, thrust forward his ears and gave utterance to a faint whinny of pleasure at the near prospect of rest and refreshment. The hand of the rider affectionately stroked and patted the long black mane, as if in silent corroboration of the animal's eager anticipations.

The young man was as fair as his mount was dark. A mass of yellow hair flowed out from under his Scot's bonnet and over his broad shoulders. A heavy blonde moustache gave him a semi-military air; a look of the cavalier; as if he were a remnant of that stricken band across the border which was fighting for King Charles against daily increasing odds; but something of jaunty self-confidence in Armstrong's manner betokened that the civil war raging in England was no concern of his, or that, if he took any interest in it, his sympathies inclined toward the winning side, as indeed was the case with many of his countrymen. His erect bearing, body straight as one of his native pines, enhanced the soldier-like appearance of the horseman, and it needed but a glance at his clear-skinned but resolute face and powerful frame to be convinced that he would prove a dangerous antagonist to meet in combat, while the radiant good-nature of his frank countenance indicated a merciful conqueror should victory fall to him, as seemed likely unless the odds were overwhelming.

Both prowess and geniality were on the instant of being put to the test as he approached the inn, where a wayfarer is usually certain of a welcome if he has but money in his pouch. A lanceman, his tall weapon held upright, stepped out into the road from the front of the closed door before which he had been standing, when he saw that the traveller was about to halt and dismount.

"Ye'll be fur dawnerin' on a bit faurer forret," hinted the sentinel in a cautious, insinuating manner, as if he were but giving expression to the other's unspoken intention.

"A wise man halts at the first public-house he comes to after the sun is down," replied Armstrong.

"Ah'm thinkin' a man's no verra wise that stops whaur he's least wanted, if them that's no wantin' him has good airn in their hauns."

"Aye, my lad, steel 's a bonny argument, rightly used. Whut's a' th' steer here, that a tired man, willin' to pay his way, is sent doon th' rod?"

Armstrong adopted for the moment a brogue as broad as that of his questioner. He flung his right leg across the horse, and now sat sideways in his saddle, an action which caused the sentinel suddenly to grip the shaft of his pike with both hands; but the equestrian making no further motion, conversing in an easy nonchalant tone, as if he had little personal interest in the discussion, the vigilance of the man on guard partially relaxed, probably thinking it as well not to provoke so excellently equipped an opponent by any unnecessary show of hostility.

"Weel, ye see, there's muckle folk in ben yonner that has mony a thing ta chatter aboot, an' that's a' Ah ken o't, except that Ah'm ta let nane inside ta disturb them."

"Whose man are you?"

"Ah belong ta th' Yerl o' Traquair."

"And a very good friend of mine the Earl of Traquair is. Will you just go inside and tell him William Armstrong is sitting here on his horse?"

"That wull Ah no, fur if th' King himsel' were ta ask, Ah munna let him by th' door. Sa jist tak a fule's advice fur yince, and gang awa' ta th' next botha afore it gets darker an' ye're like to lose yer rod amang th' hills."

"I must get something for my horse to eat. He's done, and should not be pushed further. I'll wait outside until their lordships have finished their council."

"Th' stalls are a' fou already, an' if not wi better nags, at least wi the nags o' noblemen, an' Ah'm thinkin' that's neither you nor me."

"The stalls may be fou, but my beast's empty, and I must get a feed of corn, noble or simple. Ye tell the Earl it's me and ye'll be thankit."

"Indeed, ma braw man, Ah tak' orders fra the Yerl himsel', an' fra nane else. Jist tickle yer beast wi' the spur, or Ah'll gie him a jab wi' th' point o' this spear."

The descent of young Armstrong was so instantaneous that the man-at-arms had no opportunity of carrying out his threat, or even of levelling the unwieldy weapon in his own defence. The horseman dropped on him as if he had fallen from the clouds, and the pike rang useless on the rough cobble-stones. The black horse showed no sign of fright, as might have been expected, but turned his intelligent head and calmly watched the fray as if accustomed to any eccentricity on the part of his master. And what the fine eyes of the quadruped saw was startling enough. The wide-spread limbs of the surprised soldier went whirling through the air like the arms of a windmill in a gale. Armstrong had grasped him by the waist and turned him end for end, revolving him, Catherine-wheel-wise, until the bewildered wits of the victim threatened to leave him through the action of centrifugal force. By the time the unfortunate sentinel lost all reckoning of the direction in which solid earth lay with regard to his own swiftly changing position, he found himself on his assailant's shoulder, gaping like a newly landed trout, and, thus hoisted aloft, he was carried to the closed door, which a kick from Armstrong's foot sent crashing inward. The intruder flung his burden into the nearest corner of the large room, as if he were a sack of corn; then, facing the startled audience, the young man cried:

"Strong orders should have a stronger guard than, you set, gentlemen. I hold to the right of every Scotsman to enter a public dram-shop when he pleases."

A dozen amazed men had sprung to their feet, oversetting a chair or a stool here and there behind them, and here and there a flagon before them. Eleven swords flashed out, but the upraised right hand of the chairman and his commanding voice caused the weapons to hang suspended.

"The very man! By God, the very man we want! In the Fiend's name, Will, where have you dropped from?"

"From the back of my horse a moment since, as your henchman here will bear witness, Traquair."

"Armstrong, your arrival at this juncture is providential; that's what it is, providential!"

"It must be, my Lord, for you did your best to prevent it. Your stout pikeman would not even let you know I was within call, so I just brought him in to give the message properly."

"Losh, if he knew you as well as I do, he would have thought twice or he stood in your way. Come to the table, man, and fill a flagon."

"I'll empty one with pleasure if the drawer will charge it."

"We have no drawer, Armstrong, but wait on ourselves, trusting the lugs of a cogie rather than the ears of a scullion. So I'll be your cup-bearer, Will."

"Thank you kindly, my lord, but I'll help myself, as my ancestor said to the Duke of Northumberland when he drove away the English cattle. The man who will not stretch an arm to slake a thirst deserves a dusty road all day with no bothy at the end of it." And, saying this, the young man drank long and well.

479

The sentinel had by this time got on his feet and was staring at the company like one dazed. "Where's your pike?" demanded Traquair.

"On the stanes ootside, ma lord."

"Very well, go out and lift it, and see that you hold a better grip of it when the next man comes along. Attend to Armstrong's horse, and keep an eye up and down the road."

"I'll look after my own beast, Traquair."

"No need for that, Will. We have matters of importance to discuss, and Angus here will feed the horse as well as you can do it."

"I'll eat and drink whatever's set before me, and never ask who is the cook, but I trust no man to wait on my horse. You bide by your sentry march, Angus, and I'll see to the beast."

With this Armstrong strode out of the house, the ill-used sentinel following him. As the door closed, the interrupted hum of conversation rose again.

Who the interloper might be was the burden of the inquiry.

"Armstrong's the very man for our purpose," said Traquair. "If any one can get through Old Noll's armies by craft or by force, it is Will. I had no idea he was near by, or I would never have wasted thought on any other. I have known him for years, and there's none to match him, Hielan' or Lowlan'. We need seek nae farrar if Christie's Wull is wullin'."

"I have never before heard of him," said the Reverend Alexander Henderson, of Edinburgh. "What has he done?"

"What has he not done?" asked the Earl. "The Border rings with his fame, as it has rung with the fame of his ancestors these several centuries past."

"Oh, the Border!" cried the townsman, with the contempt of his class for the supposedly ignorant condition of that wild hilly belt which girded the waist of the land. "We all know what brings a man renown on the Border.

The chief requisites are a heavy sword and a thick skull. That the proposed excursion may require a ready blade at times, I admit, but a man who depends on that will not blunder through. There are too many of his kind opposed to him in Cromwell's army. It is not a wilderness like the Border that lies between here and Oxford, but a civilized country with cities, and men of brains in them. To win through and back requires skill and diplomacy, alertness of resource, as well as the qualities of riding hard and striking swift."

"William Armstrong has all these qualities, and many more," replied Traquair.

"The sample of his conduct just presented to us savors more of violence than of tact," objected Henderson. "He comes breenging in on a private conference of his betters, carrying their sentinel on his head like a shambled sheep, and flings him in a corner. This proves him a strong man, but far from a wise one, because, for all he knew, he might have been walking into an ambuscade that would have cost him his life or liberty. It was pure luck and not foreknowledge that caused him to find a friend at our board."

"You are in the wrong there, Henderson, quite in the wrong, for you all heard him say that the sentry refused to bring in his message to me. Armstrong knew I was here, and thus was well aware he was safe enough."

Henderson shook his head, stubbornly unconvinced. He was a man of talk rather than of action, and knew he spoke well, so, being a born objector to other men's proposals, his tongue was more active than his arm. When the unexpected "breenging" had occurred, every man in the room had jumped to his feet and grasped his sword, except Henderson, who sat staring, exhibiting little of that ready resource he had been commending. Now the danger was past, he apparently thought that after-eloquence made good the absence of energy in a crisis.

Traquair, ever suave so long as he carried his point, showed no signs of irritation at this line of criticism, but made comment and gave answer in a low tone and persuasive voice. The others round the table kept silence and listened to the controversy between the man of language and the man of action, ready, doubtless, to side with whichever proved the victor. The Earl leaned his elbow on the board and gazed across at his opponent.

"Look you here, Henderson. You are willing to admit there is no such city as Edinburgh between here and the King?"

"Doubtless not."

"And I need not try to convince you that Edinburgh is second to no town in the world so far as learning, judgment, and good sense are concerned?"

"Edinburgh is not in question, my Lord."

"But you'll agree with all I say regarding it?"

"Well, there are worse places than Edinburgh."

"Cautiously uttered, but true. Very good. Perhaps you will not dispute the fact that Lord Durie is one of your most enlightened citizens?"

"Durie, Lord of Sessions? Durie's Decisions are well known in law, I am told. I have nothing to say against the man."

"There you differ from me, Henderson. I have much to say against him, be his Decisions never so good. He is, and always was, a prejudiced old fool, who, if he once got a wrong notion in his head, was proof against all reason."

"Speak no ill against those in authority over us!" cried Henderson, bristling into opposition now that a definite opinion was expressed. "For twenty years he was chosen vice-president by the best men in all Scotland, none successfully opposing him, so you cannot say ill of such an one."

"Very well, very well," coincided Traquair with suspicious haste, a faint smile parting his lips. "We will take your word for it that his legal lordship is all you say. The point I wish to establish is that Edinburgh possesses an enviable shrewdness, and that Lord Durie is one of her most esteemed citizens. Other people may hold contrary opinion, but we defer to yours, Henderson. It chanced that one man holding contrary opinion so far as his lordship was concerned, and troubled with grave doubts regarding his impartiality, had a case coming before him that involved the litigant's possessions and lands. He knew that Durie was against him, and that there was no way of getting the thrawn deevil—I beg your pardon, Henderson—this upright judge—to listen to justice. This defendant slipped a word in Armstrong's ear to the effect that it would be most admirable if there was some other presiding judge at the Court of Sessions when the case was tried. The consequence was that Lord Durie, for the time being, disappeared and was accounted dead. The case was tried before his successor, and won by the contestant I have referred to, as was but right and just. Then Lord Durie came on the scene once more, to the joy of everyone but his successor, who should have been a friend of Will's if he wished the disappearance to have been permanent."

"Ah, there you overstep the bounds of probability in order to establish a false proficiency for this ranting Borderer. 'Tis well known that Armstrong had nothing to do with the kidnapping of his lordship. The judge himself admits that the powers of evil spirited him away and kept him in a warlock's castle, hoping to lure him from the path of righteousness; but, his probity proving impregnable, they could not contend against it, and were fain to let him go again unscathed, for it is written, 'Resist the Devil and he will flee from you.'"

The Earl of Traquair leaned back and laughed aloud.

"Well, you can take my word for it that he did not flee in this instance. When the judge was enjoying an airing, as was his custom, sitting his canny horse on Leith sands, Armstrong accosted him, also on horseback, and the two entered into amiable and instructive conversation. Old Durie was so charmed with his new acquaintance that he accompanied him to the unfrequented spot known as Frigate Whins, and there Will threw his cloak over the distinguished man's head, lifted him from his horse, and made off through a section of the country known better by himself than by any other, and where he was sure he was not like to meet gossiping stragglers. At last Will deposited his burden in the lonely Tower of Graham by the water of Dryfe, and there he remained for three months, not even seeing the people who fed him, for his meat was let down to him by a rope. As the judge's horse was found wandering on the sands, people came to the conclusion that his lordship had been thrown off, stunned, and drowned, the body being carried out to sea by the tide. In due time Armstrong took the gentleman back as he had come, and flattered the auld carle by telling him that, such was his learning and piety, Satan could not prevail against him. And so the learned judge just dawnered home with this idea in his head, which he speedily-got the wise city of Edinburgh to believe."

For a wonder Henderson remained silent, but one of the others spoke up.

"I remember the incident well," he said, "and if I am not mistaken the Tower of Graham at that time belonged to your lordship."

"Yes, and it does yet," replied Traquair nonchalantly. "Armstrong, being an old friend of mine, had no hesitation in using my property without my leave, for, as he explained afterward, there was no time for consultation, the case being urgent."

"It was a most suitable place for the judge's custody," continued the other drily, "because, unless a treacherous memory misleads me, a plea regarding this very property was decided in your favour by the single vote of the Lord President, who temporarily took the place of Justice Durie during his mysterious absence."

"Sir, you are quite in the right," replied Traquair, unabashed by the evident insinuation. "It was my great good luck that the case against me was heard during Durie's absence, and, as you were doubtless about to point out, this world is full of strange coincidences which our poor finite minds fail to fathom."

"A finite mind easily probes the bottom of such a shameless conspiracy," cried Alexander Henderson sternly, bringing his fist down upon the table. "What! Kidnap the Lord President of the Sessions, from the very edge of Edinburgh in broad daylight——"

"It was drawing on to the gloaming at the time," corrected Traquair soothingly, "at least so Will informed me."

"It was nevertheless an outrageous action; a foul deed that should not go unwhipt of——"

"Gentlemen," said the Earl in a tone of authority, which seemed to recall the fact that, after all, he was the chairman of the conclave, "we are wandering from the point. At this moment Lord Durie is reported to be a dying man, and whatever evil has been done against him in the long past probably troubles him less than the injustice he may himself have been the cause of. In any case we are met here together for a certain purpose, and what is said within this circle is said in confidence, for which our plighted words to each other stand sponsor. The crux of the discussion is this. Henderson objects to my man as the most fitting for our embassy, holding him to be a rude and brainless swashbuckler. That is a definite charge. I meet it by showing that this same man befooled the wise city of Edinburgh and the most learned man within its confines. A brainless bravado would have run a dirk into Lord Durie and left his body on the sands. I wish unanimous consent to tender our present dangerous mission to William Armstrong, in the hope that he may get safely to Oxford, and, what is more important, bring us with equal safety the King's written command. If any of you have some one else to propose, whom you think may accomplish his business better than Will Armstrong, I ask you to nominate the man and give reasons for your preference."

Henderson growled in his beard, but said nothing audible. Each man looked at the others as if waiting for some one else to make further suggestion; but, as the silence was prolonged, the one who had referred to the coincidence of Durie's incarceration with Traquair's case at law, cleared his throat and said that for his part it seemed that Armstrong was the proper man for the mission. With this the others agreed, and even Henderson gave an ungracious concurrence. The Earl was about to address the company when the door opened and Armstrong himself entered.

## CHAPTER II.—SUSPICION.

Speak of the Devil, Wull," cried Traquair. "We have been talking of you, my man, and we have some employment for you if you are ready for it."

"Well, my Lord, there's no lack of that in these kittle times, for a fighting man gets civility and a welcome, whether in England or Scotland, whichever side he takes."

"I hope you are for law and the King, against riot and rebels?"

"Ye see, Traquair, I'm not just a faction man, but am standing clear, to give both sides fair play, as the De'il said when he was toasting the Elder on his fork, and changed his front to the fire. I suppose I am for the King, though I'm not so prejudiced but I can see something to be said for the other side. It seems to me that the King's not exactly as wise as his predecessor Solomon."

"That's treason," roared Henderson.

"Oh, not among friends who are most of them thinking the same thing," said Armstrong suavely. "But no, I shouldna say that, for it's likely you're all as loyal as my horse. Ye see, stranger, it's not to be expected that I should fling up my cap whenever the King's name is mentioned, for my family have stood the brunt of the battles on the Border this twothree hundred years, yet we got little thanks from any King for it."

"This is a fine enthusiastic messenger to send on important business," growled Henderson to Traquair.

"I would call your honour's attention to the fact that I am as yet no messenger at all, and if I am expected to be one it will be because of Earl Traquair and not on account of any sour Presbyterian that ever, thumped a pulpit in Edinburgh," said Armstrong calmly, quite accurately guessing the standing of the one who seemed to be the objecting element in the party.

"The crisis is this, William," broke in Traquair with visible impatience. "There are papers that we must get through to King Charles at Oxford. Then, what is much more important, we must get his signed warrant back to us before we can act to any real purpose in this ploy. The victorious rebels pretend that they are fighting for certain so-called liberties, but we have reason to know that their designs run much deeper, that they aim at nothing less than the dethronement and possible murder of the King. It is necessary to get proof of this to the King, and to obtain his sanction to certain action on our part; for if we move without his written commission, and our plans fail, we are like to get short shrift from Cromwell, who will deny us the right of belligerents. Whether the King believes this or not, the documents we wish to send him are less to the purpose than that you should bring back to us his commission, so you will know that your home-coming is much more vital to us than your out-going."

"I see. Still, if they kill me on the road there, it is not likely I will win my way back, so both journeys are equally vital to me."

"You will be travelling through a hostile country, but nevertheless will find many to favour you; for though the land is under the iron hand of Cromwell, he is far from pleasing all the people, although they may make a quiet mouth save a doubting head. Brave as you are, Will, it is on the smooth tongue rather than on the sharp sword that you must depend; for, however many silent friends we may have along the route, there are too many outspoken enemies for even you to fight your way through. Have you a good horse?"

"The best in the world."

"The pick of my stables is at your choice. Had you not better take a spare animal with you?"

"No. That would be advertising the importance of my journey. If I can get through at all, it must be by dawnering along as a cannie drover body, anxious to buy up cattle and turn an honest penny by selling them to those who want them worse than I do; a perfectly legitimate trade even during these exciting times. They all know the desire of a humble Scotsman to make a little money, though the Heavens and Kings be falling."

"That's an admirable idea, and you know the country well?"

"No one better. Indeed I'll trade my way to the very gates of Oxford if time is not too great an object with you."

"Time is an object, Armstrong, but you will have to do the best you can, and we shall await your return with what patience we may. You will tackle the job then?"

"It's just the kind of splore I like. Can you allow me three weeks or a month?"

"If you 're back inside of a month, Will, you 'll have done what I believe

487

no other man in all Scotland could do. Well, that's settled then."

"Oh, bide a wee, bide a wee," cautioned Henderson, who during this colloquy had been visibly fuming under the contemptuous reference Armstrong had uttered regarding him. "This man may be brave enough, but I doubt his judgment. He may have all the wisdom he traitorously denies to the King, but it's by no means proven."

"I did not deny wisdom to the King, Mr. Pulpiteer. I said Solomon was the wisest of men, except that he was a little daft on the marrying, and in that I'm wiser than he, for whether Cromwell catch me or no, none of the lassies have caught me yet."

"You are ribald," shouted the minister angrily, "and would add blasphemy to disloyalty. I was speaking of King Charles."

"And I was speaking of King Solomon, and speaking in a lower tone of voice as well. But while we are discussing wisdom, why are you all met here in this bothy, instead of in your own castle, Traquair? This innkeeper is a treacherous, canting dog. I know him of old."

"Henderson thought it would be safer here than at my house. I'm being watched. We conceived it would be less conspicuous if the dozen of us gathered here as if by accident."

"I wish I were as sure of your messenger as I am of the innkeeper," protested Henderson, his growing dislike of Armstrong not to be concealed. "The innkeeper is a pious man who——"

"So was Judas; and he was one of the Apostles," interrupted Armstrong flippantly, unheeding the other's anger.

"He is an enemy of your friends, the cattle-thieves," insisted Henderson.

"Is he? In that case you'll know more about him than I do, and I suppose it is policy for you to stand up for him. But, Traquair, I wonder at you! Did you search the house before you sat down here?"

"No."

"I went round the steading, and there was no guard at the back."

"Angus is keeping watch, and can see up and down the road."

"The road is the last place I would set foot on if I were a spy. You have been ranting in here at a great rate. Before I came to you I could hear every word that was said. One would think it was a Presbyterian convening, agreeing on the Scriptures. I knew Henderson's opinion of me before I opened the door."

"You look like an eavesdropper," retorted the man referred to, "and that you have a libellous ungoverned tongue is proven by every word you utter."

"Tut, tut, tut!" cried Traquair, "let us have no more bickering. This is serious business and not to be settled by bandying words. Now, Armstrong, the case stands like this. Will you——"

The Earl was interrupted by a roar from the sentinel outside, which caused every man in the room to start to his feet; but before they could move, Angus came bursting in.

"Somebody dropped from the hole on the loft above the stables, an' wuz aff ta th' wood afore I could stop him."

"To horse!" cried Traquair. "Mount instantly, and let's after him."

"It's useless, my lord," said Armstrong quietly, the only unexcited man in the group. "Ye might as well look for some particular flea in all the Hielans. He'll have a horse tied to a tree, and a thousand cavalry couldn't catch him if he knows the wilds hereabout."

"It may be just some vagrant sleeping in the straw. The loft above the stables is not the loft above this room," put in Henderson; but it was plain that he was frightened. He loved a real eavesdropper as little as did any of his comrades, and knew he had talked rather loudly at times, carried away by his fondness for opposition. Traquair stood frowning and indecisive, his hand on the hilt of his sword.

"Where's the landlord?" he asked at last. "Angus, bring him in here."

The sentinel left the room and speedily reappeared with a cowering man, evidently as panic-stricken as any of his guests.

"Have there been some stragglers about to-day?" demanded Traquair.

"Not a soul, my lord, on my oath, not a soul."

"Is there connection between the room above and the loft over the stable?"

"No possibility of it, my lord."

"What did I tell you?" said Henderson, plucking up courage again. "This turmoil is utterly without foundation."

"Dash it!" cried Armstrong with a gesture of impatience. "Will you take a man's word for a thing you can prove in a moment? Get a ladder, Angus, and speel up through the hole the spy came out at. Take a torch, an' if ye drop a lowe in the straw you'll no' be blamed for it by me. See if you can win your way through from the stables to the house."

"Go at once, Angus," commanded Traquair; then to the landlord, who showed signs of wishing to be elsewhere. "No; you stay here."

"I'm feared th' man wull set fire ta the place," whined the landlord.

"Better be feared o' the rope that will be round your neck if you have lied to us," said the Earl grimly, and as he spoke they heard the tramp of the sentinel's feet overhead.

"Is that you, Angus?" asked Traquair in an ordinary tone of voice. "Can you hear what I say?"

"Perfectly, ma lord. There's a very cunnin' trap 'tween th' stable loft an' this, that one would na hev foun' in a hurry, but the thief left it open in his sudden flight."

The lips of the landlord turned white, but he remained motionless, panting like a trapped animal, for the giant form of Armstrong stood with his back against the door, the only exit.

"Very well. Come down," said Traquair quietly. When the sentinel

490

returned, Traquair bade him get a rope and tie the innkeeper hand and foot, while the prisoner groveled for his life, his supplications meeting with no response.

"Now take him outside, Angus, and if there is any attempt on his part to move, or if there is an alarm of rescue, run him through with your pike and retreat on us. As for you, you false knave, your life will depend on your lying quiet for the moment and on what you tell us hereafter."

"Am I ta be ta'en awa', your merciful lordship?" sobbed the man, who, now that his life seemed in no immediate danger, turned his anxiety toward his property. "What'll become o' th' inn, for there's nane here to tak care o 't?"

"We'll take care o't, never fear," replied Traquair grimly.

The stalwart Angus dragged the man out, and the door was once more closed.

"I think we may venture to seat ourselves again," said Traquair, suiting the action to the word. "There's nothing more to be done, and pursuit is hopeless."

All sat down with the exception of Armstrong, who remained standing with his back to the door, gazing somewhat scornfully on the conclave.

"You will perhaps now agree with me, Henderson," continued the Earl smoothly, "that we are in no position to set up our collective wisdom as an example to William Armstrong?"

"I may at least say," returned the minister sourly, "that nothing whatever is proved. It is all surmise, suspicion, conjecture. The man who went away may well have been some lout sleeping in the straw, and no spy at all."

"There is no conjecture about the fact that the landlord lied to us. There is no surmise in my belief that he thought his trap-door was securely closed, when he lied the second time, and that the secret of the trap-door was in possession of the man who escaped. This is proof enough for me, and I think it is equally convincing to the others. Have you anything further to urge against the selection of Mr. Armstrong as our messenger?"

"Oh, very well, Traquair, have it your own way. I dare say he will do as well as another," replied Henderson with the air of one making a great concession.

"Then it's settled!" proclaimed the Earl with a sigh of relief.

But it was not.

"You will pardon me, Traquair," began Armstrong, "for you know I would be glad to forward anything you had a hand in, short of slipping my neck into a noose; but at that point I draw back. I'll not set foot on English soil now, King or no King. Henderson may go and be damned to him, for the useless, brainless clacker he is. If Cromwell hangs him, his loss will be Scotland's gain. Man, Traquair, I wonder at you! The lot of you remind me of a covey of partridges holding conference in a fox's den."

"I'm not going to defend the covey of partridges, Will; but, after all's said and done, the danger's not so much greater than it was before."

"Do you think I'm fool enough to set face south when there's a spy galloping ahead of me with full particulars of every item in my wallet? Not me! It was bad enough before, as you say; now it's impossible. That is, it is impossible for me, for the flying man knows all about me. No; the proper thing to do is to meet at your castle, or some other safe place, and choose a man whose name and description are not in the wind ahead of him."

"But I've known you to clench with quite as dangerous a task before."

"It's not the danger, Traquair, as much as the folly, that holds me back. I've been in many a foolish scramble before now, as you have hinted; but I learn wisdom with age, and thus differ from our friend Solomon."

"Will nothing change your decision?"

"Nothing; nothing in the world; not anything even you can say, my lord. I advise you to take a lad of Henderson's choosing. Any trampling ass may break an egg, but, once broken, the wisest man in the kingdom cannot place it together again. To-night's egg is smashed, Traquair."

"I cannot blame you; I cannot blame you," said the Earl dejectedly, drawing a deep sigh. Then, turning to the others, he continued, "Gentlemen, there's no more to be said. We must convene again. Would to-morrow, or the day after, be convenient for you?"

It was agreed that the meeting should take place two days from that time.

"I warn you," said the Earl to Henderson, "that I have no other candidate to propose, and will confine myself to agreeing with whatever resolution you come to."

"You are not angry with me, Traquair?" asked Armstrong.

"Not in the least, Will. I appreciate your point of view, and were I in your place I should have reached exactly the same conclusion."

"Then I must beg a bed from you to-night. I have no wish to stay in this place, and if you are bent for home, as I surmise, I'll just trot my nag alongside o' yours."

"I was this moment going to ask you, for I confess I'll ride the safer that your stout arm is near."

The company left the inn together, and in the middle of the road, before the house, they found Angus, with a torch, standing guard over a shapeless bundle huddled at his feet. The bundle was making faint pleadings to the man-at-arms, to which that warrior was listening with stolid indifference. The murmurs ceased as the group of men drew near. Traquair extended a cordial invitation to all or any to spend the night at the castle, which was the nearest house, but the others did not accept. Each man got upon his horse, and some went one direction, and some another.

"Fling your lighted torch into the loft," said Traquair to Angus, "that will prevent this woif worrying about his property. When you've done that, throw him across your horse and follow us. Has there been sign of any one else about?"

"No, ma lord," replied Angus, promptly obeying the injunction about the torch. He then tossed the howling human mass in front of his saddle, sprang into his seat, and went down the road after the two who preceded him, the flames from the burning bothy already throwing long shadows ahead.

The Earl of Traquair, chagrined at the temporary defeat of his plans, inwardly cursing the stupidity of those with whom he was compelled to act, rode moody and silent, and this reserve the young man at his side made no attempt to interrupt until they had reached a slight eminence, where the nobleman reined in his horse and looked back down the valley at the blazing steading, which now filled the hollow with its radiance.

"We will wait here till Angus overtakes us," he said. "This bonfire may collect some of the moths, and it's better travelling three than two."

"We've not far to go," said Armstrong, "and that's a blessing, for I'm on a long jaunt in the morning, and would be glad of my bed as soon as may be."

"Where are you off to?" asked the Earl indifferently, gazing anxiously down the road for a sight of his follower, who was not yet visible.

Armstrong replied with equal nonchalance, "Oh, I'm just away for Oxford, to carry a message from Lord Traquair to the King of England."

"What!" cried his lordship, nearly starting from his saddle in amazement.

"Surely my talk before these cuddies did not mislead you? I'll take your message through and bring you back an answer, if the thing's possible, but I cannot have those fools pottering and whispering in the matter. They must know nothing of my going. You will meet them two days hence, accept whomsoever they propose, and let him blunder along to a rebel gallows. It will be one blockhead out of the way, and then wise folk can do their bit travels unmolested."

"But how can I send papers with him when they'll be in your pouch?"

"Indeed, and that they will not be. This night's work compels one to a change of programme. I shall carry no papers with me. If you let me read them I'll remember every word, though they be as long as the Psalms. I'll repeat them to the King with as few slips as any man in the realm. If you have a password or sign, or if you can tell me some incident that only you and the

King know of, which will assure him that I am from you, everything else will be plain plodding. It would be folly for me, now that Cromwell's spy is on the gallop, to carry a line of writing that bears relation to politics. I'll be arrested before I'm a mile beyond the Border, so my chance of getting through will depend on the search they make. If they find nothing it is likely they'll let me go, and I must manage to get back as best I can. There's no sense in being hanged for a spy the first day I set out. I'll leave that for Henderson's man."

"You think, then, if I give the papers to him, they'll never see Oxford?"

"They'll never see Carlisle, let alone Oxford. If I were you I would give him whatever papers you wish delivered direct to Cromwell. That will put Henderson and his gang off the scent, and your information may be of much pleasure and profit to General Noll."

The Earl laughed heartily, his spirits rising surprisingly at this intimation of the young man's resolve.

"Armstrong, you're a hero. You shall read the papers to-night, and look over them again in the morning. The important matter is to get the King's commission back to us. Ah, here is Angus with his sack, so we'll say no more until we reach the castle."

## CHAPTER III.—DETENTION.

The next morning, early, William Armstrong, on Bruce, his black horse, set out for the Border with the good wishes of his host. His naturally gay demeanor was subdued, and he muttered to himself with wrinkled brow as he rode along. This unwonted abstraction was not on account of the danger which he knew lay ahead of him, but because he was committing to memory the message to the King. He carried a mass of notes, which he had written the night before, and these he consulted every now and then, for his horse required no guidance, and if it had, its rider was so accustomed to the saddle that he could have directed the animal in his sleep, for Bruce needed no tug at rein, but merely a whispered word or a touch from one knee or the other.

The night after he left Traquair's castle Armstrong slept on Scottish soil, still busy with his task of memory; then he burnt the notes in the fire that cooked his supper. It was scarcely daylight when he faced the clear and rippling Esk, and after crossing the stream to "fell English ground" he halted his horse on the southern shore and cast a long look at the hills of his native country, as one who might be taking farewell of them. Then, with a sigh, he turned to his task and sent no further glance behind.

A main road lay white and deserted before him, and the country he travelled, although in general feature similar to that he left, had nevertheless a subtle difference which always appealed to his inner sense whenever he crossed the line, but it was an evasive difference, which he would have found impossible to describe in words. The same discrepancy marked the language of the northern Englisher, which to a stranger would have seemed identical with that of his neighbours, but to Armstrong's sensitive ear the speech struck alien.

Arriving at a forking of the road, both branches tending south, he paused and pondered. Which should he take? He knew them equally well. The main road led to Carlisle, and in time of peace would have been preferable; the other, less direct, would probably carry him further in these uncertain times. The country showed no sign of the devastation of civil war, unless it was the absence of a population, and a deserted condition of the thoroughfares. That he could avoid contact with the Parliamentary forces was impossible, whichever road he took, and the question now demanding solution was not so much his direction as whether it were well to bring on his inevitable encounter with the Cromwellites sooner or later. The Carlisle route promised the speedier run into the arms of the enemy, but by the other route he would have more chance of bargaining about cattle, and thereby giving colour of truth to his statement that he was an innocent Scots drover, anxious to turn an honest penny. When questioned by an officer he could then say he had endeavoured to deal with so-and-so, and later investigation would prove the fact. But to an observer he bore the attitude of a stranger who had lost his way. This was evidently the conclusion arrived at by an object hidden in the hedge which had proved his night's lodging. The object sprang out across the ditch with a suddenness that made the horse start and snort in alarm, to be soothed by the gentle pat of its rider's hand, for the imperturbable

Armstrong seemed surprised at nothing that took place. The object had the wild, unkempt appearance of one who habitually slept out of doors. His long and matted hair, emaciated face, and ragged beard, no less than his tattered clothing, or covering rather, made up of odds and ends of various costumes, formed a combination by no means attractive. He held in his hand, grasped by the middle, a long stick, somewhat taller than himself.

"My gay gentleman," he cried cheerfully, "will you pay the price of a fool?"

"Who is the fool?" asked Armstrong with a smile. "You or me?"

"There are many of us, and someone is always paying the price. That is how I get a little money now and then. England is paying the price of a fool, and has been for some years past; paying heavily too, for all fools are not as cheap as I am."

"I asked you who the fool was?"

"Ah, that is a question you may have to answer yourself," cried the object, with a cunning leer in his shining eyes. "Beware how you answer it, for if you give the wrong answer, the price you pay is your head. 'Who is the fool?' says you. That is the point, but whoever he is, we are paying for him with fire and sword and good human lives. Wherever there's strife, look for the fool that caused it, but be cautious in naming him. Which road are you going to take, my gay gentleman?"

"I was just switherin'."

"Ah, you're from Scotland. They tell me they grow a fine crop of fools there. The road on the right leads to Carlisle, and the fool's name in that direction is the King. The safest way is the one you came, and the fool's name there is like to be Cromwell, so they tell me. Am I to get the fool's price for advice?"

"You haven 't given me any so far."

"The advice all depends on what you pay for it. Let me see the coin, then I'll show you my wares. We differ in this, that I'll take whatever you give me, but you can take my advice or not, as you please."

The horseman threw him a coin, which the object clutched in mid-air with great expertness and examined eagerly.

"Thank you, gay gentleman. The advice is to turn your fine horse end for end, and get back among the fools of your own kidney. We are always safer among our own kind."

"Are there any cattle for sale hereabout? I see none in the fields."

"Everything's for sale in England, crown, cattle, opinions, swords; oh, it's a great market for cutlery. But the price is uncertain and various."

"Well, it's cattle, not cutlery, I want to buy."

"I sometimes sell cattle myself," said the object, with a cunning look.

"It does not seem a very prosperous business then. Where do you get your stock?"

"Oh, I pick it up on the roads. You'll find no cattle on the way to Carlisle. The country is swept bare in that direction. But I can lead you to a fine herd if you make it worth my while."

"In which direction?"

"Down this way. Come along. Are you after any particular breed?"

"No. Anything there's money in."

"You're just like me," said the vagrant with a laugh, as he strode off down the unfrequented road. The object walked with incredible speed, laughing to himself now and then, and Armstrong was forced to trot his horse to keep up with him. On arriving at a slight eminence the guide waved his long arm toward a steading in the valley, which looked like a deserted group of farm buildings, and said,—"There's a fine lot of cattle down yonder."

"I can see no signs of them."

"No, no! They're well stabled. Nothing lasts in the fields nowadays.

They're not such fools as that. This herdsman knows when to keep his beasts in shelter." And with this the vagabond raised a shrill shout that echoed from the opposite hills.

"What are you crying like that for?" asked Armstrong, without showing any alarm.

"Oh, just to let the farmer know we're coming. Always give friendly warning in these parts, and then you may not get something in your inside that's hard to digest. That's a fool's advice, and costs you nothing."

"Your cry meets with no response," said Armstrong, laughing at the shallow cunning of his treacherous guide, for his keen eyes noted crouching figures making way along the other side of a hedge, and he knew that if he went down the lane, at whose junction with the road the beggar stood with repressed eagerness, he would find himself surrounded. Nevertheless he followed without betraying any knowledge of the trap he was entering.

As they neared the farmhouse a voice cried sharply, "Halt!" and an armed man sprang up from behind the hedge, cutting off retreat, if such had been attempted. While the others made through the hedge to the lane, the tattered man as nimbly put the hedge between himself and his victim, as if fearing a reprisal, laughing boisterously but rather nervously.

"Brave Captain, I've brought you a fine horse and a gay gentleman, and the two are for sale."

The man who had cried "Halt!" stepped forth from the shelter of the nearest outbuilding, a drawn sword in his hand, followed by two others with primed matchlocks, stolidly ready for any emergency. Four others closed up the rear coming down the lane. There was no mistaking the fact that the man with the drawn sword was an officer, even if the object had not addressed him as Captain, a salutation to which he paid no attention; for although his uniform showed little difference from that of his men, he had in his stern face the look of one accustomed to obedience. The horseman had drawn up at the word, and sat quite nonchalantly on his steed, as if this were an affair of no particular concern to himself.

"Who are you?" asked the captain.

"My name is William Armstrong," replied the rider simply. In spite of himself, the stolid face of the leader showed some surprise at this announcement, as if he knew the name and had not expected to hear it so frankly acknowledged.

"Where are you from?"

"I came across the Border this morning. I am a Scotsman."

"Why are you here?"

"I am a cattle-dealer, and as there is little doing in my own country I thought I would just see if business was better on this side of the line. This amusing lunatic said there was cattle for sale in the valley, and led me hither, for which service I paid him a trifle."

"And so there is, and so there is," cried the lunatic; "but the price was for my advice, not for the leading hither. I must get my pay for that yet. Aye, there's cattle for sale here, and I'm the marketman."

"Peace to your folly," said the captain, scowling. Then curtly to the horseman, "Dismount."

Armstrong sprang to the ground.

"Your sword," demanded the officer.

The weapon was handed to him.

"Do cattle-dealers in your country carry arms?"

"To tell you the truth," said the young man with a laugh, "if they did not they would carry little money home with them. I not only carry arms, but know how to use them on occasion."

"I ask to see your papers giving you permission to travel in England."

"I have none. Scotland is at peace with England, and a citizen of my country should not require papers in visiting England, any more than an

Englishman would need the same to go from one end of Scotland to the other."

"Humph," growled the captain, "you are well versed in the law. I hope you are engaged in no enterprise that is contrary to it."

"I hope not, Captain. If you are King's men, you maintain that you are upholding the law. If you are Parliamentary, you swear the same thing."

"We swear not at all."

"Then I surmise you are no King's men. But in any case, until, one or other of you have declared war against Scotland, or until Scotland has declared war against either of you, or both, you meddle with a free citizen of Scotland at your peril."

"It is perhaps wisest to indulge in no threats."

"I am not indulging in any. I am stating a plain, uncontrovertible fact, that would be held by none so stoutly as by General Cromwell himself."

"Then keep your dissertations on law until you see the General, which is like to happen before we are done with you."

"Nothing would give me greater pleasure than to have a discourse with that distinguished man. He is a fighter after my own heart, and I understand he is equally powerful in controversy."

"Search him."

To this order Armstrong not only made no objection, but assisted in its fulfilment. He took off his doublet and threw it to one of the men who approached him, then held his arms outstretched that another might, with greater ease, conduct his examination. A third paid minute attention to the saddlebags, and a fourth took the saddle itself off the horse. The search brought to light some papers which the officer scanned, gaining thereby much information regarding the price of stots, stirks, and such like, but what these articles actually were, the peruser of the paper had not the slightest idea.

"What is a stot; a weapon?" asked the captain suspiciously.

"In a way it is a weapon, or at least an engine of attack," replied William genially. "A stot is a young bull."

"Be sober in your answers, sir. This business is serious."

"I see it is. There never was much humour south of the Tweed, and you folk seem to have broad-sworded away what little you had of it."

"What is a stirk? I ask you to be careful of your answers, for they are being recorded."

"I am delighted to act as schoolmaster. A stirk is a steer or heifer between one and two years old. If my answer is not taken as an imputation on any of the solemn company here, I may add that a calf grows into a stirk."

The captain glowered angrily at the unabashed prisoner, as one in doubt whether he was experiencing a display of brazen impudence or extreme simplicity. He asked no more questions concerning the papers found, but gave them to a subordinate and directed them to be tied together. He now took from his belt a folded sheet, opened it, and read its contents with care, glancing now and then at the man before him. Apparently the comparison was to his satisfaction, and he restored the document to its place with a grunt of approval.

"Is Bates ready? Tell him to come here," he said to the subordinate, who instantly disappeared, emerging from among the outhouses shortly with a young man on a fine horse, evidently a racer before that sport was abolished. The animal was impatient to be off, but the young fellow on his back curbed its eagerness with a master hand, as one born to the saddle. The captain had employed the interval in writing a brief despatch, which he now handed to the young horseman.

"Ride hard and give that to General Cromwell as soon as you can. In case you should lose it, tell him we have got our man, who crossed the Border this morning. Say we are bringing him to Corbiton Manor, as directed, and expect to reach there before dusk."

The youth, without reply or salute, pocketed the paper, shook out the reins, and was off like the wind, Armstrong watching the pair with a glow of admiration in his eyes. Although unused to the life of a camp, he was much struck by the absence of any attempt at secrecy in the proceedings. There was no effort to bewilder the prisoner or make a mystery of the affair. That his advent had been expected was perfectly clear, and that a written description of his person had been distributed along the Border was equally evident. They had been watching for him, and now they had him. There was no military fuss about the matter, and apparently very little discipline, yet instant and unquestioned obedience without accompaniment of formal deference to authority or manifestations of salute to superiors. But underneath it all was a hint of power and efficiency. Armstrong realized that he was in the clutch of an admirably constructed human machine that knew what it wanted and went straight for it. No one had spoken except the captain, yet every man was on the alert to do what was required of him instantly, capably, and in silence.

At a word from the captain a bugle-call rang out, and its effect was soon apparent. An accoutred horse was led to the captain, who sprang into his place with the ease of one accustomed to the feat, and from the buildings appeared something like a score of mounted troopers.

"Get into your saddle," commanded the captain, addressing Armstrong.

The latter tested the buckling, which a soldier had just finished, drew up the strap a point, then, with his foot in the stirrup, turned and asked:

"Am I to consider myself a prisoner, sir?"

"Whatever questions you wish to put will be answered presently by one higher in authority than I."

"I must protest against this detention, sir."

"Your protest will doubtless be considered by the officer I referred to."

"General Cromwell, I surmise?"

"Or one delegated by him. Mount, we have far to go."

Armstrong leaped into the saddle, and the troop set off, with the captain at the head, and himself in the midst of it. There was no chance of escape, even if he meditated such an attempt, which apparently he did not. The direction tended south and east, and as the sun was setting they came to Corbiton Manor, a large country house, which was seemingly the headquarters of a considerable section of the army encamped in the neighbourhood. Into a room in this mansion Armstrong was conducted and left under guard, and he was pleased to see by the spread table that there was at least no design on the part of his captors to starve him.

## CHAPTER IV.—PREPARATION.

The mansion of Corbiton was a large and rambling structure, two stories in height for the most part, although in some places it rose to three, as in others it subsided into one. It was built partly of stone, partly of brick, and partly of timber and plaster, with many gables, and picturesque windows in the wide extending roof. Each of its owners had added to it as his needs required or his taste dictated, and now it was composed of many styles of architecture; but the jumble, as a whole, was beautiful rather than incongruous, as might have been expected. Time, moss, and ivy had blended the differing parts into one harmonious mass. The house faced the south, fronting a broad lawn that had once been smooth and level as a table, but was now cut up by horse's hoofs. A mutilated sun-dial leaned from the perpendicular in the centre. One gable contained a wide and tall mullioned window, which had formerly been filled with painted glass, but the soldiers, knowing nothing of art, and strenuous against idolatry, had smashed many of the pictured panes, but, finding that glass, whether colored or plain, kept out wind and rain, they had partially remedied the results of their own enthusiasm by stuffing the apertures with gaily-colored cloths, remnants of doublets or silken trousers, until the window was a gaudy display of brilliant rags, the odds and ends of a cavalier wardrobe; and thus the gay gable, from being an allegory of the days of chivalry, had become typical of the ruin that had overtaken the cause of the King.

Sir Richard Corbiton had been one of the first to fall in the Civil War, dashing with gallant recklessness against the pikes of the yeomen. Theoretically these coarsely garbed pikemen were the scum of the earth, cowardly dogs who, when they saw gentlemen bearing down upon them, should have turned and fled; but actually they stood grim and silent, and when the charge broke against this human rock, although many a lowly hut was then masterless, many a mansion was without an owner, Corbiton among the rest. Sir Richard, dying, paid the price of a fool, and in the struggle exacted the same tribute from others.

As evening drew on, the thin crescent of a new moon shed a faint mysterious light over the scene, as if it were a white sickle hung up in the sky, useless because there was no harvest in England to reap, save that of death. The dim lustre outlined the mansion, but failed to reveal the wounds it had received, and the aspect was one of peace, scarcely troubled by the footfall of a sentinel slouching along the grass in front, carelessly trailing his pike, with nothing of alert military manner about him. From one wing of the building came the somnolent drone of a hymn, but this was counterbalanced by the more intermittent hoarse chorus of a ribald song, mingled with a rattle of flagons from another part of the house, for the ale in the cellars was strong, and not all of the Parliamentary army were Praise-God-Bare-Bones. The torches within the house struck flamelike color from the remnants of the pictured glass in the great window, which gave a chromatic touch to an otherwise sombre scene unrelieved by the pallid half-light of the moon.

The sentinel stopped in his walk and stood for a moment by the battered sun-dial, listening. Faintly in the still night air came to him across the fields the beating of horses' hoofs on the hard road. Striding athwart the broken lawn to an oaken door, he smote it with the butt of his pike, crying,—"Peace within there; the General is coming." There was an instant hushing of the coarse song, then a laugh, and when some one in nasal tones raised the slow tune of a hymn the laughter became more uproarious, subsiding gradually, however, as voice after voice joined the drone. The sentinel now walked over to the main entrance, and said to some one within the hall,—"I think the General is coming."

The watchman now resumed his promenade, but he shouldered his weapon and marched more like a man on guard. Several officers came out of the hall and stood listening on the broken sward. From the darkness emerged three horsemen, two following a leader, a thickset man, who came somewhat stiffly to the ground, as if fatigued with hard riding. To the one who sprang to the bridle he said curtly,—"See the horse well rubbed down, and in half an hour feed him with corn," Then to his two followers, "Look to your horses first, and to yourselves afterward. Be ready in an hour."

The chief officer now stepped forward and said:

"You will surely stop the night, Excellency? Everything is prepared."

"No. Did my order to stay the execution of Wentworth reach you in time, Colonel Porlock?"

"Yes, Excellency. I would not have ventured to execute him without your sanction, although the death sentence was the unanimous finding of the court martial."

"The sentence was just. It may yet be carried out, or it may prove that the Lord has other use for him. Lead the way within."

General Cromwell gave no greeting to the different groups as he passed them, his heavy riding-boots swish-swashing against each other as he followed Colonel Porlock into the hall. He strode awkwardly, like a man more accustomed to a horse's back than a tiled floor. The Colonel led him into the great dining-room, one end of which was occupied by the shattered window, while the other was crossed by a gallery, and above all, very dim in the feeble illumination of two candles and some smoky torches, could be distinguished the knobs and projections of a timbered roof.

The vast room was almost completely bare of furniture, with the exception of a high-backed carved chair, which doubtless belonged to it, and a stout oaken table taken from some other part of the house, replacing the long hospitable board that had witnessed many a festive gathering, but which had been used for firewood by the troopers. The General gazed about the ample apartment for a moment, as one who had never seen it before, estimating his bearings with the shrewd eye of a practised soldier; then he pushed the table until it stood lengthwise with the room, instead of across, as before; glanced at the gallery and table, as if making some computation regarding their relative positions, drew up the chair and seated himself, setting the two

506

candles by the edge farthest from him.

"Has Captain Bent arrived with his prisoner?"

"Yes, Excellency. He came at sunset."

"Is he sure of his man?"

"He appears to be so, sir."

"Were any papers found on him?"

"Yes, Excellency."

"The other prisoner, Wentworth, is little more than a youth, I am told?"

"He is very young, Excellency."

"How came he to be set on an important outward post that night?"

"There was no danger of attack, and I placed him there of deliberate purpose. He was most reluctant to go, making one excuse and then another, saying he was ill, and what not. For more than a month he has been under suspicion of communicating with malignants, although we had no direct proof. He had been seen stealing away from the domain of Lord Rudby, the chief of the disaffected in the district. On the night in question he was watched, and as soon as he supposed himself alone he deserted his post, put spurs to his horse, and rode straight across country to Rudby Hall."

"And was arrested there?"

"No, Excellency. An unlooked-for event happened. He rode out from the grounds of the Hall, fighting his way, as it appeared, against a band of Rudby's followers, who were attacking him, and ran into the arms of our men, who were watching for him. The attacking party, seeing, as they supposed, an unknown force of rescuers, turned and fled. The night was very dark, and the account of what took place is confused, but Wentworth was carried back to Corbiton, tried, and condemned for deserting while on duty and holding commerce with the enemy."

"Umph! What version did Wentworth give of the affair?"

"He maintained he was no traitor, but did not give any explanation of his absence from duty."

"I thought Rudby had surrendered all arms and had taken the oath to remain neutral?"

"His men were armed with staves only, and so Wentworth, better equipped, held his own against them."

"What view did the court take of this affray?"

"They thought it merely a feint to cover the retreat of a discovered traitor. The night, as I said, was dark, and our men, being mounted, could not move silently. Knowing the house would be searched if Wentworth was hidden, this plan of seeming enmity against him was prepared beforehand, in case of discovery."

"How old a man is Rudby?"

"Nearing fifty."

"What family has he?"

"His two sons are supposed to be with the King at Oxford. There is one daughter at Rudby Hall."

"Humph! Is this the young man who is said to be a son of the late scoundrel, Strafford?"

"Yes, Excellency."

"In that very blood is hatred of the people, contumely, and all arrogance. At heart he must be a Royalist And yet—and yet——where was he brought up?"

"On the estate of Sir John Warburton, dead these some years back. Warburton was his grandfather."

"Where is the Warburton estate?"

"It adjoins the lands of Rudby."

"A-h! Is the boy's mother living?"

"No. His only relative is a sister who seems to be the most bitter King-hater in all the land."

"Is there not a chance the boy was on his way to see his sister?"

"It was thought not. She has been at liberty to visit him here, and has done so on various occasions."

"Has Wentworth ever been in action?"

"Oh yes, Excellency, and he acquitted himself bravely enough."

"No hanging back; no wavering in the face of the foe?"

"No, Excellency."

"Humph. Send Captain Bent to me with the papers. When he is gone, I wish you to bring me a trooper, some silent man who can be depended upon; an unerring marksman."

When Captain Bent arrived he handed to the General the papers he had taken from Armstrong. Cromwell examined them with great minuteness by the light of the candles, then set them in a bunch on the table without comment of any kind.

"Did your prisoner resist at all, or make any attempt at escape?"

"No, General."

"He made no protest then?"

"He said England and Scotland were at peace, that he therefore needed no passport; that his arrest was illegal, and that you would be the first to admit as much."

"Humph. Was he thoroughly searched? Are you sure he had no other papers than these?"

"Quite sure, General."

"Very good. Bring the man here. If the door is open, come in with him.

If it is shut, wait until you are called."

When the Captain left the room the Colonel entered with his trooper, who bore a matchlock. Cromwell dismissed Porlock, then said to the trooper,—"You will take your place in that gallery and remain there, making no sound. Keep your ears shut, and your eyes open. A man will be standing before me. If I raise my hand thus, you will shoot him dead. See that you make no mistake, and I warn you to shoot straight. Go."

The trooper, without a word, mounted to the gallery, and the General, rising, went round the table, standing on the other side. "Can you see plainly?" he cried to the man aloft.

"It would be better if both candles were at this end of the table, sir." Cromwell moved the farther candle to a place beside its fellow, then stood again on the spot his prisoner would occupy. "That is well, sir," said the man in the gallery. The General walked to the end of the room, threw open the door, and returned to his seat in the tall chair with the carved back.

## CHAPTER V.—EXAMINATION.

When Captain Bent entered the galleried room with his prisoner, he found Cromwell seated at the table, his head bowed over some pages of manuscript on which he was busily writing. The General did not look up for a full minute, until he had finished the sentence he was inditing, then he raised his head and said quietly to the captain: "Go."

For one brief and lamentable instant the discipline which held the captain in its bonds relaxed, and he replied in surprise,—"And leave him unguarded, sir?"

Cromwell said nothing, but a look of such devilish ferocity came into his piercing grey eyes that the captain staggered as if he had received a blow, gasped, turned, and fled. When the Commander spoke to Armstrong there was no trace of resentment or anger in his tones.

"Will you oblige me by closing that door which Captain Bent has stupidly left open? You are nearer it than I."

Armstrong with a bow did what he was requested to do, and returned

510

to his place beside the table.

"I fear I must begin with an apology, a form of speech to which I am unaccustomed. You have been stopped quite without just cause, and I trust you have met with no inconvenience or harsh treatment in consequence?"

"With neither, General Cromwell, if I am not at fault in so addressing you. I jalous there are not two such men as you in the army of the Parliament."

Cromwell paid no heed to the compliment, if such was intended, but although his voice was suave his keen eye searched the prisoner like an east wind.

"The stoppage may indeed save you further annoyance if you intend to travel about the country, for I will give you a pass likely to prevent such a mistake in future. You are in the cattle-trade, I am told?"

"Yes, General."

"'T is an honest occupation, and I am pleased to believe my army has ever been an upholder of it, paying for what it requires in sound money, even when the wages of the soldier were scant and in arrear. The requisitions and confiscations which have followed like a plague the track of the King's forces, devastating the country like the locusts of Scripture, are no accompaniment to the troopers of the Lord. It is perhaps your intention to deal with us rather than with the King's army, should you venture so far south?"

"Indeed I know little of English politics, and the man with money in his pouch, and a purchasing brain in his head, is the chap I'm looking for, be he Royalist or Parliamentarian."

"It is a commendable traffic with which I have no desire to interfere. You know of no reason, then, for your arrestment by my stupid captain, Ephraim Bent?"

"Truth to tell, your Honour, and I know a very good reason for it."

"Humph. And what is that?"

The General's brows contracted slightly, and the intensity of his gaze

511

became veiled, as if a film like that of an eagle's eye temporarily obscured it.

"Some nights since, as I was making for the English line, I stopped for refreshment at an inn where I had been accustomed to halt in my travels. To my amazement I was refused admittance by a man who stood on guard. We had a bit of a debate, which ended in my overpowering him and forcing an entrance; and which was more surprised, the dozen there gathered together, or me with their sentry under my oxter, it would be difficult to tell. Swords were drawn, and I might have come badly out of the encounter had it not been that a friend of mine among the assemblage recognized me."

A look of perplexity had overspread the grim face of the General as this apparently simple tale went on. He leaned his elbow on the table, and shaded his face with his open hand from the light of the two candles, thumb under chin, and forefinger along his temple. At this point in the discourse he interrupted: "I suppose you wish to mention no names?"

"I see no objection," continued Armstrong innocently. "I take it that the men were quite within their right in gathering there, although I contended they exceeded their right in trying to keep me out of a public-house. My friend was the Earl of Traquair. The others I did not know, and I was not introduced, but in the course of the talk I gathered that the one who had the most to say was Henderson, a minister of Edinburgh, who spoke much, as was to be expected from his trade. Well, these gentlemen, finding I was for England, asked me to carry a message to the King, but I explained that I had no wish to interfere in matters which did not concern me, and they parted to meet again somewhere else."

"Do you know where?"

"I think in Lord Traquair's own castle, but of that I am not sure."

"This is interesting. We shall, of course, try to prevent any messenger reaching the King; but I do not understand why you connect the incident at the inn with your detention."

"There was a great splore about a spy that escaped, and I have no doubt, if he saw me there, and heard the proposal made to me, he might well have brought my name and description across the Border. At least that was the way I reasoned it out with myself."

"It is very like you are right. Spies, unfortunately, seem to be necessary when a country is in a state of war. Many unjustifiable acts are then committed, including the arresting of innocent men; but I am anxious nothing shall be done that will give just cause of offence to Scotland; a God-fearing country, and a friendly. When such injustice happens, as it has happened in your case, I try to make amend. How far south do you propose to travel?"

"I may go the length of Manchester or Birmingham. The distance and the time will depend on the state of trade."

"If you will tell me places you intend to visit, I will include them in the pass I shall now write for you."

"That I cannot say just at the moment. I wish to follow trade wherever it leads me."

"Then an inclusive pass, extending as far south as Manchester, will meet your needs?"

"It will more than meet them, General," said Armstrong with supreme indifference.

The Commander took up his pen, but paused, and, still shading his face, scrutinized the man before him.

"As I am unlikely to see you again, perhaps it would be as well not to limit it to Manchester. You may wish to travel farther south when you reach that town?"

"It is barely possible."

"As you carry no message from Traquair to the King, I can write Oxford on your permit as easily as Manchester."

"Thank you, General; but Manchester will be far enough."

"I may say that we are strict about those whom we allow to journey

513

to and fro at the present time, and if you should overstep the limit of this document, you are liable to investigation and delay, and I may not be so near at hand on the next occasion."

"I quite understand, and if I wished to go farther south I would have no hesitation in begging permission of your Excellency; but I doubt if I shall even see Manchester."

"You will not be leaving Corbiton until the morning, of course?"

"No, General. I know when I am well housed."

"Then, as I have much to do, I will make out your paper later, and it will be handed to you in the morning."

"Thank you, General."

With this the Commander rose, and himself accompanied Armstrong to the door in most friendly manner. The young man, in spite of his distrust, was very favourably impressed, for there had been nothing, in Cromwell's conversation, of that cant with which he was popularly accredited. The Scot had expected to find an English Alexander Henderson; a disputatious, gruff, tyrannical leader, committing acts of oppression or cruelty, and continually appealing to his Maker for justification. But Cromwell's attitude throughout had been that of the honest soldier, with little to suggest the fervent exhorter.

After giving some laconic instructions touching the welfare of the Northerner to Captain Bent, who was hovering uneasily in the outside hall, Cromwell, bidding his enforced guest a cordial farewell, ordered Wentworth to be brought to him, and retired once more into the dim council-chamber.

With hands clasped behind him, and head bent, he strode slowly up and down the long room in deep meditation, vanishing into the gloom at the farther end, and reappearing in the limited circle of light that surrounded the two candles, for the torches had long since smoked themselves out, and there had been no replacement of them; none daring to enter that room unsummoned while the leader was within it. The watcher in the gallery felt rather than saw that there was an ominous frown on the lowered face as the

Commander waited for the second prisoner, over whom hung sentence of death.

This time a clanking of chains announced the new arrival, who was preceded by Colonel Porlock and accompanied by two soldiers, one on either side of him. The young fellow, who shuffled up to the table dragging his irons, cast an anxious look at the forbidding face of the man who was to be his final judge; in whose word lay life or death for him, and he found there little to comfort him. Cromwell seated himself once more and said gruffly: "Take off those fetters."

When the command was complied with, the General dismissed the trio and sat for some moments in silence, reading the frank open face of his opposite.

"You are to be shot at daybreak to-morrow," he began in harsh tones that echoed dismally from the raftered ceiling. This statement contained no information for the youth, but the raven's croak sent a shiver through his frame, and somehow the tidings brought a terror that had been absent before, even when sentence of death was pronounced with such solemnity by the court. There was a careless inflection in the words which showed that the speaker cared not one pin whether the human being standing before him lived or died. Allowing time to produce the impression he desired, Cromwell continued in the same strain of voice:

"I have examined the evidence, and I find your condemnation just."

The boy remembered that his father had met death bravely, asking no mercy and receiving none, and the thought nerved him. If this man had merely brought him here to make death more bitter by taunting him, it was an unworthy action; so, moistening his lips twice before they would obey his will, he spoke up.

"I have never questioned the verdict, General, nor did I make appeal."

The shaggy brows came down over Cromwell's eyes, but his face cleared perceptibly.

"You own the penalty right?"

"Sir, it is partly right and partly wrong, like most things in this world. It is right to punish me for deserting my post; it is wrong to brand me a traitor."

"Ah, you have found your voice at last, and there is some courage behind it. Desertion is an unpardonable crime. The point I press upon you is this; your life is forfeit, yet, although your fault is unpardonable, I do not say it cannot be compensated for. Even my enemies admit I am an honest trader. I will bargain with you for your life. You shall buy it of me, and I shall pay the price, even though I do not forgive the crime. We will first, if you please, clear up the charge of treachery. You were visiting your own home that night, and as it is on the farther side of Rudby Hall, your accusers naturally thought you had a rendezvous there?"

"No, General; it was my intention to have visited Rudby Hall."

"The residence of that foul malignant, Lord Rudby, so called?"

"Yes, but not to see his lordship, who is my enemy, personal as well as political."

The scowl vanished from the face of his questioner, and something almost resembling a laugh came from his firm lips.

"You are truthful, and it pleases me. Why did you make a foolish mystery of your excursions? I take the case to stand thus. Your grandfather and Rudby were neighbors, and possibly friends. You were, and are, in love with my lord's daughter, but since you belong to the cause of the people, this oppressor of the people will have naught of you. You have risked your life to see the girl, who is doubtless as silly as the rest of her class, as you will discover if I let you live. Stands the case not thus?"

"In a measure, sir, it does, saving any reflection on the lady, who——"

"Surely, surely. I know what you would say, for I was once your age and as soaked in folly. The question is, if you will risk your life for her, will you do what I ask of you to earn the girl and your life, or will you refuse, and let her go to another?"

"Sir, I will do anything for her."

"Then harken well. There was here before me, where you now stand, some moments since, the most plausible liar in the kingdom. He told me truths, which on the surface appeared to be treachery to his friend, but which he was well aware I already knew. This was to baffle me into believing him. He rides to Oxford to see the King, and in that I am willing to aid him. He may tell the King what pleases him, and those who send him,—little good will it do any of them. In return the King is to give him a commission, to be handed to certain lords in Scotland. If that commission crosses the Border, we are like to have a blaze to the north of us which I do not wish to see kindled until a year from now; then, by God——then, by God's will I shall be ready for them. We shall defeat the Scots in any case, but if this commission reaches these malcontents we cannot have the pleasure—humph!—we shall be precluded from the duty of beheading the ringleaders without bringing on ourselves the contumely of Europe. Without the King's commission they are but broilers—marauders. With this commission they will set up the claim that they are belligerents. Do you understand the position?"

"Perfectly, General."

"The commission must be intercepted at all costs. It will be your task to frustrate the intentions of the King and his Scottish nobles. But the task is more complicated than yet appears. It would be an easy matter to run this messenger through the body, and there an end. I want what he carries, but I do not wish to harm the carrier. These Scots are a clannish, troublesome, determined race. If you prick one with a sword's point, the whole nation howls. This, then, must be done quietly, so that we bring no swarm about our ears. William Armstrong is the messenger's name, and he has powerful supporters in his own country. He was stopped as soon as he crossed the Border yesterday, and brought here. He pretends to be an innocent trader in cattle, and will likely keep up that pretence. I have appeared to believe all he says, and he leaves this house to-morrow morning with a pass from my hand, giving him permission to travel as far south as Manchester, which was all he asked. I would willingly have given him safe conduct to Oxford, but he was too crafty to accept such a thing. He thinks he can make his way south from Manchester. As a matter of fact, he cannot, but I wish to make the way

517

easy for him. Of course I could give a general order that he was not to be molested, but there are reasons against this, as we have doubtless spies in our own ranks, and a general order would excite suspicion, and would probably prove useless, because this man, south of his permit's territory, will endeavour to go surreptitiously to Oxford, and by unfrequented routes. It will be your duty to become acquainted with Armstrong and win his confidence. You will accompany him to Oxford and return with him. You will be protected by a pass so broad that it will cover any disguise either of you may care to assume. It is such a pass as I have never issued before, and am not like to issue again, so I need not warn you to guard it carefully and use it only when necessary. It reads thus:"

Here the speaker took up a sheet of paper on which he had been writing, and, holding it so that the light from the candles fell upon it, read aloud:

"'Pass the bearer and one other without question or interference from Carlisle to Oxford and return.'

"The journey south will give you the opportunity to become acquainted with your man. On the northward march you must become possessed of what he carries, and when you bring it to me you receive in its stead pardon and promotion. If you do not succeed before you reach Carlisle, then I must crush him; possibly kill him as a spy. Will you undertake it?"

"'T is an ungracious office you would bestow upon me, sir. I had rather meet him in fair fight and slay him, or have him slay me, as God willed."

"There speaks youth," cried Cromwell impatiently. "This man is a treacherous, lying spy, whose life, by all the rules of war, is already forfeit. I propose to discomfit him with his own weapons. Nay, more; I willingly save him from the destruction he merits. You are set to do him the greatest service one man can offer another. If you fail, he dies. If you succeed, he has probably a long life before him. God knows I yearn to cut no man's thread where it can be avoided, but the true interests of England stand paramount. Would you condemn thousands of innocent men to agony and the horrors of prolonged war, to save the feelings of a Border ruffian who intervenes in a quarrel that should not concern him?"

518

"Sir, you are in the right, and your argument is incontestable. I accept your command willingly."

A gleam of pleasure lit the rugged face of the General, for he was flattered to believe his prowess in controversy was no less potent than his genius in war. His voice softened perceptibly as he continued: "We are enjoined by the Word to unite the wisdom of the serpent with the harmlessness of the dove. Your mission combines the two attributes, wisdom and harmlessness, for you are to beguile deceit, and yet suffer the deceiver to pass on his way scathless. You save your country, and at the same time save your country's enemy, forgiving them that persecute you. What excuse will you give to Armstrong for your desire to visit Oxford?"

"My friend, the son of Lord Rudby, is there. Although we are on opposite sides, he has none of the bitterness against me shown by his father. I will say I wish to confer with him."

"That will serve. Now this pass is for two, and you can offer to Armstrong safe conduct under your guidance, giving what plea you choose for the absence of the man who was to accompany you, and who, it may be, was supposed to have procured this pass from me. Whatever difficulties arise on the journey must be met as they advance, and in so meeting them will come into play whatever gifts of ingenuity you may possess. If you show yourself worthy and diplomatic, there is scarcely limit to what you may attain in the councils of your country. The need of the future is capable men; men earnest in welldoing, energetic in action, prompt in decision, unwavering in execution. In the hope of finding you one such, I snatch you from the scaffold. The King cravenly bent your father's neck to the block, although he had shown himself to be the one strong man in his council; I arrest the order to fire at your breast, though you are yet unproven. See that you do not disappoint me."

Cromwell folded the pass and handed it to young Wentworth. "Go. This paper is your safeguard. I shall give the order that you are to be well mounted and provided with money. Send Captain Bent to me as you pass out."

Once more alone, Cromwell wrote the pass for Armstrong, giving him permission to travel between Carlisle and Manchester. When he had finished writing, Captain Bent was standing beside the table, and to him he delivered the paper.

"You will give that to your late prisoner," he said. "He is to depart to-morrow morning, not before eight o'clock, and is to travel unmolested. You have accomplished your duties well, Captain, and your services shall not be forgotten."

The silent but gratified captain left the room with straighter shoulders than had marked his previous exit. His chief looked up at the dark gallery and called out, "Come down and report yourself to the officer of the night."

For nearly ten minutes Cromwell sat at the table in silence, save for the busy scratching of his pen. Then he rose wearily, with a deep sigh, his marked face seemingly years older than when he had entered the room. Once outside, he gave Colonel Porlock the papers he had written, and said: "The finding of the court martial is approved, but the sentence is suspended. It is possible that Wentworth may render such service to the State as will annul the sentence against him. You will give him every assistance he requires of you, and the amount of money set down in this order. Bring out my horse."

"You will surely partake of some refreshment, General, before you——"

"No. My horse; my horse."

When the animal was brought to the lawn, the General mounted with some difficulty, more like an old man than a leader of cavalry. The two silent horsemen behind him, he disappeared once more into the night, as he had come.

## CHAPTER VI.—INVALIDATION.

Nine o'clock of a summer's morning in rural England is an hour of delight if the weather be fine. The birds sing whether there be war or peace in the land; the trees and hedgerows and the flowers make a path to fairy-land of the narrow lanes; but the man who trusts to these winding thoroughfares, unless he know the country well, is like to find himself in an enchanted maze, and Armstrong, stopping his horse at an intersection, standing in his stirrups the better to view the landscape, wrinkled his brow in perplexity and felt inclined to change his tune to the wail of his countryman lost in the crypt of Glasgow Cathedral, and sing,

"I doot, I doot, I'll ne'er win out."

The sound of galloping hoof-beats to the rear caused him to sink into his saddle once more and wait patiently until he was overtaken. As his outlook had shown him the woods surrounding the mansion he had left an hour before in an entirely unexpected direction, and at a distance not at all proportionate to the time he had spent on horseback, the thought occurred to him that his late detainers had changed their minds regarding his liberation and were pursuing him, but he was fortified by the knowledge that he possessed a permit written by Cromwell's own hand, which no one in that part of England would dare to disregard. If the oncomer should prove a private marauder, of which the country doubtless had many, the horseman reposed a calm confidence in his own blade that gave sufficient repose to his manner. He turned his horse across the lane, completely barring the way, and with knuckles resting on his hip awaited whatever might ensue. Premising a friendly traveller with knowledge of the district, he was sure of a clew out of the labyrinth.

The hastening rider came round a corner, curbing his animal down to a walk on seeing the path blocked. The two horses neighed a greeting to each other. Armstrong was pleased to note that the stranger was a youth with a face as frank and beaming as the day; a face to which his friendly heart went out at once with sympathy, for it seemed glorified by the morning light, as if he were a lover sure of a warm greeting from his lass, which was indeed the hope that animated the boy. The hope had displaced a chilling dread, and the transformation made this daybreak very different from the one he had expected to face. He was riding out from under the shadow of death into the brightness of renewed life and promise.

Arriving as near the impeding horseman as he seemed to think safe, he came to a stand, and with a salutation of the hand made inquiry:

"Do you stop me, sir?"

This question carried neither challenge nor imputation, for, the times being troubled, no man could be certain that he met a friend on the highway until some declaration was forthcoming.

"Only so far as to beg of you some solution of the enigma of these roads. I am desirous of travelling southward, and seek a main highway, which I am grievously puzzled to find."

The other laughed cheerily.

"You could not have chanced on a better guide, for I was brought up some miles from this spot, although at the moment I am myself on a southern journey. We turn here to the right, but we have far to go before we reach the highway."

"The more lucky am I, then, that you have overtaken me. 'T would need a wizard to unravel this tangled skein of green passages."

"Indeed," cried the youth with a lightsome laugh, "I've often lost myself in their entanglements, and, what is more lasting, I lost my heart as well."

"There is one thing you have not lost, and that is time. You are just young enough for such nonsense as the latter losing. I am older than you, and have lost my way before now, as you may well bear witness, but I have kept my head clear and my heart whole."

"'Tis nothing to boast," said the boy, with an air of experience. "It simply means that you have not yet met the right woman. When you meet her you will be in as great a daze as that in which I found you at the cross-roads. You will think it strange that I make a confidant in so personal a matter of a total stranger, but, truth to tell, if I am to guide you to the highway, you must bear me company through Rudby Park, for I hope to get a glimpse of my fair one before I ride farther toward Oxford."

"Toward Oxford!" cried Armstrong, instinctively reining up his horse in his surprise. "Are you, then, making for Oxford?"

"Yes, I have been expecting a friend to come with me, but he is delayed, I suspect at Carlisle, so I must get on as best I can without him."

"I travel to Manchester," said Armstrong, more non-committal than the other appeared to be.

"Then I shall be happy to bear you company, if it so pleases you, until we come to the parting of our ways. That is, if you are not in haste and can wait until I have a word with my lass, in whose direction we are now tending."

To this invitation the Scotsman made no reply, and the other began to fear he had been too forward in his proposal. He rattled on, striving to cover his error in a flood of talk.

"She is the most winsome little lady in all the country side; the only daughter of Lord Rudby, who is——"

"Lord Rudby!" echoed Armstrong. "You fly high, my young sir."

"Why should I not? Although she is the sweetest angel that ever visited this glad earth, she makes no descent when she joins her hand to mine. I am Thomas Wentworth, eldest son to the late Earl of Strafford."

They had been travelling knee to knee in the narrow way, but now Armstrong pulled up and looked at his companion in amazement.

"Do you mean the Minister to the King of England?"

"Yes. There was no other."

"Then you are perhaps about to visit Charles at Oxford?"

"Ah, I have already told you more than was wise on so short an acquaintance," said Wentworth, trying another tack. "You yourself gave me a lesson in reticence a moment since, and you have not been so garrulous concerning yourself as I. I do not even know your name, although I suspect your native land lies north of us."

"Sir, I am William Armstrong, and Scotland is my country. As two swords are better than one, I shall be most glad to travel in your company. I may say, however, that I hold a pass from Cromwell himself, so, if you are a King's man, you may not wish to be my companion."

"Who journeys in Hades must have the devil's leave," answered

Wentworth jauntily. "I am myself abroad through Cromwell's permission, and I'll venture my pass is broader as well as longer than yours. 'Tis sometimes well to have a friend in the enemy's camp, and my friend pretends he can get anything from Old Noll. Read it, if you think I'm boasting."

Wentworth handed the document to the Scot, who read and returned it.

"Mine is but a limited permit compared with this. Where do you expect to encounter your comrade?"

"I fear there is little chance of seeing him until I reach Oxford, if indeed I find him there. I suspect he is detained at Carlisle. However, I travel on my own business, and he on his, so it makes little difference to me, save the lack of companionship. War throws together strange fellow-travellers, and I do not inquire too minutely into his affairs, nor he into mine."

"You go to Oxford alone then?"

"Part of the way with you, I hope. Yes; I'm tired of waiting, and so set out alone this morning, deviating from the main road and taking these lanes, the better to approach Rudby Hall without undue publicity."

"I see," said Armstrong thoughtfully; then, as he fell into a meditation, there was silence between them for some time. The theme of his reflection was the accomplishment of the task which lay before him. Here seemed a heaven-sent opportunity to win peacefully to Oxford, and perhaps to return as far north as Carlisle. Once in Carlisle, with Bruce beneath him, he could defy the whole Parliamentary army to catch him before he crossed into Scotland. Even at the first, the frank, honest face of the boy and his cheerful loquacity went far to disarm suspicion; then the announcement of his name and rank led Armstrong to the erroneous conclusion that the youth of necessity belonged to the Royal cause, forgetting that many of the nobles were on the side of the people, some of them active officers in the Parliamentary army. Circumstances combined to lull his natural shrewdness and conceal from him the danger of his position. He thought Cromwell was satisfied that the wrong man had been arrested, and believed the General had been thus deluded because no incriminating papers had been found on him. The spy of the inn must have reported that the messenger to the King would carry important documents to Oxford. The search had been thorough, but of course the most minute examination failed to discover what did not exist. Armstrong's prompt acknowledgment of his name, his explanation of the mission proposed to him, his reasons for refusal, must have had their weight with Cromwell, and if the spy were re-questioned he would necessarily corroborate most of the details given. Cromwell's complaisance in the proffering of an unasked passport appeared to be, in a way, compensation tendered for injury done, or at least interference, by his followers. Armstrong remembered that luck had often stood his friend, and the present encounter looked like another instance of it, so he resolved to journey with Wentworth as far south as Manchester, there to be guided by circumstances. Up to that point he need ask for no favour, for he had his own permit to lean upon. If the lad proved a true companion, he might then venture to propose that they should keep together under protection of the pass for two.

"Do you move on to Oxford at once, when you have seen this young lady?" asked Armstrong, breaking silence at last.

"Yes, and am willing to ride as hard as you like, if you are pressed for time."

"Oh, I'm in no hurry. He's a churl who would not wait while a lover and his lass whispered, and I shall do aught that I can to forward your adventure if there is any obstacle."

"I thank you, but there is like to be no obstacle at this time of the day. I hope to have the good fortune to find her walking in the garden. This would simplify my quest."

"Are you forbidden the house, then?"

"In a measure I am. I have my enemies within the walls, but my good friends also. If I get a word with one of the latter, difficulties will dissolve." Here the youth reined in his horse and sat for a moment anxiously scanning the landscape. A belt of tall trees bordered the lane, with thick undergrowth that seemed impenetrable to sight or movement. Over the tops of the bushes and between the trunks of the trees Armstrong gathered glimpses of a large mansion in the distance, extensive groups of chimneys being the most noticeable feature. Nearer was seen a carpet of green lawn, and beyond, the dappled glitter of the sunlight on a lake.

"Will you hold my horse?" asked the youth, almost in a whisper. "I must reconnoitre."

He sprang off his horse, and Armstrong grasped the rein.

"I hope they will not neigh," he said, as he disappeared into the undergrowth. It was evident the youth was well acquainted with his locality.

Armstrong sat silent, occasionally leaning over to stroke the neck of the steed he held in tether. He loved all animals, especially horses, and they reciprocated his affection. Suddenly the silence was shattered by a cry hoarse with rage.

"I have been watching your approach, perjured scoundrel! You shall not escape me this time."

"Sir, sir, I beseech you," came the entreating tones of Wentworth; "I cannot bear arms against you. Listen but a moment, sir."

"Draw, you dog, or die the death of one."

"Sir, I implore you; I cannot draw with you opposed. Sir, let me say a word——Oh!"

There was one clash of steel, then a brief cry of pain, and now silence again, all so quickly accomplished that first word and last were uttered in the time during which Armstrong leaped from saddle to earth. He searched hurriedly for the leafy tunnel through which Wentworth had passed, but before he found it the lad staggered into sight again, his left hand grasping his breast, his right dragging the sword, his face pale as chalk.

"He has killed me," he gasped.

"Nonsense. You would not now be on your feet if the wound were mortal. Who is your assailant?"

"No matter for that. Help me home."

"I shall first give the rogue a taste of his own surgery," cried Armstrong, drawing his blade.

But the other restrained his ardour, leaning heavily upon him.

"It is her father. Do not leave me; I faint. If—I——if I——I cannot direct you, take me down the lane; the high road. My home——the house to the right."

The victim collapsed in a heap on the sward, reddening the grass with his blood.

Armstrong was no stranger to the rough art of the leech. He undid the doublet and flung it open; tore away the waistcoat and shirt, disclosing an ebbing gash.

"Well pierced," he muttered. "An inch to the right would have done the job. The poor chap parried, but not enough; the onslaught was too fierce and sudden. The old man's intention was good, but the deflexion marred the thrust."

He staunched the wound with the torn shirt, and tied a sash tightly round the body. Taking a leathern flask from his pouch, he forced some fluid between the grey lips, and Wentworth, with a long sigh, opened his eyes.

"It's nothing to boast of," said Armstrong carelessly. "I've ridden twenty miles worse mangled. Can you sit your horse if I put you on him?"

"Oh God! oh God!" moaned the youth, near to weeping. "Fool that I was to risk all for the chance of a word."

"Tut, there's no risk. You'll be right as Edinburgh in three weeks."

"Three weeks. Oh, my God! Would he had killed me outright!"

"What is troubling you? Anything in which I can help? I see you are no coward, and it is not alone the wound that hurts. Is it this Oxford journey?"

The prone invalid made no reply, but, groaning, turned his face to the turf.

"Harken!" cried Armstrong earnestly. "Although our acquaintance is of the shortest, I would dearly love to do you a service. I will go to Oxford for you, and do there whatever you wish done."

The speaker reddened as he said this, and his conscience reproved him for thus making use of the other's infirmity, although he maintained stoutly to himself that he was honest in his proclamation.

The stricken youth was no less troubled in mind than in body, feeling himself a treacherous wretch, accidentally well punished; but he, too, inwardly braced his weakening purpose by the thought that he acted for the good of his country, an action tending toward the speedy return of peace.

"Help me to my horse," he pleaded, ignoring the proffer just made to him. "I must get home and learn whether this hurt is serious or not."

"It is far from serious, I tell you, and it means only a month's idleness. Lean you on me. There; make no exertion. I will lift you to your saddle."

The powerful Scot raised him as if he were a child, and, with a woman's tenderness, set him gently on his horse. He got into his own seat so promptly that his steadying hand was on his comrade's shoulder before the swaying body could do more than threaten a fall.

"This way, you say?"

Wentworth nodded wearily, and the two set out slowly for the high road. Despite their awkward going, the edifice they sought was soon in sight, situated in a park, to which a winding lane led from the main thoroughfare. The place seemed deserted, and as they neared it Wentworth showed a faint anxiety that he might reach his room unobserved.

"My sister must be told, of course, and a doctor brought; but I wish to avoid a rabble of gossiping servants if I can."

"I will carry you wherever you direct, and if we meet anyone we must enjoin silence. Can you indicate the position of a private door through which we may enter."

"The most private door is the most public door. The front entrance will likely be deserted. I would walk, but that we must hurry or be seen. Take me up the stair and to the second room on your right. That is always ready for me."

The Scot took the youth again in his arms and speedily laid him on his own bed. The jolting, despite the care taken, had shifted the rude bandaging, and the wound bled afresh. Armstrong, anxious for the safety of his burden, had not noticed that his own doublet was smeared with blood. With the better appliances now at hand, he did what was immediately necessary, and revived the lad's ebbing strength with a second draught from the leathern bottle. A sound of singing came to them as he finished his ministrations.

"That is Frances——my sister," breathed Wentworth with closed eyes. "Break it gently to her, and say I am not dangerously hurt. She will know what to do."

## CHAPTER VII.—DETERMINATION.

Armstrong stepped out into the hall, closing the door softly behind him. The melody was coming from the broad stairway, and ceased as the singer seemed to pause on the landing. He remembered that landing as he came up with his burden. Its whole length was lit by a row of mullioned windows, and one of these, being open, gave a view upon the green lawn in front of the house. He stood hesitating, undecided whether to advance as far as the head of the stair or await the coming of the girl where he was. Then he heard her voice evidently calling through the open window: "John, there are two saddled horses under the trees. See who has come."

Armstrong strode forward to the stairhead.

"Your pardon, madam," he said. "One of the horses is mine; the other belongs to your brother. May I ask the man to look after them?"

The girl turned quickly, her dark eyes wide with alarm. Into the mind of the intruder, looking down upon her from his elevation, flashed the words of her brother,—"It simply means you have not yet met the right woman. When you meet her, you will be in as great a daze as that in which I found you at the cross-roads."

529

"She is magnificent," he said to himself. With her mass of black hair falling in wavy cascade over her shoulders, her midnight eyes appealing and dashed with a fear that swept the colour from her cheeks, she looked a pallid goddess standing against the pictured panes.

"My brother!" she cried at last. "What of him?" Then, noticing the blood on Armstrong's coat, she gave utterance to a startled exclamation, moving a step forward and checking herself. "Is he wounded? Has there been a battle? Where is he?"

"He is wounded, but not seriously. I brought him to his own room."

Without another word she sprang up the stair, past her interlocutor, and flew along the hall, disappearing into the invalid's chamber. Armstrong thought it best not to intrude at the moment of their meeting, so passed on down the stair and out to the horses, where he found an old servitor standing guard over them, apparently at a loss what to do or how to account for their presence.

"Are you John?" asked the Scot.

"Yes, zur."

"Who is the doctor that attends on this family when any of them are ill?"

"'E be Doctor Marsden, zur, down t' th' village."

"How far away is the village?"

"'Bout dhree mile, zur."

"Very good. Get on that horse, which belongs to your master, ride to the village, and bring Doctor Marsden here as quickly as you can."

"Be Marster Tom ill, zur?"

"Yes, he is; but mind you say nothing to any one about it. Away with you."

Armstrong led his own horse to a stall in the stables, took off saddle and bridle, then went to the well and removed the stains from his clothing as well as water would do it. Going toward the house he met the girl.

"My brother says you tell him the wound is not dangerous. Is that true?" she asked.

"Quite true. I've had a dozen worse myself," he replied, with encouraging exaggeration. "But he will have to lie still for a month or more under your care."

"He says that is impossible, but I told him he shall do as the doctor orders, duty or no duty. I am going to send for Doctor Marsden, so pray pardon me."

"I have already sent for Doctor Marsden. I took that liberty, for it is better in such a case to lose no time."

"Oh, thank you!"

The girl turned and walked to the house with him. He found the patient restless and irritable. The wan whiteness of his face had given place to rising fever. His eyes were unnaturally bright, and they followed Armstrong with a haunted look in them. His visitor said nothing, but wished the doctor would make haste.

When Doctor Marsden arrived he went about his work in businesslike fashion. A physician of that day had ample experience with either gunshot or sword wounds, each being plentiful enough to arouse little curiosity respecting their origin. He brusquely turned Armstrong and the sister out of the room, after having requisitioned what materials he needed, and the two stood together in anxious and somewhat embarrassed silence on the landing, within call if either were needed. The girl was the first to speak.

"I fear my brother's case is more dangerous than you would have me suppose," she said in tremulous voice.

"Not from the wound," he answered.

"From what, then?" she asked in surprise.

"I do not know. He has something on his mind. I saw that from the moment he was hurt. He is very brave, and this accident of itself would make little impression on him. My acquaintance with him is but a few hours old, yet I know he is a fearless youth. Are you aware of a mission that takes him to Oxford?"

"I have not the least knowledge of it. I heard no hint of his going, and he said nothing of his journey when we spoke together."

"He told me he had expected a comrade who had failed him. Cromwell himself gave him a pass for two. He said he was to see the brother of his sweetheart, who is with the King in Oxford."

"That is very likely. The two were great friends always, even when they took opposite sides in this deplorable contest which is rending our distracted country."

"There must be more than friendship in this journey, otherwise Cromwell would not have given him such a pass as he holds. Then for an unknown, un-vouched-for man to enter Oxford at this moment is highly perilous, an action not to be undertaken lightly. If he go in disguise, and such a pass be found on him, not all Cromwell's army could save him. It may be he is commissioned to treat for peace, but that is unlikely. Such proposals should come from the defeated force. Depend upon it, something important hangs on this Oxford excursion, and if anything can be done to relieve his mind regarding it, this will do more toward his speedy recovery than all the leech's phlebotomy. If I can render service to him in Oxford, I shall be glad to undertake his commission."

"Do you, then, go to Oxford?" asked the girl innocently, turning her disquiet and disquieting eyes full upon him.

"I——I had no such intention when I set out," stammered Armstrong, abashed that for once his natural caution had forsaken him. "It matters little how far south I go, and I am willing to do an errand for a friend. I took him for a Royalist at first, and so saw no danger in his purpose, but if he be a Parliamentarian, then Oxford is a place to avoid."

532

"Did he not tell you he was a Parliamentarian?" questioned the girl, now alarmed in her turn.

"No. You told me so."

"I? You must be mistaken, sir; I gave you no information about my brother."

"You said his friend in the King's forces had not thought the less of him because he took the other side."

"I am distraught with anxiety about him, and gave but little heed to my words. I would have you remember only what my brother himself told you."

"You need have no fear, madam. Anything said by either of you will never be used to your hurt. I am a Scot, and have nothing to do with English strife."

Their conversation was interrupted by the opening of the door and the reappearance of the doctor. The girl could not conceal her trepidation, for the nontechnical stranger's assurances had slight weight with her.

"Thomas is doing very well; very well indeed," said the old man. "You have no cause for alarm, not the slightest, if he can but be kept quiet for some days, and rest where he is for a few weeks. You attended to him, sir, and I take it that you possess a smattering of our art."

"I have need of that knowledge, Doctor," replied Armstrong, "for those who have done me the honour to run me through rarely had the consideration to make their attack within easy call of a surgeon."

"Royal; or Parliament, sir? One likes to know before opening one's mouth."

"Neither, Doctor, I'm a Scotsman."

"Ah, that accounts for it." Then, turning to the girl, he said, "Your brother wishes to speak with you, and I have reluctantly given my consent. You will stay with him as short a time as may be, and I will be here to see that you do not overstep a reasonable limit. One word more. Do not argue with him, or dispute anything he says, no matter how absurd it may seem. Agree to any proposal he makes, even if you know it cannot be carried out. He is evidently disturbed about his duty. Soothe him, soothe him and concur. There is little use in telling a lad in his condition that duty must wait till wounds are healed, but he will recognize that fact when he is well again. Meanwhile humour him, humour him. Away, and I'll count the minutes till you are out again. I will find John and send him for a competent nurse."

Frances opened the door gently and met her brother's hungry eyes. She sat down beside him, taking his fevered hand between her cool palms.

"Oh, I'm a doomed man; a doomed man!" he groaned.

"Nonsense, Tom; the doctor quite agrees with the stranger that your wound is not dangerous."

"I was not thinking of the wound; that does not matter."

"What does, then, dear?"

"Sister, this morning at daylight I was to have been taken out and shot." The girl's hands tightened on his. "Cromwell himself reprieved me last night, but on conditions. The sentence still hangs over me, and now I'm helpless to avert it, and all through my own folly. Oh, I have been a heedless fool! With every incentive not to take risk, I have walked blindly——"

"Yes, dear, yes; but tell me how I can aid you. The stranger says he will do anything you want done in Oxford, going there specially on your errand, and he looks like a man to be trusted."

The lad drew away his hand, turned his face to the wall, and groaned again.

"Cannot you trust him?"

"Trust him!" he cried impatiently, "Frances, Frances, it is against him I am going to Oxford! The man is a spy carrying a message to the King. He is interfering in a quarrel that should be no concern of his, and his life is already forfeit, as indeed is the case with my own. But the price of my life is the thwarting of him. The King will give him a commission to be taken to the Scottish nobles. It is that document I was to rend from him, by force if necessary, by cunning if possible. I was to give him every aid to reach Oxford, but on the way back I was to gain possession of this commission and ride to Cromwell with it; then life and promotion were mine, and now I lie here helpless as a trussed fowl."

"A loathesome, treacherous task for a man to put upon the shoulders of a boy."

"But look you, Frances, 'tis but meeting treachery with treachery. Armstrong has no right in this contest, and his success means a new blaze of war with the loss of thousands of innocent lives. It means the possible triumph of the King who murdered our father and broke his pledged word to him and to you. And seeming trickery may be real mercy, as in this case it is, for if Cromwell cannot obtain the King's letter by stealthy means he will crush this Armstrong as ruthlessly as he would crush a gnat. By no possibility can this Scot ever see his land again if he holds that fatal instrument, for the whole army is watching him. But once bereft of it, he is free to go as he pleases. The simpleton thinks he has deluded Cromwell, and is blundering on through a fool's paradise that bristles with unseen swords. If I were his dearest friend I could do him no greater service than to purloin the document of doom he will carry when he turns his face north again."

"What do you wish me to do?" asked the girl in a low voice, her eyes staring into space, her hand trembling with apprehension at what she knew intuitively was to be required of her.

"Frances, dear, you once took a journey alone to London, to see our father. Again you went the same road, to aid him if you could, and failed, to our lasting grief, through the supineness of a thrice-perjured monarch. Will you refuse to set out on a shorter expedition, not for my sake only, although the saving of my worthless life will be one effect of your success, but to overturn what is perhaps the final plot of our father's slayer, who has already deluged the land with blood. Will you not help to bring more speedily that peace the kingdom yearns for, and the only peace now possible?"

"I'll do it," she said quietly, rising, stooping over, and kissing him.

He clung to her hand with the tenacity of the weak and helpless.

"Frances," he said hurriedly, "remember you are protected by Cromwell's own pass, so have no fear. In case of need the army or any part of it must stand ready to aid you if you call upon it. Old John will ride behind and look after you. Although the pass mentions two only, it is so sweeping that they will doubtless take it to include a servant. Any subordinate will hesitate before he delays one carrying so broad a permit from Cromwell himself."

"Yes, yes. I shall meet with no difficulty, you may be sure. You have already talked too much, and the doctor will censure me. Good-bye, Tom. Get speedily well, and that will be my reward, for I swear to you, by our father's memory, that my hand shall give into Cromwell's the King's parchment." Kissing him again she tore herself away from him.

"Send Armstrong to me," were his parting words to her.

Armstrong entered the room shortly after Frances had left it.

"This will never do," cried the Scot cheerily. "The doctor is in despair over the time your sister spent with you, and he is at this moment chiding her. Me he has threatened with direst penalties if I exceed a scant minute. So I shall just have to bid you farewell and be off, wishing you quick recovery."

"Armstrong," said the boy huskily. "My sister must take to the Oxford road and remedy my default. Will you be her comrade there and back?"

"As faithfully as ever belted knight attended fair lady," replied Armstrong, his eyes suddenly ablaze with joy.

"John will attend her, and I am sure your good sword will protect her if need be."

"You may take oath on that."

"I give you the pass which is safe-conduct for you both, and I think it will serve to cover John as well. If not, your own might shield him as far as Manchester."

"My own will shield me as far as Manchester, and this will, more appropriately, convey your sister and her servant."

"Yes, yes! That of course, as it should be. My head is spinning, and my thoughts are astray."

"After Manchester we will manage some way. Be not uneasy about that. I give you the word of a Scottish gentleman I will care for your sister as if she were my own."

Armstrong took the pass, which was now ominously stained red. He grasped his supposed friend by the hand, bade him farewell, and wished him quick healing. Wentworth's throat choked, for a feeling of strong liking for the man almost overpowered him, but a stinging sense of his own perfidiousness held him silent. Remorse was already biting worse than the wound in his side. The stranger turned for a moment at the door, waved his hand, and called to him to be of good cheer. A sob broke from the lad's throat, and weakly he cursed the exigiencies of war.

# BOOK III.—THE JOURNEY.

## CHAPTER I.—DISAGREEMENT.

When Armstrong left the room where the wounded boy lay he found Doctor Marsden alone, pacing up and down the long hall, visibly impatient. However, he appeared gratified that the stranger had contented himself with so short an interview.

"I think," said the Scot, "I have soothed his mind as successfully as you administered to his body. I undertook the duty which troubles him, and now he has nothing to do but get well, which I am sure will be the speedier that he is in your skilful care."

"You are very complimentary, sir, and I thank you. If you succeeded in putting his mind at ease you have taken a great weight from mine, for I like to treat corporal wounds uncomplicated by mental worry. I am expecting the nurse every moment and will just step inside until she comes."

Armstrong bade the practitioner farewell, and this proved the last he was to see of him. The young man went to the stables to feed and water Bruce, not knowing how soon he might have need of him.

Horse and man were glad to greet each other. Armstrong examined the animal with care, and was pleased to note that he was none the worse for his long and toilsome journey of the day before. The Scot found himself wondering into what part of the land he had got. Cumberland he knew, and Northumberland very thoroughly, but this district was strange to him. As a rule he was able to estimate with some exactitude the distance a horse travelled in a day, but the journey with Captain Bent had been over a rough country, in continually changing directions that had ended in bewildering him. High passes had been crossed, and deep valleys traversed with a speed that said much for the mobility of the' Parliamentary troopers. They had avoided villages, keeping through barren lands, uninhabited for the most part, until they reached the fertile and cultivated region in whose outskirts was situated the estate of Corbiton Manor. The questions he asked of his captors had invariably gone unanswered, either because the men were silent from nature or from command, or because they knew as little of the road as he did. The trend of the present morning's journey had been southeast, the country becoming more and more populous as he proceeded.

Returning to the house, he met Frances Wentworth evidently in search of him. It seemed to him she had been weeping, and there was a perceptible change in the cordiality of her manner toward him. He feared this was perhaps to be accounted for by the admiration of her beauty which his glances might have betrayed, and he resolved to be more careful in future, although it was difficult to repress the exaltation he felt at the prospect of being her companion on a long and possibly dangerous expedition.

"Has my brother spoken to you of my visit to Oxford?" she asked.

"Yes."

"Are you in great haste?"

"Not in the least."

"Would it be as convenient to you to set out tomorrow morning as this afternoon?"

"Quite. It would be better, in fact, for my horse had a hard day of it yesterday, travelling I don't know how many miles. Perhaps you can tell me where I am. I could get no information from my surly gaolers."

"You are in the southern part of Durham, near the Yorkshire border."

"We have come even farther than I thought. A day's rest will do no harm to the horse, for he little knows what is before him."

The girl seemed at a loss for a reply.

"I thank you," she said at last, somewhat primly, as she turned away. Then, pausing and hesitating a moment, she continued with face half averted,

"My brother and I are twins and perhaps the more devoted to each other on that account. I would do anything for him. I wish to stay and see the nurse installed. There are many things to think of at such an unexpected crisis, and no one to think of them but me."

"I thoroughly understand the situation, and I wish I were able to tell you how completely I sympathize with you. Although I know your brother so short a time, I am only too glad to be of the slightest assistance to him."

This gracious avowal did not appear to have the effect it merited. Some trace of a frown marred the smoothness of the girl's brow, and her lips became compressed. If a stranger is to be robbed and thwarted, it is embarrassing to hear friendly protestations from him, especially when there is no doubt about their truth. This man was evidently the soul of honest candour, and the repulsion which had sickened the girl's mind at the revolting task fate had assigned to her was increased by the genuineness of his good will.

"I thank you," she murmured again, and left him abruptly.

It was very early next morning when Armstrong stood by his black horse in the lane under the trees, waiting for his fair charge, who seemed to exercise the privilege of her sex in being late. Old John was already mounted on an animal that, besides carrying him, was pack-horse for the luggage required by the young lady on her travels. When the girl appeared, Armstrong stepped forward to offer his assistance; but he was a fraction of a second too late, for, ignoring him, she was in her saddle and away before he could utter a word. He admired the light ease with which she accomplished this act, and saw at once she was a practical horsewoman on as good terms with her steed as he was with his own. She rode down the lane to the main road, then turned south, never looking again toward the home she was leaving; hurrying, indeed, as if it were her purpose to get out of sight as soon as possible. The undulating nature of the country soon concealed Warburton Park mansion, and the trio rode on steadily, the girl in front, Armstrong following close, and Old John lagging somewhere in the rear, as if he knew that, after all, his heavily laden nag must set the pace, however briskly the more metalled cattle ahead of him started off.

After an hour of this Armstrong began to wonder where he was going. Nothing had been said to him regarding the route to be taken, and the girl went on as confidently, never turning her head, as if she and not he were to be the leader of the expedition. He laughed quietly at this, then, gathering rein, Bruce, requiring no other hint, stepped out and overtook the horse in front.

"Have you any plan marked out with reference to the roads we may take, or the towns we are to pass through or avoid?" he asked.

"Yes. We will reach York to-night, then follow the London road as far as Stamford. After that we branch southwest through Northampton to Oxford."

"It is all settled then," he said, smiling.

"I know the way well, and you told me you were a stranger. I have passed between York and London four times," she answered seriously, and with a chilling tone of finality which seemed to indicate that further discussion was unnecessary. The inflexion may have been too subtle to impress itself upon the young man, for he continued with obvious geniality,—"You have wandered far afield for one so young." To this remark the girl made no reply. Her eyes were fixed on the road ahead, and Armstrong, being at a loss to continue a one-sided conversation, found nothing further to say. He was vaguely conscious of the constraint that had come between them, for she had talked with him freely enough the day before; but he could not account for the change. He had always been accustomed to the free-spoken communion of men, and knew little of the vagaries of the other sex, whom he had ever regarded as the more talkative. He feared he had offended her by some thoughtless observation, and racked his brain trying to remember what it might have been. If it were her brother who rode beside him he would have asked him plainly where the offence lay, and would have fought him joyfully if the answer was not to his mind; but he was afraid of this dainty lady and anxious not to displease her. He began to see that he ran risk of disappointment in his anticipation of pleasure through a companionship which the other party plainly regarded as enforced and not at all to her liking.

They approached a declivity which disclosed a small hamlet at the foot of which flowed a stream.

"Do you know the name of this river?" he asked. "It is the Tees," she answered shortly.

"Then that will be Yorkshire beyond?"

"Yes."

Again he could think of nothing further to say, and inwardly chafed at his own awkwardness. He sympathized deeply with his companion, compelled to leave her only brother lying helpless from a serious wound, and thought her taciturnity arose from brooding on his peril, which in part it did. He wished he could call to his tongue some consolatory phrase, but his usually ready wit seemed to have deserted him. Yet he thought it impossible that they should journey thus gloomily the length of the land. Perhaps to-morrow would prove an amendment on to-day. And so through Yorkshire the silent progress continued.

The road was better than that to the north of the Tees, and also less deserted. They passed long trains of pack-horses travelling toward York, and occasionally met an equestrian, sometimes alone, but more often attended by one or more servants. So far they had seen nothing to show that civil war cursed the country, and no soldier had stepped forward to question their purpose in being abroad.

"This is not unlike some parts of Scotland," he said at last, in an ill-fated attempt to revive a conversation which he did not recognize as dead and beyond his power to resuscitate. The girl reined in her horse, and Bruce stopped through sympathy, old John halting, that the respectful distance he kept might not be decreased. Frances held her head high, and there was a sparkle of determination in her eye. It was best to begin right, and she would put this persistent man in his place, a task already too long delayed. And perhaps the putting of him in his place would lessen the clamour of her own conscience.

"Sir, who are you?" was her amazing inquiry.

"Me?" gasped Armstrong. "I'm a Scotsman."

"Perhaps I should have said, what are you?"

"You mean——Oh, I'm a drover—a dealer in cattle."

"Did my brother tell you who I am?"

"He told me his father was the late Earl of Strafford."

"Yesterday I was grateful to you for the aid you afforded my brother, as I should have been grateful to my servant if he had occupied your place; but I should not have forgotten the distance between that servant and myself. Strafford's daughter does not recognize a drover as her social equal. I ask you to take the position I set for you when I began this journey."

Armstrong's face became very red, and then all colour left it as this pronouncement went on. His back stiffened, and, although he spoke with measured calmness, there was a thrill of cold anger in his words.

"Do you mean, madam, that I am to ride with your servant?"

"That is what I mean."

"I have no objection in the least. From the conversations we had together he shows himself a man of knowledge and a lover of horses, which is an easy passport to my liking."

"I am glad his company is so much to your taste, and I shall be obliged to you if you fall back with him, as I wish to ride alone."

"That will I not do under command; for, although I may cherish old John's conversation, I cannot admit the claim of superiority you set up. I am a drover, I said, and so your ancient King Alfred might with equal truth have dubbed himself a baker, if old tales are true. I am William Armstrong of Gilnochie Towers, Lord of the Lands of Langholm, Dalbetht, Stapil-Gortown, Shield, and Dalblane. I can trace my lineage as far back as any noble in England, and come to my ancestral thieves as soon as they. In courtesy we Armstrongs are the equals of any Englander, and in battle we have never turned our backs on them. The castles of my clan line the river Liddel, and when I ride with my friend, the Earl of Traquair, I ride by his side and not with his followers."

"Sir, you overwhelm me with your grandeur," said the girl loftily, rejoiced to find herself in what promised to be a quarrel. She was human, and thought it would prove easier to rob an enemy than a friend. "I thought the crowns of England and Scotland were united, but I see I was mistaken. I travel with the king of Scotland, and he is doubtless on his way to Oxford to confer with his brother the king of England."

"Madam, I go to greet his Majesty, Charles, and if he dare to address me as you have done I will tell him I am more king of the Border than he is king of England, and my saying will be true."

Frances Wentworth bowed low in mock humility.

"Your Highness of the Border, will you permit me to ride in your train? I know I am not worthy, but I ask the boon that I may seek consolation in communion with my servitor."

"Madam, you may ride where you please," gruffly replied the thoroughly angered Scot, tingling with wounded pride.

"Sir, I thank you," replied the maiden, bowing again, "and I am delighted that you should exhibit to one so lowly as I, an example of that courtesy of which you just now boasted."

To this the indignant man made no reply, thus changing his former relations as regarded conversation. He urged on his horse, and she, after pausing awhile and seeing that John would approach no nearer, also went on, and thus the three kept for the day their new relative positions.

When the excitement of this verbal encounter had passed, the gratification at bringing about a rupture between them proved short-lived. Suddenly she was on the verge of tears, but strenuously repressed them, fearing he would look back, which he never did. That mood vanished, and hot anger replaced it, the more intense as she knew herself the aggressor. Nevertheless he had been boorish, she said to herself; almost brutal in his insolence. If he were a tithe of the gentleman he so blatantly proclaimed himself, he would have turned round and apologized for his rudeness, even if his anger at first had been justified. But there he rode in front of her, hand on hip and head held high, as if he were lord of the land. A beggarly Scot, proud and poor, from whose tongue flowed glibly a list of barren acres which civilized men would disdain to live upon, like the stunted lands to the north of her own home. Never turned his back indeed! If her father had been allowed a free hand, he would have chased all such braggarts home to their kennels. Even now, with his pretended independence, this Scot was travelling on his traitorous mission under the safe-conduct of the man he would betray. It was no treachery to outwit a spy, but a patriotic duty, and she would bid adieu to all qualms of conscience. And yet—and yet, he had told her brother he would treat her as his own sister, and it was they who had begged his convoy! Still, he may have eagerly seized the opportunity of the pass to get himself scathless to Oxford and back to Carlisle. Thus varying emotions surged through her heart, to be followed by anxious questionings and at last deep depression, during which her head hung and her dimmed eyes saw nothing of the road. Unheeded, the sun passed the meridian, and at last she was roused to a sense of her surroundings by the stopping of her unguided horse before a roadside inn. Armstrong, his black steed brought to a standstill across the highway, sat rigidly upright, and he said, when she thus unexpectedly looked at him with something of startled appeal in her eyes,—"We stop here for rest and refreshment."

"I need neither rest nor refreshment," she answered wearily.

"I was not thinking of you, madam, but of the horses. They have already gone too far without food, but in this benighted land there has been no opportunity of baiting them till now."

"Yes, you said it was like Scotland," she answered sharply, whipped to fresh anger again that she should have imagined he thought of her when he did not.

She sprang lightly from her horse to the ground, and, without a look at the faithful animal that had carried her so far, walked very straight to the door of the hostelry and disappeared within it.

When the time of waiting had ticked itself out on the old clock of the inn, Armstrong ordered the horses on the road again, and sent old John to warn his mistress that the way was still long to York. She came out promptly, mounting proudly without a word, and the expedition set forth as before, old John contentedly bringing up the rear. All afternoon they made their progress along the very direct road, no utterance from any one of the three. Frances grew more and more tired of this doleful journey, so woefully begun, placing the blame on her own weary shoulders for the most part, but now and then filled with a growing hatred of the stolid figure in front, who never once turned round; never once slackened the pace; never once made inquiry of any kind. What brutes men were, after all! The horses they bestrode were the better animals!

At last the nearly level rays of the evening sun glorified the towers of the grey minster, transforming them for the moment into piles of rosy marble, and the walled town was spread out before them. They came to Bootham Bar, and here, for the first time, a man-at-arms questioned their right of way. Armstrong silently presented to him the blood-stained pass, bearing the signature of the Man of Iron.

"Is he on the pack-horse of your company?"

"Yes."

"Enter."

The man-at-arms stood aside, and the trio went up the clattering street until they came to a house of entertainment once called "The King's Head," with a picture of Charles on the swaying sign, now slightly changed to represent Fairfax, a good Yorkshireman, while the lettering had been obliterated and "The Fairfax Arms" painted over it. The leader of the expedition ordered the best apartment in the house for the lady, and sat where he was while the bustling landlord assisted the fatigued traveller to dismount. Armstrong and old John saw to the disposal of the horses, then the young man walked to the minster and round it, noticing everywhere the ravages of the late siege. The town had not yet recovered its arrested prosperity, and most of the people he met were heavy-footed soldiers and citizens in sombre dress. York had been Royalist to the core, and now calamity seemed to brood over it. Armstrong made his way to a mercer's shop in the main street.

"My garments," he said to the obsequious proprietor, "are somewhat stained, and I would renew them."

"There are many changing their coats nowadays," replied the man, "and we must even cut them of the cloth most popular."

He whipped out a measuring-tape and deftly took the dimensions of his customer, muttering the numbers as he stretched his arms.

"I have no time to spare for the making of a costume, but must content myself with what lies on your shelves."

"Sir, I took you for a traveller, and am but estimating what will best become you. Your inches are just on the large side, sir, but I shall pleasure you, never fear."

He spread out on the long table some apparel in dejected brown, which, as it seemed to Armstrong, was but clumsily cut.

"You would garb me as a shepherd, I see. I come from the North, where we are not tailor's models, perhaps, but we scorn such duds as you exhibit. Cannot you furnish me with something more like what I wear?"

The mercer looked at him, hesitating for a moment, then led the way to an inner room.

"I can show you goods there is little call for, and if you are satisfied with them you take them at your own price and risk."

He closed the door and brought out from their concealment rich garments of the Cavalier fashion, which he handled gingerly, as if afraid of them.

"Ah, that's more like. Now I shall set myself out from top to toe in something suitable for riding. My horse and I are two sections of the same thing."

In the privacy of the back room the change was effected, and presently William Armstrong stood as gay and comely a man as could be found in all England, superbly attired, with filmy lace fluttering at neck and wrists. The mercer hovered before him, rubbing one hand over the other, with an artist's appreciation of the result his efforts had produced, and indeed something more glimmering behind in the depths of his appraising eye.

"You will make many a heart beat faster if you pass through the streets of York in that fashion," said the mercer.

"I doubt it. I was never one to be popular with the lasses."

"I was not thinking of women, sir, but of men who have fought and lost."

"Oh, all's not lost because York is taken! There will be a King in England for many a day yet, never you fear."

The mercer cast a timorous glance about him, then suddenly thrust forth his hand.

"You are a brave man. God make your prophecy true. I thought you came in to change your coat with the times, like the rest of us."

"Coats matter little if the heart is right," replied the Northerner, returning the proffered clasp. "You will do what you like with this discarded shell of mine, for I travel light and cannot be bothered with it. So, good-bye."

"'Ca cannie,' as your countrymen say, when once you reach the street. Avoid the soldiery and get free of York as soon as you can."

The gloom of evening was on the town when Armstrong emerged, yet he had not gone twenty steps before a stern officer planted himself square in his path.

"Who are you?" came the curt demand.

"A friend who has been looking for you. The shops are closing, and I am purposing to buy a pair of pistols like the one whose butt I can see in your belt. I may need your help to open a gunner's booth for me."

"You speak lightly."

"There is need of that when it grows dark."

"Fellow, you shall come with me and explain yourself."

"Not so. You shall come with me and do my explaining. And as the day is fading, read that while it still holds." Armstrong handed him the pass and the officer scanned it suspiciously.

"To Oxford," he muttered. "If you are not on the road between Carlisle and Oxford, you are at least in the costume for the latter sink of iniquity."

"Yes, and I have the pass to bring me there. Do you dispute it?"

"No."

"I am glad of that, for you would come into collision with Oliver Cromwell if you did. Now give me your aid toward firearms."

The officer turned with him and walked down the street, beat at the door of the gunshop, and saw the desires of the stranger fulfilled. Then he accompanied him to the door of the inn, bidding him good-night, and disappearing down the unlighted street.

The young lady was partaking of the repast prepared for her in the private parlour set aside for her use, said the landlord in answer to his guest's inquiry. On being shown to the door Armstrong knocked on the panels, and was admitted by old John, who was in attendance.

The girl sat at a table and looked up with surprise, not recognizing her visitor in his new finery, thinking some stranger had mistaken the room; but, seeing who it was as he advanced, she turned her gaze away from him and gave no greeting. If he came to apologize now, it was too late, she said to herself, and his first words showed that this was indeed his purpose.

"Madam," he said with a courtly inclination of his head, which obeisance, it flashed across the girl's mind, had been purchased with his fresh accoutering, a thought that almost brought a smile to her lips, which she hoped to keep firm. "Madam, I crave your pardon for my unseemliness of temper to-day. I am at best an uncouth person, travelling at the head of my own men, who question neither words nor acts of mine, and so have led me into the gruff habit of expecting obedience and not censure. I am no squire of dames, as there is little need to tell you, for already you know it from this day's experience of my ways; but I am deeply grieved that I fell so far short of the courtesy which is your due, and I trust you will forgive my lapse of manners."

Here was an apology indeed, that might well have called forth a generous response, and undoubtedly would have done so from a woman of the world; but Frances had been too sorely hurt by his long incivility toward her. Ladies in the romances she had read were always treated with the utmost chivalry, and, if truth must be told, she was tired and cross, so she hardened her heart, bent her proud eyes on the latticed window before her, and made no reply.

There was a few moments' silence in the room; then her punishment came in his next words.

"I had hoped we might part good friends."

"Part!" she cried in sharp terror, and those wide black eyes of hers quickly deserted the blank panes to fall upon him. She had never anticipated such an outcome of their quarrel as this, nor dreamed that it was easily possible for him to circumvent all her plans by withdrawing himself from her company. Instantly the dread consequences of such a determination on his part—and she had had a glimpse of his resoluteness—loomed up before her, every little disagreement between them sinking into nothingness before this fearful alternative. She dared not lose sight of him until her mission was accomplished, or her brother's life and her country's ruin paid the penalty of her foolishness. She must cast herself at his feet, if necessary, to retain him, and here she had jeopardized everything in an outburst of temper. A chilling fear crept into her heart that any complacency she might show him would be too late. Secretly she had rather admired his sturdy independence and pride of race, comparing it with her own vacillating purpose, ready one moment to forgive and the next to ban; but now this lofty self-respect might prove her undoing.

"I fear I overrated my power of serving you," he continued, "and I forgot for the moment how slight was my acquaintance with your family. Manchester, and not Oxford, is my destination, and I shall make for that town to-morrow before you are astir. The country is not nearly so disturbed as I expected to find it, and the roads are perfectly safe; indeed you know the route better than I. This pass is a most potent document and will open every gate. I leave it with you." He placed the paper on the table before her. "If I might venture to counsel you, I should advise you not to take it into Oxford unless you have some satisfactory plea to account for its possession."

"Have you had anything to eat since you came into York?" Her voice was as sweet as the note of a nightingale.

"No," said Armstrong with a laugh. "I had forgotten about that; a most unusual trick of memory."

"I was too angry with you at the wayside inn, and I could not touch a morsel, so I thus came famished into York. John, see if Mr. Armstrong's meal is prepared, and ask them to serve it here. I think you Scottish people possess a proverb that it is unfair, or something like that, to speak with a hungry man."

"Yes, many of our sayings pertain to eating. We are an uncouth folk, I fear."

"Indeed you are far from uncouth to-night, Mr. Armstrong. I thought it was we ladies who hurried to the mercers when we came to town, but you lost no time in the delightful quest. That was why I was so deeply offended with you when you came in. You are most ungallant not to have invited me to go with you. I could not have visited shops alone."

"You had no need to visit the shops. Nothing they sell could improve you."

"Am I so hopeless as that?" said the girl, with the sigh of the accomplished coquette, leaning back in her chair and entrancing him with her eyes.

Armstrong blushed to the roots of his flaxen hair and stammered,—"I——I meant you are perfect as it is."

She laughed merrily at his confusion, and her mirth came the heartier as she saw she was to accomplish her object; then the laugh was checked as a sudden wave of pity for him surged over her. For all his size he was a very boy in lack of guile, and a shiver ran over her as she pictured what he must think of her when he knew. The sudden tension was relieved by the arrival of old John and the servants carrying a meal hot and savoury, whose incense was a delight to the starving man.

"There," she cried, "sit down opposite me. Put this pass in safe keeping until I seek for it. You will surely not be so cruel as to desert me on the first stage of our journey?"

"Madam," said the bewitched man, "I shall do with eagerness whatever it is your pleasure to ask of me."

## CHAPTER II.—RECONCILIATION.

Another glorious summer morning greeted the pilgrims at York; a morning so clear and splendid that it seemed to have lifted the gloom which covered the captured city, as the sun might dissipate a veil of mist. In spite of her fatigue of the day before, Frances was the first afoot, and at this setting forth Armstrong and old John were the laggards, as she blithely informed them when they appeared.

As they rode away from the ancient town the girl could scarcely refrain from joining the larks in their matin song, such a strange feeling of elation filled her being. She had had her first intoxicating taste of power; the supreme power of a beautiful woman over a strong, determined man. He had come to her the night before with resolution stamped on his masterful face; came of set purpose, a course of action well marked out for himself in the long dreary ride to York, and he announced that purpose to her, catching her entirely unaware. She was without experience in the ways of men, knowing nothing of them save such enlightenment as a sister might gather from a brother, and this knowledge she saw instinctively would be of no service in the contest that so unexpectedly confronted her. As boy and girl the arguments with her brother had been of the rough-and-tumble order, where the best man won and the other sat down and cried. Armstrong had said in effect, "I leave your company," and a glance at his face left no doubt but he meant it. What instinct of heredity had placed her potent weapons silently before her; what unsuspected latent spirit of coquetry had taught her on the instant how to use them? A melting glance of the eyes; a low, lingering tone of voice; and this stubborn man was as wax in her hands. She had shorn him of his fixed intention, as Delilah had shorn Sampson of his locks; and as this simile occurred to her the spectre of her mission rose before her, and she remembered with a shudder that the parallel of Delilah held true in more senses than one. She glanced sideways at her Samson riding so easily on his splendid horse. What a noble-looking youth he was, and how well his new attire became him. Not any of the courtiers she had seen in the gay entourage of Charles in London could be compared with him. And what an ill-flavoured task was hers: to baffle him; to humiliate and defeat him; to send him crestfallen and undone to his own land! Delilah indeed! "The Philistines be upon thee, Samson!" Poor Samson! She had always been sorry for him, as she read, and now—now—hers was the role to wreck him! Again she glanced at him, and thus caught his gaze bent upon her. He smiled at her; was smiling when she turned her head.

"I can read your thoughts in your face," he said.

"Can you?" she asked in alarm.

"Yes. At first the pure sweet beauty of the morning appealed to you. You were glad to leave the shut-in streets of the town and be once more in the fresh open country. The song of the birds charmed you, and had there been no listeners your voice would have joined theirs. When first I saw you, you were singing, and that was the morning of the day before yesterday; yet it seems ages past, and I have known you all my life. It was my ill-omened fate to break upon you with evil tidings, and a remembrance of my news disturbed you a moment since. The thought of your brother came to you, and the sunshine of your face died out in sorrow for him, wishing you had news of him. Do not be concerned for him. I have seen many a wound deeper than his, and they were of small account with youth and health to contend against them."

The girl sighed and turned her face away, making no comment upon his conjectures, which were so far astray from accuracy. Why had she given no thought to her brother, whose welfare had never before been absent from her mind, yet who never before was in such danger as now? Why had a stranger's image come between them, so monopolizing her mental vision that all her pity had been for him? Delilah was the stronger woman, with no qualms of conscience to unnerve her steady hand. She remembered her kin and wasted no thought on the stranger who fell in love with her in the valley of Sorek. "And when Delilah saw that he had told her all his heart, she sent and called for the lords of the Philistines saying, 'Come up this once, for he hath shewed me all his heart.' Then the lords of the Philistines came up unto her, and brought money in their hand." Money in their hand! The price of a trusting man! Was there anything so baleful as that in all Scripture? When she presented Cromwell with the locks of Samson she would quote that sinister verse to him. Well this lord of the Philistines knew that her brother was not guilty of the treason for which he had been condemned. Cromwell came, not with money in his hand, but with life to be given or withheld, as foul play was successfully accomplished or the reverse. A helpless rage at the part assigned to her filled her heart with bitterness, and her eyes with tears.

"I wonder what valley this is we are descending?" said Armstrong.

"The valley of Sorek," said her lips before her reason could check them.

"What?" cried the young man, amazed, although the reply gave him no hint of its inner meaning. Then he saw that some strong emotion had overpowered her, against which all her struggles were in vain. Instant sympathy with her sorrow manifested itself in his action. He brought his horse close beside her, reached out and touched her hand.

"Dear heart, do not grieve," he said tenderly. "I pledge my faith your brother is better already. Would I had thought of it in time, and there might have been a horseman travelling all night to York, bringing you later tidings of him; but I am ever behindhand with my purposing, and remember a project when it is too late to put it into action. Many a fight that same backhandedness has led me into. I am for ever trusting the wrong man and laying myself open to his craft, yet am I hail-well-met with the next, learning no lesson from experience. Talking of this thrust your brother got, I remember well, two years ago, when three men who bore me no good will came to me and said the Earl of Traquair had bade them make peace with me. I was very

554

willing and struck hands with them. So off we set together, at their behest, to Traquair's Castle, that we might ratify our compact, for the Earl was a good friend of mine. We had gone near on five miles, and were chatting pleasantly together, when in the twinkling of an eye the three set on me. Three to one is no odds for an active man to grumble at if he can face them and has a rock or a tree at his back, but we were on the open plain, and I had a blade in my ribs before I could put hand to hilt. I drove Bruce at the first assailant and, ran him through as he went down. Then I cut for it till the followers were separated; so I turned on the one nearest me, gave him his dose, and chased the third man until I began to sway in my saddle. If he had but known and halted, he would have won an easy victory. Well, there were three good honest, satisfying wounds on three men,—each, I venture to say, worse than the one your brother got, and no doctor within thirty miles; yet the three of us are as hearty to-day as if we didn't know what a sword was made for. So have no fear about your brother. He'll be out and about by the time you are home again."

"Your story reminds me of the Roman tale. It was a cowardly act of your three enemies."

"I think it was rather that way. I did not heed their onslaught so much as their pretence of friendliness beforehand. Still, we mustn't be too critical when a feud is forward. Things are done then that we are sorry for afterward."

"I judge from what you say that you have forgiven the three?"

"Oh, as for that, I had forgotten all about them; it was your brother's case brought them to mind. I suppose I have forgiven them; but if I met them on the road here I'd loosen the sword in its scabbard and be prepared for blade or hand, whichever they offered. But come, we have now a level road before us. Let us gallop. There's nothing so cheers the mind as a charge on a good horse. We will make old John stir his stumps."

They set off together, and old John did his best to keep them in sight. Some fourteen miles from York they baited their horses, then pushed on through Bawtry until Tuxford came in sight more than an hour and a half after noontide, a longer stretch than Armstrong thought good for either man or beast. It was not yet five in the morning when they left York, and with the exception of a bite and sup at their only halting-place they had nothing to eat until two o'clock. Many of the numerous inns along the road were deserted and in ruins; the farther south the journey was prolonged the more evident became the traces of war, and Armstrong found that he had scant choice as to resting-places.

"I hope," said the girl, who knew the road, "that 'The Crown at Tuxford has not been blown down again. It was a good inn."

"More chance of its being blown up," replied Armstrong, flippantly. "Was it blown down once?"

"Yes, about half a century since, in a tempest, but it was rebuilt. You should have a kindly feeling for it."

"Why?"

"The Princess Margaret Tudor rested there in 1503, when she went to Scotland to marry your king."

"By my forefathers, then, the 'Crown' is a place of evil omen for me. Would that the fair Margaret had slept in it on the night of the storm."

"And now I ask, why?"

"Because her son, James V, came down to the Border, and by treachery collected the head of my clan, with about forty or more of his retainers, and hanged them, denying either trial or appeal. Jamie missed those twoscore men later in life, when his cowardly crew deserted him. We Armstrongs seem ever to have been a confiding race of simpletons, believing each man's word to be true as the steel at his side. Margaret was as false as fair, and a poor Queen for Scotland, yet here am I now risking life or liberty for one of her breed, the descendant of those fell Stuarts who never honoured woman or kept faith with man."

"Sir, what are you saying?" cried the girl, aghast at the unheeding confession into which his impetuosity had carried him.

"God! You may well ask!" said the young man, startled in his turn at the length he had gone. "Still, it does not matter, for you would be the last to betray me. I'll tell you all about it some day, and we will laugh over our march together, if you forget what I said just now. The end of our expedition is not to be the end of our acquaintance, I hope, and you live but a day's march from the Border. Will you let me take the day's march in your direction, now that I know the way?"

"I make no promise until we reach home again. Then you may not wish to make the journey."

"Little fear of that. I must see you again, if only to tell you of my luck in cattle-dealing, at which you showed such scorn yesterday."

"Do not let us speak of that. There is 'The Crown' inn; and even if the shade of the Princess Margaret does not haunt it, I am pleased to see there are people more substantial around its doors. It is not deserted.

"It is level with the times. The crown is blotted from the signboard, although some of the old gilding shines through the new paint."

It was late in the afternoon before they were on horse again, and they jogged down the road at an easy amble. Newark was passed, but they did not stop there longer than was necessary to show their permission to travel, for Newark had been a Royal town garrisoned for the King and besieged more than once. Armstrong had intended to stay the night there; but the authorities showed some reluctance in accepting a pass for two as convoy for three, and it needed all the young man's eloquence and insistance on respect for Cromwell's signature to get old John past the barriers, so when once this permission was granted he thought it well to push on clear of the place and risk the danger of camping out beside the road.

His luck still stood his friend, and at Grantham, some ten miles farther on, as the sun was setting, they came to the ancient archway of "The Angel" inn, a house that gave every indication of furnishing the best of cheer.

"At last," cried Armstrong, "we have shaken off the omens, and I find a lodging fit for you. 'The Angel' for an angel, say I, and here it is. No haunting Margaret of the past, nor inquisitive Roundhead of the present to molest us."

"I am not so sure," laughed Frances. "If ghosts walk these planks, you may wish the graceful Margaret in their stead. In one of the rooms of this house Richard III signed the death-warrant of the Duke of Buckingham. The place hints the fall of kings."

"Lord, lassie, you know too much history and too many legends of this gloomy land. I wish we were safe back in the North again."

"So do I," she said with a sigh, as he helped her down from her horse.

## CHAPTER III.—COMPANIONSHIP.

The buxom landlady of "The Angel" remembered Frances and her four former visits to the inn, so she took charge of the girl in the most motherly way, fussing over her and seeing to her comfort.

"No, nothing is changed here," she said, "though dear knows there's trouble enough in the land, and strife and what not; good men going away and never coming home again, or coming back broken and torn. I'm sure I don't know who's in the right, but somebody's deeply in the wrong, and God's heavy hand is on us all. England will never be England again, I'm thinking. I waited on the King my own self in these rooms when he went north not so long ago, and kind and gentle he was to all about him. I'm sure I don't know what he has done that his own folk should rise against him and pen him up in Oxford, as if God's Providence had ended on earth, and His anointed was no more than Jack Lorimer the sweep. And the name of God is always on their lips, but I'm thinking if they talked less of Him and were kinder to His creatures they would be fitter to meet Him when their time came. But, dearie, I must n't run on like this, for there are listening ears all about us, and a poor old body like me has been warned more than once. I fear it is not the King that is to blame, but them foreign people that's ever at his ear, and I thought little of them when they were here. There must be something fell wrong when the nobility themselves turn against him. Well I mind when the great Earl of Strafford himself came south and stayed the night here. If he had lived things would have been different, for he looked more the King than the King himself. Ah, he was a man for you! There, there, dearie, you're tired, and I go chattering along. But don't you cry again, dearie, for it's all long past and done with, and doubtless for the best, though our finite sight may not see that. What a babbling, thoughtless old wife I am; for I remember now, when you were here last, and I showed you the oriel window where Strafford sat, and told you the glint of your eye and the hold of your head reminded me of him, you sat there and wept and wept as if your heart would break. Kind-hearted you were, dearie, and I often thought of you and wondered how you were getting on. But now is not the time for tears, but for joy if ever you are to have it. I knew so comely a lass would not wander long alone, and that's a fine man you've got. I saw how it was the moment you came, for the light in his face when he helped you down from your horse comes but once in a man's lifetime and your own."

"No, no, no, no! You are wrong. He is almost a stranger to me, but is a friend of my brother. He is nothing to me."

"Do you tell me that? Well, well, we never know what the future holds for us, dearie, and unless I'm very much——"

"He was travelling this way, and my brother asked him to give me company. My brother was wounded and could not come."

"Wounded? Oh, I am grieved at that. Many a brave lad——is it dangerous?"

"They say it is not, but it frightens me."

"Yes, yes, dearie; but them that know are like to be right, and we must always hope for the best. Now here's the meal for you, and you will not get a better between York and London. Your man—ah, there I go again—the stranger is looking to his horse, no doubt, as a careful traveller should, and we will see to him when he comes in, so do not you wait."

It was late when Armstrong returned from the stables, for old John's pack-horse showed signs of distress from travelling between seventy and eighty miles that day, and as the slowest horse in the party sets the pace, the animal had to be seen to and cared for.

After his bounteous supper the young man strolled about the rambling inn, and to his surprise came upon a lonely figure in a dim alcove.

"Dear lass!" he cried, "you should have been at your rest long ago. This will never do,"—but he sat down beside her. The place was narrow and very cosy, as if the oriel window recess had been constructed for two lovers.

"I am not tired," she said, "and have much to think of, so I knew I could not sleep."

"You should sleep well after so long a day in the open air. Deep thinking is the enemy of rest, and rather useless in the main. I'll wager you're wishing for news from the North."

"Yes, I was."

"Well, see the uselessness of that."

"I know it, but how can one guide one's thoughts?"

"Oh, it can be done. They say Cromwell has the power of dropping to sleep the instant he gets half an hour to himself. He has plenty to think of, and yet he must be able to guide his thoughts or abolish them for the moment, or he could not do that."

"They say also that he has some secret power by which he gets news before any one else, and thus appears where he is most needed at the time he is least expected."

"I doubt that. He has well-trained men in his service, which is the whole secret. Do you like Cromwell?"

"I do not."

"You surprise me. I thought you were a partizan of his. You remember what I said when we were approaching this inn?"

"You said many things."

"Aye. But I said one in particular that I would have wished recalled if it had been said to any one but you. I promised to let you know all about it some day, but I've thought over the matter and I'm going to tell you now."

560

"No, no! I do not wish to hear."

"But listen a moment——"

"No! I have been trying to forget what you said."

"It is not fair to you that you should be exposed to an unknown scath. This did not occur to me when I set out, but your journey may be jeopardized because of my being deeper in dangerous projects than you have any suspicion of. So I have need to tell you my real errand in the South."

"Mr. Armstrong, I refuse to hear you. I will not be burdened with what does not concern me. Is your memory so short that you forget what has befallen yourself and your kin by trusting to strangers? I warn you to beware of me, and to treat me as if I were an enemy."

"As if I could!"

"As if you must. I have no patience with a confiding man, who needs ever to be kneeling at the confessional. I wish to know nothing of your affairs."

"At the confessional? Indeed, and you are right about that. But I have no desire to confess for confession's sake. I wished but to warn you."

"Very well; I turn the tables and warn you. I ask you to think of the injustice of what you were about to do. If you are on some secret mission, there are others besides yourself involved. It is most unfair to them that you should make a confidant of any person without their consent."

"You say sooth. If you take my hint and promptly disown me should I become involved, I am satisfied."

"I can the more readily disown you if I know nothing of the traffic you are engaged in."

"True, true!"

"They say this inn is part of what was once the monastery of the Templars, and I think the influence of these warrior priests remain in it; for I, too, was tempted to confession when you came. But we must have none of that."

"My lady, you would find me a more eager listener to a penitent than you proved to be. This alcove is like a niche in a temple, and doubtless has heard many a confidence since the Templars built it."

"It shows us a good example; it keeps silent about them."

The two were startled by a deep voice that broke in upon their discourse. They had heard no one approach, but now there stood before them at the outlet of the recess a tall, gaunt figure in the sombre garb of the Parliamentarian, as if he were the spirit of some forgotten Templar of whom they had just been speaking; indeed he seemed the modern embodiment of one of that fanatic, sinister band, for while his bearing betokened the fervid exhorter, a sword by his side indicated that he used the physical as well as the spiritual arm. His cheeks were sunken, and a two-days stubble on his chin emphasized not only the emaciation of his face, but the unhealthy clay colour of his skin.

"A word with you. Who are you? Whence come you? Whither are you bound, and to what purpose?"

"Egad!" muttered Armstrong under his breath, "here's a father-confessor indeed, and right willing to take on the task with no misgiving."

The girl wondered how long the apparition had been standing there, and rapidly ran over in her mind what had been said between herself and her companion since he came. Armstrong spoke up, and, while speaking, proffered his pass to the interloper.

"Sir, that document will possibly satisfy all your questionings." The stranger, taking it, held it near the lamp and read its brief wording.

"This answers none of my questions, except, and then by inference only, that you are perchance destined for Oxford."

"Is not the signature sufficient passport, so long as you do not find us south of Oxford or north of Carlisle? We are within the region over which the passport extends."

"For the second time I propound my inquiries."

"Then for the first time I return them to you. Who are you? Whence come you? Whither are you bound, and to what purpose?"

The man answered without the slightest show of resentment against what he must have known to be an intended impertinence.

"I am Hezekiah Benton, an humble preacher of the Word, and, if need be, a wielder of the sword. I came from Newark, and purpose returning thither, God willing, with more knowledge concerning you than you gave when you passed the gate."

"Very well, Mr. Benton, I will be equally frank, pausing to note with surprise that the signature of his Excellency General Cromwell is invalid south of Newark——"

"I said not so," interrupted the preacher.

"You imply as much by questioning after it has been shown to you."

"If you are entitled to hold this pass, you will meet no obstruction within its limits. As no persons are named upon this paper, it is my duty to satisfy my superiors that it is not misused."

"Pardon me, Mr. Benton, but has it not occurred to your superiors that if General Cromwell had wished the names known he would have set them down as fully as his own?"

Hezekiah thoughtfully scratched his stubbly chin, and was evidently nonplussed by the view so calmly presented to him. After turning the problem in his mind for a few moments, he replied: "Nevertheless you are travelling on the London road. This pass reads Carlisle to Oxford. Newark is not on the highway between these two towns."

"Admirably reasoned, Mr. Benton, and I envy those who have opportunity of hearing your discourses. They listen to good logic, I stand warrant. But the apparent mystery is soon dissolved. This paper was written by his Excellency at Corbiton Manor, in the county of Durham, at about this hour of the night three days ago, what time, if I may so put it, I was the guest of his Excellency at that place. If you will bear the county of Durham instead of the county of Northumberland in mind, you will observe I have taken the quickest route to Oxford, when the state of cross-country roads is considered. So far as the London direction is concerned, we deflect from it to-morrow at Stamford, and will rest, God permitting us, at Northampton to-morrow night. Any further questions will be as cheerfully answered, for I know you would not ask them without authority and a full explanation to give to General Cromwell, should he chance to dislike the uncovering of that which he was at some pains to conceal."

Hezekiah Benton made haste in returning the passport to the suave and eloquent man from whom he had obtained it.

"Sir, your disquisition is most complete and satisfactory. If but a tithe of it had been given at Newark I would have been saved a hurried journey, and you a cross-examination. I give you good-night, and God be with you."

"May he see you safe in Newark again, and grant you length of days to expound His Word," responded Armstrong devoutly, as he rose from his seat and bowed.

Frances rose also when their visitor had taken himself off.

"You are something of a diplomatist, Mr. Armstrong, but I fear diplomacy requires a touch of hypocrisy. Could you not have dismissed him without the benediction?"

"Why? I meant it thoroughly. I am a religious man with a creed as grim as his own; a Presbyterian. I meant every word of it. He is a good man; notice how mildly he answered my scoffing return of his own questions. He made me ashamed of my frivolity."

"A religious man, are you?"

"Yes, why not?"

"I don't know. I had not thought of you as such. Your account of another man's pass did not seem strictly accurate."

"It was true nevertheless. Every word I said was true. I never even hinted the pass belonged to me."

The girl laughed and held out her hand.

"Yet you cannot deny that he gathered a wrong impression."

"Ah, that was his fault, not mine. Hezekiah himself would tell you to possess the wisdom of the serpent as well as the harmlessness of the dove. But do not let me be too self-righteous. I will be honest with you, and admit at once that had a direct falsehood been necessary I would have used it. I was determined not to give him any name, for the pass I hold from Cromwell set Manchester as the limit, and we are now south of Manchester. I would have given the good Benton my name at York, but not at Grantham."

"You think, then, that where great events are at stake,—a man's life let us say, or a country's welfare,—one is justified in using deception?"

"Most assuredly. I should have no hesitation in trying any ruse to save my friend or serve my country. Do you not agree with me?"

"I am trying to. Yes, I do agree with you. I do! I do! I do!" she cried with a sudden fervour that surprised him, for it seemed out of proportion to the importance of the ethical question they had been discussing. He had been holding her hand all this time, and she seemed to become newly aware of that fact and hastily withdrew it, blushing as she did so. She spoke rapidly, as if to cover her confusion:

"I use the words furnished me by our visitor. I give you good-night, and God be with you,"—and she was gone before his unreadiness could frame a response.

## CHAPTER IV.—FRIENDSHIP.

Next day the three were not as early beginning their march, because Northampton was barely fifty miles distant, and the day was longer than the way. The good landlady of "The Angel," bustling and voluble, saw them off with many blessings, and wishings that God would speed them. Stamford furnished bait for their horses and a short rest for themselves. Then they took the deflecting road for Northampton, but their pack-horse limped and their progress was slow. Frances was in better spirits than was the case since the pilgrimage began, for she had now persuaded her mind, which eagerly wished to be convinced, that her future action would save the lives of two men,—Armstrong's not less than her brother's,—and so she had come to look upon her unsuspecting companion as her beneficiary rather than her victim. He himself had unknowingly been advocate against himself, and she was surprised to note how much influence his argument exerted, thinking it was because she was so anxious to be confirmed that the deed which circumstances compelled her to do had more of right than wrong in it. If he was indeed a Presbyterian, as he had said, his sympathies must, after all, lean toward the Parliamentary side rather than toward the Royal cause, and disappointment at the failure of his mission could not be very severe. She had heard him say nothing which showed enthusiasm or even concern for the King; in truth the remark which had inadvertently escaped him was to the effect that it was folly for one of his name to do service for the line of Stuart, and he had characterized the race as fair and false. Whatever motive, then, had sent him on this dangerous mission, it was neither love for the King nor loyalty toward his cause. Armstrong always spoke of himself as an outsider, having little interest in the quarrels of the English, whom he quite evidently regarded as an inferior race, easily overcome if fronted by real fighters. She smiled as she recollected his embarrassment once or twice in the midst of a diatribe against them, when he remembered just too late that he was talking to an Englishwoman. One fact, however, she failed to recognize, which was that in the intervals of conversation her mind was entirely filled with this blond Scot, to the exclusion of everything else.

The day passed pleasantly enough, even if progress was slow. Armstrong related many interesting or amusing anecdotes of the Border, and the girl came to the conclusion that life must be anything but dull in that hilly district. They partook of their noontide meal at a hospitable farm-house, for inns were few and mostly untenanted. They learned that it would probably be dark by the time they reached Northampton, but there was a new moon to light their way. They were off the main line of travel and had the road practically to themselves. At about five in the afternoon they heard the tramping of a squadron behind them, coming on at a rapid walk. Armstrong suggested that it would be well to draw into the hedge while the troopers passed, and this they did. The Scot sat easily on his horse, watching the somewhat imposing oncoming, the breastplates of the men scintillating in the declining sun, which shone full upon them. Suddenly Armstrong straightened and, unconsciously perhaps, his hand grasped that of the girl beside him.

"Have you ever seen Cromwell?" he asked.

"No."

"That is he at the head of the cavalry."

She drew away her hand, and sat there, scarcely breathing, fearful of the approaching encounter, which now could not be avoided. If Armstrong were equally perturbed he showed no sign of it, and she admired his nonchalance as she glanced momentarily at him. But her eyes turned instinctively again to the leader of the troops. There was something masterful in his very bulk; he seemed a massive man on his huge horse; power personified were horse and man. His unblinking eye faced the sun like an eagle's, and he came stolidly past them, looking neither to the right nor the left. The firm face was as inscrutable and as ruthless as that of the Sphinx.

Four and four came the men behind him; some old, but erect; the majority middle-aged; all cast in the same mould as their leader. They sat like him, and looked straight ahead like him. Polished steel on head and front, but nothing ornamental in their outfitting. No drums, no flags, no trumpets; a shining, yellow bugle at the hip of the foremost,—that was all. Everything for use, nothing for display.. Clanking past they came, four and four, four and four, in seeming endless procession; weapons, and chains at the horse's bits, jingling the only music of their march. Not a word was spoken, not a glance to one side or the other. At last the final four went by, and Frances drew a breath of relief that a menace was past and done with.

"Do you think he saw us?" she whispered, not yet daring to speak aloud,—a precaution rather absurd, for she might have shouted while they were within arm's length of her, and she would not have been heard in the trampling of the horses.

"Saw us!" echoed Armstrong, "yes, every thread of our garments. What a man! God of war, how I should like to fight him!"

"I thought you admired him."

"So I do, more than any other on earth. If I had seen him before, I doubt if I had been here."

"I understood you to say you met him at Corbiton."

"Met him, yes, by dim candle-light, smooth and courteous. But I never really saw him until now. You cannot rightly judge a man—a fighter, that is—until you have looked at him on horseback. That man knows my business. For the first time since I set out I doubt my success."

"Will you turn back?" she asked, her voice quavering.

"Oh, no! I'm his Roland. If we do not cross swords, we'll run a race, and may the best man win. But I feel strangely uncomfortable about the neck, and I think of my ancestor Johnnie and the Scottish king."

He raised his chin and moved his head from side to side, as if the rope already throttled him. Then he laughed, and she gazed at him in fascinated terror, wondering he could jest on a subject so gruesome.

"That man is likely to defeat me," he continued. "His plans are all laid, and already I feel the toils tightening around me. I am satisfied he knows every move I have made since I left him. The unseen spy is on my track, and, by my sword, I'd rather circumvent him than rule the kingdom. Wull, whaur's yer wits? Now's the time ye need them, my lad. In the first place, I dare not go through Northampton; that's clear."

"Why?"

"In my soul I'm certain a crisis awaits me there. I'll be nabbed in Northampton. Then the question, 'Why did you refuse a pass to Oxford'?"

"Did he offer you one?"

"Yes. The next question will be,' Why are you south of the limit set by yourself, travelling to Oxford on another's pass?' To that query there's no answer. I'm a self-convicted spy, and then the scaffold, according to all the rules of war."

"Pardon me if I do not follow your argument. If he has tracked you, as you think, there is no more reason he should stop you at Northampton than at Newark or Grantham. Aside from that, why did he not hold you when he had you?"

"Oh, I had not put my neck into the noose then. As for arresting me at Newark or at Grantham, I see now that such was his intention, but our friend Hezekiah failed him. It was undoubtedly Cromwell's purpose that we should have gone back with Benton."

"Still, I do not believe you. If Cromwell is as crafty as you seem to believe, it is likely he wishes you to reach Oxford. Unless that was the case, why should he have offered you the pass?"

"My lass, there are several sides to this problem, and what you say has the stamp of probability on it. Nevertheless, I'll overset his arrangements. I am the only one of us three who cannot give good excuses for being in these parts. Here is the pass which protects you and old John," he said, giving her the document. "You and he will to Oxford at your leisure. I shall gallop across country, will evade the Parliamentary lines as best I may, and will be in Oxford to-morrow morning. That will throw Old Noll a day out of his count."

"Then you leave me to meet Cromwell alone?"

"You have no need to fear the meeting. Your plea is perfect. Your brother was wounded, and you have undertaken his task. Of me or my plans you know nothing, and I was with you merely because I happened to be travelling this way, and had brought your wounded brother to his home. And here is a great warning to us all. Happy is the person who can abide by the truth; who has no secret designs to conceal. My lady, I envy you."

Frances made no reply, but sat there, bending her eyes on the ground. There could be no doubt that his new resolve was the best move in the circumstances, and she was not in a position to inform him that his night march was unnecessary, and that he would be wise to husband his horse's power until he left Oxford, for then would come his time of need.

"Well, let us get on," he cried. "I'll take the first by-road south."

Cautious old John, with his limping horse, had gone forward while they stood talking together, and now they cantered to overtake him. Frances was glad of the cessation of conversation that she might have opportunity of meditating on some argument that would retain him by her side. If he left her, she was resolved to seek out Cromwell at Northampton, tell him of her brother's disaster, and explain her own effort to make good his absence. When Cromwell was convinced that both her brother and herself had faithfully endeavoured to carry out the Commander's wishes, he might then heed her pleading that sentence be annulled, or at least suspended, until the boy had another chance of proving his loyalty to his party. She thought she should succeed in this appeal for mercy, as she was sure Cromwell himself must know her brother was not a traitor. Her meditations were interrupted by Armstrong suddenly drawing in his horse and standing up in his stirrups. She also stopped and looked inquiringly at him. A high hedge bordered the road, and he was endeavouring to peer beyond it.

"What is it?" she asked.

"I thought I caught a glint of a helmet over yonder."

They went on at a walk, and shortly after passed a road that crossed their own. Up this cross-road to the north, two troopers sat on their horses; down the road to the south were two others. As Armstrong and his companion continued west, the four troopers came out of their concealment and followed them.

"By St. Andrew, trapped! I'm trapped as completely as ever was Englishman in Tarras Moss!" muttered Armstrong.

## CHAPTER V.—AFFECTION.

The four troopers allowed the distance between themselves and the forward party neither to increase nor diminish until darkness set in, when they closed up, but said nothing. There was no further conversation between Frances and the young man. He held himself erect, and beyond the first exclamation gave no intimation that he was disturbed by the prospect before

570

him. She was victim to the most profound dejection, and was relieved when the gathering gloom allowed her pent-up tears to fall unseen. The universal silence made the situation the more impressive. The sun had gone down in a bank of cloud which now overspread the heavens, threatening a storm and obscuring the moon.

At last the lights of Northampton glimmered ahead, and shortly after a guard in front summoned them to stand. The troopers behind them also stood, but took no part in what followed. An officer examined their pass by the light of a lantern, but did not return it to them. His words seemed reassuring enough.

"You are stopping the night at Northampton?"

"Yes," replied Armstrong, although the pass had been given up by Frances, and the officer's inquiry was addressed to her.

"Have you any particular lodging in view?"

"No."

"You may meet trouble in finding a suitable abiding-place," said the officer, "more especially for the lady. Northampton is little better than a barracks at the moment. I will take you to 'The Red Lion.'" Saying this, but without waiting for any reply, he led the way with the swinging lantern. "The Red Lion" proved a much less attractive hostelry than the hospitable "Angel" at Grantham. It seemed occupied chiefly by armed men, and resembled military headquarters more than an inn.

"You will perhaps wish to see to your horses yourself," suggested the officer to Armstrong.

"Yes, after I am assured that the lady is——"

"Have no anxiety on that score. I will place her in the guardianship of the hostess, and will wait here for you."

The assurance had all the definiteness of a command, and Armstrong, without further parley, led away his own horse and hers, followed by old John.

"Come this way, madam," said the officer to Frances.

He escorted her up a stairway, and at the top turned to her and said in a low voice: "General Cromwell's commands were that you should be brought to him as soon as you arrived."

"Very well. I am ready."

He knocked at a door, and a gruff voice from within told him to enter. He opened the door and went in, followed by his prisoner.

"I have brought the woman, General. The man is under guard below." Saying this, and receiving no reply, the officer laid the pass on the table and withdrew, closing the door behind him.

Cromwell stood at the window, looking down on the dark street below, dotted with moving lights. His broad back was toward his visitor, and he did not turn round even when he addressed her. On a chair rested his polished breast-plate and steel cap, otherwise he was accoutred as he had been when she saw him on the road. His voice was hoarse.

"Who are you, wench, and what are you to this man, that you range the land brazenly together under a pass written for neither of you?"

With some difficulty the girl found her voice after two or three ineffectual attempts to speak, and said: "I am Frances Wentworth, sister to Lieutenant Wentworth of General Cromwell's army."

The General's ponderous head turned slowly, and he bent his sullen eyes upon her. She wondered Armstrong had not seen the brutal power of that countenance even by candle-light.

"Why is your brother not in your place?"

"My brother was sorely wounded the morning he set out, and now lies between life and death in our home."

"How came he wounded?"

"He met Lord Rudby, who attacked him. My brother would not defend himself, and so was thrust through the body. Armstrong brought him to our house, and the doctor says he cannot be moved for a month at least."

"Why was I not informed of this?"

"I did not know where to find you."

"You, wench, surely did not know where to find me; but your brother knew that a message to his nearest superior would find me."

"My brother, I have told you, was dangerously wounded, and had but one thing in his mind."

"What was that? Lord Rudby's daughter, most like."

The rich colour mounted in the cheeks of Frances, but she answered slowly: "It was to have done with the task you had set upon him."

"He committed it to your hands then?"

"He did."

"What was the task I set him?"

"It was to steal from Armstrong the King's commission, and to deliver the result of that theft to General Cromwell, the receiver."

"Wench, your tongue is over-sharp; a grievous fault. I pray you amend it."

"Not until I have told you I am no wench, but a lady."

"We have had too much of lady's meddling in England, and will have less of it in days to come. A wench, if she be honest, is better than a lady, who is seldom honest. Your meddling in this matter has come near to causing a serious disarrangement of great affairs. How was I to know who you were or why you travelled? Has that foolish head of yours so little understanding that, though you stopped at York, at Newark, at Grantham, you gave no officer of mine a clue to your vagabondage?"

"A woman can fulfil her duty without so much babbling of it. My foolish head never thought a great general wished his designs published from one end of England to the other."

The shaggy brows of Cromwell drew down over eyes that shot forth dull fire. He turned completely around, seemed about to speak, but did not. The flame of his glance died out, and he advanced to the table, picked up the pass, examining it critically, back and front. Then he handed it to her, saying slowly,—"If your brother had your brain without your tongue, he would advance faster than he does."

"Am I, then, to go on with this adventure?"

"Yes. You will reach Oxford to-morrow. The King will delay, and shuffle, and suspect, until our Scot is in a fine fume of impatience. For three days more I shall be in Northampton. After that for a week I shall be at Broughton Castle, some few miles west of Banbury. If you should be delayed longer in Oxford, I shall let you know where I am by means of De Courcy, who——"

"De Courcy!" exclaimed the girl.

"Yes; what do you know of him?"

"If he is the same man who was in the entourage of the King in London,—a Frenchman of that name,—I know nothing good of him."

"You cannot look for every virtue in the character of a spy, and we who are doing the Lord's work must use the tools the Lord places in our hands."

"The Lord has naught to do with De Courcy. He is a devil's man, body and soul."

Cromwell scowled at her. "What mean you by that, hussy?" he asked shortly.

"I mean that De Courcy would sell you as readily as he would the King, if there was gold to be made of the bargaining. The Philistines come with money in their hands, and they always find a De Courcy, male or female."

At this Biblical allusion the face of Cromwell cleared like magic, and she had a glimpse of another facet of his character. A certain exaltation which had nothing of hypocrisy in it radiated from his countenance, and his voice rang clear when he spoke.

"Aye, my girl, and when there is a Samson of sin to be bound and blinded, the Philistines do right to accomplish the act as best they may. Judge not, that ye be not judged. Perchance this work to which your hand is now set is not done for either God or your country."

"It will be done for my brother's life."

"Aye, truly; and that is your Philistine's wage. De Courcey toils not for the life of another, but for gold, and let him that is without sin cast the first stone. I give the wage demanded, and care nothing so that God's work be done. God's work is the one thing important, so scorn not De Courcy or any other, but seek his aid in Oxford if it be necessary to communicate with me."

"That shall I never do," muttered the girl under her breath; and if Cromwell heard he paid no heed.

"Have you given thought to your purpose?" he asked.

"I have thought of nothing else; it has never been absent from my mind."

"How do you hope to accomplish possession?"

"I expect to enact the scriptural part of the 'thief in the night,' somewhere between Oxford and Carlisle."

He had seated himself at the table, leaving her still standing before him. At these words the frown came again to his brow, and anger to his eyes.

"I do not like your iteration; it is not to the purpose, and is but womanish."

"I am a woman, and must bear the disadvantages of being so. As you have said, that matters little so that the good work be done."

"Between Oxford and Carlisle is vague. I cannot trust to a scheme so lacking in definiteness. I shall have Armstrong laid by the heels long before he reaches Carlisle. If the wench's hand fail, then comes the rough paw of the trooper immediately after. Your chance will be in Banbury, where you must contrive to have him stop for the night."

"If we leave Oxford early in the morning he will not be content to stop in Banbury, which is less than twenty-five miles away, and even on the coming hither we have covered more than double that distance each day. He will be urgent on his return."

"True, but there lies your task in management; you may fall ill, and I question if he will leave you. I can order your pass taken from you at Banbury, and a night's delay caused. You will go to the inn called 'The Banbury Arms,' at the sign of the blazoned sun. The inn-keeper will ask for your pass, and when he sees it he will place you in adjoining rooms which are fitted for your purpose. There is a communicating door, bolted on your side, invisible, except by close scrutiny, on the other. What follows will depend on your skill and quietness. Has the man any suspicion of your intention toward him?"

"None in the least. He is honest and kind."

"Ah! Do not dwell too much on his kindness in your thoughts, nor trust anything to his honesty. Make it your business to know where he keeps the King's letter, and when it is once in your possession speed at once to Broughton Castle and deliver it into my hands. I will exchange for it full pardon and a Captain's commission for your brother, and if you have further to ask my ear will be inclined toward you."

"I shall have nothing to ask except that this Scot be allowed to pass unscathed to his home."

Cromwell gazed intently at her for a moment, and she returned his look clear-eyed and unabashed. He replied slowly: "If I were willing to harm the Scot the case would be much simpler than it is. You left your home thinking only of your brother, but now the stranger occupies at least a part of your mind."

"It is natural we should feel compassion for those we injure."

A short time before the General had intimated that her tongue was an unruly member, and for a moment it seemed that her impulsive inexperience in dealing with men was about to wreck her plans, for now even the girl was shrewd enough to see that she was sowing distrust of herself in her opponent's mind by incautious utterances. Cromwell leaned back in his chair, and a look of rapt meditation crept over his features. The girl saw she had vanished from his vision, and that the grim man was alone with himself, inwardly questioning his thoughts and demanding an answer. She realized intuitively that once this answer were given, nothing she could say or do would turn him from the purpose decided upon.

"O Youth, Youth!" he murmured, "how unstable thou art! A broken reed; undependable! Give me the middle-aged; the steadfast. Youth is the flash of the burning flax; middle age the steady flame of a consuming fire. Is it not better to imprison this man secretly or hang him openly? He is a convicted spy; every law of war will uphold me. If I grasp the thistle it may sting me, but I shall uproot it. Yet——yet, why at this time bring upon me the brawling Scots? Could I be but sure——the brother risks all at the supreme moment and falls as the fool falleth. Why should she be more firm? Were I sure of her——"

"Sir, you can be sure of me," cried the girl in a panic, terror-stricken at the sight his muttered phrases conjured before her.

"What! What! What! What say you?" Cromwell shook himself as a man rudely awakened from sleep.

"I say you can be sure of me. I shall not falter."

"You will bring me this document?"

"I swear to God I will."

"Nay, nay, swear not at all. If a man's word bear him not up, he will sink when his oath alone buoys him. Wench, I will trust you; but remember this: if I am compelled to take this man through force of arms, to surround him with a troop and publicly wrench his burden from him, I must as publicly hang him, to warn the next Scot who would make the essay on Oxford. If you succeed, you save not only your brother's life, but this man's as well. Now go. Let there be no turning back from the plough to which your hand is set."

Frances retreated and let herself out of the room. On the stair-head at the end of the passage, well out of possible earshot, two soldiers stood on guard, and between them an elderly woman, who immediately advanced when she saw the girl leave the General's room.

"I am the landlady," she said. "Will you come with me?"

"I wish a word with my friend," replied Frances. The woman appeared nonplussed, and stood hesitating; but at that moment the officer who had conducted her came up the stair and approached. "I wish to speak with Mr. Armstrong," she said to him. "Where is he?"

"One moment, madam, if you please," replied the officer, knocking at the General's door. He was not bade to enter, but the single word, "Oxford," uttered in a deep voice, came from within. The subordinate appeared to understand, and with a bow to the lady said: "Mr. Armstrong is waiting below. Will you come down, or shall I ask him to come up?"

"You may tell him I wish to see him."

She walked to the head of the stair and saw Armstrong alone in the lower hall, pacing up and down with a fine swagger of Scottish indifference, which he must have been far from feeling, while the doorway was blocked by two guards holding grounded pikes. The moment the young man saw her he came bounding up the stair two steps at a time. All the guards, above and below, seemed struck with simultaneous alertness, and made a motion which, if continued, would have brought their weapons to bear on the prisoner, but a slight signal from the officer's hand brought back their former stolidity.

"Oh, Mr. Armstrong, I merely wished to know at what hour we set out to-morrow."

"Do we set out to-morrow?" he asked in a whisper. "Yes, there is no obstacle between here and Oxford. I was up so late last night, and that, with this long, dragging journey to-day, has tired me. All I wished to know was the hour for to-morrow."

"But you will have supper with me?"

"No. I can eat nothing. I am too tired."

"Now, that's strange. I'm as hungry as the Tweed at flood time. Let me persuade you."

"Thank you, but I would rest. Good-night."

In all his life he never forgot that picture of the girl at the stair-head looking down upon him. There was a pathetic droop in her attitude which was usually so firm and erect, as if the gloom of this fortress-inn oppressed her. Childlike and forlorn she seemed, and a great wave of pity surged up in his heart for her, while his arms thrilled with a yearning to enclasp and comfort her.

"Good-night!" he cried, impulsively thrusting forth his hand to her. She did not appear to notice the extended hand, and he almost imagined she shrank from it. As she went away he had one more lingering look from her, over her shoulder. A smile, sad and weary, but inexpressibly sweet, lingered on her lips.

"Good-night," she whispered.

## CHAPTER VI.—REJECTION.

There had been a lashing of rain and a clatter of thunder over Northampton in the night, as if the town were again besieged; but morning broke clear and beautiful, and when the pilgrims got out into the country again, the freshness of the air, the sparkle of the rain-drops on the trees, caused the world to seem newly made. The girl rode silent and thoughtful, but the young man was bubbling over with high spirits.

"What a wonderful magician is the morning after a rain in midsummer!" he cried. "It transforms everything and glorifies the commonest object, and it transmutes our thoughts from lead to silver. Last night, with the sky overcast and the coming storm growling in the west, when the air hung heavy and the gloom settled down upon us, every man was a lurking enemy, and that innocent tavern a place of dungeons instead of ale-cellars. This morning, hey, presto! a wave of the conjurer's wand, and every soldier is a jolly fellow and a well-wisher. I'm ashamed to confess it in this bright light, but last night I was in a panic, like a lad passing through a graveyard. Never before did my spirits sink to so low an ebb. Those kindly men bustling round to be of help to me with the horses seemed, to my distorted brain, on the watch lest I should give them the slip, and when the guards were set at the door after I had entered and was waiting for you, I thought they were so placed to keep me prisoner, and when the polite officer told me they were there every night, I actually disbelieved him. Even his own actions seemed suspicious, but now, as I look back on it, he was merely one of the few courteous persons in the Parliamentary army."

Armstrong suddenly threw back his head and laughed aloud, as if some humourous recollection had come to him.

"That poor officer must have thought me mad. When I came in from the stables I called for the landlady and asked where you were. She said you were in your room. I then requested her to find out if you would see me for a moment, and without reply she disappeared up the stair. I waited and waited, but she did not return. The officer was now by my side, chattering away about something to which I gave no attention. All at once the absurd idea struck me that you were with Cromwell, taken there by the officer, and that Old Noll was brow-beating you and threatening you, to learn something of me and what I was about."

"No one asked me anything about you or your business," said the girl.

"Of course not. I see that plainly now, but I give you my word it was real enough then. Without a word of warning I broke in on the amazed officer and shouted, 'Where is General Cromwell?' The man looked dumbfounded, as well he might; then he answered quietly enough, 'The General is in the Castle, half a mile from here.' Even then a glimmer of sense came to me, and I explained that the General had passed us that afternoon, and I wondered if he had stopped at Northampton. The officer said he had, and next moment the landlady appeared at the stair-head, and you a moment or two after. What tricks imagination can play with a man!"

"I was as anxious as you were last night, and shall always think of Northampton as the gloomiest town I ever saw."

"I am glad to be quit of it. I wonder if that officer has given us the right direction? It seems to me that we should be bearing further south for Oxford. But perhaps the road takes a turn presently."

"The road is right for the way we are going. We pass through Banbury, which is not much longer than the direct route. I intend to leave Old John at Banbury, and with him this permit, which will be a danger to carry until we turn north again. Banbury is on the straight road to Scotland, which I suppose will be the way you go on your return."

"You are right in that. I'll travel north as the crow flies if I can."

"Then what say you to making Banbury our first stop on the homeward run, after we leave Oxford, taking early to the road the next morning."

"How far is Banbury from Oxford?"

"Less than thirty miles, I think."

"Oh, we can do better than that. I must make from seventy to one hundred miles a day on my road home."

"There is sometimes real speed in apparent slowness."

"True. We shall be guided by circumstances, of course. Much will depend on the hour of the day we are done with Oxford."

Frances said nothing more, for she saw that the stop at Banbury would have to be managed from Oxford, and that it would require some tact on her part to arrange it. The ever-increasing moon was against her, for if there was much delay at Oxford, not only would Armstrong be the more impatient to get north, but night would soon be almost as light as day, and therefore travel would only be limited by the endurance of themselves and their horses. She wished Cromwell had selected some spot at least fifty miles farther away than Banbury, but, with a sigh, accepted the conditions presented to her and resolved to do her best.

At Banbury she had no difficulty in leading her unsuspicious comrade to "The Banbury Arms," and there they left Old John with his crippled horse. The landlord was a quiet, furtive-looking man, with a manner that suggested an intermittent glancing over the shoulder. Frances resolved to say nothing to him at this time, believing they had come so quickly from Northampton that she was in advance of any instructions he was to receive, but in this she was mistaken. With Cromwell to decide was to act, and some one had evidently come through in the night. While they halted, waiting the preparation of a meal, the soft-footed innkeeper, watching his opportunity, drew the girl aside and asked her if she possessed a pass; if so he would like to see it. He was very apologetic, saying all public-house keepers so near to Oxford were compelled by the military charge of the town to assure themselves that travellers who stopped with them were properly vouched for, otherwise it would be his duty to detain them and report to the local commandant. She presented the pass to him without a word, and he read it in silence, then looked at her as if he expected some comment. At last he said:

"Perhaps you intend to stop here on your return?"

"Yes. Have you received instructions already?"

"I have, and everything is prepared. Would you come up now and look at the room? Then, if for any reason I am not here when you come back, you will see that no mistake is made."

He took her to an upper room and explained to her the action of the concealed door, which moved without a sound on well-oiled hinges.

"During the night you occupy this room. I shall have a horse ready, and will be in waiting for you myself until morning. I am to show you the way to the Castle. When you see the General, perhaps you would do me the kindness to tell him that this room was prepared within two hours after I received his commands. He likes prompt service."

"I shall tell him of your promptness if I remember to do so."

"Thank you. Perhaps you will let me remind you of it when you ride to the Castle?"

"Very well."

"You will find the road to Oxford without impediment until you reach the lines of the King. I hope you will have a safe sojourn there and a speedy return."

The girl thanked him for his good wishes with what courtesy she could call to her aid, for at heart she loathed him; his smooth, oily, ingratiating manner, and his shifty glance making her shiver with repulsion. Yet, she said to herself, conscience accusing, this man was merely an assistant in a deed where she herself acted the leading part. He was a mercenary, doubtless, doing what he was bid, but against a stranger and an enemy, while she plotted against a friend and a man who trusted her. Fervently she prayed that Providence might intervene between the resolution and its accomplishment, in some way rendering her project unnecessary. There was a slight hope that the suspicious King might not receive Armstrong as the envoy of the Scots. He carried no credentials, and Charles, if he employed him, must accept the Borderer's unsupported word that he was what he declared himself to be. She feared that Charles was in such straits that he would clutch at any straw, but hoped his natural distrust would come into play, so that Armstrong might return empty-handed to Scotland, while she would be relieved of this fell betrayal, from which, as events stood, she saw no way of escape.

Glad was she to leave Banbury behind her, but tremblingly did she dread the time when she should see it again. The road, as the innkeeper had predicted, was clear, and now for the first time during that journey she was alone with her fellow traveller, Old John pottering over his lame horse in the stables of the Banbury inn.

The spirits of the young man were as high as those of the girl were low. He saw that for some reason unknown to him she was depressed, and he tried to banter her into a more cheerful frame of mind; but, this effort bringing with it indifferent success, he broke out into song, and carolled to her some of the Border ballads, both sentimental and humourous, varying his chanting with explanatory excursions into the legends that had given rise to the verses. This was more successful, for few can withstand the magic of a sympathetic voice and a good song, especially when the summer afternoon was perfect, as all the days of their march had been. The birds on either hand warbled an accompaniment; the landscape was empty of humanity, and they had the fair world to themselves. If tormenting thought would but have left her unmolested, the girl knew she would have delighted in this irresponsible outing as thoroughly as her companion enjoyed it. To all outward appearance they were in a very elysium of peace, yet they were approaching the storm centre of the most distracted country on earth, and this seemed typical of her own situation, for although an enforced calm characterized her demeanour, despair was raging in her heart.

Several times the obedient Bruce, guided by an unseen touch, edged close to her, but Armstrong could not fail to perceive that the girl shrank from his proximity, and this abashed him, silencing his song and jocularity. But a lover must be bold if he would prosper. Here was a Heaven-sent opportunity, and what more can a man ask than that? In an hour or two they would be in the midst of a thronged city, where she would meet the friends she expected to see. Who could predict what might happen? It was possible she would elect to remain in Oxford. One or more of her friends might accompany her back to Durham. Now or never was the motto. Yet he had not the least notion how he ought to begin, but thought that in such a crisis a great deal must depend on the presentation of the case. Why had he let slip so many chances of getting information on a subject that now loomed with new importance before him? There was her own brother, to take the latest instance, who would have been glad to find a confidant, and needed but the slightest encouragement that morning in the lane to dissipate all the mystery surrounding a proposal. Thomas Wentworth had solved the problem, yet he was no older than this slip of a girl riding by his side. They had gone a mile or two in silence; a silence in marked contrast to his soniferous setting out. Frances feared that her seemingly sullen indifference had offended him, and, glancing surreptitiously at him from under her long lashes, met his own eyes fixed upon her. She smiled a little and said: "Have you no more songs?"

"I have one more," he answered, speaking hurriedly, "but I have never sung it before, and am just a little in doubt how to begin. I think if I got the measure of it I could carry it on, but am not sure."

"Is it that you have been thinking about so long?"

"Yes. There is a chorus to it, and there you must help me."

"How can I if I don't know it?"

"If I can sing a song I never tried before, perhaps you could do the same with the chorus."

"Very well, let me hear the song. Is it one of those fighting ballads?"

"No. It is a love song, pure and simple."

"I like the others better. Brave and noble actions are the only deeds worthy of poetry."

"I used to think that myself, but I have come to change my mind. It seems to me now that true love is the only theme for either song or story."

"Oh!" said the girl, with a coldness that froze instantly his budding enthusiasm. She sat up straighter on her horse, and turned her face resolutely toward Oxford, as if she did not approve the tendency of the conversation. Armstrong was stricken dumb at finding his indirect course thus blocked before him. The girl was the first to speak.

"I wonder how soon we will be in sight of Oxford," she said.

"Not for a long time, I hope."

"Why do you say that? Are you not as eager as I to reach Oxford?"

"There are some important matters to be settled before we come to the end of our journey."

Frances directed upon him a look of troubled resolution. Intuitively she knew that they were come to the edge of a declaration which she had hoped might be avoided. Several times on the way the danger seemed to approach and vanish, but now the glow of his luminous eyes were not to be mistaken. In them she read a consuming love of herself which was not to be balked, yet which must be balked, and so it became now or never with her, as it was with him. Whatever words he found would be less eloquent than the glances he had before now cast upon her, and it was well to have the event over and done with.

"What important matters are to be settled?" she asked firmly.

All courage seemed to desert him under the intensity of her survey, but with the dourness of his race he urged himself forward, yet not in a direct line. Something of the military strategy with which he would approach a fortress insinuated itself into his love-making.

"We must decide in what guise you are to enter Oxford."

This remark certainly had the effect of throwing the holder of the fortress off her guard. It swept away the tribulation from her brow. After all, the case might not be so serious as she had thought, and jubilantly she welcomed the respite, for she had no wish to add a humiliation to the wrong which fate had decreed she should work upon him. She breathed a sigh of relief and said:

"What guise? I'm afraid I do not understand."

"You see, hitherto we have been shielded by a pass. Its wording was such that little inquiry was made about either of us. Now, for the first time we have no protection, and what we say to those who accost us must prove our safeguard. I shall be asked who you are. I told your brother that I would treat you as if you were my own sister, but I cannot call you my sister at Oxford."

"Why not."

"For one reason, because you go to meet friends who know that I am not your brother, and if inquiry is made we are at a disadvantage."

"True, true! I had forgotten."

"Another reason is that if we claimed such relationship no one would believe us, for your hair is as black as the raven's wing, and mine is like the yellow corn."

For the first time that day the girl laughed outright and lifted her eyes to the locks that so well became him. The simile of Samson again flashed upon her and checked her mirth, but she put the thought resolutely away from her. Armstrong laughed also, well pleased with his progress.

"I had not thought of that," she said.

"But I thought of it, and also of a way to circumvent it. If they ask who the lady is, I shall tell them she is my betrothed."

"No, no, no!" gasped the girl.

"Why not? as you asked a moment since. All's fair in love——and war. The country is at war, and we may make true the rest of the adage."

"No, no!" she repeated.

He was now close by her side and endeavoured to take her hand, but she held it from him.

"You say no because you will not act a lie, and I honour you for your truth. You are robed in truth, my beloved, as an angel is——"

"Oh, cease, cease, I beg of you!"

"Frances, this is the song that bubbles in my heart, and if my lips could worthily fulfil their prompting, I would put it to such words and such music as woman never listened to before. But, lacking eloquence, I can only say, My lady, I love you."

"And I can only say I am sorry if this be so."

"If! Why do you say if? Do you not know it to be true?"

"I know it now that you tell it to me."

"Must a man speak ere he can convey to the woman he loves the fact that he loves her?"

"If the woman love him not, he must speak, and still she finds his preference unaccountable."

"You do not love me?"

"No."

"And cannot?"

"And cannot."

"You would even rob me of all hope, the lover's guiding star?"

"If you call it robbing to take from you what should never have been possessed."

"Why should I not have possessed that hope? Is it because I am untitled, while you are the daughter of the man who was the proudest peer in England?"

"Titles have naught to do with it."

"Titles are but a breath; still, men have intrigued for them, have sold their souls for them, as others have bartered for gold. That shall I do. I thought never to beg from any man, yet for this King I stake my life, and it is but fair he should cover my wager. I will say to him, I go to Scotland on your behest, through an enemy's country. Death or treachery dog every footstep I take. I may win or lose, but if I win, then I demand the stakes, which will not take a silver penny from your depleted treasury. Make me Earl of the Southern Marches."

"You ask a just reward, but 'twould be useless as assistant to the quest you now pursue."

"Frances, no lover truly entitled to bear that dear name, thinks himself worthy of her on whom his heart is set, and I do not plead my own worthiness when I sue for your favour. But I am buoyed up by the thought that every day we live some woman marries some man, therefore are women to be persuaded, and there are none on earth but us to persuade them. Why should my fortune be worse than that of my fellows?"

"Sir, you forget or ignore that every day of our lives some woman refuses some man, and never marries him. Why should your fortune differ from that of so many of your fellows?"

"You have pierced the armour there, my girl, so I own my simile defective, and fall back on my own unworthiness, to beseech your pity on it, and point the way to that amendment which will make me deserving in your eyes."

"Sir, you force me unduly. You drive me toward confession. Pitying God is my witness that I hold naught against you."

"Then, Frances, all is well with us. An English princess, as you told me, journeyed north to marry a Scottish king. Let us furnish a quid pro quo, for the King of the Border rides south to win an English princess. Here we are on the march together to meet the descendant of Scottish prince and English princess, so we cannot do better than follow the example of his forebears."

"Sir, your precedent is unfortunate. The English princess made but a foolish wife for the royal Scot, and their descendant is a man whose word is a frail dependence. Indeed you said their house had exercised a fatal influence on yours, so beware the omens. Put not your trust in princesses, English or other."

"I put my trust on one as on an altar, and kneel before it."

"That I warn you not to do. Many a man has lost his trust through such blind folly."

"So shall not I."

"Sir, you are confident, and are likely to meet with confidence betrayed. You must accept my answer as final, and let us have an end of this fruitless and embarrassing conversation. I can never marry you."

"There is but one circumstance to prevent it."

"Then believe that circumstance exists."

"You love another?"

"I do not."

The young man laughed joyously, but no corresponding smile disturbed the set lips of the girl. He should have seen how painful this dialogue had been to her, but with a lover's selfishness he had eyes for nothing but the object of pursuit; ears for nothing but the words he hoped to compel her to say; pursuing her thus from one point of refuge to another, each abandoned in turn, with no thought but that of capture. Her face was white with dread, a whiteness made the more striking by the jet framing of her hair. Never during the conference had she looked at him since the first direct gaze when she took the resolution to have this disturbing business put at rest forever. The horses walked on unguided, her eyes on the road immediately before her. When he accused her of loving another she glanced up at him for one brief moment, and answered before she thought, wishing her reply recalled as soon as it was uttered, for if she had agreed with him, he himself had said it was at an end. Bitterly did she regret her heedless destruction of the barrier which would have separated them. Now she must erect another, more terrible, more complete, be the consequences what they may.

"Sir, you laugh. I am glad your heart is light, for mine is heavy enough. If I loved another, 't were a small matter, for the man were not likely so estimable in a woman's eyes as you are. As I have said, you drive me toward confession, and here is one bold enough for a maiden to make. I admit you please me well, and if I had loved another—a woman's affection is fickle— you were like to benefit by its transference. But there is an obstacle between us more serious than the one you proclaimed sufficient. Take that as truth, and ask me no more."

"I must be the judge of the obstacle. What is it?"

"I dare not tell you."

"Will you never tell me?"

"I shall make full confession when this war is finished, if you ask me."

"What have we to do with the war?"

"You speak as a Scot. 'T is an unnecessary question, for you know all in England are entangled in its meshes."

"But it can have nothing to do with your feeling toward me, or my adoration of you."

"You shall judge when you hear."

"Then let me hear now."

"No. Your persistence, when you see how distraught I am, dims your title of gentleman. A lady should not be coerced."

"Your censure is just; but oh, pity my despair if this obstacle be real! It cannot be real. Whatever it is it shall dissolve before my burning love as mist before the sun. Tell it to me now, that I may show you that it is the fabric of a vision."

The girl remained silent, her impetuous lover fiercely questioning her bowed head with his eyes. But as if in the interval of stillness a spectre intervened between them and brought a startled expression into his eyes, their intensity sharpened suddenly, and he said in a low voice: "Do not tell me you are already married?"

"And what if I am?" asked the girl hopelessly. "Would the knowledge that such were the case end this useless discussion?"

"No, by my salvation, it would not. If you admit but the slightest esteem for me, I will carry you to my castle in the North and hold it safe for you against the world. Are you, then, wedded?"

"I am wedded to deceit. Sir, I am not worthy your love, or that of any other honest man. If you knew what it costs me to say this, you would let these words be the last we speak in this painful debate."

"Deceit? Not worthy of any honest man? Lord save you, child of sweet innocence, if this is all that troubles you, there is nothing in our way to the church. Your eyes are limpid wells of honesty. You could not harbour a deceitful thought if you tried. I would trust my life, my honour, my very soul to your keeping, assured that———"

"O God of mercy! why do you torture me?" cried the girl in a burst of anguish, bending her head over the horse's mane. The astonished young man placed his hand affectionately on her shoulder, and felt her shudder beneath his touch.

"My dearest lass," he began, but never finished the sentence.

"Halt!" came a sharp command. Armstrong looked up like a man awakening from a dream.

"'Fore God!" he cried, wonder-stricken, "we're on the outposts of Oxford."

A ragged soldier barred the way, with musket held horizontally. An officer in a uniform that had once been gaudy, but now showed signs of hard usage, came out from the cabin at the side of the road when he heard the sentinel's challenge. Though his costume was so threadbare, he carried it with a swagger that had almost a touch of insolence in it, but this bearing melted to a debonair deference when he saw a handsome young woman before him. He lifted his hat and addressed her companion.

"Pardon me. Have you the pass-word?"

"No. I am from Scotland and bear a message to his Majesty the King."

"From Scotland? May I glance at your credentials?"

"I carry none. I have come through a hostile country; have been searched once or twice and arrested as often. Had there been writing on me I should not now be standing at the doorstep of Oxford."

"I shall do myself the honour of conducting you to the Chamberlain of his Majesty. And the lady?"

Armstrong took the girl's hand, this time without opposition on the part of its owner; it was cold as ice.

"The lady is my wife," he said boldly; then added, in a whisper heard only by herself,—"that is to be."

The officer bowed and led the way to the town.

"I wish we were in Scotland," said the young man very quietly.

"So do I," sighed the girl.

"Because what I said at the outworks would then have constituted a marriage between us, if you had replied yes."

The girl withdrew her hand from his and turned away her head.

## CHAPTER VII.—CHECKMATED.

The one on foot and the two on horseback entered the fortress which had hitherto proved impregnable, and traversed its streets until they came to "The Crown" inn. Oxford was no longer the home of learning for any art save that of war. A few students still strolled its thoroughfares, but the military man was everywhere. The colleges had been turned into barracks and arsenals; the King himself lived in Christ Church, over the towers of which floated the royal standard, now almost the only red spot in all England.

As the party came to a halt the officer turned to Armstrong. "A propitious meeting," he said, "here comes the Lord Great Chamberlain himself."

Armstrong noted the approach of a man with a countenance so remarkable that it might have been taken as typical of war. From brow to chin was drawn a long red scar, while another ran transversely across the forehead just over the eyes, so that there flamed from his face an angry cross that gave a most sinister expression to a visage which, lacking these time-healed wounds, would have been handsome. The Chamberlain stopped abruptly in his advance, his gaze riveted upon the girl, and there came into his eyes a look of such malignity that Armstrong instantly turned his glance upon his travelling companion. The girl's cheeks had gone deathly white, and she swayed blindly in her saddle, perilously near to falling. The young man sprang from his horse and caught her just in time. Bitterly he blamed himself for this unexpected collapse, cursing his persistence on the road, when he had plainly seen that some strong emotion tormented her. This mental perturbation, combined with the physical strain she had undergone during their long journey, fully accounted for the prostration of the moment at the end.

"My poor lass," he said regretfully, "I am to blame. I am a thoughtless, selfish hound to have so sorely troubled you with my insistence."

"It is not that," she whispered faintly, leaning heavily on him with the pathetic helplessness of a tired child, a dependence which sent a thrill of pity and love for her tingling to his finger-ends. "Take me in; take me in quickly. I am ill."

Now the Lord Great Chamberlain, all smiles and courtesy, stepped forward and said with authority to the innkeeper:

"The chief rooms in the house for the lady. Turn out whoever occupies them, whatever their quality."

The landlord called his wife, and Frances was given into her care.

The officer introduced the traveller to the high official: "My Lord Chamberlain, this gentleman says he has come from the Scottish nobles with a message for his Majesty. Sir, Monsieur de Courcy, Lord Great Chamberlain to the King."

Frenchman and Scot bowed to each other, the grace of the gesture being almost entirely in favour of the former, despite his marred face.

"Sir," said Armstrong to the officer, "I thank you for your guidance; and you, my lord," to De Courcy, "for your kind and prompt command with respect to the lady. She has had a long and tiring journey through a dangerous country, under continual fear of arrest, and so it is not to be wondered that a woman should succumb to the strain at the last."

"Our countries have ever been friends and allies," said De Courcy with the utmost amiability, "and I trust that we, meeting on what is to each of us foreign soil, may be animated by a like regard."

"I thank you, my lord, and, speaking for myself, admit that I have always looked with affection upon France and her brave and gallant sons."

Again De Courcy graciously inclined his head, and replied: "And believe me, sir, if you were acquainted with her daughters, your affection for the fair land would not be diminished. I regret that I have never set foot in Scotland, but hope some day that such will be my privilege. The officer who has left us did not give me your name."

"I am William Armstrong, somewhat known on the Border, a Scottish gentleman, and a loyal subject of his Majesty the King."

"Then you are very welcome in Oxford, and I am sure his Majesty wishes there were more like you in the environs thereof and the regions beyond. It is now too late to see the King to-day, and probably you are not loath to meet a night's rest after a hard day's riding. I will arrange a conference for you with his Majesty as soon as possible."

"Thank you. If I may hint that every day is of value, you will perhaps urge upon the King the danger of delay."

"I shall not fail to do so. Good-night."

For the first time in his life Armstrong left his horse to the care of others and entered the inn to inquire after the welfare of the lady who absorbed his thoughts. She sent word that she was quite recovered, but would see no one until the morrow. With this he was fain to be content, and he wandered about the town in the gathering dusk, hoping to do her a service by discovering the whereabouts of Lord Rudby's son, to whom he supposed she carried some message from her brother. He learned that this young man, who was a captain in the King's army, had been sent, it was supposed, to London, but nothing had been heard of him for a month or more, and whether he was prisoner or not, none could say. This intelligence depressed Armstrong, who feared that the girl had taken her long journey for nothing, and that the failing to find the one she sought might entail serious consequences upon her brother or herself, for each in turn had manifested great concern touching the mission she had undertaken.

Next morning his first visitor was the Lord Chamberlain, who expressed deep regret that the King was indisposed and could not see any emissary from the Scots that day. The high official spoke feelingly of the disappointment the monarch had been called upon to endure through the unmerited success of his rebellious subjects, and this statement seemed to the traveller only what was to have been expected.

During the day Armstrong was privileged in securing one brief interview with Frances. The landlord had placed two rooms at her disposal, and in the scantily furnished parlour the young man had called upon her. The improvement she had affirmed the evening before was scarcely borne out by her appearance, for she was wan and dispirited, so much so that when Armstrong announced the disappearance of Captain Rudby, the tidings did not seem to depress her more than was already the case. However, the news clung to her mind; for, as he was telling her that the King could not see him that day, she suddenly said, in a tone which showed she had not been listening, that as Captain Rudby was not in Oxford, there was no reason why she should stay. She would go on at once to Banbury, and there await the coming of Armstrong. But the young man would not hear of such a course. It was impossible, he said, that an unprotected lady in the disturbed state of the country should travel alone between Oxford and Banbury. It was not likely that he would be held from the King more than another day, and then they would both set out together. Besides, she needed all the rest she could obtain before they turned north again. The girl was too deeply dejected even to argue the question, when he so strenuously opposed her desire. It seemed that a contrary fate was tightening the coils around her, and all struggle against it was fruitless. There were unshed tears in her eyes as she glanced timidly up at him, and she had the haunted look of one who was trapped. The unforeseen meeting with De Courcy, although Cromwell's words should have prepared her for it, had completely unnerved her; that nightmare face of his confronting her whenever she closed her eyes. The past had come up before her in its most abhorrent guise. She remembered striking him fiercely with the jagged iron she happened to hold in her hand, and thought anything was justified that enabled her to escape his clutches, but that he would carry so fearful a disfiguration to his grave chilled her with fear of his vengeance; for if ever murder shone from a man's eyes it glared in his when she caught his first glance the evening before. All during the night the terrifying vision drove sleep from her couch, and she pondered on some possible method of escape, but without result. How gladly she would have confided her peril to Armstrong, did she stand in honest relation to him, but she could not bring herself to ask help from a man whom she had just rejected and whom she would shortly rob. When Armstrong mentioned the absence of Rudby, she had utterly forgotten that the ostensible reason for this Oxford journey was to see him, and for a moment it appeared that here lay a loophole of escape, but Armstrong's outspoken opposition to her plan left her with no adequate excuse for persisting in it. All force of purpose had deserted her, and it seemed impossible that it could have been she who for the sake of a father she had seen but once had braved the rage-mad Queen of England and threatened the monarch himself in his own court in the height of his power. What subtle change had come over her imperious will? What alchemy had converted the strong wine of her resolve to vapid water? It was not personal fear. She had met De Courcy before, and even when he had her at his mercy, lured into his private room, her high courage never faltered. But now her whole impulse was to call for aid from another; to have that other protect her, and to obey his slightest wish. Here was a mutability indeed for the daughter of the strenuous Strafford! This feeling was something new, something strange, something unaccountable. And that other stood before her, anxious to heal her hurt, but diagnosing wrongly, powerless to apply the soothing balm. She wished him there, for his strong presence calmed her; yet she also wished him gone, that she might collect her scattered thoughts. Absent or present, he disturbed her, and she wondered if this could be love, which she had imagined brought peace and joyous content.

During this unsatisfactory coming together, little was said by either. The girl sat in a chair by a small table, and he stood on the other side. Most of the time her head rested on her hand, and he saw she was near to tears. He censured himself again for his ill-timed avowal of the day before, but saw no method by which he could annul its consequences save by saying nothing more.

On the third day of his stay in Oxford the suave De Courcy was compelled to bewail the continued indisposition of the King. There were various important matters awaiting his Majesty's attention, he said, but nothing could be done until his recovery. Meanwhile, to pass time that must be hanging heavily on the visitor's hands, the thoughtful Frenchman suggested that Armstrong should indulge in a stroll around the fortifications. Oxford was believed to be unassailable, but De Courcy would be pleased to hear any criticisms the new-comer cared to pass upon the defences. Armstrong expressed his concurrence with this proposal, and thought at first that the obliging foreigner was to be his guide; but shortly after they set out, De Courcy introduced him to an officer who was to be his cicerone, and excused himself because of the King's illness, which had placed on his shoulders many duties that had heretofore been absent from them. As soon as the two were out of sight, De Courcy hastened back to the inn, passed up the stair, and knocked at the door of the room occupied by Frances Wentworth. On receiving permission to enter, he went in and closed the door behind him. The girl, who had expected a different caller, rose from her chair and stood silent.

"Madam, this is a meeting which I have long looked forward to with pleasant anticipation."

"Sir, I regret that I have no share in your felicity."

"Perhaps you prefer that we should meet as enemies."

"I prefer that we should not meet at all, and, knowing this, you may be good enough to make your visit as short as possible."

"I cannot find words to express my sorrow, on learning I am so unwelcome. I am sure that when last we met, I did my best to make your visit as long as I could, so why should you wish to shorten mine?"

It seemed to the girl that there was something unnecessarily shameless in his allusion to a circumstance that had so disfigured him. As she made no reply, he went on with airy nonchalance: "Will you excuse me if I lock the door, and, showing that experience is a proficient schoolmaster, I ask the extension of your forgiveness to cover the act of putting the key in my pocket. We live and learn, you know. Not that I fear any interruption, for the innocent and excellent Scot is at this moment investigating our battlements under the care of a shrewd guide, and will not return this three hours or more." The polite intruder locked the door and put the key in his pocket; then advanced toward her. She retreated to the other room, and for a moment he thought she was about to barricade herself within, but she reappeared on the instant with a jewelled dagger in her hand.

"I warn you, sir, that if you approach within striking distance I will pierce you to the heart."

The Frenchman smiled and waved his fine white hands with a gesture of inimitable grace.

"Fairest of the Wentworths," he said, "the glances of those lustrous eyes have already pierced that sensitive organ. Alas, that it is my fate they should beam upon me in anger. Well, my Lady Wentworth, you see I do not approach you, but grant my bravery the justice to believe that it is not fear of the sting that prevents my sipping the honey. May I sit down, and if I place this table between us, will you feel safer?"

"You will be safer so long as it remains between us."

"I assure you my own safety weighs but lightly with me. I implore you to be seated, for I cannot converse at ease with a lady who is standing."

"I prefer to stand. Your ingrained courtesy will then cause you to make our conference brief."

"It distresses me to say that you are prolonging the conference by standing. We have grave particulars of state policy to discuss, and I cannot begin while you are so cruel as to put me in the light——"

"Oh, very well!" cried Frances, impatiently, taking her own chair; whereupon he, elegantly gracious, seated himself opposite her, with the table between them.

"How ideally charming you look! I swear there is none to compare with you, even in that land of loveliness to which I have the honour to belong. Will you believe me when I say that there has not been a day since I last saw you, that I have not thought of you. I was angry at first, as you may well imagine, but at last I saw that I had been to blame, although I think the punishment must have obliterated my crime."

He paused for a few moments, but, she making no reply, he continued:

599

"Grief for the loss of you filled my heart. You think I come here as an enemy, but I come as a suppliant. In the folly of that time at Whitehall I refused you marriage, and I do not wonder you were wroth at me. I wish to atone for what you justly considered an insult, and am willing to marry you in the face of the world."

"I thank you."

"I shall ask no questions anent this awkward Scot who has been your courier, for I am sure you can have thought nothing of him."

"I thank you."

"You return thanks coldly, but I know that is the English nature. The fire of France is not to be expected in this northern clime, but if you say yes to my pleading, I am satisfied."

"If I wished for fire I would go down and not abroad for it. I had sooner wed the fiend from the pit than you."

De Courcy laughed lightly.

"That were a sulphurous mating indeed! Still you see how I adore you when I restate my determination to occupy the devil's place at your side before the altar. You but whet my expectation, for I should dearly love to tame you as your Shakespeare tamed his shrew."

"That you shall never do while a hand's breadth of steel will rid me of you, or myself of the world. Escape is too easy."

"Not from an Oxford dungeon, my dear. This mediaeval town furnishes us with dark pits in which there is no fire, and consequently they have a cooling effect on the hottest temperament. These are pits of which I am the fiend. My dear, you underrate my power, or overrate my patience."

"There are English gentlemen in Oxford. On what plea could you induce them to think that an English lady should be placed in a dungeon?"

"Yes, there are English gentlemen here, and some French gentlemen as well. They are unanimous in their detestation of a spy, male or female. Your man we shall hang out of hand, and there will be little difficulty about the pleasing task. I shall myself plead that your life be spared, and they will agree. Everything will be done with that beautiful legality which the English so much admire, but even from this moment you are entirely in my power, and a sensible woman should not need so much argument to convince her that the situation is hopeless."

"Armstrong is no spy."

"He may have difficulty in proving he is not. I am glad to note that you admit by inference that you are a spy."

"I can prove he is not a spy."

"Your evidence would be tainted. You are an accomplice. Besides, you could not clear him without condemning yourself."

"Such will I gladly do. I glory in that I would sacrifice myself with joy to save William Armstrong, the awkward Scot, as you called him. What would you give to hear me say this of you?"

"Much, my dear, much. Oh, I delight in you! You know how to sting without using your poniard. But I am not of a jealous nature, and love conquest for its own sake. I have told you I care nothing for the Scot, and you might easily have had him journey for the North again if you had not been so impetuous. Now I shall hang him, merely as the first step in breaking the stubborn pride which adds such zest to your overcoming."

"One word from me to Armstrong will transfer the danger to you. He will break you like a reed."

"Indeed, my dear, you do yourself injustice in threatening me. You shall have no opportunity of speaking your one word, for when next we meet, if we part now without coming to amicable arrangement, you will be on your knees to me pleading for his life."

"That will I not. I shall go to the King."

"Frances, you dishearten me, and cast grave doubts on the possession of that sound sense with which I credited you. Was your first appeal to the King for a man's life so successful that you build hopes on a second?"

"If Charles had kept his word with me then, he would not now be encaged in Oxford. He abandoned my father and clung to such as you, and not a foot of English ground remains to him but what he stands on."

"What would have happened had Strafford lived, neither you nor I can tell, and all discussion thereon is aside from our present purpose. Will you make terms with me?"

"I will not."

"You prefer the dungeon?"

"You dare not imprison me."

"Why?"

"Your master will not allow you."

The Frenchman leaned upon the table, a patient beneficent expression on his scarred features, and spoke to her gently, as one who must deal with a petulant, unreasonable child.

"My dear, let me put a quietus for ever upon your mad idea that any help is to be expected from the King. I beg you to believe that I speak the exact truth. Do you know what the King thinks of you?"

"He does not think of me at all. He has forgotten me."

"Pardon me. There you are mistaken. He thinks you came to Whitehall the day of your father's death to assassinate him. He believes that I imperilled my life to save his. The scars of your claws, however repulsive they may be to others, are to him a constant reminder of his supposed debt to me. Judge you then, my dear, what your position in Oxford would be did the King but dream you had crept surreptitiously into his stronghold. Need I say more?"

"No. But you should have paid better heed to what I said."

"What did you say?"

"I said your master would not permit you to injure me."

"But I have shown you that the King——"

"I am not speaking of the King. Your master is Oliver Cromwell."

Either the cross on his face became redder, or the sudden pallor of his other features made it appear so. Slowly he withdrew his elbows from the table and leaned back in his chair, moistening his lips, gazing on the girl with the intensity of a new-born fear. She sat motionless, returning his look without flinching.

For some moments the room was as silent as if it were deserted. At last he spoke huskily:

"What do you expect to gain by making so absurd a statement?"

The girl rose with a gesture of impatience, walked to the window and back; then to the window again, and unfastened a latch that let free a latticed sash, as if the room stifled her and she wanted air. Then she exclaimed: "Oh, let us have a truce to this fooling; I am tired of it. You say I shall beg on my knees to you, but you have mistaken your own attitude for mine. Why do I make such a statement? Because Cromwell told me in Northampton that if I met difficulty in Oxford, you, his spy, would assist me."

"Good God!"

"Aye! Good God! You did not think such a man would blab out secrets of death to a woman, but there is this to say on his behalf, that he was merely recommending one spy to another. He thought mutual safety would be their bond of union, and he was right."

"Then you knew you would meet me in Oxford? Why did you seem so distraught when the event happened? That was acting, I suppose, to fall the easier into the arms of the Scot."

"I had no need to act to bring that about. I hoped to avoid you, and would have done so but for the chance encounter. And now you see, sir, that my peril is as nothing to yours. My countrymen will not injure me; I know them better than you do, but even if it were otherwise, I have but to bend my strength to the pillars and crush you and myself in the ruins of the falling house,—an enactment, I assure you, that fits my nature better than the part of Delilah into which I am cast."

"They would not believe one self-convicted."

"Would not believe me? I dare you to put it to the test. Believe me?" She stood by the window and held up her hand. "I have but to strike open this leaded pane and cry to the officers passing in the street, 'I am the daughter of Lord Strafford, help me, for here I am caged with a French spy, a creature who has sold King and comrades for Cromwell's gold."

"In God's name, woman, do not speak so loud. There is no need for frenzy. I did but jest when I spoke of molesting you."

"I am in no jesting mood."

"You do not need to tell me that. I am quite willing to further your behests, if you but trust me and tell me what you want."

"Can you expect me to trust you?" asked the girl, coming back to the table.

He was now standing on the other side, all self-confidence gone from his attitude, speaking almost in a whisper, so anxious was he that she should have no excuse for raising her voice again.

"I suppose I have not earned your trust."

"Oh, but you have. I trust you implicitly because you stand under the shadow of the scaffold, and at a word from me the bolt is drawn. You will postpone all thought of revenge until your neck is out of the noose; of that I am very well convinced. I refuse to make terms with you, but I give my commands which you must rigidly follow unless you court calamity. You will take Armstrong to the King, and cease to block his way. You will see that we are free to leave Oxford, and are unmolested while we are within these walls. One false move and you bring your doom upon you. While we are in Oxford the rope is round your throat, so pray to the demon who aids you that we may make speedy and easy exit. Shudder to think that your fate hangs on the action of a woman, wholly unstrung, and that even a suspicious look from any officer in this garrison may instantly precipitate the disaster you apprehend."

"I implore you to be calm, madam. I swear I will carry out your orders to the letter. Do not, I beg of you, take panic at any chance word by another."

"Unlock the door and leave me. See that you do not come again."

## CHAPTER VIII.—DESTINY.

On the morning of the fourth day Armstrong was delighted to learn from De Courcy that the King had recovered and would see him at noon. The foreigner engaged the envoy in a long conversation, the object of which was to discover whether or not the girl had said anything to him of the excited conference of the day before. The unsuspecting Scot, entirely off his guard, thinking he spoke with a friend, was read by the other like an open book, and De Courcy was speedily convinced that Frances Wentworth had kept her own counsel. This gave the spy renewed confidence, and as they walked down the street together De Courcy held his head higher than had been the case when he last turned his back upon "The Crown" inn. His buoyant nature was quick to recover from depression, and his malice, fed anew from his late rebuff, set his alert mind at work to contrive some plan whereby he might salve his wounded pride and avenge himself on the girl and his favoured rival, even at some slight risk to himself. Although the danger of exposure seemed imminent enough when he was with her, he knew that as she grew calmer and reflected upon the situation she would be more and more reluctant to wreck everything in order to bring punishment upon him. He would get them out of Oxford that day if possible, but he would instill a poison in the young lover's mind that would take all sweetness from the journey.

De Courcy had offered to show Armstrong the way to the King's rooms, so that there should be no delay when the Scot set out for his appointment at twelve o'clock, and they had now entered the quadrangle of Christ Church, which was deserted save for the guards at the gate. Armstrong thanked him for his guidance, and was turning away, when the other, who seemed about to speak, glanced at the soldiers on duty, then, thinking the spot ill chosen for what he had to say, invited the Scot to his room. They went up a stair together, and entered De Courcy's apartment, the host setting out wine and asking his guest to seat himself.

"Has the lady who accompanied you quite recovered from her fatigue?" asked De Courcy, indifferently.

"Well, as I told you, I met her yesterday for a few moments only, and I am sorry she was not in the highest spirits, but she will be the better for seeing the green fields again. Like myself, she is of the country, and does not thrive within the walls of a town."

"Yes, I noticed that when she was in London."

"In London? Did you know her in London?"

"Oh, hasn't she told you of our relationship? Perhaps I should not have mentioned it."

"What do you mean by your relationship? You are French; she is pure English."

De Courcy threw back his head and laughed, unheeding and indeed unnoticing the angry colour mounting in a face that had grown suddenly stern.

"My dear comrade, there are other relationships between a young man and a handsome woman than the ties of kinship. But those days are long past, and I should never have recalled them had it not been that you two have been travelling about the country together, I make no doubt, with an innocence that recalls the sylvan days of yore."

Armstrong pushed back his chair and rose to his feet.

"Sir, the lady took her brother's place, he being unexpectedly and grievously wounded. My position has been that of true comrade to her."

"That is precisely what I have said. I said your journey was one of Arcadian innocence."

"Those were your words, but your tone bears a meaning I resent."

"You are quite in error. I will say no more about her."

"You have already said too much or too little. Tell me in plain words what this relationship was to which you have referred."

"First answer me a question. Are you betrothed to Frances Wentworth?"

"No. I told you I acted the brother's part toward her in this journey."

"Oh, we all say that; but I am not in the least curious. If you intended to marry her, then were my mouth sealed. Very well; since you will have it, and I take your word as a gentleman pledged that you will say nothing to the girl of this until you are clear of Oxford, know that I was once her betrothed. She was to have been my wife, and would have been my wife to-day had her father not fallen."

"Your wife!"

"Yes. Her father gave me permission to pay my court to her. She could not have been much more than sixteen then, and I was her first lover, a personage that a girl never forgets. At first she was frightened, but that stage did not last long. Her father's ruin changed my plans, and I refused to marry her. I announced this refusal to her in the seclusion of my own room in Whitehall and——"

"Sir, you lie!"

Armstrong's sword seemed to spring of its own will from the scabbard, and his hand drew it a-swish through the air with the hiss of a deadly serpent. The Frenchman shrugged his shoulders, but did not move. The three words of his opponent had been spoken very quietly, despite his impulsive action. De Courcy did not raise his voice as he asked: "Which of my statements do you question?"

"No matter for that. We fight on this phrase in Scotland. No man ever called me liar and lived."

"'T is a coarse phrase, I admit, and did I not represent my King—were

I as free as you—you should have had my response in steel ere this. But I cannot wreck the King in a private quarrel of my own. Whether you killed me, or I you, 't would be equally disastrous to his Majesty."

"I care nothing for the King. Draw, you poltroon, or I shall kill you where you sit."

"My dear Armstrong, I refuse to be murdered under a misapprehension on your part. I have said nothing against the girl. 'T is all your own hot blood. And indeed your brawling is the girl's greatest danger; she might well tremble if she knew your present occupation. If you run your nimble sword through me, you give the girl to the fate that befel her father."

At the first word of danger to Frances the point of Armstrongs blade sank to the floor, and he stood hesitating. A gleam of triumph glinted and died in the eye of the Frenchman. He knew he was the victor, although the chance he had run at one stage of the game almost made his heart stop beating.

"How can any action of mine jeopardize Lady Frances Wentworth?"

"If the King knew this girl was within his jurisdiction, she would be instantly arrested, tried, and condemned. She entered Whitehall the day her father was executed, for the sole purpose of murdering Charles. I prevented the carrying out of that purpose, and these scars on my face are the results of my interference with a maddened woman."

"Again, you lie, yet if she had killed you both she would have accomplished but the justice of God."

"As to the truth or falsity of my statements, regarding which you make comments of unseemly terseness, you may ask the King when you see him, or you may ask the lady herself when you get her out of Oxford. If you precipitate a turmoil here, you are like to tumble her pretty head in the basket. When this war is done with, I will go far to teach you the correct method of addressing a gentleman."

Armstrong's sword dropped into scabbard again, and he drew a breath that was a sigh. The poison was already at work. He remembered the distress of the girl on the road, and her wail, "I am not worthy the love of any honest man."

"I shall never question her or any other, but will believe her lightest word against the world when she condescends to tell me. Meanwhile I shall get her out of this thieves' den as soon as may be, and by God when I meet you——"

De Courcy had risen, and now bowed slightly to his perturbed guest.

"Sir, you shall meet me at twelve, and it will be my privilege to conduct you to his Majesty. Good morning."

He stood by the window overlooking the quadrangle and watched his late visitor cross it, staggering once as if he had partaken freely of the wine which remained untasted on the table. As the Scot disappeared under the archway De Courcy laughed.

"My fine, strutting cockerel," he muttered, "I'll lay you by the heels before two days are past. Cromwell's at Broughton, curse his tattling tongue. How many more has he told of me? Never mind. He's the coming man. The King's game is up, and I shake the dust of Oxford from my feet to-night. Saint Denis, if she had only known! Every man in Oxford distrusts me except the King."

When Armstrong was brought before Charles, a great pity filled him as he gazed for the first time on that gaunt, haggard face, the face of a beaten man with his back to the wall. He found no difficulty in convincing the King that he was a well-accredited envoy, and his Majesty inquired eagerly about the disposition of the Scottish people toward him, the number likely to take the field in his behalf, who their probable leaders were, and how soon they would be ready for the fray. All these questions Armstrong answered as hopefully as he could, in deep commiseration for a defeated man. The King commanded one of his secretaries to write out the required commission, and while this was being done Armstrong related to him the purport of the papers which he had not dared to bring with him. The names of the nobles were inserted in the document from the dictation of the Scot; then the King's seal was affixed, and Charles signed the parchment. He seemed in feverish haste to get the business done with, as if every moment lost was irreparable. When the ink was dried, and the parchment folded, Armstrong placed it in safe keeping within his vest. While thus engaged the King said a word to the secretary, who handed him a light rapier, then whispered to the messenger the single word "Kneel." The Scot flushed to think he had been wanting in the etiquette of the court, his kind heart yearning to proffer any deference which should be rendered to a monarch, more especially that he was no longer in a position to enforce homage. He dropped on one knee and bowed his head. Charles, rising, touched the rapier blade lightly upon the shoulder of the kneeling man, saying: "Rise, Sir William Armstrong, and be assured that if you bring this poor signature of mine to Scotland, there is no title in my gift you may not demand of me."

Armstrong rose, awkward as a school boy, not knowing where to look or what to say until he caught the cynical smile of De Courcy standing at the right hand of the King.

"I congratulate you, Sir William," said the Frenchman. The sight of the smile aroused the new hatred against the man which was smoldering in his heart, and he made no reply to the greeting, but said to the King: "Sire, the only thanks I can tender you is haste to the North, and may God make my arm as strong to defend this signature as my heart is true to your Majesty."

With that he turned his back upon royalty, a grievous breach in the eyes of courtiers, and fled.

"God grant it," said the King, with a sigh, as he sank once more in the seat from whence he had risen.

"There is no doubt of it," said De Courcy, softly.

"Doubt of what?" asked the King.

"The oath he took will sit lightly on his conscience. He prayed that his arm's strength might equal his heart's fealty. I distrust those who talk glibly of their hearts, and his was a most ambiguous prayer. If his heart be not true, and he made no assertion that it was, his strong arm will avail us little."

"Surely if ever honesty beamed from a man's face it was from Armstrong's. The Scots are trustworthy men."

"Some of them, your Majesty."

Uneasy suspicion came into the sunken eyes of the King as he turned them on his Chamberlain.

"What do you fear, De Courcy?"

"I have been studying the man these three days past. I accepted without question his assurances, and threw him off his guard. Cromwell loves an honest-looking envoy, and from what Armstrong said I am sure he saw Cromwell no farther away than Northampton. He was very ready with his account of his own country people, but he told us nothing about the marvellous luck that brought him safely through a hostile land, which we know to our cost is admirably patrolled. There is young Rudby, gone this month and more to Edinburgh, and yet no word of him. And this stranger expects us to believe he came over the same ground unscathed and unquestioned in less than a week."

"O God! O God! In whom can I place dependence," cried the tortured King, burying his head in his hands. Then he raised it and said with a trace of anger in his voice: "If you knew this man to be a traitor, or an emissary of that rebel, why did you bring him into our presence?"

"I could not be sure of him, your Majesty, and there was always a chance that he was loyal and might get through."

"To raise my hopes like this and then dash them to the ground!"

"Not so, your Majesty, if you will pardon me. Do you place importance on this commission?"

"The utmost importance. I know Traquair, and he will raise all Scotland for me if this commission reach him."

"Then we will mak siccar, as a famous Scot once said."

"Ah, De Courcy, that was said when a treacherous murder was intended. How will you make sure that Armstrong is honest?"

611

"I should trouble no more about Armstrong, but if you will issue a duplicate of that commission I will guarantee that it reaches the hand of Traquair. I am a Frenchman, and a subject of the French king. I carry my passport to that effect. Even if I am stopped, I shall resist search on the ground of my nationality, and Cromwell is too greatly in awe of the power of France to risk its might being thrown in the scale against him. Indeed I doubt if I could offer a greater service to your Majesty than to be captured and appeal to Louis."

The King's face cleared.

"You would not stop Armstrong then?"

"Assuredly not. If his copy gets into Cromwell's hands he may slacken his alertness and not be on the outlook for a duplicate. As I said before, there is a chance the Scot plays fair, but two commissions in the hands of Traquair will do no harm, and we mak siccar."

"You are in the right, and your advice is always of the best. How soon will you be ready to leave?"

"This very moment, your Majesty. There is no time to be lost."

"True! True! True!" Then to the secretary, "Write another. Do you remember the names?"

"Yes, your Majesty. I have them here on a slip."

De Courcy bade farewell to the King, who urged him to return as soon as horse could bring him, and went to his room to prepare for his journey, the duplicate commission following him there.

Armstrong strode to the inn, sped up the stair, and knocked at the door by the landing. Frances herself opened it, the determination on her face to refuse admission to any other than he melting into a welcome as she greeted him.

"My girl, are you ready for the North?"

"Yes, yes, ready and eager. Have you seen the King?"

"I have, and his royal signature rests over my heart."

The joy fled from the girl's face; she turned and walked with uncertain steps to the table. A hope had arisen that the venomous De Courcy would have prejudiced the King against the young man, and that the hateful task of robbery would not be required. But now this last refuge had failed. She strove not to weep.

"If you would rather not go until to-morrow," said Armstrong, "I can wait, but, lassie, I'm desperate anxious to leave Oxford as soon as possible. We will not travel farther than Banbury to-night."

"I am ready," she replied with forced firmness.

# BOOK IV.—THE RETURN

## CHAPTER I.—TENSION.

The road between Oxford and Banbury is the most peaceful of thoroughfares, laid with reasonable directness, gently undulating in parts, passing through quiet villages and a sweet country, mildly beautiful, yet to the mind of Frances Wentworth this innocent highway ever remained, as it were, a section of the broad path to perdition. In after life she never thought of it but with a creepy sensation of horror. She was compelled to traverse ground that was the scene of her lover's proposal, with the lover whom she had rejected. The futile incident, she thought, must be constantly recurring to his mind as it recurred to hers, now that they rode side by side once more along this ill-favoured highway. Even though he sat silent on his horse, more gloomy than was his wont, she guessed what he was thinking. In Oxford, God be thanked they were quit of it! a grave danger was left behind, but in Banbury awaited the cruel test. There the stage was prepared for her enactment of the part of a midnight Lady Macbeth, to rob the sleeping Scot, not of his life, but of that for which he had staked his life and for the preservation of which he stood willing to give up his life. Heretofore she had lulled an accusing conscience by telling it that her deed would preserve his life, but now that she knew him better, such solace was withdrawn from her. There was little likelihood that he would travel far beyond Banbury without discovering his loss, and, while he would never suspect her of the theft, it needed no seer to predict his course of action. He would return instantly to Oxford, and when next he was baffled it would be by Cromwell's troopers, and then, she had the General's own word for it, came condemnation and the noose.

Despondency seemed to be the portion of William Armstrong as well as of his fair companion. She surmised that he was pondering on the events which had happened when their faces were set south over this course, and in part she was right; but the thoughts which rankled in his mind were those implanted by De Courcy, and the wily Frenchman had been accurate enough in his belief that the young man's pleasure in the northward journey would be spoiled. He could not bring himself to ask any explanation from the girl, nor even tell her what De Courcy had said, for he saw that already a weight of woe oppressed her, and to that burden he would not add a pressure of the slightest word. He possessed a supreme confidence in her, and only feared that she had loved this runagate once, and that some remnant of this long-ago affection still remained. Her own words before they reached Oxford, her own action during the encounter fronting "The Crown" inn, disturbed him far more than the insinuations of the Frenchman. He strove to rid himself of these thoughts, but they were very intrusive and persistent. At last with an effort he roused himself and cried with feigned hilarity,—"Frances, we travel like two mutes. The influence of saddened Oxford is still upon us both. We are long out of sight of the town, so let us be done with all remembrance of it. The meeting with the King this morning has stirred me up to a great pity for him, but vexed meditations on his case are no help either to him or to us. The spur is the only weapon I can wield for him now, so let us gallop and cry, 'God save the King!'"

With that they raced together for a time and were the better of it. He had become almost cheerful again when the spires of Banbury came into view, and thanked fortune that the first stage of their march was safely over.

They found Old John and his pack horse both ready for the road again, and Armstrong was plainly loath to let such a fine evening slip by without further progress, but Frances seemed so wan and worn that he had not the heart to propose a more distant stopping-place, and, with a sigh, he put up his horse for the night.

While he was gone the innkeeper came furtively to Frances, and, after seeing the pass, led her to the prepared room and showed her the door.

Much against her will, Armstrong insisted upon her coming to supper with him, although she protested she had no appetite, and indeed sat opposite him most forlorn and could not touch a morsel. In vain he urged her to eat, but she shook her head, avoiding his glance and keeping her eyes downcast.

"My girl," he said anxiously, "you are completely tired. I see that you are on the point of being ill if better care is not taken. Rest here a few days, I beg of you. Eager as I am to be forward, I will stay if you wish to have me near you. Or I will push on and come back for you."

"I shall be well enough in the morning, most like. I am tired to-night."

"And dispirited too."

"Yes, and dispirited. You will excuse me, I know."

"Frances rose to her feet, but seemed so faint that she leaned against the table for support. He was by her side at once.

"My sweet lass, I am so sorry for you. Tell me what I can do for you, and on my soul, my life is yours if you require it."

"No, no! God grant you take no hurt for my sake."

He slipped his arm about her waist and would have drawn her toward him, but with more strength than he had expected her to possess she held away. His great love for her almost overcame him, and all the prudence he had gathered was scattered suddenly to the winds. "Dear, dear lass, one touch of our lips and see if all doubts do not dissolve before the contact."

Now she wrenched herself free, and would have escaped but that he sprang forward and caught her by the wrists, a grip she was to remember later in the night. In spite of this prisoning, her hands were raised to the sides of her face, and a look of such terror shot from her eyes that he feared some madness had come upon her.

"Not that! Not that!" she shrieked. "The kiss of Judas! It would kill me!"

His arms dropped paralyzed to his sides, and he stepped back a pace, amazed at the expression she had used and the terror of her utterance. Next instant he was alone, and the closed door between them. Still he stood where she had left him.

"The kiss of Judas!" he muttered. "The kiss of Judas! She loves him, thinks me his friend, trying to take Judas advantage of him because we are alone together. De Courcy spoke truth. Wae is me, she loves him, and I, blind fool——Oh God! pity that poor girl, and this insanity of passion wasted on so rank a cur!"

Frances fled to her room and threw herself on the bed in an agony of tears. This storm subsided into a gentle rain of subdued weeping, and finally ceased as she heard the heavy tramp of riding-boots in the adjoining room. She sat up in the darkness, listening intently. He closed the wooden shutters of the window, shaking them to be sure that their fastenings were secure. Then the bolts of the outer door were thrust in their places, but, this apparently failing to satisfy the doubts of the inmate, there was a sound of some heavy article of furniture being dragged across the room; then the tramping ceased and all was still. She sat there thinking of nothing; her mind seemed to be dulled by the ordeal awaiting her and the fear of it, but there was no thought of turning back or trying to avoid it. Dimly she was sorry for herself and for him, sleeping in his fancied security, yet in a set trap; but on her action this night depended her brother's life, and that outweighed all other considerations, even if her brain were alert enough to cast them in the opposite scales. Unheeding she had heard the clock in a neighbouring tower toll the hour; now it struck again and she counted the notes. Eleven! It was still too early. People slept heavier as the night wore on. She thought of their journey; of the halt at York; of their talk in the niche in the hotel of the Templars; of various incidents along the road; the march past of Cromwell's troopers, four and four, all looking straight ahead, and as she remembered them they seemed to be passing her now; passing, passing, passing; then Cromwell stopped and smote his steel breastplate with resounding clang. She lifted her head with a start, and the clang of the breastplate changed to the toll of the bell in the tower. Heavens, she had been asleep; her brother's life hanging on her drooping eyelids! One, two, three four, five, six, seven! It must be midnight, and the first five strokes had been on Cromwell's breastplate. She roused herself and attempted to take off her shoes, but her hands were trembling so she was forced to desist. She sat up again, telling herself it was better to wait until all effect of the long chiming had ceased, for the striking of twelve sometimes disturbed or awakened the soundest sleeper. The clock tower seemed dangerously near, as if it were approaching her hour by hour. At last the shoes came off, and in stockinged feet she stood by the secret door, waiting till the frightfully rapid beating of her heart should moderate. It threatened to choke her. Then she slid back the bar and drew open the door, all so smoothly oiled that there was not the whisper of a creak. She tiptoed into the cavern of blackness and silence, holding her spread hands in front of her, moving slowly with the utmost caution, step by step. In her mind she had estimated, from her earlier survey of the room, that nine steps would take her to the bed; now she realized she had taken a dozen and yet had not come to it. She stood bewildered and listened. The helplessness of a person in the pitch dark thrilled her with a new fear, upsetting all her calculations. The panic of pulsation in her throat and in her ears at first rendered any attempt at listening futile; but at last she heard his regular breathing, as peaceful as that of an infant, and it came from the other side of the room. For a moment this terrified her, and she wondered if she were really awake, or in the mazes of some baffling nightmare; but the solution came to her mind and quieted the growing agitation. It had been his bed that he dragged across the floor, and he was now sleeping against the outside door. And all his preparations were as naught, because of this midnight spectre, moving upon him! She changed her direction and, with her former stealth, came ghost-like to the edge of the couch.

His doublet was open at the throat; that was so much to the good. Like a snowflake in its coldness and its lightness, her hand stole down underneath his vest, fluttered by the slow, steady, subdued beating of his heart, running no such wild race as her own at that moment. It seemed incredible that at last her fingers closed on the parchment; but there it lay, and gently she drew it forth. Was the robbery to be so easily accomplished after all? Ah, she had congratulated herself too soon. It stuck fast; either the silken cord that bound it was caught, or the document was secured to the vest,—a contingency she had never thought of, and yet what more natural? Twice she tugged it gently, then a third time more strenuously, when it came unexpectedly away and her knuckles struck the sleeper under the chin. Instantly, like the snap of a steel trap, his fingers closed upon her wrist, and his voice rang out as wideawake and clear as ever he had spoken to her: "Frances!"

Now the racing heart stopped dead. Lucky for her that at this supreme moment all action was impossible, and that she was stricken into frozen marble. She imagined he was awake and knew her, and then the cold horror of her situation numbed thought at its source.

"Frances!" The voice came more sleepily this time, and he repeated thrice very rapidly, "Frances, Frances, Frances!" Feebly her heart had taken up its work again. She was not to die as she had feared. Sodden with drowsiness, his voice rambled on, and came to an indefinite conclusion.

"My darling, you are in danger. We must get out of Oxford. Everything, every——your safety, my dear. The King——" Then the words became indistinct and died away; but alas! the grip of iron remained on her wrist. For a long time she stood there motionless; then tried to disengage his fingers gently; but at the first movement the grasp tightened again. One o'clock struck. He slept so silently that it began to appear to her agitated brain that she was a prisoner of the dead. She came near to sinking from very weariness. Two o'clock tolled from the tower. Sometimes she fancied she slept standing there, but her five jailors did not sleep. She kept wondering in which direction lay the open door, for at times the room seemed to swim around her, thus disturbing all sense of locality. She almost laughed aloud when she thought of herself free, but groping helplessly for the open door, failing to find it, and she shuddered that even the remembrance of laughter should come to her at such a time; surely a sign of approaching frenzy. Then it seemed the fingers loosened; but hand and wrist had lost all feeling, and she could not be sure. She tottered and nearly fell; when she stood upright again she was free; he muttering to himself, and his hand slashing undirected on the mattress, as if it missed something it sought drunkenly to recover. The girl could scarce repress a cry of joy at her release. She moved eagerly in the path that should lead her to the door, but, hurrying too much, came upon his jack-boots on the floor, and fell helplessly, so overwrought that even when her feet touched them she could not draw back.

"Who's there? Who's in this room?" cried Armstrong. She was standing again, fully expecting to hear his feet on the floor; but the bell struck three, and he counted dreamily, and all was still again. When she reached her room, she closed and barred the door as silently as she had opened it. The tension relaxed, she felt she was going to swoon. Blindly she groped for her shoes, murmuring, "O God! not yet,—not yet. Give me a moment more." Finding her foot-gear at last, she dared not wait to put them on, but stole softly down the stair, steadying herself against the wall. The cool air outside struck her like the blessing of God, and soothed her whirling head. She heard a horse champing his bit, then a whisper came out of the darkness: "Is that you at last, madam?"

"Yes," she said, sinking on the doorstep, and leaning her head against the lintel, the cold stone grateful to her hot forehead.

"You are not hurt, madam?" inquired the man anxiously.

"No, no," she gasped; then, with an eldritch little laugh, "I want to put on my shoes, that's all."

## CHAPTER II.—ACQUITTANCE.

Either the moon had set, or lay behind a cloud; for the night was very dark, with no trace of morning yet visible in the east. Frances buckled on her shoes and stood up. The innkeeper led forward his horse, and would doubtless have proffered his assistance, but when she spoke he learned she was already in the saddle.

"Set me on the road to Broughton, if you please?"

"The word for to-night is 'Broughton,'" he whispered, then took the horse by the bridle and led him down the street. The girl became aware that the town was alive with unseen men; for at every corner the innkeeper breathed the word "Broughton" to some one who had challenged his progress. She realized then that Cromwell had surrounded Armstrong with a ring of flesh; a living clasp, as her own wrist had been circled earlier in the night. At last they came suddenly from the shadow of the houses into the open country, and the night seemed lighter.

"Straight on for about a league," said the innkeeper. "You will be challenged by a sentinel before you reach the castle, and he will lead you there. Remember that the word, going and returning, is 'Broughton.' Do not forget, I beg of you, to tell the General that all preparations were made to your liking;" and with that the honest man let go the rein, smote the horse on the flank, and bade her goodnight.

In spite of herself the girl experienced that exhilaration which comes of the morning air, the freshness of the country, and the movement of a spirited horse. She breathed deeply and felt as one brought newly to life again. If it were not for her upbraiding conscience and her distress of mind, she could have sung for the joy of living. But the Biblical phrase, "A thief in the night," haunted her, and brought a choking sensation to her throat. Once or twice she wavered and almost turned back; for there was still time to undo; but reflection showed her the uselessness of retreat, as the town she had left was man-environed, and, until Cromwell gave the word of release, Armstrong could no more reach its outer boundary than she could have escaped when his fingers closed upon her wrist. Her sacrifice must be complete, or all she loved were involved in common ruin. So, with the phrase ringing in her ears, "Thief in the night, Thief in the night," through the night she galloped, until her horse suddenly placed his fore feet rigid, and came to a stop so abrupt that the shock nearly unseated her.

"Who goes?" came the sharp challenge from under the trees that overshadowed the highway.

"Broughton," she answered automatically.

"Are you the woman from Banbury?"

"Yes."

"This is Broughton Castle. I will lead your horse."

They descended a slight depression and came to a drawbridge, passed under an arch in the wall, then across a level lawn, on the further edge of which stood the broad eastern front of the castle with its numerous mullioned windows, a mysterious half-light in the horizon playing on the blank panes, which recalled the staring, open eyes of a blind man. The house seemed high and sombre, with no sign of light within. The sentinel beat against the door, and it was opened at once. Muffled as had been the knocking on the oak, it awoke the alert General; for when Frances had dismounted and followed her guide into the ample hall, Cromwell stood at the head of the stair, a candle in his hand. Less mindful of his comfort than Armstrong, he had evidently slept in his boots; and, as Frances looked up at him, his strong face seemed older than when she last saw him, although but a few days had passed. The swaying flame of the candle, held on a level with his head, made the shadows come and go on his rugged features, and emphasized the deep furrows in his face. His hair was tousled, and he had the unkempt appearance of a man who had slept in his clothes. But his eyes burned down upon her, as if their fire had never been extinguished even for a moment.

"Come up," he commanded, and, as she ascended the stair, cried impatiently, "Well!"

"There is the King's commission," she said quietly, presenting the document to him. He took it without a word, turned, and entered the room; she following him. He placed the candle on a table, did not take the time to untie the silken cord that bound the royal communication, but ripped it asunder, and spread open the crinkling parchment, holding it up to the light. He read it through to the end, then cast it contemptuously on the table, muttering:

"Charles Rex! A wreck you have made of life and opportunity and country." Then to the girl. "Wench, you have done well. Would you were a man."

"The pardon for my brother, sir, if it please you."

"It is ready, and the commission as captain also. You see I trusted you."

"So did another, and through his faith he now lies undone in Banbury."

"You have not killed him?" cried Cromwell sharply, looking with something almost like alarm at the uncanny apparition. All beauty had deserted her, and her face seemed pinched and small, white as the parchment on the table, and rendered unearthly in its hue by the mass of cavern-black hair that surrounded it.

"Killed him? No! But I have killed his faith in woman, cozened him, lied to him, robbed him, to buy from you, with the name of your Maker on your lips, a life that you know was not forfeited, but which you had the power to destroy."

"Ah, yes, yes, yes! I remember your tongue of old; but it may wag harmless now, for all of me. His life was forfeited; aye, and this Scot's as well. But no matter now."

He threw before her the pardon for her brother and his commission as captain, then strode out of the room to the head of the stair again, and she heard his strenuous voice:

"Hobson!"

"Here, Excellency."

"Ride at once to the commandant at Banbury. Tell him the Scot goes free. Tell him to send word north, and see that he is not molested; but should he turn in his tracks and attempt to reach Oxford again, hold him and send word to me."

"Yes, Excellency."

"Send up a stoup of wine."

He waited at the stair-head until the wine was brought, then took it into the room and placed it on the table before her.

"Drink," he said.

"I cannot," she cried.

"Drink, drink," he shouted in a voice so harsh that it made her tremble. She lifted the flagon to her lips, and barely sipped the liquid.

"Drink!" he roared, bringing his clenched fist down on the oaken table with a force that made the very room quiver. The word had all the brutal coarseness of an oath, and it beat down her weak resolution as the storm levels the sapling. She drank deep, then let the flagon drop, raised her hands to her face, and burst into a helpless wail of weeping. Cromwell's face softened, now that he was obeyed, and he looked at this passion-swayed human flower with the air of a puzzled man. Then his huge hand patted her heaving shoulders with some attempt at gentleness.

"There, there," he said, in tones not unkindly, "do not distress yourself. You are a brave wench, and the wine will do you good, though you take it as it were a leech's draught. I meant no harshness toward you; indeed you remind me of my own daughter, who thinks her father criminal, and will shout for this foolish King in my very ears. Aye, and is as ready with the tears as any one of you, to the bewilderment of straight-going folk. I have a younger daughter who is your namesake, and I love her well. You will rest here in Broughton."

"No, no!" sobbed the girl. "I must at once to Banbury. Give me, I beg of you, a pass for my servant to the county of Durham. I would send him on to my brother without delay, so that your release may reach him as soon as may be."

"But you? You do not purpose travelling further with this Scot?"

"I have done the crime; I must not shirk the punishment."

"Tut, tut, this is woman's talk. There is no punishment. He dare not place a hand on you. You may have an escort of twenty men, who will see you safe for all the Scots that ever depredated their neighbours."

The girl dolefully shook her head.

"My punishment will take the shape of no harshness from him. It will come to me when I see his face, knowing me a thief in the night. This punishment is with me now and will be with me always."

"Woman, I do not like your bearing, touching what you have done. You did your duty by your country, God aiding you. Neither do I like your attitude towards this meddler in affairs of state. What is your relationship to him?"

"Merely that of the highwayman toward his victim."

"Sharp words again; hollow-sounding brass, and the tinkling of cymbals.

I ask you if there has been any foolish talk between you?"

"If 't were so, 't is not an affair of state, and I shall follow the example of General Cromwell and allow no meddlers in it."

A wry smile came to the lips of her questioner, and he remarked drily:

"I told you the wine would do you good."

He sat down by the table and wrote the pass for John, the servant, tying the three papers together with the discarded silk cord that had wrapped the parchment of the King. Giving her the package, he accompanied her to the head of the stair, and stood there while she descended. He did not offer her his hand, nor say any word of farewell. They needed now no candle, for the early daylight was coming through the broad eastern window. Half way down the stair she turned, and looked up at him.

"The innkeeper at Banbury did everything that was possible for a man to do in aiding me."

Cromwell made no comment on this piece of information, standing there as if he were a carven, wooden statue, part of the decoration of the hall. She completed her descent, passed outside without looking back, and mounted the horse which a soldier was holding for her. The birds were twittering in the trees, and the still water of the moat lay like molten silver in the new light. She rode up the aclivity, then galloped for Banbury, reaching the town before anyone was astir. The streets were entirely deserted, Cromwell's command having cleared them, and the invisible guards of a few hours before, whom the magic pass-word stilled, seemed as nonexistent as if they had been phantoms of a vision.

The sleepy innkeeper received the horse, and she crept up the stair of Old John's room and knocked upon it until he responded. She gave him his pass, and the two documents for her brother, and told him to set off for Durham as soon as he got his breakfast, making what haste he could to Warburton Park, he was to tell her brother that she was well and would follow shortly. Then she went to her own room, threw herself on the bed, dressed as she was, and, certain she would never enjoy innocent sleep again, slept instantly.

# CHAPTER III.—ENLIGHTENMENT.

When William Armstrong awoke, he thought he had overslept himself, for the trampling of horses sounded in the paved courtyard below. The one window of his room, over which he had drawn and fastened heavy wooden shutters the night before, let in a thread of light which showed him a new day had come, and the activity in the yard made him fear he had lain longer abed than was his custom. He was the more convinced of this in that he remembered hazily the clattering hoofs of a horse some time before, and then later, another being led out; now there appeared to be a third, and the hum of talk came up to him. His window overlooked the stable yard, and he recognized the mumble of the hostler who had assisted him yesterday. He lay still, half drowsed, the mattress most alluring to him, when suddenly he was startled wide awake by a voice he knew.

"Then I turn to the left for Broughton?"

"Yes, sir," muttered the hostler.

Armstrong leaped from his bed, placed his eye at the chink in the shutters, and peered down into the stable yard. The voice had not misled him. De Courcy, sitting on a horse, was just gathering up the reins and departing. The Scot lost no time in pulling on his boots, pushing aside the bed, unbolting the door, and making his way down the stair. What did this gaily plumaged bird of ill-omen here in the country of the Parliament, when his place was beside the King? Was there treachery afoot? It looked like it. Once outside, he saw it was still early, with the sun scarcely risen. He accosted the yawning hostler.

"Who was that man you were directing to Broughton?"

"I don 't know, sir."

"When did he arrive?"

"Last night, sir, after dark."

"Did he stop in this house?"

"Yes, sir. I thought he was a friend of yours, for he knew your horse when I was putting up his own. He asked if you were here, and I told him you were in the room over the yard."

"What is Broughton; a hamlet?"

"It is a castle, sir. Lord Say's castle, about three miles from here. General Cromwell is there now; it is his headquarters in this district."

"Cromwell!"

The young man stood stock still, his eyes gazing into vacancy. What traffic had this King's Chamberlain with Cromwell? How dared he come within the Parliamentary lines, undisguised, unless—unless——Like inspiration the whole situation flashed upon him. De Courcy knew the burden he carried, and had seen where it was placed. He was on his way to sell his secret and set the troops on the track of the messenger. He must be off at once and outride the traitor. Before De Courcy had gone his three miles, he would have traversed a dozen, and from then on it would be a race to the Scottish border.

"Is my horse fed?"

"Yes, sir."

"Get him out at once. I will arouse the others." He took three steps toward the inn, then stopped as if shot, his hand clutching his breast.

"By God, he's got the thing itself. Robbed, as I'm a sinner!"

Now the disturbance in the night stood out clear in his memory, but he wasted not a thought over it. In upon the astonished hostler he swept.

"Never mind the saddle, fellow. Spring up behind me and show me the road to Broughton. Up, I say, the horse can carry a dozen like us. Here are two gold pieces for you; guidance and a still tongue in your head is what I want."

Armstrong grasped the two pistols from the holsters, flung the hesitating hostler upon the animal's back, and leaped up in front of him.

"Which way, which way, which way?"

"Straight down the street, sir," gasped the terrified man, clasping the rider round the waist. "Now to the right, sir, and next to the left. That's it, sir. Up the hill. Ah, there's your man, jogging on ahead, leisurely enough, if it's him you seek."

"Right! Slip off; I can 't stop. God be with you!"

The hostler rolled in a heap along the ditch, staggered to his feet, feeling his limbs for broken bones, thinking his gold pieces hardly earned in such usage; then, satisfying himself that the damage was not great, hobbled back to Banbury.

De Courcy, riding easily, as the man had said, wholly unsuspicious of pursuit or any reason for it, had disappeared into a hollow when Bruce, like a thunder-cloud, came over the crest, and charged down upon him with the irresistible force of a troop of dragoons. The Frenchman, hearing too late the rumble of the hoofs, partly turned his horse across the road, the worst movement he could have made, for Bruce, with a war-neigh, came breast on, maddened with the delight of battle, and whirled opposing horse and rider over and over like a cart-wheel flung along the road from the hand of a smith. De Courcy lay partly stunned at the roadside, while his frightened steed staggered to its feet, leaped the hedge with a scream of fear, and scampered across the field to its farthest extremity. Armstrong swung himself to the ground with a quieting word to Bruce, who stood still, panting, and watching every movement of his master. A pistol in each hand, Armstrong strode over to his victim.

"You halter-dog, traitor, and scullion, give me the King's commission."

"Sir, you have killed me," moaned De Courcy faintly.

"You bribed thief, the rope is your end. You'll take no scath through honourable warfare. Disgorge!"

De Courcy, vaguely wondering how the other knew he carried it, drew from within his torn doublet the second commission signed by the King, and handed it up with a groan to the conqueror. As it was an exact duplicate of the one he had lost, even to the silken cord, the honest Scot had not the slightest doubt he had come by his own again, and the prone man was equally convinced that some one had betrayed to Armstrong his secret mission, yet for the life of him could not guess how this were possible. The young man placed the document where its predecessor had been, then said to his victim: "Had I a rope and a hangman with me, you would end your life on yonder tree. When first I learned your character, you were in some danger from my sword; a moment since you stood in jeopardy from my pistols; beware our third meeting, for if you cross my path again, I will strangle you with my naked hands, if need be."

De Courcy made no reply. He realized that this was not a time for controversy. A standing man well armed has manifest advantages over an enemy bruised and on the ground, and some thought of this came to the mind of the generous victor now that his anger was cooling. He felt that it was rather undignified to threaten a helpless adversary, and if he were a traitor to the King, let the King deal with him. So, whistling to his horse, he sprang on his back, and rode to Banbury at a slower pace than he had traversed the same highway some minutes before.

The hostler made grievous pretence that he had been all but murdered by his fall, and Armstrong examined him minutely, as he would have done with a favourite horse, pronouncing him none the worse for his tumbling, but rather the better, as he was now more supple than he had been for years. He rewarded the man lavishly, nevertheless, and gave him the recipe for a liniment good for man and beast, should after-complications ensue.

"I hope, sir," whined the man, "that you did not treat the gentleman you were in such haste to meet, as roughly as you did me."

"Very much the same," cried Armstrong, with a laugh, "but you are the better off, because I left him neither gold nor medicine; taking from him rather than bestowing."

"Ah, is that your game?" whispered the hostler, a glint of admiration lighting up his eyes. "Dang me, if I did not take thee for a gentleman of the road when first I clapped eyes on thee. Be sure I'll say naught, for I've cut a purse myself in younger days. Those times were better than now. There's too many soldiers and too few gentlemen with fat purses travelling the roads nowadays for our trade."

Again William laughed, and shook hands with the old man, as one highwayman in a good way of business might condescend to another less prosperous, and the veteran hostler boasted of his intimacy with a noted freebooter for the rest of his days.

"Rub down my horse well, while I am at breakfast," said Armstrong, and, receiving every assurance that the beast of so excellent a highwayman should get earnest attention, he went to the inn and there found Frances awaiting him.

The girl was standing by the window, which was low and long, with a valance of crimpled spotted muslin running athwart the lower half of it. A bench was fixed beneath the window, and on this bench the girl had rested a knee, while her cheek was placed against the diamond panes. The light struck her face and illuminated it strongly, and she stood so still that she seemed to form part of a tableau which might have been entitled "Watching." On the table placed in the centre of the room, breakfast was spread.

It was a jubilant man who disturbed this quiet picture by his abrupt in-coming. The early morning gallop, the excitement of contest, the flush of victory, all had their effect on his bearing, and he came in with the mien of a Saxon prince, his yellow hair almost touching the beams of the low ceiling. The two formed a striking contrast when the embodiment of elation approached the embodiment of dejection. There was a new furtiveness in the brief glance she cast upon him, and after her first startled cognizance she looked beyond him, on either side of him, over his head, or at his feet, but never turned her eyes full upon him as of yore.

"Ah, my girl," he cried, "you have not slept well. I can see that at once. This will never do; never do at all. But you are certainly looking better this morning than you did last night. Is that not so?"

"You are looking very well," she said, avoiding his question.

"Oh I've had a morning gallop already."

"What! With the ride to Scotland still before you. Is not a merciful man merciful to his horse?"

"He should be, but I may say this for Bruce; he enjoyed the ride quite as much as I did. And now I am ravenous for breakfast, and eager for the road again." He tinkled a little hand-bell that rested on the table. "We have another splendid day for it. The sunrise this morning was positively inspiring. Come, lass, and sit you down. We must get the roses back into those cheeks, and I think the ride to-day will do it; for we will be nearing the North, ever nearing the North, and you are just like me, you are yearning for the Northland, where all the men are brave and all the women fair."

"Fair and false, perhaps you would add. That was your phrase, I think."

William laughed heartily, drawing in his chair.

"Yes, about our Stuarts, not about our ladies. They are ever leal and true. And indeed many of them are dark as well as fair, and they are the best. Dark hair, fair face, and a loyal heart; there is a combination to cherish when God is good to a man and allows him to meet it."

The servant had now answered the tinkling bell, and Frances was too busy acting the housewife to make any comment on his enthusiastic description of what was to be found in the North. Her pale cheeks reddened as he spoke, and he took this for a promising sign. She was convinced that he had as yet no knowledge of his loss, and wondered when and where such knowledge would come to him. She hoped the enlightenment would be delayed until they were near the Scottish line or across it. Then she must tell him the truth at whatever cost to herself, and persuade him, if she could, not to return. When she made her confession, she would be in a position to relate all Cromwell had said to her; show him that the General had given orders which would block any backward move, and reveal his determination to hang the Scot should he entangle himself further with English politics. Yet she had the gravest doubts that these dangers would influence him. She knew him well enough to be aware that his own personal safety weighed but lightly with him, and the very opposition would determine him to try conclusions with it, unabashed by the overwhelming odds against him.

These reflections troubled her until the time they were on their horses once more, when Armstrong interrupted them by crying out:

"Where's old John?"

"I sent him on ahead long since," replied Frances.

"Good. We shall soon overtake him. Good bye, pirate!" he cried to the grinning hostler. "May I meet you on the road next time with a thousand pounds on you, and if you whisper 'Banbury' to me, I will not lift a penny of it."

"Good luck to you and your fair lady, sir," replied the enriched old man, raising his cap in salute. He wished more travellers like the brawny Scot came that way.

"Why do you call the poor man a pirate?" asked Frances.

"Oh, we're comrades!" laughed Armstrong. "He thinks me a capable, prompt, and energetic highwayman, and admitted on the quiet that he had cut a purse himself upon occasion in the days of his youth."

"And why does he think you a highwayman?"

"Ah, that would be telling. Suppose it is because I escort the fairest lady in the land? The sex have ever favoured the biggest rascals. No, I shall not incriminate myself, but shall maintain my pose of the amiable hypocrite. Here rides Will Armstrong, the honest man, if you take his own word for it. But the hostler knows better. He sees secret comings and goings, and draws his sage conclusions. Banbury! O Lord, I shall never forget Banbury! It is a place of mystery, the keeper of dark secrets and sudden rides, of midnight theft and of treachery. Ask the Broughton road, where Cromwell lies, to reveal what it knows. Things happen along that track which the King knows nothing of, and his royal signature takes journeys that he never counted upon."

"Heaven's pity! What do you mean?" moaned the girl, whitening to the lips. He laughed joyously, but checked himself when he saw the terrifying effect of his words on his companion. They were now clear of Banbury and trotting along the Coventry road. Their departure had met with no opposition, and they had seen not even a single soldier. The open country lay before them, the turrets of the town sinking in the rear.

"My foolish words have frightened you. Forget them! I am accumulating experiences that will interest you to hear when the time comes for the telling of them, but of one thing I am assured, the good Lord stands by his own, and He has shielded me since yesterday morning broke. Come, Frances, let us gallop. That, and a trust in the Lord, will remedy all the ills of man or woman."

She was glad of the respite and they set off at full speed, nevertheless her mind was sorely troubled. "What did he know, what did he know?" beat through her brain in unison with the clatter of the horse's hoofs. It was not possible that chance had brought him thus to the very centre of her guilty secret. Cromwell, treachery, midnight stealth, the Broughton road, these words and phrases tortured her. Was this, then, the line of his revenge? Did he know all, and did he purpose to keep her thus in suspense, hinting, soothing her fears, then reviving them, making her black crime the subject of jest and laughter? She cast a glance over her shoulder. Banbury had disappeared; they were alone, flying over the land. The doubt was unbearable; she would endure it no longer. Impetuously she reined her horse to a stand. "Stop!" she cried, and at the word her own horse and Bruce halted and stood. The young man turned with alarm to her agitated face.

"What do you mean by your talk of Broughton and Cromwell?"

"Oh, that is a secret! I did not intend to tell you until our journey was ended, when we could laugh over it together."

"It is no laughing matter. I must know what you mean."

"All dangers are laughable once they are past. An unknown, unsuspected danger threatened me at Banbury. It is now past and done with, and the person who plotted against me can harm me no more. There are reasons why I do not wish to mention this person's name. Barring that, I may tell you now as well as another time, if you care to listen."

"Do I know the person?"

"Oh, yes! You knew the person long before I did. It was a person I trusted, but not know to be a traitor and a thief."

It was some moments before Frances could speak, but at last she said very quietly, looking down at her horse's mane,—"Tell me the story, and I will tell you the name of the thief."

"You slept badly last night Did you hear anything?"

"I—I———I heard the clock strike the hours."

"I heard it strike three, but lay so locked in drowsiness that I knew not the Lord was calling to me. If the Seven Sleepers were melted into one, I would outsleep that one. Well, to get on, I was robbed in the night. It must have been at that hour, for I remember dimly some sort of disturbance. But Providence stood my friend. By the merest chance, it might seem, but not by chance as I believe, I saw the creature make for Broughton. 'So, here's for Broughton,' cried I, 'on the bare back of Bruce, and see if my good pistols would win back what had been stolen from me.' The Broughton road it was, and the pistols did the business." Saying this, he whisked from his pocket the King's commission, waving it triumphantly aloft. Her wide eyes drank in the amazing sight of it, slowly brimming with superstitious fear, and then she asked a duplicate of the question that had been asked of her a few hours before.

"Did you kill Cromwell?"

"Cromwell! I never saw him."

"From whom, then, did you wrench that parchment?"

"From the thief, of course. He never reached Cromwell."

"Oh, I am going mad! Who is the thief, who is the thief?"

"De Courcy, if you must know. Why does this trivial matter so disturb you? De Courcy followed us from Oxford last night, and was lodged at our inn. By some means he penetrated into my room, stole this from me, and I never missed it until I saw him ride for Broughton, and not even then, to tell the exact truth. But I remembered that he had seen me place this paper in the inside pocket of my vest, in the King's own presence, and then the whole plot came to me. Before he saw Broughton, Bruce and I were down upon him like a Highland storm on the Lowlands. 'My sword! you should have seen us! For a minute there was one whirligig of horse's legs and Frenchman, like a raree-show of acrobats struck by a whirlwind. If I had not been so angry I would have had the best laugh of my life,"—and the genial William threw back his head and made the wood echo with his merriment at the recollection. But the girl was sober enough.

"This is not the King's commission," she said quickly.

"Oh, but it is!"

"It is not. Have you read it?"

"No, but that's soon done."

He untied the cord and unfolded the sheepskin.

She leaned eagerly forward and scanned the writing, while Armstrong read it aloud.

"You see," he cried gleefully. "Of course it is the commission. There are the names of Traquair, and all the rest, just as I gave them to the secretary, and there is 'Charles Rex' in the King's own hand."

"It is a duplicate. Cromwell has the original. You never left De Courcy alive within a mile of Broughton Castle?"

"I did that very thing. Not as lively as I have seen him, yet alive nevertheless."

"Then ride, ride for the North. We have stood too long chattering here."

"All in good time, Frances. There is no more hurry than ever there was; less, indeed, for it seems to me that Cromwell, for some reason, wants to come at this by fraud and not by force. But now that De Courcy's name is mentioned between us, I ask you what you know against him more than I have told you?"

"Against him? I know everything against him. Would that you had killed him. He would sell his soul, if he has one. He robbed my dying father, and on the day of his death, when I was the only one in London who did not know he was executed, De Courcy lured me to his apartments at Whitehall under pretense of leading me to the King that I might plead for my father's life. There he attempted to entrap me, snapped in my hand the sword which I had clutched from the wall to defend myself, and I struck him twice in the face, and blinded him with his own false blood, and so escaped. Judge, then, my fear when I saw him there at Oxford."

"The truth! The truth! At last the truth!" shouted Armstrong, as if a weight had fallen from his shoulders. "The truth has a ring like honest steel, and cannot be mistaken when once you hear it. He lied to me about you in Oxford, and I called him liar, and would have proven it on him, but that he told me you were in danger. I should have killed the whelp this morning, but that he could not defend himself."

"The truth! Yes, but only part of it. He did not rob you last night."

"Nonsense! He did."

"I robbed you. I stole into your room and robbed you. I carried the original of that document to Cromwell himself, and it is now in his hands. It was the price of my brother's life. My brother was set on your track by Cromwell, and, being wounded, I took up his task. Do you understand? That was my mission to Oxford. To delude you, to rob you, and I have done it."

"Girl, you are distraught!"

"I am not. Every word I tell you is true."

"You are saying that to shield some one."

"Look, William Armstrong! For two hours and more, last night, you held me by the wrist. There is the bracelet with which you presented me,— black proof of the black guilt I confess to you."

She held her hand aloft, and the sleeve fell away from the white and rounded arm, marred only by the dark circles where his fingers had pressed.

"Do you say I did that?"

"Yes. If still you do not believe me, measure your fingers with the shadow they have cast."

She reached out her hand to him, and he took it in his left, stroking the bruised wrist with his right, but looking into her eyes all the while.

"Frances, is it this secret that stood between us?"

"Yes."

"Is this all that stood between us?"

"All! Is it not enough? All! It is a mountain of sin that bears me to the very ground."

"Why, dear lass, did you not tell me?"

"Tell you? It was from you, of all the world, I must conceal it until now."

He laughed very quietly, fondling her hand.

"Bless me, how little you know! What is quarreling King or rebellious country to me compared with you? No wonder my beating heart did not awaken me with your hand upon it, for it was co-conspirator with you, and wholly your own. Heaven mend my broken patriotism!—but if you had asked me, I would have ridden myself to Cromwell with the King's signature."

"Do you——can you forgive me, then?"

"Forgive you? You are the bravest lass in all the land,"—and with that, before she was aware or could ward off his attack if she had wished to do so, he reached impulsively forward, caught her off her horse, and held her in his arms as if she were a child, kissing her wounded wrist, her eyes, her hair, her lips. "And now, do you forgive me, Frances?"

"Oh, willingly, willingly! Trespass for trespass. 'As we forgive them that trespass against us.' But set me on my horse again, I beg of you."

"I can hardly believe you are here yet."

"Cease, cease, I beg of you! The moments are too precious for it."

"Precious they are and most preciously employed."

"Will, Will, I implore you. Do you not understand? You are jesting on the brink of the grave. De Courcy has crawled to Cromwell ere this, and that grim man is lighting the North against us. They are now on our track."

"The way is clear. There is no one in sight, and we can outride them when they come."

"They are riding across country to intercept us. Oh, let not my arms hold you back for destruction. Cromwell himself told me he would hang you if he had to take you openly."

"He dare not. Have no fear!"

"He dares anything. You do not know that man, and your condemnation, this document, rests now on the heart it would still. Cromwell will move the world to tear it from you. If you love me as you say, let us to the North at once."

Well he knew the truth of her warning, now that he understood the case, but was reluctant to let her go. The last appeal had its effect, and he placed her once more on her horse. Together they set off again, through a land that seemed silent and at peace; but it was only seeming.

## CHAPTER IV.—ENTANGLED.

There was some delay at Warwick, and the authorities proved reluctant to let them proceed farther with the journey. It was evident that the commandant had received instructions regarding the very pass they presented to him for their safe conduct, because he retired with it to the guard-house, where he remained for a time that seemed perilously long, and even when at last he came out with it he was plainly still suspicious, and in doubt regarding what action he should take. It was Frances who turned the scale in her own favour and that of her companion.

"Where did you get this pass?" the commandant asked.

"At Corbiton Manor, in the county of Durham."

"Who gave it to you?"

"It was given to me by General Cromwell's direction, and written almost in my own presence, I might say, or at least a few moments after I had been speaking with him."

"You went from Durham to Oxford?"

"Yes."

"And have come from Oxford here?"

"Yes."

"Did you travel through Banbury?"

"We stopped the night at Banbury; at 'The Banbury Arms'."

"Stopping there by the direction of General Cromwell himself," put in the girl, much to the surprise of William Armstrong. The officer looked up at her with interest.

"When did the General give you such instructions?"

"Several days ago, at Northampton."

"You saw him at Northampton?"

"Yes, and I saw him again this morning before daybreak."

"Really. And where was that?"

"At Broughton Castle, three miles west of Banbury. In my presence he told his aid to ride to Banbury, and send word North that this pass was to be honored. Has the commander at Banbury not obeyed his General's instructions?"

"Yes, he has," admitted the officer, looking with admiration on the young woman who spoke so straightforwardly; "but the communication came to me by way of Coventry, and it was somewhat vague. The messenger reached here but a scant half hour since, and he spoke of one person, not of two. May I ask your name?" he continued to the man.

"William Armstrong."

"That is right, my orders are to pass William Armstrong, holding a permit from the General, but say nothing of a lady."

"That is doubtless the messenger's mistake," said Frances confidently. "My brother is, or was, up to this morning, Lieutenant Wentworth of the Parliamentary forces in Durham. This morning General Cromwell wrote out his commission as captain, and that I brought away with me from Broughton and sent it direct to Durham by my servant. But you may detain me if you wish, or send an escort with me back to the General. It will be a more serious matter if you detain Mr. Armstrong, who is a Scotsman, and whom the General has been at some pains to further."

"Indeed, madam, I shall detain neither of you. My only excuse is that the messenger was not as clear as he might have been, and you come so close on his heels. Besides, I have had disquieting news from Birmingham. There is a rising of some sort forward. Birmingham has already been smitten sore by the King's troops, so there is little fear that the citizens have risen in his favour, but I surmise that there has been some sort of Royalist outbreak elsewhere in the North. Something is afoot, for messengers have been galloping through Alcaster to the east of us for Birmingham. You heard nothing of that further south?"

"No," said Armstrong, who nevertheless had a shrewd suspicion where the trouble lay. "If there is any Royalist rising in Birmingham I would like to avoid the place. I have no wish to get among the Royalists. Are there roads by which we can win east of Birmingham?"

"Oh, yes! I will sketch out a route for you, whereby you may reach the main highway some seven miles north of Birmingham, at Sutton Coldfield."

"I shall be much indebted to you, if you will be so good."

The officer retired to the guard-house and brought out a rude map of the district, which he gave to Armstrong after explaining it. He sent a soldier to set them on the right way when they had left the village. When the soldier had departed, and the two were once more alone, Armstrong turned in his saddle and looked back at the frowning towers of Warwick Castle, looming up through the trees, very suggestive of a prison.

"That was a narrow shave," he said, "and I have to thank you, Frances, that we have squeezed through."

The girl shook her head.

"Alas, circumstances are proving too strong for me," she said sorrowfully, "and all my old ideas of right and wrong are being flouted day and night. Just now I have used truth for the purposes of falsehood, a fault which I chided in you earlier in our journey. I wish we were free of the entanglements and might be honest once more."

"You have done well. Have no fear, and I still insist that the Lord stands by us. We cannot meet force with force, and must use what craft we are possessed of. Cromwell uses it, and so does the King. Why should we be debarred? I think we are well out of that trap, and I am wondering how many hours will elapse before the commander is sorry he let us go."

They lunched on bread and cheese at a wayside hut, and once, when they reached the top of a hill, they saw what they took to be Birmingham away to the west. The by-roads they were traversing proved to be deserted, and they resolved to keep to them rather than seek the main highway at Sutton Coldfield or elsewhere, for they considered that their comparative slowness would be more than compensated for by greater safety. This course soon proved of doubtful wisdom. Without a guide the intricate lanes were puzzling, and often came to an end without any apparent reason. When they took to the fields the soil was heavy in many cases, and fatigued their horses, besides entangling them sometimes in low-lying lands that were almost marshes. To add to their difficulties the sun became obscured in a haze, and the temperature dropped sharply, condensing the moisture in the air about them, involving them in a mist that was worse than the darkest night. Still they struggled on, leaving the direction entirely to their horses. At last they came on what appeared to be a cart track, and, following it, they arrived at a labourer's hut which faced a lane. Armstrong, without dismounting, knocked at the door with his sword, and a frightened woman, holding it ajar, answered the summons.

"We have lost our way," said the young man, throwing her a coin to bespeak good will; "can you tell us where we are?"

"Where are you going?" asked the woman, which proved a somewhat difficult question to answer.

"What is the nearest town to the north of us?"

"Lichfield."

"And how do we get to Lichfield from here?"

"Follow this lane to the cross-road, then take the lane to the left for two miles, and it will lead you into the main road. Turn to the right, and Lichfield is five or six miles further on."

"If, instead of going to the main road, we keep to this lane, where will it lead us?"

"It stops at the cross-road."

"Where will the lane turning to the right lead us?"

"I don't know."

"Is there any way to the North except by the main road?"

"I don't know."

"How long have you lived in this cottage?"

"Twenty-three years, sir."

"And you know only the way to Lichfield?"

"Yes, sir."

He thanked the woman, and they rode on through the fog. The limited knowledge of the English peasantry regarding the geography of their own district had baffled him more than once during their journey, and this was but a fair example of the ignorance he had to contend against. He resolved to take the turn to the right in preference to the leftward lane. He feared

Lichfield or any other place of similar size, and he dreaded the main road. It was impossible for Cromwell to patrol the whole country at a moment's notice, so the by-ways would be safer if less direct. Their progress had been so slow that there was ample time for a hard rider with relays of horses to have spread a warning far ahead of them, and now caution, rather than speed, was their game. These points he discussed with his companion as they rode along in the fog, and she agreed with his conclusions. Each tried to cheer the other, but both were undeniably discouraged by the conditions that surrounded them.

About a mile from the hut they came to the end of their road, with the horizontal lane at its head, extending east and west. As they turned to the right, some object loomed in the fog ahead, and there came a sharp cry:

"Who goes there?"

"To the left," whispered Armstrong, turning his horse. Frances obeyed instantly, but the man in front fired his musket into the air and raised a shout, whereupon four others sprang from the dripping bushes, and two of them seized the reins of the startled horses.

"Resistance is useless," said the soldier hanging to the rein of the plunging Bruce, "there are a hundred men along this lane."

"I have no need to resist," cried Armstrong with affected indignation, although none realized so well as he that the game was up. "We are peaceful travellers under safe-conduct from General Cromwell himself."

"The lieutenant will be here directly," said the man, and as he spoke a party of horsemen came galloping down the lane.

"Who fired that shot?" cried the officer in charge. Before an answer could be given he came upon the two captives. "Who are you?" he demanded.

"Travellers to Carlisle, who have lost their way in the mist and are seeking the high road."

"If you have a pass, let me see it."

"Here it is!"

"Your name is Armstrong, perhaps?"

"The pass does not say so."

"Do you deny it?"

"No."

"You are prisoners. Where is the bugler?"

"Here, sir."

"Sound the recall."

The man placed the bugle to his lips, and the merry notes rang out into the obscurity. All remained silent, then, like an echo from east and west, almost in unison, came a similar call; and faintly in the further distance another. The company seemed to increase mysteriously, as if pikemen were being distilled out of the fog, and after a roll-call, every name being answered, the lieutenant gave the word to march, and horse and foot set out for the west, the two prisoners in the centre of the phalanx. The head of Frances drooped, and Will rode close by her side as cheerful as ever, trying to comfort her.

"Clever man, this Cromwell," he whispered with admiration in his tones. "You see what he has done? He has run thin lines across the country as fast as horses could gallop, stringing out the local men as they went along. We have probably blundered through one or two of these lines, but were bound to be caught sooner or later, unless we made for the coast on either side, and that would but have delayed things a bit, for there was little chance of us getting ship with all ports in his hands. It serves me right. I should have killed De Courcy and then galloped for it. However, the Lord stands by us, Frances; never forget that."

"It doesn't look much like it," said the girl despondently.

"Oh, well, nothing looks like itself in this accursed fog. Why could n't we have had this mist on the road from York? Still, I don't think it would have made any difference, once Cromwell's riders got to the north of us. Resourceful man, Oliver. I like him."

"And I don't. Yet you are supposed to be against him, and I am supposed to be for him. I fear him; I fear him."

"Oh, there's no danger; not the slightest for either of us. You have done your task, and have done it well. I am the blunderer. But I stand on my status as a Scot, and I will argue the matter out with him. The man I tumbled into the ditch was the King's Chamberlain, and not a Parliamentarian, and a foreigner at that. The document I am supposed to carry was not given to me by the King, but taken by force from a minion of the King, and a Frenchman. I have assaulted no Englishman, and Cromwell knew I was travelling on this pass. He cannot deny that he wrote it, and for exactly the purpose it has served. Oh, I shall have a beautiful legal argument with Old Noll, and will upset him with his own law. I'm in no danger; neither are you."

"I trust it will appear so."

"It cannot appear otherwise. He was trying to frighten you when he said he would hang me. He is a sly, capable dog, who will be satisfied with having beaten me, and will not court trouble with my countrymen by hanging even a Borderer. It cost one of our Kings his throne to do the like of that."

This conversation, with which there was no interference on the part of their captors, was brought to a conclusion by their arrival at the main road. Here a halt was called and the bugle was sounded, again to be answered, as before, from different directions. "Dismount," said the officer to Armstrong, whereupon the latter, without a word, sprang to the ground. Against the next move he protested, but his opposition was unavailing and indeed unreplied to. The officer gave the lady and the two horses in charge of a party of six, with orders to take them to Lichfield and install them in the cathedral. A guard was to be set at the door, and no communication was to be allowed with any one outside. Orders from headquarters were to the effect that the lady was to be treated with every deference, and these orders were impressed upon the six men. The detached squad disappeared down the road in the fog, and Armstrong stood disconsolate and angry, but helpless, surrounded by troopers.

The monotony of waiting was relieved by the frequent arrival of companies from the east and from the west, who did not stay at the cross-roads, however, but marched south toward Sutton Coldfield and Birmingham. Thus the little company standing at arms was continually augmented, and continually reduced to its original size. It was waiting for some one higher in command than the mild lieutenant, and nearly two hours passed before this man, set in authority, arrived. Armstrong heard the trampling of horse to the south, and presently the sound of voices became quite audible through the fog. There seemed to be a dispute going forward, which was something unusual in the Parliamentary forces, where, if discipline appeared lax, instant obedience was invariably required.

"I tell you, Colonel, I am to take charge of the lady and escort her to Cromwell."

"I have no orders to that effect."

"I have come direct from Cromwell, and those were his orders."

"I do not take orders from you. I hold written instructions relating to both the man and the woman, and these I shall carry out."

"You will be wise to hang the man on the nearest tree, and take his papers to Cromwell."

To this there was no reply, and Armstrong now knew that De Courcy had not been so badly hurt as he had pretended, for he had taken a long ride to the North since then. The prisoner recognized his voice long before his cavalier costume emerged from the mist. De Courcy had not changed his apparel, and it formed a strange contrast to the Parliamentary uniform, as indeed did Armstrong's own dress.

"Ah, my young friend," cried De Courcy, the moment he recognized the prisoner, "you had your laugh in the morning, and I have mine in the evening."

"There is a time for everything," replied Armstrong indifferently, "and my time for laughing is in the morning. It is brighter then."

"Yes, it looks rather dark for you at the moment, and you seem less merry than when I met you earlier."

"Oh, there were more amusing things happening then, that's all. How's your horse?"

"We are neither of us the worse for our encounter. Do n't you wish you could say the same for yourself?"

"I do, and I thank you for your sympathy."

"Have you sent the woman to Lichfield?" asked the officer-in-chief of his subordinate.

"Yes, Colonel; some two hours ago."

"Very well. We will relieve you of your prisoner. Take your men to Birmingham."

"Is there any truth in the Royalist rising there, Colonel?"

"None in the least. Have you heard anything?"

"Nothing but a rumor that there was an outbreak of some sort. I heard that a detachment from Lichfield was to leave for Birmingham."

"We will turn it back if we meet it. Good night!" At the word the lieutenant and his men marched off to the south, and Armstrong was taken in charge by the squadron of horse. A trooper was dismounted and his steed given to Armstrong, of whom no questions were asked, as he had expected. They seemed very sure of their man. The cavalry set off to the North, and De Courcy rode close beside his enemy, taking a delight in taunting him. To this enforced companionship the Scot objected and made appeal to the colonel.

"Sir, am I your prisoner, or do I belong to this renegade King's man? Who is in authority here,—you, or this Frenchman?"

To this the colonel made no reply, nor did he order De Courcy to the rear, probably not wishing to offend one who seemed to be a friend of Cromwell's. The angry Scot was forced to make the best of it in silence, while the Frenchman, very polite and jocular, pressed ironic services upon him, asked after the girl, and said he would use his influence with Cromwell to have a silken rope used at the coming execution of so distinguished a spy. It is ill to tamper with a Border temper, as the Frenchman soon discovered. Armstrong slipped his knife from his belt and held it in readiness, when his attention was drawn to the trampling of an approaching host in front of them, and he remembered that here was coming the troop from Lichfield, which expected to meet a body of the King's men if the rumour from Birmingham were true. The rumour had no doubt been started by the riding North in hot haste of this courtier now at his side, at a time when such costume was not seen outside Oxford. Besides, the country was in a constant state of alarm, and the wildest tales were current, whose constant contradiction by afterevents did nothing to allay ever-recurring panic. Armstrong quietly gathered up his reins, watched his opportunity, and, instead of running his blade between the ribs of De Courcy, jabbed the point into the flank of the Frenchman's horse.

## CHAPTER V.—SANCTUARY.

However graceful the Frenchman might be on foot, and no one denied his elegance of bearing, he was but an amateur on horseback, and when his steed unexpectedly plunged forward he relinquished the reins and grasped the mane. For one brief moment the attention of the troop was diverted toward the unexplained antics of the maddened horse and the imminent overthrow of its rider. It is one of the defects of human nature that man is prone to laugh when he sees a fellow creature in some predicament from which his own superior skill leaves him free. Every man in the company was a faultless rider, and nothing their horses could do would have been any embarrassment to them. To see this dandified foreigner, whom at heart they despised in any case, crouching like a gaudily dressed monkey on a frolicsome dog, and screaming for help, was too much for even the saddest of them, and a roar of laughter went up which did nothing toward quieting the injured and frightened quadruped. If it had been the horse of Armstrong that had begun these dancings, his guards would have been instantly on the alert for an attempted escape, but at the very moment their eyes should have been on the Scot their attention was withdrawn. Armstrong did not laugh, but, thrusting back his knife, whipped out his sword, and struck De Courcy's horse twice with the broad of it. His own steed leaped forward under the prick of the spur, and before the colonel could give a word of command the two had disappeared in the fog ahead. Even then the colonel, who was the only man that had his wits about him, did not think there was the least chance of escape, for he had heard the troop coming toward him, and Armstrong must run directly into it. He rose in his stirrups to give the alarm to those ahead, when all heard a ringing shout: "Charge, cavaliers! God save the King! To hell with the Roundheads! Charge!"

Out of the fog came a spattering fire, then a volley. Two horses and three men went down, while the other troopers hastily unslung their carbines and fired down the street without waiting for the word of command.

"Stop, you fools!" yelled the colonel, "you are shooting your own men." Then to the oncomers he roared a like warning, which was drowned in another volley. The Lichfield men were not to be taken in, even if they had heard the warning. With their own eyes they had seen two cavaliers burst upon them out of the fog with a strident cry for the King. De Courcy, coming first, they concentrated upon him, and he went down before them. Armstrong, swinging his sword, smiting right and left, bellowing like a fiend in true cavalier style, a very Prince Rupert come again, dashed at the weakest spot, and his impetuosity carried all before him.

"Never mind him," cried the leader, as some would have pursued. "Fire, and break their charge," and fire they did right stoutly, until a maddened officer, with a bravery that scorned the bullets around him, galloped along their front, waving his sword and commanding them to stop.

"You are killing your own men! There are no Royalists, but an interfering fool of a Frenchman and an escaped Scot. Back to Lichfield!" Nevertheless, a battle is not quelled at a word, and the brave colonel pressed through among them and galloped in pursuit of his late prisoner.

Once clear of the clash, Armstrong was not sparing of a horse that belonged to someone else. At great risk to his neck he raced through the blind fog, sword in hand, ready for further opposition should he meet it. He emerged from the fog with a suddenness that startled him. The sun had set, and there, barely a mile away, stood out against the darkening sky the great red bulk of the cathedral with its war-broken towers, and the little town huddled at its feet. At the same moment he became aware that some one was thundering after him, and again he dug the cruel spurs into the labouring horse. A glance over his shoulder showed him the colonel breaking through the bank of fog, and he thought of turning and fighting him on the run, but the sound of firing had ceased, and he knew the colonel would prove a stouter combatant than the Frenchman, so he hurried on. Aside from this, Lichfield had been roused by the sound of the guns, and he saw the long narrow street that lay between him and the cathedral becoming alive with pikemen, and knew he would have his work cut out for him if he was to get safely through the town. As soon as he came within earshot he shouted to them: "Barricade the street! The King is upon us. I have just escaped. Our men are on the retreat. Defend the town to the south. Barricade! Barricade!" Thus he clattered through Lichfield, shouting.

Soldiers are so accustomed to the word of command that they obey first and think after, if at all. Seeing a rider in the costume of a cavalier come tearing down upon them, they made hasty preparation for stopping him; but his tone of authority was so well assumed that they gave way before him, and began the running out of carts and whatever other obstructions they could lay their hands upon, to make the way difficult for the oncoming colonel, who swore as loudly at their stupidity as if he were the King's own.

"What are you about, you accursed clodhoppers? Don't you know a King's man when you see one? Leave that rubbish and follow me to the cathedral."

Armstrong's horse, nearly done, staggered over the bridge and up the slight incline that led to the cathedral precincts. Across the grounds surrounding the church had been raised a great earthwork, and the battered west front of the sacred building showed that war had been no respecter of sculptured beauty. A lone pikeman paced up and down before the cathedral door, but paused as he saw this impetuous rider, whose horse had stumbled and fallen at the top of the rubbish heap.

"What do you there?" shouted Armstrong, springing nimbly from his

650

fallen horse. "Did n't you hear the firing? Down to the street and help your comrades; the town is attacked! Run!"

"I was told to stand here," objected the bewildered guard.

"Run, confound you! Do you question the word of an officer?"

The man, trailing his pike, ran, and disappeared down the street.

"Frances, Frances, are you within? Open the small door; it is I, Armstrong."

"Yes, yes, I knew you would come," he heard her say, and then followed the welcome rattle of the bolts. But they must be speedily drawn if they were to clear the way for a man hard pressed. Over the barricade surged a wave of pikemen, twoscore or more, the mounted colonel behind them, urging them on with pungent oaths.

"Sanctuary! Sanctuary!" shouted Armstrong, raising his sword aloft, standing under the arched doorway, steadfast as one of the stone knights beside him.

"Sanctuary be damned!" cried the colonel, urging his horse up the embankment. "Down on him, you dogs, and take him dead or alive!"

In spite of the cursing of the colonel; in spite of the battered condition of the great church; in spite of the deadening influence of the war, the cry of "Sanctuary" struck home to many of the hearts there opposed to the fugitive, and the pike-topped crest of the human wave paused for one brief instant, yet it was enough. Before the wave broke and fell, the small door gave and swung inward. As the pikes rattled against it, Armstrong had the bars and bolts in their places again.

"Break down that door!" he heard the colonel roar outside, while the impetuous William clasped the girl in his arms and kissed her.

"Lord, lassie, I'm glad to meet you again, although it's just dark enough in this place for the seeing of any one."

The young woman shook herself free.

"We wasted too much time at that before. Let it be a lesson to us. This place is a stable. Our horses are well fed, and the saddles are still on them."

"But is there a way out?"

"Yes, a small door in the northeast corner. Come."

"It will be guarded, surely."

"No. I think they wanted me to escape, for they went out that way after barring the front door. But they did n't think you would be with me when I took my leave. Come quickly, or they will be round to it from the front."

"I doubt it. The colonel is a Birmingham man and a powerful swearer, who knows nothing of this church—or any other, I think. The men will not remember the back door until it is too late, and then I pity them; they will hear language from the colonel."

The two made their way to the farther end of the cathedral, where the horses were stalled. The vast nave was dark and would soon be black as a cellar until the moon rose. It was used as a military storehouse, as a stable, and as a dormitory for troops when the accommodation in the town was overtaxed. As Armstrong and his companion stumbled over obstructions toward the horses, the spacious chamber rang with the impact of timber against the stubborn doors. Frances, knowing the geography of the place, led the way with her horse, and Armstrong followed with his. Once outside, there was more light than he wished for, but their way to the rear was clear, and, mounting, he took the lead, crossing an alpine ridge which had done duty during the siege, and taking a somewhat terrifying leap down to the greensward of the field at the back of the cathedral. Then they ran north through a slight valley, and, for the moment, were safe from observation.

"The moon will be up soon," said the young man, "and I do n't know whether to welcome it or fear it."

"We shall do neither, as we have no influence one way or another, and must bear its disadvantages or the reverse, as chance wills. Now tell me what happened. How did you escape?"

652

The tale was soon told, half humorously, as if it were an escapade rather than an escape, and the narrator wound up with a determination to avoid the main road in future.

"There I do not agree with you," she said. "I have been alone in that cathedral some three hours or more, and have had time to think. You said we blundered into the ambuscade, and so we did. You have hewn your way out by a marvellous combination of luck and prowess, but such exploits are not to be depended upon. You must use your mind, as well as your right arm and the swiftness of your horse, if you are to win Scotland."

"Frances, you discourage me: I looked upon my escape rather as a triumph of wit than of muscle. The setting of the Roundheads at each other's throats in the mist seemed an inspiration, and the cry of 'Sanctuary' gave me just the moment of time that was needed. Your estimate of me is that of the Reverend Henderson of Edinburgh, who held I had barely sense enough to direct a stout blow."

"No, no, I give you full credit for great ingenuity, but we stumbled upon, the Parliamentarians with no plans made. Everything has been done on the spur of the moment, and has not been thought out before the crisis came. A few chance remarks got us clear at Warwick; while inspiration and a fog were your safety at Lichfield, and even then by one brief instant of time. The recurrence of such strokes of luck and good management are not to be looked for. Some time the moment needed will go against us, and then all is lost."

"True enough. What do you propose?"

"I propose we take to the main road again, which must be near at hand on our left."

"You forget we have no pass from Cromwell now. The lieutenant has it."

"You will have a pass for yourself the moment you are north of Manchester, which cannot be more than fifty miles away. We must get over those miles as speedily as possible; therefore the main road is our route."

"Yes, if it were practicable; surely danger lies thick along the main road."

"I do not think so. While in the cathedral I heard troop after troop of men going northward. They will carry the news of your capture, but not of your escape. Until they beat in the door of the cathedral and search the place thoroughly, no messenger will be sent North. We are ahead of them once more, with the news of your capture travelling in front of us. We will keep ahead so long as we ride fast and until we stop somewhere for the night; then they having relays of horses, while we have only our own, will pass us. We cannot ride all night, or we shall kill our horses; but We can cover a good deal of the ground between here and Manchester. Once north of Manchester I think you are fairly safe. So I propose we ride now for the main road, and keep going as long as our horses are able to travel."

"Agreed; but, following your own instructions, what are we to say when we are stopped? We have no pass, so how am I to account for myself?"

"You are a Roundhead soldier, sent on to Manchester by the colonel at Lichfield."

"I look like a Roundhead soldier!" cried William, with a laugh.

"You will. It is always well to have some one in a travelling party who can think. Have you not noticed the load you carry behind your saddle?" Armstrong turned. The rising moon displayed a steel cap that looked like an overturned pot and a bundle of cloth, all neatly strapped on.

"The cathedral is a storehouse for uniforms and accoutrements enough to fit out a regiment. I selected the largest suit I could find, with cloak and cap, and belted them to your saddle. Now I shall hold your horse while you go into the thicket and change your raiment. Conceal your cavalier costume as well as you can, so that, if they trace us over this fog-sodden turf, which is likely, they will get no hint of your new appearance. It might be well to climb a tree and tie your discarded shell among the leaves, with the straps that bind the bundle to your horse, and be careful to leave neither the King's message nor your purse with your finery."

It was a happy omen for future domestic peace that the huge man did at once and without question what the comparatively fragile young woman bade him, she holding his horse while he made the rapid change. When he emerged, the horse plunged, and she had some ado to hold him until he heard his master's voice and laugh.

"Yea, verily, this is a transformation indeed," cried Armstrong, looking at himself in the moonlight. "My name is Hezekiah, and the steel cap is a thought on the small side, but the rest o' the duds are not so bad."

"The cap was the largest I could find," laughed the girl, "and will fit closely enough when your locks are shorn."

"Oh. Must I sacrifice this vanity of Absalom as well?"

"Surely. If I am to be your Delilah, I must fulfill my duty. I searched the whole cathedral for that which would do the work of shears, but could find nothing. However, the first cottage we come to will supply us with a suitable instrument. Now mount, and let us away."

They speedily came upon the main road, and cantered on through the beautiful night, determined to put fifty miles, or thereabout, between themselves and Lichfield, but before they had accomplished half that distance Armstrong saw that the girl was completely exhausted in spite of her disclaimers, for, aside from the tiresome day's travel, she had had little sleep the night before. It was most tempting to push on, for the night was perfect and the road was good. Even though they passed through several villages they were not questioned. Soldiers in drab cloaks and steel caps were too common on the road to cause comment, and they were, as yet, in advance of any news of escape.

At last they came to a farmhouse near the roadside, and Armstrong beat up the inmates, bringing a woman's head to an opened window. At first she would admit no one at that hour of the night, but the moon shining on the steel cap and the long cloak apparently gave her confidence. Her husband was in the south with Cromwell, she said. She could make a place in the house for the lady, but the soldier would find better accommodation than he was accustomed to in an outhouse. With this Armstrong expressed himself as amply satisfied. They dismounted, and he led away the horses. He found a place for them in a shed, examined them, and rubbed them down with care. Having satisfied himself that they were none the worse for their long journey, he attended to their wants and flung down some bundles of straw for his own night's lodging. He began to think he must go supperless, or run the risk of foraging in an unknown pantry, if he could find entrance, when he saw Frances approach from the house with a loaf of bread and a lump of cheese on a trencher, and a measure of ale. He met her half way and relieved her of the load. Under her arm she carried some cumbrous weapon, which she brought out when he assumed the burden of the provender.

"It is a pair of sheep-shears, which the woman tells me is all she has, but I assured her they were most suitable for my purpose. Now sit on this stone here in the moonlight and be shorn; for we must set out in the daylight without those long locks of yours. You look too much like the King, even with your cloak and steel cap."

The girl laughed softly as she said this, and snapped the big shears menacingly. He sat on the stone like the obedient young man he was, shook out his lion's mane, and in a few moments was bereft of it. The girl stood back and surveyed her work, laughing, but nevertheless with a tinge of regret in her laughter.

"Oh, it's a pity!" she cried. "All the King's horses and all the King's men are not worth the sacrifice. I hope it will grow again, for, if not, the Philistines be upon thee, Samson. Your dearest friend would n 't know you now."

Armstrong smiled ruefully and passed his hand in anxious doubt over his cropped head.

"I suppose it will grow again, unless my dearest friend refuses to acknowledge me with this curtailment, when I shall become bald through grief at her defection."

"I make no promises, if you mean me. I shall very likely reconsider. You are never the man who cast a glamour over me at Oxford and elsewhere. I fear I am no true Parliamentarian after all, but I shall not come to a decision until I see you in the daylight. Perhaps the cap will be an improvement, but

I doubt it."

He squeezed on the cap, which was still too small.

"By the bones of my ancestors, it will need Peter, the blacksmith of Gilnockie, to get this off again!"

"That is worse and worse," urged his tormentor. "I cannot bear the sight any longer, or it will drive sleep away from me. Good night, my poor, shorn Samson,"—and she was off before he could spring up and intercept her.

## CHAPTER VI.—EXPEDIENCE.

Great is the recuperative power of youth, and shortly after sunrise the two were on the road again, refreshed and with high courage, to face the outcome of another long ride. They had travelled farther than their estimate of the night before, and so found themselves but little more than twenty miles south of Manchester. In the night the weather had undergone another change, and the sun was hidden, while now and then a scurry of rain passed over them. To the North the outlook was black and lowering. They were approaching the land of storm.

"I have made up my mind," said Frances, "that we must part. No, it is not on account of that cropped head of yours, but rather to save it."

"I have been thinking myself that it is wrong you should share my danger, when there is nothing to hinder you from going across country to your own home."

"I shall not go across my country until I have seen you safely into your own. But, as you know, the swearing colonel and his men are not looking for me. Perhaps they think I took the opportunity left open to get away from the cathedral; but on the other hand, if wise, they must have looked for our horses' tracks, and then they learned we left Lichfield together. I propose to act as your scout. I shall ride a mile or two ahead, and if I am stopped, you will strike to the right or to the left, and avoid the danger if you can. On every elevation I reach I will stand for a few moments. If my horse faces west, the way between us is safe; if he faces east, there is danger."

"Frances, I would rather run the risk and have your company."

"I am sure you would, but"—and she laughed—"now that you are clipped, you are the one who is beautiful, and I the one who is wise. It is really to your advantage that I should see as little of my Roundhead lover as possible, and you would be foolish to detain me, for I cannot help glancing at you now and then, and whenever I do, I sigh for the cavalier who wooed me yesterday. Women are not so changeable as they say, and I am constant to my first adorer."

To this William made no reply, gazing somewhat gloomily at the storm away on the horizon.

"There, there," she cried, riding alongside and touching his hand. "I have offended his vanity, and he doesn't like to be laughed at. Poor boy, you little know what is in store for you. Don't you understand you will have enough of my company in the days to come, and may well spare some of it now? I shall not disown my promise if you remind me of it when your love-locks are over your shoulders again. But, seriously, my plan is a good one unless you have a better to propose. We must quit the main road now, and avoid Manchester as we avoided Birmingham, but we should have a care that we do not ride into another ambuscade, and if I go first that may be prevented."

"When I see you interfered with, I will just gallop to your assistance."

"You shall do nothing so foolish. No one in England is going to injure me; but you are not safe until you are over the Scottish line. We shall be north of Manchester in three or four hours, and then you have your own pass. You are really a most creditable Roundhead. After Manchester we can travel in company again, if you wish. Have you anything better to propose?"

"Yes. I propose we stay together and take our chances."

"Good bye," she cried gaily, touching up her horse, then, over her shoulder as she galloped off, "Remember. West, safety; east, danger."

Armstrong had not only to curb his own inclination, but his horse as well, who viewed with evident disapproval the departure of his mate. At the summit of the first hill the girl turned her horse across the road facing west, waved her hand to him, and disappeared over the crest. And thus the journey went on; sometimes two miles between them, sometimes less. Manchester was seen and left in the rear. He now tried to catch up with her, but she kept valorously ahead, as if she were some fabled siren luring the poor man on. For a time he lost sight of her, then, as he mounted a hill, saw her standing on a crest a mile away, like an equestrian statue against an inky sky; but this time her horse faced the east, and he thought she was motioning with her handkerchief in that direction. She stood there until he sent his horse over the hedge and made in the direction of a forest, then the darkness seemed to swallow her up. He skirted the edge of the wood. Rain was now coming down heavily, but before it blotted out the landscape he passed the head of a valley and saw dimly through the downpour a large encampment of white tents. A man in drab on a black charger stood little chance of being seen against the dark forest from the encampment, but he moved on as rapidly as he could, knowing that if a lull came in the deluge he ran great risk of detection by the outposts. Some distance on he stood for a time under the trees, blessing the long cloak, which formerly he had maligned for its ugliness, for now it proved of good material and waterproof. The girl had evidently gone directly down into the camp, and he was at a loss what to do. Duty called him to press forward to the North, but duty is often an ill-favoured jade whose strident voice is outdistanced by the soft whisper of a beautiful woman. Armstrong dared not shout, and the deluge formed an impenetrable curtain whichever way he turned. He skirted the wood for some time, then crossed the fields to the west until he came to the road which trended North from the camp. Here he stood in the rain, and wondered whether she was detained, or whether she had already passed the spot he now occupied. They had made no arrangement for meeting again in case they should lose sight of each other, and he blamed himself for his negligence on this important point. One thing was certain. It was useless to stand here until he was dissolved. Even his stout-hearted horse had assumed an attitude of the utmost dejection, with drooping head, the water pouring off every part of him. Should the weather clear, which he was compelled to confess there seemed little likelihood of it doing, he was in danger so near the camp. He resolved to turn North, go on until he reached some place of shelter, and there wait. Progress was slow, for the lane had become a quagmire. The forest which he had skirted extended now to the west, and the road became a woodland track, but just where it began to penetrate into the wilderness there shone upon him a ray of hope. From an overhanging branch of the first tree hung a limp and dripping white rag, tied by one on horseback in such a position that it might brush the face of a rider passing that way. He took it down, and it proved to be a lady's handkerchief. If he had followed the edge of the wood, he could hardly have missed it; if he came along the lane he was almost certain to see it. He thrust this token under his cloak and chirruped to his discouraged horse. When something like a mile had been cast behind him, his horse neighed, and was answered by another further ahead. Then he came to a forester's hut, and in an open shed, sheltered from the storm, stood the companion of Bruce, who showed lively pleasure at the encounter.

Inside the hut a cheerful sight met his eyes. A fire of faggots blazed on the hearth, and before it stood a radiant young woman, arranging the brands to their better burning with the tip of her boot. On a high stool was spread her steaming cloak. In a far corner sat the old forester and his wife, frowning on their visitor and their newly arrived guest; for strangers were viewed with universal suspicion by high and low, little good ever coming of them in the minds of the peasantry, while the chance of danger was always present; danger whether hospitality was proffered or withheld. There was more likelihood of entertaining devils unaware than angels, and well the afflicted poor knew it.

However, less risk lay in succoring a steel cap than a feathered hat, so the moment the dripping horseman shoved in the door, the old woman rose and began to set out a meal of dark bread and swine's flesh, boiled and cold.

"Ah, here you are at last," cried the girl. "I was beginning to fear I should have to go back to the camp for you. Did you find my token?"

"Yes."

"Give it to me."

"Not so. Findings are keepings. You cannot prove your right to the property."

"Alas, honest travellers are few, as these good people seem to think.

Throw off your cloak. Here is a wooden hook by the fire that I have kept for it. Draw up your stool and eat. I was so hungry that I didn't wait. You see what it is to possess a good conscience once more."

"I possess a good appetite any way."

"Then sit down, and I shall be your waiting-maid."

"What news have you?"

"Hush! Great news, for I am the very princess of scouts. One thing at a time, however, and the one thing now is this black bread, which is like the old woman here, better than it looks. We can get nothing for our horses at this place, so must set out again as soon as possible, in spite of the rain."

When he had finished his meal and stood again with her before the fire, she whispered to him: "You must not pay these people too lavishly. They are somewhat near the camp, and although they do not seem over talkative it is better to run no risks. Bargain with them; be as a very Jew in computation."

"I'll do better than that. I'll be a very Scot, and so save money."

Once on the road again, she gave him her budget of news.

"You are a hero, William Armstrong. England is ringing with your exploits, and I never dreamed with what a valorous knight of old I travelled. It seems you stormed Warwick Castle and took it. You passed unseen through cordons of troops, and it is suspected you have dealings with the Devil, who travels beside you in the guise of a female, as is right and proper, and who appears and disappears at her will. Single-handed, you scattered two armies at Lichfield——"

"Oh, give the Devil her due!"

"With her aid, of course; that is always understood. You attacked Lichfield cathedral and captured it, and there is much disapproval among the peasantry that Cromwell had formerly dismantled it, for they think that if this had not been done the holy belongings of the place would have baffled you. The cathedral now reeks of sulphur, and you escaped in a whirl of flame amid a storm of bullets. They know that nothing will prevail against you but a silver pellet, and even that must be well aimed. So I am not sure but I have been mistaken in disguising you, for if any Cavalier shows himself in the North, the inhabitants are like to take him for Satan and fly from him."

"Then they are not good Christians, for they are told to resist the Devil and he will flee from them. You think, then, that my fiendish character will protect me?"

"Not so; but you have nothing to fear between here and Carlisle. I thought you said De Courcy had been killed?"

"He went down, and I supposed him shot, but was in too much of a hurry to inquire."

"He and others rode to the North last night, and they are now between us and Carlisle."

"He has as many lives as a cat. If that is the case, why do you say the road to Carlisle is clear?"

"Because from Carlisle to Newcastle, right across England, the cordon is to be stretched, and from Carlisle west to the coast. Before we can reach there; a line of men, almost within touching distance of each other, will extend from sea to sea, and all traffic North will be stopped. A thousand pounds is on your head, and Cromwell thinks to stay you, not with silver, but with gold. The General himself is on his way North, to see that you are trapped, or to be ready for any outbreak of the Scots should you win through."

"I fear I have been unable to convince Oliver that I am the devil, since he takes such excellent human means of frustrating me. A thousand pounds! And yet you held that first day I was of slight value!"

"I have confessed my error since. The camp I visited is breaking up to-day, and moving on to Carlisle. Twenty-three thousand men, I was told, but, being mostly foot, there is no chance of their overtaking us."

"Well, the North looks black with more than rain, though goodness knows there is enough of that. I wish I were in Glasgow."

"What do you propose to do?"

"You are the plan-maker of this foray. What do you propose to do, or have you thought of that yet?"

"I have not only thought of it, but have received instructions on it. I have heard the officers discuss what should be done, but I want to hear your conclusions first."

"Very well. The line runs from the west coast to Newcastle. At Newcastle I am more than forty miles from Scotland at the nearest point, while at Carlisle I am less than ten. Every step east I go, I am placing myself more and more at a disadvantage, yet I might go east simply because of this, and because they know that I know that they know I am on the road to Carlisle. Having fallen into one ambush, they will imagine me on the constant outlook for another. Going free for so long, they might even count on my increasing carelessness, but shrewd men would not lippen to that Knowing I am singlehanded and can make no stand, they will expect me to creep through at night, either east or west of Carlisle, and as near as may be to that place, trusting to the short distance and the fleetness of my horse in a race for the Scottish Border. I am a hillsman, accustomed to threading my way through a wild country, with a keen eye for an enemy. I have avoided all the big towns, Birmingham, Manchester, and the like, so they will not expect me to risk either Newcastle or Carlisle. Night will be the time when they are greatly on the alert, especially if this storm continues. Very well again. Who am I, if questioned? I am a trooper of Cromwell's own horse, sent North from Warwick, having seen this escaped devil of a Scot, and therefore the more likely to identify him. I have become detached from my company in the storm. I will ride into Carlisle in broad daylight, and ask where the Warwick horse are to be found. They were ordered to Carlisle, I shall say. I shall not avoid the commander, but will seek for him. Then, if I can saunter over the bridge, it's 'Hoorah for Scotland,' and may the best hoofs win."

"Good," cried the girl, "and well reasoned. They all agreed that Carlisle was the weakest link in the chain."

"Did they so? Then that makes me hesitate. If those in Carlisle think it

663

the weakest link, they will strengthen it."

"The officer's plan was not so bold as yours. Of course they did not know you were travelling in the likeness of one of themselves. They thought you would abandon your horse before you came to Carlisle, creep into that town after dark, avoid the bridge, which is sure to be well guarded, swim the Eden, and be across the Scottish border by daylight. There are two defects in your own proposal; your accent is not that of Warwickshire, and De Courcy is sure to be in Carlisle and may recognize you. Besides this, you may meet some one who knows the Warwick regiments, and you are not even acquainted with the name of the captain of your supposed company. I think the night attempt more like to prosper."

"In the night every one is on the alert, and a Roundhead cannot be distinguished from a cavalier, so there is closer scrutiny. I can enact the stupid trooper to perfection, having natural gifts toward stupidity. There is a risk, of course, but this is a risky journey at best. If I once get over the bridge at Carlisle, I'll beat all England in a race for the Border."

"I hope you will. I said I would see you across into Scotland, but I am convinced that purpose is futile, and I shall prove but a danger to you. A Warwick trooper on duty does not wander over the country a-squiring of dames. I have given you good advice and a Roundhead's equipment, and have acted as your scout, so I must not imperil your mission by hanging to the skirt of that sopping cloak. To-night we shall likely reach Yorkshire, and to-morrow I bid you God speed and make across the county to my own home."

"Indeed, lass, I have come so to depend on you, I shall be but a lost sheep, shorn at that, if you leave me."

"The wind is tempered to all such, and if you depend on your own wit you are likely to prosper. But you should have some care for me. It is my own safety I am thinking of."

Although the day was far from being one that incited toward hilarity, Armstrong laughed, and turned his dripping face up to the storm. The girl joined him, but with less of merriment in her tones.

"You will never persuade me," he said, "that there is a tinge of selfishness about you, or that you ever think of yourself when there is a friend to think of."

"There is worse to come," she went on. "I must beg of you to sacrifice that moustache. You will never get through Carlisle with that on your lip. Anyone who has ever seen you before would recognize you now, in spite of cloak and cap."

"Madam, you ask too much. The kingdom of England may fall, but this moustache, never."

"Really," laughed the girl. "If you saw it at this moment you would not be so proud of it. It has drooped and wilted in the rain like a faded flower. 'Twere better done away with, for it will mark you out from the smooth-faced troopers who throng Carlisle."

William somewhat wistfully wrung the water from it, and attempted to draw it out across his cheeks.

"Madam, I suspect your design. One by one you have depleted me of what goes to make up a Borderer, and gradually you have reduced me to the commonplace level of those crop-eared villains who are fighting against their King. Then, when I come to you and say, 'I beseech you to fulfill your promise to me,' you will reply, 'Away, Hezekiah, I know you not.'"

"'T is near to that point now, and a little more or less will make slight difference with me, while it will greatly aid your passage through Carlisle."

"Would it not be well to have my ears cropped also?"

"They are somewhat prominent, now that your locks are gone. I wish I had brought those shears with me. You see now why I must leave you. Oh, the vanity of man! The self-conceit of woman is a molehill compared with a mountain. But take courage, William. I shall not be near you when the deed is done, and the moustache sacrificed, and you will wait in Scotland until it grows again. Perhaps by that time our English troubles will be finished, and thus Armstrong and England will be their true selves at the same moment."

They had long since reached the main road and were making way as well as they could through the mud. The rain had not ceased, nor did it show any sign of ceasing. It needed frivolous talk to keep the spirits up in such weather. The young woman was earnest enough in her resolve to further his disguise by the means she had suggested, but to this she could not get Armstrong to say either yea or nay. He changed the subject.

"You never told me how you managed to get so much information in the camp. Did they let you pass unquestioned?"

"It happened that I knew the officer in charge, and he knew me, and was rather apologetic in his demeanour toward me, for he was one of those of the court-martial who condemned my brother, I told him, truly enough, that I had been to see Cromwell and had obtained his complete pardon. That I had seen the General at Northampton, where he had made me a promise, and again at Broughton Castle, where he had redeemed it. I was now on my way home; that was all. The officer was very glad indeed to hear of my success, and said, what was also true, that he had deeply regretted the condemnation, but that the court could not do otherwise with the evidence before it. He had no suspicion that I was the female fiend who accompanied the man they sought, and as the talk was all of this man I could not help but hear, and was indeed very glad to listen."

As evening drew on, conversation lagged, and they rode silently together, keeping doggedly to the work in hand, in spite of the flagging energies of their horses and their own bedraggled weariness. The rain fell with pitiless steadiness, and darkness came on early, with no chance of a moon being visible that night. The welcome light of a town twinkled ahead at last, and they resolved to stop there unless the risk threatened to be overwhelming. At the outskirts they learned that they had reached Clitheroe, and that "The Star" inn offered fair accommodation for man and beast. They were not to reach Yorkshire that night, and had accomplished less than thirty miles from Manchester. They dismounted at "The Star," two very water-soaked persons, and their reception was far from being particularly cordial.

"Are you one of the troopers billeted here tonight?" asked the host, who appeared not over pleased to welcome such enforced guests.

"No, I pay for my accommodation. I am an officer of the Warwick horse."

"I was warned this morning to keep all the room I had for a company from Manchester."

"Then that need not trouble you. They will not be here to-night. They did not strike camp until this afternoon, later than they expected. Should any arrive who have a better right here than I, I will turn out, at whatever time of the night it is necessary. I want two rooms, and a sitting-room with a big fire. And get us a hot supper as soon as you can. There is good stabling for the horses, I hope?"

"The best in Lancashire. You are on this hide-and-seek business, I suppose?"

The landlord had become wonderfully genial, now that there was the prospect of good orders and gold ahead.

"What hide-and-seek business?"

"This slippery Scot. Have you got him yet?"

"No. It is thought he has made for the coast."

"Never you fear, sir. I know that kind of cattle, and have had them staying with me many's the time. He'll take to the hills, and you mark my word, unless you hold hands across England, you'll not catch him, and even then you'll have to look well to your feet, or he'll slip through between them."

"I hardly, see how a man on horseback can do that."

"You mark my word, they'll be looking for a man on horseback, and he'll be sneaking through the grass; then they'll be looking in the grass, and he's whistled to his horse and is off over the hills. I know they chaps, and have played blind man's buff with them myself. You mark my word, that lad is in Scotland before to-morrow night, and laughing at you all."

"Oh, I hope not!"

"You try to catch an eel by diving after it, and all you get is a wetting."

"Well, I'm wet enough now, landlord, and have caught no eel yet, so if you'll order a brisk fire going, we will see what we can do in the way of eels tomorrow."

It proved that Armstrong was quite right about the non-arrival of the Manchester contingent, and his deep slumber was not disturbed by any notice to quit. All night long the rain lashed down, but at daybreak it ceased, although the heavy clouds hung low in the sky. After a good breakfast the two set out, and were not molested or questioned as they passed from under the shadow of the castle at Clitheroe.

## CHAPTER VII.—VICTORY.

Despite the night's rest, the horses were stiff after the long struggle with rain and mud the day before. If the situation was to be saved by a race, there seemed little chance of success with animals so tired and discouraged. With the exception of the departure from Oxford, the riders were more silent and melancholy than at any other time during their journey together. They had discussed the case in all its bearings the previous night, before the blazing fire, and had come to the conclusion that it would be safer to part. Armstrong was now in a country that he knew reasonably well, and he had no need to ask his direction from any chance comer, which was an advantage to a fugitive. They had agreed to deflect toward the east and bid good-bye to each other at Kirby Stephen, he striking northwest to Penrith, and she taking the main road east, entering Durham at Barnard Castle. There was no blinking the fact that while a Parliamentarian trooper might pass through this land unquestioned, especially as so many soldiers were making their way North, a trooper with a beautiful young woman of aristocratic appearance would certainly cause comment and excite curiosity. The nearer they came to Carlisle, the greater would be the danger of embarrassing questions. They had a wild country to traverse, bleak hills and moorland, and the roads as bad as they could be; but although they left Clitheroe at five o'clock it was past noontide before they reached Kirby Stephen, a distance of less than forty miles. They had met no one, and so far as the morning section of the journey was concerned, the road to Scotland was clear enough. At the squalid inn of Kirby Stephen they partook of what each thought was their last meal together for a long time to come, and then, in spite of her protests, he accompanied her east out of the town and into the lonely hill country. At last she pulled up her horse, and impetuously thrust out her right hand, dashing away some tear-drops from her long lashes with her left.

"Good bye," she cried, the broken voice belieing the assumed cheerfulness of the tone. "I cannot allow you to come farther. You must now bid farewell to your scout."

"Dear lass, it breaks my heart to part with you in this way," stammered William, engulphing her small hand in both of his, then drawing her to him. "It shames my manhood to let you go this wild road alone. I must see you to your own door, in spite of all the Cromwells that ever broke their country's laws."

"No, no!" she pleaded. "We went over all that last night, and settled it. I am safe enough. It is you who are in danger. You will come to me when this trouble is passed and done with."

"By Saint Andrew, I'll come to you as soon as this letter is in Traquair's hands."

"Again, no, no! Cromwell is a hard man, and if you steal through his cordon you must not come within his power in a hurry."

"No fear, lass, he dare not touch me. Once my foot's in Scotland, I'm like that ancient chap you told me of; I draw virtue from the soil and am unassailable. Cromwell wants nothing of me when this packet escapes him. I'll turn back from Traquair the moment I give it to him."

"I do not permit such folly; remember that." She wept a little, then laughed a little. "I do not wish to see you until your hair is grown again. My Scottish Samson, you must come to me with flowing locks, as when I first saw you, so that I may forget I have been your Delilah."

For answer he kissed her protesting lips again and again, then she hid her face in his sombre cloak and sobbed quietly. The patient horses, now accustomed to any vagaries on the part of their owners, stood quietly close together.

"Good-bye, good-bye, good-bye," she cried breathlessly, then whisked herself from him and was gone, never looking back, but waving her hand as she rode. He sat motionless as she had left him. At the top of the distant hill, outlined against the dark sky, she drew in and stood. Dimly he saw the flutter of something white in her waving hand, and he drew from his breast her own handkerchief and waved in return. He pressed his hand across his eyes, and, when he saw more clearly, only the blank sky and the bare hilltop confronted him.

"Now curse the man who tries to stop me," growled Armstrong through his set teeth. "I have been too mild with these ruffians. I'll break him across the pommel of my saddle as if he were a rotten spear."

The rain began to fall once more as he passed again through Kirby Stephen, but he paid slight heed to it and pushed on to Penrith, where he bought a day's provender, so that he would have no need to make request for food as he neared the danger spot. Just before darkness set in, the sky cleared somewhat, and he saw ahead of him the gloomy bulk of Carlisle castle. He turned aside from the main road, and before the night became black found quarters for himself in a barn that contained some fodder for his horse. He threw himself down on the fragrant hay and slept peacefully.

In the morning the rain was again falling steadily. He reconnoitered his position. There was no dwelling near, and he determined to let his horse rest all that day and the next night, so that he should be in trim for anything that might happen when the pinch came. A day more or less could make little difference with the effectual guarding of the bridge, which was now doubtless held as strongly as it could be. He was convinced that success must depend ultimately on the speed of his horse, and he could not enter the contest with an exhausted animal. Bruce was never so carefully tended as on the day before the crisis, and as his intelligent head turned toward his master, he seemed to know that something unusual was afoot. On the second day Armstrong thought it best not to enter Carlisle too early in the morning. He wished to mingle with a crowd and not to ride the streets alone. The second night in the barn, with the rest of the day and night before, had left both himself and his horse fit to face anything that might ensue. The day was fine; the clouds had cleared away, and the sun was shining on the sodden ground. When he came in sight of the main road he saw what appeared to be an army marching North. He halted at the cross-road, in doubt regarding his next move. The men, in a long line, were on foot, trudging sullenly, wearily forward, water-soaked and mud-covered. No man looked up or seemed to take an interest in anything but the dismal work in hand. Far on toward the gates of Carlisle rode a group of horsemen, and at the rear another squad of mounted men encouraged the laggards to keep up for a little longer. Armstrong sat on his horse until the latter company was abreast of him.

"That is Carlisle ahead, I hope," said one of the officers.

"Yes," answered Armstrong. "Is this the Manchester contingent?"

"Yes. Brutal weather we've had," growled the officer.

"It was that," assented William, cheerfully, falling into line with them, "but it seems on the mend."

"Aye, now that our march is finished."

"Oh, you are likely to go farther afield, across country, when you reach Carlisle."

"I suppose so," replied the officer, gruffly, not too good-natured over the prospect. No one asked Armstrong who he was, and the elaborate fiction he had prepared to account for himself was not called for. The troopers were worn out by their contest with the elements and the roads, and all curiosity was dead in them. There stood Carlisle in front, and that was enough. The foot soldiers struggled on, in no definite order of formation, each doing the best he could. The officers rode silent behind them. Thus they all marched into Carlisle without question, and in their company the man the army was seeking. After a slight delay and pause in the streets the new troops moved on to the castle. Armstrong found no difficulty in falling behind, being thus free of the town. He knew every turn of every street and lane in the place as well as he knew the inside of his own pocket. He resolved to ride leisurely to the bridge, cut through the guard, if it did not prove too strong, and then trust to the spur. The town was thronged with military, but no one paid the slightest attention to him. As he jogged along very nonchalantly, more contented with the prospect than a few days before he would have thought possible, Bruce awoke the echoes by neighing loudly.

"Now, old man, what did you that for?" whispered William.

He looked ahead and was stricken speechless for the moment by seeing Frances Wentworth on her horse, without doubt a prisoner, two troopers riding on either side of her, and a young officer in front. She had unquestionably seen him, for her brow was wrinkled with anxiety; but her eyes gazed steadily past him into the distance. As he made toward the party they flashed one look of appeal upon him, which said as plainly as words, "For Heaven's sake, ride on and do not recognize me!"—but the young man was oblivious to everything except the fact that she was in some trouble.

"Where are you going with this lady?" he demanded of the officer.

"You may well ask," said the man, in no accent of pleasure. "We have come across country to Carlisle under orders from one in authority, and now we must hale her back to Durham, where General Cromwell is stationed; and those are the orders of some one else."

"But it is all a mistake," cried William.

"That's what I'm telling you," said the man, with a short laugh.

"This lady is the sister of Captain Wentworth of our army."

"So she says. Others say she is the woman who was with the Scotch renegade. I know nothing of it and care less. I obey orders."

"Sir," said Frances, coldly, "I beg you not to interfere. It is a mistake that will be explained in due time, but these men must do as they are told. That much you should know."

Although her words were spoken harshly enough, her eloquent eyes were bringing him to his senses and a realization of the unwisdom and futility of his behaviour. Before he could speak again, a sharp voice behind him rang out: "Why are you loitering there? Get on with you!"

Without turning, he knew who the speaker was, and if he had not, the gleam of fear in the girl's eyes might have warned him of peril.

"This man questions my orders," said the officer.

"No man has a right to question your orders. Who is he?"

Armstrong was edging away, but De Courcy spurred the horse he rode in a semicircle to cut off his retreat. Instantly the Frenchman raised a shout that echoed through the streets of the town, and arrested every foot within hearing.

"The Scot! The Scot!" he roared. "Stop that man; never mind the woman. After him. Sound the signal and close the bridge. The thousand pounds are mine, by God!"

Now Bruce was doing his best down the main street of Carlisle. A dozen shots spattered fire harmlessly, and a big bell began to toll. Armstrong was well ahead of the troopers who followed him, and he gained ground at every stride. The pursuers were continually augmented from each lane and alley, and came thundering after the flying man like a charge of cavalry. A turn in the road brought the bridge in sight, and Armstrong saw it was guarded only at the end nearest him, and that merely by two lone pikemen. He would mow them down like grass, he said to himself, as he drew his sword.

"Stand aside," he yelled. "The Scot is loose, and we're after him."

The men jumped aside, glad they were not called upon to arrest such a progress as they beheld coming down upon them. It was apparently one of their own officers who commanded them, and there was neither time to think or question. As the horse's hoofs struck the bridge, the deep crash of a cannon boomed from the castle, and before the fugitive reached the centre there arose at the other end of the bridge—he could not guess from whence they came—a troop of horse, as if the thunder of the gun had called the company

673

magically from the earth. Bruce stopped on the crown of the bridge, at a touch of the rein, quivering with excitement, raised his head, and gave a snort of defiance at the blockade ahead of him. Armstrong glanced back; the bridge had closed on him like a trap, both ends stopped by forces impossible for one man to contend against.

"That cannon-shot did it. Well planned," he growled to himself, his horse now drawn across the bridge, alert for the word of command whatever it might be. Below, the swollen Eden, lipping full from bank to bank, rolled yellow and surly to the sea. Right and left, at either end of the bridge, stood a mass of steel-clad men, impregnable as the walls of the castle itself. De Courcy sprang off his horse and advanced with a valour which Armstrong, sitting there, apparently calm, had not given him credit for.

"He's my man," he cried. "Shoot him dead if he raises his hand." Then to the Scot. "Surrender quietly. You have no chance. A score of muskets are turned on you."

"If they shoot, some of them will wing you. Better warn them not to fire," replied Armstrong mildly, as if proffering to a friend advice which did not concern himself.

"Do you surrender?"

"Come and take me, if you are anxious for the thousand pounds. It's worth the money."

The Frenchman hesitated, edging cautiously along the parapet, so that if his friends shot he would be as much as possible aside from the line of fire. Seemingly his confidence in their marksmanship had not been augmented by Armstrong's warning.

"If you raise your hand to a weapon," said De Courcy, "they will fire on you, and I cannot stop them. They will not wait my word."

"I know. I shall not raise my hand."

The Frenchman dashed forward and seized the bridle of Bruce.

"Come quietly," he shouted.

"I will," said Armstrong. He leaned forward; said sharply to his horse, "Over, my lad!" and smote him a rising blow on the shoulder with his open hand. The horse raised his powerful front, and stood poised for a moment like a statue, then launched himself into space. As De Courcy felt his feet leave the stones, he let go the rein and fell sprawling on the parapet, but Armstrong leaned over and grasped him by the loose folds of his doublet.

"Come down with me, you traitor!" he cried. There was a scream of terror, and the next instant the river roared in Armstrong's ears. When he came to the surface he shook his head like a spaniel, swept the water from his eyes, and looked aloft at the great bridge. The parapet was lined with troopers, all stricken motionless, as if they had been transformed to stone. De Courcy, one moment afloat, shrieked for help, then sank again. Armstrong knew that the paralysis on the bridge would not last long, and he turned his horse toward the bank of raw clay.

"No one in command up there, apparently," he muttered. "We must make the most of it, old man."

The panting horse, breathing laboriously, essayed the bank and slipped back. Armstrong let loose his sodden cloak and flung it on the flood, turning the horse that he might take the ascent at an angle. The crowd still stared at him as if it were a show they had come out to see. Bruce, his feet once more on firm ground, shook his mane and gave forth a wild whinny of delight. Now the voice of command came in a blast of anger from the bridge.

"After him, you fools! What are you staring at?"

"Too late, my lads, I think," ventured William, as he leaped his horse across the ditch that divided the fields from the road. Once the followers came near him, and he turned in his saddle, threatening them with his pistols, and they, forgetting that his powder was water-soaked, fell back.

The troopers found no difficulty in believing that a man who jumped his horse over Carlisle bridge into the Eden was directly aided by the devil, as had been rumoured, and they made no doubt the powder would soon dry on such a pit-scorched favourite as he. They felt sure he could put the pistols to deadly use in case of need.

From the moment Bruce struck his hoofs on the road the horses behind had no chance of overtaking him. They fell farther and farther to the rear, and at last the silvery Esk gleamed ahead, while all along, since pursuit grew hopeless, William had been feasting his eyes on the blue hills of Scotland. He walked his horse through the Esk, but it, too, had been swollen by the rains, and Bruce again had to swim for it before he reached the other side. William sprang to the ground, flung his arms round the neck of his sterling companion, laying his cheek against that of the horse.

"You've won the race, my boy. All the credit is to you, and Bruce, my lad, poets will sing of you." Then, with a choking in his throat, he knelt down and kissed the soil, the sensible horse looking on in wonder. As the young man rose to his feet and saw, on the other side of the Esk, the troopers lining up, his mood changed, and he laughed aloud. Drawing forth his leathern bottle, he held it aloft and shouted to them: "Come over, lads, and I'll give you a drink. Don't be feared; none o' the water got into this."

But the officer dared not cross the boundary, Cromwell's orders had been strict, so he and his men stood glum, making no response to the generous invitation.

"Well, here's to us a'," cried William, raising the bottle to his lips.

"And now, my friends," he continued, replacing the flask and springing into the saddle, "don't be so down in the mouth. You've seen a Scotchman run, which was more than your ancestors saw at Bannockburn."

And with that he rode for Traquair Castle.

## CHAPTER VIII.—ACCOMPLISHMENT.

As evening drew on, the old warder of Traquair Castle beheld a sight that caused him to rub his eyes in the fear that they were misleading him. A horseman bearing the guise of a Roundhead trooper, his steel cap glittering, approached the ancient stronghold. That such a man dared set foot on Scottish soil and ride thus boldly to the home of the most noted Royalist on the Border seemed incredible, but the warder was not to be caught napping, and he gave orders that the gates be closed and guarded, for the Border was ever a land of surprises, and one must take all precaution. Doubtless this lone trooper had a company concealed somewhere, and was advancing to parley, although he carried no flag of truce. He came on with a fine air of indifference, and stopped when he found his way barred, sitting carelessly on his horse with an amused smile on his lips.

"What's yer wull, surr?" demanded the warder from the wall.

"That's it," replied the horseman.

"Whut's it? I dinna unnerstaun' ye."

"Wull's ma name," said the rider with an accent as broad as that of his questioner. "Wuz that no' whut ye were spierin'? Dinna staun glowerin' there, Jock Tamson, like an oolet or a gowk. Can ye no' see Ah'm English? Gang awa' and tell yer maister that a freen o' Crummle's at th' door an' craves a word wi' him."

"Dod!" cried the Bewildered warder, scratching his head, "if ye hae a tongue like that on ye since ye crossed the Border, ye've made the maist o' yer time."

"Is the Yerl o' Traquair in?"

"He's jist that."

"Then rin awa' an' gi'e ma message, for Ah'm wet an' tired an' hungry."

The warder sought Traquair in his library, where he sat, an anxious man, with many documents spread out on a table before him.

"Yer lordship, there's a soldier in the uniform of the English rebels at th' gates, wha says he's a freen o' Crummle's, and begs a word wi' ye."

"Ah!" said the Earl, frowning, "they've caught poor Armstrong, then, and now, in addition to our troubles, we'll need to bargain with that fiend Noll to save his neck. Everything is against us."

"He may be an Englisher, but he's got a Scotch accent as broad as th'

Tweed."

"He's one of our countrymen fighting for Cromwell, and therefore thought by that shrewd villain the better emissary. Bring him in."

"There may be others o' his like in hiding, ma Lord."

"Close the gates after him, then, and keep a strict watch. There's no danger on that score yet, but lippen to nothing. This man's just come to strike a bargain, an' I'm afraid we must dance to the tune he pipes. Bring him in."

When William and the warder came in together, a moment or two passed before the Earl recognized his visitor, then he sprang forward and held out both his hands.

"In God's name, Armstrong, is this you?" he cried. "What have they done to you? Save us all! Who has shorn and accoutred you like this?"

"The necessities of the chase, Traquair. This is a disguise, and although you saw through it, I'm happy to think I deluded Jock Tamson there."

"Losh!" cried Tamson, peering forward, "ye'll never threep doon ma throat that this is Wull Armstrong."

"Sir William, if you please, Tamson," corrected the new knight. "The title was bestowed upon me by his Majesty himself, and I shall expect that deference from the lower orders, Tamson, which the designation calls for. Still, Jock, I'll forgive your familiarity if you'll help me off with this helmet, that seems glued to my skull."

The old man grasped the edges of the steel cap with both his hands when Armstrong bent his head. He braced his foot against that of the helmet-wearer, and pulled with all his might, but his strength was unequal to the task.

"Lord pity us!" growled Will, "catch me ever putting my head in a trap like this again. I'll have to take it off with a boot-jack."

"Bring in Angus," laughed the Earl, "he'll pull either the helmet or the head off you."

The huge Angus came lumbering in after the warder, who went in search of him.

"Have you had your supper, Angus?" asked the Earl.

"Yes, ma lord."

"Then let us see what strength it's given you. Tug this iron pot from Armstrong's head."

Angus, bracing himself as the warder had done, jerked ineffectually several times.

"Pull, ye deevil," cried Armstrong. "Ye've no more strength than a three-year-old wean."

"Ah'm feart to thraw yer neck," protested Angus.

"Never mind the neck. Being hanged by Cromwell is as nothing to this. Pull, ye gomeral! Am I to go about with my head in a metal bucket all my life? Pull!"

Angus put forth his strength, and the helmet gave way with unexpected suddenness, whereupon Angus sat down on the floor with a thud like an earthquake, the steel cap in his lap. Traquair slapped his thigh and roared till the rafters rang.

"Will, you'll be an inch taller after that. I never saw the like of it. I've heard that a man's head grows with new honors placed upon him, but I had no idea it was so bad as that. Man, where's your hair? And did they chop it off with a battle-axe? If that's a fair example of barber's work in England, I'm glad I live in Scotland."

Armstrong rubbed his shorn head slowly with his open palm.

"A barber may have other qualities than expertness with the shears," he said.

"The trick of the shears is surely the chief equipment for the trade."

"Yes. You're in the right. My hair was cut in a stable-yard under the moonlight, with great haste and blunt blades. We will see what your own poll-man can do in still shortening the result. I have been hotly chased, Traquair, and hair-cutting was the least drawback that troubled me. I think my tailoring is even worse than my barbering, and there, also, you must stand my friend. Is the Castle tailor out of work?"

"My whole wardrobe is at your disposal, Will."

"Nothing in it would fit me, and I am a thought particular about a new dress, as I have lost all self-respect in this one. I may borrow a hat from you, if you have one of the latest fashion, with a fine feather on it."

"Aha! What's come over you, Will? Some lady in the Court of Charles? You didn't fash much over your clothes in the old days."

"I don't fash much now, as you may see by my array. Still, it is n't duds, but food that is the first necessity. I've had nothing all day but a hurried drink out of the Eden. It was as thick as brose, and about the same colour, but not so sustaining."

"They're preparing supper for you now, and I'll bear you company when it's ready. I'm eager to hear what befell. So the King knighted you. Deed, he might have gone farther than that and made you a marquis or a duke at the same cost."

"Oh, he offered me anything in his gift if I brought the commission safely through to you,—a promise that I'm thinking I'll never trouble him to redeem. Nevertheless, here's the packet, a little damp, but none the worse for that."

He placed the cause of all the trouble on the table, and Traquair turned it over and over in his hands, with no great delight in its possession, as the messenger thought. The Earl sighed as he opened it at last and slowly perused its contents in silence, laying it on the table again when he had finished.

"You're a wonderful man, William," he said. "If every one in Scotland did his duty as thoroughly as you do it, we would soon place the King on his throne again."

"Is there more trouble brewing?"

680

"More trouble, and the old trouble, and the new trouble. Every one pulling his own way, and in all directions, thinking only of himself, and never by any chance of the interests of the whole."

"May I tell Cromwell that? He seemed at some pains to intercept a billet that you receive but lightly."

"Tell Cromwell! You're never going to write to that scoundrel?"

"I intend to see him before the week is past."

"What! You're not such a fool as to put yourself in Cromwell's clutch again?"

"Just that."

"Will, I wonder at you. Angus got the steel bonnet off you with some work, but no man in Scotland can get Cromwell's rope off your neck if once you thrust your head through the noose."

"Cromwell's not such a fool as to hang me. If he did, it would but unite your wavering hosts like an invasion of Scotland."

"It would be a heavy price to pay for union, Will."

"The price will never be paid. Cromwell knows what he wants, and he does n't want me now, however anxious he was for my company this morning."

"Have you actually seen him?"

"I met him the first day I crossed the Border. I saw him once again, and I travelled over most of England on a pass from his own hand. Cromwell and I have a mutual respect for each other by this time, but there are some matters of difference between us that I think will best be settled by word of mouth, so I'm off day after to-morrow to foregather with him. I cannot go sooner, because my new gear will not be ready, and I want to give the General time to withdraw his troops from across the country, so that I may come on him in other fettle than as a prisoner."

"Who is the woman, Will? I knew you would go clean daft when you met her."

"Never you mind. As the Border is a land of nobility and romance, we will call her an Earl's daughter to please you."

"More like some peasant girl who assisted you to escape from your enemies."

"Well, whoever she is, Traquair, I'll make her Mrs. Armstrong when I get the chance."

"Lady Armstrong, you mean. You're forgetting your new dignity. Surely if the case stands thus you will ask the King to fulfill his promise and make you a baron at the least."

"That will I not. I'll trouble the badgered man no further."

"I know the ways of the sex better than you do, and I warrant you the lady will give you no rest until the title's yours, whenever she knows you have earned it and have had the offer of it."

"She thinks less of these things than I do, even."

"Then she is no peasant lass."

"I never said she was."

At this point, greatly to the delight of Armstrong, whose answers were becoming more and more short, his supper was announced, and Traquair with his arm over the shoulder of his guest, led him to the dining-room.

The tailor came when supper was finished, and measured his new customer, received minute directions concerning the garments, and retired protesting he would do his best in the limited time allowed him. The barber operated as well as he could on a head that began to nod in spite of the efforts of its owner. Sleep laid its heavy hand on Armstrong, and the voice of Traquair sounded distant and meaningless, something resembling the rush of Eden water in his ears, whereupon William nearly got those useful members cropped in earnest. At last he found himself in his room, and, for the first time since he left that hospitable mansion, enjoyed the luxury of lying between clean sheets with his clothes off. Then he slept as dreamlessly as his ancestors.

# CHAPTER IX.—MATRIMONY.

A night, and a day, and a night rejuvenated the tired man and his horse. Clothed and in his right mind he was once more the gallant Borderer, ready to face whatever fortune had in store for him; on this occasion, so Traquair said, more superbly attired than ever had been the case before; but Armstrong held that this was merely interested praise of the Castle tailor. Traquair endeavoured to persuade him not to trust himself again on English soil, but his advice was unheeded, as is usually the fate of unasked counsel. Traquair wished him to take a bodyguard of a score or more, but Armstrong pointed out that unless he had an army at his back able to defeat Cromwell's forces all other assistance was useless. He risked everything upon his belief in Cromwell's common sense, and from this position nothing Traquair said could turn him. The Earl rode with him as far as the Esk, and there bade him good luck and God speed.

When Armstrong had once gone over a road, he needed no other guide than his own memory and instinct of direction. He made directly for the farmsteading where first he had been arrested, and found it deserted; then took the route over which his captors had conducted him, expecting to reach Corbiton Manor before darkness set in. This plan was frustrated by the fact that he had allowed too scant time for the cordon across the country to be withdrawn. Cromwell was indeed calling in his men, and massing them at Carlisle, Newcastle, and Hexham, which latter town Armstrong's own ancestors had frequently pillaged. He learned of this movement from chance wayfarers, and was on the alert not to fall within the scope of any marching company. There was evidently no secret about Cromwell's intentions, and the Scot surmised that the General wished his plans to be well spread over the land, and thus overawe the Northerners in any hostile projects they might think of undertaking, showing his readiness to crush them if they ventured to set foot across the Border.

About mid-day Armstrong caught sight of the first large body of men, and he was compelled to hide for several hours in a depression on the moor until they and the danger were past. This delay retarded his arrival at Corbiton Manor until after nightfall, when the full moon shone upon the ancient mansion, instead of the silver crescent which hung in the western sky when last he visited the place. It seemed incredible that the space of time could have been so short, for the events of a life were crowded into the interval. As he approached the ancient house, the challenge of a sentinel brought him to a stand, and called from the hall several officers.

"Is Cromwell here?" asked the newcomer.

"This is the headquarters of his Excellency, General Cromwell," said one of the officers, with some severity in his tone, a rebuke to the questioner's off-hand method of designation.

"That's the man I mean," replied Armstrong. "I never heard there were two of the name or the kind. Well; tell him that William Armstrong, who carried the commission from the King to Scotland, is here, and requires a private conference with him."

The strong moonlight was shining on the back of the horseman, and in the faces of the officers. The latter did not obey the injunction laid upon them, but their leader gave, instead, a brief command, and in a moment two dozen pikemen surrounded the rider, who laughed heartily and said: "My lads, you are too late. You should have done that trick several days since. Oliver will give you no thanks for it now. Go in and tell him I am here, and send some one to take charge of my horse while I talk with him."

The chief officer hesitated for a moment, then turned and disappeared within the mansion, while Armstrong dismounted and gave to the soldier who took his horse minute instructions touching the treatment of the animal.

"You are all good horsemen," said the visitor, in his most genial accents, "and will doubtless respect Bruce here, whatever you think of his master; for this is the charger that louped over the parapet of Carlisle bridge, and, after that, beat the best you had in your cavalry in a race for the Border. If your chief should come to a disagreement with me, take care of the horse at least, for you have n't another like him."

The horse was led away, palpably admired by all the men, for some of them stroked and patted his flank, speaking soothingly to him. William stood with his hands in his pockets, the centre of a ring of armed men, his gay dress in striking contrast to the more sober uniform of his guards. Cromwell was taking his time making up his mind, and the young man thought this delay was not an encouraging sign. He had thrust his head between the lion's jaws, and the minutes that passed before he could know whether the brute was going to bite or not were irksome to him especially as there was now nothing to do but await the issue. At last the officer reappeared, dismissed the guard, and said curtly to the prisoner: "Follow me."

Armstrong was ushered into the huge room which he remembered so well, and found Cromwell sitting alone at the table, as if he had never left it. Even the two candles stood where they had been placed before, but the face of the seated man seemed more inscrutable, more stern, than he recollected it. This was the leader of the Ironsides on the Northampton road, rather than the urbane man who had pretended to believe the story of the search for cattle.

Armstrong swept off his feathered hat most courteously as he approached the table, bowed, and, standing at ease on the spot he had formerly occupied, said: "Good evening, General!" The General lifted his heavy eyes to the cropped head, now glistening in the light, and although his firm mouth remained immobile, the slightest suspicion of a twinkle scintillated for one brief moment in his searching glance.

"Good evening. You wished to see me?"

"Yes, General, and have come from Scotland this very day for no other purpose."

"You are out of employment, perhaps, and are looking for re-engagement?"

"Well, General, if I was, you are the man I should come to for a recommendation. In a manner of speaking, you are in the right. I have been riding hard this while back for other folk, and now I have taken a bit of journey on my own account. You see my case is——"

"I will state the case," interrupted Cromwell, menacingly. "You stood here and lied to me."

"You sat there and did the same by me."

"You stood here and lied to me. You came as a spy, mixing with affairs that did not concern you."

"Pardon me, General. I took service for my King, and you will be good enough to remember that Charles is King of Scotland, even if it pleases you to forget that he is King of England, and that he will be, till he dies, your King as well as mine."

"He is King of Oxford solely."

"Very well. Let me tell you, you'll find that same Oxford a very hard nut to crack if you attempt to take it by assault. I went carefully around the fortifications, and would seek no better job than to hold it against you and your whole army. There would be many a cropped head low before you got mine in your clutches," and William passed his hand sympathetically over his denuded crown, as had become a custom with him. His questioner bent forward with more of eagerness than he had hitherto shown, all thought of the indictment he was heaping up seeming to pass from his mind.

"Where is its weakest spot?" he said, as one expert might seek counsel from another who had personal experience of the subject.

"That is the beauty of it. There is no weakest spot."

"Is there not? We shall never need to take it by assault, but if that were thought best, it might be attacked from the south."

Armstrong raised his eyes to the ceiling and meditated for a moment.

"I think you're right," he said, "but it would cost a'wheen o' men."

"Yes; better men than are within its walls, and they shall not be sacrificed. I can wait, and the King cannot. You delivered the King's message to Traquair?"

"Yes. That's what I went for."

"And you have the impudence to come to me, thinking I will allow you to return?"

"Say confidence, rather. I am very sure you will allow me to return."

"Yes, confidence is the word, but with a mixture of impudence as well; the malt and the hops. It never crossed your mind that it was a dungeon you were approaching?"

"I thought if you did anything, it would be hanging."

"And why not?"

"Because my death by rope would be just the little fillip that Scotland needs at the present moment. You thraw my neck, and the Scots are at yours before I am fairly happit in the ground."

"You look upon yourself as important to your countrymen, then?"

"I do nothing of the kind. Man, I wonder at both you and the King. Neither of you understand the Scottish nature in the least. If the King had any comprehension, he would have had the heather afire years since. A man may dawner about Scotland all his life, hungry and athirst, cold and in rags, getting fewer kickshaws than kicks, none paying heed or anything else to him, but let him die the death of a martyr, and his tired bones are more potent than ten thousand live men. Ma sang! I'd like to see ye hang me! There's poor Traquair, at his wit's end for discouragement through dissension among the people and their leaders. You hang me, and you've done the trick for him."

Cromwell leaned back in his chair, his lids partially closed, but they could not veil the look of admiration he cast upon the man standing before him, who spoke enthusiastically of his own execution as if it were rather a good joke on his opponent. For some moments the General kept silence, then he said abruptly:

"Will you take a commission in my army?"

"I will not."

"I thought you were a fighter."

"I am, but I prefer to engage under Traquair's banner if he raises it."

"Against me?"

"Just that."

"And you think I will let you go?"

"I'll take my oath on it."

"You are right. The way is clear to Scotland, to Oxford, or where you please. What have you come to me for?"

"For Frances Wentworth."

"I thought as much. In this I cannot oblige you. With you I have nothing to do, and you are at liberty. That wench of Wentworth's stands on a different footing, inasmuch as she has proved traitor to her own. I shall do nothing to injure her, but she shall taste captivity until she confesses her error."

"She is no traitor, but did well the work you set for her."

"I set no work for her. 'Twas given to her brother, and his folly brought her into the business."

"You gave your consent at Northampton; thus I say you set her to the task, and well she performed it. If your men had done your bidding as faithfully, I had never crossed the Esk."

"She connived at your escape from Lichfield, and elsewhere."

"True, but she was a free woman then, having fulfilled her duty to you."

"You are quibbling. She is a traitor, and more honest than you; she admits it."

"I say she is a true woman," cried Armstrong, red anger flushing his brow. The hot Border blood sprang into mastery for the first time during their controversy, and he failed to note that Cromwell remained cold as at the beginning, and might be negotiated with, if he had remembered the commander's resolve to enlist the Scot in his service. But before the General could give hint of a bargain, the impetuosity of the younger man left him only the choice of killing the Scot where he stood, or apparently succumbing to him, a most dangerous alternative had Armstrong to deal with one less schooled in the repression of his feelings than Cromwell. The ill-advised Borderer dropped his hat silently to the floor, flashed forth his sword, and presented it at his opponent's throat.

"They tell me you wear concealed armour,"—his voice was quiet in its intensity, almost a whisper,—"but that will not help you. No human power can avail you at this moment, for if you cry out my blade advances, and a bit of your backbone sticks to the point of it. You see I cannot help myself, but must kill you unless I get your promise."

Cromwell sat rigid, not a muscle of face or body moving. The sword was held as steady as a beam of the roof.

"I implore you to heed me," continued the young man, seeing the other did not intend to speak. "I implore you, as if I were on my bended knees before you, and my life in your hands, instead of yours in mine. Will you let the great affairs of state be jeopardized to thwart two lovers? With you slain, the King wins, for there is none in England can fill your place. Have you sons and daughters of your own that your heart goes out to? Think of them, and be kind to us."

"Will you marry the girl?"

"Surely, surely."

"Here, before you depart together?"

"Here and now, if there is one to knot us."

"You know that a promise given under coercion does not hold?"

"I know it well, but the word of General Cromwell is enough for me, once it is passed, however given."

"Then take down your sword; I promise, and am well rid of you both."

With a deep sigh of relief Armstrong sheathed his sword and lifted his hat from the floor. Cromwell rose from his chair and paced twice up and down the long room between the great moonlit windows and the table. He paused in his march, looked up at the dim gallery, and said: "Cobb, come down."

To Armstrong's amazement, who thought he had been alone with the General, he heard lurching heavy steps come clumping down the wooden stair, and a trooper, with primed musket in his hand, stood before his master.

"Cobb, why did you not shoot this man dead when you saw him draw his sword?"

"Because, Excellency, you did not give the signal."

"If I had, what then?"

"He was a dead man before he could move an arm, or your finger was on the table again."

"You have done well. That is what I like; exact obedience, and no panic. Keep your lips closed. Go and tell your colonel to come here."

The man withdrew, and Cromwell resumed his walk, making no comment on the brief dialogue. William blew a long whistle, then he laughed a little.

When the colonel came in, Cromwell turned to him and said: "Is that malignant brawler, chaplain to Lord Rudby, in the cells yet?"

"Yes, Excellency."

"Tell your men to clear out the chapel at once and light it. There are some stores in it, I think, and bring the reverend greybeard to me."

In a few moments the colonel returned, accompanied by an aged clergyman, who, despite his haggard and careworn look and bent shoulders, cast a glance of hatred at the General, which seemed to entitle him to the epithet Cromwell had bestowed upon him. To this silent defiance Cromwell paid no attention, but said to him:

"Sir, you may earn your liberty to-night by marrying two young people in the chapel."

690

"That will I not," returned the clergyman stoutly, "and all your tyranny cannot compel me to do so."

"The wench," continued Cromwell, unmoved, "you already know. She is Frances Wentworth, daughter of the late Earl of Strafford. The groom stands here before you; William Armstrong, a Scot, who has but lately carried a message from the man Charles, at Oxford, to Traquair on the Border. I should hang him, but he prefers the noose you can tie to the one my hands might prepare."

The old clergyman looked at Armstrong with an interest he had not displayed on entering the room.

"Have you, then, seen his gracious Majesty, the King?"

"Yes, reverend sir, and but a few days ago."

"And carried his message safe through these rebellious hordes now desecrating the land?"

"There was some opposition, but I won through, thanks to my horse."

"And thanks, no doubt, to your own loyal courage. God bless you, sir, and God save the King. The lady you have chosen is worthy of you, as you of her. In God's shattered temple, I will marry you, if its walls remain."

When the colonel came in with Frances, the girl turned a frightened look upon the group as she saw who stood there.

"Oh," she cried impulsively, "I told you not to come."

"'Tis you who are to obey, not he," said Cromwell harshly. "He has come for you. Will you marry him?"

The girl allowed her eyes to seek the floor, and did not answer him. Even in the candle-light her cheeks burned rosy red.

"Come, come," cried Cromwell impatiently, "yes, or no, wench."

"I will not have her so addressed by any," spoke up Armstrong, stoutly stepping forward; but the girl flashed a glance from her dark eyes on the commander.

"Yes," she said, with decision, then directed her look on her lover, and so to the floor again.

"Are there candles in the chapel?"

"Yes, Excellency," replied the colonel.

"Bring some of the officers,—I think witnesses are needed,—and your regimental book, if there is signing to be done. 'Twill hold them as fast as the parish register, I warrant." Then to the clergyman, "Follow me, sir, and the rest of you."

With that Cromwell strode out and led the way to the chapel, so hastily converted from a storehouse to its former purpose. The old divine took his place with the young people before him, the group of officers in the dimness near the door. Cromwell, however, stood near the girl.

"Slip off one of your rings and give it to this pastor," he whispered to her. "We are short of such gear here, and I doubt if your man ever thought of it."

Frances, without a word, selected from the number on her fingers that which had been her mother's wedding-ring, and handed it to the clergyman.

"Dearly beloved, we are gathered together here in the sight of God, and in the face of this congregation, to join together this Man and this Woman in holy Matrimony; which is an honourable estate, instituted of God in the time of man's innocency, signifying unto us the mystical union that is betwixt Christ and his Church; which holy estate Christ adorned and beautified with his presence, and first miracle that he wrought in Cana of Galilee."

As the sonorous words resounded in the ancient chapel, the old man straightened himself, the former anger in his face gave way to a benignant expression, and his attitude took on all the grave dignity of his calling. He went on with the service until he came to the words:

"Who giveth this woman to be married to this man?"

Cromwell stepped forward and said brusquely, "I do."

692

The clergyman seemed to have forgotten the Commander's presence, and now paused when it was recalled to him; then he went on to the end, and added, in a voice trembling with emotion: "God bless you, my children, sworn to love and cherish each other in this time of hatred and war. May you live to see what my aged eyes may never behold,—peace upon this distracted land, and the King upon an unchallenged throne."

"Amen, and amen!" said the deep voice of Cromwell, "provided the word 'righteous' is placed before the word 'King'."

Once more on horseback, and clear of Corbiton Manor, her hand stole into his.

"Well," he said, "which way?"

"If you are willing, I will take the way known to me, and lead you to my home; to-morrow you may take the way known to you, and lead me to yours."

"Frances, I am ready to follow wherever you lead." And so they went forth together in the glamour of the moonlight.

### THE END

# About Author

**Robert Barr** (16 September 1849 – 21 October 1912) was a Scottish-Canadian short story writer and novelist.

### Early years in Canada

Robert Barr was born in Barony, Lanark, Scotland to Robert Barr and Jane Watson. In 1854, he emigrated with his parents to Upper Canada at the age of four years old. His family settled on a farm near the village of Muirkirk. Barr assisted his father with his job as a carpenter, and developed a sound work ethic. Robert Barr then worked as a steel smelter for a number of years before he was educated at Toronto Normal School in 1873 to train as a teacher.

After graduating Toronto Normal School, Barr became a teacher, and eventually headmaster/principal of the Central School of Windsor, Ontario in 1874. While Barr worked as head master of the Central School of Windsor, Ontario, he began to contribute short stories—often based on personal experiences, and recorded his work. On August 1876, when he was 27, Robert Barr married Ontario-born Eva Bennett, who was 21. According to the 1891 England Census, the couple appears to have had three children, Laura, William, and Andrew.

In 1876, Barr quit his teaching position to become a staff member of publication, and later on became the news editor for the Detroit Free Press. Barr wrote for this newspaper under the pseudonym, "Luke Sharp." The idea for this pseudonym was inspired during his morning commute to work when Barr saw a sign that read "Luke Sharp, Undertaker." In 1881, Barr left Canada to return to England in order to start a new weekly version of "The Detroit Free Press Magazine."

### London years

In 1881 Barr decided to "vamoose the ranch", as he called the process of immigration in search of literary fame outside of Canada, and relocated to London to continue to write/establish the weekly English edition of the Detroit Free Press. During the 1890s, he broadened his literary works, and started writing novels from the popular crime genre. In 1892 he founded the magazine The Idler, choosing Jerome K. Jerome as his collaborator (wanting, as Jerome said, "a popular name"). He retired from its co-editorship in 1895.

In London of the 1890s Barr became a more prolific author—publishing a book a year—and was familiar with many of the best-selling authors of his day, including :Arnold Bennett, Horatio Gilbert Parker, Joseph Conrad, Bret Harte, Rudyard Kipling, H. Rider Haggard, H. G. Wells, and George Robert Gissing. Barr was well-spoken, well-cultured due to travel, and considered a "socializer."

Because most of Barr's literary output was of the crime genre, his works were highly in vogue. As Sherlock Holmes stories were becoming well-known, Barr wrote and published in the Idler the first Holmes parody, "The Adventures of "Sherlaw Kombs" (1892), a spoof that was continued a decade later in another Barr story, "The Adventure of the Second Swag" (1904). Despite those jibes at the growing Holmes phenomenon, Barr remained on very good terms with its creator Arthur Conan Doyle. In Memories and Adventures, a serial memoir published 1923–24, Doyle described him as "a volcanic Anglo—or rather Scot-American, with a violent manner, a wealth of strong adjectives, and one of the kindest natures underneath it all".

In 1904, Robert Barr completed an unfinished novel for Methuen & Co. by the recently deceased American author Stephen Crane entitled The O'Ruddy, a romance.Despite his reservations at taking on the project, Barr reluctantly finished the last eight chapters due to his longstanding friendship with Crane and his common-law wife, Cora, the war correspondent and bordello owner.

### Death

The 1911 census places Robert Barr, "a writer of fiction," at Hillhead, Woldingham, Surrey, a small village southeast of London, living with his wife, Eva, their son William, and two female servants. At this home, the author died from heart disease on 21 October 1912.

## Writing Style

Barr's volumes of short stories were often written with an ironic twist in the story with a witty, appealing narrator telling the story. Barr's other works also include numerous fiction and non-fiction contributions to periodicals. A few of his mystery stories and stories of the supernatural were put in anthologies, and a few novels have been republished. His writings have also attracted scholarly attention. His narrative personae also featured moral and editorial interpolations within their tales. Barr's achievements were recognized by an honorary degree from the University of Michigan in 1900.

His protagonists were journalists, princes, detectives, deserving commercial and social climbers, financiers, the new woman of bright wit and aggressive accomplishment, and lords. Often, his characters were stereotypical and romanticized.

Barr wrote fiction in an episode-like format. He developed this style when working as an editor for the newspaper Detroit Press. Barr developed his skill with the anecdote and vignette; often only the central character serves to link the nearly self-contained chapters of the novels. (Source: Wikipedia)

# NOTABLE WORKS

In a Steamer Chair and Other Stories (Thirteen short stories by one of the most famous writers in his day -1892)

"The Face And The Mask" (1894) consists of twenty-four delightful short stories.

In the Midst of Alarms (1894, 1900, 1912), a story of the attempted Fenian invasion of Canada in 1866.

From Whose Bourne (1896) Novel in which the main character, William Brenton, searches for truth to set his wife free.

One Day's Courtship (1896)

Revenge! (Collection of 20 short stories, Alfred Hitchcock-like style, thriller with a surprise ending)

The Strong Arm

A Woman Intervenes (1896), a story of love, finance, and American journalism.

Tekla: A Romance of Love and War (1898)

Jennie Baxter, Journalist (1899)

The Unchanging East (1900)

The Victors (1901)

A Prince of Good Fellows (1902)

Over The Border: A Romance (1903)

The O'Ruddy, A Romance, with Stephen Crane (1903)

A Chicago Princess (1904)

The Speculations of John Steele (1905)

The Tempestuous Petticoat (1905–12)

A Rock in the Baltic (1906)

The Triumphs of Eugène Valmont (1906)

The Measure of the Rule (1907)

Stranleigh's Millions (1909)

The Sword Maker (Medieval action/adventure novel, genre: Historical Fiction-1910)

The Palace of Logs (1912)

"The Ambassadors Pigeons" (1899)

"And the Rigor of the Game" (1892)

"Converted" (1896)

"Count Conrad's Courtship" (1896)

"The Count's Apology" (1896)

"A Deal on Change " (1896)

"The Exposure of Lord Stanford" (1896)

"Gentlemen: The King!"

"The Hour-Glass" (1899)

"An invitation" (1892)

" A Ladies Man"

"The Long Ladder" (1899)

"Mrs. Tremain" (1892)

" Transformation" (1896)

"The Understudy" (1896)

" The Vengeance of the Dead" (1896)

"The Bromley Gibbert's Story" (1896)

" Out of Thun" (1896)

"The Shadow of Greenback" (1896)

"Flight of the Red Dog" (fiction)

"Lord Stranleigh Abroad" (1913)

"One Day's Courtship and the Herald's of Fame" (1896)

"Cardillac"

"Dr. Barr's Tales"

"The Triumphs of Eugene Valmont"